THE DANGER
AND
TWICE SHY

Also by Dick Francis in Pan Books

DEAD CERT
NERVE
FOR KICKS
ODDS AGAINST
FLYING FINISH
BLOOD SPORT
FORFEIT
ENQUIRY
RAT RACE
BONECRACK
SMOKESCREEN
SLAY-RIDE
KNOCK DOWN
HIGH STAKES
IN THE FRAME
RISK
TRIAL RUN
WHIP HAND
REFLEX

BANKER
THE DANGER
PROOF
BREAK IN
BOLT
HOT MONEY
THE EDGE
STRAIGHT
LONGSHOT
COMEBACK
DRIVING FORCE
DECIDER
WILD HORSES
COME TO GRIEF
TO THE HILT
10lb PENALTY
FIELD OF THIRTEEN
SECOND WIND
SHATTERED

THE SPORT OF QUEENS (autobiography)

LESTER: The Official Biography

DICK FRANCIS OMNIBUS ONE:
Long Shot, Straight, High Stakes

DICK FRANCIS OMNIBUS TWO:
Forfeit, Risk, Reflex

DICK FRANCIS OMNIBUS THREE:
Slay-Ride, Banker, Proof

DICK FRANCIS OMNIBUS FOUR:
Enquiry, Rat Race, Smokescreen

SID HALLEY OMNIBUS:

Dick Francis has written forty-one international bestsellers and is widely acclaimed as one of the world's finest thriller writers. His awards include the Crime Writers' Association's Cartier Diamond Dagger for his outstanding contribution to the crime genre, and an honorary Doctorate of Humane Letters from Tufts University of Boston. In 1996 Dick Francis was made a Mystery Writers of America Grand Master for a lifetime's achievement and in 2000 he received a CBE in the Queen's Birthday Honours list.

Dick Francis

THE DANGER
AND
TWICE SHY

PAN BOOKS

The Danger first published 1983 by Michael Joseph.
First published in paperback by Pan Books 1984
Twice Shy first published 1981 by Michael Joseph.
First published in paperback by Pan Books 1982.

This omnibus edition published 2003 by Pan Books
an imprint of Pan Macmillan Ltd
Pan Macmillan, 20 New Wharf Road, London N1 9RR
Basingstoke and Oxford
Associated companies throughout the world
www.panmacmillan.com

ISBN 0 330 43673 2

1 3 5 7 9 8 6 4 2

A CIP catalogue record for this book is available from
the British Library.

Printed and bound in Great Britain by
Mackays of Chatham plc, Chatham, Kent

THE DANGER

Liberty Market Ltd is fictional, though similar organisations exist. No one who has helped me with the background of this book wants to be mentioned, but my thanks to them just the same.

I acknowledge my debt also to *Kidnap and Ransom: The Response* by Richard Clutterbuck.

Kidnapping is a fact of life. Always has been, always will be. Extorting a ransom is an age-old pastime, less risky and more lucrative than robbing banks.

Kidnapping, twentieth-century style, has meant train loads and 'plane loads of hostages, athletes killed in company at Munich, men of substance dying lonely deaths. All kidnappers are unstable, but the political variety, hungry for power and publicity as much as money, make quicksand look like rock.

Give me the straightforward criminal any day, the villain who seizes and says pay up or else. One does more or less know where one is, with those.

Kidnapping, you see, is my business.

My job, that is to say, as a partner in the firm of Liberty Market Ltd, is both to advise people at risk how best not to be kidnapped, and also to help negotiate with the kidnappers once a grab has taken place: to get the victim back alive for the least possible cost.

Every form of crime generates an opposing force, and to fraud, drugs and murder one could add the Kidnap Squad, except that the kidnap squad is unofficial and highly discreet . . . and is often *us.*

ITALY

CHAPTER ONE

There was a God-awful cock-up in Bologna.

I stood as still as possible while waves of cold rage and fiery anxiety jerked at my limbs and would have had me pacing.

Stood still . . . while a life which might depend on me was recklessly risked by others. Stood still among the ruins of a success nearly achieved, a freedom nearly won, safety within grasp.

The most dangerous, delicate stage of any kidnap is the actual handing over of the ransom, because it is then, at the moment of collection, that someone, somehow, must step out of the shadows . . . and a kidnapper comes to his waterhole with more caution than any beast in the jungle.

One suspicion, one sight or glint of a watcher, is encugh to send him scuttling away; and it is afterwards, seething with fright and in a turmoil of vengeful anger, that he can most easily kill. To bungle the drop is to escalate the threat to the victim a hundredfold.

Alessia Cenci, twenty-three years old, had by that

time been in the hands of kidnappers for five weeks, three days, ten hours, and her life had never been closer to forfeit.

Enrico Pucinelli climbed grim-faced through the rear door of the ambulance in which I stood: a van, more accurately, which looked like an ambulance from the outside but whose darkly tinted windows concealed a bench, a chair, and a mass of electronic equipment within.

'I was off duty,' he said. 'I did not give those orders.'

He spoke in Italian, but slowly, for my sake. As men, we got on very well. As linguists, speaking a little of each other's language but understanding more, we had to take time. We spoke to each other carefully, each in our own tongue, and listened with attention, asking for repetition whenever necessary.

He was the carabinieri officer who had been leading the official investigations. He had agreed throughout on the need for extreme care and for the minimum of visible involvement. No emblazoned cars with busily flashing lights had driven to or from the Villa Francese, where Paolo Cenci waited with white face for news of his daughter. No uniformed men had been in evidence in any place where hostile eyes could watch. Not while Pucinelli himself had been able to prevent it.

He had agreed with me that the first priority was the girl's safety, and only the second priority the catching of the kidnappers. Not every policeman by any means saw things that way round, the hunting instincts of law enforcers everywhere being satisfied solely by the capture of their prey.

Pucinelli's colleague-on-duty on that devastating evening, suddenly learning that he could pounce with fair ease on the kidnappers at the moment they picked up the ransom, had seen no reason to hold back. Into the pregnant summer darkness, into the carefully negotiated, patiently damped-down moment of maximum quiet, he had sent a burst of men with batons waving, lights blazing, guns rising ominously against the night sky, voices shouting, cars racing, sirens wailing, uniforms running . . . all the moral aggression of a righteous army in full pursuit.

From the dark stationary ambulance a long way down the street I had watched it happen with sick disbelief and impotent fury. My driver, cursing steadily, had started the engine and crawled forward towards the mêlée, and we had both quite clearly heard the shots.

'It is regretted,' Pucinelli said with formality, watching me.

I could bet it was. There had been so many carabinieri on the move in the poorly-lit back street that, unsure where to look precisely, they had missed their target altogether. Two dark-clad men, carrying the suitcase which contained the equivalent of six hundred and fifty thousand pounds, had succeeded in reaching a hidden car, in starting it and driving off before the lawmen noticed; and certainly their attention had been more clearly focused, as was my own, on the sight of the young man spilling head-first from the car which all along had been plainly in everyone's view, the car in which the ransom had been carried to this blown-open rendezvous.

The young man, son of a lawyer, had been shot. I could see the crimson flash on his shirt and the weak flutter of his hand, and I thought of him, alert and confident, as we'd talked before he set off. Yes, he'd said, he understood the risk, and yes, he would follow their instructions absolutely, and yes, he would keep me informed by radio direct from the car to the ambulance. Together we had activated the tiny transmitter sewn into the handle of the suitcase containing the ransom money and had checked that it was working properly as a homer, sending messages back to the radar in the ambulance.

Inside the ambulance that same radar tracker was showing unmistakably that the suitcase was on the move and going rapidly away. I would without doubt have let the kidnappers escape, because that was best for Alessia, but one of the carabinieri, passing and catching sight of the blip, ran urgently towards the bull-like man who with blowing whistle appeared to be chiefly in charge, shouting to him above the clamour and pointing a stabbing finger towards the van.

With wild and fearful doubt the officer looked agonisedly around him and then shambled towards me at a run. With his big head through the window of the cab he stared mutely at the radar screen, where he read the bad news unerringly with a pallid outbreak of sweat.

'Follow,' he said hoarsely to my driver, and brushed away my attempt at telling him in Italian why he should do no such thing.

The driver shrugged resignedly and we were on our way with a jerk, accompanied, it seemed to me, by a veritable posse of wailing cars screaming through the empty streets of the industrial quarter, the factory workers long ago gone home.

'Since midnight,' Pucinelli said, 'I am on duty. I am again in charge.'

I looked at him bleakly. The ambulance stood now in a wider street, its engine stilled, the tracker showing a steady trace, locating the suitcase inside a modern lower-income block of flats. In front of the building, at an angle to the kerb, stood a nondescript black car, its overheated engine slowly cooling. Around it, like a haphazard barrier, the police cars were parked at random angles, their doors open, headlights blazing, occupants in their fawn uniforms ducking into cover with ready pistols.

'As you see, the kidnappers are in the front apartment on the third floor,' Pucinelli said. 'They say they have taken hostage the people who live there and will kill them, and also they say Alessia Cenci will surely die, if we do not give them safe passage.'

I had heard them shouting from the open window, and had hardly needed the repetition.

'In a short time the listening bug will be in position,' Pucinelli said, glancing uneasily at my rigid face. 'And soon we will have to tap on the telephone. We have men on the staircase outside. They are fixing them.'

I said nothing.

'My men say you would have let the kidnappers get away . . . taking the money with them.'

'Of course.'

We looked at each other unsmilingly, almost foes where recently we'd been allies. He was thin and about forty, give or take. Dark and intense and energetic. A communist in a communist city, disapproving of the capitalist whose daughter was at risk.

'They had shot the boy who drove the car,' he said. 'We could not possibly let them escape.'

'The boy took his chances. The girl must still be saved.'

'You English,' he said. 'So cold.'

The anger inside me would have scorched asbestos. If his men hadn't tried their abortive ambush, the boy would not have been shot. He would have walked away unharmed and left the ransom in the car, as he'd been instructed.

Pucinelli turned his attention to the benchful of bolted-down radio receivers, turning a few knobs and pressing switches. 'I am sending a man in here to receive messages,' he said. 'I will be here also. You can stay, if you wish.'

I nodded. It was too late to do anything else.

It had been absolutely against my instincts and my training to be anywhere near the dropping point of the ransom, yet Pucinelli had demanded my presence there in return for a promise of his force's absence.

'You can go in our van,' he said. 'Our radio van. Like an ambulance. Very discreet. You go. I'll send you a driver. When the kidnappers take the suitcase, you follow it. You can tell us where they're hiding. Then, when the girl is free, we'll arrest them. OK?'

'When the girl is free, I will tell you where they took the money.'

He had narrowed his eyes slightly, but had clapped me on the shoulder and agreed to it, nodding. 'The girl first.'

Not knowing, as one never does, precisely when the kidnappers would set the handing-over procedure rolling, Pucinelli had stationed the van permanently in the garage at the Villa Francese, with the driver living in the house. Four days after we'd signalled to the kidnappers that the agreed money had been collected and was ready for them, they had sent their delivery instructions: and as promised between Pucinelli and myself, I had telephoned his office to tell him the drop was about to start.

Pucinelli had not been there, but we had planned for that contingency.

In basic Italian I had said, 'I am Andrew Douglas. Tell Enrico Pucinelli immediately that the ambulance is moving.'

The voice at the other end had said it understood.

I now wished with all my heart that I had not kept my promise to give Pucinelli that message; but cooperation with the local police was one of the firm's most basic policies.

Pucinelli's own trust in me, it now turned out, had not been so very great. Perhaps he had known I would rather have lost track of the suitcase than give away my presence near the drop. In any case, both the suitcase's homer, and a further homer in the van, had been trackable from Pucinelli's own official car. The colleague-on-duty, receiving my message, had not consulted Pucinelli but had simply set out with a maximum task force, taking Pucinelli's staff car and chasing personal glory. Stupid, swollen-headed, lethal human failing.

How in God's name was I going to tell Paolo Cenci? And who was going to break it to the lawyer that his bright student son had been shot?

'The boy who was driving,' I said to Pucinelli. 'Is the boy alive?'

'He's gone to hospital. He was alive when they took him. Beyond that, I don't know.'

'His father must be told.'

Pucinelli said grimly, 'It's being done. I've sent a man.'

This mess, I thought, was going to do nothing at all for the firm's reputation. It was positively my job to help to resolve a kidnap in the quietest way possible, with the lowest of profiles and minimum action. My job to calm, to plan, to judge how little one could get a kidnapper to accept, to see that negotiations were kept on the coolest, most businesslike footing, to bargain without angering, to get the timing right. My brief, above all, to bring the victim home.

I had by that time been the advisor-on-the-spot in fifteen kidnaps, some lasting days, some weeks, some several months. Chiefly because kidnappers usually do release their victims unharmed once the ransom is in their hands, I hadn't so far been part of a disaster; but Alessia Cenci, reportedly one of the best girl jockeys in the world, looked set to be my first.

'Enrico,' I said, 'don't talk to these kidnappers yourself. Get someone else, who has to refer to you for decisions.'

'Why?' he said.

'It calms things down. Takes time. The longer they go on talking the less likely they are to kill those people in the flat.'

He considered me briefly. 'Very well. Advise me. It's your job.'

We were alone in the van and I guessed he was sorely ashamed of his force's calamity, otherwise he would never have admitted such a tacit loss of face. I had realised from shortly after my first arrival at the villa that as officer-in-charge he had never before had to deal with a real kidnapper, though he had carefully informed me that all carabinieri were instructed in the theory of kidnap response, owing to the regrettable frequency of that crime in Italy. Between us, until that night, his theory and my experience had done well enough, and it seemed that he did still want the entente to go on.

I said, 'Telephone that flat direct from here. Tell the kidnappers you are arranging negotiations. Tell them they must wait for a while. Tell them that if they tire of the waiting they may telephone you. Give them a number . . . you have a line in this van?'

He nodded. 'It's being connected.'

'Once their pulses settle it will be safer, but if they are pressed too hard to start with they may shoot again.'

'And my men would fire . . .' He blinked rapidly and went outside, and I could hear him speaking to his forces through a megaphone. 'Do not return fire. I repeat, do not shoot. Await orders before firing.'

He returned shortly, accompanied by a man unrolling a wire, and said briefly, 'Engineer.'

The engineer attached the wire to one of the switch boxes and passed Pucinelli an instrument which looked a cross between a microphone and a handset. It appeared to lead a direct line to the flat's telephone because after a pause Pucinelli was clearly conversing with one of the kidnappers. The engineer, as a matter of course, was recording every word.

The Italian was too idiomatic for my ears, but I understood at least the tone. The near-hysterical shouting from the kidnapper slowly abated in response to Pucinelli's determined calmness and ended in a more manageable agitation. To a final forceful question

Pucinelli, after a pause, answered slowly and distinctly, 'I don't have the authority. I have to consult my superiors. Please wait for their reply.'

The result was a menacing, grumbling agreement and a disconnecting click.

Pucinelli wiped his hand over his face and gave me the tiniest flicker of a smile. Sieges, as I supposed he knew, could go on for days, but at least he had established communications, taking the first vital step.

He glanced at the engineer and I guessed he was wanting to ask me what next, but couldn't because of the engineer and his recordings.

I said, 'Of course you will be aiming searchlights at those windows soon so that the kidnappers will feel exposed.'

'Of course.'

'And if they don't surrender in an hour or two, naturally you'd bring someone here who's used to bargaining, to talk to them. Someone from a trades union, perhaps. And after that a psychiatrist to judge the kidnappers' state of mind and tell you when he thinks is the best time to apply most pressure, to make them come out.' I shrugged deprecatingly. 'Naturally you know that these methods have produced good results in other hostage situations.'

'Naturally.'

'And of course you could tell them that if Alessia Cenci dies, they will never get out of prison.'

'The driver . . . they'll know they hit him . . .'

'If they ask, I am sure you would tell them he is alive. Even if he dies, you would of course tell them he is still alive. One wouldn't want them to think they had nothing to lose.'

A voice spluttered suddenly from one of the so far silent receivers, making both the engineer and Pucinelli whirl to listen. It was a woman's voice, gabbling, weeping, to me mostly unintelligible but, in gist, again plain enough.

The kidnapper's rough voice sliced in over hers, far too angry for safety, and then, in a rising wail, came a child's voice, crying, then another, calling 'Mama! Papa! Mama!'

'God,' Pucinelli said, 'children! There are children, too, in that flat.' The thought appalled him. In one instant he cared more for them than he had in five weeks for the girl, and for the first time I saw real concern in his olive face. He listened intently to the now-jumbled loud voices crowding through from the bug on the flat, a jumble finally resolving into a kidnapper yelling at the woman to give the children some biscuits to shut them up, or he personally would throw them out of the window.

The threat worked. Comparative quietness fell. Pucinelli took the opportunity to begin issuing rapid orders by radio to his own base, mentioning searchlights, negotiator, psychiatrist. Half the time he looked upward to the third floor windows, half down to the cluttered street outside: both, from our side of the van's darkly tinted glass, unrealistically dim. Not dark enough, however, for him not to catch sight of something which displeased him mightily and sent him speeding out of the van with a shout. I followed the direction of his agitation and felt the same dismay: a photographer with flashlight had arrived, first contingent of the press.

For the next hour I listened to the voices from the flat, sorting them gradually into father, mother, two children, a baby, and two kidnappers, one, the one who had talked on the telephone, a growling bass, the other a more anxious tenor.

It was the tenor, I thought, who would more easily surrender: the bass the more likely killer. Both, it appeared, were holding guns. The engineer spoke rapidly with Pucinelli, who then repeated everything more slowly for my benefit: the kidnappers had locked the mother and three children in one of the bedrooms, and had mentioned ropes tying the father. The father moaned occasionally and was told violently to stop.

In the street the crowd multiplied by the minute, every apartment block in the neighbourhood, it seemed, emptying its inhabitants to the free show on the doorstep. Even at two in the morning there were hordes of children oozing round every attempt of the carabinieri to keep them back, and everywhere, increasingly, sprouted the cameras, busy lenses pointing at the windows, now shut, where drama was the tenor kidnapper agreeing to warm the baby's bottle in the kitchen.

I ground my teeth and watched a television van pull

up, its occupants leaping out with lights, cameras, microphones, setting up instant interviews, excitedly telling the world.

The kidnapping of Alessia Cenci had until that time been a piano affair, the first shock news of her disappearance having made the papers, but only briefly, for most editors all over the world acknowledged that reporters glued to such stories could be deadly. A siege in a public street, though, was everyone's fair game; and I wondered cynically how long it would be before one of the fawn-uniformed law-enforcers accepted a paper gift in exchange for the fact of just whose ransom was barricaded there, three flights up.

I found myself automatically taking what one might call a memory snapshot, a clear frozen picture of the moving scene outside. It was a habit from boyhood, then consciously cultivated, a game to while away the boring times I'd been left in the car while my mother went into shops. Across the road from the bank I used to memorise the whole scene so that if any bank robbers had rushed out I would have been able to tell the police about all the cars which had been parked nearby, make, colour, and numbers, and describe all the people in the street at the time. Get-away cars and drivers would never have got away unspotted by eagle-eyed ten-year-old Andrew D.

No bank robbers ever obliged me, nor smash-and-grabbers outside the jewellers, nor baby snatchers from prams outside the bakers, nor muggers of the elderly collecting their pensions, nor even car thieves trying for unlocked doors. A great many innocent people had come under my sternly suspicious eye – and though I'd grown out of the hope of actually observing a crime, I'd never lost the ability of freeze-frame recall.

Thus it was that from behind the darkened glass, after a few moments' concentration, I had such a sharp mind's-eye picture that I could have described with certainty the numbers of windows in the block of flats facing, the position of each of the carabinieri cars, the clothes of the television crew, the whereabouts of each civilian inside the police circle, even the profile of the nearest press photographer, who was hung with two cameras but not at that moment taking pictures. He had a roundish head with smooth black hair, and a brown leather jacket with gold buckles at the cuffs.

A buzzer sounded sharply inside the van and Pucinelli lifted the handset which was connected with the flat's telephone. The bass-voiced kidnapper, edgy with waiting, demanded action; demanded specifically a safe passage to the airport and a light aircraft to fly him, and his colleage and the ransom, out.

Pucinelli told him to wait again, as only his superiors could arrange that. Tell them to bloody hurry, said the bass. Otherwise they'd find Alessia Cenci's dead body in the morning.

Pucinelli replaced the handset, tight-lipped.

'There will be no aeroplane,' he said to me flatly. 'It's impossible.'

'Do what they want,' I urged. 'You can catch them again later, when the girl is free.'

He shook his head. 'I cannot make that decision. Only the highest authority . . .'

'Get it, then.'

The engineer looked up curiously at the fierceness in my voice. Pucinelli, however, with calculation was seeing that shuffling off the decision had seductive advantages, so that if the girl did die it couldn't be held to be his fault. The thoughts ticked visibly behind his eyes, coming to clarity, growing to a nod.

I didn't know whether or not his superiors would let the kidnappers out; I only knew that Enrico couldn't. It was indeed a matter for the top brass.

'I think I'll go back to the Villa Francese,' I said.

'But why?'

'I'm not needed here, but there . . . I might be.' I paused fractionally. 'But I came from there in this van. How, at this time of night, can I get a car to take me back there quietly?'

He looked vaguely at the official cars outside, and I shook my head. 'Not one of those.'

'Still the anonymity . . .?'

'Yes,' I said.

He wrote a card for me and gave me directions.

'All-night taxi, mostly for late drunks and unfaithful husbands. If he is not there, just wait.'

I let myself out through the cab, through the door on the dark side, away from the noisy, brightly-lit embroilment in the street, edging round behind the gawpers, disentangling myself from the public scene, heading for the unremarked shadows, my most normal sphere of work.

With one corner behind me the visible nightmare faded, and I walked fast through the sleeping summer streets, even my shoes, from long custom, making no clatter in the quiet. The taxi address lay beyond the far side of the old main square, and I found myself slowing briefly there, awed by the atmosphere of the place.

Somewhere in or near that aged city a helpless young woman faced her most dangerous night, and it seemed to me that the towering walls, with their smooth closed faces, embodied all the secrecy, the inimity and the implacability of those who held her.

The two kidnappers, now besieged, had been simply the collectors. There would be others. At the very least there would be guards still with her; but also, I thought, there was the man whose voice over five long weeks had delivered instructions, the man I thought of as HIM.

I wondered if he knew what had happened at the drop. I wondered if he knew yet about the siege, and where the ransom was.

Above all, I wondered if he would panic.

Alessia had no future, if he did.

CHAPTER TWO

Paolo Cenci was doing the pacing I had stifled in myself: up and down his tiled and pillared central hall, driven by intolerable tension. He broke from his eyes-down automatic-looking measured stride and came hurrying across as soon as he saw me walking through from the kitchen passage.

'Andrew!' His face was grey in the electric light. 'What in God's name has happened? Giorgio Traventi has telephoned me to say his son has been shot. He telephoned from the hospital. They are operating on Lorenzo at this minute.'

'Haven't the carabinieri told you . . .?'

'No one has told me anything. I am going mad with anxiety. It is five hours since you and Lorenzo set out. For five hours I've been waiting.' His hoarse voice shook over the gracefully accented English, the emotion raw and unashamed. At fifty-six he was a strong man at the height of his business ability, but the past weeks had made appalling demands on his mental stamina, and even his hands now trembled often. I saw so much of this distress in my job; and no matter how rich, no matter how powerful, the victim's family suffered in direct simple ratio to the depth of their love. Alessia's mother was dead: Alessia's father felt anguish enough for two.

With compassion I drew him into the library, where he sat most evenings, and with my own anger, I suppose, apparent, told him the details of the disaster. He sat with his head in his hands when I'd finished, as near to weeping as I'd seen him.

'They'll kill her . . .'

'No,' I said.

'They are animals.'

There had been enough bestial threats during the past weeks for me not to argue. The assaults on her body the kidnappers had promised should Cenci not obey their instructions had been brutally calculated to break any father's nerve, and my assurances that threats were more common than performance hadn't comforted him to any extent. His imagination was too active, his fear too relentlessly acute.

My relationship with victims' families was something like that of a doctor's: called in in an emergency, consulted in a frightening and unsettling situation, looked to for miracles, leant on for succour. I'd set off on my first solo advisory job without any clear idea of the iron I would need to grow in my own core, and still after four years could quake before the demands made on my strength. Never get emotionally involved, I'd been told over and over during my training, you'll crack up if you do.

I was thirty. I felt, at times, a hundred.

Paolo Cenci's numbness at the nature and extent of the disaster began turning before my eyes to anger and, not surprisingly, to resentment against myself.

'If you hadn't told the carabinieri we were about to hand over the ransom, this wouldn't have happened. It's your fault. Yours. It's disgraceful. I should never have called you in. I shouldn't have listened to you. Those people warned me all along that if I brought in the carabinieri they would do unspeakable things to Alessia, and I let you persuade me, and I should not have done, I should have paid the ransom at once when they first demanded it, and Alessia would have been free weeks ago.'

I didn't argue with him. He knew, but in his grief was choosing not to remember, that to raise the ransom at first demanded had been impossible. Rich though he was, the equivalent of six million pounds sterling represented the worth not only of his whole estate but in addition of a large part of his business. Nor, as I'd forcefully told him, had the kidnappers ever expected him to pay that much: they were simply bludgeoning him with a huge amount so that anything less would seem a relief.

'Everything that Alessia has suffered has been your fault.'

Barring, presumably, the kidnap itself.

'Without you, I would have got her back. I would have paid. I would have paid anything . . .'

To pay too much too soon was to make kidnappers think they had underestimated the family's resources, and sometimes resulted in the extortion of a second ransom for the same victim. I had warned him of that, and he had understood.

'Alessia is worth more to me than everything I possess. I wanted to pay . . . you wouldn't let me. I should have done what I thought best. I would have given everything . . .'

His fury bubbled on, and I couldn't blame him. It often seemed to those who loved that literally no price was too great to pay for the safe return of the loved one, but I'd learned a great deal about the unexpected faces of stress over the past four years, and I'd seen that for the future health of the family's relationships it was essential that one member had not in fact cost the rest everything. After the first euphoria, and when the financial loss had begun to bite, the burden of guilt on the paid-for victim became too great, and the resentment of the payers too intense, and they too began to feel guilt for their resentment, and could eventually hate the victim for love of whom they had beggared themselves.

To save the victims' future equilibrium had gradually become to me as important as their actual physical freedom, but it was an aim I didn't expect Paolo Cenci at that moment to appreciate.

The telephone at his elbow started ringing, making him jump. He put out his hand towards it and then hesitated, and with a visible screwing-up of courage lifted the receiver to his ear.

'Ricardo! . . . Yes . . . yes . . . I understand. I will do that now, at once.' He put down the receiver and rose galvanically to his feet.

'Ricardo Traventi?' I asked, standing also. 'Lorenzo's brother?'

'I must go alone,' he said, but without fire.

'You certainly must not. I will drive you.'

I had been acting as his chauffeur since I had arrived, wearing his real chauffeur's cap and navy suit, while that grateful man took a holiday. It gave me the sort of invisibility that the firm had found worked best: kidnappers always knew everything about a household they had attacked, and a newcomer too officiously visiting alarmed them. A kidnapper was as nervous as a stalking fox and tended to see dangers when they didn't exist, let alone when they did. I came and went to the villa through the servants' entrance, taking it for granted that everything else would be noted.

Cenci's fury had evaporated as quickly as it had grown, and I saw that we were back to some sort of trust. I was grateful both for my sake and his that he would still accept my presence, but it was with some diffidence that I asked, 'What did Ricardo say?'

'They telephoned . . .' No need to ask who 'they' were. 'They' had been telephoning Traventi's house with messages all along, taking it for granted that there was an official tap on the telephones to the Villa Francese. That the Traventis' telephone was tapped also, with that family's reluctant permission, seemed to be something 'they' didn't know for certain.

'Ricardo says he must meet us at the usual place. He says he took the message because his parents are both at the hospital. He doesn't want to worry them. He says he will come on his scooter.'

Cenci was already heading towards the door, sure that I would follow.

Ricardo, Lorenzo's younger brother, was only eighteen, and no one originally had intended the two boys to be involved. Giorgio Traventi had agreed, as a lawyer, to act as a negotiator between Paolo Cenci and the kidnappers. It was he who took messages, passed them on, and in due course delivered the replies. The kidnappers themselves had a negotiator . . . HIM . . . with whom Giorgio Traventi spoke.

At times Traventi had been required to pick up packages at a certain spot, usually but not always the same place, and it was to that place that we were now headed. It had become not just the post-box for proof of Alessia's still being alive, or for appeals from her, or demands from HIM, or finally, earlier that evening, for the instructions about where to take the ransom, but also the place where Giorgio Traventi met Paolo Cenci, so that they could consult together in private. Neither had been too happy about the carabinieri overhearing their every word on the telephone and I had to admit that their instincts had been right.

It was ironic that at the beginning Giorgio Traventi had been approached by Cenci and his own lawyer simply because Traventi did not know the Cenci family well, and could act calmly on their behalf. Since then the whole Traventi family had become determined on Alessia's release, until finally nothing could have dissuaded Lorenzo from carrying the ransom himself. I hadn't approved of their growing emotional involvement – exactly what I had been warned against myself – but had been unable to stop it, as all of the Traventis had proved strong-willed and resolute, staunch allies when Cenci needed them most.

Indeed, until the carabinieri's ambush, the progress of negotiations had been, as far as was possible in any kidnap, smooth. The demand for six million had been cooled to about a tenth of that, and Alessia, on that afternoon at least, had been alive, unmolested and sane, reading aloud from the day's newspaper onto tape, and saying she was well.

The only comfort now, I thought, driving Cenci in his Mercedes to meet Ricardo, was that the kidnappers were still talking. Any message at all was better than an immediate dead body in a ditch.

The meeting place had been carefully chosen – by HIM – so that even if the carabinieri had had enough plain-clothes men to watch there day and night for weeks on end, they could have missed the actual delivery of the message: and indeed it was pretty clear that this had happened at least once. To confuse things during the period of closest continual watch, the messages had been delivered somewhere else.

We were heading for a motorway restaurant several miles outside Bologna, where even at night people came and went anonymously, travellers unremembered, different every hour of every day. Carabinieri who sat for too long over a coffee could be easily picked out.

Messages from HIM were left in a pocket in a cheap, grey, thin plastic waterproof, to be found hanging from a coat-rack inside the restaurant. The row of pegs was passed by everyone who went in or out of the cafeteria-style dining-room, and we guessed that the nondescript garment was in its place each time before the collect-the-message telephone call was made.

Traventi had taken the whole raincoat each time, but they had never been useful as clues. They were of a make sold throughout the region in flat, pocket-sized envelopes as a handy insurance against sudden rain-storms. The carabinieri had been given the four raincoats so far collected from the restaurant, and the one from the airport and the one from the bus station. All had been new, straight out of the packet, wrinkled from being folded, and smelling of the chemicals they were made from.

The messages had all been on tape. Regular-issue cassettes, sold everywhere. No fingerprints on anything.

Everything exceedingly careful; everything, I had come to think, professional.

Each tape had contained proof of Alessia's being alive. Each tape contained threats. Each tape carried a response to Traventi's latest offer. I had advised him to offer only two hundred thousand at first, a figure received by HIM with fury, faked or real. Slowly, with hard bargaining, the gap between demand and credibility had been closed, until the ransom was big enough to be worth HIS trouble, and manageable enough not to cripple Cenci entirely. At the point where each felt comfortable if not content, the amount had been agreed.

The money had been collected: Italian currency in used everyday notes, fastened in bundles with rubber bands and packed in a suitcase. Upon its safe delivery, Alessia Cenci would be released.

Safe delivery . . . ye gods.

The motorway restaurant lay about equidistant from Bologna and the Villa Francese, which stood in turreted idyllic splendour on a small country hillside, facing south. By day the road was busy with traffic, but at four in the morning only a few solitary pairs of headlights flooded briefly into our car. Cenci sat silent beside me, his eyes on the road and his mind heaven knew where.

Ricardo on his scooter arrived before us in the car park, though if anything he had had further to travel. Like his brother he was assertively intelligent, his eyes full now of the aggression brought on by the shooting, the narrow jaw jutting, the lips tight, the will to fight shouting from every muscle. He came across to the car as we arrived and climbed into the back seat.

'The bastards,' he said intensely. 'Lorenzo's state is critical, Papa says.' He spoke Italian, but distinctly, like all his family, so that I could nearly always understand them.

Paolo Cenci made a distressed gesture with his hands, sparing a thought for someone else's child. 'What is the message?' he said.

'To stand here by the telephones. He said I was to bring you, to speak to him yourself. No negotiator, he said. He sounded angry, very angry.'

'Was it the same man?' I asked.

'I think so. I've heard his voice on the tapes, but I've never spoken to him before. Always Papa speaks to him. Before tonight he wouldn't speak to anyone but Papa, but I told him Papa was at the hospital with Lorenzo and would be there until morning. Too late, he said. I must take the message myself. He said that you, Signor Cenci, must be alone. If there were any more carabinieri, he said, you wouldn't see Alessia again. They wouldn't return even her body.'

Cenci trembled beside me. 'I'll stay in the car,' I said. 'In my cap. They'll accept that. Don't be afraid.'

'I'll go with you,' Ricardo said.

'No.' I shook my head. 'Ricardo too might be taken for carabinieri. Better stay here with me.' I turned to

Cenci. 'We'll wait. Have you any *gettoni* if he asks you to call him back?'

He fished vaguely through his pockets, and Ricardo and I gave him some of the necessary tokens; then he fumbled with the door handle and stood up, as if disoriented, in the car park.

'The telephones are near the restaurant,' Ricardo said. 'In the hall just outside. I have telephoned from there often.'

Cenci nodded, took a grip on the horrors, and walked with fair steadiness to the entrance.

'Do you think there will be someone watching?' Ricardo said.

'I don't know. We cannot take the risk.' I used the Italian word for danger, not risk, but he nodded comprehension. It was the third time I'd worked in Italy: time I spoke the language better than I did.

We waited a long time, not speaking much. We waited so long that I began to fear either that no call would come to Cenci at all, that the message had been a retributive piece of cruelty, or even worse, that it had been a ruse to lure him away from his house while something dreadful took place in it. My heart thumped uncomfortably. Alessia's elder sister, Ilaria, and Paolo Cenci's sister, Luisa, were both upstairs in the villa, asleep.

Perhaps I should have stayed there . . . but Cenci had been in no state to drive. Perhaps I should have awoken his gardener in the village, who drove sometimes on the chauffeur's days off . . . Perhaps, perhaps.

The sky was already lightening to dawn when he returned, the shakiness showing in his walk, his face rigid as he reached the car. I stretched over and opened the door for him from the inside, and he subsided heavily into the passenger seat.

'He rang twice.' He spoke in Italian, automatically. 'The first time, he said wait. I waited . . .' He stopped and swallowed. Cleared his throat. Started again with a better attempt at firmness. 'I waited a long time. An hour. More. Finally, he telephoned. He says Alessia is still alive but the price has gone up. He says I must pay two thousand million lire in two days.'

His voice stopped, the despair sounding in it clearly. Two thousand million lire was approaching a million pounds.

'What else did he say?' I asked.

'He said that if anyone told the carabinieri of the new demand, Alessia would die at once.' He seemed suddenly to remember that Ricardo was in the car, and turned to him in alarm. 'Don't speak of this meeting, not to anyone. Promise me, Ricardo. On your soul.'

Ricardo, looking serious, promised. He also said he would go now to the hospital, to join his parents and get news of Lorenzo, and with a further passionate assurance of discretion he went over to his scooter and putputted away.

I started the car and drove out of the car park.

Cenci said dully, 'I can't raise that much. Not again.'

'Well,' I said, 'you should eventually get back the money in the suitcase. With luck. That means that the real extra is . . . um . . . seven hundred million lire.'

Three hundred thousand pounds. Said quickly, it sounded less.

'But in two days . . .'

'The banks will lend it. You have the assets.'

He didn't answer. So close on the other collection of random used notes, this would be technically more difficult. More money, much faster. The banks, however, would read the morning papers – and raising a ransom was hardly a process unknown to them.

'What are you to do, when you've collected it?' I asked.

Cenci shook his head. 'He told me . . . But this time I can't tell you. This time I take the money myself . . . alone.'

'It's unwise.'

'I must do it.'

He sounded both despairing and determined, and I didn't argue. I said merely, 'Will we have time to photograph the notes and put traces on them?'

He shook his head impatiently. 'What does it matter now? It is Alessia only that is important. I've been given a second chance . . . This time I do what he says. This time I act alone.'

Once Alessia was safe – if she were so lucky – he would regret he'd passed up the best chance of recovering at least part of the ransom and of catching the kidnappers. Emotion, as so often in kidnap situations, was stampeding common sense. But one couldn't, I supposed, blame him.

Pictures of Alessia Cenci, the girl I had never seen, adorned most rooms in the Villa Francese.

Alessia Cenci on horses, riding in races round the world. Alessia the rich girl with the hands of silk and a temperament like the sun (a fanciful newspaper report had said), bright, warm, and occasionally scorching.

I knew little about racing, but I'd heard of her, the glamour girl of the European tracks who nevertheless could really ride: one would have to have averted one's eye from newspapers pretty thoroughly not to. There seemed to be something about her that captivated the daily scribblers, particularly in England, where she raced often; and in Italy I heard genuine affection in every voice that spoke of her. In every voice, that is to say, except for that of her sister Ilaria, whose reaction to the kidnap had been complex and revealing.

Alessia in close-up photographs wasn't particularly beautiful: thin, small-featured, dark-eyed, with short head-hugging curls. It was her sister, by her side in silver frames, who looked more feminine, more friendly, and more pretty. Ilaria in life however was not particularly any of those things, at least not in the present horrific family circumstances. One couldn't tell what happiness might do.

She and her aunt Luisa still slept when Cenci and I returned to the villa. All was quiet there, all safe. Cenci walked straight into the library and poured a large amount of brandy into a tumbler, indicating that I should help myself to the same. I joined him, reflecting that seven in the morning was as good a time as any to get drunk.

'I'm sorry,' he said. 'I know it's not your fault. The carabinieri . . . do what they want.'

I gathered he was referring back to the anger he'd poured on me that last time we'd sat in those same two chairs. I made a vague don't-think-about-it gesture and let the brandy sear a path to my stomach, a shaft of vivid feeling going down through my chest. It might not have been wise, but the oldest tranquilliser was still the most effective.

'Do you think we'll get her back?' Cenci asked. 'Do you really think so?'

'Yes.' I nodded. 'They would be starting again more or less from scratch if they meant to kill her. They don't want to harm her, as I've told you all along. They only want you to believe they will . . . and yes, I do think it's a good sign they still have the nerve to bargain, with two of their number besieged by the carabinieri.'

Cenci looked blank. 'I'd forgotten about those.'

I hadn't; but then the ambush and the siege were imprinted in my mind as memories, not reports. I had wondered, through most of the night, whether the two collectors had been carrying walkie-talkie radios, and whether HE had known of the débâcle at almost the moment it happened, not simply when neither his colleagues nor the money turned up.

I thought that if I were HIM I'd be highly worried about those two men, not necessarily for their own sakes, but for what they knew. They might know where Alessia was. They might know who had planned the operation. They had to know where they'd been expected to take the money. They might be hired hands . . . but trusted enough to be collectors. They might be full equal partners, but I doubted it. Kidnap gangs tended to have hierarchies, like every other organisation.

One way or another those two were going to fall into the grasp of the carabinieri, either talking or shot. They themselves had promised that if they didn't go free, Alessia would die, but apparently HE had said nothing like that to Cenci. Did that mean that HIS priority was money, that he was set on extorting only what he almost certainly could – money from Cenci – and not what he almost as certainly couldn't – the return of his friends? Or did it mean that he didn't have radio contact with his colleagues, who had made the threat in faith more than promise . . . or did it mean that by radio he had persuaded the colleagues to barricade themselves in and make the fiercest threats continually, staying out of the carabinieri's clutches long enough for HIM to spirit

Alessia away to a new hide-out, so that it wouldn't matter if the colleagues finally did talk, they wouldn't know the one thing worth telling?

'What are you thinking?' Cenci asked.

'Of hope,' I said; and thought that the kidnappers in the flat probably didn't have contact by radio after all, because they hadn't made any reference to it during the hour I'd listened to them via the bug. But then HE might guess about bugs . . . if HE was that clever . . . and have told them to switch off after his first burst of instructions.

If I'd been HIM, I'd have been in touch with those collectors from the moment they set out . . . but then there weren't so many radio frequencies as all that, and the possibility of being overheard was high. But there were codes and pre-arranged phrases . . . And how did you pre-arrange a message which said the carabinieri have swarmed all over us and we've shot the man who brought the ransom?

If they hadn't taken the ransom with its homing transmitter, they would probably have escaped. If they hadn't been fanatical about taking the ransom, they wouldn't have shot the driver to get it.

If the carabinieri had acted stupidly, so had the kidnappers, and only as long as HE didn't decide after all to cut his losses was there any positive hope. I still thought that hope to be frail. One didn't however admit it to the victim's dad.

Cenci anyway had tears at last running down his

cheeks, released, I guessed, by the brandy. He made no sound, nor tried to brush them away or hide them. Many a man would have come to that stage sooner, and in my own experience, most victims' parents did. Through outrage, anger, anxiety and grief, through guilt and hope and pain, the steps they trod were the same. I'd seen so many people in despair that sometimes a laughing face would jolt me.

The Paolo Cenci I knew was the man sitting opposite, who hadn't smiled once in my sight. He had attempted at first to put up a civilised front, but the mask had soon crumbled as he got used to my presence, and it was the raw man whose feelings and strengths and blindnesses I knew. The urban successful man-of-the-world looking out with genial wisdom from the portrait in the drawing-room, he was the stranger.

For his part, after his first blink at my not being in his own age group, he had seemed to find me compatible on all counts. His cry for help had reached our office within a day of Alessia's disappearance, and I had been on his back-doorstep the next; but forty-eight hours could seem a lifetime in that sort of nightmare and his relief at my arrival had been undemanding. He would very likely have accepted a four-armed dwarf with blue skin, not just a five-ten thin frame with ordinary dark hair and washed-out grey eyes: but he was, after all, paying for my help, and if he really hadn't liked me he had an easy way out.

His original call to our office had been brief and

direct. 'My daughter has been kidnapped. I telephoned Tomasso Linardi, of the Milan Fine Leather Company, for advice. He gave me your name . . . he says it was your firm which got him safely home and helped the police trace the kidnappers. I need your help now myself. Please come.'

Tomasso Linardi, owner of the Milan Fine Leather Company, had himself been held to ransom two years earlier, and it wasn't surprising that Paolo Cenci should have known him, as Cenci too was in the leather business, heading a corporation with world-wide trade. Half the Italian shoes imported into England, he had told me, had passed in the uncut leather stage through his firm.

The two men incidentally had proved to have a second and more tenuous factor in common, an interest in horses; Cenci of course because of Alessia's jockeyship, and Linardi because he had owned a majority share in a racetrack. This holding in a fashionable, profit-making piece of flat land had been one of the things sold to raise his ransom, much to his sorrow when on his release he found out. In his case, although some of his kidnappers had been arrested a month later, only a small part of the million-pound ransom had been recovered. The seven million which had at first been strongly demanded would have meant losing his business as well, so on the whole he had been relieved, resigned, and obviously content enough with Liberty Market to recommend us to the next guy in trouble.

I had shared the Linardi assignment with another partner. We'd found Linardi's wife less than distraught about her husband and furious about the cost of getting him back. His mistress had wept buckets, his son had usurped his office chair, his cook had had hysterics, his sisters had squabbled and his dog had pined. The whole thing had been conducted with operative histrionics fortissimo, leaving me finally feeling I'd been swamped by a tidal wave.

In the Villa Francese, a much quieter house, Paolo Cenci and I sat for a further half-hour, letting the brandy settle and thinking of this and that. At length, his tears long dried, he sighed deeply and said that as the day had to be faced he would change his clothes, have breakfast and go to his office. I would drive him no doubt as usual. And I could photograph the new ransom money, as before. He had been thinking, and of course I was right, it was the best chance of getting any of it back.

Breakfast in that formal household was eaten in the dining-room: coffee, fruit and hot breads against murals of shepherdesses à la Marie Antoinette.

Ilaria joined us there, silently as usual, assembling her own preferences onto her plate. Her silences were a form of aggression; a positive refusal, for instance, to say good-morning to her father even out of good manners. He seemed to be used to it, but I found it extraordinary, especially in the circumstances, and especially as it seemed there was no animosity or discord between them. Ilaria lived a privileged life which included no gainful occupation: mostly travel, tennis, singing lessons, shopping and lunches, thanks to her father's money. He gave, she received. I wondered sometimes if it was resentment at this dependency that made her so insistently refuse to acknowledge it even to the extent of behaving sweetly, but she had apparently never wanted or sought a job. Her Aunt Luisa had told me so, with approval.

Ilaria was a fresh-looking twenty-four, curved, not skinny, with brown wavy hair superbly cut and frequently shampooed. She had a habit of raising her eyebrows and looking down her nose, as she was now doing at her coffee cup, which probably reflected her whole view of life and would undoubtedly set into creases before forty.

She didn't ask if there was any news of Alessia: she never did. She seemed if anything to be angry with her sister for being kidnapped, though she hadn't exactly said so. Her reaction however to my suggestion that she should not go so predictably at set times to the tennis court and in fact should go away altogether and stay with friends, because kidnappers if feeling frustrated by delays had been known to take a second speeding-up bite at the same family, had been not only negative but acid. 'There wouldn't be the same agonised fuss over me.'

Her father had looked aghast at her bitterness, but both she and I saw in his face that what she'd said was true, even if he had never admitted it to himself. It would in fact have been very much easier to abduct Ilaria, but even as a victim she had been passed over in favour of her famous little sister, her father's favourite. She had continued, with the same defiance as in her silences, to go at the same time to the same places, an open invitation to trouble. Cenci had begged her not to, to no avail.

I wondered if she even positively wanted to be taken, so that her father would have to prove his love for her, as for Alessia, by selling precious things to get her back.

Because she hadn't asked, we hadn't told her the evening before that that was the night for paying the ransom. Let her sleep, Cenci had said, contemplating his own wakeful ordeal and wishing to spare her. 'Perhaps Alessia will be home for breakfast,' he'd said.

He looked at Ilaria now and with great weariness told her that the hand-over had gone wrong, and that another and bigger ransom had to be collected for Alessia.

'Another . . .' She stared at him in disbelief, cup stopping halfway to her mouth.

'Andrew thinks we may get the first one back again, but meanwhile . . .' He made an almost beseeching gesture with his hand. 'My dear, we are going to be poorer. Not just temporarily, but always. This extra demand is a grave setback. . . . I have decided to sell the house on Mikonos, but even that will not be enough. Your mother's jewels must go, also the collection of snuff boxes. The rest I must raise on the worth of this house and this estate, and if we do not recover the first ransom I will be paying interest on the loan out of the receipts from the olives, which will leave nothing over. The land I sold in Bologna to raise the first ransom will not now be providing us with any revenue, and we have to live on what I make in the business.' He shrugged slightly. 'We'll not starve. We'll continue to live here. But there are the pensions for our retired servants, and the allowances for my uncles' widows, which they live on . . . It is going to be a struggle, my dear, and I think you should know, and be prepared.'

She looked at him with absolute shock, and I thought that until that moment she hadn't realised that paying a ransom was a very cruel business.

CHAPTER THREE

I drove Cenci to his office and left him there to his telephone and his grim task with the banks. Then, changing from chauffeur's uniform into nondescript trousers and sweater, I went by bus and foot to the street where the siege might still be taking place.

Nothing, it seemed, had changed there. The dark-windowed ambulance still stood against the kerb on the far side of the road from the flats, the carabinieri's cars were still parked helter-skelter in the same positions with fawn uniforms crouching around them, the television van still sprouted wires and aerials, and a commentator was still talking into camera.

Daylight had subtracted drama. Familiarity had done the same to urgency. The scene now looked not frightening but peaceful, with figures moving at walking pace, not in scurrying little runs. A watching crowd stood and stared bovinely, growing bored.

The windows on the third floor were shut.

I hovered at the edge of things, hands in pockets, hair tousled, local paper under arm, looking, I hoped, not too English. Some of the partners in Liberty Market were stunning at disguises, but I'd always found a slouch and vacant expression my best bet for not being noticed.

After a while during which nothing much happened I wandered off in search of a telephone, and rang the number of the switchboard inside the ambulance.

'Is Enrico Pucinelli there?' I asked.

'Wait.' Some mumbling went on in the background, and then Pucinelli himself spoke, sounding exhausted.

'Andrew? Is it you?'

'Yes. How's it going?'

'Nothing has altered. I am off duty at ten o'clock for an hour.'

I looked at my watch. Nine thirty-eight. 'Where are you eating?' I said.

'Gino's.'

'OK,' I said, and disconnected.

I waited for him in the brightly-lit glass-and-tile-lined restaurant that to my knowledge served fresh pasta at three in the morning with good grace. At eleven it was already busy with early lunches, and I held a table for two by ordering loads of fettucine that I didn't want. Pucinelli, when he arrived, pushed away his cooling plateful with horror and ordered eggs.

He had come, as I knew he would, in civilian clothes, and the tiredness showed in black smudges under his eyes and in the droop of his shoulders.

'I hope you slept well,' he said sarcastically.

I moved my head slightly, meaning neither yes nor no.

'I have had two of the top brass on my neck in the van all night,' he said. 'They can't make up their fat minds about the aeroplane. They are talking to Rome. Someone in the government must decide, they say, and no one in the government wanted to disturb his sleep to think about it. You would have gone quite crazy, my friend. Talk, talk, talk, and not enough action to shit.'

I put on a sympathetic face and thought that the longer the siege lasted, the safer now for Alessia. Let it last, I thought, until she was free. Let HIM be a realist to the end.

'What are the kidnappers saying?' I asked.

'The same threats. The girl will die if they and the ransom money don't get away safely.'

'Nothing new?'

He shook his head. His eggs came with rolls and coffee, and he ate without hurry. 'The baby cried half the night,' he said with his mouth full. 'The deep-voiced kidnapper keeps telling the mother he'll strangle it if it doesn't shut up. It gets on his nerves.' He lifted his eyes to my face. 'You always tell me they threaten more than they do. I hope you're right.'

I hoped so to. A crying baby could drive even a temperate man to fury. 'Can't they feed it?' I said.

'It has colic.'

He spoke with familiarity of experience, and I wondered vaguely about his private life. All our dealings had been essentially impersonal, and it was only in flashes, as now, that I heard the man behind the policeman.

'You have children?' I asked.

He smiled briefly, a glimmer in the eyes. 'Three sons, two daughters, one . . . expected.' He paused. 'And you?'

I shook my head. 'Not yet. Not married.'

'Your loss. Your gain.'

I laughed. He breathed deprecatingly down his nose as if to disclaim the disparagement of his lady. 'Girls grow into mamas,' he said. He shrugged. 'It happens.'

Wisdom, I thought, showed up in the most unexpected places. He finished his eggs as one at peace with himself, and drank his coffee. 'Cigarette?' he asked, edging a packet out of his shirt pocket. 'No. I forgot. You don't.' He flicked his lighter and inhaled the first lungful with the deep relief of a dedicated smoker. Each to his own release: Cenci and I had found the same thing in brandy.

'During the night,' I said, 'did the kidnappers talk to anyone else?'

'How do you mean?'

'By radio.'

He lifted his thin face sharply, the family man retreating. 'No. They spoke only to each other, to the hostage family, and to us. Do you think they have a radio? Why do you think that?'

'I wondered if they were in touch with their colleagues guarding Alessia.'

He considered it with concentration and indecisively shook his head. 'The two kidnappers spoke of what was happening, from time to time, but only as if they were talking to each other. If they were also transmitting on a radio and didn't want us to know, they are very clever. They would have to guess we are already listening to every word they say.' He thought it over a bit longer and finally shook his head with more certainty. 'They are not clever. I've listened to them all night. They are violent, frightened, and . . .' he searched for a word I would understand '. . . ordinary.'

'Average intelligence?'

'Yes. Average.'

'All the same, when you finally get them out, will you look around for a radio?'

'You personally want to know?'

'Yes.'

He looked at me assessingly with a good deal of professional dispassion. 'What are you not telling me?' he said.

I was not telling him what Cenci passionately wished to keep private, and it was Cenci who was paying me. I might advise full consultation with the local law, but only that. Going expressly against the customer's wishes was at the very least bad for future business.

'I simply wonder,' I said mildly, 'if the people guarding Alessia know exactly what's going on.'

He looked as if some sixth sense was busy doubting me, so to take his mind off it I said, 'I dare say you've thought of stun grenades as a last resort?'

'Stun?' He didn't know the word. 'What's stun?'

'Grenades which more or less knock people out for a short while. They produce noise and shock waves, but do no permanent damage. While everyone is semi-conscious, you walk into the flat and apply handcuffs where they're needed.'

'The army has them, I think.'

I nodded. 'You are part of the army.'

'Special units have them. We don't.' He considered. 'Would they hurt the children?'

I didn't know. I could see him discarding stun grenades rapidly. 'We'll wait,' he said. 'The kidnappers cannot live there for ever. In the end, they must come out.'

Cenci stared morosely at a large cardboard carton standing on the desk in his office. The carton bore stick-on labels saying FRAGILE in white letters on red, but the contents would have survived any drop. Any drop, that is, except one to kidnappers.

'Fifteen hundred million lire,' he said. 'The banks arranged for it to come from Milan. They brought it straight to this office, with security guards.'

'In that box?' I asked, surprised.

'No. They wanted their cases back . . . and this box

was here.' His voice sounded deathly tired. 'The rest comes tomorrow. They've been understanding and quick, but the interest they're demanding will cripple me.'

I made a mute gesture of sympathy, as no words seemed appropriate. Then I changed into my chauffeur's uniform, carried the heavy carton to the car, stowed it in the boot, and presently drove Cenci home.

We ate dinner late at the villa, though meals were often left unfinished according to the anxiety level of the day. Cenci would push his plate away in revulsion, and I sometimes thought my thinness resulted from never being able to eat heartily in the face of grief. My suggestion that Cenci might prefer my not living as family had been met with emphatic negatives. He needed company, he said, if he were to stay sane. I would please be with him as much as possible.

On that evening, however, he understood that I couldn't be. I carried the FRAGILE box upstairs to my room, closed the curtains, and started the lengthy task of photographing every note, flattening them in a frame of non-reflecting glass, four at a time of the same denomination. Even with the camera on a tripod, with bulk film, cable release and motor drive, the job always took ages. It was one that I did actually prefer not to leave to banks or the police, but even after all the practice I'd had I could shift only about fifteen hundred notes an hour. Large ransoms had me shuffling banknotes in my dreams.

It was Liberty Market routine to send the undeveloped films by express courier to the London office, where we had simple developing and printing equipment in the basement. The numbers of the notes were then typed into a computer, which sorted them into numerical order for each denomination and then printed out the lists. The lists returned, again by courier, to the advisor in the field, who, after the victim had been freed, gave them to the police to circulate to all the country's banks, with a promise that any teller spotting one of the ransom notes would be rewarded.

It was a system which seemed to us best, principally because photography left no trace on the notes. The problem with physically marking them was that anything the banks could detect, so could the kidnappers. Banks had no monopoly, for instance, in scans to reveal fluorescence. Geiger counters for radioactive pin dots weren't hard to come by. Minute perforations could be seen as easily by any eyes against a bright light, and extra lines and marks could be spotted by anyone's magnification. The banks, through simple pressure of time, had to be able to spot tracers easily, which put chemical invisible inks out of court. Kidnappers, far more thorough and with fear always at their elbows, could test obsessively for everything.

Kidnappers who found tracers on the ransom had to be considered lethal. In Liberty Market, therefore, the markings we put on notes were so difficult to find that we sometimes lost them ourselves, and they were certainly unspottable by banks. They consisted of transparent microdots (the size of the full stops to which we applied them) which when separated and put under a microscope revealed a shadowy black logo of L and M, but through ordinary magnifying glasses appeared simply black. We used them only on larger denomination notes, and then only as a back-up in case there should be any argument about the photographed numbers. To date we had never had to reveal their existence, a state of affairs we hoped to maintain.

By morning, fairly dropping from fatigue, I'd photographed barely half, the banks having taken the 'small denomination' instruction all too literally. Locking all the money into a wardrobe cupboard I showered and thought of bed, but after breakfast drove Cenci to the office as usual. Three nights I could go without sleep. After that, zonk.

'If the kidnappers get in touch with you,' I said, on the way, 'you might tell them you can't drive. Say you need your chauffeur. Say . . . um . . . you've a bad heart, something like that. Then at least you'd have help, if you needed it.'

There was such an intense silence from the back seat that at first I thought he hadn't heard, but eventually he said, 'I suppose you don't know, then.'

'Know what?'

'Why I have a chauffeur.'

'General wealth, and all that,' I said.

'No. I have no licence.'

I had seen him driving round the private roads on his estate in a jeep on one or two occasions, though not, I recalled, with much fervour. After a while he said, 'I choose not to have a licence, because I have epilepsy. I've had it most of my life. It is of course kept completely under control with pills, but I prefer not to drive on public roads.'

'I'm sorry,' I said.

'Forget it. I do. It's an inconvenience merely.' He sounded as if the subject bored him, and I thought that regarding irregular brain patterns as no more than a nuisance was typical of what I'd gleaned of his normal business methods: routine fast and first, planning slow and thorough. I'd gathered from things his secretary had said in my hearing that he'd made few decisions lately, and trade was beginning to suffer.

When we reached the outskirts of Bologna he said, 'I have to go back to those telephones at the motorway restaurant tomorrow morning at eight. I have to take the money in my car. I have to wait for him . . . for his instructions. He'll be angry if I have a chauffeur.'

'Explain. He'll know you always have a chauffeur. Tell him why.'

'I can't risk it.' His voice shook.

'Signor Cenci, he wants the money. Make him believe you can't drive safely. The last thing he wants is you crashing the ransom into a lamppost.'

'Well . . . I'll try.'

'And remember to ask for proof that Alessia is alive and unharmed.'

'Yes.'

I dropped him at the office and drove back to the Villa Francese, and because it was what the Cenci chauffeur always did when he wasn't needed during the morning, I washed the car. I'd washed the damn car so often I knew every inch intimately, but one couldn't trust kidnappers not to be watching; and the villa and its hillside, with its glorious views, could be observed closely by telescope from a mile away in most directions. Changes of routine from before to after a kidnap were of powerful significance to kidnappers, who were often better detectives than detectives, and better spies than spies. The people who'd taught me my job had been detectives and spies and more besides, so when I was a chauffeur, I washed cars.

That done I went upstairs and slept for a couple of hours and then set to again on the photography, stopping only to go and fetch Cenci at the usual hour. Reporting to his office I found another box on the desk, this time announcing it had been passed by customs at Genoa.

'Shall I carry it out?' I asked.

He nodded dully. 'It is all there. Five hundred million lire.'

We drove home more or less in silence, and I spent the evening and night as before, methodically clicking until I felt like a zombie. By morning it was done, with the microdots applied to a few of the fifty-thousand lire notes, but not many, through lack of time. I packed all the rubber-banded bundles into the FRAGILE box and humped it down to the hall to find Cenci already pacing up and down in the dining-room, white with strain.

'There you are!' he exclaimed. 'I was just coming to wake you. It's getting late. Seven o'clock.'

'Have you had breakfast?' I asked.

'I can't eat.' He looked at his watch compulsively, something I guessed he'd been doing for hours. 'We'd better go. Suppose we were held up on the way? Suppose there was an accident blocking the road?'

His breathing was shallow and agitated, and I said diffidently, 'Signor Cenci, forgive me for asking, but in the anxiety of this morning . . . have you remembered your pills?'

He looked at me blankly. 'Yes. Yes, of course. Always with me.'

'I'm sorry . . .'

He brushed it away. 'Let's go. We must go.'

The traffic on the road was normal: no accidents. We reached the rendezvous half an hour early, but Cenci sprang out of the car as soon as I switched off the engine. From where I'd parked I had a view of the entrance across a double row of cars, the doorway like the mouth of a beehive with people going in and out continually.

Cenci walked with stiff legs to be lost among them, and in the way of chauffeurs I slouched down in my seat and tipped my cap forward over my nose. If I wasn't careful, I thought, I'd go to sleep . . .

Someone rapped on the window beside me. I opened my eyes, squinted sideways, and saw a youngish man in a white open-necked shirt with a gold chain round his neck making gestures for me to open the window.

The car, rather irritatingly, had electric windows: I switched on the ignition and pressed the relevant button, sitting up slightly while I did it.

'Who are you waiting for?' he said.

'Signor Cenci.'

'Not Count Rieti?'

'No. Sorry.'

'Have you seen another chauffeur here?'

'Sorry, no.'

He was carrying a magazine rolled into a cylinder and fastened by a rubber band. I thought fleetingly of one of the partners in Liberty Market who believed one should never trust a stranger carrying a paper cylinder because it was such a handy place to stow a knife . . . and I wondered, but not much.

'You're not Italian?' the man said.

'No. From Spain.'

'Oh.' His gaze wandered, as if seeking Count Rieti's chauffeur. Then he said absently in Spanish, 'You're a long way from home.'

'Yes,' I said.

'Where do you come from?'

'Andalucia.'

'Very hot, at this time of year.'

'Yes.'

I had spent countless school holidays in Andalucia, staying with my divorced half-Spanish father who ran a hotel there. Spanish was my second tongue, learned on all levels from kitchen to penthouse: any time I didn't want to appear English, I became a Spaniard.

'Is your employer having breakfast?' he asked.

'I don't know.' I shrugged. 'He said to wait, so I wait.'

His Spanish had a clumsy accent and his sentences were grammatically simple, as careful as mine in Italian.

I yawned.

He could be a coincidence, I thought. Kidnappers were normally much too shy for such a direct approach, keeping their faces hidden at all costs. This man could be just what he seemed, a well-meaning citizen carrying a magazine, looking for Count Rieti's chauffeur and with time to spare for talking.

Could be. If not, I would tell him what he wanted to know: if he asked.

'Do you drive always for Signor . . . Cenci?' he said casually.

'Sure,' I said. 'It's a good job. Good pay. He's considerate. Never drives himself, of course.'

'Why not?'

I shrugged. 'Don't know. He hasn't a licence. He has to have someone to drive him always.'

I wasn't quite sure he had followed that, though I'd spoken pretty slowly and with a hint of drowsiness. I yawned again and thought that one way or another he'd had his ration of chat. I would memorise his face, just in case, but it was unlikely . . .

He turned away as if he too had found the conversation finished, and I looked at the shape of his round smooth head from the side, and felt most unwelcome tingles ripple all down my spine. I'd seen him before . . . I'd seen him outside the ambulance, through the tinted glass, with cameras slung from his neck and gold buckles on the cuffs of his jacket. I could remember him clearly. He'd appeared at the siege . . . and he was here at the drop, asking questions.

No coincidence.

It was the first time I'd ever knowingly been physically near one of the shadowy brotherhood, those foes I opposed by proxy, whose trials I never attended, whose ears never heard of my existence. I slouched down again in my seat and tipped my cap over my nose and thought that my partners in London would emphatically disapprove of my being in that place at that time. The low profile was down the drain.

If I'd seen him, he'd seen me.

It might not matter: not if he believed in the Spanish chauffeur who was bored with waiting. If he believed in the bored Spanish chauffeur, he'd forget me. If he hadn't believed in the bored Spanish chauffeur I would quite likely be sitting there now with a knife through my ribs, growing cold.

In retrospect I felt distinctly shivery. I had not

remotely expected such an encounter, and at first it had only been habit and instinct, reinforced by true tiredness, that had made me answer him as I had. I found it definitely scary to think that Alessia's life might have hung on a yawn.

Time passed. Eight o'clock came and went. I waited as if asleep. No one else came to my still open window to ask me anything at all.

It was after nine before Cenci came back, half-running, stumbling, sweating. I was out of the car as soon as I saw him, politely opening a rear door and helping him in as a chauffeur should.

'Oh my God,' he said. 'I thought he wouldn't telephone. . . . It's been so long.'

'Is Alessia all right?'

'Yes . . . yes . . .'

'Where to, then?'

'Oh . . .' He drew in some calming breaths while I got back behind the wheel and started the engine. 'We have to go to Mazara, about twenty kilometres south. Another restaurant . . . another telephone. In twenty minutes.'

'Um . . .' I said. 'Which way from here?'

He said vaguely, 'Umberto knows,' which wasn't especially helpful, as Umberto was his real chauffeur, away on holiday. I grabbed the road map from the glove compartment and spread it on the passenger seat beside me, trying unsuccessfully to find Mazara while pulling in a normal fashion out of the car park.

The road we were on ran west to east. I took the first major-looking turn towards the south, and as soon as we were out of sight of the motorway drew into the side and paused for an update on geography. One more turn, I thought, and there would be signposts: and in fact we made it to Mazara, which proved to be a little more than a crossroads, with breathing time to spare.

On the way Cenci said, 'Alessia was reading from today's paper . . . on tape, it must have been, because she just went on reading when I spoke to her . . . but to hear her voice . . .'

'You're sure it was her?'

'Oh yes. She started as usual with one of those memories of her childhood that you suggested. It was Alessia herself, my darling, darling daughter.'

Well, I thought. So far, so good.

'He said . . .' Cenci gulped audibly. 'He said if there are homers this time in the ransom he'll kill her. He says if we are followed . . . if we don't do exactly as he says . . . if anything . . . *anything* goes wrong, he'll kill her.'

I nodded. I believed it. A second chance was a partial miracle. We'd never get a third.

'You promise,' he said, 'that he'll find nothing on the notes?'

'I promise,' I said.

At Mazara Cenci ran to the telephone, but again he was agonisingly kept waiting. I sat as before in the car, stolidly patient, as if the antics of my employer were of little interest, and surreptitiously read the map.

The restaurant at this place was simply a café next to a garage, a stop for coffee and petrol. People came and went, but not many. The day warmed up under the summer sun, and as a good chauffeur should I started the purring engine and switched on the air-conditioning.

He returned with his jacket over his arm and flopped gratefully into the cool.

'Casteloro,' he said. 'Why is he doing this?'

'Standard procedure, to make sure we're not followed. He'll be doubly careful because of last time. We might be chasing about all morning.'

'I can't stand it,' he said; but he could, of course, after the last six weeks.

I found the way to Casteloro and drove there: thirty-two kilometres, mostly of narrow, straight, exposed country roads. Open fields on both sides. Any car following us would have shown up like a rash.

'He made no trouble about you,' Cenci said. 'I said straight away that I'd brought my chauffeur because I have epilepsy, that it was impossible for me to drive, to come alone. He just said to give you instructions and not explain anything.'

'Good,' I said, and thought that if HE were me he'd check up with Alessia about the epilepsy, and be reassured.

At Casteloro, a small old town with a cobbled central

square full of pigeons, the telephone Cenci sought was in a café, and this time there was no delay.

'Return to Mazara,' Cenci said with exhaustion.

I reversed the car and headed back the way we had come, and Cenci said, 'He asked me what I had brought the money in. I described the box.'

'What did he say?'

'Nothing. Just to follow instructions or Alessia would be killed. He said they would kill her . . . horribly.' His voice choked and came out as a sob.

'Listen,' I said, 'they don't want to kill her. Not now, not when they're so close. And did they say what "horribly" meant? Were they . . . specific?'

On another sob he said, 'No.'

'They're frightening you,' I said. 'Using threats to make sure you'd elude the carabinieri, even if up to now you'd been letting them follow you.'

'But I haven't!' he protested.

'They have to be convinced. Kidnappers are very nervous.'

It was reassuring though, I thought, that they were still making threats, because it indicated they were serious about dealing. This was no cruel dummy run: this was the actual drop.

Back at the Mazara crossroads there was another lengthy wait. Cenci sat in the café, visible through the window, trembling over an undrunk cup of coffee. I got out of the car, stretched, ambled up and down a bit, got back in, and yawned. Three unexceptional cars filled with petrol and the garage attendant scratched his armpits.

The sun was high, blazing out of the blue sky. An old woman in black cycled up to the crossroads, turned left, cycled away. Summer dust stirred and settled in the wake of passing vans, and I thought of Lorenzo Travventi, who had driven the last lot of ransom and now clung to life on machines.

Inside the café Cenci sprang to his feet, and after a while came back to the car in no better state than before. I opened the rear door for him as usual and helped him inside.

'He says . . .' He took a deep breath. 'He says there is a sort of shrine by the roadside between here and Casteloro. He says we've passed it twice already . . . but I didn't notice . . .'

I nodded. 'I saw it.' I closed his door and resumed my own seat.

'Well, there,' Cenci said. 'He says to put the box behind the shrine, and drive away.'

'Good,' I said with relief. 'That's it, then.'

'But Alessia . . .' he wailed. 'I asked him, when will Alessia be free, and he didn't answer, he just put the telephone down . . .'

I started the car and drove again towards Casteloro.

'Be patient,' I said gently. 'They'll have to count the money. To examine it for tracers. Maybe, after last time, to leave it for a while in a place they can observe, to make sure no one is tracking it by homer. They won't free Alessia until they're certain they're safe, so I'm afraid it means waiting. It means patience.'

He groaned on a long breath. 'But they'll let her go . . . when I've paid . . . they'll let her go, won't they?'

He was asking desperately for reassurance, and I said, 'Yes,' robustly: and they would let her go, I thought, if they were satisfied, if they were sane, if something unforeseen didn't happen and if Alessia hadn't seen their faces.

About ten miles from the crossroads, by a cornfield, stood a simple stone wayside shrine, a single piece of wall about five feet high by three across, with a weather-beaten foot-high stone madonna offering blessings from a niche in front. Rain had washed away most of the blue paint of her mantle, and time or vandals had relieved her of the tip of her nose, but posies of wilting flowers lay on the ground before her, and someone had left some sweets beside her feet.

The road we were on seemed deserted, running straight in each direction. There were no woods, no cover, no obstructions. We could probably be seen for miles.

Cenci stood watching while I opened the boot, lugged out the box, and carried it to the back of the shrine. The box had just about been big enough to contain the whole ransom, and there it stood on the dusty earth, four-square, brown and ordinary, tied about with thick string to make carrying easier and cheerfully labelled with red. Almost a million pounds. The house on Mikonos, the snuff box collection, his dead wife's jewellery, the revenue forever from the olives.

Cenci stared at it blindly for a few moments, then we both returned to the car and I reversed and drove away.

CHAPTER FOUR

For the rest of that day, Saturday, and all Sunday, Cenci walked slowly round his estate, came heavily home, drank too much brandy and lost visible weight.

Ilaria, silently defiant, went to the tennis club as usual. Luisa, her aunt, drifted about in her usual wispy fashion, touching things as if to make sure they were still there.

I drove to Bologna, sent off the films, washed the car. Lorenzo still breathed precariously on his machines and in the meagre suburban street the two kidnappers remained barricaded in the third-floor flat, with talk going on from both sides, but no action, except a delivery of milk for the baby and bread and sausage for the others.

On the Sunday evening Ilaria came into the library where I was watching the news on television. The scene in the street looked almost exactly the same, except that there was no crowd, long discouraged from lack of excitement, and perhaps fewer fawn uniforms. The television coverage had become perfunctory: repetitive as-you-were sentences only.

'Do you think they'll release her?' Ilaria said, as the screen switched away to politicians.

'Yes, I think so.'

'When?'

'Can't tell.'

'Suppose they've told the carabinieri they'll keep her until those men in the flat go free? Suppose the ransom isn't enough?'

I glanced at her. She'd spoken not with dread but as if the question didn't concern her beyond a certain morbid interest. Her face was unstudiedly calm. She appeared really not to care.

'I talked to Enrico Pucinelli this morning,' I said. 'By then they hadn't said anything like that.'

She made a small, noncommittal puffing noise through her nose and changed the television channel to a tennis match, settling to watch with concentration.

'I'm not a bitch, you know,' she said suddenly. 'I can't help it if I don't fall down and kiss the ground she walks on, like everyone else.'

'And six weeks is a long time to keep up the hair-tearing?'

'God,' she said, 'you're on the ball. And don't think I'm not glad you're here. Otherwise he would have leant on me for everything he gets from you, and I'd have ended up despising him.'

'No,' I said.

'Yes.'

Her eyes had been on the tennis throughout.

'How would you behave,' I said, 'if you had a son, and he was kidnapped?'

The eyes came round to my face. 'You're a righteous sod,' she said.

I smiled faintly. She went resolutely back to the tennis, but where her thoughts were, I couldn't tell.

Ilaria spoke perfect idiomatic English, as I'd been told Alessia did also, thanks to the British widow who had managed the Cenci household for many years after the mother's death. Luisa, Ilaria and Alessia ran things between them nowadays, and the cook in exasperation had complained to me that nothing got done properly since dear Mrs Blackett had retired to live with her brother in Eastbourne.

The next morning, during the drive to the office, Cenci said, 'Turn round, Andrew. Take me home. It's no good, I can't work. I'll sit there staring at the walls. I hear people talk but I don't listen to what they say. Take me home.'

I said neutrally, 'It might be worse at home.'

'No. Turn round. I can't face a new week in the office. Not today.'

I turned the car and drove back to the villa, where he telephoned to his secretary not to expect him.

'I can't think,' he said to me, 'except of Alessia. I think of her as she was as a little girl, and at school, and learning to ride. She was always so neat, so small, so full of life . . .' He swallowed, turned away and walked into the library, and in a few seconds I heard bottle clink against glass.

After a while I went after him.

'Let's play backgammon,' I said.

'I can't concentrate.'

'Try.' I got out the board and set up the pieces, but the moves he made were mechanical and without heart. He did nothing to capitalise on my shortcomings, and after a while simply fell to staring into space, as he'd done for hour after hour since we'd left the money.

At about eleven the telephone at his elbow brought him out of it, but sluggishly.

'Hello? . . . Yes, Cenci speaking . . .' He listened briefly and then looked at the receiver with an apathetic frown before putting it back in its cradle.

'What was it?' I said.

'I don't know. Nothing much. Something about my goods being ready, and to collect them. I don't know what goods . . . he rang off before I could ask.'

I breathed deeply. 'Your telephone's still tapped,' I said.

'Yes, but what's that . . .' His voice died as his eyes widened. 'Do you think . . . ? Do you really?'

'We could see,' I said. 'Don't bank on anything yet. What did he sound like?'

'A gruff voice.' He was uncertain. 'Not the usual one.'

'Well . . . let's try, anyway. Better than sitting here.'

'But where? He didn't say where.'

'Perhaps . . . where we left the ransom. Logical place.'

Hope began swelling fast in his expression and I said hastily, 'Don't expect anything. Don't believe. You'll never be able to stand it, if she isn't there. He may mean somewhere else . . . but I think we should try there first.'

He tried to take a grip on things but was still hectically optimistic. He ran through the house to where the car stood waiting near the back door, where I'd parked it. Putting on my cap I followed him at a walk, to find him beckoning frantically and telling me to hurry. I climbed behind the wheel stolidly and thought that someone had known Cenci was at home when he was normally in the office. Perhaps there was still a watcher. In any case, I reckoned that until Alessia was safely home, a chauffeur in all things was what I needed to be.

'Do hurry,' Cenci said. I drove out of the gates without rush. 'For God's sake, man . . .'

'We'll get there. Don't hope . . .'

'I can't help it.'

I drove faster than usual, but it seemed an eternity to him; and when we pulled up by the shrine there was no sign of his daughter.

'Oh no . . . oh no.' His voice was cracking. 'I can't . . . I can't . . .'

I looked at him anxiously, but it was normal crushing grief, not a heart attack, not a fit.

'Wait,' I said, getting out of the car. 'I'll make sure.'

I walked round to the back of the shrine, to the

spot where we'd left the ransom, and found her there, unconscious, curled like a foetus, wrapped in a grey plastic raincoat.

Fathers are odd. The paramount emotion filling Paolo Cenci's mind for the rest of that day was not joy that his beloved daughter was alive, safe, and emerging unharmed from a drugged sleep, but fear that the press would find out she had been more or less naked.

'Promise you won't say, Andrew. Not to anyone. Not at all.'

'I promise.'

He made me promise at least seven separate times, though in any case it wasn't necessary. If anyone told, it would be Alessia herself.

Her lack of clothes had disturbed him greatly, especially as he and I had discovered when we tried to pick her up that her arms weren't through the sleeves of the raincoat, and the buttons weren't buttoned. The thin grey covering had slid right off.

She had the body of a child, I thought. Smooth skin, slender limbs, breasts like buds. Cenci had strangely been too embarrassed to touch her, and it had been I, the all-purpose advisor, who'd steered her arms through the plastic and fastened her more discreetly inside the folds. She had been light to carry to the car, and I'd lain her on her side on the rear seat, her knees bent, her curly head resting on my rolled-up jacket.

Cenci sat beside me in front: and it was then that he'd started exacting the promise. When we reached the villa he hurried inside to reappear with a blanket, and I carried her up to her half-acre bedroom in woolly decency.

Ilaria and Luisa were nowhere to be found. Cenci discarded the cook as too talkative and finally asked in a stutter if I would mind very much substituting clothes for the raincoat while he called the doctor. As I'd seen her already once, he said. As I was sensible. Astonished but obliging I unearthed a shift-like dress and made the exchange, Alessia sleeping peacefully throughout.

She was more awkward than anything else. I pulled the blue knitted fabric over her head, fed her hands through the armholes, tugged the hem down to her knees and concentrated moderately successfully on my own non-arousal. Then I laid her on top of the bed-clothes and covered her from the waist down with the blanket. Her pulse remained strong and regular, her skin cool, her breathing easy: sleeping pills, probably, I thought; nothing worse.

Her thin face was calm, without strain, long lashes lying in half-moon fringes on taut cheeks. Strong eye-brows, pale lips, hollows along the jaw. Hair tousled, clearly dirty. Let her sleep, I thought: she'd have little peace when she woke up.

I went downstairs and found Cenci again drinking brandy, standing up.

'Is she all right?' he said.

'Fine. Just fine.'

'It's a miracle.'

'Mm.'

He put down the glass and began to weep. 'Sorry. Can't help it,' he said.

'It's natural.'

He took out a handkerchief and blew his nose. 'Do all parents weep?'

'Yes.'

He put in some more work with the handkerchief, sniffed a bit, and said, 'You lead a very odd life, don't you?'

'Not really.'

'Don't say she had no clothes on. Promise me, Andrew.'

'I promise.'

I said I'd have to tell Pucinelli she was safe, and, immediately alarmed, he begged for the promise again. I gave it without impatience, because stress could come out in weird ways and the return of the victim was never the end of it.

Pucinelli was fortunately on duty in the ambulance, though presumably I could have spread the news directly via the wire-tappers.

'She's home,' I said laconically. 'I'm in the villa. She's upstairs.'

'Alessia?' Disbelief, relief, a shading of suspicion.

'Herself. Drugged but unharmed. Don't hurry, she'll probably sleep for hours. How's the siege going?'

'Andrew!' The beginnings of exasperation. 'What's been going on?'

'Will you be coming here yourself?'

A short pause came down the line. He'd told me once that I always put suggestions into the form of questions, and I supposed that it was true that I did. Implant the thought, seek the decision. He knew the tap was on the telephone, he'd ordered it himself, with every word recorded. He would guess there were things I might tell him privately.

'Yes,' he said. 'I'll be coming.'

'And of course you'll have a great lever now with those two kidnappers in the flat, won't you? And – um – will you bring the ransom money straight here when you lay your hands on it? It does, of course, belong to Signor Cenci.'

'Of course,' he said dryly. 'But it may not be my decision.'

'Mm. Well . . . I photographed all the notes, of course.'

A pause. 'You're wicked, you know that?'

'Things have disappeared out of police custody before now.'

'You insult the carabinieri!' He sounded truly affronted, loyally angry.

'Certainly not. Police stations are not banks. I am sure the carabinieri would be pleased to be relieved of the responsibility of guarding so much money.'

'It is evidence.'

'The rest of the kidnappers, of course, are still free, and no doubt still greedy. The money could be held safe from them under an official seal in a bank of Signor Cenci's choosing.'

A pause. 'It's possible that I may arrange it,' he said stiffly, not quite forgiving. 'No doubt I will see you at the villa.'

I put the telephone down with a rueful smile. Pucinelli himself I trusted, but not all law-enforcers automatically. In South American countries particularly, where I had worked several times, kidnappers regularly bribed or threatened policemen to look the wrong way, a custom scarcely unknown elsewhere. Kidnappers had no scruples and seldom any mercy, and many a policeman had had to choose between his duty and the safety of wife and children.

Within ten minutes Pucinelli was back on the line.

'Just to tell you . . . things are moving here. Come if you want. Come into the street from the west, on this side. I'll make sure you get through.'

'Thanks.'

The partners wouldn't have approved, but I went. I'd studied many case-histories of sieges and been to lectures by people involved in some of them, but I'd never been on the spot before at first hand: too good a chance to miss. I changed from Spanish chauffeur to nondescript onlooker, borrowed the family's runabout, and was walking along the Bologna street in record time.

Pucinelli had been as good as his word: a pass awaiting me at the first barrier saw me easily through to the still-parked ambulance. I went into it as I'd left, through the nearside passenger door, and found Pucinelli there with his engineer and three men in city suits.

'You came,' he said.

'You're kind.'

He gave me a small smile and briefly introduced me to the civilians: negotiator, psychiatrist, psychiatrist.

'These two medical gentlemen have been advising us about the changing mental state of the kidnappers.' Pucinelli spoke formally; they nodded gravely back.

'Mostly their mental state has been concerned with the baby,' Pucinelli said. 'The baby has cried a lot. Apparently the milk we sent in upset its stomach even worse.'

As if on cue the bug on the flat produced the accelerating wail of the infant getting newly into its stride, and from the faces of the five men in front of me it wasn't only the kidnappers who were finding the sound a frazzle.

'Forty minutes ago,' Pucinelli said, turning down the baby's volume, 'the deep-voiced kidnapper telephoned here and said they would come out if certain conditions were met. No aeroplane – they've abandoned that. They want only to be sure they aren't shot. In about twenty minutes . . . that's one hour from when they telephoned . . . they say the mother will leave with the baby. Then one of the kidnappers will come out. There are to be no carabinieri anywhere in the flats. The stairs must be clear, also the front door and the pavement outside. The mother and baby will come out into the road, followed by the first kidnapper. He will have no gun. If he is taken peacefully, one of the children will leave, and after an interval, the father. If the second kidnapper is then sure he will be safe, he will come out with the second child in his arms. No gun. We are to arrest him quietly.'

I looked at him. 'Did they discuss all this between themselves? Did you hear them plan it, on the bug?'

He shook his head. 'Nothing.'

'They telephoned you very soon after Alessia was home.'

'Suspiciously soon.'

'You'll look for the radio?' I said.

'Yes.' He sighed. 'We have been monitoring radio frequencies these past few days. We've had no results, but I have thought once or twice before this that the kidnappers were being instructed.'

Instructed, I thought, by a very cool and bold intelligence. A pity such a brain was criminal.

'What do they plan to do with the money?' I asked.

'Leave it in the flat.'

I glanced at the screen which had shown the whereabouts of the homer in the ransom suitcase, but it was dark. I leant over and flicked the on-off switch, and the trace obligingly appeared, efficient and steady. The suitcase, at least, was still there.

I said, 'I'd like to go up there, as Signor Cenci's representative, to see that it's safely taken care of.'

With suppressed irritation he said, 'Very well.'

'It's a great deal of money,' I said reasonably.

'Yes . . . yes, I suppose it is.' He spoke grudgingly, partly, I guessed, because he was himself honest, partly because he was a communist. So much wealth in one man's hands offended him, and he wouldn't care if Cenci lost it.

Across the street the flat's windows were still closed. All the windows of all the flats were closed, although the day was hot.

'Don't they ever open them?' I asked.

Pucinelli glanced across at the building. 'The kidnappers open the windows sometimes for a short while when we switch off the searchlights at dawn. The blinds are always drawn, even then. There are no people now in any of the other flats. We moved them for their own safety.'

Down on the road there was little movement. Most of the official cars had been withdrawn, leaving a good deal of empty space. Four carabinieri crouched with guns behind the pair still parked, their bodies tense. Metal barriers down the street kept a few onlookers at bay, and the television van looked closed. One or two photographers sat on the ground in its shade, drinking beer from cans. On the bug the colicky crying had stopped, but no one seemed to be saying very much. It was siesta, after all.

Without any warning a young woman walked from the flats carrying a baby and shielding her eyes against the brilliance of the sunlight. She was very dishevelled and also heavily pregnant.

Pucinelli glanced as if stung at his wristwatch, said 'They're early,' and jumped out of the van. I watched him through the dark glass as he strode without hesitation towards her, taking her arm. Her head turned towards him and she began to fall, Pucinelli catching the baby and signalling furiously with his head to his men behind the cars.

One scurried forward, hauled the fainting woman unceremoniously to her feet and hustled her into one of the cars. Pucinelli gave the baby a sick look, carried it at arm's length in the wake of its mother, and, having delivered it, wiped his hands disgustedly on a handkerchief.

The photographers and the television van came to life as if electrified, and a young plump man walked three steps out of the flats and slowly raised both hands.

Pucinelli, now sheltering behind the second car, stretched an arm through the window, removed a loudhailer, and spoke through it.

'Lie face down on the road. Legs apart. Arms outstretched.'

The plump young man wavered a second, looked as if he would retreat, and finally did as he was bid.

Pucinelli spoke again. 'Stay where you are. You will not be shot.'

There was a long breath-holding hush. Then a boy came out; about six, in shorts, shirt and bright blue and white training shoes. His mother frantically waved to him through the car window, and he ran across to her, looking back over his shoulder at the man on the ground.

I switched up the volume to full on the bug on the flat, but there was still no talking, simply a few grunts and unidentifiable movements. After a while these ended, and shortly afterwards another man walked out into the street, a youngish man this time, with his hands tied behind his back. He looked gaunt and tottery, with stubbled chin, and he stopped dead at the sight of the spreadeagled kidnapper.

'Come to the cars,' Pucinelli said through the loud-hailer. 'You are safe.'

The man seemed unable to move. Pucinelli, again exposing his whole body to the still-present threat of the guns in the flat, walked calmly across the road, took him by the arm, and led him behind the car holding his wife.

The psychiatrists watching beside me shook their heads over Pucinelli, not approving such straight-forward courage. I picked up a pair of binoculars which were lying on the bench and focused them on the opposite windows, but nothing stirred. Then I scanned the onlookers at the barriers down the street, and took in a close-up of the photographers, but there was no sign of the man from the motorway car park.

I put down the glasses, and time gradually stretched out, hot and silent, making me wonder, making everyone wonder if by some desperate mischance at the last minute the surrender had gone wrong. There was no sound from the bug. There was stillness in the street. Forty-six minutes had passed since the mother and baby had emerged.

Pucinelli spoke through the loudhailer with firmness but not aggression. 'Bring out the child. You will not be hurt.'

Nothing happened.

Pucinelli repeated his instructions.

Nothing.

I thought of guns, of desperation, of suicide, murder and spite.

Pucinelli's voice rang out. 'Your only hope of ever being released from prison is to come out now as arranged.'

No result.

Pucinelli's hand put the loudhailer through the car's window and reappeared holding a pistol. He pushed the pistol through his belt in the small of his back, and without more ado walked straight across the street and in through the door of the flats.

The psychiatrists gasped and made agitated motions with their hands and I wondered if I would ever have had the nerve, in those circumstances, to do what Pucinelli was doing.

There were no shots; none that we could hear. No sounds at all, just more long-drawn-out quiet.

The carabinieri behind the cars began to grow dangerously restive for lack of their leader and to look at each other for guidance, waving their guns conspicuously. The engineer in the van was muttering ominously under his breath, and there was still silence from the bug. If nothing happened soon, I thought, there could be another excited, destructive, half-cocked raid.

Then, suddenly there was a figure in the doorway: a strong burly man carrying a little girl like a feather on one arm.

Behind him came Pucinelli, gun nowhere in sight. He pointed to the first kidnapper, still spreadeagled, and the big man with a sort of furious resignation walked over to him and put the small child on the ground. Then he lowered his bulk into the same outstretched attitude, and the little girl, only a toddler, stood looking at him for a moment and then lay down and copied him, as if it were a game.

The carabinieri burst like uncorked furies from behind the cars and bristling with guns and handcuffs descended on the prone figures with no signs of loving-kindness. Pucinelli watched while the kidnappers were marched to the empty car and the child returned to her parents, then came casually back to the open door of the ambulance as if he'd been out for a stroll.

He thanked the negotiator and the psychiatrists from there, and jerked his head to me to come out and follow him. I did: across the road, in through the door of the flats and up the stone staircase beyond.

'The big man,' Pucinelli said, 'was up there,' he pointed, 'right at the top, sixth floor, where the stairs lead to the roof. It took me some time to find him. But we had barricaded that door, of course. He couldn't get out.'

'Was he violent?' I asked.

Pucinelli laughed. 'He was sitting on the stairs with the little girl on his knee, telling her a story.'

'What?'

'When I went up the stairs with my pistol ready he said to put it away, the show was over, he knew it. I told him to go down into the street. He said he wanted to stay where he was for a while. He said he had a child of his own of that age and he'd never be able to hold her on his knee again.'

Sob stuff, I thought. 'What did you do?' I asked.

'Told him to go down at once.'

The 'at once' however had taken quite a long time. Pucinelli like all Italians liked children, and even carabinieri, I supposed, could be sentimental.

'That poor deprived father,' I said, 'abducted someone else's daughter and shot someone else's son.'

'Your head,' Pucinelli said, 'is like ice.'

He led the way into the flat that had been besieged for four and a half days, and the heat and stink of it were indescribable. Squalor took on a new meaning. Apart from the stench of sweat and the decomposing remains of meals there were unmentionable heaps of cloth and rags and newspaper in two of the three small rooms: the baby, incontinent at both ends, had done more than cry.

'How did they stand it?' I wondered. 'Why didn't they wash anything?'

'The mother wanted to. I heard her asking. They wouldn't let her.'

We searched our way through the mess, finding the ransom suitcase almost immediately under a bed. As far as I could tell, the contents were untouched: good news for Cenci. Pucinelli gave the packets of notes a sour look and poked around for the radio.

The owners of the flat had one themselves, standing openly on top of a television set, but Pucinelli shook his head over it, saying it was too elementary. He started a methodical search, coming across it eventually inside a box of Buttoni in a kitchen cupboard.

'Here we are,' he said, brushing off pasta shells. 'Complete with earplug for private listening.' A smallish but elaborate walkie-talkie, aerial retracted.

'Don't disturb the frequency,' I said.

'I wasn't born yesterday. And nor was the man giving the instructions, I shouldn't think.'

'He might not have thought of everything.'

'Maybe not. All criminals are fools sometimes, otherwise we'd never catch them.' He wound the cord with its earpiece carefully around the radio and put it by the door.

'What range do you think that has?' I asked.

'Not more than a few miles. I'll find out. But too far, I would think, to help us.'

There remained the pistols, and these were easy: Pucinelli found them on a windowsill when he let up one of the blinds to give us more light.

We both looked down from the window. The ambulance and the barriers were still there, though the drama had gone. I thought that the earlier host of official cars and of highly armed men crouching behind them must have been a fearsome sight. What with that threat ever present and the heat, the baby, the searchlights and the stench, their nerves must have been near exploding point the whole time.

'He could have shot you any time,' I said, 'when you walked out across the street.'

'I reckoned he wouldn't.' He spoke unemotionally. 'But when I was creeping up the stairs . . .' he smiled fractionally, '. . . I did begin to wonder.'

He gave me a cool and comradely nod and departed, saying he would arrange transit for the ransom and send his men to collect and label the pistols and radio.

'You'll stay here?' he asked.

I pinched my nose. 'On the stairs outside.'

He smiled and went away, and in due course people arrived. I accompanied the ransom to the bank of Pucinelli's choosing, followed it to the vaults and accepted bank and carabinieri receipts. Then, on my way back to collect the Cenci runabout, I made a routine collect call to my firm in London. Reports from advisors-in-the-field were expected regularly, with wisdom from the collective office mind flowing helpfully back.

'The girl's home,' I said. 'The siege is over, the first ransom's safe, and how are my snaps doing on the second?'

'Lists with you tomorrow morning.'

'Right.'

They wanted to know how soon I'd be back.

'Two or three days,' I said. 'Depends on the girl.'

CHAPTER FIVE

Alessia woke in the evening, feeling sick. Cenci rushed upstairs to embrace her, came down damp-eyed, said she was still sleepy and couldn't believe she was home.

I didn't see her. Ilaria slept all night on an extra bed in Alessia's room at her aunt Luisa's suggestion, and did seem genuinely pleased at her sister's return. In the morning she came down with composure to breakfast and said that Alessia felt ill and wouldn't get out of the bath.

'Why not?' Cenci said, bewildered.

'She says she's filthy. She's washed her hair twice. She says she smells.'

'But she doesn't,' he protested.

'No. I've told her that. It makes no difference.'

'Take her some brandy and a bottle of scent,' I said.

Cenci looked at me blankly but Ilaria said, 'Well, why not?' and went off on the errand. She had talked more easily that morning than at any breakfast before, almost as if her sister's release had been also her own.

Pucinelli arrived mid-morning with a note-taking

aide, and Alessia came downstairs to meet him. Standing there beside him in the hall I watched the tentative figure on the stairs and could clearly read her strong desire to retreat. She stopped four steps from the bottom and looked behind her, but Ilaria, who had gone up to fetch her, was nowhere to be seen.

Cenci went forward and put his arm round her shoulders, explaining briefly who I was, and saying Pucinelli wanted to know everything that happened to her, hoping for clues to lead him to arrests.

She nodded slightly, looking pale.

I'd seen victims return with hectic jollity, with hysteria, with apathy; all with shock. Alessia's state looked fairly par for the circumstances: a mixture of shyness, strangeness, weakness, relief and fear.

Her hair was still damp. She wore a T-shirt, jeans and no lipstick. She looked a defenceless sixteen, recently ill; the girl I'd seen undressed. What she did not look was the glossy darling of the European racetracks.

Cenci led her to the library, and we scattered around on chairs.

'Tell us,' Pucinelli said. 'Please tell us what happened, from the beginning.'

'I . . . it seems so long ago.' She spoke mostly to her father, looking seldom at Pucinelli and not at all at me; and she used Italian throughout, though as she spoke slowly with many pauses, I could follow her with ease. Indeed it occurred to me fleetingly that I'd soaked in a good deal more of the language than I'd arrived with, and more than I'd noticed until then.

'I'd been racing here on our local track . . . but you know that.'

Her father nodded.

'I won the six o'clock race, and there was an objection . . .'

More nods, both from Cenci and Pucinelli. The note-taking aide, eyes down to the task, kept his shorthand busily flowing.

'I drove home. I was thinking of England. Of riding Brunelleschi in the Derby . . .' She broke off. 'Did he win?'

Her father looked blank. At the time, shortly after her disappearance, he'd have been unlikely to notice an invasion of Martians in the back yard.

'No,' I said. 'Fourth.'

She said 'Oh,' vaguely, and I didn't bother to explain that I knew where the horse had finished simply because it was she who had been going to ride it. Ordinary curiosity, nothing more.

'I was here . . . in sight of the house. Not far from the gate. I slowed down, to turn in . . .'

The classic spot for kidnaps; right outside the victim's house. She had a red sports car, besides, and had been driving it that day with the roof down, as she always did in fine weather. Some people, I'd thought when I'd heard it, made abduction too simple for words.

'There was a car coming towards me . . . I waited for

it to pass, so that I could turn . . . but it didn't pass, it stopped suddenly between me and the gate . . . blocking the way.' She paused and looked anxiously at her father. 'I couldn't help it, Papa. I really couldn't.'

'My dear, my dear . . .' He looked surprised at the very thought. He didn't see, as I did, the iceberg tip of the burden of guilt, but then he hadn't seen it so often.

'I couldn't think what they were doing,' she said. 'Then all the car doors opened at once, and there were four men . . . all wearing horrid masks . . . truly horrible . . . devils and monsters. I thought they wanted to rob me. I threw my purse at them and tried to reverse to get away backwards . . . and they sort of leapt into my car . . . just jumped right in . . .' She stopped with the beginnings of agitation and Pucinelli made small damping-down motions with his hands to settle her.

'They were so fast,' she said, her voice full of apology. 'I couldn't do anything . . .'

'Signorina,' Pucinelli said calmly, 'there is nothing to be ashamed of. If kidnappers wish to kidnap, they kidnap. Even all Aldo Moro's guards couldn't prevent it. And one girl alone, in an open car . . .' He shrugged expressively, finishing the sentence without words, and for the moment at least she seemed comforted.

A month earlier, to me in private, he had said that any rich girl who drove around in an open sports car was inviting everything from mugging to rape. 'I'm not saying they wouldn't have taken her anyway, but she was stupid. She made it easy.'

'There's not much fun in life if you're twenty-three and successful and can't enjoy it by driving an open sports car on a sunny day. What would you advise her to do, go round in a middle-aged saloon with the doors locked?'

'Yes,' he had said. 'So would you, if your firm was asked. That's the sort of advice you'd be paid for.'

'True enough.'

Alessia continued, 'They put a hood of cloth right over my head . . . and then it smelled sweet . . .'

'Sweet?' Pucinelli said.

'You know. Ether. Chloroform. Something like that. I simply went to sleep. I tried to struggle . . . They had their hands on my arms . . . sort of lifting me . . . nothing else.'

'They lifted you out of the car?'

'I think so. I suppose so. They must have done.'

Pucinelli nodded. Her car had been found a bare mile away, parked on a farm track.

'I woke up in a tent,' Alessia said.

'A tent?' echoed Cenci, bewildered.

'Yes . . . well . . . it was inside a room, but I didn't realise that at first.'

'What sort of tent?' Pucinelli asked. 'Please describe it.'

'Oh . . .' she moved a hand weakly, 'I can describe every stitch of it. Green canvas. About two and a half metres square . . . a bit less. It had walls . . . I could stand up.'

A frame tent.

'It had a floor. Very tough fabric. Grey. Waterproof, I suppose, though of course that didn't matter . . .'

'When you woke up,' Pucinelli asked, 'what happened?'

'One of the men was kneeling on the floor beside me, slapping my face. Quite hard. Hurry up, he was saying. Hurry up. When I opened my eyes he grunted and said I must just repeat a few words and I could go back to sleep.'

'Was he wearing a mask?'

'Yes . . . a devil face . . . orange . . . all warts.'

We all knew what the few words had been. We'd all listened to them, over and over, on the first of the tapes.

'This is Alessia. Please do as they say. They will kill me if you don't.' A voice slurred with drugs, but alarmingly her own.

'I knew what I said,' she said. 'I knew when I woke up properly . . . but when I said them, everything was fuzzy. I couldn't see the mask half the time . . . I kept switching off, then coming back.'

'Did you ever see any of them without masks?' Pucinelli asked.

A flicker of a smile reached the pale mouth. 'I didn't see any of them again, even in masks. Not at all. No one. The first person I saw since that first day was Aunt Luisa . . . sitting by my own bed . . . sewing her tapestry, and I thought . . . I was dreaming.' Tears unexpectedly appeared in her eyes and she blinked them slowly away.

'They said . . . if I saw their faces, they would kill me. They told me not to try to see them . . .' She swallowed. 'So . . . I didn't . . . try.'

'You believed them?'

A pause. Then she said 'Yes' with a conviction that brought understanding of what she'd been through vividly to life. Cenci, although he had believed the threats himself, looked shattered. Pucinelli gravely assured her that he was sure she had been right: and so, though I didn't mention it, was I.

'They said . . . I would go home safely . . . if I was quiet . . . and if you would pay for my release.' She was still trying not to cry. 'Papa . . .'

'My dearest . . . I would pay anything.' He was himself close to tears.

'Yes,' Pucinelli said matter-of-factly. 'Your father paid.'

I glanced at him. 'He paid,' he repeated, looking steadily at Cenci. 'How much, and where he paid it, only he knows. In no other way would you be free.'

Cenci said defensively, 'I was lucky to get the chance, after your men . . .'

Pucinelli cleared his throat hurriedly and said, 'Let's get on. Signorina, please describe how you have lived for the past six weeks.'

'I didn't know how long it was, until Aunt Luisa told me. I lost count . . . there were so many days, I had no way of counting . . . and then it didn't seem to matter much. I asked why it was so long, but they didn't answer. They never answered any questions. It wasn't worth asking . . . but sometimes I did, just to hear my own voice.' She paused. 'It's odd to talk as much as this. I went days without saying anything at all.'

'They talked to you, though, Signorina?'

'They gave me orders.'

'What orders?'

'To take in the food. To put out the bucket . . .' She stopped, then said, 'It sounds so awful, here in this room.'

She looked round at the noble bookcases stretching to the high ceiling, at the silk brocaded chairs, at the pale Chinese carpet on the marble-tiled floor. Every room in the house had the same unselfconscious atmosphere of wealth, of antique things having stood in the same places for decades, of treasures taken for granted. She must have been in many a meagre room in her racing career, but she was seeing her roots, I guessed, with fresh eyes.

'In the tent,' she said resignedly, 'there was a piece of foam for me to lie on, and another small piece for a pillow. There was a bucket . . . an ordinary bucket, like out of a stable. There was nothing else.' She paused. 'There was a zip to open one side of the tent. It would open only about fifty centimetres . . . it was jammed above that. They told me to unzip it, and I would find food . . .'

'Could you see anything of the room outside the tent?' Pucinelli asked.

She shook her head. 'Beyond the zip there was just more tent . . . but folded a bit, I think . . . I mean, not properly put up like another room . . .' She paused. 'They told me not to try to get into it.' Another pause. 'The food was always where I could reach it easily, just by the zip.'

'What was the food?' Cenci asked, deeply concerned.

'Pasta.' A pause. 'Sometimes warm, sometimes cold. Mixed with sauce. Tinned, I think. Anyway . . .' she said tiredly, 'it came twice a day . . . and the second lot usually had sleeping pills in it.'

Cenci exclaimed in protest, but Alessia said, 'I didn't mind . . . I just ate it . . . it was better really than staying awake.'

There was a silence, then Pucinelli said, 'Was there anything you could hear, which might help us to find where you were held?'

'Hear?' She glanced at him vaguely. 'Only the music.'

'What music?'

'Oh . . . tapes. Taped music. Over and over, always the same.'

'What sort of music?'

'Verdi. Orchestral, no singing. Three-quarters of that, then one-quarter of pop music. Still no singing.'

'Could you write down the tunes in order?'

She looked mildly surprised but said, 'Yes, I should think so. All that I know the names of.'

'If you do that today, I'll send a man for the list.'

'All right.'

'Is there anything else at all you can think of?'

She looked dully at the floor, her thin face tired with the mental efforts of freedom. Then she said, 'About four times they gave me a few sentences to read aloud, and they told me each time to mention something that had happened in my childhood, which only my father would know about, so that he could be sure I was still . . . all right.'

Pucinelli nodded. 'You were reading from daily papers.'

She shook her head. 'They weren't newspapers. Just sentences typed on ordinary paper.'

'Did you keep those papers?'

'No . . . they told me to put them out through the zip.' She paused. 'The only times they turned the music off was when I made the recordings.'

'Did you see a microphone?'

'No . . . but I could hear them talk clearly through the tent, so I suppose they recorded me from outside.'

'Would you remember their voices?'

An involuntary shudder shook her. 'Two of them, yes. They spoke most – but there were others. The one who made the recordings . . . I'd remember him. He was just . . . cold. The other was beastly . . . He seemed to enjoy it . . . but he was worse at the beginning . . . or at least perhaps I got used to him and didn't care. Then there was one sometimes who kept apologising . . . "Sorry, Signorina" . . . when he told me the food was there. And another who just grunted . . . None of them ever answered, if I spoke.'

'Signorina,' Pucinelli said, 'if we play you one of the tapes your father received, will you tell us if you recognise the man's voice?'

'Oh . . .' She swallowed. 'Yes, of course.'

He had brought a small recorder and copies of the tapes with him, and she watched apprehensively while he inserted a cassette and pressed a button. Cenci put out a hand to grasp one of Alessia's, almost as if he could shield her from what she would hear.

'Cenci,' HIS voice said. 'We have your daughter Alessia. We will return her on payment of one hundred and fifty thousand million lire. Listen to your daughter's voice.' There was a click, followed by Alessia's slurred words. Then, 'Believe her. If you do not pay, we will kill her. Do not delay. Do not inform the carabinieri, or your daughter will be beaten. She will be beaten every day you delay, and also . . .' Pucinelli pressed the stop button decisively, abruptly and mercifully shutting off the worse, the bestial threats. Alessia anyway was shaking and could hardly speak. Her nods were small and emphatic. 'Mm . . . yes . . .'

'You could swear to it?'

'. . . Yes . . .'

Pucinelli methodically put away the recorder. 'It is the same male voice on all the tapes. We have had a voice print made, to be sure.'

Alessia worked saliva into her mouth. 'They didn't

beat me,' she said. 'They didn't even threaten it. They said nothing like that.'

Pucinelli nodded. 'The threats were for your father.'

She said with intense anxiety, 'Papa, you didn't pay that much? That's everything . . . you couldn't.'

He shook his head reassuringly. 'No, no, nothing like that. Don't fret . . . don't worry.'

'Excuse me,' I said in English.

All the heads turned in surprise, as if the wallpaper had spoken.

'Signorina,' I said, 'were you moved from place to place at all? Were you in particular moved four or five days ago?'

She shook her head. 'No.' Her certainty however began to waver, and with a frown she said, 'I was in that tent all the time. But . . .'

'But what?'

'The last few days, there was a sort of smell of bread baking, sometimes, and the light seemed brighter . . . but I thought they had drawn a curtain perhaps . . . though I didn't think much at all. I mean, I slept so much . . . it was better . . .'

'The light,' I said, 'it was daylight?'

She nodded. 'It was quite dim in the tent, but my eyes were so used to it . . . They never switched on any electric lights. At night it was dark, I suppose, but I slept all night, every night.'

'Do you think you could have slept through a move,

if they'd taken the tent from one room in one place and driven it to another place and set it up again?'

The frown returned while she thought it over. 'There was one day not long ago I hardly woke up at all. When I did wake it was already getting dark and I felt sick . . . like I did when I woke here yesterday . . . and oh,' she exclaimed intensely, 'I'm so glad to be here, so desperately grateful . . . I can't tell you. . . .' She buried her face on her father's shoulder and he stroked her hair with reddening eyes.

Pucinelli rose to his feet and took a formal leave of father and daughter, removing himself, his note-taker and myself to the hall.

'I may have to come back, but that seems enough for now.' He sighed. 'She knows so little. Not much help. The kidnappers were too careful. If you learn any more, Andrew, you'll tell me?'

I nodded.

'How much was the ransom?' he said.

I smiled. 'The list of the notes' numbers will come here today. I'll let you have them. Also, do you have the Identikit system, like in England?'

'Something like it, yes.'

'I could build a picture of one of the other kidnappers, I think. Not the ones in the siege. If you like.'

'If I like! Where did you see him? How do you know?'

'I've seen him twice. I'll tell you about it when I come in with the lists.'

'How soon?' he demanded.

'When the messenger comes. Any time now.'

The messenger obligingly arrived while Pucinelli was climbing into his car, so I borrowed the Fiat runabout again and followed him to his headquarters.

Fitting together pieces of head with eyes and mouth, chin and hairline, I related the two sightings. 'You probably saw him yourself, outside the ambulance, the night the siege started,' I said.

'I had too much to think of.'

I nodded and added ears. 'This man is young. Difficult to tell . . . not less than twenty-five, though. Lower thirties, probably.'

I built a full face and a profile, but wasn't satisfied, and Pucinelli said he would get an artist in to draw what I wanted.

'He works in the courts. Very fast.'

A telephone call produced the artist within half an hour. He came, fat, grumbling, smelling of garlic and scratching, and saying that it was siesta, how could any sane man be expected to work at two in the afternoon? He stared with disillusion at my composite efforts, fished out a thin charcoal stick, and began performing rapid miracles on a sketch pad. Every few seconds he stopped to raise his eyebrows at me, inviting comment.

'Rounder head,' I said, describing it with my hands. 'A smooth round head.'

The round head appeared. 'What next?'

'The mouth . . . a fraction too thin. A slightly fuller lower lip.'

He stopped when I could think of no more improvements and showed the results to Pucinelli. 'This is the man as your English friend remembers him,' he said, sniffing. 'Memories are usually wrong, don't forget.'

'Thanks,' Pucinelli said. 'Go back to sleep.'

The artist grumbled and departed, and I said, 'What's the latest on Lorenzo Traventi?'

'Today they say he'll live.'

'Good,' I said with relief. It was the first time anyone had been positive.

'We've charged the two kidnappers with intent to kill. They are protesting.' He shrugged. 'So far they are refusing to say anything about the kidnap, though naturally we are pointing out that if they lead us to other arrests their sentences will be shorter.' He picked up the artist's drawings. 'I'll show them these. It will shock them.' A fleeting look of savage pleasure crossed his face: the look of a born policeman poised for a kill. I'd seen it on other faces above other uniforms, and never despised it. He deserved his satisfaction, after the strains of the past week.

'The radio,' Pucinelli said, pausing as he turned away.

'Yes?'

'It could transmit and receive on aircraft frequencies.'

I blinked. 'That's not usual, is it?'

'Not very. And it was tuned to the international

emergency frequency . . . which is monitored all the time, and which certainly did not pick up any messages between kidnappers. We checked at the airport this morning.'

I shook my head in frustration. Pucinelli went off with eagerness to his interrogations, and I returned to the villa.

Alessia said, 'Do you mind if I ask you something?'

'Fire away.'

'I asked Papa but he won't answer, which I suppose anyway is an answer of sorts.' She paused. 'Did I have any clothes on, when you found me?'

'A plastic raincoat,' I said matter-of-factly.

'Oh.'

I couldn't tell whether the answer pleased her or not. She remained thoughtful for a while, and then said, 'I woke up here in a dress I haven't worn for years. Aunt Luisa and Ilaria say they don't know how it happened. Did Papa dress me? Is that why he's so embarrassed?'

'Didn't you expect to have clothes on?' I asked curiously.

'Well . . .' She hesitated.

I lifted my head. 'Were you naked . . . all the time?'

She moved her thin body restlessly in the armchair as if she would sink into it, out of sight. 'I don't want . . .' she said; and broke off, swallowing, while in my mind I finished the sentence. Don't want everyone to know.

'It's all right,' I said. 'I won't say.'

We were sitting in the library, the evening fading to dark, the heat of the day diminishing; freshly showered, casually dressed, waiting in the Cenci household routine to be joined by everyone for a drink or two before dinner. Alessia's hair was again damp, but she had progressed as far as her lipstick.

She gave me short glances of inspection, not sure of me.

'Why are you here?' she said. 'Papa says he couldn't have got through these weeks without you, but . . . I don't really understand.'

I explained my job.

'An advisor?'

'That's right.'

She thought for a while, her gaze wandering over my face and down to my hands and up again to my eyes. Her opinions were unreadable, but finally she sighed, as if making up her mind

'Well . . . advise me too,' she said. 'I feel very odd. Like jet lag, only much worse. Time lag. I feel as if I'm walking on tissue paper. As if nothing's real. I keep wanting to cry. I should be deliriously happy . . . why aren't I?'

'Reaction,' I said.

'You don't know . . . you can't imagine . . . what it was like.'

'I've heard from many people what it's like. From people like you, straight back from kidnap. They've told me. The first bludgeoning shock, the not being able to believe it's happening. The humiliation, forced on you precisely to make you afraid and defenceless. No bathrooms. Sometimes, no clothes. Certainly no respect. No kindness or gentleness of any sort. Imprisonment, no one to talk to, nothing to fill the mind, just uncertainty and fear . . . and guilt. . . . Guilt that you didn't escape at the beginning, guilt at the distress brought on your family, guilt at what a ransom will cost . . . and fear for your life . . . if the money can't be raised . . . or if something goes wrong . . . if the kidnappers panic.'

She listened intently, at first with surprise and then with relief. 'You do know. You do understand. I haven't been able to say. . . . I don't want to upset them . . . and also . . . also . . .'

'Also you feel ashamed,' I said.

'Oh.' Her eyes widened. 'I . . . Why do I?'

'I don't know, but nearly everyone does.'

'Do they?'

'Yes.'

She sat quiet for a while, then she said, 'How long will it take . . . for me to get over it?'

To that there was no answer. 'Some people shake it off almost at once,' I said. 'But it's like illness, or a death . . . you have to grow scar tissue.'

Some managed it in days, some in weeks, some in years; some bled for ever. Some of the apparently strong disintegrated most. One couldn't tell, not on the day after liberation.

Ilaria came into the room in a stunning scarlet and gold toga and began switching on the lamps.

'It was on the radio news that you're free,' she said to Alessia. 'I heard it upstairs. Make the most of the peace, the paparazzi will be storming up the drive before you can blink.'

Alessia shrank again into her chair and looked distressed. Ilaria, it occurred to me uncharitably, had dressed for such an event: another statement about not wanting to be eclipsed.

'Does your advice stretch to paparazzi?' Alessia asked weakly, and I nodded. 'If you like.'

Ilaria patted the top of my head as she passed behind my chair. 'Our Mr Fixit. Never at a loss.'

Paolo Cenci himself arrived with Luisa, the one looking anxious, the other fluttery, as usual.

'Someone telephoned from the television company,' Cenci said. 'They say a crew is on the way here. Alessia, you'd better stay in your room until they've gone.'

I shook my head. 'They'll just camp on your doorstep. Better, really, to get it over.' I looked at Alessia. 'If you could possibly . . . and I know it's hard . . . make some sort of joke, they'll go away quicker.'

She said in bewilderment, 'Why?'

'Because good news is brief news. If they think you had a really bad time, they'll keep on probing. Tell them the kidnappers treated you well, say you're glad to be home, say you'll be back on the racecourse very soon. If they ask you anything which it would really distress you to answer, blank the thoughts out and make a joke.'

'I don't know . . . if I can.'

'The world wants to hear that you're all right,' I said. 'They want to be reassured, to see you smile. If you can manage it now it will make your return to normal life much easier. The people you know will greet you with delight . . . they won't find meeting you uncomfortable, which they could if they'd seen you in hysterics.'

Cenci said crossly, 'She's not in hysterics.'

'I know what he means,' Alessia said. She smiled wanly at her father. 'I hear you're paying for the advice, so we'd better take it.'

Once mobilised, the family put on a remarkable show, like actors on stage. For Ilaria and Luisa it was least difficult, but for Cenci the affable host role must have seemed bizarre, as he admitted the television people with courtesy and was helpful about electric plugs and moving furniture. A second television crew arrived while the first was still setting up, and after that several cars full of reporters, some from international news agencies, and a clatter of photographers. Ilaria moved like a scarlet bird among them, gaily chatting, and even Luisa was appearing gracious, in her unfocused way.

I watched the circus assemble from behind the almost closed library door, while Alessia sat silent in her armchair, developing shadows under her eyes.

'I can't do it,' she said.

'They won't expect a song and dance act. Just be . . . normal.'

'And make a joke.'

'Yes.'

'I feel sick,' she said.

'You're used to crowds,' I said. 'Used to people staring at you. Think of being . . .' I groped, '. . . in the winner's circle. Lots of fuss. You're used to it, which gives you a shield.'

She merely swallowed, but when her father came for her she walked out and faced the barrage of flashlights and questions without cracking. I watched from the library door, listening to her slow, clear Italian.

'I'm delighted to be home with my family. Yes, I'm fine. Yes, I hope to be racing again very soon.'

The brilliant lighting for the television cameras made her look extra pale, especially near the glowing Ilaria, but the calm half-smile on her face never wavered.

'No, I never saw the kidnappers' faces. They were very . . . discreet.'

The newsgatherers reacted to the word with a low growing rumble of appreciation.

'Yes, the food was excellent . . . if you liked tinned pasta.'

Her timing was marvellous: this time she reaped a full laugh.

'I've been living in the sort of tent people take on holiday. Size? A single bedroom . . . about that size.

Yes . . . quite comfortable . . . I listened to music, most of the time.'

Her voice was quiet, but rock-steady. The warmth of the newsmen towards her came over clearly now in their questions, and she told them an open sports car had proved a liability and she regretted having caused everyone so much trouble.

'How much ransom? I don't know. My father says it wasn't too much.'

'What was the worst thing about being kidnapped?' She repeated the question as if herself wondering, and then, after a pause, said, 'Missing the English Derby, I guess. Missing the ride on Brunelleschi.'

It was the climax. To the next question she smiled and said she had a lot of things to catch up with, and she was a bit tired, and would they please excuse her?

They clapped her. I listened in amazement to the tribute from the most cynical bunch in the world, and she came into the library with a real laugh in her eyes. I saw in a flash what her fame was all about: not just talent, not just courage, but style.

ENGLAND

CHAPTER SIX

I spent two more days at the Villa Francese and then flew back to London; and Alessia came with me.

Cenci, crestfallen, wanted her to stay. He hadn't yet returned to his office, and her deliverance had not restored him to the man-of-the-world in the picture. He still wore a look of ingrained anxiety and was still making his way to the brandy at unusual hours. The front he had raised for the media had evaporated before their cars were out through the gate, and he seemed on the following day incapably lethargic.

'I can't understand him,' Ilaria said impatiently. 'You'd think he'd be striding about, booming away, taking charge. You'd think he'd be his bossy self again. Why isn't he?'

'He's had six terrible weeks.'

'So what? They're over. Time for dancing, you'd think.' She sketched a graceful ballet gesture with her arm, gold bracelets jangling. 'Tell you the truth, I was goddam glad she's back, but the way Papa goes on, she might just as well not be.'

'Give him time,' I said mildly.

'I want him the way he was,' she said. 'To be a man.'

When Alessia said at dinner that she was going to England in a day or two, everyone, including myself, was astonished.

'Why?' Ilaria said forthrightly.

'To stay with Popsy.'

Everyone except myself knew who Popsy was, and why Alessia should stay with her, and I too learned afterwards. Popsy was a woman racehorse trainer, widowed, with whom Alessia usually lodged when in England.

'I'm unfit,' Alessia said. 'Muscles like jelly.'

'There are horses here,' Cenci protested.

'Yes, but . . . Papa, I want to go away. It's fantastic to be home, but . . . I tried to drive my car out of the gate today and I was shaking. . . . It was stupid. I meant to go to the hairdressers. My hair needs cutting so badly. But I just couldn't. I came back to the house, and look at me, still curling onto my shoulders.' She tried to laugh, but no one found it funny.

'If that's what you want,' her father said worriedly.

'Yes. . . . I'll go with Andrew, if he doesn't mind.'

I minded very little. She seemed relieved by her decisions, and the next day Ilaria drove her in the Fiat to the hairdresser, and bought things for her because she couldn't face shops, and brought her cheerfully home. Alessia returned with short casual curls and a slight case of the trembles, and Ilaria helped her pack.

On that evening I tried to persuade Cenci that his family should still take precautions.

'The first ransom is still physically in one suitcase, and until the carabinieri or the courts, or whatever, free it and allow you to use it to replace some of the money you borrowed from Milan, I reckon it's still at risk. What if the kidnappers took you . . . or Ilaria? They don't often hit the same family twice, but this time . . . they might.'

The horror was too much. He had crumbled almost too far.

'Just get Ilaria to be careful,' I said hastily, having failed to do that myself. 'Tell her to vary her life a bit. Get her to stay with friends, invite friends here. You yourself are much safer because of your chauffeur, but it wouldn't hurt to take the gardener along for a while, he has the shoulders of an ox and he'd make a splendid bodyguard.'

After a long pause, and in a low voice, he said, 'I can't face things, you know.'

'Yes, I do know,' I agreed gently. 'Best to start, though, as soon as you can.'

A faint smile. 'Professional advice?'

'Absolutely.'

He sighed. 'I can't bear to sell the house on Mikonos. My wife loved it.'

'She loved Alessia too. She'd think it a fair swap.'

He looked at me for a while. 'You're a strange young

man,' he said. 'You make things so clear.' He paused. 'Don't you ever get muddled by emotion?'

'Yes, sometimes,' I said. 'But when it happens . . . I try to sort myself out. To see some logic.'

'And once you see some logic, you act on it?'

'Try to.' I paused. 'Yes.'

'It sounds . . . cold.'

I shook my head. 'Logic doesn't stop you feeling. You can behave logically, and it can hurt like hell. Or it can comfort you. Or release you. Or all at the same time.'

After a while, he said, stating a fact, 'Most people don't behave logically.'

'No,' I said.

'You seem to think everyone could, if they wanted to?'

I shook my head. 'No.' He waited, so I went on diffidently, 'There's genetic memory against it, for one thing. And to be logical you have to dig up and face your own hidden motives and emotions, and of course they're hidden principally because you don't want to face them. So . . . um . . . it's easier to let your basement feelings run the upper storeys, so to speak, and the result is rage, quarrels, love, jobs, opinions, anorexia, philanthropy . . . almost anything you can think of. I just like to know what's going on down there, to pick out why I truly want to do things, that's all. Then I can do them or not. Whichever.'

He looked at me consideringly. 'Self-analysis . . . did you study it?'

'No. Lived it. Like everyone does.'

He smiled faintly. 'At what age?'

'Well . . . from the beginning. I mean, I can't remember not doing it. Digging into my own true motives. Knowing in one's heart of hearts. Facing the shameful things . . . the discreditable impulses . . . Awful, really.'

He picked up his glass and drank some brandy. 'Did it result in sainthood?' he said, smiling.

'Er . . . no. In sin, of course, from doing what I knew I shouldn't.'

The smile grew on his lips and stayed there. He began to describe to me the house on the Greek island that his wife had loved so, and for the first time since I'd met him I saw the uncertain beginnings of peace.

On the aeroplane Alessia said, 'Where do you live?'

'In Kensington. Near the office.'

'Popsy trains in Lambourn.' She imparted it as if it were a casual piece of information. I waited, though, and after a while she said, 'I want to keep on seeing you.'

I nodded. 'Any time.' I gave her one of my business cards, which had both office and home telephone numbers, scribbling my home address on the back.

'You don't mind?'

'Of course not. Delighted.'

'I need . . . just for now . . . I need a crutch.'

'De luxe model at your service.'

Her lips curved. She was pretty, I thought, under all the strain, her face a mingling of small delicate bones and firm positive muscles, smooth on the surface, taut below, finely shaped under all. I had always been attracted by taller, softer, curvier girls, and there was nothing about Alessia to trigger the usual easy urge to the chase. All the same I liked her increasingly, and would have sought her out if she hadn't asked me first.

In bits and pieces over the past two days she had told me many more details of her captivity, gradually unburdening herself of what she'd suffered and felt and worried over; and I'd encouraged her, not only because sometimes in such accounts one got a helpful lead towards catching the kidnappers, but also very much for her own sake. Victim therapy, paragraph one: let her talk it all out and get rid of it.

At Heathrow we went through immigration, baggage claims and customs in close proximity, Alessia keeping near to me nervously and trying to make it look natural.

'I won't leave you,' I assured her, 'until you meet Popsy. Don't worry.'

Popsy was late. We stood and waited, with Alessia apologising twice every five minutes and me telling her not to and, finally, like a gust of wind, a large lady arrived with outstretched arms.

'My darling,' she said, enveloping Alessia, 'a bloody crunch on the motorway. Traffic crawling past like snails. Thought I'd never get here.' She held Alessia away from her for an inspection. 'You look marvellous. What an utterly drear thing to happen. When I heard you were safe I bawled, absolutely bawled.'

Popsy was forty-fiveish and wore trousers, shirt and padded sleeveless waistcoat in navy, white and olive green. She had disconcertingly green eyes, a mass of fluffy greying hair, and a personality as large as her frame.

'Popsy . . .' Alessia began.

'My darling, what you need is a large steak. Look at your arms . . . matchsticks. The car's just outside, probably got some traffic cop writing a ticket, I left it on the double yellows, so come on, let's go.'

'Popsy, this is Andrew Douglas.'

'Who?' She seemed to see me for the first time. 'How do you do.' She thrust out a hand, which I shook. 'Popsy Teddington. Glad to know you.'

'Andrew travelled with me . . .'

'Great,' Popsy said. 'Well done.' She had her eyes on the exit, searching for trouble.

'Can we ask him to lunch on Sunday?' Alessia said.

'What?' The eyes swivelled my way, gave me a quick assessment, came up with assent. 'OK darling, anything you like.' To me she said, 'Go to Lambourn, ask anybody, they'll tell you where I live.'

'All right,' I said.

Alessia said, 'Thank you,' half under her breath, and

allowed herself to be swept away, and I reflected bemusedly about irresistible forces in female form.

From Heathrow I went straight to the office, where Friday afternoon was dawdling along as usual.

The office, a nondescript collection of ground floor rooms along either side of a central corridor, had been designed decades before the era of open-plan, half-acre windows and Kew Gardens rampant. We stuck to the rabbit hutches with their strip lighting because they were comparatively cheap; and as most of us were partners, not employees, we each had a sharp interest in low overheads. Besides, the office was not where we mostly worked. The war went on on distant fronts: headquarters was for discussing strategy and writing up reports.

I dumped my suitcase in the hutch I sometimes called my own and wandered along the row, both to announce my return and to see who was in.

Gerry Clayton was there, making a complicated construction in folded paper.

'Hello,' he said. 'Bad boy, Tut tut.'

Gerry Clayton, tubby, asthmatic, fifty-three and bald, had appointed himself father-figure to many wayward sons. His speciality was insurance, and it was he who had recruited me from a firm at Lloyd's, where I'd been a water-treading clerk looking for more purpose in life.

'Where's Twinkletoes?' I said. 'I may as well get the lecture over.'

'Twinkletoes, as you so disrespectfully call him, went to Venezuela this morning. The manager of Luca Oil got sucked.'

'Luca Oil?' My eyebrows rose. 'After all the work we did for them, setting up defences?'

Gerry shrugged, carefully knifing a sharp crease in stiff white paper with his thumbnail. 'That work was more than a year ago. You know what people are. Dead keen on precautions to start with, then perfunctory, then dead sloppy. Human nature. All any self-respecting dedicated kidnapper has to do is wait.'

He was unconcerned about the personal fate of the abducted manager. He frequently said that if everyone took fortress-like precautions and never got themselves – in his word – sucked, we'd all be out of a job. One good kidnapping in a corporation encouraged twenty others to call us in to advise them how to avoid a similar embarrassment; and as he regularly pointed out, the how-not-to-get-sucked business was our bread and butter and also some of the jam.

Gerry inverted his apparently wrinkled heap of white paper and it fell miraculously into the shape of a cockatoo. When not advising anti-kidnap insurance policies to Liberty Market clients he sold origami patterns to a magazine, but no one grudged his paper-folding in the office. His mind seemed to coast along while he creased and tucked, and would come up often as if from nowhere with highly productive business ideas.

Liberty Market as a firm consisted at that time of thirty-one partners and five secretarial employees. Of the partners, all but Gerry and myself were ex-S.A.S., ex-police, or ex-something-ultra-secret in government departments. There were no particular rules about who did which job, though if possible everyone was allowed their preferences. Some opted for the lecture tour full-time, giving seminars, pointing out dangers; all the how-to-stay-free bit. Some sank their teeth gratefully into the terrorist circuit, others, like myself, felt more useful against the simply criminal. Everyone in between times wrote their own reports, studied everyone else's, manned the office switchboard year round and polished up their techniques of coercive bargaining.

We had a Chairman (the firm's founder) for our Monday morning state-of-the-nation meetings, a Co-ordinator who kept track of everyone's whereabouts, and an Adjuster – Twinkletoes – to whom partners addressed all complaints. If their complaints covered the behaviour of any other partner, Twinkletoes passed the comments on. If enough partners disapproved of one partner's actions, Twinkletoes delivered the censure. I wasn't all that sorry he'd gone to Venezuela.

This apparently shapeless company scheme worked in a highly organised way, thanks mostly to the ingrained discipline of the ex-soldiers. They were lean, hard, proud and quite amazingly cunning, most of them preferring to deal with the action of the after-kidnap affairs. They were, in addition, almost paranoid about secrecy, as also the ex-spies were, which to begin with I'd found oppressive but had soon grown to respect.

It was the ex-policemen who did most of the lecturing, not only advising on defences but telling potential kidnap targets what to do and look for if they were taken, so that their captors could be in turn captured.

Many of us knew an extra like photography, languages, weaponry and electronics, and everyone could use a wordprocessor, because no one liked the rattle of typewriters all day long. No one was around the office long enough for serious feuds to develop, and the Co-ordinator had a knack of keeping incompatibles apart. All in all it was a contented ship which everyone worked in from personal commitment, and, thanks to the kidnappers, business was healthy.

I finished my journey along the row of hutches, said a few hellos, saw I was pencilled in with a question mark for Sunday midnight on the switchboard roster, and came at length to the big room across the far end, the only room with windows to the street. It just about seated the whole strength if we were ever there together, but on that afternoon the only person in it was Tony Vine.

''Lo,' he said. 'Hear you made an effing balls of it in Bologna.'

'Yeah.'

'Letting the effing carabinieri eff up the R.V.'

'Have you tried giving orders to the Italian army?'

He sniffed as a reply. He himself was an ex-S.A.S. sergeant, now nearing forty, who would never in his service days have dreamed of obeying a civilian. He could move across any terrain in a way that made a chameleon look flamboyant, and he had three times tracked and liberated a victim before the ransom had been paid, though no one, not even the victim, was quite sure how. Tony Vine was the most secretive of the whole tight-lipped bunch, and anything he didn't want to tell didn't get told.

It was he who had warned me about knives inside rolled-up magazines, and I'd guessed he'd known because he'd carried one that way himself.

His humour consisted mostly of sarcasm, and he could hardly get a sentence out without an oiling of fuck, shit and piss. He worked nearly always on political kidnaps because he, like Pucinelli, tended to despise personal and company wealth.

'If you're effing poor,' he'd said to me once, 'and you see some capitalist shitting around in a Roller, it's not so effing surprising you think of ways of levelling things up. If you're down to your last bit of goat cheese in Sardinia, maybe, or short of beans in Mexico, a little kidnap makes effing sense.'

'You're romantic,' I'd answered. 'What about the poor Sardinians who steal a child from a poor Sardinian village, and grind all the poor people there into poorer dust, forcing them all to pay out their pitiful savings for a ransom?'

'No one's effing perfect.'

For all that he'd been against me joining the firm in the first place, and in spite of his feeling superior in every way, whenever we'd worked together it had been without friction. He could feel his way through the psyches of kidnappers as through a minefield, but preferred to have me deal with the families of the victims.

'When you're with them, they stay in one effing piece. If I tell them what to do, they fall to effing bits.'

He was at his happiest cooperating with men in uniform, among whom he seemed to command instant recognition and respect. Good sergeants ran the army, it was said, and when he wanted to he had the air about him still.

No one was allowed to serve in the S.A.S. for an extended period, and once he'd been bounced out because of age, he'd been bored. Then someone had murmured in his ear about fighting terrorists a different way, and Liberty Market had never regretted taking him.

'I put you in for Sunday midnight on the blower, did you see, instead of me?' he said.

I nodded.

'The wife's got this effing anniversary party organised, and like as not by midnight I'll be pissed.'

'All right,' I said.

He was short for a soldier: useful for passing as a woman, he'd told me once. Sandy-haired, blue-eyed and light on his feet, he was a fanatic about fitness, and it was he who had persuaded everyone to furnish (and use) the iron-pumping room in the basement. He never said much about his origins: the tougher parts of London, from his accent.

'When did you get back?' I asked. 'Last I heard you were in Colombia.'

'End of the week.'

'How was it?' I said.

He scowled. 'We winkled the effing hostages out safe, and then the local strength got excited and shot the shit out of the terrorists, though they'd got their effing hands up and were coming out peaceful.' He shook his head. 'Never keep their bullets to themselves, those savages. Effing stupid, the whole shitting lot of them.'

Shooting terrorists who'd surrendered was, as he'd said, effing stupid. The news would get around, and the next bunch of terrorists, knowing they'd be shot if they did and also shot if they didn't, would be more likely to kill their victims.

I had missed the Monday meeting where that débâcle would have been discussed, but meanwhile there was my own report to write for the picking over of Bologna. I spent all Saturday on it and some of Sunday morning, and then drove seventy-five miles westward to Lambourn.

Popsy Teddington proved to live in a tall white house

near the centre of the village, a house seeming almost suburban but surprisingly fronting a great amount of stabling. I hadn't until that day realised that racing stables could occur actually inside villages, but when I remarked on it Poppy said with a smile that I should see Newmarket, they had horses where people in other towns had garages, greenhouses and sheds.

She was standing outside when I arrived, looming over a five-foot man who seemed glad of the interruption.

'Just see to that, Sammy. Tell them I won't stand for it,' she was saying forcefully as I opened the car door. Her head turned my way and a momentary 'who-are-you?' frown crossed her forehead. 'Oh yes, Alessia's friend. She's around the back, somewhere. Come along.' She led me past the house and behind a block of stabling, and we arrived suddenly in view of a small railed paddock, where a girl on a horse was slowly cantering, watched by another girl on foot.

The little paddock seemed to be surrounded by the backs of other stables and other houses, and the grass within it had seen better days.

'I hope you can help her,' Popsy said straightly, as we approached. 'I've never known her like this. Very worrying.'

'How do you mean?' I asked.

'So insecure. She wouldn't ride out yesterday with the string, which she always does when she's here, and now look at her, she's supposed to be up on that horse, not watching my stable girl riding.'

'Has she said much about what happened to her?' I asked.

'Not a thing. She just smiles cheerfully and says it's all over.'

Alessia half turned as we drew near, and looked very relieved when she saw me.

'I was afraid you wouldn't come,' she said.

'You shouldn't have been.'

She was wearing jeans and a checked shirt and lipstick, and was still unnaturally pale from six weeks in dim light. Popsy shouted to the girl riding the horse to put it back in its stable. 'Unless, darling, you'd like . . .' she said to Alessia. 'After all?'

Alessia shook her head. 'Tomorrow, I guess.' She sounded as if she meant it, but I could see that Popsy doubted. She put a motherly arm round Alessia's shoulders and gave her a small hug. 'Darling, do just what you like. How about a drink for your thirsty traveller?' To me she said, 'Coffee? Whisky? Methylated spirits?'

'Wine,' Alessia said. 'I know he likes that.'

We went into the house: dark antique furniture, worn Indian rugs, faded chintz, a vista of horses through every window.

Popsy poured Italian wine into cut crystal glasses with a casual hand and said she would cook steaks if we were patient. Alessia watched her disappear kitchenwards and said uncomfortably, 'I'm a nuisance to her. I shouldn't have come.'

'You're quite wrong on both counts,' I said. 'It's obvious she's glad to have you.'

'I thought I'd be all right here . . . That I'd feel different. I mean, that I'd feel all right.'

'You're sure to, in a while.'

She glanced at me. 'It bothers me that I just can't . . . shake it off.'

'Like you could shake off double septic pneumonia?'

'That's different,' she protested.

'Six weeks of no sunlight, no exercise, no decent food and a steady diet of heavy sleeping pills is hardly a recipe for physical health.'

'But . . . it's not just . . . physical.'

'Still less can you just shake off the non-physical.' I drank some wine. 'How are your dreams?'

She shuddered. 'Half the time I can't sleep. Ilaria said I should keep on with the sleeping pills for a while, but I don't want to, it revolts me to think of it. . . . But when I do sleep . . . I have nightmares . . . and wake up sweating.'

'Would you like me,' I said neutrally, 'to introduce you to a psychiatrist? I know quite a good one.'

'No.' The answer was instinctive. 'I'm not mad, I'm just . . . not right.'

'You don't need to be dying to go to a doctor.'

She shook her head. 'I don't want to.'

She sat on a large sofa with her feet on a coffee table, looking worried.

'It's you that I want to talk to, not some shrink. You understand what happened, and to some strange doctor it would sound exaggerated. You know I'm telling the truth, but he'd be worrying half the time if I wasn't fantasising or dramatising or something and be looking for ways of putting me in the wrong. I had a friend who went to one . . . She told me it was weird, when she said she wanted to give up smoking he kept suggesting that she was unhappy because she had repressed incestuous longings for her father.' She ended with an attempt at a laugh, but I could see what she meant. Psychiatrists were accustomed to distortion and evasion, and looked for them in the simplest remark.

'I do think all the same that you'd be better off with expert help,' I said.

'You're an expert.'

'No.'

'But it's you I want . . . Oh dear,' she broke off suddenly, looking most confused. 'I'm sorry. . . . You don't want to. . . . How stupid of me.'

'I didn't say that. I said . . .' I too stopped. I stood up, walked over, and sat next to her on the sofa, not touching. 'I'll untie any knots I can for you, and for as long as you want me to. That's a promise. Also a pleasure, not a chore. But you must promise me something too.'

She said, 'What?' glancing at me and away.

'That if I'm doing you no good, you will try someone else.'

'A shrink?'

'Yes.'

She looked at her shoes. 'All right,' she said; and like any psychiatrist I wondered if she were lying.

Popsy's steaks came tender and juicy, and Alessia ate half of hers.

'You must build up your strength, my darling,' Popsy said without censure. 'You've worked so hard to get where you are. You don't want all those ambitious little jockey-boys elbowing you out, which they will if they've half a chance.'

'I telephoned Mike,' she said. 'I said . . . I'd need time.'

'Now my darling,' Popsy protested. 'You get straight back on the telephone and tell him you'll be fit a week today. Say you'll be ready to race tomorrow week, without fail.'

Alessia looked at her in horror. 'I'm too weak to stay in the saddle . . . let alone race.'

'My darling, you've all the guts in the world. If you want to, you'll do it.'

Alessia's face said plainly that she didn't know whether she wanted to or not.

'Who's Mike?' I asked.

'Mike Noland,' Popsy said. 'The trainer she often rides for in England. He lives here, in Lambourn, up the road.'

'He said he understood,' Alessia said weakly.

'Well of course he understands. Who wouldn't? But all the same, my darling, if you want those horses back, it's you that will have to get them.'

She spoke with brisk, affectionate commonsense, hallmark of the kind and healthy who had never been at cracking point. There was a sort of quiver from where Alessia sat, and I rose unhurriedly to my feet and asked if I could help carry the empty dishes to the kitchen.

'Of course you can,' Popsy said, rising also, 'and there's cheese, if you'd like some.'

Alessia said horses slept on Sunday afternoons like everyone else, but after coffee we walked slowly round the yard anyway, patting one or two heads.

'I can't possibly get fit in a week,' Alessia said. 'Do you think I should?'

'I think you should try sitting on a horse.'

'Suppose I've lost my nerve.'

'You'd find out.'

'That's not much comfort.' She rubbed the nose of one of the horses absentmindedly, showing at least no fear of its teeth. 'Do you ride?' she asked.

'No,' I said. 'And . . . er . . . I've never been to the races.'

She was astonished. 'Never?'

'I've watched them often on television.'

'Not the same at all.' She laid her own cheek briefly against the horse's. 'Would you like to go?'

'With you, yes, very much.'

Her eyes filled with sudden tears, which she blinked away impatiently. 'You see,' she said. 'That's always happening. A kind word . . . and something inside me melts. I do try . . . I honestly do try to behave decently, but I know I'm putting on an act . . . and underneath there's an abyss . . . with things coming up from it, like crying for nothing, for no reason, like now.'

'The act,' I said, 'is Oscar class.'

She swallowed and sniffed and brushed the unspilt tears away with her fingers. 'Popsy is so generous,' she said. 'I've stayed with her so often.' She paused. 'She doesn't exactly say "Snap out of it" or "Pull yourself together", but I can see her thinking it. And I expect if I were someone looking at me, I'd think it too. I mean, she must be thinking that here I am, free and undamaged, and I should be grateful and getting on with life, and that far from moping I should be full of joy and bounce.'

We wandered slowly along and peered into the shadowy interior of a box where the inmate dozed, its weight on one hip, its ears occasionally twitching.

'After Vietnam,' I said, 'when the prisoners came home, there were very many divorces. It wasn't just the sort of thing that happened after the war in Europe, when the wives grew apart from the husbands just by living, while for the men time stood still. After Vietnam it was different. Those prisoners had suffered dreadfully, and they came home to families who expected them to be joyful at their release.'

Alessia leant her arms on the half-door, and watched the unmoving horse.

'The wives tried to make allowances, but a lot of the men were impotent, and would burst into tears in public, and many of them took offence easily . . . and showed permanent symptoms of mental breakdown. Hamburgers and coke couldn't cure them, nor going to the office nine to five.' I fiddled with the bolt on the door. 'Most of them recovered in time and lead normal lives, but even those will admit they had bad dreams for years and will never forget clear details of their imprisonment.'

After a while she said, 'I wasn't a prisoner of war.'

'Oh yes, just the same. Captured by an enemy through no fault of your own. Not knowing when – or whether – you would be free. Humiliated . . . deprived of free will . . . dependent on your enemy for food. All the same, but made worse by isolation . . . by being the only one.'

She put the curly head down momentarily on the folded arms. 'All they ever gave me, when I asked, were some tissues, and I begged . . . I begged . . . for those.' She swallowed. 'One's body doesn't stop counting the days, just because one's in a tent.'

I put my arm silently round her shoulders. There were things no male prisoner ever had to face. She cried quietly, with gulps and small compulsive sniffs, and after a while simply said, 'Thank you,' and I said, 'Any time,' and we moved on down the line of boxes knowing there was a long way still to go.

CHAPTER SEVEN

Manning the office switchboard day and night was essential because kidnappers kept anti-social hours; and it was always a partner on duty, not an employee, for reasons both of reliability and secrecy. The ex-spies feared 'moles' under every secretarial desk and positive-vetted the cleaner.

That particular Sunday night was quiet, with two calls only: one from a partner in Ecuador saying he'd discovered the local police were due to share in the ransom he was negotiating and asking for the firm's reactions, and the second from Twinkletoes, who wanted a copy of the set of precautions we'd drawn up for Luca Oil.

I made a note of it, saying, 'Surely Luca Oil have one?'

'The kidnappers stole it,' Twinkletoes said tersely. 'Or bribed a secretary to steal it. Anyway, it's missing, and the manager was abducted at the weakest point of his daily schedule, which I reckon was no coincidence.'

'I'll send it by courier straight away.'

'And see who's free to join me out here. This will be a

long one. It was very carefully planned. Send me Derek, if you can. And oh . . . consider yourself lucky I'm not there to blast you for Bologna.'

'I do,' I said, smiling.

'I'll be back,' he said darkly. 'Goodnight.'

I took one more call, at nine in the morning, this time from the head of a syndicate at Lloyd's which insured people and firms against kidnap. Much of our business came direct from him, as he was accustomed to make it a condition of insurance that his clients should call on our help before agreeing to pay a ransom. He reckoned we could bring the price down, which made his own liability less; and we in return recommended him to the firms asking our advice on defences.

'Two English girls have been snatched in Sardinia,' he said. 'The husband of one of them insured her against kidnap for her two weeks' holiday as he wasn't going to be with her, and he's been on to us. It seems to have been a fairly unplanned affair – the girls just happened to be in the wrong place, and were ambushed. Anyway, the husband is distraught and wants to pay what they're asking, straight away, so can you send someone immediately?'

'Yes,' I said. 'Er . . . what was the insurance?'

'I took a thousand pounds against two hundred thousand. For two weeks.' He sighed. 'Win some, lose some.'

I took down names and details and checked on flights to Sardinia, where in many regions bandits took, ransomed and released more or less as they pleased.

'Very hush-hush,' the Lloyd's man had said. 'Don't let it get to the papers. The husband has pressing reasons. If all goes well she'll be home in a week, won't she, and no one the wiser?'

'With a bit of luck,' I agreed.

Bandits had nowhere to keep long-term prisoners and had been known to march their victims miles over mountainsides daily, simply abandoning them once they'd been paid. Alessia, I thought, would have preferred that to her tent.

The partners began arriving for the Monday conference and it was easy to find one with itchy feet ready to go instantly to Sardinia, and easy also to persuade Derek to join Twinkletoes at Luca Oil. The Co-ordinator wrote them in on the new week's chart and I gave the request from the partner in Ecuador to the Chairman.

After about an hour of coffee, gossip and reading reports the meeting began, the bulk of it as usual being a review of work in progress.

'This business in Ecuador,' the Chairman said. 'The victim's an American national, isn't he?'

A few heads nodded.

The Chairman pursed his lips. 'I think we'll have to advise that corporation to use local men and not send any more from the States. They've had three men captured in the last ten years, all Americans . . . you'd think they'd learn.'

'It's an American-owned corporation,' someone murmured.

'They've tried paying the police themselves,' another said. 'I was out there myself last time. The police took the money saying they would guard all the managers with their lives, but I reckon they also took a cut of the ransom then, too. And don't forget, the corporation paid a ransom of something like ten million dollars . . . plenty to spread around.'

There was a small gloomy silence.

'Right,' the Chairman said. 'Future advice, no Americans. Present advice?' He looked around. 'Opinions, anyone?'

'The kidnappers know the corporation will pay in the end,' Tony Vine said. 'The corporation can't afford not to.'

All corporations had to ransom their captured employees if they wanted anyone ever to work overseas for them in future. All corporations also had irate shareholders, whose dividends diminished as ransoms rose. Corporations tended to keep abductions out of the news, and to write the ransoms down as a 'trading loss' in the annual accounts.

'We've got the demand down to ten million again,' Tony Vine said. 'The kidnappers won't take less, they'd be losing face against last time, even if – especially if – they're a different gang.'

The Chairman nodded. 'We'll advise the corporation to settle?'

Everyone agreed, and the meeting moved on.

The Chairman, around sixty, had once been a soldier himself, and like Tony felt comfortable with other men whose lives had been structured, disciplined and official. He had founded the firm because he'd seen the need for it; the action in his case of a practical man, not a visionary. It had been a friend of his, now dead, who had suggested partnerships rather than a hierarchy, advising the sweeping away of all former ranks in favour of one new one: equal.

The Chairman was exceptionally good-looking, a distinctly marketable plus, and had an air of quiet confidence to go with it. He could maintain that manner in the face of total disaster, so that one always felt he would at any moment devise a brilliant victory-snatching solution, even if he didn't. It had taken me a while, when I was new there, to see that it was Gerry Clayton who had that sort of mind.

The Chairman came finally to my report, photocopies of which most people had already read, and asked if any partners would like to ask questions. We gained always from what others had learned during a case, and I usually found question time very fruitful – though better when not doing the answering.

'This carabinieri officer . . . er . . . Pucinelli, what sort of a personal relationship could you have with him? What is your estimate of his capabilities?' It was a notoriously pompous partner asking; Tony would have said, 'How did you get on with the sod? What's he like?'

'Pucinelli's a good policeman,' I said. 'Intelligent, bags of courage. He was helpful. More helpful, I found, than most, though never stepping out of the official line. He hasn't yet . . .' I paused. 'He hasn't the clout to get any higher, I don't think. He's a second-in-command in his region, and I'd say that's as far as he'll go. But as far as his chances of catching the kidnappers are concerned, he'll be competent and thorough.'

'What was the latest, when you left?' someone asked. 'I haven't yet had time to finish your last two pages.'

'Pucinelli said that when he showed the drawings of the man I'd seen to the two kidnappers from the siege, they were both struck dumb. He showed them to them separately, of course, but in each case he said you could clearly see the shock. Neither of them would say anything at all and they both seemed scared. Pucinelli said he was going to circulate copies of the drawings and see if he could identify the man. He was very hopeful, when I left.'

'Sooner the better,' Tony said. 'That million quid will be laundered within a week.'

'They were a pretty cool lot,' I said, not arguing. 'They might hold it for a while.'

'And they might have whisked it over a border and changed it into francs or schillings before they released the girl.'

I nodded. 'They could have set up something like that for the first ransom, and been ready.'

Gerry Clayton's fingers as usual were busy with any

sheet of paper within reach, this time the last page of my report. 'You say Alessia Cenci came to England with you. Any chance she'll remember any more?' he asked.

'You cannot rule it out, but Pucinelli and I both went through it with her pretty thoroughly in Italy. She knows so little. There were no church bells, no trains, no close aeroplanes, no dogs . . . she couldn't tell whether she was in city or country. She thought the faint smell she was conscious of during the last few days might have been someone baking bread. Apart from that . . . nothing.'

A pause.

'Did you show the drawings to the girl?' someone asked. 'Had she ever seen the man, before the kidnap?'

I turned to him. 'I took a photostat to the villa, but she hadn't ever seen him that she could remember. There was absolutely no reaction. I asked if he could have been one of the four who abducted her, but she said she couldn't tell. None of her family or anyone in the household knew him. I asked them all.'

'His voice . . . when he spoke to you outside the motorway restaurant . . . was it the voice on the tapes?'

'I don't know,' I admitted. 'I'm not good enough at Italian. It wasn't totally different, that's all I could say.'

'You brought copies of the drawings and the tapes back with you?' the Chairman asked.

'Yes. If anyone would like . . .?'

A few heads nodded.

'Anything you didn't put in the report?' the Chairman asked. 'Insignificant details?'

'Well. . . . I didn't include the lists of the music. Alessia wrote what she knew, and Pucinelli said he would try to find out if they were tapes one could buy in shops, ready recorded. Very long shot, even if they were.'

'Do you have the lists?'

'No, afraid not. I could ask Alessia to write them again, if you like.'

One of the ex-policemen said you never knew. The other ex-policemen nodded.

'All right,' I said. 'I'll ask her.'

'How is she?' Gerry asked.

'Just about coping.'

There were a good many nods of understanding. We'd all seen the devastation, the hurricane's path across the spirit. All of us, some oftener than others, had listened to the experiences of the recently returned: the de-briefing, as the firm called it, in its military way.

The Chairman looked around for more questions but none were ready. 'All finished? Well, Andrew, we can't exactly sack you for coming up with pictures of an active kidnapper, but driving a car to the drop is not on the cards. Whether or not it turns out well this time, don't do it again. Right?'

'Right,' I said, neutrally; and that, to my surprise, was the full extent of the ticking-off.

*

A couple of days later the partner manning the switchboard called me down the corridor, where I was wandering with a cup of coffee in search of anything new.

'Andrew? Call for you from Bologna. I'll put it through to your room.'

I dumped the coffee and picked up the receiver, and a voice said 'Andrew? This is Enrico Pucinelli.'

We exchanged hellos, and he began talking excitedly, the words running together in my ear.

'Enrico,' I shouted. 'Stop. Speak slowly. I can't understand you.'

'Hah.' He sighed audibly and began to speak clearly and distinctly, as to a child. 'The young one of the kidnappers has been talking. He is afraid of being sent to prison for life, so he is trying to make bargains. He has told us where Signorina Cenci was taken after the kidnap.'

'Terrific,' I said warmly. 'Well done.'

Pucinelli coughed modestly, but I guessed it had been a triumph of interrogation.

'We have been to the house. It is in a suburb of Bologna, middle-class, very quiet. We have found it was rented by a father with three grown sons.' He clicked his tongue disgustedly. 'All of the neighbours saw men going in and out, but so far no one would know them again.'

I smiled to myself. Putting the finger on a kidnapper was apt to be unhealthy anywhere.

'The house has furniture belonging to the owner, but

we have looked carefully, and in one room on the upper floor all the marks where the furniture has stood on the carpet for a long time are in slightly different places.' He stopped and said anxiously, 'Do you understand, Andrew?'

'Yes,' I said. 'All the furniture has been moved.'

'Correct.' He was relieved. 'The bed, a heavy chest, a wardrobe, a bookcase. All moved. The room is big, more than big enough for the tent, and there is nothing to see from the window except a garden and trees. No one could see into the room from outside.'

'And have you found anything useful . . . any clues in the rest of the house?'

'We are looking. We went to the house for the first time yesterday. I thought you would like to know.'

'You're quite right. Great news.'

'Signorina Cenci,' he said, 'has she thought of anything else?'

'Not yet.'

'Give her my respects.'

'Yes,' I said. 'I will indeed.'

'I will telephone again,' he said. 'I will reverse the charges again, shall I, like you said? As this is private, between you and me, and I am telephoning from my own house?'

'Every time,' I said.

He said goodbye with deserved satisfaction, and I added a note of what he'd said to my report.

*

By Thursday morning I was back in Lambourn, chiefly for the lists of music, and I found I had arrived just as a string of Popsy's horses were setting out for exercise. Over her jeans and shirt Popsy wore another padded waistcoat, bright pink this time, seeming not to notice that it was a warm day in July; and her fluffy grey-white hair haloed her big head like a private cumulus cloud.

She was on her feet in the stable-yard surrounded by scrunching, skittering quadrupeds, and she beckoned when she saw me, with a huge sweep of her arm. Trying not to look nervous and obviously not succeeding, I dodged a few all-too-mobile half-tons of muscle and made it to her side.

The green eyes looked at me slantwise, smiling. 'Not used to them, are you?'

'Er . . .' I said. 'No.'

'Want to see them on the gallops?'

'Yes, please.' I looked round at the riders, hoping to see Alessia among them, but without result.

The apparently disorganised throng suddenly moved off towards the road in one orderly line, and Popsy jerked her head for me to follow her into the kitchen; and at the table in there, coffee cup in hand, sat Alessia.

She still looked pale, but perhaps now only in contrast to the outdoor health of Popsy, and she still looked thin, without strength. Her smile when she saw me started in the eyes and then curved to the pink lipstick; an uncomplicated welcome of friendship.

'Andrew's coming up on the Downs to see the schooling,' Popsy said.

'Great.'

'You're not riding?' I asked Alessia.

'No . . . I . . . anyway, Popsy's horses are jumpers.'

Popsy made a face as if to say that wasn't a satisfactory reason for not riding them, but passed no other comment. She and I talked for a while about things in general and Alessia said not much.

We all three sat on the front seat of a dusty Land Rover while Popsy drove with more verve than caution out of Lambourn and along a side road and finally up a bumpy track to open stretches of grassland.

Away on the horizon the rolling terrain melted into blue haze, and under our feet, as we stepped from the Land Rover, the close turf had been mown to two inches. Except for a bird call or two in the distance there was a gentle enveloping silence, which was in itself extraordinary. No drone of aeroplanes, no clamour of voices, no hum of faraway traffic. Just wide air and warm sunlight and the faint rustle from one's own clothes.

'You like it, don't you?' observed Popsy, watching my face.

I nodded.

'You should be up here in January with the wind howling across. Though mind you, it's beautiful even when you're freezing.'

She scanned a nearby valley with a hand shading her

eyes. 'The horses will be coming up from there at half-speed canter,' she said. 'They'll pass us here. Then we'll follow them up in the Land Rover to the schooling fences.'

I nodded again, not reckoning I'd know a half-speed canter from a slow waltz, but in fact when the row of horses appeared like black dots from the valley I soon saw what speed she meant. She watched with concentration through large binoculars as the dots became shapes and the shapes flying horses, lowering the glasses only when the string of ten went past, still one behind the other so that she had a clear view of each. She pursed her mouth but seemed otherwise not too displeased, and we were soon careering along in their wake, jerking to a stop over the brow of the hill and disembarking to find the horses circling with tossing heads and puffing breath.

'See those fences over there?' said Popsy, pointing to isolated timber and brushwood obstacles looking like refugees from a racecourse. 'Those are schooling fences. To teach the horses how to jump.' She peered into my face, and I nodded. 'The set on this side, they're hurdles. The far ones are . . . er . . . fences. For steeplechasers.' I nodded again. 'From the start of the schooling ground up to here there are six hurdles – and six fences – so you can give a horse a good work-out if you want to, but today I'm sending my lot over these top four only, as they're not fully fit.'

She left us abruptly and strode over to her excited

four-legged family, and Alessia with affection said, 'She's a good trainer. She can see when a horse isn't feeling right, even if there's nothing obviously wrong. When she walks into the yard all the horses instantly know she's there. You see all the heads come out, like a chorus.'

Popsy was despatching three of the horses towards the lower end of the schooling ground. 'Those three will come up over the hurdles,' Alessia said. 'Then those riders will change onto three more horses and start again.'

I was surprised. 'Don't all of the riders jump?' I asked.

'Most of them don't ride well enough to teach. Of those three doing the schooling, two are professional jockeys and the third is Popsy's best lad.'

Popsy stood beside us, binoculars ready, as the three horses came up over the hurdles. Except for a ratatatat at the hurdles themselves it was all very quiet, mostly, I realised, because there was no broadcast commentary as on television, but partly also because of the Doppler effect. The horses seemed to be making far more noise once they were past and going away.

Popsy muttered unintelligibly under her breath and Alessia said 'Borodino jumped well,' in the sort of encouraging voice which meant the other two hadn't.

We all waited while the three schooling riders changed horses and set off again down the incline to the starting point – and I felt Alessia suddenly stir beside me and take a bottomless breath – moving from there into a small, restless, aimless circle. Popsy glanced at her but said nothing, and after a while Alessia stopped her circling and said, 'Tomorrow . . .'

'Today, here and now,' Popsy interrupted firmly, and yelled to a certain Bob to come over to her at once.

Bob proved to be a middle-aged lad riding a chestnut which peeled off from the group and ambled over in what looked to me a sloppy walk.

'Hop off, will you?' Popsy said, and when Bob complied she said to Alessia, 'OK, just walk round a bit. You've no helmet so I don't want you breaking the speed limit, and besides old Paperbag here isn't as fit as the others.'

She made a cradle for Alessia's knee and threw her casually up into the saddle, where the lady jockey landed with all the thump of a feather. Her feet slid into the stirrups and her hands gathered the reins, and she looked down at me for a second as if bemused at the speed with which things were happening. Then as if impelled she wheeled her mount and trotted away, following the other three horses down the schooling ground.

'At last,' Popsy said. 'And I'd begun to think she never would.'

'She's a brave girl.'

'Oh yes.' She nodded. 'One of the best.'

'She had an appalling time.'

Popsy gave me five seconds of the direct green eyes.

'So I gather,' she said, 'from her refusal to talk about it. Let it all hang out, I told her, but she just shook her head and blinked a couple of tears away, so these past few days I've stopped trying to jolly her along, it was obviously doing no good.' She raised the binoculars to watch her three horses coming up over the hurdles and then swung them back down the hill, focusing on Alessia.

'Hands like silk,' Popsy said, 'God knows where she got it from, no one else in the family knows a spavin from a splint.'

'She'll be better now,' I said, smiling. 'But don't expect . . .'

'Instant full recovery?' she asked, as I paused.

I nodded. 'It's like a convalescence. Gradual.'

Popsy lowered the glasses and glanced at me briefly. 'She told me about your job. What you've done for her father. She says she feels safe with you.' She paused. 'I've never heard of a job like yours. I didn't know people like you existed.'

'There are quite a few of us . . . round the world.'

'What do you call yourself, if people ask?'

'Safety consultant, usually. Or insurance consultant. Depends how I feel.'

She smiled. 'They both sound dull and worthy.'

'Yes . . . er . . . that's the aim.'

We watched Alessia come back up the hill, cantering now, but slowly, and standing in the stirrups. Though of course I'd seen them do it, I'd never consciously noted before then that that was how jockeys rode, not sitting in the saddle but tipped right forward so their weight could be carried over the horse's shoulder, not on the lower spine. Alessia stopped beside Bob, who took hold of the horse's reins, and she dismounted by lifting her right leg forward over the horse's neck and dropping lightly, feet together, to the ground: a movement as graceful and springy as ballet.

A different dimension, I thought. The expertise of the professional. Amazing to the non-able, like seeing an artist drawing.

She patted the horse's neck, thanked Bob and came over to us, slight in shirt and jeans, smiling.

'Thanks,' she said to Popsy.

'Tomorrow?' Popsy said. 'With the string?'

Alessia nodded, rubbing the backs of her thighs. 'I'm as unfit as marshmallow.'

With calmness she watched the final trio of horses school, and then Popsy drove us again erratically back to her house, while the horses walked, to cool down.

Over coffee in the kitchen Alessia rewrote the lists of the music she listened to so often, a job she repeated out of generosity, and disliked.

'I could hum all the other tunes that I don't know the titles of,' she said. 'But frankly I don't want to hear them ever again.' She pushed the list across: Verdi, as before, and modern gentle songs like 'Yesterday' and 'Bring in the Clowns', more British and American in origin than Italian.

'I did think of something else,' she said hesitantly. 'I dreamed it, the night before last. You know how muddled things are in dreams . . . I was dreaming I was walking out to race. I had silks on, pink and green checks, and I know I was supposed to be going to ride, but I couldn't find the parade ring, and I asked people, but they didn't know, they were all catching trains or something and then someone said, "At least an hour to Viralto," and I woke up. I was sweating and my heart was thumping, but it hadn't been a nightmare, not a bad one anyway. Then I thought that I'd actually heard someone say "at least an hour to Viralto" at that minute, and I was afraid there was someone in the room. . . . It was horrible, really.' She put a hand on her forehead, as if the clamminess still stood there. 'But of course, when I woke up properly, there I was in Popsy's spare bedroom, perfectly safe. But my heart was still thumping.' She paused, then said, 'I think I must have heard one of them say that, when I was almost asleep.'

'This dream,' I asked slowly, considering, 'was it in English . . . or Italian?'

'Oh.' Her eyes widened. 'I was riding in England, Pink and green checks . . . one of Mike Noland's horses. I asked the way to the parade ring in English . . . they were English people, but that voice saying "at least an hour to Viralto", that was Italian.' She frowned. 'How awfully odd. I translated it into English in my mind, when I woke up.'

'Do you often go to Viralto?' I asked.

'No. I don't even know where it is.'

'I'll tell Pucinelli,' I said, and she nodded consent.

'He found the house you were kept in most of the time,' I said neutrally.

'Did he?' It troubled her. 'I . . . I don't want . . .'

'You don't want to hear about it?'

'No.'

'All right.'

She sighed with relief. 'You never make me face things. I'm very grateful. I feel . . . I still feel I could be pushed over a cliff . . . break down, I suppose . . . if too much is forced on me. And it's absolutely ridiculous – I didn't cry at all, not once, when I was . . . in that tent.'

'That's thoroughly normal, and you're doing fine,' I said. 'And you look fabulous on a horse.'

She laughed. 'God knows why it took me so long. But up on the Downs . . . such a gorgeous morning . . . I just felt . . .' She paused. 'I love horses, you know. Most of them, anyway. They're like friends . . . but they live internal lives, secret, with amazing instincts. They're telepathic . . . I suppose I'm boring you.'

'No,' I said truthfully, and thought it was horses, not I, who would lead her finally back to firm ground.

She came out to the car with me when I left and kissed me goodbye, cheek to cheek, as if I'd known her for years.

CHAPTER EIGHT

'Viralto?' Pucinelli said doubtfully. 'It's a village off one of the roads into the mountains. Very small. No roads in the village, just alleyways between houses. Are you sure she said Viralto?'

'Yes,' I said. 'Is it one of those hill-top villages with houses all stuck together with red tiled roofs and blinding white walls without windows? All on slopes, shut in and secret?'

'Like that, yes.'

'Would it be an hour's drive from Bologna? From the house where Alessia was kept?'

'I suppose so . . . If you knew the way. It is not on a main road.'

'And . . . er . . . would it have a bakery?'

After the faintest of pauses he said smoothly, 'My men will be up there at once, searching thoroughly. But Andrew, it would not be usual to take a kidnapped person there. In these villages everyone knows everyone. There is no room to hide a stranger.'

'Try Viralto on the kidnapper who told you about the first house,' I said.

'You can be sure I will,' he said happily. 'He has now confessed that he was one of the four in masks who abducted Alessia. He also sometimes sat in the house at night to guard her, but he says he never spoke to her, she was always asleep.' He paused. 'I have asked him several times every day for the name of the man in the drawings. He says the man's name is Giuseppe. He says that's what he called him and he doesn't know any other name for him. This may be true. Maybe not. I keep asking. Perhaps one day he will tell me different.'

'Enrico,' I said diffidently, 'you are an expert investigator. I hesitate to make a suggestion . . .'

A small laugh travelled by wire from Bologna. 'You don't hesitate very often.'

'Then . . . before you go to Viralto, shall we get Paolo Cenci to offer a reward for the recovery of any of the ransom money? Then you could take that promise and also the drawings of "Giuseppe" with you . . . perhaps?'

'I will also take photographs of our kidnappers and of Alessia,' he said. 'Signor Cenci will surely agree to the reward. But . . .' he paused, 'Viralto . . . was only a word in a dream.'

'A word which caused sweating and an accelerated heartbeat,' I said. 'It frightened her.'

'Did it? Hmm. Then don't worry, we'll sweep through the village like the sirocco.'

'Ask the children,' I said.

He laughed. 'Andrew Machiavelli Douglas . . . every child's mother would prevent us.'

'Pity.'

When we'd finished talking I telephoned to Paolo Cenci, who said 'willingly' to the reward, and then again to Pucinelli to confirm it.

'I am making a leaflet for photocopying,' he said. 'The reward offer and all the pictures. I'll call you if there are any results.'

'Call me anyway.'

'Yes, all right.'

He called me again on the following day, Friday, in the evening, while I happened to be on duty at the switchboard.

'I've been up in that damned village all day,' he said exhaustedly. 'Those people . . . they shut their doors and their faces and their minds.'

'Nothing?' I asked with disappointment.

'There's something,' he said, 'but I don't know what. The name of Viralto was a shock to the kidnapper who talks, but he swears it means nothing to him. He swears it on his dead mother's soul, but he sweats while he swears. He is lying.' He paused. 'But in Viralto . . . we found nothing. We went into the bakery. We threatened the baker, who also keeps the very small grocery store. There is nowhere near his bakehouse that Alessia could have been hidden, and we searched everywhere. He gave us permission. He said he had nothing to hide.

He said he would have known if Alessia had been brought to the village; he says he knows everything. He says she was never there.'

'Did you believe him?' I asked.

'I'm afraid so. We asked at every single house. We did even ask one or two children. We found nothing; we heard nothing. But . . .'

'But . . .?' I prompted.

'I have looked at a map,' he said, yawning. 'Viralto is up a side road which goes nowhere else. But if when one gets to the turn to Viralto one drives past it, straight on, that road goes on up into the mountains and although it is not a good road it crosses the Apennines altogether and then descends towards Firenze. Above Viralto there is a place which used to be a castle but is now a hotel. People go there to walk and enjoy the mountains. Perhaps the Signorina didn't hear enough . . . perhaps it was at least an hour to Viralto, and longer still to wherever they planned to go? Tomorrow,' he paused, sighing, 'tomorrow I am off duty. Tomorrow I expect I will however be on duty after all. I'll go up to the hotel and blow the sirocco through that.'

'Send some of your men,' I suggested.

After a definite pause he said levelly, 'I have given instructions that no one is to act again in this case in any way without my being there in person.'

'Ah.'

'So I will telephone again tomorrow, if you like.'

'Tomorrow I'll be here from four until midnight,' I said gratefully. 'After that, at home.'

In the morning, Saturday, Popsy telephoned while I was pottering round my flat trying to shut my eyes to undone chores.

'Something the matter?' I asked, interpreting the tone of her hello.

'Sort of. I want your help. Can you come?'

'This instant, or will tomorrow do? I have to be in the office, really, by four.'

'On Saturday afternoon?' she sounded surprised.

''Fraid so.'

She hesitated. 'Alessia didn't ride out with the string yesterday because of a headache.'

'Oh . . . and today?'

'Today she didn't feel like it. Look,' she said abruptly, 'I'd say the idea scared her, but how can it, you saw how she rode?' The faint exasperation in her voice came over clearly, accompanying the genuine concern. When I didn't answer immediately she demanded, 'Are you there?'

'Yes. Just thinking.' I paused. 'She wasn't scared of the horses or of riding, that's for sure. So perhaps she's scared . . . and I don't think that's the right word, but it'll do for now . . . of being closed in, of being unable to escape . . . of being in the string. Like a sort of claustrophobia, even though it's out in the open air. Perhaps that's why she wouldn't go in the string before, but felt all right on her own, up on the Downs.'

She thought it over, then said, 'Perhaps you're right. She certainly wasn't happy yesterday . . . she spent most of the day in her room, avoiding me.'

'Popsy . . . don't press her. She needs you very badly, but just as someone there . . . and undemanding. Tell her not to try to go out with the string until she can't bear not to. Say it's fine with you, you're glad to have her, she can do what she likes. Would that be OK? Could you say that? And I'll come down tomorrow morning.'

'Yes, yes, and yes,' she said sighing. 'I'm very fond of her. Come to lunch and wave your wand.'

Pucinelli telephoned late in the evening with the news: good, bad and inconclusive.

'The Signorina was right,' he said first, sounding satisfied. 'She was taken past Viralto, up to the hotel. We consulted the manager. He said he knew nothing, but we could search all the outbuildings, of which there are very many, most used for storage, but once living quarters for servants and carriage horses and farm animals. In one of the old animal feed lofts we found a tent!' He broke off for dramatic effect, and I congratulated him.

'It was folded,' he said. 'But when we opened it, it was the right size. Green canvas walls, grey floor-covering, just as she said. The floor of the loft itself was of wood, with hooks screwed into it, for the tent ropes.' He paused. 'In the house in the suburbs, we think they tied the tent ropes to the furniture.'

'Mm,' I said encouragingly.

'The loft is in a disused stable yard which is a small distance behind the hotel kitchens. It is perhaps possible she could smell baking . . . the hotel bakes its own bread.'

'Terrific,' I said.

'No, not terrific. No one there saw her. No one is saying anything. The stores of the hotel are kept in the outbuildings and there are great stocks of household items there, also cold stores for vegetables and meat, and a huge freezer room . . . vans make deliveries to these storerooms every day. I think the Signorina could have been taken to the hotel in a van, and no one would have paid much attention. There are so many outbuildings and courtyards at the back . . . garages, garden equipment stores, furniture stores for things not in use, barns full of useless objects which used to be in the old castle, ancient cooking stoves, old baths, enough rubbish to fill a town dump. You could hide for a month there. No one would find you.'

'No luck, then, with the pictures of the kidnapper?' I said.

'No. No one knew him. No one knew the two we have in jail. No one knew anything.' He sounded tired and discouraged.

'All the same,' I said, 'you do have the tent. And it's pretty certain that one of the kidnappers knew the hotel fairly well, because that loft doesn't sound like a place you'd find by accident.'

'No.' He paused. 'Unfortunately the Vistaclara has many people staying there and working there. One of the kidnappers might have stayed there, or worked there, in the past.'

'Vistaclara . . . is that the name of the hotel?' I asked.

'Yes. In the past there were horses in the stable yard, but the manager says they no longer have them, not enough people want to ride in the hills, they prefer now to play tennis.'

Horses, I thought vaguely.

'How long ago did they have horses?' I asked.

'Before the manager came. I could ask him, if you like. He said the stable yard was empty when he started, about five years ago. It has been empty ever since. Nothing has been stored there in case one day it would again be profitable to offer riding for holidays.'

'Pony trekking,' I said.

'What?'

'Riding over hills on ponies. Very popular in some parts of Britain.'

'Oh,' he said without enthusiasm. 'Anyway, there were grooms once and a riding instructor, but now they have a tennis pro instead . . . and he didn't know any of the kidnappers in our pictures.'

'It's a big hotel, then?' I said.

'Yes, quite. People go there in the summer, it is cooler than on the plains or on the coast. Just now there are thirty-eight on the staff besides the manager, and there are rooms for a hundred guests. Also a restaurant with views of the mountains.'

'Expensive?' I suggested.

'Not for the poor,' he said. 'But also not for princes. For people who have money, but not for the jet-set. A few of the guests live there always . . . old people, mostly.' He sighed. 'I asked a great many questions, as you see. No one at all, however long they had lived there, or been employed there, showed any interest in our pictures.'

We talked it over for a while longer but without reaching any conclusion except that he would try 'Vistaclara' on the talkative kidnapper the next day: and on that next day, Sunday, I drove down again to Lambourn.

Alessia had by that time been free for nearly two weeks and had progressed to pink varnish on her nails. A lifting of the spirits, I thought.

'Did you buy the varnish?' I asked.

'No . . . Popsy did.'

'Have you been shopping yet on your own?'

She shook her head. I made no comment, but she said, 'I suppose you think I ought to.'

'No. Just wondered.'

'Don't press me.'

'No.'

'You're as bad as Popsy.' She was looking at me almost with antagonism, something wholly new.

'I thought the varnish looked pretty,' I said equably.

She turned her head away with a frown, and I drank the coffee Popsy had poured before she'd walked out round her yard.

'Did Popsy ask you to come?' Alessia said sharply.

'She asked me to lunch, yes.'

'Did she complain that I've been acting like a cow?'

'No,' I said. 'Have you?'

'I don't know. I expect so. All I know is that I want to scream. To throw things. To hit someone.' She spoke indeed as if a head of steam was being held in tight by slightly precarious will-power.

'I'll drive you up to the Downs.'

'Why?'

'To scream. Kick the tyres. So on.'

She stood up restlessly, walked aimlessly round the kitchen and then went out of the door. I followed in a moment and found her standing halfway to the Land Rover, irresolute.

'Go on, then,' I said. 'Get in.' I made a questioning gesture to where Popsy stood, pointing to the Land Rover, and from the distance collected a nod.

The keys were in the ignition. I sat in the driver's seat and waited, and Alessia presently climbed in beside me.

'This is stupid,' she said.

I shook my head, started the engine, and drove the

way we'd gone three days earlier, up to the silence and the wide sky and the calling birds.

When I braked to a stop and switched off, Alessia said defensively, 'Now what? I can't just . . . scream.'

'If you care to walk off along there on your own and see if you want to, I'll wait here.'

Without looking at me directly she did exactly as I'd said, sliding down from the Land Rover and walking away. Her narrow figure diminished in the distance but stayed in sight, and after a fair while she came slowly back. She stopped with dry eyes at the open window beside me and said calmly, 'I can't scream. It's pointless.'

I got out of the Land Rover and stood on the grass near her. I said, 'What is it about riding in the string which makes you feel trapped?'

'Did Popsy say that?'

'No, she just said you didn't want to.'

She leaned against the front wing of the Land Rover, not looking at me.

'It's nonsense,' she said, 'I don't know why. On Friday I got dressed to go. I wanted to go . . . but I felt all churned up. Breathless. Worse than before my first big race . . . but the same sort of feeling. I went downstairs, and it got much worse. Stifling. So I told Popsy I had a headache . . . which was nearly true . . . and yesterday it was just the same. I didn't even go downstairs . . . I felt so wretched, but I just couldn't . . .'

I pondered, then said, 'Start from getting up. Think of riding clothes. Think of the horses. Think of riding through the streets. Think of everything separately, one by one, and then say at what thought you begin to feel . . . churned up.'

She looked at me dubiously, but blinked a few times as she went through the process and then shook her head. 'I don't feel churned now. I don't know what it is . . . I've thought of everything. *It's the boys.*' The last three words came out as if impelled; as if unpremeditated and from the depths.

'The boys?'

'The lads.'

'What about them?'

'Their eyes.' The same erupting force.

'If you rode at the back they wouldn't see you,' I said.

'I'd think of their eyes.'

I glanced at her very troubled face. She was taking me out of my depth, I thought. She needed professional help, not my amateur common sense.

'Why their eyes?' I said.

'Eyes . . .' she spoke loudly, as if the words themselves demanded violence. 'They watched me. I knew they did. When I was asleep. They came in and watched.'

She turned suddenly towards the Land Rover and did actually kick the tyre.

'They came in. I know they did. I hate . . . I hate . . . I can't bear . . . their eyes.'

I stretched out, put my arms round her and pulled

her against my chest. 'Alessia . . . Alessia . . . It doesn't matter. What if they did?'

'I feel . . . filthy . . . dirty.'

'A kind of rape?' I said.

'Yes.'

'But not . . .?'

She shook her head silently and conclusively.

'How do you know they came in?' I said.

'The zip,' she said. 'I told you I knew every stitch of the tent . . . I knew how many teeth in the zip. And some days, it would be open higher than others. They undid the zip . . . and came in . . . and fastened it at a different level . . . six or seven teeth higher, ten lower . . . I dreaded it.'

I stood holding her, not knowing what to say.

'I try not to care,' she said. 'But I dream . . .' She stopped for a while, then said, 'I dream about eyes.'

I rubbed one of my hands over her back, trying to comfort. 'Tell me what else,' I said. 'What else is unbearable?'

She stood quiet for so long with her nose against my chest that I thought there might be nothing, but finally, with a hard sort of coldness, she said, 'I wanted him to like me. I wanted to please him. I told Papa and Pucinelli that his voice was cold . . . but that was . . . at the beginning. When he came each time with the microphone, to make the tapes, I was . . . ingratiating.' She paused. 'I . . . loathe . . . myself. I am . . . hateful . . . and dreadfully . . . *unbearably* . . . ashamed.'

She stopped talking and simply stood there, and after a while I said, 'Very often people who are kidnapped grow to like their kidnappers. It isn't even unusual. It's as if a normal human being can't live without some sort of friendly contact. In ordinary criminal prisons, the prisoners and warders grow into definitely friendly relationships. When a lot of hostages are taken, some of them always make friends with one or more of the terrorists holding them. Hostages sometimes beg the police who are rescuing them not to harm their kidnappers. You mustn't, you shouldn't, blame yourself for trying to make the man with the microphone like you. It's normal. Usual. And . . . how did he respond?'

She swallowed. 'He called me . . . dear girl.'

'Dear girl,' I said myself, meaning it. 'Don't feel guilty. You are normal. Everyone tries to befriend their kidnappers to some extent, and it's better that they should.'

'Why?' The word was muffled, but passionate.

'Because antagonism begets antagonism. A kidnapped person who can make the kidnappers like her is much safer. They'll be less likely to harm her . . . and more careful, for her own sake, not to let her see their faces. They wouldn't want to kill someone they'd grown to like.'

She shivered.

'And as for coming in to see you when you were asleep . . . maybe they looked on you with friendship . . .

Maybe they wanted to be sure you were all right, as they couldn't see you when you were awake.'

I wasn't sure whether I believed that last bit myself, but it was at least possible: and the rest was all true.

'The lads are not the kidnappers,' I said.

'No, of course not.'

'Just other men.'

She nodded her smothered head.

'It's not the lads' eyes you dream about.'

'No.' She sighed deeply.

'Don't ride with the string until you feel OK about it. Popsy will arrange a horse for you up on the Downs.' I paused. 'Don't worry if tomorrow you still feel churned up. Knowing the reason for feelings doesn't necessarily stop them coming back.'

She stood quiet for a while and then disconnected herself slowly from my embrace, and without looking at my face said, 'I don't know where I'd be without you. In the nut-house, for sure.'

'One day,' I said mildly, 'I'll come to the Derby and cheer you home.'

She smiled and climbed into the Land Rover, but instead of pointing its nose homewards I drove on over the hill to the schooling ground.

'Where are you going?' she said.

'Nowhere. Just here.' I stopped the engine and put on the brakes. The flights of hurdles and fences lay neat and deserted on the grassy slope, and I made no move to get out of the car.

'I've been talking to Pucinelli,' I said.

'Oh.'

'He's found the second place, where you were kept those last few days.'

'Oh.' A small voice, but not panic-stricken.

'Does the Hotel Vistaclara mean anything to you?'

She frowned, thought, and shook her head.

'It's up in the mountains,' I said, 'above the place called Viralto, that you told me about. Pucinelli found the green tent there, folded, not set up, in a loft over a disused stable yard.'

'Stables?' She was surprised.

'Mm.'

She wrinkled her nose. 'There was no smell of horses.'

'They've been gone five years,' I said. 'But you said you could smell bread. The hotel makes its own, in the kitchens. The only thing is . . .' I paused, '. . . why just bread? Why not all cooking smells?'

She looked forward through the windscreen to the peaceful rolling terrain and breathed deeply of the sweet fresh air, and calmly, without strain or tears, explained.

'At night when I had eaten the meal one of them would come and tell me to put the dish and the bucket out through the zip. I could never hear them coming because of the music. I only knew they were there when they spoke.' She paused. 'Anyway, in the morning when I woke they would come and tell me to take the bucket in again . . . and at that point it would be clean and empty.' She stopped again. 'It was then that I could smell the bread, those last few days. Early . . . when the bucket was empty.' She fell silent and then turned her head to look at me, seeking my reaction.

'Pretty miserable for you,' I said.

'Mm.' She half smiled. 'It's incredible . . . but I got used to it. One wouldn't think one could. But it was one's own smell, after all . . . and after the first few days I hardly noticed it.' She paused again. 'Those first days I thought I'd go mad. Not just from anxiety and guilt and fury . . . but from boredom. Hour after hour of nothing but that damned music . . . no one to talk to, nothing to see . . . I tried exercises, but day after day I grew less fit and more dopey, and after maybe two or three weeks I just stopped. The days seemed to run into each other, then. I just lay on the foam mattress and let the music wash in and out, and I thought about things that had happened in my life, but they seemed far away and hardly real. Reality was the bucket and pasta and a polystyrene cup of water twice a day . . . and hoping that the man with the microphone would think I was behaving well . . . and like me.'

'Mm,' I said. 'He liked you.'

'Why do you think so?' she asked, and I saw that curiously she seemed glad at the idea, that she still wanted her kidnapper to approve of her, even though she was free.

'I think,' I said, 'that if you and he had felt hate for

each other he wouldn't have risked the second ransom. He would have been very much inclined to cut his losses. I'd guess he couldn't face the thought of killing you . . . because he liked you.' I saw the deep smile in her eyes and decided to straighten things up in her perspective. No good would come of her falling in love with her captor in fantasy or in retrospect. 'Mind you,' I said, 'he gave your father an appalling time and stole nearly a million pounds from your family. We may thank God he liked you, but it doesn't make him an angel.'

'Oh . . .' She made a frustrated, very Italian gesture with her hands. 'Why are you always so . . . so sensible?'

'Scottish ancestors,' I said. 'The dour sort, not the firebrands. They seem to take over and spoil the fun when the quarter of me that's Spanish aches for flamenco.'

She put her head on one side, half laughing. 'That's the most I've ever heard you say about yourself.'

'Stick around,' I said.

'I don't suppose you'll believe it,' she said, sighing deeply and stretching her limbs to relax them, 'but I am after all beginning to feel fairly sane.'

CHAPTER NINE

July crept out in a drizzle and August swept in with a storm in a week of little activity in the London office but a good deal in Italy.

Pucinelli telephoned twice to report no progress and a third time, ecstatically, to say that Cenci's offer of a reward had borne results. The offer, along with the kidnappers' pictures, had been posted in every possible public place throughout Bologna and the whole province around; and an anonymous woman had telephoned to Paolo Cenci himself to say she knew where a part of the ransom could be found.

'Signor Cenci said she sounded spiteful. A woman scorned. She told him it would serve "him" right to lose his money. She wouldn't say who "he" was. In any case, tomorrow Signor Cenci and I go to where she says the money can be found, and if she is right, Signor Cenci will post a reward to her. The address to send the reward is a small hotel, not high class. Perhaps we will be able to find the woman and question her.'

On the following evening he sounded more moderately elated.

'It is true we found some of the money,' he said. 'But unfortunately not very much, when you think of the whole amount.'

'How much?' I asked.

'Fifty million lire.'

'That's . . . er . . .' I did rapid sums, 'nearly twenty-five thousand pounds. Hm . . . The loot of a gang member, not a principal, wouldn't you say?'

'I agree.'

'Where did you find it?' I asked.

'In a luggage locker at the railway station. The woman told Signor Cenci the number of the locker, but we had no key. We had a specialist to open the lock for us.'

'So whoever left the money thinks it's still there?'

'Yes. It is indeed still there, but we have had the lock altered. If anyone tries to open it, he will have to ask for another key. Then we catch him. We've set a good trap. The money is in a soft travel bag, with a zip. The numbers on the notes match the photographs. There is no doubt it is part of the ransom. Signor Cenci has sent a reward of five million lire and we will try to catch the woman when she collects it. He is disappointed, though, as I am, that we didn't find more.'

'Better than nothing,' I said. 'Tell me how you get on.'

There were two usual ways to deal with 'hot' money,

of which the simplest was to park the loot somewhere safe until the fiercest phase of investigation was over. Crooks estimated the safety margin variously from a month to several years, and were then fairly careful to spend the money far from home, usually on something which could instantly be resold.

The second, more sophisticated method, most used for large amounts, was to sell the hot money to a sort of fence, a professional who would buy it for about two-thirds of its face value, making his profit by floating it in batches onto the unsuspecting public via the operators of casinos, markets, fair-grounds, racecourses or anywhere else where large amounts of cash changed hands quickly. By the time the hot money percolated back to far-flung banks the source of it couldn't be traced.

Some of Paolo Cenci's million quid could have been lopped by a third in such laundering, some could have been split between an unknown number of gang members, and some could have been spent in advance on outgoings, such as renting the suburban house. The expenses of a successful kidnapping were high, the ransom never wholly profit. All the same, despite its risks, it was the fastest way to a fortune yet devised, and in Italy particularly the chances of being detected and caught were approximately five per cent. In a country where no woman could walk in the streets of Rome with a handbag over her arm for fear of having it razored off by thieves on motorcycles, kidnapping was regarded as a fact of life, like ulcers.

Pucinelli telephoned two days later in a good mood to report that the woman who had collected the reward had been followed home without challenge and had proved to be the wife of a man who had served two terms in jail for raids on liquor stores. Neighbours said the man was known for chasing girls, his wife hot-bloodedly jealous. Pucinelli thought that an arrest and search of the man on suspicion would present no problems, and the next evening reported that the search had revealed the luggage locker ticket in the man's wallet. The man, identified as Giovanni Santo, was now in a cell and pouring out information like lava from a volcano.

'He is stupid,' Pucinelli said disparagingly. 'We've told him he will spend his whole life in jail if he doesn't co-operate, and he's shit scared. He has told us the names of all the kidnappers. There were seven of them altogether. Two we already have, of course, and now Santo. At this minute we have men picking up three others.'

'And Giuseppe?' I asked, as he stopped.

'Giuseppe,' he said reluctantly 'is not one of them. Giuseppe is the seventh. He was the leader. He recruited the others, who were all criminals before. Santo doesn't know Giuseppe's real name, nor where he came from, nor where he's gone. I'm afraid in this instance Santo speaks the truth.'

'You've done marvels,' I said.

He coughed modestly. 'I've been lucky. And Andrew . . . between us privately I will admit it . . . it has been most helpful to talk to you. It clears things in my mind to tell them to you. Very odd.'

'Carry right on,' I said.

'Yes. It's a pleasure,' he said; and he telephoned three days later to say they now had all six gang members in custody and had recovered a further hundred million lire of Cenci's money.

'We have also taken recordings of all six men and had voice prints made and analysed, but none of them is the voice on the tapes. And none of them is the man you saw, of whom we have the picture.'

'Giuseppe,' I said. 'On the tapes.'

'Yes,' he agreed gloomily. 'None of them knew him before. He recruited one as a stranger in a bar, and that one recruited the other five. We will convict the six, there's no doubt, but it's hollow without Giuseppe.'

'Mm.' I hesitated. 'Enrico, isn't it true that some of the students who joined the Red Brigades in their hot-headed youth grew out of it and became ordinary blameless citizens?'

'I've heard so, but of course they keep the past secret.'

'Well . . . it just struck me a day or two ago that Giuseppe might have learned the techniques of kidnapping from the Red Brigades, when he was a student, perhaps, or even as a member.'

Pucinelli said doubtfully, 'Your Identikit pictures don't match anyone with a criminal record.'

'I just wondered if it might be worthwhile to show

those pictures to ex-students of about the same age, say twenty-five to forty, at perhaps some sort of students' reunion? It's a faint chance, anyway.'

'I'll try,' he said. 'But the Red Brigades, as I'm sure you know, are organised in small cells. People in one cell can't identify people in other cells because they never meet them.'

'I know it's a long shot and involves a lot of probably fruitless work,' I agreed.

'I'll think about it.'

'OK.'

'All the universities are closed for summer vacations.'

'So they are,' I said. 'But in the autumn . . .'

'I will think about it,' he said again. 'Goodnight, friend. Sleep well.'

Alessia heard from her father about the recovery of some of the ransom and from me of the capture of six of the kidnappers.

'Oh,' she said blankly.

'Your man with the microphone isn't among them.'

'Oh.' She looked at me guiltily, hearing, as I did, the faint relief in her voice. We were sitting in Popsy's minute tree-shaded garden where four lounging chairs squeezed onto a square of grass and low stone surrounding walls failed to obscure views of stableyard on three sides. We were drinking iced coffee in the heat wave which had followed the storms, clinking the cubes and being watched politely by equine heads peering in rows over half-doors.

I had invited myself down on my day off, a move neither Alessia nor Popsy had objected to, and I'd found Popsy alone when I arrived, as usual out in her yard.

'Hello,' she said, as I drew up. 'Sorry about the wet.' She was standing in green gumboots, hose in hand, watering the lower hind leg of a large chestnut horse. Bob held its head. Its eyes blinked at me as if bored. The water ran in a stream across the yard to a drain. 'It's got a leg,' Popsy said, as if that explained things.

I stifled a desire to say that as far as I could see it had four.

'Alessia walked along to the shops,' she said. 'She won't be long.' She squelched away and turned off a tap, flinging the hose in loose coils beside it. 'That'll do for now, Bob,' she said. 'Get Jamie to roll up that hose.' She dried her hands on the seat of her trousers and gave me a bright blaze from the green eyes.

'She rides, you know,' she said as Bob led the watered horse off to an empty box, 'but only up on the Downs. She goes up and down with me in the Land Rover. We don't discuss it. It's routine.'

'How is she otherwise?'

'Much happier, I'd say.' She grinned hugely and clapped me lightly on the shoulder. 'Don't know how anyone so cold can bring someone else to life.'

'I'm not cold,' I protested.

'No?' She considered me quizzically. 'There's a

feeling of iron about you. Like a rod. You don't smile much. You're not intimidating . . . but I'm sure you could be, if you tried.'

I shook my head.

'Do you ever get drunk?' she said.

'Not often.'

'Never, more like.' She waved a hand towards the kitchen. 'Like a drink? It's so bloody hot.'

We went into a cool interior with her shaking off her gumboots on the doorstep, and she brought white wine from the refrigerator in the kitchen in fawn socks.

'I'll bet for instance,' she said, pouring, 'that you never get helpless giggles or sing vulgar songs or generally make an ass of yourself.'

'Often.'

She gave me an 'oh yeah' look and settled her large self comfortably onto a kitchen chair, putting her heels up on the table.

'Well, sometimes,' I said.

She drank some wine cheerfully. 'What makes you giggle, then?' she asked.

'Oh . . . one time I was with an Italian family during a kidnap and they all behaved like a comic soap opera at the top of their voices, and it was painful. I had to go upstairs sometimes to stop myself laughing . . . awful giggles over and over, when really the whole thing was deadly dangerous. I had terrible trouble. My face was aching with the effort of keeping it straight.'

'Like wanting to explode in church,' Popsy said, nodding.

'Just like that.'

We sipped the cold wine and regarded each other with friendliness, and in a moment or two Alessia appeared with a bag of groceries and a welcoming smile. There was colour in her cheeks at last, and a sort of rebirth taking place of the girl she must have been before. I could see a great difference in even the carriage of her head; self respect returning to straighten the spine.

I got up at the sight of her and kissed her cheek in greeting and she put the groceries on the table and gave me a positive hug.

'Hi,' she said. 'Please note, I've been shopping. That's the third time. We are now back in business . . . no nerves, not to speak of.'

'Terrific.'

She poured herself some wine and the three of us amicably ate lunch, and it was afterwards, when Popsy had gone off to her office to do paperwork, that I told Alessia in the garden about the new arrests.

'Do you think they'll catch him . . . the man with the microphone?' she asked.

'He called himself Giuseppe,' I said, 'though that's almost certainly not his name. The six kidnappers knew him just as Giuseppe, and none of them knows anything else. I think he's cool and intelligent, and I'm afraid Pucinelli won't find him, or the bulk of your ransom.'

She was quiet for a while and then said, 'Poor Papa. Poor all of us. I love the house on Mikonos . . . so full of brilliant light, right by the sapphire sea . . . Papa says the money so far recovered won't be enough to save it. He says he keeps postponing putting it up for sale, just hoping . . . but it's not just its value, there's the upkeep, and the fares there two or three times a year. It was always a luxury, even before.' She paused. 'Part of my childhood. Part of my life.'

'Giuseppe took it,' I said.

She stirred slightly and finally nodded. 'Yes, you are right.'

We drank the iced coffee. Time passed tranquilly.

'I thought of going to the races next week,' she said. 'To Brighton. Mike Noland runs a lot of horses there, because he used to train in Sussex, and many of his owners still live there. I may as well go and talk to them . . . show them I'm still alive.'

'If I went,' I said, 'would I be in your way?'

She smiled at the still-watching horses. 'No, you wouldn't.'

'Which day?'

'Wednesday.'

I thought of switchboard schedules. 'I'll fix it,' I said.

Gerry Clayton having agreed with a thoroughly false martyred expression to sit in for me from four to midnight, I drove early to Lambourn to collect Alessia, pausing only for coffee and encouragement from Popsy before setting off on the three-hour trek to Brighton.

'I could have got a lift,' Alessia said. 'You didn't have to come all this huge way round.'

'Sure,' I said.

She sighed, but not apparently with regret. 'Half a dozen trainers or jockeys will be driving from here to Brighton.'

'Bully for them.'

'So I could always get a lift back.'

I looked at her sideways. 'I'll drive you unless you definitely prefer not.'

She didn't answer; just smiled. We drove to Brighton and talked of many things for which there had never been peace enough before; of likes and dislikes, places, books, people; cabbages and kings.

It was the first time, I thought, that I had seen her in a skirt: if one excepted, of course, the dress I had pulled over her unconscious head. A vision of her lean nakedness rose unbidden; an agreeable memory, to be honest. For Brighton she had covered the basics with a neat pale-coffee-coloured dress, and wore big gold earrings under the short curls.

Her reappearance on a racecourse was greeted with a warmth that almost overwhelmed her, with everyone who saw her seemingly intent on hugging her until her bones cracked. She introduced me vaguely many times but no one took any notice. The eyes were only for her, devouring her with curiosity, but also with love.

'Alessia! How super!'

'Alessia! Fantastic!'

'Alessia! Marvellous . . . smashing . . . delirious . . . terrific . . .'

She need not have doubted that Mike Noland's owners would notice her re-emergence. At least four widely-grinning couples assured her that as soon as she was fit they would be thrilled to have her back in their saddles. Mike Noland himself, big and fifty, told her it was time to leave Popsy's jumpers and come to ride work on the two-year-olds; and passing bright-silked jockeys, I was interested to see, greeted her with genuine pleasure under more casual greetings.

'Hello Alessia, how's it going?'

'How ya doing?'

'Well done; glad you're back.'

'Get your boots on, Cenci.'

Their direct camaraderie meant a lot to her. I could see the faint apprehension of the outward journey vanishing minute by minute, replaced by the confidence of being at home. She kept me beside her all the same, glancing at me frequently to check I was still there and never moving a step without being sure I followed. One might have thought of it as courtesy except for what had gone before.

I saw little enough of the races themselves, and nor did she, from the press of people wanting to talk; and the afternoon was cut short, as far as I was concerned, by a message broadcast over the loudspeakers after the fourth event.

'Would Mr Andrew Douglas please go to the Clerk of the Course's office. Mr Andrew Douglas, please, go to the Clerk of the Course's office.'

Alessia, looking worried, said she'd show me where the office was, and told me that messages of that sort nearly always meant bad news. 'I hope it's not . . . Papa,' she said. 'Popsy would ask for you . . . so as not to frighten me.'

We went quickly to the Clerk's office, brushing away the non-stop clutching greetings with quick smiles. Alessia's anxiety deepened with every step, but when we arrived at the office the Clerk of the Course himself put her fears to rest.

'I'm so sorry, Mr Douglas,' he said to me, 'but we have a distressing message for you. Please would you ring this number . . .?' He handed me a slip of paper. 'Your sister has had a bad accident. I'm so sorry.'

Alessia said 'Oh!' faintly, as if not sure whether to be glad or horrified, and I put a hand comfortingly on her arm.

'There's a more private telephone just over there,' the Clerk said, pointing to a small alcove at the rear. 'Do use it. How splendid, Miss Cenci, to see you back.'

She nodded vaguely and followed me across the room. 'I'm so sorry . . .' she said.

I shook my head. I had no sister. The number on the

slip of paper was that of the office. I dialled the number and was answered by Gerry Clayton.

'It's Andrew,' I said.

'Thank God. I had to tell all sorts of lies before they'd put out a call for you.'

'What happened?' I said with an amount of agitation appropriate to the circumstances.

He paused, then said, 'Can you be overheard?'

'Yes.'

The Clerk himself was listening with half an ear and Alessia with both. Two or three other people were looking my way.

'Right. I won't expect comments. There's been a boy kidnapped from the beach at West Wittering. That's about an hour's drive along the coast from Brighton, I'd guess. Go over there pronto and talk to the mother, will you?'

'Where is she?' I said.

'In the Breakwater Hotel, Beach Road, climbing the walls. I promised her we'd have someone with her in two hours, and to hang on. She's incoherent, most unhelpful. We had a telephone call from Hoppy at Lloyd's, the father got in touch with his insurers and got passed along a chain to us. The father's had instructions to stay by his home telephone. Tony Vine's on his way to him now. Can you take down the number?'

'Yes, hang on.' I fumbled for pen and paper. 'Fire away.'

He read out the father's number. 'His name is John

Nerrity.' He spelled it. 'The child's name is Dominic. Mother's Miranda. Mother and son were alone in the hotel on holiday, father busy at home. Got all that?'

'Yes.'

'Get her to agree to the police.'

'Yes.'

'Hear from you later? Sorry about your day at the races.'

'I'll go at once,' I said.

'Break a leg.'

I thanked the Clerk of the Course and left his office with Alessia still looking distressed on my behalf.

'I'll have to go,' I said apologetically. 'Can you possibly get a lift back to Lambourn? With Mike Noland, perhaps?'

Even though she had herself earlier suggested it, she looked appalled at the idea and vigorously shook her head. Panic stood quite clear in her eyes.

'No,' she said. 'Can't I come with you? Please . . . I won't be a nuisance. I promise. I could help . . . with your sister.'

'You're never a nuisance, but I can't take you.' I looked down at her beseeching face, at the insecurity still so close to the surface. 'Come out to the car with me, away from these crowds, and I'll explain.'

We walked through the gates and along to the car park, and I said, 'I haven't any sisters. There was no crash. I have to go on a job . . . a child's been kidnapped, and I have to go to his mother . . . so dearest Alessia, we must find Mike Noland. You'll be safe with him. You know him well.'

She was horrified and apologetic and also shaking. 'Couldn't I comfort the mother?' she said. 'I could tell her . . . her child will come back . . . as I did?'

I hesitated, knowing the suggestion stemmed from her not wanting to go home with Mike Noland but also thinking that perhaps it made sense. Perhaps Alessia would indeed be good for Miranda Nerrity.

I looked at my watch. 'Mrs Nerrity's expecting me,' I said indecisively, and she interrupted sharply, 'Who? Who did you say?'

'Nerrity. Miranda Nerrity. But . . .'

Her mouth had literally fallen open. 'But I know her,' she said. 'Or at least, I've met her . . . Her husband is John Nerrity, isn't he?'

I nodded, nonplussed.

'Their horse won the Derby,' Alessia said.

I lifted my head.

Horses.

So many horses.

'What is it?' Alessia said. 'Why do you look so . . . bleak?'

'Right,' I said, not directly answering. 'Get in the car. I'd be glad for you to come, if you really mean it. But there's a good chance we won't be going back to Lambourn tonight. Would you mind that?'

For answer she slid into the front passenger seat and

closed the door, and I walked round to climb in beside her.

As I started the engine and drove out of the gate she said, 'The Nerritys' horse won the Derby last year. Ordinand. Don't you remember?'

'Um . . .' No, actually, I didn't.

'It wasn't one of the really greats,' she said assessingly, 'or at least no one thought so. He was an outsider. Thirty-three to one. But he's been winning this year quite well.' She stopped. 'I can't bear to think of that child.'

'His name's Dominic,' I said. 'Haul the map out of the glove compartment and find the fastest route to Chichester.'

She reached for the map. 'How old is he?'

'Don't know.'

We sped westwards through Sussex in the golden afternoon and came eventually to the Breakwater Hotel, right on the pebbly beach at West Wittering.

'Look,' I said, putting on brakes and pulling off my tie. 'Behave like a holidaymaker. Walk into the hotel slowly. Smile. Talk to me. Don't seem worried. OK?'

She looked at me with puzzlement turning to comprehension. 'Do you think . . . someone's watching?'

'Someone usually is,' I said astringently. 'Always take it for granted that someone is. Kidnappers post watchers to make sure the police don't arrive in huge numbers.'

'Oh.'

'So we're on holiday.'

'Yes,' she said.

'Let's go in.'

We climbed, stretching, out of the car, and Alessia wandered a few steps away from the hotel to look out to the English Channel, shading her eyes and speaking to me over her shoulder. 'I'm going in for a swim.'

I put my arm round her shoulders and stood beside her for a few seconds, then with me saying teasingly 'Mind the jellyfish' we walked through the hotel's glass entrance doors into a wide armchair-scattered lounge. A few people sat around drinking tea, and a girl in a black dress was moving to and fro behind a polished brown counter labelled 'Reception'.

'Hello,' I said, smiling. 'We think a friend of ours is staying here. A Mrs Nerrity?'

'And Dominic,' Alessia said.

'That's right,' the girl said calmly. She looked at a guest list. 'Room sixty-three . . . but they're probably still on the beach. Lovely day, isn't it?'

'Gorgeous,' Alessia agreed.

'Could you give their room a ring?' I asked. 'Just in case.'

The girl obligingly turned to the switchboard and was surprised at receiving an answer. 'Pick up the 'phone,' she said, pointing to a handset on the counter, and I lifted the receiver with an appropriate smile.

'Miranda?' I said. 'This is Andrew Douglas.'

'Where are you?' a small voice said tearfully.

'Downstairs, here in the hotel.'

'Oh . . . Come up . . . I can't bear . . .'

'On my way,' I said.

The girl gave us directions which we followed to a room with twin beds, private bathroom, view of the sea. Miranda Nerrity opened her door to us with swollen eyes and a clutched, soaking handkerchief and said between gulps, 'They said . . . the man in London said . . . you would get Dominic back . . . he promised me . . . Andrew Douglas will get him back . . . he always does, he said . . . don't worry . . . but how can I not worry? Oh my God . . . my baby . . . Get him back for me. Get him back.'

'Yes,' I said gently. 'Come and sit down.' I put my arm round her shoulders this time, not Alessia's, and guided her over to one of the armchairs. 'Tell us what happened. Then we'll make a plan to get him back.'

Miranda took a very small grip on things, recognising Alessia with surprise and pointing to a piece of paper which lay on one of the beds.

'A little girl gave it to me,' she said, the tears rolling. 'She said a man had asked her. Oh dear . . . oh dear . . .'

'How old was the little girl?' I asked.

'What? Oh . . . eight . . . something like that . . . I don't know.'

Alessia knelt beside Miranda to comfort her, her own face pale again and taut with strain, and I picked up the sheet of paper and unfolded it, and read its brutal block-lettered message.

WE'VE TAKEN YOUR KID. GIVE YOUR OLD MAN A BELL. TELL HIM TO GO HOME. WE'LL TELL YOUR HUBBY WHAT WE WANT. DON'T GO SQUAWKING AROUND. TELL NO ONE AT ALL, SEE. IF YOU WANT TO SEE YOUR KID AGAIN DON'T GO TO THE POLICE. WE'LL TIE A PLASTIC BAG OVER HIS HEAD IF YOU GET THE POLICE. SAVVY?

I lowered the page. 'How old is Dominic?' I asked.

'Three and a half,' Miranda said.

CHAPTER TEN

Miranda, twenty-six, had long blonde hair falling from a centre parting and on other occasions might have been pretty. She still wore a bathing suit with a towelling robe over, and there was still sand on her legs from the beach. Her eyes were glazed behind the puffed eyelids as if too much devastated emotion had put a film over them to repel reality, and she made vague pointless movements with her hands as if total inactivity was impossible.

Out of habit I carried with me a flat container like a cigarette case, which contained among other things a small collection of pills. I took out the case, opened it, and sorted out a strip of white tablets in foil.

'Take one of these,' I said, fetching water in a toothmug and sliding a pill from its wrapper.

Miranda simply swallowed as instructed. It was Alessia who said, 'What are you giving her?'

'Tranquilliser.'

'Do you carry those round with you always?' she asked incredulously.

'Mostly,' I nodded. 'Tranquillisers, sleeping pills, aspirins, things for heart attacks. First aid, that all.'

Miranda drank all the water.

'Do they have room service in this hotel?' I asked.

'What?' she said vaguely. 'Yes, I suppose so . . . They'll be bringing Dominic's supper soon . . .' The idea of it reduced her to fresh deep sobs, and Alessia put her arm round her and looked shattered.

I telephoned to room service for tea, strong, as soon as possible, for three. Biscuits? Certainly biscuits. Coming right away, they said: and with very little delay the tray arrived, with me meeting the maid at the door and thanking her for her trouble.

'Mrs Nerrity, drink this,' I said, putting down the tray and pouring tea for her. 'And eat the biscuits.' I poured another cup for Alessia. 'You too,' I said.

The girls each drank and ate like automatons, and slowly in Miranda the combined simple remedies of tranquilliser, caffeine and carbohydrate took the worst edge off the pain so that she could bear to describe what happened.

'We were on the sand . . . with his bucket and spade . . . making a sandcastle. He loves making sandcastles . . .' She stopped and swallowed, tears trickling down her cheeks. 'A lot of the sand was wet, and I'd left our things up on the shingle . . . towels, a beach chair, our lunch box, packed by the hotel, Dominic's toys . . . It was a lovely hot day, not windy like usual . . . I went up to sit on the chair . . . I was watching him all the time, he was only thirty yards away . . . less, less . . . squatting, playing with his bucket and spade, patting the sandcastle . . . I was watching him all the time, I really was.' Her voice tapered off into a wail, the dreadful searing guilt sounding jagged and raw.

'Were there a lot of people on the beach?' I asked.

'Yes, yes there were . . . it was so warm . . . But I was watching him, I could see him all the time . . .'

'And what happened?' I said.

'It was the boat . . .'

'What boat?'

'The boat on fire. I was watching it. Everyone was watching it. And then . . . when I looked back . . . he wasn't there. I wasn't scared. It was less than a minute . . . I thought he'd be going over to look at the boat . . . I was looking for him . . . and then the little girl gave me the note . . . and I read it . . .'

The awfulness of that moment swept over her again like a tidal wave. The cup and saucer rattled and Alessia took them from her.

'I shouted for him everywhere . . . I ran up and down . . . I couldn't believe it . . . I couldn't . . . I'd seen him such a short time ago, just a minute . . . and then I came up here . . . I don't know how I got up here . . . I telephoned John . . . and I've left all our things . . . on the beach.'

'When is high tide?' I said.

She looked at me vaguely. 'This morning . . . The tide had just gone out . . . the sand was all wet . . .'

'And the boat? Where was the boat?'

'On the sand.'

'What sort of boat?' I asked.

She looked bewildered. 'A sailing dinghy. What does it matter? There are millions of sailing dinghies round here.'

But millions of sailing dinghies didn't go on fire at the exact moment that a small child was kidnapped. A highly untrustworthy coincidence of timing.

'Both of you drink more tea,' I said. 'I'll go down and fetch the things from the beach. Then I'll ring Mr Nerrity . . .'

'No,' Miranda interrupted compulsively. 'Don't. Don't.'

'But we must.'

'He's so angry,' she said piteously. 'He's . . . livid. He says it's my fault . . . He's so angry . . . you don't know what he's like . . . I don't want to talk to him . . . I can't.'

'Well,' I said. 'I'll telephone from another place. Not this room. I'll be as quick as I can. Will you both be all right?'

Alessia nodded, although she was herself shaking, and I went downstairs and found a public telephone tucked into a private corner of the entrance hall.

Tony Vine answered from John Nerrity's number.

'Are you alone?' I asked.

'No. Are you?'

'Yes. What's the score?'

'The pinchers have told him he'll get his boy safe . . . on conditions.'

'Such as?'

'Five million.'

'For God's sake,' I said, 'has he got five million?' The Breakwater Hotel, nice enough, wasn't a millionaire's playground.

'He's got a horse,' Tony said baldly.

A horse.

Ordinand, winner of the Derby.

'Ordinand?' I said.

'No slouch, are you? Yeah, Ordinand. The pinchers want him to sell it at once.'

'How did they tell him?' I asked.

'On the telephone. No tap, of course, at that point. He says it was a rough voice full of slang. Aggressive. A lot of threats.'

I told Tony about the block-lettered note. 'Same level of language?'

'Yeah.' Tony's occasional restraint in the matter of eff this and eff that was always a source of wonder, but in fact he seldom let rip in front of clients. 'Mr Nerrity's chief, not to say sole, asset, as I understand it, is the horse. He is . . . er . . .'

'Spitting mad?' I suggested.

'Yeah.'

I half smiled. 'Mrs Nerrity is faintly scared of him.'

'Not in the least surprising.'

I told Tony how the kidnap had been worked and

said I thought the police ought to investigate the dinghy very fast.

'Have you told the local fuzz anything yet?'

'No. Miranda will take a bit of persuading. I'll do it next. What have you told them from your end?'

'Nothing so far. I tell Mr Nerrity we can't help him without the police, but you know what it's like.'

'Mm. I'll call you again, shortly.'

'Yeah.' He put his receiver down and I strolled out of the hotel and rolled my trouser legs up to the knees on the edge of the shingle, sliding down the banks of pebbles in great strides towards the sand. Once there I took off shoes and socks and ambled along carrying them, enjoying the evening sun.

There were a few breakwaters at intervals along the beach, black fingers stretching stumpily seawards, rotten in places and overgrown with molluscs and sea-weed. Miranda's chair, towels and paraphernalia were alone on the shingle, most other people having packed up for the day; and not far away there was still a red plastic bucket and a blue plastic spade on the ground beside a half-trampled sandcastle. The British seaside public, I reflected, were still remarkably honest.

The burnt remains of the dinghy were the focal point for the few people still on the sand, the returning tide already swirling an inch deep around the hull. I walked over there as if drawn like everyone else, and took the closest possible look, paddling, like others, to see inside the shell.

The boat had been fibreglass and had melted as it burned. There were no discernible registration numbers on what was left of the exterior, and although the mast, which was aluminium, had survived the blaze and still pointed heavenward like an exclamation mark, the sail, which would have born identification, lay in ashes round its foot. Something in the scorched mess might tell a tale – but the tide was inexorable.

'Shouldn't we try to haul it up to the shingle?' I suggested to a man paddling like myself.

He shrugged. 'Not our business.'

'Has anyone told the police?' I said.

He shrugged again. 'Search me.'

I paddled round to the other side of the remains and tried another more responsible-looking citizen but he too shook his head and muttered about being late already, and it was two fourteen-sized boys, overhearing, who said they would give me a hand, if I liked.

They were strong and cheerful. They lifted, strained, staggered willingly. The keel slid up the sand leaving a deep single track and between us we manhandled it up the shingle to where the boys said the tide wouldn't reach it to whisk it away.

'Thanks,' I said.

They beamed. We all stood hands on hips admiring the result of our labours and then they too said they had to be off home to supper. They loped away, vaulting a breakwater, and I collected the bucket and spade and all Miranda's belongings and carried them up to her room.

Neither she nor Alessia was in good shape, and Alessia, if anything, seemed the more relieved at my return. I gave her a reassuring hug, and to Miranda I said, 'We're going to have to get the police.'

'No.' She was terrified. 'No . . . no . . .'

'Mm.' I nodded. 'Believe me, it's best. The people who've taken Dominic don't want to kill him, they want to sell him back to you safe and sound. Hold on to that. The police will be very helpful and we can arrange things so that the kidnappers won't know we've told them. I'll do that. The police will want to know what Dominic was wearing on the beach, and if you have a photograph, that would be great.'

She wavered helplessly. 'John said . . . keep quiet, I'd done enough damage . . .'

I picked up the telephone casually and got through again to her husband's number. Tony again answered.

'Andrew,' I said.

'Oh.' His voice lost its tension; he'd been expecting the kidnappers.

'Mrs Nerrity will agree to informing the police on her husband's say-so.'

'Go ahead then. He understands we can't act for him without. He . . . er . . . doesn't want us to leave him. He's just this minute decided, when he heard the 'phone ring.'

'Good. Hang on . . .' I turned to Miranda. 'Your husband says we can tell the police. Do you want to talk to him?'

She shook her head violently. 'OK.' I said to Tony. 'Let's get started and I'll call you later.'

'What was the kid wearing?' he asked.

I repeated the question to Miranda and between new sobs she said red bathing trunks. Tiny towelling trunks. No shoes, no shirt . . . it had been hot.

Tony grunted and rang off, and as unhurriedly as I could I asked Miranda to put some clothes on and come out driving with me in my car. Questioning, hesitant and fearful she nevertheless did what was needed, and presently, having walked out of the hotel in scarf and sunglasses between Alessia and myself, sat with Alessia in the rear seats as I drove all three of us in the direction of Chichester.

Checks on our tail and an unnecessary detour showed no one following, and with one pause to ask directions I stopped the car near the main police station but out of sight of it, round a corner. Inside the station I asked for the senior officers on duty, and presently explained to a chief inspector and a CID man how things stood.

I showed them my own identification and credentials, and one of them, fortunately, knew something of Liberty Market's work. They looked at the kidnappers' threatening note with the blankness of shock, and rapidly paid attention to the account of the death of the dinghy.

'We'll be on to that straight away,' said the chief inspector, stretching a hand to the telephone. 'No one's reported it yet, as far as I know.'

'Er . . .' I said. 'Send someone dressed as a seaman. Gumboots. Seaman's sweater. Don't let them behave like policemen, it would be very dangerous for the child.'

The chief inspector drew back from the telephone, frowning. Kidnapping in England was so comparatively rare that very few local forces had any experience of it. I repeated that the death threat to Dominic was real and should be a prime consideration in all procedure.

'Kidnappers are full of adrenalin and easily frightened,' I said. 'It's when they think they're in danger of being caught that they kill . . . and bury . . . the victim. Dominic really is in deadly danger, but we'll get him back safe if we're careful.'

After a silence the CID officer, who was roughly my own age, said they would have to call in his super.

'How long will that take?' I asked. 'Mrs Nerrity is outside in my car with a woman friend, and I don't think she can stand very much waiting. She's highly distressed.'

They nodded. Telephoned. Guardedly explained. The super, it transpired to their relief, would speed back to his office within ten minutes.

Detective Superintendent Eagler could have been born to be a plain-clothes cop. Even though I was expecting him I gave the thin, harmless-looking creature who came into the room no more than a first cursory glance. He had wispy balding hair and a scrawny neck rising from an ill-fitting shirt. His suit looked old and saggy and his manner seemed faintly apologetic. It was only when the other two men straightened at his arrival that with surprise I realised who he was.

He shook my hand, not very firmly, perched a thin rump on one corner of the large official desk, and asked me to identify myself. I gave him one of the firm's business cards with my name on. With neither haste nor comment he dialled the office number and spoke, I supposed, to Gerry Clayton. He made no remark about whatever answers Gerry gave him, but merely said 'Thanks' and put down the receiver.

'I've studied other cases,' he said directly to me and without more preamble. 'Lesley Whittle . . . and others that went wrong. I want no such disasters on my patch. I'll listen to your advice, and if it seems good to me, I'll act on it. Can't say more than that.'

I nodded and again suggested seamen-lookalikes to collect the dinghy, to which he instantly agreed, telling his junior to doll himself up and take a partner, without delay.

'Next?' he asked.

I said, 'Would you talk to Mrs Nerrity in my car, not in here? I don't think she should be seen in a police station. I don't think even that I should walk with you directly to her. I could meet you somewhere. One may be taking precautions quite unnecessarily, but some kidnappers are very thorough and suspicious, and one's never quite sure.'

He agreed and left before me, warning his two colleagues to say nothing whatever yet to anyone else.

'Especially not before the press blackout has been arranged,' I added. 'You could kill the child. Seriously; I mean it.'

They gave earnest assurances, and I walked back to the car to find both girls near to collapse. 'We're going to pick someone up,' I said. 'He's a policeman, but he doesn't look like it. He'll help to get Dominic back safely and to arrest the kidnappers.' I sighed inwardly at my positive voice, but if I couldn't give Miranda even a shred of confidence, I could give her nothing. We stopped for Eagler at a crossroads near the cathedral, and he slid without comment into the front passenger seat.

Again I drove a while on the look-out for company, but as far as I could see no kidnappers had risked it. After a few miles I stopped in a parking place on the side of a rural road, and Eagler got Miranda again to describe her dreadful day.

'What time was it?' he said.

'I'm not sure . . . After lunch. We'd eaten out lunch.'

'Where was your husband, when you telephoned him?'

'In his office. He's always there by two.'

Miranda was exhausted as well as tearful. Eagler, who was having to ask his questions over the clumsy barrier of the front seats, made a sketchy stab at patting her hand in a fatherly way. She interpreted the intention behind the gesture and wept the harder, choking over the details of red swimming trunks, no shoes, brown eyes, fair hair, no scars, suntanned skin . . . they'd been at the seaside for nearly two weeks . . . they were going home on Saturday.

'She ought to go home to her husband tonight,' I said to Eagler, and although he nodded, Miranda vehemently protested.

'He's so angry with me . . .' she wailed.

'You couldn't help it,' I said. 'The kidnappers have probably been waiting their chance for a week or more. Once your husband realises . . .'

But Miranda shook her head and said I didn't understand.

'That dinghy,' Eagler said thoughtfully, 'the one which burnt . . . had you seen it on the beach on any other day?'

Miranda glanced at him vaguely as if the question were unimportant. 'The last few days have been so windy . . . we haven't sat on the beach much. Not since the weekend, until today. We've mostly been by the pool, but Dominic doesn't like that so much because there's no sand.'

'The hotel has a pool?' Eagler asked.

'Yes, but last week we were always on the beach . . . Everything was so simple, just Dominic and me.' She spoke between sobs, her whole body shaking.

Eagler glanced at me briefly. 'Mr Douglas, here,' he said to Miranda, 'he says you'll get him back safe. We all have to act calmly, Mrs Nerrity. Calm and patience, that's the thing. You've had a terrible shock, I'm not trying to minimise it, but what we have to think of now is the boy. To think calmly for the boy's sake.'

Alessia looked from Eagler to me and back again. 'You're both the same,' she said blankly. 'You've both seen so much suffering . . . so much distress. You both know how to make it so that people can hold on . . . It makes the unbearable . . . possible.'

Eagler gave her a look of mild surprise, and in a totally unconnected thought I concluded that his clothes hung loosely about him because he'd recently lost weight.

'Alessia herself was kidnapped,' I explained to him. 'She knows too much about it.' I outlined briefly what had happened in Italy, and mentioned the coincidence of the horses.

His attention focused in a thoroughly Sherlockian manner.

'Are you saying there's a positive significance?'

I said, 'Before Alessia I worked on another case in Italy in which the family sold their shares in a race-course to raise the ransom.'

He stared. 'You do, then, see a . . . a thread?'

'I fear there's one, yes.'

'Why fear?' Alessia asked.

'He means,' Eagler said, 'that the three kidnaps have

been organised by the same perpetrator. Someone normally operating within the racing world and consequently knowing which targets to hit. Am I right?'

'On the button,' I agreed, talking chiefly to Alessia. 'The choice of target is often a prime clue to the identity of the kidnappers. I mean . . . to make the risks worthwhile, most kidnappers make sure in advance that the family or business actually can pay a hefty ransom. Of course every family will pay what they can, but the risks are just as high for a small ransom as a large, so it makes more sense to aim for the large. To know, for instance, that your father is much richer than the father of most other jockeys, girls or not.'

Alessia's gaze seemed glued to my face. 'To know . . . that the man who owns Ordinand has a son . . .?' She stopped, the sentence unfinished, the thought trotting on.

'Yes,' I said.

She swallowed. 'It costs just as much to keep a bad horse in training as a good one. I mean, I do clearly understand what you're saying.'

Miranda seemed not to have been listening but the tears had begun to dry up, like a storm passing.

'I don't want to go home tonight,' she said in a small voice. 'But if I go . . . Alessia, will you come with me?'

Alessia looked as if it were the last thing she could face and I answered on her behalf, 'No, Mrs Nerrity, it wouldn't be a good idea. Have you a mother, or a sister . . . someone you like? Someone your husband likes?'

Her mordant look said as much as words about the current state of her marriage, but after a moment or two she said faintly, 'I suppose . . . my mother.'

'That's right,' Eagler said paternally. 'Now would you two ladies just wait a few minutes while I walk a little way with Mr Douglas?'

'We won't be out of sight,' I said.

All the same they both looked as insecure as ever as we opened the front doors and climbed out. I looked back as we walked away and waggled a reassuring hand at their two anxious heads showing together from the rear seat.

'Very upsetting,' Eagler observed as we strolled away. 'But she'll get her kid back, with a bit of luck, not like some I've dealt with. Little kids snatched at random by psychos and murdered . . . sexual, often. Those mothers . . . Heartbreaking. Rotten. And quite often we know the psychos. Know they'll probably do something violent one day. Kill someone. We can often arrest them within a day of the body being found. But we can't prevent them. We can't keep them locked up for ever, just in case. Nightmare, those people. We've got one round here now. Time bomb waiting to go off. And some poor kid, somewhere, will be cycling along, or walking, at just the wrong time, just the wrong place. Some woman's kid. Something triggers the psycho. You never know what it is. Something small. Tips them over. After, they don't know why they've done it, like as not.'

'Mm,' I said. 'Worse than kidnappers. With them there's always hope.'

During his dissertation he'd given me several sideways glances: reinforcing his impressions, I thought. And I too had been doing the same, getting to know what to expect of him, good or bad. Occasionally someone from Liberty Market came across a policeman who thought of us as an unnecessary nuisance encroaching on their jealously guarded preserves, but on the whole they accepted us along the lines of if you want to understand a wreck, consult a diver.

'What can you tell me that you wouldn't want those two girls to hear?' he asked.

I gave him a small smile; got reserved judgement back.

'The man who kidnapped Alessia,' I said, 'recruited local talent. He recruited one, who roped in another five. The carabinieri have arrested those six, but the leader vanished. He called himself Giuseppe, which will do for now. We produced a drawing of him and flooded the province with it, with no results. I'll let you have a copy of it, if you like,' I paused. 'I know it's a long shot. This horse thing may be truly and simply a coincidence.'

Eagler put his head on one side. 'File it under fifty-fifty, then.'

'Right. And there's today's note . . .'

'Nothing Italian about that, eh?' Eagler looked

genial. 'But local talent? Just the right style for local talent, wouldn't you say?'

'Yes, I would.'

'Just right for an Italian leaning over the local talent's shoulder saying in broken English "tell her to telephone her husband, tell her not to inform the police".' He smiled fleetingly. 'But that's all conjecture, as they say.'

We turned as of one accord and began to stroll back to the car.

'The girl jockey's a bit jumpy still,' he said.

'It does that to them. Some are jumpy with strangers for ever.'

'Poor girl,' he said, as if he hadn't thought of freedom having problems; victims naturally being vastly less interesting than villains to the strong arm of the law.

I explained about Tony Vine being at that moment with John Nerrity, and said that Nerrity's local force would also by now know about Dominic. Eagler noted the address and said he would 'liaise'.

'I expect Tony Vine will be in charge from our point of view,' I said. 'He's very bright, if you have any dealings with him.'

'All right.'

We arranged that I would send the photostats of Giuseppe and a report on Alessia's kidnapping down to him on the first morning train; and at that point we were back at the car.

'Right then, Mr Douglas.' He shook my hand limply as if sealing a bargain, as different from Pucinelli as a tortoise from a hare; one wily, one sharp, one wrinkled in his carapace, one leanly taut in his uniform, one always on the edge of his nerves, one avuncularly relaxed.

I thought that I would rather be hunted by Pucinelli, any day.

CHAPTER ELEVEN

John Nerrity was a heavily-built man of medium height with greying hair cut neat and short; clipped moustache to match. On good days I could imagine him generating a fair amount of charm, but on that evening I saw only a man accustomed to power who had married a girl less than half his age and looked like regretting it.

They lived in a large detached house on the edge of a golf course near Sutton, south of London, only about three miles distant from where their four-legged wonder had made a fortune on Epsom Downs.

The exterior of the house, in the dusk of our arrival, had revealed itself as thirties-developed Tudor, but on a restrained and successful scale. Inside, the carpets wall-to-wall looked untrodden, the brocade chairs un-sat-on, the silk cushions unwrinkled, the paper and paint unscuffed. Unfaded velvet curtains hung in stiff regular folds from beneath elaborate pelmets, and upon several glass and chromium coffee tables lay large glossy books, unthumbed. There were no photographs and no flowers, and the pictures had been chosen to occupy wall-space, not the mind; the whole thing more like a shop-window than the home of a little boy.

John Nerrity was holding a gin and tonic with ice clinking and lemon slice floating, a statement in itself of his resistance to crisis. I couldn't imagine Paolo Cenci organising ice and lemon six hours after the first ransom demand: it had been almost beyond him to pour without spilling.

With Nerrity were Tony Vine, wearing his most enigmatic expression, and another man, sour of mouth and bitter of eye, who spoke with Tony's accent and looked vaguely, in his flannels and casual sweater, as if he'd been out for a stroll with his dog.

'Detective Superintendent Rightsworth,' Tony said, introducing him deadpan. 'Waiting to talk to Mrs Nerrity.'

Rightsworth gave me barely a nod, and that more of repression than of acknowledgement. One of those, I thought. A civilian-hater. One who thought of the police as 'us' and the public as 'them', the 'them' being naturally inferior. It always surprised me that policemen of that kind got promoted, but Rightsworth was proof enough that they did. The old ridiculous joke of 'Where do the police live? In Letsby Avenue,' crossed my mind; and Popsy would have appreciated my struggle to keep a straight face.

Alessia and Miranda had come into the sitting room close together and a step behind me, as if using me as a riot shield: and it was clear from John Nerrity's face that the first sight of his wife prompted few loving, comforting or supportive feelings.

He gave her no kiss. No greeting. He merely said, as if in a continuing conversation, 'Do you realise that Ordinand isn't mine to sell? Do you realise we're in hock to the limit? No, you don't. You can't do anything. Not even something simple like looking after a kid.'

Miranda crumpled behind me and sank to the floor. Alessia and I bent to help her up, and I said to Miranda's ear, 'People who are frightened are often angry and say things that hurt. He's as frightened as you are. Hang on to that.'

'What are you mumbling about?' Nerrity demanded. 'Miranda, for Christ's sake get up, you look a wreck.' He stared with disfavour at the ravaged face and untidy hair of his son's mother, and with only the faintest flicker of overdue compassion said impatiently, 'Get up, get up, they say it wasn't your fault.'

She would always think it had been, though; and so would he. Few people understood how persistent, patient, ingenious and fast committed kidnappers could be. Whomever they planned to take, they took.

Rightsworth said he wanted to ask Mrs Nerrity some questions and guided her off to a distant sofa, followed by her bullish husband with his tinkling glass.

Alessia sat in an armchair as if her legs were giving way, and Tony and I retreated to a window seat to exchange quiet notes.

'He . . .' Tony jerked his head towards Nerrity, 'has

been striding up and down here wearing holes in the effing carpet and calling his wife an effing cow. All sorts of names. Didn't know some of them myself.' He grinned wolfishly. 'Takes them like that, sometimes, of course.'

'Pour the anger on someone that won't kick back?'

'Poor little bitch.'

'Any more demands?' I asked.

'Zilch. All pianissimo. That ray of sunshine Rightsworth brought a suitcase full of bugging gear with him from the telephone blokes but he didn't know how to use half of it, I ask you. I fixed the tap on the 'phone myself. Can't bear to see effing amateurs mucking about.'

'I gather he doesn't like us,' I said.

'Rightsworth? Despises the ground we walk on.'

'Is it true John Nerrity can't raise anything on the horse?'

I'd asked very quietly, but Tony looked round to make sure neither the Nerritys nor Rightsworth could hear the answer. 'He was blurting it all out, when I got here. Seems his effing business is dicky and he's pledged bits of that horse to bail him out. Borrowed on it, you might say. All this bluster, I reckon it's because he hasn't a hope of raising the wherewithal to get his nipper back, he's in a blue funk and sending his effing underpants to the laundry.'

'What did he say about our fee?'

'Yeah.' Tony looked at me sideways. 'Took him in the

gut. He says he can't afford us. Then he begs me not to go. He's not getting on too effing well with Rightsworth, who would? So there he is, knackered every which way and taking it out on the lady wife.' He glanced over at Miranda who was again in tears. 'Seems she was his secretary. That's her photo, here on this table. She was a knockout, right enough.'

I looked at the glamorous studio-lit portrait; a divinely pretty face with fine bones, wide eyes and the hint of a smile. A likeness taken just before marriage, I guessed, at the point of her maximum attraction, before life rolled on and trampled over the heady dreams.

'Did you tell him we'd help him for nothing?' I asked.

'No, I effing didn't. I don't like him, to be honest.'

We sometimes did, as a firm, work for no pay: it depended on circumstances. All the partners agreed that a family in need should get help regardless, and none of us begrudged it. We never charged enough anyway to make ourselves rich, being in existence on the whole to defeat extortion, not to practise it. A flat fee, plus expenses: no percentages. Our clients knew for sure that the size of the ransom in no way affected our own reward.

The telephone rang suddenly, making everyone in the room jump. Both Tony and Rightsworth gestured to Nerrity to answer it and he walked towards it as if it were hot. I noticed that he pulled his stomach in as the muscles tightened and saw his breath become shallow. If the room had been silent I guessed we would actually have heard his heart thump. By the time he stretched out an unsteady hand to pick up the receiver Tony had the recorder running and the amplifier set so that everyone in the room could hear the caller's words.

'Hello,' Nerrity said hoarsely.

'Is that you, John?' It was a woman's voice, high and anxious. 'Are you expecting me?'

'Oh.' Miranda jumped to her feet in confusion. 'It's Mother. I asked her . . .' Her voice tailed off as her husband held out the receiver with the murderous glare of a too-suddenly released tension, and she managed to take it from him without touching him skin to skin.

'Mother?' she said, waveringly. 'Yes, please do come. I thought you were coming . . .'

'My dear girl, you sounded so flustered when you telephoned earlier. Saying you wouldn't tell me what was wrong! I was worried. I don't like to interfere between you and John, you know that.'

'Mother, just come.'

'No, I . . .'

John Nerrity snatched the telephone out of his wife's grasp and practically shouted, 'Rosemary, just come. Miranda needs you. Don't argue. Get here as fast as you can. Right?' He crashed the receiver down in annoyance, and I wondered whether or not the masterfully bossy tone would indeed fetch the parent. The telephone rang again almost immediately and Nerrity snatched it up in fury, saying 'Rosemary, I told you . . .'

'John Nerrity, is it?' a voice said. Male, loud,

aggressive, threatening. Not Rosemary. My own spine tingled. Tony hovered over the recording equipment, checking the quivering needles.

'Yes,' Nerrity said breathlessly, his lungs deflating.

'Listen once. Listen good. You'll find a tape in a box by your front gate. Do what it says.' There was a sharp click followed by the dialling tone, and then Tony, pressing buttons, was speaking to people who were evidently telephone engineers.

'Did you get the origin of the second call?' he asked. We read the answer on his face. 'OK,' he said resignedly. 'Thanks.' To Nerrity he said, 'They need fifteen seconds. Better than the old days. Trouble is, the crooks know it too.'

Nerrity was on his way to the front door and could presently be heard crunching across his gravel.

Alessia was looking very frail indeed. I went down on my knees by her chair and put my arms protectively around her.

'You could wait in another room,' I said. 'Watch television. Read a book.'

'You know I can't.'

'I'm sorry about all this.'

She gave me a rapid glance. 'You tried to get me to go home to Popsy. It's my own fault I'm here. I'm all right. I won't be a nuisance, I promise.' She swallowed. 'It's all so odd . . . to see it from the other side.'

'You're a great girl,' I said. 'Popsy told me so, and she's right.'

She looked a small shade less fraught and rested her head briefly on my shoulder. 'You're my foundations, you know,' she said. 'Without you the whole thing would collapse.'

'I'll be here,' I said. 'But seriously it would be best if you and Miranda went into the kitchen and found some food. Get her to eat. Eat something yourself. Carbohydrate. Biscuits, cake – something like that.'

'Fattening,' she said automatically: the jockey talking.

'Best for your bodies just now, though. Carbohydrates are a natural tranquilliser. It's why unhappy people eat and eat.'

'You do know the most extraordinary things.'

'And also,' I said, 'I don't want Miranda to hear what's on the tape.'

'Oh.' Her eyes widened as she remembered. 'Pucinelli switched off that tape . . . so I couldn't hear.'

'Yes. It was horrid. So will this be. The first demands are always the most frightening. The threats will be designed to pulverise. To goad Nerrity into paying anything, everything, very quickly, to save his little son. So dearest Alessia, take Miranda into the kitchen and eat cake.'

She smiled a shade apprehensively and walked over to Miranda, who was sobbing periodically in isolated gulps, like hiccups, but who agreed listlessly to making a cup of tea. The two girls went off to their haven, and Nerrity crunched back with a brown cardboard box.

Rightsworth importantly took charge of opening it, telling everyone else to stand back. Tony's eyebrows were sardonic. Rightsworth produced a pair of clear plastic gloves and methodically put them on before carefully slitting with a penknife the heavy adhesive tape fastening the lid.

Opening the box Rightsworth first peered inside, then put an arm in and brought out the contents: one cassette tape, in plastic case, as expected.

Nerrity looked at it as if it would bite and waved vaguely at an ornate stretch of gilt and padded wall unit, some of whose doors proved to be screening a bank of expensive stereo. Rightsworth found a slot for the cassette, which he handled carefully with the plastic gloves, and Nerrity pushed the relevant buttons.

The voice filled the room, harsh, thunderous, uncompromising.

'Now, you, Nerrity, you listen good.'

I took three quick strides and turned down the volume, on the grounds that threats fortissimo would sound even worse than threats should. Tony nodded appreciatively, but Rightsworth was irritated. The voice went on, more moderate in decibels, immoderate in content.

'We nicked your kid, Nerrity, and if you want your heir back in one piece you do what you're told like a good boy. Otherwise we'll take our knife out, Nerrity, and slash off something to persuade you. Not his hair, Nerrity. A finger maybe. Or his little privates. Those for sure. Understand, Nerrity? No messing about. This is for real.

'Now you got a horse, Nerrity. Worth a bit, we reckon. Six million. Seven. Sell it, Nerrity. Like we said, we want five million. Otherwise your kid suffers. Nice little kid, too. You don't want him screaming, do you? He'll scream with what we'll do to him.

'You get a bloodstock agent busy. We'll wait a week. One week, seven days. Seven days from now, you get that money ready in used notes, nothing bigger than twenty. We'll tell you where to leave it. You do what we tell you, or it's the castration. We'll send you a tape of what it sounds like. Slash. Rip. Scream.

'And you keep away from the police. If we think you've called in the Force, your kid's for the plastic bag. Final. You won't get his body back. *Nothing*. Think about it.

'Right, Nerrity. That's the message.'

The voice stopped abruptly and there was a numb minute of silence before anyone moved. I'd heard a score of ransom demands, but always, every time, found them shocking. Nerrity, like many a parent before him, was poleaxed to his roots.

'They can't . . .' he said, his mouth dry, the words gagging.

'They can,' Tony said flatly, 'but not if we manage it right.'

'What did they say to you this afternoon?' I asked. 'What's different?'

Nerrity swallowed. 'The . . . the knife. That part. Before, he just said "five million for your kid". And I said I hadn't got five million. . . . He said, "you've got a horse, so sell it." That was all. And no police, he said that too. Five million, no police, or the boy would die. He said he'd be getting in touch. I began to shout at him . . . he just rang off.'

Rightsworth took the cassette out of the recorder and put it in its box, putting that in its turn in the cardboard carton, all with exaggerated care in the plastic gloves. He would be taking the tape, he said. They would maintain the tap on Mr Nerrity's telephone, he said. They would be working on the case, he said.

Nerrity, highly alarmed, begged him to be careful; and begging didn't come easy, I thought, to one accustomed to bully. Rightsworth said with superiority that every care would be taken, and I could see Tony thinking, as I was, that Rightsworth was treating the threats too pompously and was not, in consequence, a brilliant detective.

When he had gone, Nerrity, his first fears subsiding, poured himself another stiff gin and tonic, again with ice and lemon. He picked the ice out of a bucket with a pair of tongs. Tony watched with incredulity.

'Drink?' he said to us as an afterthought.

We shook our heads.

'I'm not paying that ransom,' he said defensively. 'For one thing, I can't. The horse is due to be sold in any case. It's four years old, and going to stud. I don't need to get a blood-stock agent, it's being handled already. Some of the shares have already been sold, but I'll hardly see a penny. Like I said, I've got business debts.' He took a deep drink. 'You may as well know, that horse is the difference to me between being solvent and bankrupt. Biggest stroke of luck ever, the day I bought it as a yearling.' He swelled slightly, giving himself a mental pat on the back, and we could both see an echo of the expansiveness with which he must have waved many a gin and tonic while he recounted his good fortune.

'Isn't your business,' I said, 'a limited company? If you'll excuse my asking?'

'No, it isn't.'

'What is your business?' Tony asked him casually.

'Importer. Wholesale. One or two wrong decisions . . .' He shrugged. 'Bad debts. Firms going bankrupt, owing me money. On my scale of operations it doesn't take much of a recession to do a damned lot of damage. Ordinand will clear everything. Set me to rights. Fund me for future trading. Ordinand is a bloody miracle.' He made a furious chopping gesture with his free hand. 'I'm damned if I'm going to throw away my entire life for those bloody kidnappers.'

He'd said it, I thought. He'd said aloud what had been festering in his mind ever since Miranda's 'phone call. He didn't love his son enough for the sacrifice.

'How much is Ordinand worth?' Tony said unemotionally.

'They got it right. Six million, with luck. Forty shares at a hundred and fifty thousand each.' He drank, the ice clinking.

'And how much do you need to straighten your business?'

'That's a bloody personal question!'

Tony said patiently, 'If we're going to negotiate for you, we have to know just what is or isn't possible.'

Nerrity frowned at his lemon slice, but then said, 'Four and a half, thereabouts, will keep me solvent. Five would clear all debts. Six will see me soundly based for the future.'

Tony glanced about him at the over-plush room. 'What about this house?'

Nerrity looked at him as if he were a financial baby. 'Every brick mortgaged,' he said shortly.

'Any other assets?'

'If I had any other bloody assets I'd have cashed them by now.'

Tony and I exchanged glances, then Tony said, 'I reckon we might get your kid back for less than half a million. We'll aim lower of course. First offer, a hundred thousand. Then take it from there.'

'But they won't . . . they said . . .' Nerrity stopped, floundering.

'The best thing,' I said, 'would be to get yourself onto the City pages of the newspapers. Go into print telling the world there's nothing like a Derby winner for keeping the bailiffs out.'

'But . . .'

'Yes,' I interrupted. 'Maybe not in the normal way good for business. But your creditors will be sure they'll be paid, and the kidnappers will be sure they won't. Next time they get in touch, they'll demand less. Once they acknowledge to themselves that the proceeds will be relatively small compared with their first demand, that's what they'll settle for. Better than nothing, sort of thing.'

'But they'll harm Dominic . . .'

I shook my head. 'It's pretty doubtful, not if they're sure they'll make a profit in the end. Dominic's their only guarantee of that profit. Dominic, alive and whole. They won't destroy or damage their asset in any way if they're convinced you'll pay what you can. So when you talk to the press, make sure they understand – and print – that there'll be a margin over, when Ordinand is sold. Say that the horse will wipe out all your debts and then some.'

'But . . .' he said again.

'If you have any difficulty approaching the City editors, we can do that for you,' I said.

He looked from Tony to me with the uncertainty of a commander no longer in charge.

'Would you?' he said.

We nodded. 'Straight away.'

'Andrew will do it,' Tony said. 'He knows the City. Cut his teeth at Lloyd's, our lad here.' Neither he nor I explained how lowly my job there had been. 'Very smooth, our Andrew, in his city suit,' Tony said.

Nerrity looked me up and down. I hadn't replaced my tie, although I'd long unrolled my trousers. 'He's young,' he said disparagingly.

Tony silently laughed. 'As old as the pyramids,' he said. 'We'll get your nipper back, don't you fret.'

Nerrity said uncomfortably, 'It's not that I don't like the boy. Of course I do.' He paused. 'I don't see much of him. Five minutes in the morning. He's in bed when I get home. Weekends . . . I work, go to the races, go out with business friends. Don't have much time for lolling about.'

Not much inclination, either, I diagnosed.

'Miranda dotes on him,' Nerrity said, as if that were no virtue. 'You'd have thought she could keep her eyes on him for five minutes, wouldn't you? I don't see how she could have been so bloody stupid.'

I tried explaining about the determination of kidnappers, but it seemed to have no effect.

'It was her idea to have the kid in the first place,' Nerrity grumbled. 'I told her it would spoil her figure. She went on and on about being lonely. She knew what my life was like before she married me, didn't she?'

From the other side, I thought. From the office side, where his life was most intense, where hers was busy and fulfilled.

'Anyway, we had the kid.' He made another sharply frustrated gesture. 'And now . . . this.'

Miranda's mother arrived conveniently at that point, and shortly afterwards I put Alessia in my car and talked to Tony quietly in the garden.

'Thursday, tomorrow,' I said. 'Wittering's a seaside place. Good chance the same people will be on the beach tomorrow as today, wouldn't you think?'

'The Super in Chichester, would he buy that?' Tony asked.

'Yes, I'm sure.'

'I wouldn't mind a day myself of sitting on the effing pebbles.'

'The tide's going out in the mornings,' I said. 'How about if you take the stuff down to Eagler on the train, and I'll join you for a paddle when I've buzzed up the City?'

He nodded. 'See you at the Breakwater Hotel, then?'

'Yeah. Tell them at Reception that we're taking over Miranda's room. She's booked in until Saturday. Tell them the boy's ill, she's had to take him home, we're her brothers, we've come down to collect her clothes and her car . . . and pay her bill.'

'I don't know that sitting around in the Breakwater too long will do much good.'

I grinned in the darkness. 'Makes a change from the switchboard, though.'

'You're an effing rogue, I always knew it.'

He vanished into the shadows without noise, departing on foot to his distantly parked car, and I climbed in beside Alessia and pointed our nose towards Lambourn.

I asked if she were hungry and would like to stop somewhere for a late dinner, but she shook her head. 'Miranda and I ate cornflakes and toast until our eyes crossed. And you were right, she seemed a bit calmer by the time we left. But oh . . . when I think of that little boy . . . so alone, without his mother . . . I can't bear it.'

I spent the next morning in Fleet Street swearing various business-page editors to secrecy and enlisting their aid, and then drove back to West Wittering, reflecting that I'd spent at least twelve of the past thirty hours with my feet on the pedals.

Arriving at the Breakwater in jeans and sports shirt, I found Tony had checked in and left a message that he was out on the beach. I went down there and came across him sitting on a gaudy towel, wearing swimming trunks and displaying a lot of impressive keep-fit muscle. I dropped down beside him on a towel of my own and watched the life of the beach ebb and flow.

'Your Eagler already had the same idea,' Tony said. 'Half the holidaymakers on this patch of sand are effing plain clothes men quizzing the other half. They've been out here since breakfast.'

It appeared that Tony had got on very well with Eagler. Tony considered he had 'constructive effing ideas', which was Tony's highest mark of approval.

'Eagler's already sorted out what arson device was used to fire the dinghy. The dinghy was stolen, what a surprise.'

Some small children were digging a new sandcastle where Dominic's had been wiped out by the tide.

'A little girl of about eight gave Miranda the kidnapper's note,' I said. 'What do you bet she's still here?'

Without directly answering Tony rose to his feet and loped down onto the sand, where he was soon passing the time of day with two agile people kicking a football.

'They'll look for her,' he said, returning. 'They've found plenty who saw the boat. Some who saw who left it. The one with the green shorts has a stat of Giuseppe in his pocket, but no luck with that, so far.'

The two boys who had helped me carry the boat up from the grasp of the tide came by and said hello, recognising me.

'Hi,' I said. 'I see the boat's gone, what was left of it.'

One of them nodded. 'We came back along here after supper and there were two fishermen types winching it onto a pickup truck. They didn't know whose it was. They said the coastguards had sent them to fetch it into a yard in Itchenor.'

'Do you live here?' I asked.

They shook their heads. 'We rent a house along there for August.' One of them pointed eastwards, along the beach. 'We come every year. Mum and Dad like it.'

'You're brothers?' I asked.

'Twins, actually. But fraternal, as you see.'

They picked up some pebbles and threw them at an empty Coke can for target practice, and presently moved off.

'Gives you a thought or two, doesn't it?' Tony said.

'Yes.'

'Eagler wanted to see us anyway at about five,' he said. 'In the Silver Sail café in that place the boy mentioned. Itchenor. Sounds like some disgusting effing disease.'

The football-kicker in green shorts was presently talking to a little girl whose mother bustled up in alarm and protectively shepherded her nestling away.

'Never mind,' Tony said. 'That smashing bit of goods in the pink bikini over there is a policewoman. What'll you bet green-shorts will be talking to her in two effing ticks?'

'Not a pebble,' I said.

We watched while green-shorts got into conversation with pink-bikini. 'Nicely done,' Tony said approvingly. 'Very natural.'

The pink-bikini girl stopped looking for shells exclusively and started looking for small girls as well, and I took my shirt off and began turning a delicate shade of lobster.

No dramas occurred on the beach. The hot afternoon warmed to tea-time. The football-kickers went off across the breakwaters and the pink-bikini went in for a swim. Tony and I stood up, stretched, shook and folded our towels, and in good holidaymaker fashion got into my car and drove westwards to Itchenor.

Eagler, inconspicuous in an open-necked shirt, baggy grey flannels and grubby tennis shoes, was drinking tea in the Silver Sail and writing a picture postcard.

'May we join you?' I asked politely.

'Sit down, laddie, sit down.'

It was an ordinary sort of café: sauce bottles on the tables, murals of sailing boats round the walls, brown tiled floor, plastic stacking chairs in blue. A notice by a cash desk stated 'The best chips on the coast' and a certain warm oiliness in the atmosphere tended to prove their popularity.

'My WPC found your girl child,' Eagler said, sticking a stamp on his postcard. 'Name of Sharon Wellor, seven years old, staying in a guest house until Saturday. She couldn't describe the man who asked her to deliver the note. She says he gave her some fruit pastilles, and she's scared now because her mother's always told her never to take sweets from strangers.'

'Did she know whether he was old or young?' I asked.

'Everyone over twenty is old to a seven-year-old,' Eagler said. 'She told my WPC where she's staying, though, so perhaps we'll ask again.' He glanced at us. 'Come up with any more ideas, have you?'

'Yeah,' Tony said. 'Kidnappers often don't transport their victims very far from their snatching point. Lowers the risk.'

'In holiday resorts,' I said mildly, 'half the houses are for rent.'

Eagler fiddled aimlessly with his teaspoon. 'Thousands of them,' he said dryly.

'But one of them might have been rented sometime last week.'

We waited, and after a while he nodded. 'We'll do the legwork. Ask the travel agents, estate agents, local papers.' He paused, then said without emphasis, 'The kid may have been taken off in a boat.'

Tony and I paid fast attention.

'There was a motor-boat there,' Eagler said. 'One of those putt-putt things for hire by the hour. My detective constables were told that when the dinghy went on fire the other boat was bobbing round in the shallows with no one in it, but a man in swimming trunks was standing knee-deep in the water holding on to it by the bows. Then, our informants said, the dinghy suddenly went up in flames, very fast, with a whoosh, and everyone ran towards it, naturally. Our informants said that afterwards the motor-boat had gone, which they thought perfectly normal as its time was probably up.' He stopped, looking at us neutrally but with a smile of satisfaction plainly hovering.

'Who were your informants?' I asked.

The smile almost surfaced. 'A ten-year-old canal digger and his grandmother.'

'Very reliable,' I said.

'The boat was blue, clinker built, with a number seventeen in white on its bow and stern.'

'And the man?'

'The man was a man. They found the boat more interesting.' He paused again. 'There's a yard here in Itchenor with boats like that for hire. The trouble is they've got only ten. They've never had one with seventeen on it, ever.'

'But who's to know?' Tony said.

'Look for a house with a boat-shed,' I murmured.

Eagler said benignly, 'It wouldn't hurt, would it, to find the kid?'

'If they spot anyone looking they'll be off in a flash,' I said, 'and it would be dangerous for the boy.'

Eagler narrowed his eyes slightly at our alarm. 'We'll go round the agencies,' he said. 'If we turn up anything likely on paper we won't surround it without telling you first. How's that?'

We both shook our heads.

'Better to avoid raids and sieges if possible,' I said.

Tony said to Eagler, 'If you find a likely house on paper, let me suss it out. I've had all sorts of experience at this sort of thing. I'll tell you if the kid's there. And if he is, I'll get him out.'

CHAPTER TWELVE

There was an urgent message from the office at the Breakwater Hotel for me to telephone Alessia, which I did.

'Miranda's distracted . . . she's in pieces,' she said, sounding strung up herself beyond sympathy to near snapping point. 'It's awful. . . . She's telephoned me three times, crying terribly, begging me to get you to do something . . .'

'Sweet Alessia,' I said. 'Take three deep breaths and sit down if you're standing up.'

'Oh . . .' Her cough of surprise had humour in it, and after a pause she said, 'All right. I'm sitting. Miranda's dreadfully frightened. Is that better?'

'Yes,' I said, half smiling. 'What's happened?'

'Superintendent Rightsworth and John Nerrity are making a plan and won't listen to Miranda, and she's desperate to stop them. She wants you to make them see they mustn't.' Her voice was still high and anxious, the sentences coming fast.

'What's the plan?' I asked.

'John is going to pretend to do what the kidnappers tell him. Pretend to collect the money. Then when the pretend money is handed over, Superintendent Rightsworth will jump on the kidnappers and make them say where Dominic is.' She gulped audibly. 'That's what went wrong . . . with me . . . in Bologna . . . isn't it?'

'Yes,' I said, 'an ambush at the R.V. is to my mind too high a risk.'

'What's the R.V.?'

'Sorry. Rendezvous. The place where the ransom is handed over.'

'Miranda says John doesn't want to pay the ransom and Superintendent Rightsworth is telling him not to worry, he doesn't need to.'

'Mm,' I said. 'Well, I can see why Miranda's upset. Did she talk to you from the telephone in her own house?'

'What? Oh, my goodness, it's tapped, isn't it, with the police listening to every word?'

'It is indeed,' I said dryly.

'She was up in her bedroom. I suppose she didn't think. And, heavens . . . she said John was regretting calling in Liberty Market, because you were advising him to pay. Superintendent Rightsworth has assured him the police can take care of everything, there's no need to have outsiders putting their oar in.'

The phrase had an authentic Rightsworth ring.

'Miranda says John is going to tell Liberty Market he

doesn't want their help any more. He says it's a waste of money . . . and Miranda's frantic.'

'Mm,' I said. 'If she telephones you again, try to remind her the 'phone's tapped. If she has any sense she'll ring you back from somewhere else. Then reassure her that we'll do our best to change her husband's mind.'

'But how?' Alessia said, despairing.

'Get our Chairman to frighten him silly, I dare say,' I said. 'And I never said that. It's for your ears only.'

'Will it work?' Alessia said doubtfully.

'There are also people who can overrule Rightsworth.'

'I suppose there are.' She sounded happier with that. 'Shall I tell Miranda to telephone directly to you in your office?'

'No,' I said. 'I'll be moving about. When you've heard from her, leave a message again for me to call you, and I will.'

'All right.' She sounded tired. 'I haven't been able to think of anything else all day. Poor Miranda. Poor, poor little boy. I never really understood until now what Papa went through because of me.'

'Because of your kidnappers,' I said, 'and for love of you, yes.'

After a pause she said, 'You're telling me again . . . I must feel no guilt.'

'That's right,' I said. 'No more guilt than Dominic.'

'It's not easy. . . .'

'No,' I agreed. 'But essential.'

She asked if I would come to lunch on Sunday, and I said yes if possible but not to count on it.

'You will get him back alive, won't you?' she said finally, none of the worry dissipated; and I said 'Yes,' and meant it.

'Goodbye, then . . .'

'Goodbye,' I said, 'and love to Popsy.'

Liberty Market, I reflected, putting down the receiver, might have an overall success rate as high as ninety-five per cent, but John Nerrity seemed to be heading himself perilously towards the other tragic five. Perhaps he truly believed, perhaps even Rightsworth believed, that an ambush at the drop produced the best results. And so they did, if capturing some of the kidnappers was the prime overriding aim.

There had been a case in Florida, however, when the police had ambushed the man who picked up the ransom and shot him down as he ran to escape, and only because the wounded man relented and told where his victim was a few seconds before he slid into a final coma, had they ever found the boy alive. He had been left in the boot of a parked car, and would slowly have suffocated if the police had fired a fraction straighter.

I told Tony of Nerrity's plans and he said disgustedly, 'What is he, an effing optimist?' He bit his thumbnail. 'Have to find that little nipper, won't we?'

'Hope to God.'

'Better chance in this country than anywhere else, of course.'

I nodded. Among well-meaning peoples, like the British, kidnappers were disadvantaged. Their crime was reviled, not tolerated, and the population not afraid of informing. Once the victim was safely home, the trace-and-capture machinery had proved excellent.

Finding the hide-out before the pay-off was easier in Britain than in Italy, but still dauntingly difficult: and most successes along that line had come from coincidence, from nosey neighbours, and from guessing who had done the kidnap because of the close knowledge inadvertently revealed of the victim's private life.

'No one knew my daughter was going to be at that dance except her boy-friend,' one grief-stricken father had told us: and sure enough her apparently shattered boy-friend had organised the extortion – that time without the girl's knowledge, which wasn't always so. Collusion with the 'victim' had to be considered every time, human greed being what it was. The girl in that case had been found and freed without a ransom being paid, but she'd had a worse time in captivity than Alessia and the last I'd heard she was being treated for deep prolonged depression.

'I think I'll just nosey around a bit where the boats are,' Tony said. 'Can I borrow your car? You can use Miranda's if you're desperate. Do you mind if I go home later for some gear? I'll see you at effing breakfast.'

'Don't crunch it,' I said, giving him the keys.

'As if I would.'

I spent the evening eating the hotel's very reasonable dinner and packing Miranda's belongings. Dominic's clothes, quiet and folded, filled a neat small suitcase. I put his cuddly toys, a teddy and a Snoopy, in beside them, and shut the lid: and thought of him, so defenceless, so frightened, and knew that it was because of people like him and Alessia that what I was doing was a job for life.

In view of John Nerrity's change of heart I guessed he wouldn't be too pleased with the morning newspapers' money columns, where the financial editors had done him proud. The word 'Nerrity' sprang out in large black letters from every page I'd visited, which were mostly of the sort that I guessed the writer of the kidnap note would read.

'Nerrity Home and Dried', 'Nerrity's Nag to the Rescue', 'Nerrity Floats on Stud' they said, and 'Nerrity Solvent by Short Head'. To kidnappers nervously scanning the press for signs of police activity, the bad news couldn't be missed. Creditors were zeroing in on the Ordinand proceeds, and there would be precious little left for other sharks.

Eagler telephoned me in Miranda's room while I was still reading. 'These papers. . . . Is this your doing?' he asked.

'Er, yes.'

He chuckled. 'I thought I detected the fine hand. Well, laddie, we're doing a spot of rummaging around the classifieds in the local rags of a week to two weeks ago, and we're checking through all the properties to rent. We'll have a partial list for you any time today.' He paused. 'Now I'm putting a lot of faith in your friend Tony Vine, and I want to be sure it's not misplaced.'

'He's an ex-S.A.S.,' I said. 'A sergeant.'

'Ah.' He sounded relieved.

'He prefers working at night.'

'Does he now?' Eagler was almost purring. 'I should have a fairly complete list for you by late this afternoon. Will you fetch it?'

We arranged time and place, and rang off; and when I went downstairs to breakfast Tony was walking in through the front door, yawning.

Over bacon, eggs and kippers he recounted what he'd found. 'Did you know there's a whole internal water system behind the coast here? Itchenor Creek goes all the way to Chichester. But there's a lock some way up, and our fellows didn't go through it.' He chewed. 'I hired a rowing boat. Sneaked around a bit. Reckon it's an effing needle in a haystack we're after. There's dozens, hundreds of likely houses. Holiday flats. Chalets. You name it. And on top of that the water goes clear to somewhere called Hayling Island, with thousands more little bungalows, and there are uncountable places where a car could have met the boat and taken the nipper anywhere.'

I gloomily ate some toast and told him about Eagler's impending list.

'OK then,' Tony said. 'I'll swim this morning, sleep this afternoon, work tonight, OK?'

I nodded and passed him one of the newspapers. Tony read the financial news over the rim of his cup of tea. 'You hit the effing bullseye. No one could miss it,' he said.

Nerrity himself certainly hadn't missed it. Gerry Clayton telephoned to say that Nerrity was furious and insisting we dropped the case. He wanted nothing more to do with Liberty Market.

'He admitted he'd agreed to your getting the story into the papers,' Gerry said. 'But he didn't think it would happen so quickly, and he had intended to cancel it.'

'Too bad.'

'Yes. So officially you and Tony can break off and come home.'

'No,' I said. 'We're working for Mrs Nerrity now. She specifically asked for us to continue.'

Gerry's voice had a smile in it. 'I thought you might, but it makes it all a damn sight more tricky. Both of you . . . take care.'

'Yeah,' I said. 'Fold some nice paper. Try a boat.'

'Boat?'

'A boat to thrust a small boy into so that you can put a tarpaulin or some such over him, a boat to chug noisily away over the breaking waves so that no one can hear him crying out.'

'Is that how it was done?' Gerry asked soberly.

'We think so, yes.'

'Poor little blighter,' Gerry said.

Tony and I in true holiday-making fashion spent the morning in or out of water, although the day was not so warm nor the beach so fruitfully crowded. The policewoman, now in a white bikini, came to splash with us in the shallows but said she hadn't been able to find anyone who had seen Dominic carried off. 'Every single person seems to have been looking at the dinghy,' she said disgustedly. 'And all we know about that is that it was stranded on the sand when the tide went out, and it had a large piece of paper taped to the seat saying "Don't touch the boat, we'll be back for it soon." '

'Didn't someone say they'd seen who left it?' I asked.

'Well, yes, but that was a boy playing up on the shingle, and all he could say was that they were two men in shorts and bright orange rainproof sailing jackets, who had pulled the dinghy up the sand a bit and been busy round it for a while and then had walked off northwest along the beach. The boy went down to the dinghy soon afterwards and read the note, and after that he went off to get an icecream. He wasn't here in the afternoon when it went up in flames, much to his disgust. When he came back it was burnt and black.'

The policewoman was shivering in the rising breeze and turning a pale shade of blue. 'Time for a sweater and thick socks,' she said cheerfully. 'And I might as well chat up the ancient ladies living in the Haven Rest Home along there.' She pointed. 'They've nothing to do but look out of the windows.'

Tony and I picked up our belongings and moved to the shelter of the hotel, and in the afternoon while the clouds thickened overhead he slept undisturbed in Miranda's bed.

At five I drove to Chichester to collect the list of rentals from Eagler: he came to meet me himself, looking insignificant and slow, and climbed into the passenger seat at my side.

'These top eleven are the most promising,' he said, pointing. 'They are collected from all the agencies we could think of. They are all holiday homes on or near the water and they were all rented at the last minute. The weather was so bad in July and at the beginning of August that there were more properties than usual available, and then when it turned warmer there was a rush.'

I nodded. 'Miranda herself decided to come here only a few days in advance. The hotel had had cancellations because of the weather, and could take her.'

'I wonder what would have happened if she hadn't come?' Eagler said thoughtfully.

'They'd have grabbed him at home.'

'You'd have thought they'd have found it easier to wait until he was back there.'

'Kidnappers don't try to make things easy for

themselves,' I said mildly. 'They plan to the last inch. They spend money. They're obsessional. There's never anything casual about a kidnap. Kidnappers would see a good chance of success while the child was in charge of his mother alone down here, and I bet once they'd done the planning they waited day after day for the right minute. If it hadn't presented itself they would have followed Miranda home and thought up a new plan. Or perhaps have reverted to a former plan which hadn't so far borne fruit. You never can tell. But if they wanted him, they would have got him in the end.'

'How would they have known she was coming here?' Eagler asked.

'Kidnappers watch,' I said. 'They're obsessional about that, too. What conclusion would you come to if you saw Miranda load suitcases and a beach chair into her car, strap Dominic into his seat, and drive away waving?'

'Hm.'

'You'd follow,' I said.

'I expect so.'

'Miranda in her nice red car, driving at a moderate speed, as mothers do with their children in the back.'

'True,' he said. He stirred. 'Anyway, the next bunch of houses on the list are all at least one street away from the water, and the last lot are further inland, but still in the coastline villages. Beyond that . . .' He stopped, looking doubtful. 'This whole section of Sussex is one big holiday area.'

'We'll try these,' I said.

'I've some good men,' Eagler suggested. 'They could help.'

I shook my head. 'They might just possibly enquire of one of the kidnappers themselves if they'd heard a child crying. That's happened before. The kidnapper said no, and the child turned up dead on some waste ground a week later. It happened in Italy. The police caught the kidnappers in the end, and the kidnappers said they'd panicked when they found the police were so close to their hideout.'

Eagler stroked thumb and forefinger down his nose. 'All right,' he said. 'We'll do it your way.' He glanced at me sideways. 'But to be honest, I don't think you'll succeed.'

Tony, back at the hotel, wasn't particularly hopeful either. He looked judiciously at the first eleven addresses and said he would first locate them by land and then approach by rowing boat, and those eleven alone would take him all night. He said he would take my car, which still had his gear stowed in it, and he'd be back in the morning.

'Sleep tomorrow, try again tomorrow night,' he said. 'That brings us to Sunday. Hope those effing kidnappers meant it about giving Nerrity a week to collect the dough. They might be twitchy after the newspapers. Might advance the time of the drop. Hope effing not.'

He ate little for dinner and drove away when it was getting dark. I telephoned Alessia for news of Miranda, but except for her having come out of the house to call Alessia, nothing much had happened. Miranda continued to be distraught. The kidnappers had not been in touch again. John Nerrity still appeared to have faith in the ambush plan and had said he thought Miranda's near-collapse excessive.

'I wonder how he would have reacted if it had been Ordinand who'd been kidnapped?' I said.

Alessia nearly laughed. 'Don't talk of it. And it's been done.'

'Without success,' I agreed. 'Enough to put the horse-nappers off for life.'

'Would your firm work to free a horse?' she asked curiously.

'Sure. Extortion is extortion, however many legs the victim has. Ransoms can be negotiated for anything.'

'Paintings?'

'Anything anyone cares about.'

'Like "I'll give you your ball back if you pay me a penny"?'

'Exactly like that.'

'Where are you?' she said. 'Not at home . . . I tried there.'

'An evening off,' I said. 'I'll tell you when I see you.'

'Do come on Sunday.'

'Yes, I'll try.'

We spent more time than necessary saying goodbye. I thought that I could easily have talked to her all evening, and wished vaguely that she felt secure enough to travel and drive alone.

Tony came back soon after dawn, waking me from a shallow sleep.

'There are two possibles out of those eleven places,' he said, stripping off for a shower. 'Nine of them are occupied by bona-fide effing holidaymakers. I went into four to make absolutely sure, but there they were, tucked up nice and unsuspecting, dads, mums, grannies and kids, all regular law-abiding citizens.'

Tony's skill, as he immodestly said, would make any professional night burglar look like a herd of elephants. 'A creeper as good as me,' I'd heard him say, 'can touch a person in bed and get them to turn over to stop them snoring. I could take the varnish off their nails, let alone the wallets from under the pillows. Good thing I'm effing honest.'

I waited while he stepped into the shower and sluiced lavishly about. 'There's two of those places,' he said, reappearing eventually and towelling his sandy-brown hair, 'that gave me bad vibes. One of them's got some sort of electronic gadget guarding the door: it sent my detection gear into a tizzy. I'd guess it's one of those do-it-yourself alarms you can buy anywhere to stop hotel creepers fitting you up while you're sleeping off the mickey the barman slipped you.' He dried his neck. 'So

I left a couple of bugs on that one, and we'll go back soon and listen in.'

He wrapped the towel round his body like a sarong and sat on Miranda's bed. 'The other one's got no electronic gadgets that I could see, but it's three storeys high. Boatshed on the ground floor. Empty. Just water and effing fish. Above that, rooms overlooking the creek. Above that, more rooms. There's a sort of scrubby paved garden on two sides. Not much cover. I didn't fancy going in. Anyway I stuck two bugs on it, one on each of the upper floors. So we'll listen to them as well.'

'Cars?' I said.

'Can't tell.' He shook his head. 'Neither place has a garage. There were cars along the streets.' He stood up and began to dress. 'Come on then,' he said. 'Get out of the effing pit, and let's go fishing.'

He meant it literally, it seemed. By eight-thirty we were out on Itchenor Creek in the chilly morning in his rented rowing boat, throwing lines with maggots on hooks over the side.

'Are you sure this is the right bait?' I said.

'Who cares? Bass swallow bare hooks sometimes, silly buggers.'

He paddled the boat along like a born waterman with one oar in a loop of rope over the stern. No creaking rowlocks, he explained. Ultra-silent travel: high on the S.A.S. curriculum.

'The tide was low at five this morning,' he said. 'You

can't get a boat ashore at low tide in a lot of places, so if they landed the kid from that motor-boat it was probably somewhere where there's water at half-tide. Both our possibles qualify, just.'

Our rowing boat drifted along on slowly flooding water. The fish disdained the maggots and there was a salty smell of seaweed.

'We're just coming to the place with the electronic bulldog,' Tony said. 'Hold this aerial so it looks like a fishing rod.' He untelescoped about six feet of thin silvery rod and handed it over, and I found there was a line tied to the end of it with a small weight. 'Chuck the weight in the water,' he said, bending down to fiddle with the radio receiver in what looked like a fishing-gear box. 'Keep your eyes on the briny and pin back the lugs.'

I did all of those things but nothing much happened. Tony grunted and did some fine tuning, but in the end he said, 'The lazy so-and-so's aren't awake. The bugs are working. We'll come back when we've checked the other house.'

I nodded and he paddled a good way northwards before stopping again to deploy the lines. Again we drifted on the tide, apparently intent on catching our breakfast, and Tony bent to his knobs.

The voice when it came nearly tipped me out of the boat.

'Give the little bleeder his breakfast and tape off his noise if he starts whining.'

The voice – unmistakably the voice – which we had heard on the tape in John Nerrity's house. Not over loud, but crystal clear.

'My God,' I said numbly, not believing it.

'Bingo,' Tony said with awe. 'Holy effing hell.'

A different voice on the tape said, 'He won't eat it. What's the point of taking it up there?'

'Son,' said the first voice with exaggerated patience, 'do we want our little goldmine to starve to death? No we don't. Take him his bread and jam, and shut up.'

'I don't like this job,' the second voice complained. 'Straight up, I don't.'

'You were keen enough when I put you up for it. Good work, you said; those were your words.'

'I didn't reckon on the kid being so . . .'

'So what?'

'So stubborn.'

'He's not that bad. Pining, most like. You concentrate on the payola and get up the bleeding stairs.'

Tony flipped a couple of switches and for a while we sat in silence listening to the faint slap of the water against our own drifting boat; and then the second voice, sounding much more distant, said, 'Here you are, kid, eat this.'

There was no audible reply.

'Eat it,' the voice said with irritation, and then, after a pause, 'I'd stuff it down your throat if you were mine, you snotty little sod.'

Tony said 'Charming' under his breath and began to

pull in the lines. 'Heard enough, haven't we? That second bug is on the top floor, facing the street.'

I nodded. Tony reversed his switches and the second voice, downstairs again, said, 'He's just lying there staring, same as usual. Gives me the willies. Sooner we're shot of him, the better.'

'Patience,' the first voice said, as if humouring an idiot. 'You got to let the man sell his horse. Stands to reason. One week we gave him. One week is what he'll get.'

'We're not collecting the five million, though, are we?' He sounded aggrieved. 'Not a chance.'

'We were never going to get five million, stupid. Like Peter said, you demand five to frighten the dads and take half a million nice and easy, no bones broken.'

'What if Nerrity calls in the Force, and they jump us?'

'No sign of them, is there? Be your age. Terry and Kevin, they'd spot the law the minute it put its size twelves over the doorstep. Those two, they got antennae where you've got eyes. No one at the hotel. No one at the house in Sutton. Right?'

The second voice gave an indistinguishable grumble, and the first answered. 'Peter knows what he's doing. He's done it before. He's an expert. You just do what you're bleeding told and we'll all get rich, and I've had a bellyful of your grousing, I have, straight up.'

Tony put the single oar over the stern of the boat and without fuss or hurry paddled us off towards where we'd set out, against the swirling incoming tide. I rolled up the fishing lines and unbaited the hooks, my fingers absentminded while my thoughts positively galloped.

'Don't let's tell Eagler until . . .' I said.

'No,' Tony answered.

He looked across at me, half-smiling. 'And let's not tell the Chairman either,' I said. 'Or Gerry Clayton.'

Tony's smile came out like the sun. 'I was afraid you'd insist.'

'No.' I paused. 'You watch from the water and I'll watch from the land, OK? And this evening we'll tell Eagler. On our terms.'

'And the low profile can rest in effing peace.'

'You just get that vacuum pump purring like a cat and don't fall off any high walls.'

'In our report,' Tony said, 'we will write that the police found the hideout.'

'Which they did,' I said reasonably.

'Which they did,' he repeated with satisfaction.

Neither Tony nor I were totally committed to the advice-only policy of the firm, though we both adhered to it more or less and agreed that in most circumstances it was prudent. Tony with his exceptional skills tended always to be more actively involved than I, and his reports were peppered with phrases like 'it was discovered' and 'as it happened' and never with the more truthful 'I planted a dozen illegal bugs and heard . . .' or 'I let off a smoke canister and under its cover . . .'

Tony steered the boat back to where we'd left the car

and rapidly set up a duplicate receiver to work through the car's aerial.

'There you are,' he said, pointing. 'Left switch for the lower floor bug, middle switch for the top floor. Don't touch the dials. Right switch, up for me to talk to you, down for you to talk to me. OK?'

He dug around in the amazing stores he called his gear and with a nod of pleasure took out a plastic lunch box. 'Long-term subsistence supplies,' he said, showing me the contents. 'Nut bars, beef jerky, vitamin pills – keep you fighting fit for weeks.'

'This isn't the South American outback,' I said mildly.

'Saves a lot of shopping, though.' He grinned and stowed the lunch box in the rowing boat along with a plastic bottle of water. 'If the worst should happen and they decide to move the kid, we're in dead trouble.'

I nodded. Trouble with the law, with Liberty Market and with our own inescapable guilt.

'And let's not forget,' he added slowly, 'that somewhere around we have Terry and Kevin and Peter, all with their antennae quivering like effing mad, and you never know whether that crass bastard Rightsworth won't drive up to Nerrity's house with his blue light flashing.'

'He's not that crazy.'

'He's smug. Self satisfied. Just as dangerous.'

He put his head on one side, considering. 'Anything else?'

'I'll go back to the hotel, pay the bill, collect the cases.'

'Right. Give me a buzz when you're on station.' He stepped into the boat and untied its painter. 'And, by the way, do you have a dark sweater? Black, high neck?'

'Yes, I brought one.'

'Good. See you tonight.'

I watched him paddle away, a shortish figure of great physical economy, every movement deft and sure. He waved goodbye briefly, and I turned the car and got on with the day.

CHAPTER THIRTEEN

The hours passed slowly with the mixture of tension and boredom that I imagined soldiers felt when waiting for battle. Half of the time my pulse rate was up in the stratosphere, half the time I felt like sleep. At only one point did the watch jerk from stand-by to nerve-racking, and that was at midday.

For most of the morning I had been listening to the bug on the lower of the two floors, not parking the whole time in one place but moving about and stopping for a while in any of the streets within range. The two kidnappers had repeated a good deal of what we'd already heard; grouse, grouse, shut up.

Dominic at one point had been crying.

'The kid's whining,' the first voice said.

I switched to the top floor bug and heard the lonely heart-breaking grizzle, the keening of a child who'd lost hope of being given what he wanted. No one came to talk to him, but presently his voice was obliterated by pop music, playing loudly.

I switched to the lower bug again and felt my muscles go into knots.

A new voice was speaking. '. . . a bloke sitting in a car a couple of streets away, just sitting there. I don't like it. And he's a bit like one of the people staying in the hotel.'

The first-voice kidnapper said decisively, 'You go and check him out, Kev. If he's still there, come right back. We're taking no bleeding risks. The kid goes down the chute.'

The second-voice kidnapper said, 'I've been sitting at this ruddy window all morning. There's been no one in sight here, sussing us out. Just people walking, not looking.'

'Where did you leave the car?' Kevin demanded. 'You've moved it.'

'It's in Turtle Street.'

'That's where this bloke is sitting.'

There was a silence among the kidnappers. The bloke sitting in the car in Turtle Street, his heart lurching, started his engine and removed himself fast.

A red light on Tony's radio equipment began flashing, and I pressed the switch to talk to him. 'I heard,' I said. 'Don't worry, I'm on my way. Talk to you when I can.'

I drove a mile and pulled up in the car park of a busy pub, and bent my ears to catch the much fainter transmissions.

'The bloke's gone,' a voice eventually said.

'What do you reckon, Kev?'

The reply was indistinguishable.

'There hasn't been a smell of the Force. Not a flicker.' The first-voice kidnapper sounded as if he were trying to reassure himself as much as anyone else. 'Like Peter said, they can't surround this place without us seeing, and it takes eight seconds, that's all, to put the kid down the chute. You know it, I know it, we practised. There's no way the police would find anything here but three blokes having a bleeding holiday and a little gamble on the cards.'

There were some more indecipherable words, then the same voice. 'We'll both watch, then. I'll go upstairs, ready. You, Kev, you walk round the bleeding town and see if you can spot that bloke about. If you see him, give us a bell, then we'll decide. Peter won't thank us if we panic. We got to give the goods back breathing, that's what he said. Otherwise we get nothing, savvy, and I don't want to have gone through all this aggravation for a hole in the bleeding pocket.'

I couldn't hear the replies, but first-voice seemed to have prevailed. 'Right then. Off you go, Kev. See you later.'

I went inside the pub where I was parked and ate a sandwich with fingers not far from trembling. The low profile, I judged, had never been more justified or more essential, and I'd risked Dominic's life by not sticking to the rules.

*

The problem with dodging Kevin was that I didn't know what he looked like while he could spot me easily, and probably he knew the colour, make and number of my car. Itchenor was too small for handy hiding places like multi-storey parks. I concluded that as I couldn't risk being seen I would have to give the place a miss altogether, and drove by a roundabout route to reach Itchenor Creek at a much higher point, nearer Chichester. I could no longer hear the bugs, but hoped to reach Tony down the water; and he responded to my first enquiry with a faint voice full of relief.

'Where are you?' he demanded.

'Up the creek.'

'You've said it.'

'What's happened in the house?'

'Nothing. Whatever that chute is, the goods have not yet gone down it. But they're still quivering like effing jellyfish.' He paused. 'Effing bad luck, them having their car in that street.'

He was excusing me. I was grateful. I said, 'I'd been there only ten minutes.'

'Way it goes. Kev is back with them, incidentally.'

'I'll be here, if you need me.'

'OK,' he said. 'And by the way, it was the one called Peter who picked the goods up. Sweet as a daisy, they said. Peter 'phones them every day and apparently might go there himself tomorrow or the day after. Pity we can't wait.'

'Too risky.'

'Yeah.'

We agreed on a time and place for me to meet him, and switched off to conserve the power packs he had with him in the boat. Listening to the bugs was far more important and, besides, drained the batteries less.

There was always the slight chance with radio that someone somewhere would be casually listening on the same channel, but I reviewed what we'd said and thought it wouldn't have enlightened or alarmed anyone except the kidnappers themselves, even if we had, on the whole, sounded like a couple of thieves.

I stayed by the water all afternoon, in or near the car, but heard no more from Tony, which was in itself a sign that the status was still quo. At a few minutes to five I drove inland to the nearest telephone box and put a call through to Eagler.

He was off duty, the station said. What was my name?

Andrew Douglas.

In that case, would I ring the following number?

I would, and did, and he answered immediately. What a terrific change, I thought fleetingly, from my disaster with Pucinelli's second in command.

'Can your men work at night?' I said.

'Of course.'

'Tony found the kidnappers,' I said.

'I don't believe it!'

'It should be possible for you to arrest them.'

'Where are they?'

'Er,' I said. 'They are extremely alert, watching for any sign of police activity. If you turn up there too soon it would be curtains for the boy. So would you – um – act on our suggestions, without questioning them, and positively, *absolutely* not altering the plan in any way?'

There was a fair pause, then he said, 'Am I allowed to approve this plan, or not?'

'Er . . . not.'

Another pause. 'Take it or leave it?'

'I'm afraid so.'

'Hm.' He deliberated. 'The kidnappers on your terms, or not at all?'

'Yes,' I said.

'I hope you know what you're doing, laddie.'

'Mm,' I said.

A final pause, then he said, 'You're on. All right. What's the plan?'

'You need enough men to arrest at least three people,' I said. 'Can you get them to your Chichester main police station by one in the morning?'

'Certainly.' He sounded almost affronted. 'Plain clothes or in uniform?'

'I don't think it will matter.'

'Armed or not?'

'It's up to you. We don't know if the kidnappers have guns.'

'Right. And where are my men to go?'

'I'll call you with directions after one o'clock.'

He snorted. 'Not very trusting, are you?'

'I do trust you,' I said. 'Otherwise I wouldn't be setting this up for you at all.'

'Well, well,' he said. 'The iron man in the kid glove, just as I rather suspected. All right, laddie, your trust won't be misplaced, and I'll play fair with you. And I'll tear the both of you to shreds if you bungle it.'

'It's a deal,' I said thankfully. 'I'll call you at the station.'

I went back to the water to wait but heard no squeak from Tony; and long after it had grown dark I drove to where we'd agreed to meet, and transferred him and his equipment from boat to car.

'They simmered down a bit in the house,' he said. 'They had a 'phone call from Peter, whoever he is, and that seemed to steady them a bit. Pity I couldn't have fixed a tap on the telephone. Anyway, Peter apparently told them to carry on with the look-out and not dump the boy unless they could see the police outside.' He grinned. 'Which I hope they won't do.'

'No.' I stowed the power packs from the boat beside a large, amorphous canvas bag. 'Our friend Eagler promised. Also . . .' I hesitated, 'I've thought of another safeguard.'

'Tricky, aren't we?' Tony said, when I told him. 'But yes, we can't afford a balls-up. Want a nut bar? Good as dinner.'

I ate a nut bar and we sat quietly and waited, and a good while after one o'clock I telephoned Eagler and told him when and where to bring – and conceal – his men.

'Tell them to be silent,' I said. 'Not just quiet. Silent. No talking. No noisy feet. Absolutely silent.'

'All right.'

'Wait for us, for Tony and me. We will come to meet you. We may be a long time after you get there, we're not sure. But please wait. Wait in silence.'

'That's all you're telling me?' he said doubtfully.

'We'll tell you the rest when we meet you. But it's essential to get the timing right . . . so will you wait?'

'Yes,' he said, making up his mind.

'Good. We'll see you, then.'

I put the receiver down and Tony nodded with satisfaction.

'All right, then,' he said. 'How are your nerves?'

'Lousy. How are yours?'

'To be honest,' he said, 'when I'm doing this sort of thing I feel twice as alive as usual.'

I drove us gently back to Itchenor and parked in a row of cars round the corner from the kidnappers' house. There was only one street lamp, weak and away on a corner, which pleased Tony particularly, as he wanted time for us to develop night vision. He produced a tube of make-up and blacked his face and hands, and I tuned into the bugs again for a final check-up.

There was no noise from either of them.

I looked at my watch. Two-fifteen. Eagler's men were

due to be in position by two-thirty. With luck the kidnappers would be asleep.

'Black your face,' Tony said, giving me the tube. 'Don't forget your eyelids. If you hear anyone walking along the street, squat in a corner and close your eyes. It's almost impossible to see anyone in the shadows who's doing that. Standing up and moving with your eyes open and gleaming, that's playing silly buggers.'

'All right.'

'And be patient. Silence takes time.'

'Yes.'

He grinned suddenly, the white teeth satanic in the darkened face. 'What's the good of years of training if you never put them to effing use?'

We got out of the car into the quiet deserted street, and from the large shapeless canvas bag in the boot Tony extracted his intricate and lovingly-tended harness. I held the supple black material for him while he slid his arms through the armholes and fastened the front from waist to neck with a zip. It changed his shape from lithe normality to imitation hunchback, the power packs on his shoulders lumpy and grotesque.

The harness itself was a mass of pockets, both patched on and hanging, each containing something essential for Tony's purpose. Everything was in pockets because things which were merely clipped on, as in a climber's harness, clinked and jingled and also threw off gleams of light. Everything Tony used was matt black and if possible covered in slightly tacky binding, for a good grip. I'd been utterly fascinated the first time he'd shown me his kit, and had also felt privileged, as he kept its very existence private from most of the partners, for fear they would ban its use.

'OK?' he said.

I nodded. He seemed to have no trouble breathing, but my own lungs appeared to have stopped. He had gone in, though, with his bare hands in many a land where to be discovered was death, and I dare say a caper in an English seaside village seemed a picnic beside those.

He pressed an invisible knob somewhere up by his neck, and there was a small muffled whine as the power came on, steadying to a faint hiss inaudible at two paces.

'Fine, then,' he said. 'Bring the bag.'

I took the canvas bag out of the boot and quietly shut and locked the door. Then without any fuss we walked in our black clothes as far as the corner, where Tony seemed to melt suddenly into shadow and disappear. I counted ten as agreed, slid to my knees, and with caution and thumping heart took my first dim view of the target.

'Always kneel,' Tony had said. 'Look-outs look at head height, not near the ground.'

The house's paved garden, weed-grown, was in front of me, but dimly perceived, even with night-accustomed eyes. 'Move to the house wall, on the right-hand side,' Tony had said. 'Bend double, head down. When you get there, stand up, face the wall, stay in any deep shadow you can find.'

'Right.'

I followed his instructions, and no one shouted, no one set up a clamour in the house.

Above me on the wall I could see, looking up, a dark irregular shadow where no one would expect a man to be. No one except people like Tony, who was climbing the bare walls with sucker clamps fastened on by a battery-powered vacuum pump. Tony – who could go up a tower block, for whom two storeys were a doddle.

I seemed all the same to wait for several centuries, my heart thudding in my chest. No one walked along the road; no insomniacs, no people humouring importunate dogs. Sussex-by-the-sea was fast asleep and dreaming, with only policemen, Liberty Market and perhaps kidnappers wide awake.

Something hit me gently in the face. I put my hand up to catch it and fastened my fingers round the dangling length of black nylon rope.

'Tie the bag on, give the rope two tugs, I'll pull it up,' Tony had said.

I obeyed his instructions, and the canvas hold-all disappeared into the darkness above.

I waited, heart racing worse than ever. Then suddenly the bag was down with me again, but heavy, not empty. I took it into my arms and gave two more tugs on the rope. The rope itself dropped down into the shadows round my feet, and I began to pull it in awkwardly, my arms full of bag.

I didn't hear Tony come down. His skill was truly amazing. One second he wasn't there, the next moment he was, stowing the last of the released clamps into voluminous pockets. He felt for the rope I was trying to wind in and had it collected into the holdall in a flash. Then he touched me on the arm, and we both left the scrubby garden, me hunched double over my burden and Tony already sliding out of his harness. Once in the road and out of any possible sight of the house I stood upright and grasped the bag by both handles, carrying it in one hand as one normally would.

'Here,' Tony said quietly, 'rub this over your face.' He gave me something moist and cold, a sort of sponge, with which I wiped away a good deal of the blacking, and I could see that he too was doing the same.

We reached the car on silent feet.

'Don't slam the doors,' Tony said, dumping his harness onto the front passenger seat. 'We'll close them properly later.'

'OK.'

I took the bag with me into the rear seats and removed its precious contents: one very small boy, knees bent to his chest, lying on his back, with coils of black nylon rope falling over his legs. He was more than normally asleep but not totally unconscious: unwakeably drowsy. Uncombed blond-brown curls outlined his head, and across his mouth there was a wide band of medicated sticky tape. I wrapped him in the rug I always kept in the car, and laid him along the back seat.

'Here,' Tony said, passing me a bottle and a tiny cloth over from the front seats. 'This'll clean the adhesive off.'

'Did they do this?' I said.

'No, I did. Couldn't risk the kid waking up and bawling.' He started the car and drove off in one fluid movement, and I pulled the plaster off gently and cleaned the stickiness away.

'He was asleep,' Tony said. 'But I gave him a whiff of ether. Not enough to put him right out. How does he look?'

'Dopey.'

'Fair enough.'

He drove quietly to where I'd told Eagler to take his men, which was to another of the eleven houses on his list; to the one which had had the electronic anti-burglar device, a good half-mile away.

Tony stopped the car short of the place, then got out and walked off, and presently returned with Eagler himself, alone. When I saw them coming I got out of the car myself, and for a moment in the dim light Eagler looked bitterly disappointed.

'Don't worry,' I said. 'He's here, in the car.'

Eagler bent to look as I opened a rear door gently, and then, relieved, straightened up. 'We're taking him straight to his mother,' I said. 'She can get her own doctor. One the boy knows.'

'But . . .'

'No buts,' I said. 'What he absolutely doesn't want is a police station full of bright lights, loud voices and assorted officials. Fair's fair, we got the boy, you get the kidnappers. You also get the media coverage, if you don't mind. We want our two selves and Liberty Market left out of it completely. We're useful only as long as we're unknown, both to the general public and especially to all prospective kidnappers.'

'All right, laddie,' he said, listening and capitulating paternally. 'I'll stick to the bargain. Where do we go?'

Tony gave him directions.

'I left a canister of tear-gas there,' he said cheerfully. 'I took it as a precaution, but I didn't need it myself. It had a timer on it.' He looked at his watch. 'I set it to go off seven minutes from now. There's enough in it to fill the house, more or less, so if you wait another five to ten minutes you should have a nice easy task. The air will be OK to breathe about then, but their eyes will be streaming . . . that is, if they haven't already come out.'

Eagler listened enigmatically, neither objecting nor commending.

'The kid was on the top floor,' Tony said. 'He was wearing one of those harness things they put in prams. He was tied to the bed with it. I cut it off him, it's still there. Also there's some floorboards up. Mind your PCs don't fall down the hole. God knows where they'd get to.' He fished into the car and brought five cassette tapes out of the glove compartment. 'These make good listening. You play them to your friends when you have them in the nick. No one's going to confess where they came from. Bugging other people's conversations ain't gentlemanly. Andrew and I never saw these recordings before.'

Eagler took the tapes, looking faintly bemused.

'That's about all then,' Tony said. 'Happy hunting.'

He slid into the car behind the steering wheel, and before I followed him, I said to Eagler, 'The kidnappers' leader is due to join them tomorrow or the day after. I don't suppose he'll come, now, but he might telephone . . . if the news doesn't break too soon.'

Eagler bent down as I manoeuvred myself into the rear seat. 'Thanks, laddie,' he said.

'And to you,' I answered. 'You're the best.'

Tony started the car, waved to Eagler as he closed the rear door and without more fuss we were away and on the road, taking a direction opposite to the kidnappers' house, set fair for safety.

'Wow,' Tony said, relaxing five miles on. 'Not a bad bit of liberating, though I say it myself.'

'Fantastic,' I said, 'and if you go round any more corners at that speed Dominic will fall off the seat.'

Tony glanced back to where I was awkwardly jammed sideways to let Dominic lie stretched out, and decided to stop the car for rearrangements, which included removing more thoroughly the black from our faces and stowing Tony's gear tidily in the boot. When we set off again I had Dominic on my lap with his head cradled against my shoulder, and he was half grasping the cuddly teddy which I'd taken from his suitcase.

His eyes opened and fell shut occasionally, but even when it was clear the ether had worn off, he didn't wake. I wondered for a while if he'd been given sleeping pills like Alessia, but later concluded it was only the middle-of-the-night effect on the extremely young, because towards the end of the journey I suddenly found his eyes wide open, staring up at my face.

'Hello, Dominic,' I said.

Tony looked over briefly. 'He's awake?'

'Yes.'

'Good.'

I interpreted the 'good' to be satisfaction that the patient had survived the anaesthetic. Dominic's eyes slid slowly in Tony's direction and then came back to watch mine.

'We're taking you to your mother,' I said.

'Try mummy,' Tony said dryly.

'We're taking you to your mummy,' I said.

Dominic's eyes watched my face, unblinking.

'We're taking you home,' I said. 'Here's your teddy. You'll soon be back with your mummy.'

Dominic showed no reaction. The big eyes went on watching.

'You're safe,' I said. 'No one will hurt you. We're taking you home to your mummy.'

Dominic watched.

'Talkative kid,' Tony said.

'Frightened out of his wits.'

'Yeah, poor little bugger.'

Dominic was still wearing the red swimming trunks in which he'd been stolen away. The kidnappers had added a blue jersey, considerably too large, but no socks or shoes. He had been cold to the touch when I'd taken him out of the holdall, but his little body had warmed in the rug to the point where I could feel his heat coming through.

'We're taking you home,' I said again.

He made no reply but after about five minutes sat upright on my lap and looked out of the car window. Then his eyes came round again to look at mine, and he slowly relaxed back into his former position in my arms.

'Nearly there,' Tony said. 'What'll we do? It's only four. She'll pass effing out if we give her a shock at this time of night.'

'She might be awake,' I said.

'Yeah,' he said. 'Worrying about the kid. I suppose she might. Here we are, just down this road.'

He turned in through the Nerrity gates, the wheels crunching on the gravel: stopped right beside the front door, and got out and rang the bell.

A light went on upstairs and after a considerable wait the front door opened four inches on a chain.

'Who is it?' John Nerrity's voice said. 'What on earth do you want at this hour?'

Tony stepped closer into the light coming through the crack.

'Tony Vine.'

'Go away.' Nerrity was angry. 'I've told you . . .'

'We brought your kid back,' Tony said flatly. 'Do you want him?'

'What?'

'Dominic,' Tony said with mock patience. 'Your son.'

'I . . .' he floundered.

'Tell Mrs Nerrity,' Tony said.

I imagined he must have seen her behind her husband, because very shortly the front door opened wide and Miranda stood there in a nightgown, looking gaunt. For a moment she hovered as if terrified, not daring to believe it, and I climbed out of the car with Dominic hanging on tight.

'Here he is,' I said, 'safe and sound.'

She stretched out her arms and Dominic slid from my embrace to hers, the rug dropping away. He wrapped his little arms round her neck and clung with his legs like a limpet, and it was as if two incomplete bodies had been fused into one whole.

Neither of them spoke a word. It was Nerrity who did all the talking.

'You'd better come in, then,' he said.

Tony gave me a sardonic look and we stepped through into the hall.

'Where did you find him?' Nerrity demanded. 'I haven't paid the ransom . . .'

'The police found him,' Tony said. 'In Sussex.'

'Oh.'

'In conjunction with Liberty Market,' I added smoothly.

'Oh.' He was nonplussed, not knowing how to be grateful or how to apologise or how to say he might have been wrong in giving us the sack. Neither of us helped him. Tony said to Miranda, 'Your car's still at the hotel, but we brought all your gear – your clothes, chair, and so on – back with us.'

She looked at him vaguely, her whole consciousness attuned to the limpet.

'Tell Superintendent Rightsworth the boy's back,' I said to Nerrity.

'Oh . . . yes.'

Dominic, seen by electric light, was a nice-looking child with a well-shaped head on a slender stalk of a neck. He had seemed light in my arms but Miranda leant away from his weight as he sat on her hip, the two of them still entwined as if with glue.

'Good luck,' I said to her. 'He's a great kid.'

She looked at me speechlessly, like her son.

Tony and I unloaded their seaside stuff into the hall and said we would telephone in the morning to check if everything was all right; but later, when Nerrity had finally come up with a strangled thank you and shut his door on us, Tony said, 'What do you think we'd better do now?'

'Stay here,' I said decisively. 'Roughly on guard. There's still Terry and Peter unaccounted for, and maybe others. We'd look right idiots if they walked straight in and took the whole family hostage.'

Tony nodded. 'Never think the enemy have ceased hostilities, even though they've effing surrendered. Vigilance is the best defence against attack.' He grinned. 'I'll make a soldier of you yet.'

CHAPTER FOURTEEN

For one day there was peace and quiet. Tony and I went to the office for a few hours and wrote a joint report, which we hoped would be acceptable to the assembled partners on the following morning. Apart from being misleading about the order in which Dominic's escape and the entry of the gladiators had occurred, we stuck fairly closely to the truth: as always it was in the wording itself that the less orthodox activities were glossed over.

'We deduced that the child was being held in the upper storey,' he wrote, without saying how the deduction had been made. 'After the child had been freed, Superintendent Eagler was of the opinion that he (the child) should be reunited with his parents as soon as possible, and consequently we performed the service.'

On the telephone Eagler had allayed our slightly anxious enquiries.

'Don't you fret. We took them without a fight. They were coughing and crying all over the place.' His voice smiled. 'There were three of them. Two were on the top storey running about, absolutely frantic, looking for the kid and not being able to see for tears. They kept saying he'd fallen down the chute.'

'Did you find the chute?' I asked curiously.

'Yes. It was a circular canvas thing like they have for escapes from aircraft. It slanted from the hole in the floorboards into a small cupboard on the floor below. The door of the cupboard had been bricked up and wallpapered and there was a wardrobe standing in front of it. All freshly done, the cement wasn't thoroughly dried. Anyway, they could have slid the boy down the chute and replaced the chunk of floorboards and put a rug over the trapdoor, and no ordinary search would have found him.'

'Would he have survived?' I asked.

'I should think so, yes, as long as they'd taken him out again, but to do that they'd have to have unbricked the doorway.'

'All rather nasty,' I said soberly.

'Yes, very.'

Tony and I put Eagler's account of the chute into our report and decided not to tell Miranda.

Eagler also said that none of the kidnappers was talking; that they were tough, sullen, and murderously angry. None of them would give his name, address or any other information. None of them had said a single word that could with propriety be taken down and used in evidence. All their utterances had been of the four-letter variety, and they had been sparing even with those.

'We've sent their prints to the central registry, of course, but with no results so far.' He paused. 'I've been listening to your tapes. Red hot stuff. I'll pry open these fine oysters with what's on them, never fear.'

'Hope they utter pearls,' I said.

'They will, laddie.'

Towards midday I telephoned to Alessia to postpone the lunch invitation and was forgiven instantly.

'Miranda telephoned,' she said. 'She told me you brought Dominic home. She can't speak for tears, but at least this time they're mostly happy.'

'Mostly?' I said.

'John and that policeman, Superintendent Rightsworth, both insisted on Dominic being examined by a doctor, and of course Miranda didn't disagree, but she says they are talking now of treatment for him, not because of his physical state, which isn't bad, but simply because he won't talk.'

'What sort of treatment?'

'In hospital.'

'They can't be serious!' I said with alarm.

'They say Miranda can go with him, but she doesn't like it. She's trying to persuade everyone to let Dominic stay at home with her in peace for a few days. She says she's sure he'll talk to her, if they're alone.'

I reflected that once the news of his kidnap and return hit the public consciousness there would be little enough peace for a while, but that otherwise her instincts were right on the button.

I said, 'Do you think you could persuade John Nerrity, referring to your own experiences, that to be carted off to hospital among strangers would be desperately disturbing for Dominic now, even if Miranda went with him, and could make him worse, not better.'

There was silence. Then she said slowly, 'If Papa had sent me to a hospital, I would have gone truly mad.'

'People sometimes do awful things with the best intentions.'

'Yes,' she said faintly. 'Are you at home?'

'No. In the office. And – about lunch, I'm very sorry . . .'

'Another day will do fine,' she said absently. 'I'll talk to John and ring you back.'

She telephoned back when Tony and I had finished the report and he'd gone home to a well-earned sleep.

'John was very subdued, you'd be surprised,' she said. 'All that self-importance was in abeyance. Anyway, he's agreed to give Dominic more time, and I've asked Miranda and Dominic down to Lambourn tomorrow. Popsy's such a darling. She says it's open house for kidnap victims. She also suggested you should come as well, if you could, and I think . . . I do think it would be the best ever thing . . . if you could.'

'Yes, I could,' I said. 'I'd like to, very much.'

'Great,' she said; then, reflectively, 'John sounded pleased, you know, that Miranda and Dominic would be out of the house. He's so odd. You'd think he'd be delirious with joy, having his son back, and he almost seemed . . . annoyed.'

'Think of your own father's state after you got home.'

'Yes, but . . .' She broke off. 'How very strange.'

'John Nerrity,' I said neutrally, 'is like one of those snowstorm paperweights, all shaken up, with bits of guilt and fear and relief and meanness all floating around in a turmoil. It takes a while after something as traumatic as the last few days for everything in someone's character to settle, like the snowstorm, so to speak, and for the old pattern to reassert itself.'

'I'd never thought of it like that.'

'Did he realise,' I asked, 'that the press will descend on him, as they did on you?'

'No, I don't think so. Will they?'

''Fraid so. Sure to. Someone down in Sussex will have tipped them off.'

'Poor Miranda.'

'She'll be fine. If you ring her again, tell her to hold onto Dominic tight through the interviews and keep telling him in his ear that he's safe and that all the people will go away soon.'

'Yes.'

'See you tomorrow,' I said.

Dominic was a big news item on breakfast television and near-headlines in the newspapers. Miranda, I was glad to see, had met the cameras with control and happiness, the wordless child seeming merely shy. John Nerrity, head back, moustache bristling, had confirmed that the sale of his Derby winner would go through as planned, though he insisted he was nowhere near bankruptcy; that the story had been merely a ploy to confound the kidnappers.

They all asked who had rescued his son.

The police, John Nerrity said. No praise was too high.

Most people in the office, having seen the coverage, read Tony's and my report with interest, and we both answered questions at the Monday session. Gerry Clayton's eyebrows rose a couple of times, but on the whole no one seemed to want to enquire too closely into what we had done besides advise. The Chairman concluded that even if Nerrity stuck to his guns and refused to pay a fee it shouldn't worry us. The deliverance of Dominic, he said contentedly, had been tidily and rapidly carried out at little cost to the firm. Liaison with the police had been excellent. Well done, you two chaps. Any more business? If not, we'll adjourn.

Tony adjourned to the nearest pub and I to Lambourn, arriving later than I would have liked.

'Thank goodness,' Alessia said, coming out of the house to meet me. 'We thought you'd got lost.'

'Held up in the office.' I hugged her with affection.

'No excuse.'

There was a new lightness about her: most encouraging. She led me through the kitchen to the more formal drawing room where Dominic sat watchfully on Miranda's lap and Popsy was pouring wine.

'Hello,' Popsy said, giving me a welcoming kiss, bottle in one hand, glass in the other. 'Out with the wand, it's badly needed.'

I smiled at her green eyes and took the filled glass. 'Pity I'm not twenty years younger,' she said. I gave her an 'oh yeah' glance and turned to Miranda.

'Hello,' I said.

'Hello.' She was quiet and shaky, as if ill.

'Hello, Dominic.'

The child stared at me gravely with the big wide eyes. Blue eyes, I saw by daylight. Deep blue eyes.

'You looked terrific on the box,' I said to Miranda. 'Just right.'

'Alessia told me . . . what to do.'

'Alessia told her to dress well, to look calm and to pretend everything was normal,' Popsy said. 'I heard her. She said it was a good lesson she'd learned from you, and Miranda might as well benefit.'

Popsy had made an informal lunch in the kitchen, of which Miranda ate little and Dominic nothing, and afterwards she drove us all up to the Downs in her Land Rover, thinking instinctively, I reckoned, that as it was there that Alessia felt most released, so would Dominic also.

'Has Dominic eaten anything at all since we brought him back?' I asked on the way.

'Only milk,' Miranda said. 'He wouldn't touch even

that until I tried him with one of his old bottles.' She kissed him gently. 'He always used to have his bedtime milk in a bottle, didn't you, poppet? He only gave it up six months ago.'

We all in silence contemplated Dominic's regression to babyhood, and Popsy put the brakes on up by the schooling fences.

'I brought a rug,' she said. 'Let's sit on the grass.'

She and the two girls sat, with Dominic still clinging to his mother, and I leaned against the Land Rover and thought that Popsy was probably right: the peace of the rolling hills was so potent it almost stretched out and touched you.

Miranda had brought a toy car, and Alessia played with it, wheeling it across the rug, up Miranda's leg and onto Dominic's. He watched her gravely for a while without smiling and finally hid his face in his mother's neck.

Miranda said, her mouth trembling, 'Did they . . . did they hurt him? He hasn't any bad bruises, just little ones . . . but what did they do, what did they do to make him like this?'

I squatted beside her and put an arm round her shoulder, embracing Dominic also. He looked at me with one eye from under his mother's ear, but didn't try to squirm away.

'They apparently kept him fastened to a bed with a sort of harness you get in prams. I didn't see it, but I was told. I don't think the harness would have hurt him. He would have been able to move a little – sit up, kneel, lie down. He refused to eat any food and he cried sometimes because he was lonely.' I paused. 'It's possible they deliberately frightened him more than they had to, to keep him quiet.' I paused again. 'There was a hole in the floorboards. A big hole, big enough for a child to fall through.' I paused again. 'They might have told Dominic that if he made a lot of noise they'd put him down the hole.'

Miranda's whole body shuddered and Dominic let out a wail and clung to his mother with frenzy. It was the first sound I'd heard him utter, and I wasn't going to waste it.

'Dominic,' I said firmly. 'Some nice policemen have filled up that hole so that no little boys can fall down it. The three men who took you away in a boat are not coming back. The policemen have locked them up in prison. No one is going to take you to the seaside.' I paused. 'No one is going to stick any more tape on your mouth. No one is going to be angry with you and call you horrid names.'

'Oh, darling,' Miranda said in distress, hugging him.

'The hole is all filled in,' I said. 'There is no hole any more in the floor. Nobody can fall down it.'

The poor little wretch would have nightmares about it perhaps all his life. Any person who could find a prevention for nightmares, I often thought, would deserve a Nobel prize.

I stood up and said to Alessia and Popsy, 'Let's go for

a stroll,' and when they stood up I said to Dominic, 'Give your mummy lots of kisses. She cried all the time, when those horrid men took you. She needs a lot of kisses.'

She needed the kisses her husband hadn't given her, I thought. She needed the comfort of strong adult arms. She was having to generate strength enough to see herself and Dominic through alone, and it still seemed to me a toss-up whether she'd survive triumphantly or end in breakdown.

Popsy, Alessia and I walked slowly over to one of the schooling fences and stood there talking.

'Do you think you did right, reminding him of the hole in the floor?' Popsy asked.

'Splinters have to come out,' I said.

'Or the wound festers?'

'Yes.'

'How did you know what they threatened?'

'I didn't know. I just guessed. It was so likely, wasn't it? The hole was there. He was crying. Shut up you little bleeder or we'll put you down it.'

Popsy blinked. Alessia swallowed. 'Tell Miranda,' I said to her, 'that it takes a long time to get over something as awful as being kidnapped. Don't let her worry if Dominic wets the bed and clings to her. Tell her how it's been with you. How insecure it made you feel. Then she'll be patient with Dominic once the first joy of having him back has cooled down.'

'Yes, I'll tell her.'

Popsy looked from Alessia to me and back again, but said nothing, and it was Alessia herself who half smiled and gave voice to Popsy's thought.

'I've clung to you all right,' she said to me, looking briefly over to Miranda and then back. 'When you aren't here, and I feel panicky, I think of you, and it's a support. I'll tell Miranda that too. She needs someone to cling to herself, poor girl.'

'You make Andrew sound like a sort of trellis for climbing plants,' Popsy said. We walked again, as far as the next schooling fence, and stopped, looking out across the hills. High cirrus clouds curled in feathery fronds near the sun, omen of bad weather to come. We'd never have found Dominic, I thought, if it had rained the day after he was taken and there had been no canal-digger with his grandmother on the beach.

'You know,' Alessia said, suddenly stirring, 'it's time for me to go back to racing.' The words came out as if unpremeditated and seemed to surprise her.

'My darling!' Popsy exclaimed. 'Do you mean it?'

'I think I mean it at this moment,' Alessia said hesitantly, smiling nervously. 'Whether I mean it tomorrow morning is anyone's guess.'

We all saw, however, that it was the first trickle through the dike. I put my arms round Alessia and kissed her: and in an instant it wasn't a gesture of congratulation but something much fiercer, something wholly different. I felt the fire run through her in return and then drain away, and I let go of her thinking that the basement had taken charge of me right and proper.

I smiled. Shrugged my shoulders. Made no comment.

'Did you mean that?' Alessia demanded.

'Not exactly,' I said. 'It was a surprise.'

'It sure was.' She looked at me assessingly and then wandered away on her own, not looking back.

'You've pruned her off the trellis,' Popsy said, amused. 'The doctor kissed the patient; most unprofessional.'

'I'll kiss Dominic too if it will make you feel better.'

She took my arm and we strolled in comradely fashion back to the Land Rover and the rug. Miranda was lying on her back, dozing, with Dominic loosely sprawled over her stomach. His eyes, too, were shut, his small face relaxed, the contours rounded and appealing.

'Poor little sweetheart,' Popsy murmured. 'Pity to wake them.'

Miranda woke naturally when Alessia returned, and with Dominic still asleep we set off on the short drive home. One of the bumps in the rutted Down track must have roused him, though, because I saw him half sit up in Miranda's arms and then lie back, with Miranda's head bent over him as if to listen.

Alessia gave me a wild look and she too bent her head to listen, but I could hear nothing above the sound of the engine, and anyway it didn't seem to me that Dominic's lips were moving.

'Stop the car,' Alessia said to Popsy, and Popsy, hearing the urgency, obeyed.

Dominic was humming.

For a few seconds the low noise went on: randomly, I thought at first, though certainly not on one note.

'Do you know what that is?' Alessia said incredulously, when the child stopped. 'I simply don't believe it.'

'What, then?' I said.

For answer she hummed the phrase again, exactly as Dominic had done. He sat up in Miranda's arms and looked at her, clearly responding.

'He knows it!' Alessia exclaimed. 'Dominic knows it.'

'Yes, darling,' Popsy said patiently. 'We can see he does. Can we drive on now?'

'You don't understand,' Alessia said breathlessly. 'That's out of *Il Trovatore*. The Soldiers' Chorus.'

My gaze sharpened on her face. 'Do you mean . . .' I began.

She nodded. 'I heard it five times a day for six weeks.'

'What are you talking about?' Miranda asked. 'Dominic doesn't know any opera. Neither John nor I like it. Dominic only knows nursery rhymes. He picks those up like lightning. I play them to him on cassettes.'

'Holy hell,' I said in awe. 'Popsy, drive home. All is fine.'

With good humour Popsy restarted the car and took us back to the house, and once there I went over to my car to fetch my briefcase and carry it into the kitchen.

'Miranda,' I said, 'I'd like Dominic to look at a picture.'

She was apprehensive but didn't object. She sat at the kitchen table with Dominic on her lap, and I took out one of the photostats of Giuseppe and laid it face up on the table, Miranda watched Dominic anxiously for a frightened reaction, but none came. Dominic looked at the face calmly for a while and then turned away and leaned against Miranda, his face to her neck.

With a small sigh I put the picture back in the case and accepted Popsy's offer of a universal cup of tea.

'*Ciao, bambino*,' Dominic said.

My head and Alessia's snapped round as if jerked by strings.

'What did you say?' Alessia asked him, and Dominic snuggled his face deeper into Miranda's neck.

'He said "*Ciao, bambino*",' I said.

'Yes . . . that's what I thought.'

'Does he know any Italian?' I asked Miranda.

'Of course not.'

'Goodbye, baby,' Popsy said. 'Isn't that what he said?'

I took the picture of Giuseppe out of the case again and laid it on the table.

'Dominic, dear little one,' I said, 'what was the man called?'

The great eyes swivelled my way, but he said nothing.

'Was his name . . . Michael?' I asked.

Dominic shook his head: a fraction only, but a definite negative.

'Was his name David?'

Dominic shook his head.

'Was his name Giuseppe?'

Dominic's eyes didn't waver. He shook his head.

I thought a bit. 'Was his name Peter?'

Dominic did nothing except look at me.

'Was his name Dominic?' I said.

Dominic almost smiled. He shook his head.

'Was his name John?'

He shook his head.

'Was his name Peter?'

Dominic was still for a long time; then, slowly, very slightly, he nodded.

'Who's Peter?' Alessia asked.

'The man who took him for a ride in a boat.'

Dominic stretched out a hand and briefly touched the pictured face with one finger before drawing back.

'*Ciao, bambino*,' he said again, and tucked his head against his mother.

One thing was crystal clear, I thought. It wasn't Giuseppe-Peter who had most frightened Dominic. The baby, like Alessia herself, had liked him.

Eagler said, 'I thought the boy wouldn't talk. Superintendent Rightsworth told me he'd tried, but the child was in shock, and the mother was being obstructive about treatment.'

'Mm,' I said. 'Still, that was yesterday. Today Dominic has positively identified the photostat as being one of the kidnappers, known to him as Peter.'

'How reliable do you think the kid is?'

'Very. He certainly knew him.'

'All right. And this Peter – and I suppose he's the one the kidnappers are talking about on those tapes – he's Italian?'

'Yes. Dominic had learned two words from him: *ciao, bambino*.'

'Luv-a-duck,' Eagler said quaintly.

'It seems also,' I said, 'as if Giuseppe-Peter has a fondness for Verdi. Alessia Cenci said her kidnappers played three of Verdi's operas to her, over and over. Dominic is humming the Soldiers' Chorus from *Il Trovatore*, which was one of them. Did you by any chance find a cassette player in that house?'

'Yes, we did.' He sounded as if nothing ever again would surprise him. 'It was up in the room where the kid was kept. There were only two tapes there. One was pop music, and yes, laddie, the other was Verdi. *Il Trovatore*.'

'It's conclusive, then, isn't it?' I said. 'We have a practitioner.'

'A what?'

'Practitioner. Sorry; it's what in Liberty Market we

call a man who kidnaps on a regular basis. Like a safe-breaker or a con-man. His work.'

'Yes,' Eagler agreed. 'We have a practitioner; and we have you. I wonder if Giuseppe-Peter knows of the existence of Liberty Market.'

'His constant enemy,' I said.

Eagler almost chuckled. 'I dare say you made things too hot for him in his part of Italy, flooding the place with what is obviously a recognisable portrait. It would be ironic if he'd decided to move to England and came slap up against you all over again. He'd be speechless if he knew.'

'I dare say he'll find out,' I said. 'The existence of Liberty Market isn't a total secret, even though we don't advertise. Any kidnapper of experience would hear of us sometime. Perhaps one of these days there'll be a ransom demand saying no police and no Liberty Market either.'

'I meant you, personally, laddie.'

'Oh.' I paused. 'No, he wouldn't know that. He saw me once, in Italy, but not here. He didn't know then who I worked for. He didn't even know I was British.'

'He'll have a fit when he finds his picture all over England too.' Eagler sounded cheerfully smug. 'Even if we don't catch him, we'll chase him back where he came from in no time.'

'You know,' I said tentatively, 'you and Pucinelli might both flash that picture about among horse people, not just put it up in police stations. Many crooks are ostensibly sober citizens, aren't they? Both of the kidnaps that we're sure are his work are to do with racing. They're the people who'd know him. Someone, somewhere, would know him. Perhaps the racing papers would print it?'

'It's a pity I can't compare notes with your friend Pucinelli,' Eagler said. 'I sometimes think police procedures do more to prevent the exchange of information than to spread it. Even in England it's hard enough for one county to get information from another county, let alone talk to regional coppers in Europe.'

'I don't see why you can't. I can tell you his 'phone number. You could have an interpreter this end, standing by.'

'Ring Italy? It's expensive, laddie.'

'Ah.' I detected also in his voice the reluctance of many of the British to make overseas calls: almost as if the process itself was a dangerous and difficult adventure, not just a matter of pressing buttons.

'If I want to know anything particular,' Eagler said, 'I'll ask you to ask him. Things I learn from you come under the heading of information received, origin unspecified.'

'So glad.'

He chuckled. 'We had our three kidnappers in court this morning: remanded in custody for a week. They're still saying nothing. I've been letting them stew while I listened to all the tapes, but now, tonight, and with what you've just told me, I'll bounce them out of their socks.'

CHAPTER FIFTEEN

Eagler opened his oysters, but they were barren of pearls. He concluded, as Pucinelli had done, that none of the arrested men had known Giuseppe-Peter before the day he recruited one of them in a pub.

'Does Giuseppe-Peter speak English?' I asked.

'Yes, apparently, enough to get by. Hewlitt understood him, right enough.'

'Who's Hewlitt?'

'Kidnapper. The voice on the ransom tape. Voice prints made and matched. Hewlitt has a record as long as your arm, but for burglary, not anything like this. The other two are in the same trade; housebreaking, nicking silver and antiques. They finally gave their names, once they saw we'd got them to rights. Now they're busy shoving all the blame onto Peter, but they don't know much about him.'

'Were they paid at all?' I asked.

'They say not, but they're lying. They got some on account, must have. Stands to reason.'

'I suppose Giuseppe-Peter didn't telephone the house in Itchenor, did he?'

There was dead silence from Eagler. Embarrassment, I diagnosed.

'He did,' I suggested, 'and got a policeman?'

'Well . . . there was one call from someone unknown.'

'But you got a recording?'

'All he said,' said Eagler resignedly, 'was "Hello". My young PC thought it was someone from the station and answered accordingly, and the caller rang off.'

'Can't be helped,' I said.

'No.'

'Did Hewlitt say how Giuseppe-Peter knew of him? I mean, you can't go up to a perfect stranger in a British pub and proposition them to kidnap.'

'On that subject Hewlitt is your proverbial silent stone. There's no way he's going to say who put him up. There's some things, laddie, one just can't find out. Let's just say that there are a lot of Italians in London, where Hewlitt lives, and there's no way he's going to point the finger at any of them.'

'Mm,' I said. 'I do see that.'

I telephoned Alessia to ask how she was feeling and found her full of two concerns: the first, her own plans for a come-back race, and second, the predicament of Miranda and Dominic.

'Miranda's so miserable and I don't know how to

help her,' she said. 'John Nerrity's being thoroughly unreasonable in every way, and he and Miranda are now sleeping in different rooms, because he won't have Dominic sleeping in the room with them, and Dominic won't sleep by himself.'

'Quite a problem,' I agreed.

'Mind you, I suppose it's difficult for both of them. Dominic wakes up crying about five times every night, and won't go to sleep again unless Miranda strokes him and talks to him, and she says she's getting absolutely exhausted by it, and John is going on and on about sending Dominic to hospital.' She paused. 'I can't ask Popsy to have her here to stay. I simply don't know what to do.'

'Hm. . . . How much do you like Miranda?'

'Quite a lot. More than I expected, to be honest.'

'And Dominic?'

'He's a sweetheart. Those terrific eyes. I love him.'

I paused, considering, and she said, 'What are you thinking? What should Miranda do?'

'Is her mother still with her?'

'No. She has a job and doesn't seem to be much help.'

'Does Miranda have any money except what John gives her?'

'I don't know. But she was his secretary.'

'Yeah. Well . . . Miranda should take Dominic to a doctor I know of, and she should go and stay for a week near someone supportive like you that she can be with for a good deal of every day. And I don't know how much of that is possible.'

'I'll make it possible,' Alessia said simply.

I smiled at the telephone. She sounded so whole, her own problems submerged under the tidal wave of Dominic's.

'Don't let Miranda mention my name to her husband in connection with any plan she makes,' I said. 'I'm not in favour with him, and if he knew I'd suggested anything he'd turn it down flat.'

'But you brought Dominic back!'

'Much to his embarrassment. He'd sacked us two days earlier.'

She laughed. 'All right. What's the name of the doctor?'

I told her, and also told her I'd telephone the doctor myself, to explain the background and verify Dominic's need.

'You're a poppet,' Alessia said.

'Oh sure. What was it you said about going racing?'

'I rode out with the string today and yesterday, and I can't understand why I didn't do it sooner. I'm riding work for Mike Noland tomorrow, and he says if I'm fit and OK he'll give me a ride next week at Salisbury.'

'Salisbury . . . races?' I said.

'Yes, of course.'

'And, um, do you want an audience?'

'Yes, I do.'

'You've got it.'

She said goodbye happily and in the evening rang me at home in my flat.

'It's all fixed,' she said. 'Miranda said your doctor sounded a darling, and she's taking Dominic there first thing tomorrow. Then she's coming straight down here to Lambourn. I've got her a room in a cottage owned by a retired nanny, who I went to see, and who's pleased with the whole idea, and John raised no objections, absolutely the contrary, he's paying for everything.'

'Terrific,' I said, with admiration.

'And Popsy wants you down again. And so does Miranda. And so do I.'

'I give in, then. When?'

'Soon as you can.'

I went on the following day and also twice more during the following week. Dominic slept better because of a mild liquid sleeping draught in his nightly bottle of milk and progressed to eating chocolate drops and, later, mashed banana. The ex-nanny patiently took away rejected scrambled eggs and fussed over Miranda in a way which would have worn my nerves thin but in that love-deprived girl produced a grateful dependency.

Alessia spent much of every day with them, going for walks, shopping in the village, all of them lunching most days with Popsy, sunbathing in the cottage garden.

'You're a clever clogs, aren't you?' Popsy said to me on my third visit.

'How do you mean?'

'Giving Alessia something so worthwhile to do.'

'It was accidental, really.'

'And encouraged.'

I grinned at her. 'She looks great, doesn't she?'

'Marvellous. I keep thinking about those first days when she was so deathly pale and shaky. She's just about back to her old self now.'

'Has she driven anywhere yet, on her own?'

Popsy glanced at me. 'No. Not yet.'

'One day she will.'

'And then?'

'Then she'll fly . . . away.'

I heard in my voice what I hadn't intended or expected to be there: a raw sense of loss. It was all very well mending birds' broken wings. They could take your heart off with them when you set them free.

She wouldn't need me, I'd always known it, once her own snowstorm had settled. I could have tried, I supposed, to turn her dependence on me into a love affair, but it would have been stupid: cruel to her, unsatisfactory to me. She needed to grow safely back to independence and I to find a strong and equal partner. The clinging with the clung-to wasn't a good proposition for long-term success.

We were all at that moment out in Popsy's yard, with Alessia taking Miranda slowly round and telling her about each horse as they came to it. Dominic by then had developed enough confidence to stand on the ground, though he hung onto Miranda's clothes permanently with one hand and needed lifting to her hip at the approach of any stranger. He had still not said anything else, but day by day, as the fright level slowly declined, it became more likely that he soon would.

Popsy and I strolled behind the two girls and on an impulse I squatted down to Dominic's height and said, 'Would you like a ride on my shoulders?'

Miranda encouragingly swept up Dominic and perched him on me with one leg past each ear.

'Hold on to Andrew's hair,' Alessia said, and I felt the little fingers gripping as I stood upright.

I couldn't see Dominic's face, but everyone else was smiling, so I simply set off very slowly past the boxes, so he could see the inmates over the half doors.

'Lovely horses,' Miranda said, half anxiously. 'Big horses, darling, look.'

We finished the tour of the yard in that fashion and when I lifted Dominic down he stretched up his arms to go up again. I hoisted him onto my left arm, my face level with his. 'You're a good little boy,' I said.

He tucked his head down to my neck as he'd done so often with Miranda, and into my receptive ear he breathed one very quiet word, 'Andrew.'

'That's right,' I said equally quietly, 'and who's that?' I pointed at Miranda.

'Mummy.' The syllables weren't much more than a whisper, but quite clear.

'And that?' I said.

'Lessia.'

'And that?'

'Popsy.'

'Very good.' I walked a few steps with him away from the others. He seemed unalarmed. I said in a normal voice, 'What would you like for tea?'

There was a fairly long pause, then he said, 'Chocolate,' still quietly.

'Good. You shall have some. You're a very good boy.'

I carried him further away. He looked back only once or twice to check that Miranda was still in sight, and I reckoned that the worst of his troubles were over. Nightmares he would have, and bouts of desperate insecurity, but the big first steps had been taken, and my job there too was almost done.

'How old are you, Dominic?' I asked.

He thought a bit. 'Three,' he said, more audibly.

'What do you like to play with?'

A pause. 'Car.'

'What sort of car?'

He sang, 'Dee-dah, dee-dah, dee-dah,' into my ear very clearly on two notes, in exact imitation of a police car's siren.

I laughed and hugged him. 'You'll do,' I said.

Alessia's return to race-riding was in some respects unpromising, as she came back white-faced after finishing last.

The race itself, a five-furlong sprint for two-year-olds, had seemed to me to be over in a flash. Hardly had she cantered down to the start, a bent figure in shining red silks, than the field of eighteen were loaded into the stalls and set running. The red silks had shown briefly and been swamped, smothered by a rainbow wave which left them slowing in the wake. The jockey sat back onto her saddle the moment she passed the winning post, stopping her mount to a walk in a few strides.

I went to where all except the first four finishers were being dismounted, where glum-faced little groups of owners and trainers listened to tale after tale of woe and disaster from impersonal jockeys whose minds were already on the future. I heard snatches of what they were saying while I waited unobtrusively for Alessia.

'Wouldn't quicken when I asked him . . .'

'Couldn't act on the going . . .'

'Got bumped . . . shut in . . . squeezed out.'

'Still a baby . . .'

'Hanging to the left . . .'

Mike Noland, without accompanying owners, noncommittally watched Alessia approaching, then patted his horse's neck and critically inspected its legs. Alessia struggled to undo the buckles on the girths, a service Noland finally performed for her, and all I heard her say to him was 'Thanks. . . . Sorry,' which he received with a nod and a pat on the shoulder; and that seemed to be that.

Alessia didn't spot me standing there and hurried away towards the weighing-room; and it was a good twenty minutes before she emerged.

She still looked pale. Also strained, thin, shaky and miserable.

'Hi,' I said.

She turned her head and stopped walking. Managed a smile. 'Hello.'

'What's the matter?' I said.

'You saw.'

'I saw that the horse wasn't fast enough.'

'You saw that every talent I used to have isn't there any more.'

I shook my head. 'You wouldn't expect a prima ballerina to give the performance of a lifetime if she'd been away from dancing for three months.'

'This is different.'

'No. You expected too much. Don't be so . . . so cruel to yourself.'

She gazed at me for a while and then looked away, searching for another face. 'Have you seen Mike Noland anywhere?' she said.

'Not since just after the race.'

'He'll be furious.' She sounded desolate. 'He'll never give me another chance.'

'Did he expect the horse to win?' I asked. 'It started at about twelve to one. Nowhere near favourite.'

Her attention came back to my face with another flickering smile. 'I didn't know you betted.'

'I didn't. I don't. I just looked at the bookies' boards, out of interest.'

She had come from Lambourn with Mike Noland,

and I had driven from London. When I'd talked to her before she went to change for the race she'd been nervously expectant: eyes wide, cheeks pink, full of small movements and half smiles, wanting a miracle.

'I felt sick in the parade ring,' she said. 'I've never been like that before.'

'But you didn't actually vomit . . .'

'Well, no.'

'How about a drink?' I suggested. 'Or a huge sandwich?'

'Fattening,' she said automatically, and I nodded and took her arm.

'Jockeys whose talents have vanished into thin air can eat all the sandwiches they want,' I said.

She pulled her arm away and said in exasperation, 'You . . . you always make people see things straight. All right. I'll admit it. Not every vestige of talent is missing, but I made a rotten showing. And we'll go and have a . . . a small sandwich, if you like.'

Some of the blues were dispersed over the food, but not all, and I knew too little about racing to judge whether her opinion of herself was fair. She'd looked fine to me, but then so would almost anyone have done who could stand in the stirrups while half a ton of thoroughbred thundered forward at over thirty miles an hour.

'Mike did say something on the way here about giving me a ride at Sandown next week if everything was OK today, and I don't suppose he will, now.'

'Would you mind very much?'

'Yes, of course,' she said passionately. 'Of course I'd mind.' She heard both the conviction and the commitment in her voice, and so did I. Her head grew still, her eyes became more peaceful, and her voice, when she spoke again, was lower in pitch. 'Yes, I'd mind. And that means I still want to be a jockey more than anything on earth. It means that I've got to work harder to get back. It means that I must put these last three months behind me, and get on with living.' She finished the remains of a not very good chicken sandwich and sat back in her chair and smiled at me. 'If you come to Sandown, I'll do better.'

We went eventually in search, Alessia said, of an honest opinion from Mike Noland; and with the forthrightness I was coming to see as normal among the racing professionals he said, 'No, you were no good. Bloody bad. Sagging all over the place like a sponge. But what did you expect, first time back, after what you've been through? I knew you wouldn't win. I doubt if that horse could have won today anyway, with Fred Archer incarnate in the saddle. He might have been third . . . fourth.' He shrugged. 'On the form book he couldn't have touched the winner. You'll do better next time. Sure to. Sandown, right?'

'Right,' Alessia said faintly.

The big man smiled kindly from the height of his fifty years and patted her again on the shoulder. 'Best girl jockey in Europe,' he said to me. 'Give or take a dozen or two.'

'Thanks so much,' Alessia said.

I went to Sandown the following week and to two more race meetings the week after, and on the third of those days Alessia won two races.

I watched the applause and the acclaim and saw her quick bright smiles as she unsaddled her winners, saw the light in her eyes and the certainty and speed of her movements, saw the rebirth of the skills and the quality of spirit which had taken her before to the heights. The golden girl filled to new stature visibly day by day and on the morning after her winners the newspapers printed her picture with rapturous captions.

She still seemed to want me to be there; to see me, specifically, waiting. She would search the surrounding crowds with her eyes and stop and smile when she saw me. She came and went from Lambourn every time with Mike Noland and spent her free minutes on the racecourse with me, but she no longer grasped me physically to save herself from drowning. She was afloat and skimming the waves, her mind on far horizons. She had begun to be, in the way she most needed to be, happy.

'I'm going home,' she said one day.

'Home?'

'To Italy. To see Papa. I've been away so long.'

I looked at the fine-boned face, so healthy now, so brown, so full of poise, so intimately known.

'I'll miss you,' I said.

'Will you?' She smiled into my eyes. 'I owe you a debt I can't pay.'

'No debt,' I said.

'Oh yes.' Her voice took it for granted. 'Anyway, it's not goodbye for ever, or anything dramatic like that. I'll be back. The Flat season will be finished here in a few weeks, but I'll definitely be riding here some of the time next summer.'

Next summer seemed a long way away.

'Alessia,' I said.

'No.' She shook her head. 'Don't say whatever's in your mind. You carry on giving a brilliant imitation of a rock, because my foundations are still shaky. I'm going home to Papa . . . but I want you to know you're only a telephone call away . . . some days I wake up sweating . . .' She broke off. 'I'm not making sense.'

'You are indeed,' I assured her.

She gave me a brief but searching inspection. 'You never need telling twice, do you? Sometimes you don't need telling once. Don't forget me, will you?'

'No,' I said.

She went to Italy and my days seemed remarkably empty even though my time was busily filled.

Nerrity's near-loss of Ordinand had caused a huge

flutter in the dovecotes of owners of good-as-gold horses and I, in conjunction with our chummy insurance syndicate at Lloyd's, was busy raising defences against copy-cat kidnaps.

Some owners preferred to insure the animals themselves against abduction, but many saw the point of insuring their wives and children. I found myself invited to ring the front door bell of many an imposing pile and to pass on the Chairman's considered judgements, the Chairman in some erroneous way having come to consider me an expert on racing matters.

The Lloyd's syndicate did huge new business, and into every contract they wrote as usual a stipulation that in the case of 'an event', the advice of Liberty Market should be instantly sought. You scratch my back, I'll scratch yours: both the syndicate and Liberty Market were purring.

The Jockey Club showed some interest. I was despatched to their offices in Portman Square in London to discuss the problems of extortion with the Senior Steward, who shook my hand firmly and asked whether Liberty Market considered the danger a real one.

'Yes,' I said moderately. 'There have been three kidnaps in the racing world recently: man in Italy who owned a racecourse, Alessia Cenci, the girl jockey, whom you must know about, and John Nerrity's son.'

He frowned. 'You think they're connected?'

I told him how positively the latter two were connected and his frown deepened.

'No one can tell whether this particular man will try again now that the Nerrity venture has ended in failure,' I said, 'but the idea of forcing someone to sell a valuable horse may be seductive enough to attract imitators. So yes, we do think owners would be prudent to insure against any sort of extortion involving their horses.'

The Senior Steward watched my face unsmilingly. He was a thick-set man, maybe sixty, with the same natural assumption of authority as our Chairman, though not with the same overpowering good looks. Morgan Freemantle, Senior Steward, top authority of the huge racing industry, came across as a force of more power than charm, more intelligence than kindness, more resolution than patience. I guessed that in general people respected him rather than liked him, and also that he was probably good news for the health of the racing world.

He had said he had heard of our existence from a friend of his who was an underwriter at Lloyd's, and that he had since made several enquiries.

'It seems your firm is well-regarded,' he told me austerely. 'I must say I would have seen no need for such an organisation, but I now learn there are approximately two hundred kidnaps for ransom in the world each year, not counting tribal disturbances in Africa, or political upheavals in Central and South America.'

'Er . . .' I said.

He swept on. 'I am told there may be many more occurrences than those actually reported. Cases where families or firms settle in private and don't inform the police.'

'Probably,' I agreed.

'Foolish,' he said shortly.

'Most often, yes.'

'I understand from the Police Commissioners that they are willing to work with your firm whenever appropriate.' He paused, and added almost grudgingly, 'They have no adverse criticism.'

Bully for them, I thought.

'I think we can say, therefore,' Morgan Freemantle went on judiciously, 'that if anything further should happen to anyone connected with racing, you may call upon the Jockey Club for any help it is within our power to give.'

'Thank you very much,' I said, surprised.

He nodded. 'We have an excellent security service. They'll be happy to work with you also. We in the Jockey Club,' he informed me regretfully, 'spend a great deal of time confounding dishonesty, because unfortunately racing breeds fraud.'

There didn't seem to be an answer to that, so I gave none.

'Let me know, then, Mr . . . er . . . Douglas,' he said, rising, 'if your firm should be engaged by anyone in racing to deal with a future circumstance which might come within our province. Anything, that is to say, which might affect the stability of racing as a whole. As extortion by means of horses most certainly does.'

I stood also. 'My firm could only advise a client that the Jockey Club should be informed,' I said neutrally. 'We couldn't insist.'

He gave me a straight considering stare. 'We like to know what's going on in our own backyard,' he said. 'We like to know what to defend ourselves against.'

'Liberty Market will always cooperate as fully as possible,' I assured him.

He smiled briefly, almost sardonically. 'But you, like us, don't know where an enemy may strike, or in what way, and we find ourselves wishing for defences we never envisaged.'

'Mm,' I said. 'Life's like that.'

He shook my hand again firmly and came with me from his desk to the door of his office.

'Let's hope we've seen an end to the whole thing. But if not, come to see me.'

'Yes,' I said.

I telephoned to the Villa Francese one evening and my call was answered by Ilaria.

'Hello, Mr Fixit,' she said with amusement. 'How's it going?'

'Every which way,' I said. 'And how are you?'

'Bored, wouldn't you know?'

'Is Alessia there?' I asked.

'The precious girl is out visiting with Papa.'

'Oh . . .'

'However,' Ilaria said carefully, 'she should be back by ten. Try again later.'

'Yes. Thank you.'

'Don't thank me. She is out visiting Lorenzo Traventi, who has made a great recovery from his bullets and is now looking particularly ravishing and romantic and is kissing her hand at every opportunity.'

'Dear Ilaria,' I said. 'Always so kind.'

'Shit,' she said cheerfully, 'I might tell her you called.'

She did tell her. When I rang again, Alessia answered almost immediately.

'Sorry I was out,' she said. 'How's things?'

'How are they with you?' I asked.

'Oh . . . fine. Really fine. I mean it. I've ridden in several races since I've been back. Two winners. Not bad. Do you remember Brunelleschi?'

I thought back. 'The horse you didn't ride in the Derby?'

'That's right. Spot on. Well, he was one of my winners last week, and they're sending him to Washington to run in the International, and believe it or not but they've asked me to go too, to ride him.' Her voice held both triumph and apprehension in roughly equal amounts.

'Are you going?' I said.

'I . . . don't know.'

'Washington DC?' I asked. 'America?'

'Yes. They have an international race every year there at Laurel racecourse. They invite some really super horses from Europe to go there – pay all their expenses, and those of the trainers and jockeys. I've never been, but I've heard it's great. So what do you think?'

'Go, if you can,' I said.

There was a small silence. 'That's the whole thing, isn't it? If I can. I almost can. But I have to decide by tomorrow at the latest. Give them time to find someone else.'

'Take Ilaria with you,' I suggested.

'She wouldn't go,' she said positively, and then more doubtfully. 'Would she?'

'You can but ask.'

'Yes. Perhaps I will. I do wish, though, that you could go, yourself. I'd sail through the whole thing if I knew you were there.'

'Not a chance,' I said regretfully. 'But you will be all right.'

We talked for a while longer and disconnected, and I spent some time wondering if I could, after all, wangle a week off and blow the fare, but we were at that time very shorthanded in the office, Tony Vine having been called away urgently to Brazil and four or five partners tied up in a multiple mess in Sardinia. I was constantly taking messages from them on the switchboard in between the advisory trips to racehorse owners, and even Gerry Clayton's folded birds of paradise had given way to more orthodox paperwork.

Nothing happens the way one expects.

Morgan Freemantle, Senior Steward of the Jockey

Club, went to Laurel for a week to be the guest of honour of the president of the racecourse, a courtesy between racing fraternities.

On the second day of his visit he was kidnapped.

WASHINGTON D.C.

CHAPTER SIXTEEN

The Chairman sent me round to the Jockey Club, where shock had produced suspended animation akin to the waxworks.

For a start there were very few people in the place and no one was quite sure who was in charge; a flock without its leader. When I asked which individual had received the first demand from the kidnappers I was steered to the office of a stiff-backed middle-aged woman in silk shirt and tweed skirt who looked at me numbly and told me I had come at a bad time.

'Mrs Berkeley?' I enquired.

She nodded, her eyes vague, her thoughts elsewhere, her spine rigid.

'I've come about Mr Freemantle,' I said. It sounded rather as if I'd said 'I've come about the plumbing', and I had difficulty in stifling a laugh. Mrs Berkeley paid more attention and said, 'You're not the man from Liberty Market, are you?'

'That's right.'

'Oh.' She inspected me. 'Are you the person who saw Mr Freemantle last week?'

'Yes.'

'What are you going to do about it?'

'Do you mind if I sit down?' I asked, indicating the chair nearest to me, beside her polished desk.

'By all means,' she said faintly, her voice civilised upper class, her manner an echo of country house hostess. 'I'm afraid you find us . . . disarranged.'

'Could you tell me what messages you have actually received?' I said.

She looked broodingly at her telephone as if it were itself guilty of the crime. 'I am taking all incoming calls to the Senior Steward's private number on this telephone during his absence. I answered . . . There was an American voice, very loud, telling me to listen carefully . . . I felt disembodied, you know. It was quite unreal.'

'The words,' I said without impatience. 'Do you remember the words?'

'Of course I do. He said the Senior Steward had been kidnapped. He said he would be freed on payment of ten million English pounds sterling. He said the ransom would have to be paid by the Jockey Club.' She stared at me with the shocked gaze still in her eyes. 'It's impossible, you know. The Jockey Club doesn't have that sort of money. The Jockey Club are administrators. There are no . . . assets.'

I looked at her in silence.

'Do you understand?' she said. 'The Jockey Club are just people. Members. Of a club.'

'Rich members?' I asked.

Her mouth, half open, stopped moving.

'I'm afraid,' I said neutrally, 'that kidnappers usually couldn't care less where the money comes from or who it hurts. We'll get the demand down to far below ten million pounds, but it may still mean that contributions will be sought from racing people.' I paused. 'You didn't mention any threats. Were there any threats?'

She nodded slowly. 'If the ransom wasn't paid, Mr Freemantle would be killed.'

'Straight and simple?'

'He said . . . there would be another message later.'

'Which you haven't yet received?'

She glanced at a round-faced clock on a wall where the hands pointed to four-thirty.

'The call came through just after two,' she said. 'I told Colonel Tansing. He thought it might have been a hoax, so we telephoned to Washington. Mr Freemantle wasn't in his hotel. We got through to the public relations people who are looking after his trip and they said he hadn't turned up yesterday evening at a reception and they didn't know where he'd gone. Colonel Tansing explained about the ransom demand and they said they would tell Eric Rickenbacker – that's the president of the racecourse – and Mr Rickenbacker would get the police on to it straight away.'

'Was there any mention of not going to the police, on your ransom-demand call?'

She shook her head slowly. 'No.'

She had a firm, tidy-looking face with brown wavy hair greying at the sides; the sort of face that launched a thousand pony clubs and church bazaars, worthy, well-intentioned, socially secure. Only something of the present enormity could have produced her current rudderlessness, and even that, I judged, would probably transform to brisk competence very soon.

'Has anyone told the British police?' I asked.

'Colonel Tansing thought it best to contact your Chairman first,' she said. 'Colonel Tansing, you see, is . . .' She paused as if seeking for acceptable words. 'Colonel Tansing is the deputy licensing officer, whose job is mainly the registration of racehorse owners. No one of any seniority is here this afternoon, though they were this morning. No one here now really has the power to make top-level decisions. We're trying to find the Stewards . . . they're all out.' She stopped rather blankly. 'No one expects this sort of thing, you know.'

'No,' I agreed. 'Well, the first thing to do is to tell the police here and get them to put a tap on all the Jockey Club's telephones, and after that to get on with living, and wait.'

'Wait?'

I nodded. 'While the ransom negotiations go on. I don't want to alarm you, but it may be some time before

Mr Freemantle comes home. And what about his family? His wife? Has she been told?'

She said glumly, 'He's a widower.'

'Children?'

'He has a daughter,' she said dubiously, 'but I don't think they get on well. I believe she lives abroad . . . Mr Freemantle never mentions her.'

'And, excuse me,' I said, 'is Mr Freemantle himself . . . er . . . rich?'

She looked as if the question were in ultra-poor taste but finally answered. 'I have no idea. But anyone who becomes Senior Steward must be considered to have personal funds of some sort.'

'Ten million?' I asked.

'Certainly not,' she said positively. 'By many standards he is moderate in his expenditure.' Her voice approved of this. 'He dislikes waste.'

Moderate spending habits and a dislike of waste turned up often enough in the most multi of millionaires, but I let it go. I thanked her instead and went in search of Colonel Tansing, who proved to be a male version of Mrs Berkeley, courteous, charming and shocked to near immobility.

In his office I telephoned the police and got things moving there and then asked him who was the top authority at the Jockey Club in Mr Freemantle's absence.

'Sir Owen Higgs,' he said. 'He was here this morning. We've been trying to reach him . . .' He looked slightly apprehensive. 'I'm sure he will agree we had to call you in.'

'Yes,' I said reassuringly. 'Can you arrange to record all calls on all your telephones? Separately from and in addition to the police?'

'Shall be done,' he said.

'We have a twenty-four-hour service at Liberty Market, if you want us.'

He clasped my hand. 'The Jockey Club is one of the most effective organisations in Britain,' he said apologetically. 'This business had just caught us on the hop. Tomorrow everything will swing into action.'

I nodded and departed, and went back to the Liberty Market offices reflecting that neither the Colonel nor Mrs Berkeley had speculated about the victim's present personal sufferings.

Stunned disbelief, yes. Tearful sympathetic devotion, no.

Sir Owen Higgs having formally engaged Liberty Market's services, I set off to Washington the following morning, and by early afternoon, their time, was driving a rented car towards Laurel racecourse to talk to Eric Rickenbacker, its president.

The racecourse lay an hour's drive away from the capital city along roads ablaze with brilliant trees, golden, red, orange, tan – nature's last great flourish of trumpets before winter. The first few days of November:

warm, sunny and windless under a high blue sky. The sort of day to lift the spirits and sing to. I felt liberated, as always in America, a feeling which I thought had something to do with the country's own vastness, as if the wide-apartness of everything flooded into the mind and put spaces between everyday problems.

Mr Rickenbacker had left instructions about me at the raceclub entrance: I was to be conveyed immediately to his presence. Not so immediately, it transpired, as to exempt me from being stamped on the back of the hand with an ultraviolet dye, normally invisible to the eye but transformed to a glowing purple circular pattern under special lamps. My pass into the Club, it was explained: without it I would be stopped at certain doorways. A ticket one couldn't lose or surreptitiously pass to a friend, I thought. It would wash off, they said.

Mr Rickenbacker was in the president's domain, a retreat at the top of the grandstand, reached by elevator, hand-checks, a trudge through the Members' lounge, more checks, an inconspicuous doorway and a narrow stair. At the top of the stair, a guardian sitting at a table. I gave my name. The guardian checked it against a list, found it, ticked it, and let me through. The president's private dining room, built on three levels, looked out across the course through acres of glass, with tables for about a hundred people; but it was almost empty.

The only people in the place were sitting round one of the furthest tables on the lowest level. I walked over and down, and they looked up enquiringly at my approach. Six men, four women, dressed for tidy racing.

'Mr Rickenbacker?' I said generally.

'Yes?'

He was a big man with thick white hair, quite clearly tall even though sitting down. His eyes had the reflecting brilliance of contact lenses and his skin was pale and smooth, immensely well-shaven.

'I'm Andrew Douglas,' I said briefly.

'Ah.' He stood up and clasped my hand, topping me by a good six inches. 'These are friends of mine.' He indicated them with a small gesture but made none of the usual detailed introductions, and to them he said, 'Excuse me, everyone, I have some business with Mr Douglas.' He waved to me to follow him and led the way up deep-carpeted steps to a yet more private eyrie, a small room beyond, above, behind his more public dining room.

'This is a goddam mess,' he said forcefully, pointing me to an armchair. 'One minute Morgan was telling me about John Nerrity's troubles, and the next . . .' He moved his arms frustratedly. 'We've heard nothing ourselves from any kidnappers. We've told the police both here and in Washington of the ransom demand received in London, and they've been looking into Morgan's disappearance. How much do you know about that?'

'Nothing,' I said. 'Please tell me.'

'Do you want a drink?' he said. 'Scotch? Champagne?'

'No, thank you.'

'We have a public relations firm that handles a lot of things here for us. This is a social week, you follow me? We have a lot of overseas visitors. There are receptions, press conferences, sponsors' parties. We have guests of honour – Morgan was one of those – for whom we arrange transport from the hotel to the racecourse, and to the various receptions, you follow?'

I nodded.

'The public relations firm hires the cars from a limousine service. The cars come with drivers, of course. The public relations firm tells the limousine service who to pick up from where, and where to take them, and the limousine service instructs its drivers, you follow me?'

'Yes,' I said.

'Morgan was staying at the Ritz Carlton, you follow? We put him in there, it's a nice place. The racecourse is picking up the tab. Morgan was supposed to join us at a reception in Baltimore the evening before last. The reception was for the press . . . many overseas sportswriters come over for our big race, and I guess we do everything we can to make them feel welcome.'

'Mm,' I said, understanding. 'World coverage of a sports event is good for the gate.'

He paused a fraction before nodding. Maybe I shouldn't have put it so baldly; but the public-relations-promotions bandwagon generated business and business generated jobs, and the artificial roundabout bought real groceries down the line.

'Morgan didn't arrive at the reception,' Rickenbacker said. 'He was expected . . . he had assured me he would be there. I know he intended to say he was glad to be representing British racing, and to tell the press of some of the plans the English Jockey Club is making for the coming year.'

'He was going to speak?' I said. 'I mean, make a speech?'

'Yes, didn't I make that clear? We always have three or four speakers at the press party, but very short and informal, you follow, just a few words of appreciation, that sort of thing. We were surprised when Morgan didn't show, but not disturbed. I was myself surprised he hadn't sent a message, but I don't know him well. We met just three days ago. I wouldn't know if he would be careful about courtesies, you follow?'

'Yes,' I said. 'I follow.'

He smoothed a muscular hand over the white hair. 'Our public relations firm told the limousine service to pick Morgan up from the Ritz Carlton and take him to the Harbor Room in Baltimore.' He paused. 'Baltimore is nearer to this racetrack than Washington is, you follow me, so a majority of the press stay in Baltimore.' He paused again, giving me time for understanding. 'The Ritz Carlton report a chauffeur coming to the front desk, saying he had been assigned to collect Morgan. The front desk called Morgan, who came down, left his key, and went out with the chauffeur. And that's all. That's all anyone knows.'

'Could the front desk describe the chauffeur?' I asked.

'All they could positively remember was that he wore a chauffeur's uniform and cap. He didn't say much. They think he may have spoken with some sort of non-American accent, but this is a polyglot city and no one took much notice.'

'Mm,' I said. 'What happened to the real chauffeur?'

'The real . . .? Oh, no, nothing. The Ritz Carlton report a second chauffeur appeared. They told him Morgan had already been collected. The chauffeur was surprised, but not too much. With an operation of this size going on there are always mix-ups. He reported back to his service, who directed him to another assignment. The limousine service thought Morgan must have taken a ride with a friend and not told them. They were philosophical. They would charge the racetrack for their trouble. They wouldn't lose.'

'So no one was alarmed,' I said.

'Of course not. The public relations firm called the Ritz Carlton in the morning – that was yesterday – and the front desk said Morgan's key was there, he must already have gone out. No one was alarmed until we had the call from your Colonel Tansing asking about a hoax.' He paused. 'I was at home eating breakfast.'

'Rather a shock,' I said. 'Have all these pressmen woken up yet to the story under their noses?'

With a first faint glimmer of humour he said that

things were at the unconfirmed rumour stage, the whole hive buzzing.

'It'll put your race on the world map like nothing else will,' I said.

'I'm afraid so.' He looked undecided about the worth of that sort of publicity, or more probably about the impropriety of dancing up and down with commercial glee.

'You told the police,' I said.

'Sure. Both here in Laurel and in Washington. The people in Washington are handling it.'

I nodded and asked which police, specifically: there were about five separate forces in the capital.

'The Metropolitan Police,' he said. 'Sure, the FBI and the Missing Persons Bureau have taken an interest, but they've sorted it out that it's the Metropolitan Police's baby. The man in charge is a Captain Kent Wagner. I told him you were coming. He said I could send you along, if you wanted.'

'Yes, please.'

He took a wallet from an inner pocket and removed a small white card. 'Here you are,' he said, handing it over. 'And also . . .' he sorted out another card, 'this is my home number. If I've left the racetrack, you can call me there.'

'Right.'

'Tomorrow morning we have the Press Breakfast,' he said. 'That's when all the overseas owners and trainers and jockeys meet downstairs here in the club.' He paused. 'We have a Press Breakfast before most big races in America . . . have you been to one before?'

'No,' I said.

'Come tomorrow. You'll be interested. I'll arrange passes for you.'

I thanked him, not sure whether I could manage it. He nodded genially. A small thing like the abduction of Britain's top racing executive was not, it seemed, going to dent the onward steamrollering of the week's serious pleasures.

I asked him if I could make a call to Liberty Market before I went to the police in Washington, and he waved me generously to the telephone.

'Sure. Go right ahead. It's a private line. I'll do everything possible to help, you know that, don't you? I didn't know Morgan himself real well, and I guess it couldn't be thought this racetrack's fault he was kidnapped, but anything we can do . . . we'll give it our best shot.'

I thanked him and got through to London, and Gerry Clayton answered.

'Don't you ever go home?' I said.

'Someone has to mind the store,' he said plaintively: but we all knew he lived alone and was lonely away from the office.

'Any news from the Jockey Club?' I asked.

'Yeah, and how. Want me to play you the tape they got by Express Mail?'

'Fire away.'

'Hang on.' There was a pause and a few clicks, and then an American voice, punchy and hard.

'If you Brits at the Jockey Club want Freemantle back, listen good. It's going to cost you ten million English pounds sterling. Don't collect the money in notes. You're going to pay in certified bankers' checks. You won't get Freemantle back until the checks are clear. You've got one week to collect the bread. In one week you'll get more instructions. If you fool around, Freemantle will lose his fingers. You'll get one every day, Express Mail, starting two weeks from now.

'No tricks. You in the Jockey Club, you've got money. Either you buy Freemantle back, or we kill him. That's a promise. We take him out. And if you don't come up with the bread, you get nothing, you don't even get his corpse. If we kill him, we kill him real slow. Make him curse you. Make him scream. You hear us? He gets no tidy single shot. He dies hard. If we kill him, you'll get his screams on tape. If you don't want that, you're going to have to pay.

'Freemantle, he wants to talk to you. You listen.'

There was a pause on the line, then Freemantle's own voice, sounding strong and tough and incredibly cultured after the other.

'If you do not pay the ransom, I will be killed. I am told this is so, and I believe it.'

Click. 'Did you get all that?' Gerry Clayton's voice said immediately.

'Yeah.'

'What do you think?'

'I think it's our man again,' I said. 'For sure.'

'Right. Same feel.'

'How long will you be on the switchboard?' I asked.

'Until midnight. Seven p.m., your time.'

'I'll probably ring again.'

'OK. Happy hunting.'

I thanked Rickenbacker and drove off to Washington, and after a few false trails found Captain of Detectives Kent Wagner in his precinct.

The Captain was a walking crime deterrent, big of body, hard of eye, a man who spoke softly and reminded one of cobras. He was perhaps fifty with flat-brushed dark hair, his chin tucked back like a fighting man; and I had a powerful impression of facing a wary, decisive intelligence. He shook my hand perfunctorily, looking me over from head to foot, summing up my soul.

'Kidnappers never get away with it in the United States,' he said. 'This time will be no exception.'

I agreed with him in principle. The American record against kidnappers was second to none.

'What can you tell me?' he asked flatly, from his look not hoping much.

'Quite a lot, I think,' I said mildly.

He eyed me for a moment, then opened the door of his glass-walled office and asked across an expanse of desks, 'Ask Lieutenant Stavoski to step in here, if you please.'

One of the many blue-uniformed men rose to his feet

and went on the errand, and through the windows I watched the busy, orderly scene, many people moving, telephones ringing, voices talking, typewriters clacking, computer screens flicking, cups of coffee on the march. Lieutenant Stavoski, when he came, was a pudgy man in the late thirties with a large drooping moustache and no visible doubts about himself. He gave me a disillusioned stare; probably out of habit.

The Captain explained who I was. Stavoski looked unimpressed. The Captain invited me to give. I obligingly opened my briefcase and brought out a few assorted articles, which I laid on his desk.

'We think this is definitely the third, and probably the fourth, of a series of kidnappings instigated by one particular person,' I said. 'The Jockey Club in England has today received a tape from the kidnappers of Morgan Freemantle, which I've arranged for you to hear now on the telephone, if you like. I've also brought with me the ransom-demand tapes from two of the other kidnaps.' I pointed to them as they lay on the desk. 'You might be interested to hear the similarities.' I paused slightly. 'One of the tapes is in Italian.'

'Italian?'

'The kidnapper himself is Italian.'

Neither of them particularly liked it.

'He speaks English,' I said, 'but in England he recruited an English national to utter his threats, and on today's tape the voice is American.'

Wagner pursed his lips. 'Let's hear today's tape then.'

He gave me the receiver from his telephone and pressed a few preliminary buttons. 'This call will be recorded,' he said. 'Also all our conversations from now on.'

I nodded and got through to Gerry Clayton, who gave the kidnapper a repeat performance. The aggressive voice rasped out loudly through the amplifier in Captain Wagner's office, both the policemen listening with concentrated disgust.

I thanked Gerry and disconnected, and without a word Wagner held out a hand to me, his eyes on the tapes I'd brought. I gave him the Nerrity one, which he fitted into a player and set going. The sour threats to Dominic, the cutting off of fingers, the screams, the non-return of the body, all thundered into the office like an echo. The faces of Wagner and Stavoski both grew still and then judicious and finally convinced.

'The same guy,' Wagner said, switching off. 'Different voice, same brain.'

'Yes,' I said.

'Get Patrolman Rossellini in here,' he told the Lieutenant and it was Stavoski, this time, who put his head out of the door and yelled for the help. Patrolman Rossellini, large-nosed, young, black-haired, very American, brought his Italian grand-parentage to bear on the third of the tapes and translated fluently as it went along. When it came to the last of the series of threats to Alessia's body his voice faltered and stopped, and he glanced uneasily around, as if for escape.

'What is it?' Wagner demanded.

'The guy says,' Rossellini said, squaring his shoulders to the requirement, 'well, to be honest, Captain, I'd rather not say.'

'The guy roughly said,' I murmured, coming to the rescue, 'that bitches were accustomed to dogs and that all women were bitches.'

Wagner stared. 'You mean—?'

'I mean,' I said, 'that that threat was issued to reduce her father to pulp. There seems to have been no intention whatsoever of carrying it out. The kidnappers never threatened anything like it to the girl herself, nor anything indeed about daily beatings. They left her completely alone.'

Patrolman Rossellini went away looking grateful, and I told Wagner and Stavoski most of what had happened in Italy and England and in what ways the similarities of the two kidnappings might be of use to them now. They listened silently, faces impassive, reserving comments and judgement to the end.

'Let's get this straight,' Wagner said eventually, stirring. 'One: this Giuseppe-Peter is likely to have rented a house in Washington, reasonably near the Ritz Carlton, within the last eight weeks. That, as I understand it, is when Morgan Freemantle accepted Eric Rickenbacker's invitation.'

I nodded. 'That was the date given us by the Jockey Club.'

'Two: there are likely to be at least five or six kidnappers involved, all of them American except Giuseppe-

Peter. Three: Giuseppe-Peter has an inside edge on racecourse information and therefore must be known to people in that world. And four,' with a touch of grim humour, 'at this moment Morgan Freemantle may be getting his ears blasted off by Verdi.'

He picked up the photocopy likeness of Giuseppe-Peter.

'We'll paper the city with this,' he said. 'If the Nerrity kid recognised him, anyone can.' He gave me a look in which, if there wasn't positive friendship, one could at least read a sheathing of poison fangs.

'Only a matter of time,' he said.

'But . . . er . . .' I said diffidently, 'you won't, of course, forget that if he sees you getting close, he'll kill Morgan Freemantle. I'd never doubt he means that part. Kill him and bury him. He'd built a tomb for little Dominic that might not have been found for years.'

Wagner looked at me with speculation. 'Does this man Giuseppe-Peter frighten you?'

'As a professional adversary, yes.'

Both men were silent.

'He keeps his nerve,' I said. 'He thinks. He plans. He's bold. I don't believe a man like that would turn to this particular crime if he were not prepared to kill. Most kidnappers will kill. I'd reckon Giuseppe-Peter would expect to kill and get away with it, if killing were necessary. I don't think he would do it inch by inch, as the tape threatened. But a fast kill to cut his losses, to escape, yes, I'd bet on it.'

Kent Wagner looked at his hands. 'Has it occurred to you, Andrew, that this Giuseppe-Peter may not like you personally one little bit?'

I was surprised by his use of my first name but took it thankfully as a sign of a working relationship about to begin; and I answered similarly, 'Kent, I don't think he knows I exist.'

He nodded, a smile hovering, the connection made, the common ground acknowledged.

CHAPTER SEVENTEEN

Silence from the kidnappers, indignation from the about-to-be-dunned members of the Jockey Club and furore from the world's sporting press: hours of horrified talk vibrating the air-waves, but on the ground overnight a total absence of action. I went to the Press Breakfast in consequence with a quiet conscience and a light heart, hoping to see Alessia.

The raceclub lounges were packed when I arrived, the decibel count high. Glasses of orange juice sprouted from many a fist, long-lensed cameras swinging from many a shoulder. The sportswriters were on their feet, moving, mingling, agog for exclusives, ears stretching to hear conversations behind them. The majority, knowing each other, clapped shoulders in passing. Trainers held small circular conferences, the press heads bending to catch vital words. Owners stood around looking either smug or bemused according to how often they'd attended this sort of shindig; and here and there, like gazelles among the herd, like a variation of the species, stood short light-boned creatures, heads thrown back, being deferred to like stars.

'Orange juice?' someone said, handing me a glass.

'Thanks.'

I couldn't see Rickenbacker, nor anyone I knew.

No Alessia. The gazelles I saw were all male.

I wandered about, knowing that without her my presence there was pointless; but it had seemed unlikely that she would miss taking her place among her peers.

I knew she'd accepted Laurel's invitation, and her name was plainly there at the breakfast, on a list pinned to a notice board on an easel, as the rider of Brunelleschi. I read through the list, sipping orange juice. Fourteen runners; three from Britain, one from France, one from Italy, two from Canada, two from Argentina, all the rest home-grown. Alessia seemed to be the only jockey who was a girl.

Presumably at some sort of signal the whole crowd began moving into a large side room, in which many oblong tables were formally laid with flowers, tablecloths, plates and cutlery. I had vaguely assumed the room to be made ready for lunch, but I'd been wrong. Breakfast meant apparently not orange juice on the wing, but bacon and eggs, waitresses and hot breads.

I hung back, thinking I wouldn't stay, and heard a breathless voice by my left ear saying incredulously, 'Andrew?' I turned. She was there after all, the thin face strong now and vivid, the tilt of the head confident. The dark bubble curls shone with health, the eyes below them gleaming.

I hadn't been sure what I felt for her, not until that moment. I hadn't seen her for six weeks and before that I'd been accustomed to thinking of her as part of my job; a rewarding pleasure, a victim I much liked, but transient, like all the others. The sight of her that morning came as almost a physical shock, an intoxicant racing in the bloodstream. I put out my arms and hugged her, and felt her cling to me momentarily with savagery.

'Well . . .' I looked into her brown eyes. 'Want a lover?'

She gasped a bit and laughed, and didn't answer. 'We're at a table over there,' she said, pointing deep into the room. 'We were sitting there waiting. I couldn't believe it when I saw you come in. There's room for you at our table. A spare place. Do join us.'

I nodded and she led the way: and it wasn't Ilaria who had come with her from Italy, but Paolo Cenci himself. He stood up at my approach and gave me not a handshake but an immoderate Italian embrace, head to head, his face full of welcome.

Perhaps I wouldn't have recognised him, this assured, solid, pearl-grey suited businessman, if I'd met him unexpectedly in an American street. He was again the man I hadn't known, the competent manager in the portrait. The shaky wreckage of five months earlier had retreated, become a memory, an illness obliterated by recovery. I was glad for him and felt a stranger with him, and would not in any way have referred to the anxieties we had shared.

He himself had no such reservations. 'This is the man who brought Alessia back safely,' he said cheerfully in Italian to the three other people at the table, and Alessia, glancing briefly at my face said, 'Papa, he doesn't like us to talk about it.'

'My darling girl, we don't often, do we?' He smiled at me with intense friendship. 'Meet Bruno and Beatrice Goldoni,' he said in English. 'They are the owners of Brunelleschi.'

I shook hands with a withdrawn-looking man of about sixty and a strained-looking woman of a few years younger, both of whom nodded pleasantly enough but didn't speak.

'And Silvio Lucchese, Brunelleschi's trainer,' Paolo Cenci said, introducing the last of the three.

We shook hands quickly, politely. He was dark and thin and reminded me of Pucinelli; a man used to power but finding himself at a disadvantage, as he spoke very little English very awkwardly, with an almost unintelligible accent.

Paolo Cenci waved me to the one empty chair, between Alessia and Beatrice Goldoni, and when all in the room were seated a hush fell on the noisy general chatter and Rickenbacker, followed by a few friends, made a heralded entrance, walking in a modest procession down the whole room, heading for the top table facing everyone else.

'Welcome to Laurel racecourse,' he said genially, reaching his centre chair, his white hair crowning his height like a cloud. 'Glad to see so many overseas friends here this morning. As I expect most of you have now heard, one of our good friends is missing. I speak of course of Morgan Freemantle, Senior Steward of the British Jockey Club, who was distressfully abducted here two days ago. Everything possible is being done to secure his early release and of course we'll keep you all informed as we go along. Meanwhile, have a good breakfast, and we'll all talk later.'

A flurry of waitresses erupted all over the place, and I suppose I ate, but I was conscious only of my stirred feelings for Alessia, and of her nearness, and of the question she hadn't answered. She behaved to me, and I dare say I to her, with civil calm. In any case, since everyone else was talking in Italian, my own utterances were few, careful, and limited in content.

It seemed that the Goldonis were enjoying their trip, though one wouldn't have guessed it from their expressions.

'We are worried about the race tomorrow,' Beatrice said. 'We always worry, we can't help it.' She broke off. 'Do you understand what I'm saying?'

'I understand much more than I speak.'

She seemed relieved and immediately began talking copiously, ignoring repressive looks from her gloomier husband. 'We haven't been to Washington before. Such a spacious, gracious city. We've been here two days . . . we leave on Sunday for New York. Do you know New York? What should one see in New York?'

I answered her as best I could, paying minimal attention. Her husband was sporadically discussing Brunelleschi's prospects with Lucchese as if it were their fiftieth reiteration, rather like the chorus of a Greek play six weeks into its run. Paolo Cenci told me five times he was delighted to see me, and Alessia ate an egg but nothing else.

An ocean of coffee later the day's real business began, proving to be short interviews with all the trainers and jockeys and many of the owners of the following day's runners. Sportswriters asked questions, Rickenbacker introduced the contestants effusively, and everyone learned more about the foreign horses than they'd known before or were likely to remember after.

Alessia interpreted for Lucchese, translating the questions, slightly editing the answers, explaining in one reply that Brunelleschi didn't actually mean anything, it was the name of the architect who'd designed a good deal of the city of Florence; like Wren in London, she said. The sportswriters wrote it down. They wrote every word she uttered, looking indulgent.

On her own account she said straightforwardly that the horse needed to see where he was going in a race and hated to be shut in.

'What was it like being kidnapped?' someone asked, transferring the thought.

'Horrible.' She smiled, hesitated, said finally that she felt great sympathy for Morgan Freemantle and hoped sincerely that he would soon be free.

Then she sat down and said abruptly, 'When I heard about Morgan Freemantle I thought of you, of course . . . wondered if your firm would be involved. That's why you're here, isn't it? Not to see me race.'

'Both,' I said.

She shook her head. 'One's work, one's luck.' She sounded merely practical. 'Will you find him, like Dominic?'

'A bit unlikely,' I said.

'It brings it all back,' she said, her eyes dark.

'Don't . . .'

'I can't help it. Ever since I heard . . . when we got to the track this morning . . . I've been thinking of him.'

Beatrice Goldoni was talking again like a rolling stream, telling me and also Alessia, who must have heard it often before, what a terrible shock it had been when dear Alessia had been kidnapped, and now this poor man, and what a blessing that I had been able to get dear Alessia back . . . and I thought it colossally lucky she was speaking in her own tongue, which I hoped wouldn't be understood by the newspaper ears all around.

I stopped her by wishing her firmly the best of luck in the big race, and by saying my farewells to the whole party. Alessia came with me out of the dining room and we walked slowly across the bright club lounge to look out across the racecourse.

'Tomorrow,' I said, 'they'll be cheering you.'

She looked apprehensive more than gratified. 'It depends how Brunelleschi's travelled.'

'Isn't he here?' I asked, surprised.

'Oh yes, but no one knows how he feels. He might be homesick . . . and don't laugh, the tap water here tastes vile to me, God knows what the horse thinks of it. Horses have their own likes and dislikes, don't forget, and all sorts of unimaginable factors can put them off.'

I put my arm round her tentatively.

'Not here,' she said.

I let the arm fall away. 'Anywhere?' I asked.

'Are you sure . . .?'

'Don't be silly. Why else would I ask?'

The curve of her lips was echoed in her cheekbones and in her eyes, but she was looking at the track, not at me.

'I'm staying at the Sherryatt,' I said. 'Where are you?'

'The Regency. We're all there: the Goldonis, Silvio Lucchese, Papa and I. All guests of the racecourse. They're so generous, it's amazing.'

'How about dinner?' I said.

'I can't. We've been invited by the Italian ambassador . . . Papa knows him . . . I have to be there.'

I nodded.

'Still,' she said. 'We might go for a drive or something

this afternoon. I don't truthfully want to spend all day here on the racecourse. We were here yesterday . . . all the foreign riders were shown what we'll be doing. Today is free.'

'I'll wait for you here, then, on this spot.'

She went to explain to her father but returned immediately saying that everyone was about to go round to the barns and she couldn't get out of that either, but they'd all said I was very welcome to go with them, if I'd like.

'Barns?' I said.

She looked at me with amusement. 'Where they stable the horses on American racecourses.'

In consequence I shortly found myself, along with half the attendance from the breakfast, watching the morning routines on the private side of the tracks; the feeding, the mucking-out, the grooming, the saddling-up and mounting, the breezes (short sharp canters), the hot-walking (for cooling off from exercise), the sand-pit rolling, and all around, but constantly shifting, the tiny individual press conferences where trainers spoke prophesies like Moses.

I heard the trainer of the home-based horse that was favourite saying confidently, 'We'll have the speed all the way to the wire.'

'What about the foreign horses?' one of the reporters asked. 'Is there one to beat you?'

The trainer's eye wandered and lit on Alessia, by

my side. He knew her. He smiled. He said gallantly, 'Brunelleschi is the danger.'

Brunelleschi himself, in his stall, seemed unimpressed. Silvio Lucchese, it appeared, had brought the champion's own food from Italy so that the choosy appetite should be unimpaired. And Brunelleschi had, it seemed, 'eaten up' the evening before (a good sign), and hadn't kicked his stable-lad, as he did occasionally from displeasure. Everyone patted his head with circumspection, keeping their fingers away from his strong white teeth. He looked imperious to me, like a bad-tempered despot. No one asked what he thought of the water.

'He's nobody's darling,' Alessia said out of the owners' earshot. 'The Goldonis are afraid of him, I often think.'

'So am I,' I said.

'He puts all his meanness into winning.' She looked across with rueful affection at the dark tossing head. 'I tell him he's a bastard, and we get on fine.'

Paolo Cenci seemed pleased that Alessia would be spending most of the day with me. He, Lucchese and Bruno Goldoni intended to stay for the races. Beatrice, with a secret, sinful smile of pleasure, said she was going to the hotel's hairdresser, and, after that, shopping. Slightly to my dismay Paolo Cenci suggested Alessia and I should give her a lift back to Washington to save the limousine service doubling the journey, and accordingly we passed the first hour of our day with the voluble lady saying nothing much at great length. I had an overall impression that separation, even temporary, from her husband, had caused an excited rise in her spirits, and when we dropped her at the Regency she had twin spots of bright red on her sallow middle-aged cheeks and guilt in every line of her heavy face.

'Poor Beatrice, you'd almost think she was meeting a lover,' Alessia said smiling, as we drove away, 'not just going shopping.'

'You, on the other hand,' I observed, 'are not blushing a bit.'

'Ah,' she said. 'I haven't promised a thing.'

'True.' I stopped the car presently in a side street and unfolded a detailed map of the city. 'Anything you'd like to see?' I asked. 'Lincoln Monument, White House, all that?'

'I was here three years ago, visiting. Did all the tours.'

'Good . . . Do you mind then, if we just drive around a bit? I want to put . . . faces . . . onto some of these street names.'

She agreed, looking slightly puzzled, but after a while said, 'You're looking for Morgan Freemantle.'

'For possible districts, yes.'

'What are possible?'

'Well . . . not industrial areas. Not decayed housing. Not all-black neighbourhoods. Not parks, museums or government offices. Not diplomatic residential areas . . . embassies and their offices. Not blocks of flats with janitors. Not central shopping areas, nor banking areas, nor schools or colleges, nowhere with students.'

'What's left?'

'Private housing. Suburbs. Anywhere without prying neighbours. And at a guess, somewhere north or west of the centre, because the Ritz Carlton is there.'

We drove for a good long while, methodically sectioning the sprawling city according to the map, but concentrating most and finally on the north and west. There were beauties to the place one couldn't guess from the tourist round, and miles and hosts of residential streets where Morgan Freemantle could be swallowed without trace.

'I wonder if we've actually been past him,' Alessia said at one point. 'Gives me the shivers, not knowing. I can't bear to think of him. Alone . . . dreadfully alone . . . somewhere close.'

'He might be further out,' I said. 'But kidnappers don't usually go for deserted farmhouses or places like that. They choose more populated places, where their comings and goings aren't noticeable.'

The scale of it all, however, was daunting, even within the radius I thought most likely. Analysis of recent rentals wouldn't come up this time with just eleven probables: there would be hundreds, maybe one or two thousand. Kent Wagner's task was impossible, and we would have to rely on negotiation, not a second miracle, to get Morgan Freemantle safe home.

We were driving up and down some streets near

Washington Cathedral, simply admiring the houses for their architecture: large old sprawling houses with frosting of white railings, lived-in houses with signs of young families. On every porch, clusters of Halloween pumpkins.

'What are those?' Alessia said, pointing at the grinning orange faces of the huge round fruits on the steps outside every front door.

'It was Halloween four days ago,' I said.

'Oh yes, so it was. You don't see those at home.'

We passed the Ritz Carlton on Massachusetts Avenue and paused there, looking at the peaceful human-scaled hotel with its blue awnings from where Morgan had been so unceremoniously snatched, and then coasted round Dupont Circle and made our way back to the more central part. Much of the city was built in radii from circles, like Paris, which may have made for elegance but was a great recipe for getting lost: we'd chased our tails several times in the course of the day.

'It's so vast,' Alessia said, sighing. 'So confusing. I'd no idea.'

'We've done enough,' I agreed. 'Hungry?'

It was three-thirty by then, but time meant nothing to the Sherryatt Hotel. We went up to my room on the twelfth floor of the anonymous, enormous, bustling pile and we ordered wine and avocado shrimp salad from room service. Alessia stretched lazily on one of the armchairs and listened while I telephoned Kent Wagner.

Did I realise, he asked trenchantly, that the whole goddam population of North America was on the move through Washington D.C., and that a list of rentals would bridge the Potomac.

'Look for a house without pumpkins,' I said.

'What?'

'Well, if you were a kidnapper, would you solemnly carve Halloween faces on pumpkins and put them on the front steps?'

'No, I guess not.' He breathed out in the ghost of a chuckle. 'Takes a limey to come up with a suggestion as dumb as that.'

'Yeah,' I said. 'I'll be at the Sherryatt this evening and at the races tomorrow, if you should want me.'

'Got it.'

I telephoned next to Liberty Market, but nothing much had developed in London. The collective fury of the members of the Jockey Club was hanging over Portman Square in a blue haze and Sir Owen Higgs had retreated for the weekend to Gloucestershire. Hoppy at Lloyd's was reported to be smiling cheerfully as in spite of advising everyone else to insure against extortion the Jockey Club hadn't done so itself. Apart from that, nix.

The food arrived and we ate roughly jockey-sized amounts. Then Alessia pushed her plate away and, looking at her wine glass, said, 'Decision time, I suppose.'

'Only for you,' I said mildly. 'Yes or no.'

Still looking down she said, 'Would no . . . be acceptable?'

'Yes, it would,' I said seriously.

'I . . .' She took a deep breath. 'I want to say yes, but I feel . . .' She broke off, then started again. 'I don't seem to want . . . since the kidnap . . . I've thought of kissing, of love, and I'm dead . . . I went out with Lorenzo once or twice and he wanted to kiss me . . . his mouth felt like rubber to me.' She looked at me anxiously, willing me to understand. 'I did love someone passionately once, years ago, when I was eighteen. It didn't last beyond summer . . . We both simply grew up . . . but I know what it's like, what I should feel, what I should want . . . and I don't.'

'Darling Alessia.' I stood up and walked to the window, thinking that for this battle I wasn't strong enough, that there was a limit to controlled behaviour, that what I myself longed for now was warmth. 'I do truly love you in many ways,' I said, and found the words coming out an octave lower than in my normal voice.

'Andrew!' She came to her feet and walked towards me, searching my face and no doubt seeing there the vulnerability she wasn't accustomed to.

'Well . . .' I said, struggling for lightness; for a smile; for Andrew the unfailing prop. 'There's always time. You ride races now. Go shopping. Drive your car?'

She nodded.

'It all took time,' I said. I wrapped my arms around

her lightly and kissed her forehead. 'When rubber begins feeling like lips, let me know.'

She put her head against my shoulder and clung to me for help as she had often clung before; and it was I, really, who wanted to be enfolded and cherished and loved.

She rode in the race the next day, a star in her own firmament.

The racecourse had come alive, crowds pressing, shouting, betting, cheering. The grandstands were packed. One had to slide round strangers to reach any goal. I had my hand stamped and checked and my name taken and ticked, and Eric Rickenbacker welcomed me busily to the biggest day of his year.

The president's dining room, so echoingly empty previously, spilled over now with chattering guests all having a wow of a time. Ice clinked and waitresses passed with small silver trays and a large buffet table offered crab cakes to aficionados.

Paolo Cenci was there with the Goldonis and Lucchese, all of them looking nervous as they sat together at one of the tables. I collected a glass of wine from an offered trayful and went over to see them, wishing them well.

'Brunelleschi kicked his groom,' Paolo Cenci said.

'Is that good or bad?'

'No one knows,' he said.

I kept the giggle in my stomach. 'How's Alessia?' I asked.

'Less worried than anyone else.'

I glanced at the other faces: at Lucchese, fiercely intense, at Bruno Goldoni, frowning, and at Beatrice, yesterday's glow extinguished.

'It's her job,' I said.

They offered me a place at their table but I thanked them and wandered away, too restless to want to be with them.

'Any news from London?' Eric Rickenbacker said in my ear, passing close.

'None this morning.'

He clicked his tongue, indicating sympathy. 'Poor Morgan. Should have been here. Instead . . .' He shrugged resignedly, moving away, greeting new guests, kissing cheeks, clapping shoulders, welcoming a hundred friends.

The Washington International was making the world's news. Poor Morgan, had he been there, wouldn't have caused a ripple.

They saved the big race until ninth of the ten on the card, the whole afternoon a titillation, a preparation, with dollars flooding meanwhile into the Pari-mutuel and losing tickets filling the trashcans.

The whole of the front of the main stands was filled in with glass, keeping out the weather, rain or shine. To one slowly growing used to the rigours of English courses the luxury was extraordinary but, when I commented on it, one of Rickenbacker's guests said reasonably that warm betters betted, cold betters stayed at home. A proportion of the day's take at the Pari-mutuel went to the racecourse: racegoer comfort was essential.

For me the afternoon passed interminably, but in due course all the foreign owners and trainers left the president's dining room to go down nearer the action and speed their horses on their way.

I stayed in the eyrie, belonging nowhere, watching the girl I knew so well come out onto the track; a tiny gold and white figure far below, one in a procession, each contestant led and accompanied by a liveried outrider. No loose horses on the way to the post, I thought. No runaways, no bolters.

A trumpet sounded a fanfare to announce the race. A frenzy of punters fluttered fistfuls of notes. The runners walked in procession across in front of the stands and cantered thereafter to the start, each still with an escort. Alessia looked from that distance identical with the other jockeys: I wouldn't have known her except for the colours.

I felt, far more disturbingly than on the English tracks, a sense of being no part of her real life. She lived most intensely there, on a horse, where her skill filled her. All I could ever be to her as a lover, I thought, was a support: and I would settle for that, if she would come to it.

The runners circled on the grass, because the one and

a half mile International was run on living green turf, not on dirt. They were fed into the stalls on the far side of the track. Lights still flickered on the Pari-mutuel, changing the odds: races in America tended to start when the punters had finished, not to any rigid clock.

They were off, they were running, the gold and white figure with them, going faster than the wind and to my mind crawling like slow motion.

Brunelleschi, the brute who kicked, put his bad moods to good use, shouldering his way robustly round the first bunched-up bend, forcing himself through until there was a clear view ahead. Doesn't like to be shut in, Alessia had said. She gave him room and she held him straight: they came past the stands for the first time in fourth place, the whole field close together. Round the top bend left-handed, down the back stretch, round the last corner towards home.

Two of the leaders dropped back: Brunelleschi kept on going. Alessia swung her stick twice, aimed the black beast straight at the target and rode like a white and gold arrow to the bull.

She won the race, that girl, and was cheered as she came to the winners' enclosure in front of the stands. She was photographed and filmed, her head back, her mouth laughing. As Brunelleschi stamped around in his winner's garland of laurels (what else?) she reached forward and gave his dark sweating neck a wide-armed exultant pat, and the crowd again cheered.

I wholeheartedly shared in her joy: and felt lonely.

They all came up to the dining room for champagne – winners, losers, and Eric Rickenbacker looking ecstatic.

'Well done,' I said to her.

'Did you see?' She was high, high with achievement.

'Yes, I did.'

'Isn't it fantastic?'

'The day of a lifetime.'

'Oh, I do love you,' she said, laughing, and turned away immediately, and talked with animation to a throng of admirers. Ah, Andrew, I thought wryly, how do you like it? And I answered myself: better than nothing.

When I finally got back to the hotel the message button was flashing on my telephone. My office in England had called when I was out. Please would I get through to them straight away.

Gerry Clayton was on the switchboard.

'Your Italian friend rang from Bologna,' he said. 'The policeman, Pucinelli.'

'Yes?'

'He wants you to telephone. I couldn't understand him very well, but I think he said he had found Giuseppe-Peter.'

CHAPTER EIGHTEEN

By the time I got the message it was three in the morning, Italian time. On the premise, however, that the law neither slumbered nor slept I put the call through straight away to the carabinieri, and was answered by a yawning Italian who spoke no English.

Pucinelli was not there.

It was not known when Pucinelli would be there next.

It was not known if Pucinelli was in his own house.

I gave my name, spelling it carefully letter by letter but knowing it would look unpronounceable to most Italians.

I will telephone again, I said; and he said, 'Good.'

At one in the morning, Washington time, I telephoned Pucinelli's own home, reckoning his family would be shaping to breakfast. His wife answered, children's voices in the background, and I asked for her husband, in Italian.

'Enrico is in Milan,' she said, speaking slowly for my sake. 'He told me to give you a message.' A short pause with paper noises, then: 'Telephone this house at fourteen hours today. He will return by that time. He says it is very important, he has found your friend.'

'In Milan?' I asked.

'I don't know. Enrico said only to ask you to telephone.'

I thanked her and disconnected, and slept fitfully while four thousand miles away Pucinelli travelled home. At fourteen hours, two p.m. his time, eight a.m. in Washington, I got through again to his house and found he had been called out on duty the minute he returned.

'He is sorry. Telephone his office at seventeen hours.'

By that time, I reckoned, my fingernails would be bitten to the knuckle. My stomach positively hurt with impatience. I ordered breakfast from room service to quieten it and read the Washington Sunday papers and fidgeted, and finally at eleven I got him.

'Andrew, how are you?' he said.

'Dying of suspense.'

'What?'

'Never mind.'

'Where are you?' he said. 'Your office said America.'

'Yes. Washington. Have you really found Giuseppe-Peter?'

'Yes and no.'

'What do you mean?'

'You remember,' he said, 'that we have been enquiring all the time among horse people, and also that we were going to try some students' reunions, to see if anyone recognised him from the drawing.'

'Yes, of course,' I said.

We had drifted automatically into our normal habit of speaking two languages, and it seemed just as satisfactory as ever.

'We have succeeded in both places. In both worlds.' He paused for effect and sounded undeniably smug. 'He lives near Milan. He is thirty-four now. He went to Milan University as a student and joined radical political groups. It is believed he was an activist, a member of the Red Brigades, but no one knows for sure. I was told it was a fact, but there was no true evidence. Anyway, he did not continue in political life after he left university. He left without sitting his final examinations. The university asked him to leave, but not because of his radical opinions. They made him leave because he forged cheques. He was not prosecuted, which I think is a mistake.'

'Mm,' I agreed, riveted.

'So then I had his name. And almost immediately, the same day that I learned it, we had the information from the horse people. They say he is not well known in the horse world, he never goes to the races, he is the black sheep of a well-regarded family, and is banished from their house. No one seems to be absolutely certain in detail why this is, but again there are many rumours that it is to do with fraud and forging cheques. Everyone believes the father repaid every penny to keep the family name out of the disgrace.'

'But the horse world told you this?'

'Yes. In the end, someone recognised him. Our men were very diligent, very persistent.'

'They're to be congratulated,' I said sincerely.

'Yes, I agree.'

'What is his name?' I asked. It hardly seemed to matter, but it would be tidier to give him the proper label.

'His father owns racehorses,' Pucinelli said. 'His father owns the great horse Brunelleschi. Giuseppe-Peter's real name is Pietro Goldoni.'

Washington D.C. seemed to stand still. Suspended animation. I actually for a while stopped breathing. I felt stifled.

'Are you there, Andrew?' Pucinelli said.

I let out a long breath. 'Yes . . .'

'No one has seen Pietro Goldoni since the summer. Everyone thinks he went abroad and hasn't come back.' He sounded pleased. 'It fits the timetable, doesn't it? We chased him out of Italy and he went to England.'

'Er . . .' I said faintly, 'have you heard about Morgan Freemantle? Did you read anything in the papers yesterday or today, see anything on television?'

'Who? I have been so busy in Milan. Who is Morgan Freemantle?'

I told him. I also said, 'Bruno and Beatrice Goldoni have been here all this week in Washington. I have talked to them. Brunelleschi won the big International race here yesterday afternoon. Alessia Cenci rode it.'

There was the same sort of stunned breathless silence from his end as there had been from mine.

'He is there,' he said finally. 'Pietro Goldoni is in Washington.'

'Yeah.'

'You of course knew that.'

'I assumed that Giuseppe-Peter was here, yes.'

He paused, considering. 'In what way is it best that I inform the American police of his identity? It may be that my superiors would want to consult . . .'

'If you like,' I said politely, 'I myself will first tell the police captain in charge of things here. The captain might be pleased to talk to you then direct. There's an Italian-speaker in his force who could translate for you both.'

Pucinelli was grateful and careful not to sound it. 'That would be excellent. If you would arrange it, I am sure it would be helpful.'

'I'll do it at once,' I said.

'It is Sunday,' he said, almost doubtfully.

'But you yourself are working,' I pointed out. 'And I'll reach him, somehow.'

He gave me his schedule of times on and off duty, which I wrote down.

'You've done marvels, Enrico,' I said warmly, near the end. 'I do congratulate you. It must be worth promotion.'

He laughed shortly, both pleased and unhopeful. 'This Goldoni has still to be caught.' A thought struck him. 'In which country, do you think, will he be brought to trial?'

'On his past record,' I said dryly, 'nowhere. He'll skip to South America as soon as the police get near him here, and next year maybe a polo player will be snatched from out of a chukka.'

'What?'

'Untranslatable,' I said. 'Goodbye for just now.'

I telephoned immediately to Kent Wagner's headquarters and by dint of threats and persuasion finally tracked him to the home of his niece, who was celebrating her birthday with a brunch.

'Sorry,' I said; and explained at some length.

'Jesus Christ,' he said. 'Who is this guy Pucinelli?'

'A good cop. Very brave. Talk to him.'

'Yeah.'

I gave him the telephone numbers and Enrico's schedule. 'And the Goldonis are going to New York,' I said. 'Mrs Goldoni told me. I think they're going today. They've been staying here at the Regency.'

'I'll get onto it at once. Will you be at the Sherryatt still?'

'Yes, I'm there now.'

'Stay by the 'phone.'

'OK.'

He grunted. 'Thanks, Andrew.'

'A pleasure, Kent,' I said, meaning it. 'Just catch him. He's all yours.'

As soon as I put the receiver down there was a knock on the door, and I was already opening it before it occurred to me that perhaps I should start to be careful. It was only the maid, however, on my doorstep; short, dumpy, middle-aged and harmless, wanting to clean the room.

'How long will you be?' I said, looking at the trolley of fresh linen and the large vacuum cleaner.

She said in Central-American Spanish that she didn't understand. I asked her the same question in Spanish. Twenty minutes, she said stolidly. Accordingly I lifted the telephone, asked the switchboard to put any calls through to me in the lobby temporarily, and went downstairs to wait.

To wait . . . and to think.

I thought chiefly about Beatrice Goldoni and her excited guilt. I thought of her son, banished from his father's house. I thought it highly likely that it wasn't a lover Beatrice had been sneaking off to meet in Washington that Friday, but a still-beloved black sheep. He would have set it up himself, knowing she was there for the race, and still feeling, on his part, affection.

For a certainty she didn't know he was the kidnapper of Alessia and Freemantle. She hadn't that sort of guile. She did know, however, that it had been I who'd negotiated Alessia's ransom, because at that Friday breakfast Paolo Cenci had told her. What else he had told her, heaven knew. Maybe he had told her also about Dominic: it wouldn't have been unreasonable. Many people didn't understand why Liberty Market liked to keep quiet about its work, and saw no great harm in telling.

I had myself driven Beatrice into Washington; and she talked, always, a lot. Chatter, chatter . . . we're here with the Cencis, you remember Alessia who was kidnapped? And there's a young man with her, the one who came to Italy to get her back safely . . . he's here because of this other kidnapping . . . and Paolo Cenci told us he rescued a little boy Dominic in England . . . Alessia was there too . . . chatter, chatter, chatter.

I stood up from the lobby sofa, went to the desk, and said I was checking out; would they please prepare my bill. Then I got through again to Kent Wagner, who said I'd just caught him, he was leaving the brunch.

'You sure as hell broke up my day,' he said, though sounding philosophical. 'Thought of something else?'

I said I was leaving the Sherryatt, and why.

'Jee-sus,' he said. 'Come down to headquarters; I'll put you into a good place where Goldoni would never find you. It's sure prudent to assume that he does now know you exist.'

'Might be safer,' I agreed. 'I'm on my way.'

The desk said my account would be ready when I came down with my gear. The twenty minutes was barely up, but when I stepped out of the lift I saw the maid pushing her trolley away down the passage. I unlocked my door and went in.

There were three men there, all in high-domed peaked caps and white overalls, with International Rug Co. Inc. on chests and backs. They had pushed some of the furniture to the walls and were unrolling a large Indian-type rug in the cleared free centre.

'What . . .' I began. And I thought: it's Sunday.

I spun on my heel to retreat, but it was already too late.

A fourth man, International Rug Co. Inc. on his chest, was blocking the doorway; advancing, stretching out his arms, thrusting me forcefully backwards into the room.

I looked into his eyes . . . and knew him.

I thought in lightning flashes.

I thought: I've lost.

I thought: I'm dead.

I thought: I meant to win. I thought I would win. I thought I'd find him and get him arrested and stop him, and it never seriously occurred to me it could be this way round.

I thought: I'm a fool, and I've lost. I thought I would win, and Brunelleschi . . . the danger . . . has beaten me.

Everything happened very fast, in a blur. A sort of canvas bag came down over my head, blocking out sight. I was tripped and tossed by many hands to the floor. There was a sharp sting in my thigh, like a wasp. I was conscious of being turned over and over, realised dimly that I was being rolled up like a sausage in the Indian rug.

It was the last thing I thought for quite a long while.

I woke up out of doors, feeling cold.

I was relieved to wake up at all, but that said, could find little else of comfort.

For a start, I had nothing on.

Sod it, I thought furiously. True to bloody form. Just like Alessia. Morgan Freemantle – he too, I dared say, was currently starkers.

Liberty Market's own private unofficial training manual, issued to each partner on joining, spelled it out: 'immediate and effective domination and demoralisation of the victim is achieved by depriving him/her of clothes.'

Dominic had had clothes; they'd even added a jersey to his tiny shorts. Dominic, on the other hand, was too little to find anything humiliating in nakedness. There would have been no point.

The only thing to do was to try to think of myself as dressed.

I was sitting on the ground; ground being loamy earth covered with fallen leaves. I was leaning against the tree from which most of the said leaves appeared to have descended: a small tree with a smooth hard trunk no more than four inches in diameter.

The view was limited on every side by growths of

evergreen; mostly, it seemed to me ironically, of laurel. I was in a small clearing, with only one other youthful tree for company. Beech trees, perhaps, I thought.

The main and most depressing problem was the fact of being unable to walk away on account of having something that felt like handcuffs on my wrists, on the wrong side of the tree trunk, behind my back.

It was quiet in the clearing, but beyond I could hear the muffled, constant roar which announced itself as city. Wherever I was, it wasn't far out. Not nearly as far, for instance, as Laurel. More like a mile or two . . . in a suburb.

I opened my mouth and yelled at the top of my lungs the corny old word 'Help.' I yelled it many times. Consistently negative results.

The sky, so blue for the race-week, was clouding over: grey, like my thoughts.

I had no idea what time it was. My fingers, exploring discovered I had no watch.

I could stand up.

I stood.

I could kneel down: didn't bother.

I could circle round the tree.

I did that. The surrounding greenery was similar from all angles.

The branches of the tree spread from just above my head, narrow hard arms ending in smaller offshoots and twigs. A good many tan-coloured leaves still clung there. I tried shaking them off, but my efforts hardly wobbled them and they stubbornly remained.

I sat down again and thought a good many further unwelcome thoughts, chief among them being that in the Liberty Market office I would never live this day down . . . if ever I lived to tell.

Getting myself kidnapped . . . bloody stupid.

Embarrassing to a degree.

I thought back. If Pucinelli had been easier to reach I would have learned about the Goldoni family sooner, and I would have been long gone by the time the International Rug Co Inc. arrived at the Sherryatt with their rug.

If I hadn't gone back upstairs to fetch my things . . .

If, if, if.

I thought of the face of Giuseppe-Peter-Pietro Goldoni coming through my bedroom door: intent, determined, a soldier in action, reminding me in his speed and neatness of Tony Vine. He had himself taken Dominic from the beach, and in a mask had been there personally to seize Alessia. It was possible to imagine that it had been he who had announced himself as the chauffeur to collect Morgan Freemantle; and if so the actual act of successful abduction could be almost as potent a satisfaction to him as the money it brought.

If I understood him, I wondered, would I be better equipped? I'd never negotiated face to face with a kidnapper before: always through proxies. The art of coercive bargaining, Liberty Market training manual, chapter six. Hard to be coercive while at the present disadvantage.

Time passed. Aeroplanes flew at intervals overhead and a couple of birds came crossly to inspect the stranger in their territory. I sat not uncomfortably, trying to shape my mind to the possibility of remaining where I was for some time.

It began to rain.

The tree gave little shelter, but I didn't particularly mind. The drops spattered through the dying leaves in a soft shower, fresh and interesting on my skin. I'd never been out in the rain before with no clothes on, that I could remember. I lifted my face up, and opened my mouth, and drank what came my way.

After a while the rain stopped, and it grew dark. All night, I thought coldly.

Well. All night, then. Face it. Accept it. It's not so hard.

I was strong and healthy and possessed of a natural inborn stamina which had rarely been tested anywhere near its limits. The restriction to my arms was loose and not unbearable. I could sit there for a long time without suffering. I guessed, in fact, that I would have to.

The greatest discomfort was cold, to which I tried to shut my mind, joined, as the night advanced, by a desire for a nice hot dinner.

I tried on and off to rub the handcuffs vigorously against the treetrunk to see if the friction would do anything spectacularly useful like sawing the wood right through. The result of such labours was a slight roughening of the tree's surface and a more considerable roughening of the skin inside my arms. Small the tree-trunk might be, but densely, forbiddingly solid.

I slept on and off, dozing quite deeply and toppling sideways once, waking later with my nose on the dead leaves and my shoulders stretched and aching. I tried to find a more comfortable way of lying, but everything was compromise: sitting was the best.

Waiting, shivering, for dawn, I began to wonder seriously for the first time whether he intended simply to leave me to the elements until I died.

He hadn't killed me in the hotel. The injection in my thigh which had put me unconscious could just as easily have been fatal, if death had been what he intended. A body in a rug could have been carried out of a hotel as boldly dead as unconscious. If he'd simply wanted me out of his life, why was I still in it?

If he'd wanted revenge . . . that was something else.

I'd told Kent Wagner confidently that Giuseppe-Peter wouldn't kill by inches . . . and perhaps I'd been wrong.

Well, I told myself astringently, you'll just have to wait and see.

Daylight came. A grey day, the clouds lower, scurrying, full of unhappy promise.

Where's the Verdi?, I thought. I wouldn't mind an orchestral earful. Verdi . . . Giuseppe Verdi.

Oh well. Giuseppe . . . It made sense.

Peter was his own name – Pietro – in English.

Coffee wouldn't be bad, I thought. Ring room service to bring it.

The first twenty-four hours were the worst for a kidnap victim: chapter one, Liberty Market training manual. From my own intimate viewpoint, I now doubted it.

At what would have been full daylight except for the clouds, he came to see me.

I didn't hear him approach, but he was suddenly there, half behind me, stepping round one of the laurels: Giuseppe-Peter-Pietro Goldoni, dressed in his brown leather jacket with the gold buckles at the cuffs.

I felt as if I had known him forever, yet he was totally alien. There was some quality of implacability in his approach, a sort of mute violence in the way he walked, a subtle arrogance in his carriage. His satisfaction at having brought me to this pass was plain to see, and the hairs rose involuntarily all up my spine.

He stopped in front of me and looked down.

'Your name is Andrew Douglas,' he said in English. His accent was pronounced, and like all Italians he had difficulty with the unfamiliar Scots syllables, but his meaning was clear.

I looked back at him flatly and didn't reply.

Without excitement but with concentration he returned me look for look, and I began to sense in him the same feeling about me as I had about him. Professional curiosity, on both sides.

'You will make a tape recording for me,' he said finally.

'All right.'

The ready agreement lifted his eyebrows: not what he'd expected.

'You do not ask . . . who I am?'

I said, 'You're the man who abducted me from the hotel.'

'What is my name?' he asked.

'I don't know,' I said.

'It is Peter.' A very positive assertion.

'Peter.' Inclined my head, acknowledging the introduction. 'Why am I here?'

'To make a tape recording.'

He looked at me sombrely and went away, his head round and dark against the sky, all his features long familiar because of the picture. I'd nearly got him right, I thought. Maybe in the line of the eyebrows I'd been wrong: his were straighter at the outer edge.

He was gone for a period I would have guessed at as an hour, and he returned with a brown travelling bag slung from one shoulder. The bag looked like fine leather, with gold buckles. All of a piece.

From his jacket he produced a large sheet of paper which he unfolded and held for me to read.

'This is what you will say,' he said.

I read the message, which had been written in laborious block capitals by an American, not by Giuseppe-Peter himself. It said:

I AM ANDREW DOUGLAS, UNDERCOVER COP, YOU IN THE FUCKING JOCKEY CLUB, LISTEN GOOD. YOU'VE GOT TO SEND THE TEN MILLION ENGLISH POUNDS, LIKE WE SAID. THE CERTIFIED CHECK'S GOT TO BE READY TUESDAY. SEND IT TO ACCOUNT NUMBER ZL327/42806, CREDIT HELVETIA, ZURICH, SWITZERLAND. WHEN THE CHECK IS CLEARED, YOU GET FREEMANTLE BACK. NO FINGERS MISSING. THEN SIT TIGHT. IF ANY COPS COME IN, I WON'T BE MAKING IT. IF EVERYTHING IS ON THE LEVEL AND THE BREAD IS SATISFACTORY, YOU'LL BE TOLD WHERE TO FIND ME. IF ANYONE TRIES TO BLOCK THE DEAL AFTER FREEMANTLE GOES LOOSE, I'LL BE KILLED.

He tucked the paper inside the front of his jacket and began to pull a tape recorder from the leather bag.

'I'm not reading that,' I said neutrally.

He stopped in mid-movement. 'You have no choice. If you don't read it, I will kill you.'

I said nothing, simply looked at him without challenge; trying to show no worry.

'I will kill you,' he said again: and I thought yes, perhaps, but not for that.

'It's bad English,' I said. 'You could have written it better yourself.'

He let the tape recorder's weight fall back into the bag. 'Are you telling me,' he asked with incredulity, 'that you are not reading this because of the style literary?'

'Literary style,' I said. 'Yes.'

He turned his back on me while he thought, and after a while turned back.

'I will change the words,' he said. 'But you will read only what I say. Understand? No . . .' he searched for the words but said finally in Italian, 'no code words. No secret signals.'

I thought that if I kept him speaking English it might fractionally reduce my disadvantage, so I said, 'What did you say? I don't understand.'

He narrowed his eyes slightly. 'You speak Spanish. The maid at the hotel said you were a Spanish gentleman. I think you also speak Italian.'

'Very little.'

He pulled the paper from his jacket and found a pen, and, turning the sheet over, began to write a new version for me, supporting it on the bag. When he'd finished, he showed it to me, holding it so that I could read.

In elegant handwriting the note now said:

I AM ANDREW DOUGLAS. JOCKEY CLUB, COLLECT TEN MILLION ENGLISH POUNDS. TUESDAY, SEND CERTIFIED BANKER'S DRAFT TO ACCOUNT NUMBER ZL327/42806, CREDIT HELVETIA, ZURICH, SWITZERLAND. WHEN THE BANK CLEARS THE DRAFT, MORGAN FREEMANTLE RETURNS. AFTER THAT, WAIT. POLICE MUST NOT INVESTIGATE. WHEN ALL IS PEACE, I WILL BE FREE. IF THE MONEY IS NOT ABLE TO BE TAKEN OUT OF THE SWISS BANK, I WILL BE KILLED.

'Well,' I said. 'It's much better.'

He reached again for the tape recorder.

'They won't pay ten million,' I said.

His hand paused again. 'I know that.'

'Yes. I'm sure you do.' I wished I could rub an itch on my nose. 'In the normal course of events you would expect a letter to be sent to your Swiss account number from the Jockey Club, making a more realistic proposal.'

He listened impassively, sorting the words into Italian, understanding. 'Yes,' he said.

'They might suggest paying a ransom of one hundred thousand pounds,' I said.

'That is ridiculous.'

'Perhaps fifty thousand more, to cover your expenses.'

'Still ridiculous.'

We looked at each other assessingly. In the normal course of events negotiation of a ransom price was not conducted like this. On the other hand, what was there to prevent it?

'Five million,' he said.

I said nothing.

'It must be five,' he said.

'The Jockey Club has no money. The Jockey Club is just a social club, made up of people. They aren't all rich people. They cannot pay five million. They do not have five million.'

He shook his head without anger. 'They are rich. They have five million, certainly. I know.'

'How do you know?' I asked.

His eyelids flickered slightly, but all he said again was, 'Five million.'

'Two hundred thousand. Positively no more.'

'Ridiculous.'

He stalked away and disappeared between the laurel bushes, and I guessed he wanted to think and not have me watch him at it.

The Swiss bank account was fascinating, I thought: and clearly he intended to move the money more or less at once from ZL327/42806 to another account number, another bank even, and wanted to be sure the Jockey Club hadn't thought of a way of stopping him or tracing him, or laying a trap. As some of England's top banking brains could be found either in or advising the Jockey Club, his precautions made excellent sense.

One victim in return for the ransom itself.

One victim in return when the ransom had disappeared into further anonymity.

Morgan Freemantle for money, Andrew Douglas for time.

No drops to be ambushed by excitable carabinieri: no stacks of tatty – and photographed – notes. Just numbers, stored electronically, sophisticated and safe. Subtract the numbers from the gentlemen of the Jockey Club, add the total, telex it to Switzerland.

With his money in Zurich, Giuseppe-Peter could lose

himself in South America and not be affected by its endemic inflation, Swiss francs would ride any storm.

Alessia's ransom, at a guess, had gone to Switzerland the day it had been paid, changed into francs, perhaps, by a laundryman. Same for the racecourse owner, earlier. Even with the Dominic operation showing a heavy loss, Giuseppe-Peter must have amassed an English million. I wondered if he had set a target at which he would stop, and I wondered also whether once a kidnapper, always a kidnapper, addicted: in his case, for ever and ever.

I found I still thought of him as Giuseppe-Peter, from long habit. Pietro Goldoni seemed a stranger.

He came back eventually and stood in front of me, looking down.

'I am a businessman,' he said.

'Yes.'

'Stand up when you talk to me.'

I thrust away the first overwhelming instinct to refuse. Never antagonise your kidnapper: victim lesson number two. Make him pleased with you, making him like you; he will be less ready to kill you.

Sod the training manual, I thought mordantly: and stood up.

'That's better,' he said. 'Every time I am here, stand up.'

'All right.'

'You will make the recording. You understand what I

wish to say. You will say it.' He paused briefly. 'If I do not like what you say, we will start again.'

I nodded.

He pulled the black tape recorder from the leather bag and switched it on. Then he plucked the sheet of instructions from his jacket pocket, shook it open, and held it, with his own version towards me, for me to read. He gestured to me to start, and I cleared my voice and said as unemotionally as I could manage:

'This is Andrew Douglas. The ransom demand for Morgan Freemantle is now reduced to five million pounds—'

Giuseppe-Peter switched off the machine.

'I did not tell you to say that,' he said intensely.

'No,' I agreed mildly. 'But it might save time.'

He pursed his lips, considered, told me to start again, and pressed the record buttons.

I said:

'This is Andrew Douglas. The ransom demand for Morgan Freemantle is now reduced to five million pounds. This money is to be sent by certified banker's draft to the Credit Helvetia, Zurich, Switzerland, to be lodged in account number ZL327/42806. When that account has been credited with the money, Morgan Freemantle will be returned. After that there are to be no police investigations. If there are no investigations, and if the money in the Swiss bank account has been paid clear of all restrictions and may be moved to other accounts without stoppage, I will be freed.'

I halted. He pressed the stop buttons and said, 'You have not finished.'

I looked at him.

'You will say that unless these things happen, you will be killed.'

His dark eyes looked straight at mine; level, at my own height. I saw only certainty. He pressed the start buttons again and waited.

'I am told,' I said in a dry voice, 'that unless these conditions are met, I will be killed.'

He nodded sharply and switched off.

I thought: he will kill me anyway. He put his tape recorder into one section of his bag and began feeling into another section for something else. I had the most dreadful lurch of fear in my gut and tried with the severest physical will to control it. But it wasn't a gun or a knife that he brought out of the bag: it was a cola bottle containing a milky-looking liquid.

The reaction was almost as bad. In spite of the chilly air, I was sweating.

He appeared not to have noticed. He was unscrewing the cap and looking in the bag for what proved to be a fat, plastic, gaily-striped drinking straw.

'Soup,' he said. He put the straw into the bottle and offered it to my mouth.

I sucked. It was chicken soup, cold, fairly thick. I drank all of it quite fast, afraid he would snatch it away.

He watched without comment. When I'd finished he threw the straw on the ground, screwed the top on the bottle and replaced it in the bag. Then he gave me another long, considering, concentrated stare, and abruptly went away.

I sat down regrettably weakly on the loamy ground.

God dammit it, I thought. God dammit to hell.

It is in myself, I thought, as in every victim; the hopeless feeling of indignity, the sickening guilt of having been snatched.

A prisoner, naked, alone, afraid, dependent on one's enemy for food . . . all the classic ingredients of victim-breakdown syndrome. The training manual come to life. Knowing so well what it was like from other people's accounts didn't sufficiently shield one from the shock of the reality.

In the future I would understand what I was told not just in the head but with every remembered pulse.

If there were a future.

CHAPTER NINETEEN

Rain came again, at first in big heavy individual drops, splashing with sharp taps on the dead leaves, and then quite soon in a downpour. I stood up and let the rain act as a shower, soaking my hair, running down my body, cold and oddly pleasant.

I drank some of it again, getting quite good at swallowing without choking. How really extraordinary I must look, I thought, standing there in the clearing getting wet.

My long-ago Scottish ancestors had gone naked into battle, whooping and roaring down the heather hillsides with sword and shield alone and frightening the souls out of the enemy. If those distant clansmen, Highland-born in long-gone centuries, could choose to fight as nature made them, then so should I settle for the same sternness of spirit in this day.

I wondered if the Highlanders had been fortified before they set off by distillations of barley. It would give one more courage, I thought, than chicken soup.

It went on raining for hours, heavily and without

pause. Only when it again began to get dark did it ease off, and by then the ground round the tree was so wet that sitting on it was near to a mud bath. Still, having stood all day, I sat. If it rained the next day, I thought wryly, the mud would wash off.

The night was again long and cold, but not to the point of hypothermia. My skin dried when the rain stopped. Eventually, against all the odds, I again went to sleep.

I spent the damp dawn and an hour or two after it feeling grindingly hungry and drearily wondering whether Giuseppe-Peter would ever come back: but he did. He came as before, stepping quietly, confidently, through the laurel screen, wearing the same jacket, carrying the same bag.

I stood up at his approach. He made no comment; merely noted it. There was a fuzz of moisture on his sleek hair, a matter of a hundred per cent humidity rather than actual drizzle, and he walked carefully, picking his way between puddles.

It was Tuesday, I thought.

He had brought another bottle of soup, warm this time, reddish-brown, tasting vaguely of beef. I drank it more slowly than on the day before, moderately trusting this time that he wouldn't snatch it away. He waited until I'd finished, threw away the straw, screwed the cap on the bottle, as before.

'You are outside,' he said unexpectedly, 'while I make a place inside. One more day. Or two.'

After a stunned moment I said, 'Clothes . . .'

He shook his head. 'No.' Then, glancing at the clouds, he said, 'Rain is clean.'

I almost nodded, an infinitesimal movement, which he saw.

'In England,' he said, 'you defeated me. Here, I defeat you.'

I said nothing.

'I have been told it was you, in England. You who found the boy.' He shrugged suddenly, frustratedly, and I guessed he still didn't know how we'd done it. 'To take people back from kidnap, it is your job. I did not know it was a job, except for the police.'

'Yes,' I said neutrally.

'You will never defeat me again,' he said seriously.

He put a hand into the bag and brought out a much-creased, much-travelled copy of the picture of himself, which, as he unfolded it, I saw to be one of the original printing, from way back in Bologna.

'It was you, who drew this,' he said. 'Because of this, I had to leave Italy. I went to England. In England, again this picture. Everywhere. Because of this I came to America. This picture is here now, is it not?'

I didn't answer.

'You hunted me. I caught you. That is the difference.'

He was immensely pleased with what he was saying.

'Soon, I will look different. I will change. When I have the ransom I will disappear. And this time you will not send the police to arrest my men. This time I will stop you.'

I didn't ask how. There was no point.

'You are like me,' he said.

'No.'

'Yes . . . but between us, I will win.'

There could always be a moment, I supposed, in which enemies came to acknowledge an unwilling respect for each other, even though the enmity between them remained unchanged and deep. There was such a moment then: on his side at least.

'You are strong,' he said, 'like me.'

There seemed to be no possible answer.

'It is good to defeat a strong man.'

It was the sort of buzz I would have been glad to give him.

'For me,' I said, 'are you asking a ransom?'

He looked at me levelly and said, 'No.'

'Why not?' I asked; and thought, why ask, you don't want to know the answer.

'For Freemantle,' he said merely, 'I will get five million pounds.'

'The Jockey Club won't pay five million pounds,' I said.

'They will.'

'Morgan Freemantle isn't much loved,' I said. 'The members of the Jockey Club will resent every penny screwed out of them. They will hold off, they'll argue, they'll take weeks deciding whether each member should contribute an equal amount, or whether the rich should give more. They will keep you waiting . . . and every day you have to wait, you risk the American police finding you. The Americans are brilliant at finding kidnappers . . . I expect you know.'

'If you want food you will not talk like this.'

I fell silent.

After a pause he said, 'I expect they will not pay exactly five million. But there are many members. About one hundred. They can pay thirty thousand pounds each, of that I am sure. That is three million pounds. Tomorrow you will make another tape. You will tell them that is the final reduction. For that, I let Freemantle go. If they will not pay, I will kill him, and you also, and bury you here in this ground.' He pointed briefly to the earth under our feet. 'Tomorrow you will say this on the tape.'

'Yes,' I said.

'And believe me,' he said soberly, 'I do not intend to spend all my life in prison. If I am in danger of it, I will kill, to prevent it.'

I did believe him. I could see the truth of it in his face.

After a moment I said, 'You have courage. You will wait. The Jockey Club will pay when the amount is not too much. When they can pay what their conscience . . . their guilt . . . tells them they must. When they can shrug and grit their teeth, and complain . . . but pay . . . that's what the amount will be. A total of about one quarter of one million pounds, maximum, I would expect.'

'More,' he said positively, shaking his head.

'If you should kill Freemantle, the Jockey Club would regret it, but in their hearts many members wouldn't grieve. If you demand too much, they will refuse, and you may end with nothing . . . just the risk of prison . . . for murder.' I spoke without emphasis, without persuasion: simply as if reciting moderately unexciting facts.

'It was you,' he said bitterly. 'You made me wait six weeks for the ransom for Alessia Cenci. If I did not wait, did not reduce the ransom . . . I would have nothing. A dead girl is no use . . . I understand now what you do.' He paused. 'This time, I defeat you.'

I didn't answer. I knew I had him firmly hooked again into the kidnapper's basic dilemma: whether to settle for what he could get, or risk holding out for what he wanted. I was guessing that the Jockey Club would grumble but finally pay half a million pounds, which meant five thousand dollars per member, if it was right about their numbers. At Liberty Market we would, I thought, have advised agreeing to that sort of sum; five per cent of the original demand. The expenses of this kidnap would be high: trying too hard to beat the profit down to zero would be dangerous to the victim.

With luck, I thought, Giuseppe-Peter and I would in the end negotiate a reasonable price for Morgan Freemantle, and the Senior Steward would return safely home: and that, I supposed, was what I had basically come to America to achieve. After that . . . for myself . . . it depended on how certain Giuseppe-Peter was that he could vanish . . . and on how he felt about me . . . and on whether he considered me a danger to him for life.

Which I would be. I would be.

I didn't see how he could possibly set me free. I wouldn't have done, if I had been he.

I thrust the starkly unbearable thought away. While Morgan Freemantle lived in captivity, so would I . . . probably.

'Tomorrow,' Giuseppe-Peter said, 'when I come, you will say on the tape that one of Freemantle's fingers will be cut off next week on Wednesday, if three million pounds are not paid before then.'

He gave me another long calculating stare as if he would read my beliefs, my weaknesses, my fears, my knowledge; and I looked straight back at him, seeing the obverse of myself, seeing the demon born in every human.

It was true that we were alike, I supposed, in many ways, not just in age, in build, in physical strength. We organised, we plotted, and we each in our way sought battle. The same battle . . . different sides. The same primary weapons . . . lies, threats and fear.

But what he stole, I strove to restore. Where he wantonly laid waste, I tried to rebuild. He crumbled his victims, I worked to make them whole. His satisfaction lay in taking them, mine in seeing them free. The obverse of me . . .

As before he turned away abruptly and departed, and I was left with an urge to call after him, to beg him to stay, just to talk. I didn't want him to go. I wanted his company, enemy or not.

I was infinitely tired of that clearing, that tree, that mud, that cold, those handcuffs. Twenty-four empty hours stretched ahead, a barren landscape of loneliness and discomfort and inevitable hunger. It began raining again, had slanting stuff driven now by a rising wind, and I twisted my hands to grip the tree, hating it, trying to shake it, to hurt it, furiously venting on it a surge of raw, unmanageable despair.

That wouldn't do, I thought coldly, stopping almost at once. If I went that way, I would crack into pieces. I let my hands fall away. I put my face blindly to the sky, eyes shut, and concentrated merely on drinking.

A leaf fell into my mouth. I spat it out. Another fell on my forehead. I opened my eyes and saw that most of the rest of the dead leaves had come down.

The wind, I thought. But I took hold of the tree again more gently and shook it, and saw a tremor run up through it to the twigs. Three more leaves fell off, fluttering down wetly.

Two days ago the tree had immovably resisted the same treatment. Instead of shaking it again I bumped my back against it several times, giving it shocks. I could feel movement in the trunk that had definitely not been there before: and under my feet, under the earth, something moved.

I scraped wildly at the place with my toes and then circled the tree and sat down with a rush, rubbing with my fingers until I could feel a hard surface come clear. Then I stood round where I'd been before, and bumped hard against the trunk, and looked down and saw what I'd uncovered.

A root.

One has to be pretty desperate to try to dig up a tree with one's fingernails, and desperate would be a fair description of Andrew Douglas that rainy November morning.

Let it pour, I thought. Let this sodden soaking glorious rain go on and on turning my prison into a swamp. Let this nice glorious fantastic loamy mud turn liquid . . . Let this stubborn little tree not have a tap root its own height.

It rained. I hardly felt it. I cleared the mud from the root until I could get my fingers round it, to grasp. I could feel it stretching away sideways, tugging against my tug.

Standing up I could put my foot under it; a knobbly dark sinew as thick as a thumb, tensing and relaxing when I leant my weight against the tree trunk.

I've got all day, I thought, and all night.

I have no other chance.

*

It did take all day, but not all night.

Hour by hour it went on raining, and hour by hour I scraped away at the roots with toes and fingers, baring more of them, burrowing deep. The movement I could make in the trunk slowly grew from a tremble to a protesting shudder, and from a shudder to a sway.

I tested my strength against the tree's own each time in a sort of agony, for fear Giuseppe-Peter would somehow see the branches moving above the laurels and arrive with fearsome ways to stop me. I scraped and dug and heaved in something very near frenzy, and the longer it went on the more excruciatingly anxious I became. Given time I would do it. Given time . . . Oh God, give me time.

Some of the roots tore free easily, some were heartbreakingly stubborn. Water filled the hole as I dug, blocking what I could see, hindering and helping both at the same time. When I felt one particularly thick and knotty root give up the contest the tree above me lurched as if in mortal protest, and I stood up and hauled at it with every possible muscle, pushing and pulling, wrenching, thudding, lying heavily against the trunk, digging in with my heels, feeling the thrust through calves and thighs; then yanking the tree this way and that, sideways, like a pendulum.

A bunch of beleagured roots gave way altogether and the whole tree suddenly toppled, taking me down with it in rough embrace, its branches crashing in the rain onto a bed of its own brown leaves, leaving me breathless and exultant . . . and still . . . still . . . fastened.

Every single root had to be severed before I could get my arms out from under them, but I doubt if barbed wire would have stopped me at that point. Scratching and tugging, hands down in water, kneeling and straining, I fought for that escape as I'd never thought to fight in my life; and finally I felt the whole root mass shift freely, a tangled clump of blackly-sprouting woody tentacles, their grip on the earth all gone. Kneeling and jerking I got them up between my arms, up to my shoulders . . . and rolled free into a puddle, ecstatic.

It took not so very much longer to thread myself through my own arms, so to speak, bottom first then one leg at a time, so that I ended with my hands in front, not behind my back; an unbelievable improvement.

It was still raining and also, I realised, beginning to get dark. I went shakily over to the laurels on the opposite side of the clearing from where Giuseppe-Peter had appeared, and edged slowly, cautiously, between two of the glossy green bushes.

No people.

I took a deep breath, trying to steady myself, trying to make my knees work efficiently instead of wanting to buckle. I felt strained and weak and in no shape for barefoot country rambles, but none of it mattered. Nothing mattered at all beside the fact of being free.

I could hear only wind and rain. I went on and came shortly to a sketchy fence made of strands of wire strung between posts. I climbed through and walked on and suddenly reached the top of an incline, the wood sloping away in front: and down there, through the trees, there were lights.

I went down towards them. I'd been naked so long that I'd stopped thinking about it, which was somewhat of a mistake. I was concerned only to get away from Giuseppe-Peter, feeling that he still might find me gone and chase after me. I was thinking only, as I approached what turned out to be a very substantial house, that I'd better make sure it wasn't where Giuseppe-Peter was actually staying before I rang the doorbell.

I didn't get as far as ringing the bell. An outside light was suddenly switched on, and the door itself opened on a chain.

A pale, indistinguishable face inspected me and a sharp, frightened female voice said, 'Get away. Get away from here.'

I started to say 'Wait,' but the door closed with a slam, and while I hovered indecisively it opened again to reveal the business end of a pistol.

'Go away,' she said. 'Get away from here, or I'll shoot.'

I thought she might. I looked down at myself and didn't altogether blame her. I was streaked with mud and handcuffed and bare: hardly a riot as a visitor on a darkening November evening.

I backed away, looking as unaggressive as I could,

and presently felt it safe to slide away again into the trees and reconsider my whole boring plight.

Clearly I needed some sort of covering, but all that was to hand easily were branches of evergreen laurel. Back to Adam and Eve, and all that. Then I'd got to get a householder – a different one – to talk to me without shooting first. It might not have been too difficult in the Garden of Eden, but in twentieth-century suburban Washington D.C., a proper poser.

Further down the hill there were more lights. Feeling slightly foolish I picked up a twig of laurel and held it, and walked down towards the lights, feeling my way as it grew darker, stubbing my toes on unseen stones. This time, I thought, I would go more carefully and look for something to wrap round me before I tackled the door: a sack, a trash bag . . . absolutely anything.

Again events overtook me. I was slithering in darkness under a sheltering canopy-roof past double garage doors when a car came unexpectedly round a hidden driveway, catching me in its lights. The car braked sharply to a stop and I took a step backwards, bravely ready to bolt.

'Stop right there,' a voice said, and a man stepped out of the car, again bearing a pistol. Did they all, I thought despairingly, shoot strangers? Dirty naked unshaven handcuffed strangers . . . probably, yes.

This native wasn't frightened, just masterful. Before he could say anything else I opened my mouth and said loudly, 'Please get the police.'

'What?' He came three paces nearer, looking me up and down. 'What did you say?'

'Please get the police. I escaped. I want . . . er . . . to turn myself in.'

'Who are you?' he demanded.

'Look,' I said. 'I'm freezing cold and very tired, and if you telephone Captain Wagner he'll come and get me.'

'You're not American,' he said accusingly.

'No. British.'

He came nearer to me, still warily holding the gun. I saw that he was of middle age with greying hair, a worthy citizen with money, used to decision. A businessman come home.

I told him Wagner's telephone number. 'Please,' I said. 'Please . . . call him.'

He considered, then he said, 'Walk along there to that door. No tricks.'

I walked in front of him along a short path to his impressive front door, the rain stopping now, the air damp.

'Stand still,' he said. I wouldn't have dreamt of doing anything else.

Three orange pumpkin faces rested on the steps, grinning up at me evilly. There was the sound of keys clinking and the lock being turned. The door swung inward, spilling out light.

'Turn round. Come in here.'

I turned. He was standing inside his door, waiting for me, ready with the gun.

'Come inside and shut the door.'

I did that.

'Stand there,' he said, pointing to a spot on a marble-tiled hallway, in front of a wall. 'Stand still . . . wait.'

He took his eyes off me for a few seconds while he stretched a hand through a nearby doorway; it re-appeared holding a towel.

'Here.' He threw it to me; a dry fluffy handtowel, pale green with pink initials. I caught it, but couldn't do much with it, short of laying it on the ground and rolling.

He made an impatient movement of his head.

'I can't . . .' I said, and stopped. It was all too damn bloody much.

He parked the pistol, came towards me, wrapped the towel round my waist and tucked the ends in, like a sarong.

'Thank you,' I said.

He put the pistol near an adjacent telephone and told me to repeat the number of the police.

Kent Wagner, to my everlasting gratitude, was in his headquarters half an hour after he should have gone off duty.

My unwilling host said to him, 'There's a man here says he escaped . . .'

'Andrew Douglas,' I interrupted.

'Says his name is Andrew Douglas.' He held the receiver suddenly away from his ear as if the noise had hurt the drum. 'What? He says he wants to give himself up. He's here, in handcuffs.' He listened for a few seconds and then with a frown came to put the receiver into my hands. 'He wants to talk to you,' he said.

Kent's voice said into my ear. 'Who is this?'

'Andrew.'

'Jee . . . sus.' His breath came out wheezing. 'Where are you?'

'I don't know. Wait.' I asked my host where I was. He took the receiver temporarily back and gave his address, with directions. 'Three miles up Massachusetts Avenue from Dupont Circle, take a right onto 46th Street, make a right again on to Davenport Street, a quarter mile down there, in the woods.' He listened, and gave me back the receiver.

'Kent,' I said, 'bring some men and come very quickly. Our friend is near here.'

'Got it,' he said.

'And Kent . . . bring some trousers.'

'What?'

'Pants,' I said tersely. 'And a shirt. And some shoes, size ten English.'

He said disbelievingly, 'You're not . . .?'

'Yeah. Bloody funny. And a key for some handcuffs.'

My host, looking increasingly puzzled, took the receiver back and said to Kent Wagner, 'Is this man dangerous?'

What Kent swore afterwards that he said was, 'Take good care of him,' meaning just that, but my host interpreted the phrase as 'beware of him' and kept me standing there at gunpoint despite my protestations that I was not only harmless but positively benign.

'Don't lean against the wall,' he said. 'My wife would be furious to find blood on it.'

'Blood?'

'You're covered in scratches.' He was astonished. 'Didn't you know?'

'No.'

'What did you escape from?'

I shook my head wearily and didn't explain, and waited what seemed an age before Kent Wagner rang the doorbell. He came into the hall half grinning in anticipation, the grin widening as he saw the pretty towel but then suddenly dying to grimness.

'How're you doing?' he said flatly.

'OK.'

He nodded, went outside and presently returned with clothes, shoes and impressive metal cutters which got rid of the handcuffs with a couple of clips. 'These aren't police issue handcuffs,' he explained. 'We've no keys to fit.'

My host lent me his cloakroom to dress in, and when I came out I thanked him, handing over the towel.

'Guess I should have given you a drink,' he said vaguely; but I'd just seen myself in a looking glass, and I reckoned he'd dealt with me kindly.

CHAPTER TWENTY

'You're not doing that,' Kent said.

'Yes I am.'

He gave me a sidelong look. 'You're in no shape . . .'

'I'm fine.' A bit tattered as to fingers and toes, but never mind.

He shrugged, giving in. We were out in the road by the police cars, silent as to sirens and lit only by parking lights, where I'd been telling him briefly what had happened.

'We'll go back the way I came,' I said. 'What else?'

He told his men, shadowy in the cars, to stay where they were and await orders, and he and I went up through the woods, up past the house I'd waited in, and up past the one with the frightened lady: up to the top of the slope, over onto flat ground and through the wire fence.

We were both quiet, our feet softly scuffling on the sodden leaves. The rain had stopped. Behind broken clouds the moon sailed serene. The light was enough to see by, once we were used to it.

'Somewhere here,' I said, half whispering. 'Not far.'

We went from laurel clump to laurel clump and found the familiar clearing. 'He came from that way,' I said, pointing.

Kent Wagner looked at the uprooted tree for a frozen moment but without discernible expression, and then delicately, cautiously, we passed out of the laurel ring, merging with the shadows, a couple of cats stalking.

He wasn't as good as Tony Vine, but few were. I was conscious just that he would be a good companion in a dark alley, and that I wouldn't have gone back up there without him. He, for his part, had explained that his job was chiefly indoors now, in his office, and he was pleased for once to be outside with the action.

He was carrying a gun like a natural extension of his right hand. We went forward slowly, testing every step, aware of the chance of trip-alarms. There were a good many laurels here among a whole bunch of younger trees and we could get no distant view, but approximately fifty paces from the clearing we caught a glimpse of a light.

Kent pointed to it with the gun. I nodded. We inched in that direction, very careful now, conscious of risk.

We saw no look-outs, which didn't mean there weren't any. We saw the front of a modern split-level house looking perfectly harmless and ordinary, with lights on downstairs and curtains half drawn.

We went no closer. We retreated into the first line of

trees and followed the line of the driveway from the house to the road. At the roadside there was a mailbox on a post, the mailbox bearing the number 5270. Kent pointed to it and I nodded, and we walked along the road in what he confidently assured me was the direction of the city. As we went he said, 'I heard the tape you made. Your company relayed it to us from London this morning. Seems the Jockey Club had got it by express courier.'

'My company,' I said wryly, 'were no doubt displeased with me.'

'I talked with some guy called Gerry Clayton. All he said was that while you were alive and negotiating it was OK.'

'Nice.'

'They did seem to want you back; can't think why.'

We walked on, not hurrying.

'I talked to the Goldonis,' he said. 'Parents.'

'Poor people.'

I felt him shrug. 'He was furious. She was all broken up. Seems she did see her son, did tell him about you. But no use to us. She met him by the Potomac, they walked about a bit, then went to some quiet restaurant for lunch. He'd telephoned her in their hotel to fix it . . . never told her where he was staying, himself.'

'It figured.'

'Yeah.'

A step or two further on he stopped, parked the gun in his belt and unclipped a hand radio instead.

'Turn around,' he said to his men in the police cars. 'Go back to 45th Street, make a left, make another left into Cherrytree, and crawl along there until you reach me. No sirens. No, repeat, no noise. Understood?'

The policemen answered in regulation jargon and Kent pushed down the telescopic aerial of his radio and stuck the black box on his belt.

We stood waiting. He watched me calmly in the moonlight, a hard man offering parity. I felt at ease with him, and grateful.

'Your girl-friend,' he said casually, 'will be one happy lady to have you back.'

'Alessia?'

'The jockey,' he said. 'White face, huge eyes, hardly could speak for crying.'

'Well,' I said, 'she knows what it's like to be kidnapped.'

'Yeah, so I heard. I was talking to her this afternoon. In addition she said she didn't know she loved you that way. Does that make sense? She said something about regretting saying no.'

'Did she?'

He glanced with interest at my face. 'Good news, is it?'

'You might say so.'

'Something about prisoners coming home impotent from Vietnam.'

'Mm,' I said, smiling, 'I told her that.'

'Glad it makes sense to you.'

'Thanks,' I said.

'She's still at the Regency Hotel,' Kent said. 'She said she wasn't leaving until you were free.'

I made no immediate reply, and after a pause he said, 'I didn't tell her you wouldn't make it. That if you did, it would be a miracle.'

'They happen,' I said; and he nodded.

'Once in a while.'

We looked back along the road to where I'd escaped from.

'The house back there is three and a half miles in a pretty direct route from the Ritz Carlton,' he said. 'And . . . did you notice? No pumpkins.' He was smiling in the semi-darkness, his teeth gleaming like Halloween.

He checked things pretty thoroughly, however, when his cars came, climbing into the back of one of them, with me beside him, and flicking through sheets and sheets of computer print-out. The print-out, I discovered, was of properties offered for rental, during the past eight weeks, not only in the District of Columbia itself but in adjacent Arlington and parts of Maryland and Virginia. It seemed to me to have entailed a prodigious amount of work: and again, like Eagler's efforts, it produced results.

Kent growled a deep syllable of satisfaction and showed me one particular sheet, pointing to the lines:

⁂ *5270 Cherrytree Street, 20016, Rented October 16, period 26 weeks, full rental period.*

He picked up a map already folded to the right page and showed me where we were.

'There's the house you called from, on Davenport Street. We walked a block up diagonally through the woods to Cherrytree, which is parallel with Davenport. The woods are part of American University park.'

I nodded.

He heaved himself out of the car to talk to his men, and presently we were riding back in the direction of 5270, driving slowly with side lights only.

Kent and Lieutenant Stavoski, who'd come in the second car, were in full agreement with each other that a sudden all-out raid was best, but a raid on their own well-prepared terms. They sent two policemen through the woods to approach from the rear but stay out of sight, and positioned the cars also out of sight of the house, but ready.

'You stay out here,' Kent said to me. 'You keep out, understand?'

'No,' I said. 'I'll find Freemantle.'

He opened his mouth and closed it again, and I knew that like all policemen he'd been concentrating almost exclusively on capturing the villains. He looked assessingly at me for a moment and I said, 'I'm going in, don't argue.'

He shook his head in resignation and didn't try any further to stop me, and it was he and I, as before, who made the first approach, quiet as cobwebs, to the house with no pumpkins.

In the shadow of a laurel I touched his arm and pointed, and he stiffened when he saw what I was showing him: a man standing in an upstairs unlit window, smoking a cigarette.

We stayed quiet, watching. So did the man, unalarmed.

'Shit,' Kent said.

'There's always the back.'

Behind bushes we slithered our way. The windows facing rearwards to the woodland looked merely blank.

'What do you think?' I asked.

'Got to be done.' The gun was back in his hand, and there was both apprehension and resolution in his voice. 'Ready?'

'Yes.'

Ready, if that included a noisy heart and difficulty in breathing.

We left the shelter of the bushes at the nearest point to the house and crept from shadow to shadow to what was evidently the kitchen door. The door was double; an outer screen against insects, an inner door made half of glass. Kent put his hand on the screen door latch and pulled it open, and tried the handle of the main door beneath.

Unsurprisingly, locked.

Kent pulled the radio from his belt, extended the aerial, and said one single word, 'Go.'

Before he'd finished returning the radio to his belt there was a sudden skin-crawling crescendo of sirens from in front of the house, and even at the rear one could see the reflection of the revolving lights racing forwards. Then there were searchlights flooding and voices shouting incomprehensibly through megaphones: and by that time Kent had smashed the glass panel of the door and put a hand inside to undo the lock.

There was pandemonium in the house as well as out. Kent and I with the two rear patrolmen on our heels raced through the kitchen and made straight for the stairs, sensing as much as seeing two men pulling guns to oppose the invasion. Stavoski's men seemed to have shot the lock off the front door: in a half glimpse after the staccato racket I saw the blue uniforms coming into the hall and then I was round the bend of the stairs, heading for the upper level.

Still quiet up there, comparatively. All doors except one were open. I made for it, running, and Kent behind me cried agonisedly, 'Andrew, don't do that.'

I looked back for him. He came, stood out of the line of fire of the door for a second, then leaped at it, giving it a heavy kick. The door crashed open, and Kent with gun ready jumped through and to one side, with me following.

The light inside was dim, like a child's nightlight, shadowy after the bright passage outside. There was a tent in the room, greyish-white, guy ropes tied to pieces of furniture: and standing by the tent, hurrying to unfasten the entrance, to go for his hostage, stood Giuseppe-Peter.

He whirled round as we went in.

He too held a gun.

He aimed straight in our direction, and fired twice. I felt a fierce sting as one bullet seared across the skin high on my left arm, and heard the second one fizz past my ear . . . and Kent without hesitation shot him.

He fell flat on his back from the force of it, and I went over to him, dropping to my knees.

It was Kent who opened the tent and went in for Morgan Freemantle. I heard the Senior Steward's slow sleepy voice, and Kent coming and saying the victim was doped to the eyeballs and totally unclothed, but otherwise unharmed.

I was trying with no success at all to wad a handful of folded tent against my enemy's neck, to stop the scarlet fountain spurting there. The bullet had torn too much away; left nothing to be done.

His eyes were open, but unfocused.

He said in Italian, 'Is it you?'

'Yes,' I said, in his tongue.

The pupils slowly sharpened, the gaze steadying on my face.

'I couldn't know,' he said. 'How could I have known . . . what you were . . .'

I knelt there trying to save his life.

He said, 'I should have killed you then . . . in

Bologna . . . when you saw me . . . I should have put my knife . . . into . . . that Spanish . . . chauffeur.'

'Yes,' I said again. 'You should.'

He gave me a last dark look, not admitting defeat, not giving an inch. I watched him with unexpected regret. Watched him until the consciousness went out of his eyes, and they were simply open but seeing nothing.

TWICE SHY

With love and thanks to my son Felix
An excellent shot who teaches physics

PART ONE

JONATHAN

CHAPTER ONE

I told the boys to stay quiet while I went to fetch my gun.

It usually worked. For the five minutes that it took me to get to the locker in the common-room and to return to the class-room, thirty fourteen-year-old semi-repressed hooligans could be counted on to be held in a state of fragile good behaviour, restrained only by the promise of a lesson they'd actually looked forward to. Physics in general they took to be unacceptably hard mental labour, but what happened when a gun spat out a bullet . . . that was *interesting*.

Jenkins delayed me for a moment in the common-room: Jenkins with his sour expression and bad-tempered moustache, telling me I could teach momentum more clearly with chalk on a blackboard, and that an actual firearm was on my part simply self-indulgent dramatics.

'No doubt you're right,' I said blandly, edging round him.

He gave me his usual look of frustrated spite. He

hated my policy of always agreeing with him, which was, of course, why I did it.

'Excuse me,' I said, retreating, 'Four A are waiting.'

Four A, however, weren't waiting in the hoped-for state of gently simmering excitement. They were, instead, in collective giggles fast approaching mild hysteria.

'Look,' I said flatly, sensing the atmosphere with one foot through the door, 'steady down, or you'll copy notes . . .'

This direst of threats had no result. The giggles couldn't be stifled. The eyes of the class darted between me and my gun and the blackboard, which was still out of my sight behind the open door, and upon every young face there was the most gleeful anticipation.

'OK,' I said, closing the door, 'so what have you writ—'

I stopped.

They hadn't written anything.

One of the boys stood there, in front of the blackboard, straight and still: Paul Arcady, the wit of the class. He stood straight and still because, balanced on his head, there was an apple.

The giggles all around me exploded into laughter, and I couldn't myself keep a straight face.

'Can you shoot it off, sir?'

The voices rose above a general hubbub.

'William Tell could, sir.'

'Shall we call an ambulance, sir, just in case?'

'How long will it take a bullet to get through Paul's skull, sir?'

'Very funny,' I said repressively, but indeed it *was* very funny, and they knew it. But if I laughed too much I'd lose control of them, and control of such a volatile mass was always precarious.

'Very clever, Paul,' I said. 'Go and sit down.'

He was satisfied. He'd produced his effect perfectly. He took the apple off his head with a natural elegance and returned in good order to his place, accepting as his due the admiring jokes and the envious catcalls.

'Right then,' I said, planting myself firmly where he had stood, 'by the end of this lesson you'll all know how long it would take for a bullet travelling at a certain speed to cross a certain distance . . .'

The gun I had taken to the lesson had been a simple air-gun, but I told them also how a rifle worked, and why in each case a bullet or a pellet came out fast. I let them handle the smooth metal: the first time many of them had seen an actual gun, even an air-gun, at close quarters. I explained how bullets were made, and how they differed from the pellets I had with me. How loading mechanisms worked. How the grooves inside a rifle barrel rotated the bullet, to send it out spinning. I told them about air friction, and heat.

They listened with concentration and asked the questions they always did.

'Can you tell us how a bomb works, sir?'

'One day,' I said.

'A nuclear bomb?'

'One day.'

'A hydrogen . . . cobalt . . . neutron bomb?'

'One day.'

They never asked how radio waves crossed the ether, which was to me a greater mystery. They asked about destruction, not creation; about power, not symmetry. The seed of violence born in every male child looked out of every face, and I knew how they were thinking, because I'd been there myself. Why else had I spent countless hours at their age practising with a .22 cadet rifle on a range, improving my skill until I could hit a target the size of a thumbnail at fifty yards, nine times out of ten. A strange, pointless, sublimated skill, which I never intended to use on any living creature, but had never since lost.

'Is it true, sir,' one of them said, 'that you won an Olympic medal for rifle shooting?'

'No, it isn't.'

'What, then, sir?'

'I want you all to consider the speed of a bullet compared to the speed of other objects you are all familiar with. Now, do you think that you could be flying along in an aeroplane, and look out of the window, and see a bullet keeping pace with you, appearing to be standing still just outside the window?'

The lesson wound on. They would remember it all

their lives, because of the gun. Without the gun, whatever Jenkins might think, it would have faded into the general dust they shook from their shoes every afternoon at four o'clock. Teaching, it often seemed to me, was as much a matter of image-jerking as of imparting actual information. The facts dressed up in jokes were the ones they got right in exams.

I liked teaching. Specifically I liked teaching physics, a subject I suppose I embraced with passion and joy, knowing full well that most people shied away in horror. Physics was only the science of the unseen world, as geography was of the seen. Physics was the science of all the tremendously powerful invisibilities – of magnetism, electricity, gravity, light, sound, cosmic rays . . . Physics was the science of the mysteries of the universe. How could *anyone* think it dull?

I had been for three years head of the physics department of the East Middlesex Comprehensive, with four masters and two technicians within my domain. My future, from my present age of thirty-three, looked like a possible deputy headmastership, most likely with a move involved, and even perhaps a headship, though if I hadn't achieved that by forty I could forget it. Headmasters got younger every year; mostly, cynics suggested, because the younger the man they appointed, the more the authorities could boss him about.

I was, all in all, contented with my job and hopeful

of my prospects. It was only at home that things weren't so good.

Four A learned about momentum and Arcady ate his apple when he thought I wasn't looking. My peripheral vision after ten years of teaching was, however, so acute that at times they thought I could literally see out of the back of my head. It did no harm: it made control easier.

'Don't drop the core on the floor, Paul,' I said mildly. It was one thing to let him eat the apple – he'd deserved it – but quite another to let him think I hadn't seen. Keeping a grip on the monsters was a perpetual psychological game, but also priority number one. I'd seen stronger men than myself reduced to nervous breakdowns by the hunting-pack instincts of children.

When the end-of-lesson bell rang, they did me the ultimate courtesy of letting me finish what I was saying before erupting into the going-home stampede. It was, after all, the last lesson on Friday – and God be thanked for weekends.

I made my way slowly round the four physics laboratories and the two equipment rooms, checking that everything was in order. The two technicians, Louisa and David, were dismantling and putting away all apparatus not needed on Monday, picking Five E's efforts at radio-circuitry to pieces and returning the batteries, clips, bases and transistors to the countless racks and drawers in the equipment rooms.

'Shooting anyone special?' Louisa said, eyeing the gun which I was carrying with me.

'Didn't want to leave it unattended.'

'Is it loaded?' Her voice sounded almost hopeful. By late Friday, she was always in the state in which one never asked her for an extra favour: not, that is, unless one was willing to endure a weepy ten minutes of 'you don't realise how much this job entails', which, on most occasions, I wasn't. Louisa's tantrums, I reckoned, were based on her belief that life had cheated her, finding her at forty as a sort of storekeeper (efficient, meticulous and helpful) but not a Great Scientist. 'If I'd gone to college . . .' she would say, leaving the strong impression that if she had, Einstein would have been relegated. I dealt with Louisa by retreating at the warning signs of trouble, which was maybe weak, but I had to live with her professionally, and bouts of sullenness made her slow.

'My list for Monday!' I said, handing it to her.

She glanced disparagingly down it. 'Martin has ordered the oscilloscopes for third period.'

The school's shortage of oscilloscopes was a constant source of friction.

'See what you can manage,' I said.

'Can you make do with only two?'

I said I supposed so, smiled, hoped it would keep fine for her gardening, and left for home.

I drove slowly with the leaden feeling of resignation clamping down, as it always did on the return journey.

Between Sarah and me there was no joy left; no springing love. Eight years of marriage, and nothing to feel but a growing boredom.

We had been unable to have children. Sarah had hoped for them, longed for them, pined for them. We'd been to every conceivable specialist and Sarah had had countless injections and pills and two operations. My own disappointment was bearable, though none the less deep. Hers had proved intractable and finally disabling in that she had gone into a state of permanent depression from which it seemed nothing could rescue her.

We'd been told by encouraging therapists that many childless marriages were highly successful, husband and wife forging exceptionally strong bonds through their misfortune, but with us it had worked in reverse. Where once there had been passion there was now politeness; where plans and laughter, now a grinding hopelessness; where tears and heartbreak, silence.

I hadn't been enough for her, without babies. I'd been forced to face the fact that to her motherhood mattered most, that marriage had been but the pathway, that many a man would have done. I wondered unhappily from time to time how soon she would have divorced me had it been I who had proved infertile: and it was profitless also to guess that we would have been contented enough for ever if she herself had been fulfilled.

I dare say it was a marriage like many another. We

never quarrelled. Seldom argued. Neither of us any longer cared enough for that; and as a total, prolonged way of life it was infinitely dispiriting.

It was a homecoming like thousands of others. I parked outside the closed garage doors and let myself into the house with arms full of air-gun and exercise books. Sarah, home as usual from her part-time job as a dentist's receptionist, sat on the sofa in the sitting-room reading a magazine.

'Hullo,' I said.

'Hullo. Good day?'

'Not bad.'

She hadn't looked up from her pages. I hadn't kissed her. Perhaps for both of us it was better than total loneliness, but not much.

'There's ham for supper,' she said. 'And coleslaw. That all right?'

'Fine.'

She went on reading; a slim fair-haired girl, still arrestingly pretty but now with a settled resentful expression. I was used to it, but in flashes suffered unbearable nostalgia for the laughing eagerness of the early days. I wondered sometimes if she noticed that the fun had gone out of me, too, although I could sometimes feel it still bubbling along inside, deeply buried.

On that particular evening I made an effort (as I did more and more rarely) to jog us out of our dimness.

'Look, let's just dump everything and go out to dinner. Maybe to Florestan's, where there's dancing.'

She didn't look up. 'Don't be silly.'

'Let's just go.'

'I don't want to.' A pause. 'I'd rather watch television.' She turned a page and added with indifference, 'And we can't afford Florestan's prices.'

'We could, if you'd enjoy it.'

'No, I wouldn't.'

'Well,' I sighed, 'I'll make a start on the books, then.'

She nodded faintly. 'Supper at seven.'

'All right.'

I turned to go.

'There's a letter for you from William,' she said with boredom in her voice. 'I put it upstairs.'

'Oh? Well, thanks.'

She went on reading, and I took my stuff up to the third and smallest of our three bedrooms, which I used as a sort of study-cum-office. The estate agent who had shown us the house had brightly described the room as 'just right for the nursery', and had nearly lost himself the sale. I'd annexed the place for myself and made it as masculine as possible, but I was aware that for Sarah the spirit of unborn children still hovered there. She rarely went in. It was slightly unusual that she should have put the letter from my brother on my desk.

It said:

Dear Jonathan,
Please can I have thirty pounds? It's for going to the farm at half-term. I wrote to Mrs Porter, and she'll have me. She says her rates have gone up because of inflation. It can't be for what I eat, as she mostly gives me bread and honey. (No complaints.) Also actually I need some money for riding, in case they won't let me earn any more rides at the stables by mucking out, they were a bit funny about it last time, something to do with the law and exploiting juveniles, I ask you. Roll on sixteen. Anyway, if you could make it fifty quid it would be fine. If I can earn my riding, I'll send the extra twenty back, because if you don't want your heavy dough lifted at this high-class nick you have to have it embedded in concrete. Half-term is a week on Friday, early this term, so could you send it pronto?

Did you notice that Clinker did win the Wrap-Up 'chase at Stratford? If you don't want me to be a jockey, how about a tipster?

Hope you are well. And Sarah.

William.

P.S. Can you come for sports day, or for Blah-Blah day? I've got a prize for two plus two, you'll be astounded to hear.

Blah-Blah day was Speech Day, at which the school prizes were handed out. I'd missed every one of William's for one reason or another. I would go this time, I thought. Even William might sometimes feel lonely with no one close to him ever to see him collect his prizes, which he did with some monotony.

William went to public school thanks to a rich godfather who had left him a lot of money in trust 'for his education and vocational training, and good luck to the little brat'. William's trustees regularly paid his fees to the school and maintenance for clothes and etceteras to me, and I passed on cash to William as required. It was an arrangement which worked excellently on many counts, not least that it meant that William didn't have to live with Sarah and me. Her husband's noisy and independent-minded brother was not the child she wanted.

William spent his holidays on farms, and Sarah occasionally said that it was most unfair that William should have more money than I had and that William had been spoiled rotten from the day my mother had discovered she was pregnant again at the age of forty-six. Sarah and William, whenever they met, behaved mostly with wary restraint and only occasionally with direct truth. William had learned very quickly not to tease her, which was his natural inclination, and she had accepted that doling out sarcastic criticism invited a cutting response. They circled each other, in consequence, like exactly matched opponents unwilling to declare open war.

For as long as he could remember William had been irresistibly attracted to horses and had long affirmed his intention to be a jockey, of which Sarah strongly and I mildly disapproved. Security, William said, was a dirty word. There were better things in life than a safe job. Sarah and I, I suppose, were happier with pattern and order and achievement. William increasingly as he grew through thirteen, fourteen, and now fifteen, seemed to hunger for air and speed and uncertainty. It was typical of him that he proposed to spend the week's mid-term break in riding horses instead of working for the eight 'O' Level exams he was due to take immediately afterwards.

I left his letter on my desk to remind myself to send him a cheque and unlocked the cupboard where I kept my guns.

The air-gun that I'd taken to school was little more than a toy and needed no licence or secure storage, but I also owned two Mauser 7.62s, an Enfield No. 4 7.62 and two Anschütz .22s around which all sorts of regulations bristled, and also an old Lee Enfield .303 dating back from my early days which was still as lethal as ever if one could raise the ammunition for it. The little I had, I hoarded, mostly out of nostalgia. There were no more .303 rounds being made, thanks to the army switching to 7.62 mm in the sixties.

I put the air-gun back in its rack, checked that everything was as it should be, and locked the doors on the familiar smell of oil.

The telephone bell rang downstairs and Sarah answered it. I looked at the pile of exercise books which would all have to be read and corrected and handed out to the boys again on Monday, and wondered why I didn't have a fixed-hours job that one didn't have to take home. It wasn't only for the pupils that homework was a drag.

I could hear Sarah's telephone-answering voice, loud and bright.

'Oh. Hullo, Peter. How nice . . .'

There was a long pause while Peter talked, and then from Sarah a rising wail.

'Oh, *no*! Oh, my *God*! Oh, no, Peter . . .' Horror, disbelief, great distress. A quality, anyway, which took me straight downstairs.

Sarah was sitting stiffly upright on the sofa, holding the telephone at the end of its long cord. 'Oh no,' she was saying wildly. 'It can't be true. It just *can't*.'

She stared at me unseeingly, neck stretched upwards, listening with even her eyes.

'Well, of course . . . of course we will . . . Oh, Peter, yes, of course . . . yes, straight away. Yes . . . yes . . . we'll be there . . .' She glanced at her watch. 'Nine o'clock. Perhaps a bit later. Will that do? . . . All right then . . . and Peter, give her my love . . .'

She clattered the receiver down with shaking hands.

'We'll have to go,' she said. 'Peter and Donna—'

'Not tonight,' I protested. 'Whatever it is, not tonight. I'm damned tired and I've got all those books . . .'

'Yes, at once, we must go at once.'

'It's a hundred miles.'

'I don't *care* how far it is. We must go *now*. *Now!*'

She stood up and practically ran towards the stairs. 'Pack a suitcase,' she said. 'Come on.'

I followed her more slowly, half exasperated, half moved by her urgency. 'Sarah, hold on a minute, what exactly has happened to Peter and Donna?'

She stopped four stairs up, and looked down at me over the bannister. She was already crying, her whole face screwed into agonised disorder.

'Donna.' The words were indistinct. 'Donna . . .'

'Has she had an accident?'

'No . . . not . . .'

'What, then?'

The question served only to increase the tears. 'She . . . needs . . . me.'

'You go, then,' I said, feeling relieved at the solution. 'I can manage without the car for a few days. Until Tuesday anyway. Monday I can go by bus.'

'No. Peter wants you, too. He begged me . . . both of us.'

'Why?' I said, but she was already running again up the stairs, and wouldn't answer.

I won't like it, I thought abruptly. Whatever had happened she knew that I wouldn't like it and that my instincts would all be on the side of non-involvement. I followed her upwards with reluctance and found her already gathering clothes and toothpaste onto the bed.

'Donna has parents, hasn't she?' I said. 'And Peter, too? So if something terrible's happened, why in God's name do they need *us*?'

'They're our friends.' She was rushing about, crying and gulping and dropping things. It was much, much more than ordinary sympathy for any ill that might have befallen Donna: there was a quality of extravagance that both disturbed and antagonised.

'It's beyond the bounds of friendship,' I said, 'to go charging off to Norfolk hungry and tired and not knowing why. And I'm not going.'

Sarah didn't seem to hear. The haphazard packing went ahead without pause and the tears developed into a low continous grizzle.

Where once we had had many friends, we now had just Donna and Peter, notwithstanding that they no longer lived five miles away and played squash on Tuesdays. All our other friends from before and after marriage had either dropped away or coupled and bred; and it was only Donna and Peter who, like us, had produced no children. Only Donna and Peter, who never talked nursery, whose company Sarah could bear.

She and Donna had once been long-time flat-mates. Peter and I, meeting for the first time as their subsequent husbands, had got on together amicably enough for the friendship to survive the Norfolk removal, though it was by now more a matter of birthday cards and telephone calls than of frequent house-to-house visits. We had spent a boating holiday together once on the canals. 'We'll do it again next year,' we'd all said: but we didn't.

'Is Donna ill?' I asked.

'No . . .'

'I'm not going.' I said.

The keening grizzle stopped. Sarah looked a mess, standing there with vague reddened eyes and a clumsily folded night-dress. She stared down at the pale green froth that she wore against the chill of separate beds and the disastrous news finally burst out of her.

'She was arrested,' she said.

'Donna . . . arrested?' I was astounded. Donna was mouselike. Organised. Gentle. Apologetic. Anything but likely to be in trouble with the police.

'She's home now,' Sarah said. 'She's . . . Peter says she's . . . well . . . *suicidal*. He says he can't cope with it.' Her voice was rising. 'He says he needs us . . . *now* . . . this minute. He doesn't know what to do. He says we're the only people who can help.'

She was crying again. Whatever it was, was too much.

'What,' I said slowly, 'has Donna done?'

'She went out shopping,' Sarah said, trying at last to speak clearly. 'And she stole . . . She stole . . .'

'Well, for heaven's sake,' I said, 'I know it's bloody for them, but thousands of people shoplift. So why all this excessive drama?'

'You don't listen,' Sarah shouted. 'Why don't you *listen*?'

'I—'

'She stole a *baby*.'

CHAPTER TWO

We went to Norwich.

Sarah had been right. I didn't like the reason for our journey. I felt a severe aversion to being dragged into a highly charged emotional situation where nothing constructive could possibly be done. My feelings of friendship towards Peter and Donna were nowhere near strong enough. For Peter, perhaps. For Donna, definitely not.

All the same, when I thought of the tremendous forces working on that poor girl to impel her to such an action, it occurred to me that perhaps the unseen universe didn't stop at the sort of electro-magnetics that I taught. Every living cell, after all, generated electric charges: especially brain cells. If I put baby-snatching on a par with an electric storm, I could be happier with it.

Sarah sat silently beside me for most of the way, recovering, re-adjusting, preparing. She said only once what must have been in both our minds.

'It could have been me.'

'No,' I said.

'You don't know . . . what it's like.'

There was no answer. Short of having been born female and barren, there was no way of knowing. I had been told about five hundred times over the years in various tones from anguish to spite that I didn't know what it was like, and there was no more answer now than there had been the first time.

The long lingering May evening made the driving easier than usual, although going northwards out of London in the Friday night exodus was always a beast of a journey.

At the far, far end of it lay the neat new box-like house with its big featureless net-curtained windows and its tidy oblong of grass. One bright house in a street of others much the same. One proud statement that Peter had reached a certain salary-level and still aspired to future improvement. A place and a way of life that I understood and saw no harm in: where William would suffocate.

The turmoil behind the uninformative net curtains was much as expected in some ways and much worse in others.

The usually meticulously tidy interior was in much disarray, with unwashed cups and mugs making wet rings on every surface and clothes and papers scattered around. The trail, I came to realise, left by the in-and-out tramp of officialdom over the past two days.

Peter greeted us with gaunt eyes and the hushed

voice of a death in the family; and probably for him and Donna what had happened was literally hurting them worse than a death. Donna herself sat in a silent huddle at one end of the big green sofa in their sitting-room and made no attempt to respond to Sarah when she rushed to her side and put her arms round her in almost a frenzy of affection.

Peter said helplessly, 'She won't talk . . . or eat.'

'Or go to the bathroom?'

'*What?*'

Sarah looked up at me with furious reproach, but I said mildly, 'If she goes off to the bathroom when she feels the need, it's surely a good sign. It's such a *normal* act.'

'Well, yes,' Peter said limply. 'She does.'

'Good, then.'

Sarah clearly thought that this was another prime example of what she called my general heartlessness, but I had meant only to reassure. I asked Peter what exactly had taken place, and as he wouldn't tell me in front of Donna herself we removed to the kitchen.

In there, too, the police and medics and court officials and social workers had made the coffee and left the dishes. Peter seemed not to see the mess that in past times would have set both him and Donna busily wiping up. We sat at the table with the last remnants of daytime fading to dusk, and in that gentle light he slowly unlocked the horrors.

It was on the previous morning, he said, that Donna

had taken the baby from its pram and driven off with it in her car. She had driven seventy odd miles north-east to the coast, and had at some point abandoned the car with the baby inside it, and had walked off along the beach.

The car and the baby had been traced and found within hours, and Donna herself had been discovered sitting on the sand in pouring rain, speechless and stunned.

The police had arrested her, taken her to the station for a night in the cells, and paraded her before a magistrate in the morning. The bench had called for psychiatric reports, set a date for a hearing a week ahead and, despite protests from the baby's mother, set Donna free. Everyone had assured Peter she would only be put on probation, but he still shuddered from their appalling future of ignominy via the press and the neighbourhood.

After a pause, and thinking of Donna's trancelike state, I said, 'You told Sarah she was suicidal.'

He nodded miserably. 'This afternoon I wanted to warm her. To put her to bed. I ran the bath for her.' It was a while before he could go on. It seemed that the suicide attempt had been in deadly earnest; he had stopped her on the instant before she plunged herself and her switched-on hair-drier into the water. 'And she still had all her clothes on,' he said.

It seemed to me that what Donna urgently needed was some expert and continuous psychiatric care in a comfortable private nursing-home, all of which she was probably not going to get.

'Come on out for a drink,' I said.

'But I *can't*.' He was slightly trembling all the time, as if his foundations were in an earthquake.

'Donna will be all right with Sarah.'

'But she might try . . .'

'Sarah will look after her.'

'But I can't face . . .'

'No,' I said. 'We'll buy a bottle.'

I bought some Scotch and two glasses from a philosophical publican just before closing time, and we sat in my car to drink in a quiet tree-lined street three miles from Peter's home. Stars and street lights between the shadowy leaves.

'What are we going to do?' he said despairingly.

'Time will pass.'

'We'll never get over it. How can we? It's bloody impossible.' He choked on the last word and began to cry like a boy. An outrush of unbearable, pent-up, half-angry grief.

I took the wobbling glass out of his hand. Sat and waited and made vague sympathetic noises and wondered what to God I would have done if, like she said, it had been Sarah.

'And to happen now,' he said at length, fishing for a handkerchief to blow his nose, 'of all times.'

'Er . . . oh?' I said.

He sniffed convulsively and wiped his cheeks. 'Sorry about that.'

'Don't be.'

He sighed. 'You're always so calm.'

'Nothing like this has happened to me.'

'I'm in a mess,' he said.

'Well, it'll get better.'

'No, I mean, besides Donna. I didn't know what to do . . . before . . . and now, after, I can't even *think*.'

'What sort of mess? Financial?'

'No. Well, not exactly.' He paused uncertainly, needing a prompt.

'What then?'

I gave him his glass back. He looked at it vaguely, then drank most of the contents in one mouthful.

'You don't mind if I burden you?' he said.

'Of course not.'

He was a couple of years younger than I, the same age as both Donna and Sarah; and all three of them, it had sometimes seemed to me, saw me not only as William's elder brother but as their own. At any rate it was as natural to me as to Peter that he should tell me his troubles.

He was middling tall and thin and had recently grown a lengthy moustache which had not given him the overpoweringly macho appearance he might have been aiming for. He still looked an ordinary inoffensive competent guy who went around selling his computer know-how to small businesses on weekdays and tinkered with his boat on Sundays.

He dabbed his eyes again and for several minutes took slow deep calming breaths.

'I got into something which I wish I hadn't,' he said.

'What sort of thing?'

'It started more or less as a joke.' He finished the last inch of drink and I stretched across and poured him a refill. 'There was this fellow. Our age, about. He'd come up from Newmarket, and we got talking in that pub you bought the whisky from. He said it would be great if you could get racing results from a computer. And we both laughed.'

There was a silence.

'Did he know you worked with computers?' I said.

'I'd told him. You know how one does.'

'So what happened next?'

'A week later I got a letter. From this fellow. Don't know how he got my address. From the pub, I suppose. The barman knows where I live.' He took a gulp from his drink and was quiet for a while, and then went on, 'The letter asked if I would like to help someone who was working out a computer program for handicapping horses. So I thought, why not? All handicaps for horse races are sorted out on computers, and the letter sounded quite official.'

'But it wasn't?'

He shook his head. 'A spot of private enterprise. But I still thought, why not? Anyone is entitled to work out his own program. There isn't such a thing as *right* in handicapping unless the horses pass the post in the exact order that the computer weighted them, which they never do.'

'You know a lot about it,' I said.

'I've learnt, these past few weeks.' The thought brought no cheer. 'I didn't even notice I was neglecting Donna, but she says I've hardly spoken to her for ages.' His throat closed and he swallowed audibly. 'Perhaps if I hadn't been so occupied . . .'

'Stop feeling guilty,' I said. 'Go on about the handicapping.'

After a while he was able to.

'He gave me pages and pages of stuff. Dozens of them. All handwritten in diabolical handwriting. He wanted it organised into programs that any fool could run on a computer.' He paused. 'You do know about computers.'

'More about microchips than programming, which isn't saying much.'

'The other way round from most people, though.'

'I guess so,' I said.

'Anyway, I did them. Quite a lot of them. It turned out they were all much the same sort of thing. They weren't really very difficult, once I'd got the hang of what the notes all meant. It was understanding those which was the worst. So, anyway, I did the programs and got paid in cash.' He stopped and moved restlessly in his seat, glum and frowning.

'So what is wrong?' I asked.

'Well, I said it would be best if I ran the programs a few times on the computer he was going to use, because so many computers are different from each other, and although he'd told me the make of computer he'd be using and I'd made allowances, you never can really tell you've got no bugs until you actually try things out on the actual type of machine. But he wouldn't let me. I said he wasn't being reasonable and he told me to mind my own business. So I just shrugged him off and thought if he wanted to be so stupid it was his own affair. And then these other two men turned up.'

'What other two men?'

'I don't know. They just sneered when I asked their names. They told me to hand over to them the programs I'd made on the horses. I said I had done. They said they were nothing to do with the person who'd paid for the job, but all the same I was to give them the programs.'

'And did you?'

'Well, yes – in a way.'

'But, Peter – ' I said.

He interrupted, 'Yes, I know, but they were so bloody *frightening*. They came the day before yesterday – it seems years ago – in the evening. Donna had gone out for a walk. It was still light. About eight o'clock, I should think. She often goes for walks . . .' He trailed off again and I gave his glass a nudge with the bottle. 'What?' he said. 'Oh no, no more, thanks. Anyway, they came, and they were so *arrogant*, and they said I'd regret it if I didn't give them the programs. They said Donna was a pretty little missis, wasn't she, and they were sure I'd like her to stay that way.' He swallowed. 'I'd never have believed . . . I mean, that sort of thing doesn't *happen* . . .'

It appeared, however, that it had.

'Well,' he said, rallying, 'what I gave them was all that I had in the house, but it was really only first drafts, so to speak. Pretty rough. I'd written three or four trial programs out in long-hand, like I often do. I know a lot of people work on typewriters or even straight onto a computer, but I get on better with pencil and rubber, so what I gave them *looked* all right, especially if you didn't know the first thing about programming, which I should think they didn't, but not much of it would run as it stood. And I hadn't put the file names on anyway, or any REMS or anything, so even if they de-bugged the programs they wouldn't know what they referred to.'

Disentangling the facts from the jargon, it appeared that what he had done had been to deliver to possibly dangerous men a load of garbage, knowing full well what he was doing.

'I see,' I said slowly, 'what you meant by a mess.'

'I'd decided to take Donna away for a few days, just to be safe. I was going to tell her as a nice surprise when I got home from work yesterday, and then the police turned up in my office, and said she'd taken . . . taken . . . Oh Christ, how *could* she?'

I screwed the cap onto the bottle and I looked at my watch. 'It's getting on for midnight,' I said. 'We'd better go back.'

'I suppose so.'

I paused with my hand on the ignition key. 'Didn't you tell the police about your two unpleasant visitors?' I said.

'No, I didn't. I mean, how could I? They've been in and out of the house, and a policewoman too, but it was all about Donna. They wouldn't have listened, and anyway . . .'

'Anyway what?'

He shrugged uncomfortably. 'I got paid in cash. Quite a lot. I'm not going to declare it for tax. If I told the police . . . well, I'd more or less have to.'

'It might be better,' I said.

He shook his head. 'It would cost me a lot to tell the police, and what would I gain? They'd make a note of what I said and wait until Donna got bashed in the face before they did anything. I mean, they can't go around guarding everyone who's been vaguely threatened night and day, can they? And as for guarding *Donna* – well, they weren't very nice to her, you know. Really rotten, most of them were. They made cups of tea for each other and spoke over her head as if she was a lump of wood. You'd think she'd poked the baby's eyes out, the way they treated her.'

It didn't seem unreasonable to me that official sympathy had been mostly on the side of the baby's frantic mother, but I didn't say so.

'Perhaps it would be best, then,' I said, 'if you did take Donna away for a bit, straight after the hearing. Can you get leave?'

He nodded.

'But what she really needs is proper psychiatric care. Even a spell in a mental hospital.'

'No,' he said.

'They have a high success rate with mental illness nowadays. Modern drugs, and hormones, and all that.'

'But she's not—' He stopped.

The old taboos died hard. 'The brain is part of the body,' I said. 'It's not separate. And it goes wrong sometimes, just like anything else. Like the liver. Or the kidneys. You wouldn't hesitate if it was her kidneys.'

He shook his head, however, and I didn't press it. Everyone had to decide things for themselves. I started the car and wheeled us back to the house, and Peter said as we turned into the short concrete driveway that Donna was unusually happy on their boat, and he would take her away on that.

The weekend dragged on. I tried surreptitiously now and then to mark the inexorable exercise books, but the telephone rang more or less continuously and, as answering it seemed to be the domestic chore I was best fitted for, I slid into a routine of chat. Relatives, friends, press, officials, busybodies, cranks and stinkers, I talked with the lot.

Sarah cared for Donna with extreme tenderness and devotion and was rewarded with wan smiles at first and, gradually, low-toned speech. After that came hysterical tears, a brushing of hair, a tentative meal, a change of clothes, and a growth of invalid behaviour.

When Peter talked to Donna it was in a miserable mixture of love, guilt and reproach, and he found many an opportunity of escaping into the garden. On Sunday morning he went off in his car at pub-opening time and returned late for lunch, and on Sunday afternoon I said with private relief that I would now have to go back home ready for school on Monday.

'I'm staying here,' Sarah said. 'Donna needs me. I'll ring my boss and explain. He owes me a week's leave anyway.'

Donna gave her the by now ultra-dependent smile she had developed over the past two days, and Peter nodded with eager agreement.

'OK,' I said slowly, 'but take care.'

'What of?' Sarah said.

I glanced at Peter, who was agitatedly shaking his head. All the same, it seemed sensible to take simple precautions.

'Don't let Donna go out alone,' I said.

Donna blushed furiously and Sarah was instantly angry, and I said helplessly, 'I didn't mean . . . I meant keep her safe . . . from people who might want to be spiteful to her.'

Sarah saw the sense in that and calmed down, and a short while later I was ready to leave.

I said goodbye to them in the house because there seemed to be always people in the street staring at the windows with avid eyes, and right at the last minute Peter thrust into my hand three cassettes for playing in the car if I should get bored on the way home. I glanced at them briefly: *The King and I, Oklahoma*, and *West Side Story*. Hardly the latest rave, but I thanked him anyway, kissed Sarah for appearances, kissed Donna ditto, and with a regrettable lightening of spirits took myself off.

It was on the last third of the way home, when I tried *Oklahoma* for company, that I found that what Peter had given me wasn't music at all, but quite something else.

Instead of 'Oh What a Beautiful Morning', I got a loud vibrating scratchy whine interspersed with brief bits of one-note plain whine. Shrugging, I wound the tape forward a bit, and tried again.

Same thing.

I ejected the tape, turned it over, and tried again. Same thing. Tried *The King and I* and *West Side Story*. All the same.

I knew that sort of noise from way back. One

couldn't forget it, once one knew. The scratchy whine was made by two tones alternating very fast so that the ear could scarcely distinguish the upper from the lower. The plain whine indicated an interval with nothing happening. On *Oklahoma*, fairly typically, the stretches of two-tone were lasting anywhere from ten seconds to three minutes.

I was listening to the noise a computer produced when its programs were recorded onto ordinary cassette tape.

Cassettes were convenient and widely used, especially with smaller computers. One could store a whole host of different programs on cassette tapes, and simply pick out whichever was needed, and use it: but the cassettes were still, all the same, just ordinary cassettes, and if one played the tape straightforwardly in the normal way on a cassette player, as I had done, one heard the vibrating whine.

Peter had given me three sixty-minute tapes of computer programs: and it wasn't so very difficult to guess what those programs would be about.

I wondered why he had given them to me in such an indirect way. I wondered, in fact, why he had given them to me at all. With a mental shrug I shovelled the tapes and their misleading boxes onto the glove shelf and switched on the radio instead.

*

School on Monday was a holiday after the green-house emotions in Norfolk, and Louisa-the-technician's problems seemed moths' wings beside Donna's.

On Monday evening, while I was watching my own choice on the television and eating cornflakes and cream with my feet on the coffee table, Peter telephoned.

'How's Donna?' I said.

'I don't know where she'd be without Sarah.'

'And you?'

'Oh, pretty fair. Look, Jonathan, did you play any of those tapes?' His voice sounded tentative and half apologetic.

'A bit of all of them,' I said.

'Oh. Well, I expect you'll know what they are?'

'Your horse-handicapping programs?'

'Yes . . . er . . . Will you keep them for me for now?' He gave me no chance to answer and rushed on, 'You see, we're hoping to go off to the boat straight after the hearing on Friday. Well, we do have to believe Donna will get probation, even the nastiest of those officials said it would be so in such a case, but obviously she'll be terribly upset with having to go to court and everything and so we'll go away as soon as we can, and I didn't like the thought of leaving those cassettes lying around in the office, which they were, so I went over to fetch them yesterday morning, so I could give them to you. I mean, I didn't really think it out. I could have put them in the bank, or anywhere.

I suppose what I really wanted was to get those tapes right out of my life so that if those two brutes came back asking for the programs I'd be able to say I hadn't got them and that they'd have to get them from the person I made them for.'

It occurred to me not for the first time that for a computer programmer Peter was no great shakes as a logical thinker, but maybe the circumstances were jamming the circuits.

'Have you heard from those men again?' I asked.

'No, thank God.'

'They probably haven't found out yet.'

'Thanks very much,' he said bitterly.

'I'll keep the tapes safe,' I said. 'As long as you like.'

'Probably nothing else will happen. After all, I haven't done anything illegal. Or even faintly wrong.'

The 'if-we-don't-look-at-the-monster-he'll-go-away' syndrome, I thought. But maybe he was right.

'Why didn't you tell me what you were giving me?' I enquired. 'Why *The King and I* dressing, and all that?'

'What?' His voice sounded almost puzzled, and then cleared to understanding. 'Oh, it was just that when I got home from the office, you were all sitting down to lunch, and I didn't get a single chance to catch you away from the girls, and I didn't want to have to start explaining in front of them, so I just shoved them into those cases to give to you.'

The faintest twitch of unease crossed my mind, but I smothered it. Peter's world since Donna took the baby had hardly been one of general common sense and normal behaviour. He had acted pretty well, all in all, for someone hammered from all directions at once, and over the weekend I had felt an increase of respect for him, quite apart from liking.

'If you want to play those programs,' he said, 'you'll need a Grantley computer.'

'I don't suppose . . .' I began.

'They might amuse William. He's mad on racing, isn't he?'

'Yes, he is.'

'I spent so much time on them. I'd really like to know how they work out in practice. I mean, from someone who knows horses.'

'All right,' I said. But Grantley computers weren't scattered freely round the landscape and William had his exams ahead, and the prospect of actually using the programs seemed a long way off.

'I wish you were still here,' he said. 'All the telephone calls, they're really getting me down. And did you have any of those poisonous abusive beastly voices spitting out hate against Donna, when you were answering?'

'Yes, several.'

'But they've never even *met* her.'

'They're unbalanced. Just don't listen.'

'What did you say to them?'

'I told them to take their problems to a doctor.'

There was a slightly uncomfortable pause, then he said explosively, 'I wish to God Donna had gone to a doctor.' A gulp. 'I didn't even *know* . . . I mean, I knew she'd wanted children, but I thought, well, we couldn't have them, so that was that. I never *dreamed* . . . I mean, she's always so quiet and wouldn't hurt a fly. She never showed any signs . . . We're pretty fond of each other, you know. Or at least I thought . . .'

'Peter, stop it.'

'Yes . . .' A pause. 'Of course, you're right. But it's difficult to think of anything else.'

We talked a bit more, but only covering the same old ground, and we disconnected with me feeling that somehow I could have done more for him than I had.

Two evenings later, he went down to the river on his two-berth cabin cruiser, filling its tanks with water and fuel, installing new cooking-gas cylinders and checking that everything was in working order for his trip with Donna.

He had been telling me earlier that he was afraid the ship's battery was wearing out and that if he didn't get a new one they would run it down flat with their lights at night and in the morning find themselves unable to start the engine. It had happened once before, he said.

He wanted to check that the battery still had enough life in it.

It had.

When he raised the first spark, the rear half of the boat exploded.

CHAPTER THREE

Sarah told me.

Sarah on the telephone with the stark over-controlled voice of exhaustion.

'They think it was gas, or petrol vapour. They don't know yet.'

'Peter . . .'

'He's dead,' she said. 'There were people around. They saw him moving . . . with his clothes on fire. He went over the side into the water . . . but when they got him out . . .' A sudden silence, then, slowly, 'We weren't there. Thank God Donna and I weren't there.'

I felt shaky and slightly sick. 'Do you want me to come?' I said.

'No. What time is it?'

'Eleven.' I had undressed, in fact, to go to bed.

'Donna's asleep. Knock-out drops.'

'And how . . . how is she?'

'Christ, how would you expect?' Sarah seldom spoke in that way: a true measure of the general awfulness. 'And Friday,' she said, 'the day after tomorrow, she's due in court.'

'They'll be kind to her.'

'There's already been one call, just now, with some beastly woman telling me it served her right.'

'I'd better come,' I said.

'You can't. There's school. No, don't worry. I can cope. The doctor at least said he'd keep Donna heavily sedated for several days.'

'Let me know, then, if I can help.'

'Yes,' she said. 'Goodnight, now. I'm going to bed. There's a lot to do tomorrow. Goodnight.'

I lay long awake in bed and thought of Peter and the unfairness of death: and in the morning I went to school and found him flicking in and out of my mind all day.

Driving home I saw that his cassettes were still lying in a jumble on the glove shelf. Once parked in the garage, I put the tapes back into their boxes, slipped them in my jacket pocket, and carried my usual burden of books indoors.

The telephone rang almost at once, but it was not Sarah, which was my first thought, but William.

'Did you send my cheque?' he said.

'*Hell*, I forgot.' I told him why, and he allowed that forgetting in such circs could be overlooked.

'I'll write it straight away, and send it direct to the farm.'

'OK. Look, I'm sorry about Peter. He seemed a nice guy, that time we met.'

'Yes.' I told William about the computer tapes, and about Peter wanting his opinion on them.

'Bit late now.'

'But you still might find them interesting.'

'Yeah,' he said without much enthusiasm. 'Probably some nutty betting system. There's a computer here somewhere in the maths department. I'll ask what sort it is. And look, how would it grab you if I didn't go to university?'

'Badly.'

'Yeah. I was afraid so. Anyway, work on it, big brother. There's been a lot of guff going on this term about choosing a career, but I reckon it's the career that chooses *you*. I'm going to be a jockey. I can't help it.'

We said goodbyes and I put the receiver down thinking that it wasn't much good fighting to dissuade someone who at fifteen already felt that a vocation had him by the scruff of the neck.

He was slim and light: past puberty but still physically a boy, with the growth into man's stature just ahead. Perhaps nature, I thought hopefully, would take him to my height of six feet and break his heart.

Sarah rang almost immediately afterwards, speaking crisply with her dentist's-assistant voice. The shock had gone, and the exhaustion. She spoke to me with edgy bossiness, a left-over, I guessed, from a very demanding day.

'It seems that Peter should have been more careful,' she said. 'Everyone who owns a boat with an inboard engine is repeatedly told not to start up until they are sure that no gas or petrol or petrol vapour has accumulated in the bilge. Boats blow up every year. He must have known. You wouldn't think he would be so stupid.'

I said mildly, 'He had a great deal else on his mind.'

'I suppose he had, but all the same everyone says . . .'

If you could blame a man for his own death, I thought, it diminished the chore of sympathy. 'It was his own fault . . .' I could hear the sharp voice of my aunt over the death of her neighbour . . . 'He shouldn't have gone out with that cold.'

'The insurance company,' I said to Sarah, 'may be trying to wriggle out of paying all they might.'

'What?'

'Putting the blame onto the victim is a well-known ploy.'

'But he should have been more careful.'

'Oh, sure. But for Donna's sake, I wouldn't go around saying so.'

There was a silence which came across as resentful. Then she said, 'Donna wanted me to tell you . . . She'd rather you didn't come here this weekend. She says she could bear things better if she's alone with me.'

'And you agree?'

'Well, yes, frankly, I do.'

'OK, then.'

'You don't mind?' She sounded surprised.

'No. I'm sure she's right. She relies on you.' And too much, I thought. 'Is she still drugged?'

'Sedated.' The word was a reproof.

'Sedated, then.'

'Yes, of course.'

'And for the court hearing tomorrow?' I asked.

'Tranquillisers,' Sarah said decisively. 'Sleeping pills after.'

'Good luck with it.'

'Yes,' she said.

She disconnected almost brusquely, leaving me with the easement of having been let off an unpleasant task. Once upon a time, I supposed, we would have clung together to help Donna. At the beginning our reactions would have been truer, less complicated, less distorted by our own depressions. I mourned for the dead days, but undoubtedly I was pleased not to be going to spend the weekend with my wife.

On the Friday I went to school still with the computer tapes in my jacket pocket and, feeling that I owed it to Peter at least to try to play them, sought out one of the maths masters in the common-room. Ted Pitts, short-sighted, clear-headed, bi-lingual in English and algebra.

'That computer you've got tucked away somewhere

in a cubby hole in the maths department,' I said, 'it's your especial baby, isn't it?'

'We all use it. We teach the kids.'

'But it's you who plays it like Beethoven while the rest are still at chopsticks?'

He enjoyed the compliment in his quiet way. 'Maybe,' he said.

'Could you tell me what make it is?' I asked.

'Sure. It's a Harris.'

'I suppose,' I said unhopefully, 'that you couldn't run a tape on it that was recorded on a Grantley?'

'It depends,' he said. He was earnest and thoughtful, twenty-six, short on humour, but full of good intentions and ideals of fair play. He suffered greatly under the sourly detestable Jenkins who was head of the maths department and extracted from his assistants the reverential attitude he never got from me.

'The Harris has no language built into it,' Ted said. 'You can feed it any computer language, Fortran, Cobol, Algol, Z-80, Basic, you name it, the Harris will take it. Then you can run any programs written in those languages. But the Grantley is a smaller affair which comes already pre-programmed with its own form of Basic. If you had a Grantley Basic language tape, you could feed it into our Harris's memory, and then you could run Grantley Basic programs.' He paused. 'Er, is that clear?'

'Sort of.' I reflected. 'How difficult would it be to get a Grantley Basic language tape?'

'Don't know. Best to write to the firm direct. They might send you one. And they might not.'

'Why might they not?'

He shrugged. 'They might say you'd have to buy one of their computers.'

'For heaven's sake,' I said.

'Yeah. Well, see, these computer firms are very awkward. All the smaller personal computers use Basic, because it's the easiest language and also one of the best. But the firms making them all build in their own variations, so that if you record your programs from their machines, you can't run them on anyone else's. That keeps you faithful to *them* in the future, because if you change to another make, all your tapes will be useless.'

'What a bore,' I said.

He nodded. 'Profits getting the better of common sense.'

'Like all those infuriatingly incompatible video-recorders.'

'Exactly. But you'd think the computer firms would have more sense. They may hang on to their own customers by force, but they're sure as Hades not going to persuade anyone else to switch.'

'Thanks anyway,' I said.

'You're welcome.' He hesitated. 'Do you actually have a tape that you want to use?'

'Yes.' I fished in my pocket and produced *Oklahoma*. 'This one and two others. Don't be misled by the packaging, it's got computer noise all right on the tape.'

'Were they recorded by an expert or an amateur?'

'An expert. Does it make any difference?'

'Sometimes.'

I explained about Peter making the tapes for a client who had a Grantley, and I added that the customer wouldn't let Peter try out the programs on the machine they were designed to run on.

'Oh, really?' Ted Pitts seemed happy with the news. 'In that case, if he was a conscientious and careful chap, it's just possible that he recorded the machine language itself on the first of the tapes. TOMS can be very touchy. He might have thought it would be safer.'

'You've lost me,' I said. 'What are TOMS?'

'Computers.' He grinned. 'Stands for Totally Obedient Moron.'

'You've made a joke,' I said disbelievingly.

'Not mine, though.'

'So why should it be safer?'

He looked at me reproachfully, 'I thought you knew more about computers than you appear to.'

'It's ten years at least since I knew more. I've forgotten and they've changed.'

'It would be safer,' he said patiently, 'because if the client rang up and complained that the program wouldn't run, your friend could tell them how to stuff into their computer a brand-new version of its own language, and then your friend's programs would run from that. Mind you,' he added judiciously, 'you'd use up an awful lot of computer space putting the language in. You might not have much room for the actual programs.'

He looked at my expression, and sighed.

'OK,' he said. 'Suppose a Grantley has a 32K store, which is a pretty normal size. That means it has about forty-nine thousand store-slots, of which probably the first seventeen thousand are used in providing the right circuits to function as Basic. That would leave you about thirty-two thousand store-slots for punching in your programs. Right?'

I nodded. 'I'll take it on trust.'

'But then if you feed in the language all over again it would take another seventeen thousand store-slots, which would leave you with under fifteen thousand store-slots to work with. And as you need one store-slot for every letter you type, and one for every number, and one for every space, and comma, and bracket, you wouldn't be able to do a great deal before all the store-slots were used and the whole thing was full up. And at that point the computer would stop working.' He smiled. 'So many people think computers are bottomless pits. They're more like bean bags. Once they're full you have to empty the beans out before you can start to fill them again.'

'Is that what you teach the kids?'

He looked slightly confused. 'Er . . . yes. Same words. One gets into a rut.'

The bell rang for afternoon registration and he stretched out his hand for the tape. 'I could try that,' he said, 'if you like.'

'Yes. If it isn't an awful bother.'

He shook his head encouragingly, and I gave him *The King and I* and *West Side Story* for good measure.

'Can't promise it will be today,' he said. 'I've got classes all afternoon and Jenkins wants to see me at four.' He grimaced. 'Jenkins. Why can't we call him Ralph and be done with it?'

'There's no hurry,' I said, 'with the tapes.'

Donna got her probation.

Sarah reported, again sounding tired, that even the baby's mother had quietened down because of Peter being killed, and Donna had gently wept in court, and even some of the policemen had been fatherly.

'How is she?' I said.

'Miserable. It's just hitting her, I think, that Peter's really gone.' Her voice sounded sisterly, motherly, protective.

'No more suicide?' I asked.

'I don't think so, but the poor darling is so *vulnerable*. So easily hurt. She says it's like living without skin.'

'Have you enough money?' I said.

'That's just like you!' she exclaimed. 'Always so damned practical.'

'But . . .'

'I've got my bank card.'

I hadn't wanted to wallow too long in Donna's emotions and it had irritated her. We both knew it. We knew each other too well.

'Don't let her wear you out,' I said.

Her voice came back, still sharp, 'I'm perfectly all right. There's no question of wearing me out. I'm staying here for a week or two longer at least. Until after the inquest and the funeral. And after that, if Donna needs me. I've told my boss, and he understands.'

I wondered fleetingly whether I might not become too fond of living alone if she were away a whole month. I said, 'I'd like to be there at the funeral.'

'Yes. Well, I'll let you know.'

I got a tart and untender goodnight: but then my own to her hadn't been loving. We wouldn't be able to go on, I thought, if ever the politeness crumbled.

The building had long been uninhabited, and we were only a short step from demolition.

On Saturday I put the Mausers and the Enfield No. 4 in the car and drove to Bisley and let off a lot of bullets over the Surrey ranges.

During the past few months, my visits there had become less constant, partly of course because there was no delight during the winter in pressing one's stomach to the cold earth, but mostly because my intense love of the sport seemed to be waning.

I had been a member of the British rifle team for several years but now never wore any of the badges to prove it. I kept quiet in the bar after shooting and listened to others analyse their performances and spill the excitement out of their systems. I didn't like talking of my own scores, present or past.

A few years back, I had taken the sideways jump of entering for the Olympics, which was a competition for individuals and quite different from my normal pursuits. Even the guns were different (at that time all small bore) and all the distances the same (300 metres). It was a world dominated by the Swiss, but I had shot luckily and well in the event and had finished high for a Briton in the placings, and it had been marvellous. The day of a lifetime; but it had faded into memory, grown fuzzy with time passing.

In the British team, which competed mostly against the old Commonwealth countries and often won, one shot 7.62 mm guns at varying distances – 300, 500, 600, 900 and 1,000 yards. I had always taken immense delight in accuracy, in judging wind velocity and air temperature and getting the climatic variables exactly right. But now, both internally and externally, the point of such skill was fading.

The smooth elegant Mausers that I cherished were already within sight of being obsolete. Only long-distance assassins, these days, seemed to need totally accurate rifles, and *they* used telescopic sights, which were banned and anathema to target shooters. Modern armies tended to spray out bullets regardless. None of the army rifles shot absolutely straight and in addition, every advance in effective killing-power was a loss to aesthetics. The present standard issue self-loading rifle, with its gas-powered feed of twenty bullets per magazine and its capability of continuous fire, was already a knobby untidy affair with half of it made of plastic for lightness. On the horizon was a rifle without a stock, unambiguously designed to be shot from waist level if necessary with no real pretence at precise aim: a rifle with infra-red sights for night use, all angular protuberances. And beyond cordite and lead, what? Neutron missiles fired from ground launchers which would halt an invading tank army literally in its tracks. A new sort of battery which would make hand-held ray guns possible.

The marksman's special skill was drifting towards sport, as archery had, as swordplay had, as throwing the javelin and the hammer had; the commonplace weapon of one age becoming the Olympic medal of the next.

I didn't shoot very well on that particular afternoon and found little appetite afterwards for the camaraderie in the clubhouse. The image of Peter stumbling over the side of his boat on fire and dying made too many things seem irrelevant. I was pledged to shoot in the Queen's Prize in July and in a competition in

Canada in August, and I reflected driving home that if I didn't put in a little more practice I would disgrace myself.

The trips overseas came up at fairly regular intervals, and because of the difficulties involved in transporting guns from one country to another, I had had built my own design of carrying case. About four feet long and externally looking like an ordinary extra-large suitcase, it was internally lined with aluminium and divided into padded shock-absorbing compartments. It held everything I needed for competitions, not only three rifles but all the other paraphernalia: score-book, eardefenders, telescope, rifle sling, shooting glove, rifle oil, cleaning rod, batman jag, roll of flannelette patches, cleaning brush, wool mop for oiling the barrel ammunition, thick jersey for warmth, two thin olive-green protective boiler suits and a supporting canvas and leather jacket. Unlike many people, I usually carried the guns fully assembled and ready to go, legacy of having missed my turn once through traffic hold-ups, a firearm still in pieces and fingers trembling with haste. I was not actually supposed to leave them with the bolt in place, but I often did. Only when the special gun suitcase went onto aeroplanes did I strictly conform to regulations, and then it was bonded and sealed and hedged about with red tape galore; and perhaps also because it didn't look like what it was, I'd never lost it.

Sarah, who had been enthusiastic at the beginning

and had gone with me often to Bisley, had in time got tired of the bang bang bang, as most wives did. She had tired also of my spending so much time and money and had been only partly mollified by the Games. All the jobs I applied for, she had pointed out crossly, let us live south of London, convenient for the ranges. 'But if I could ski,' I'd said, 'it would be silly to move to the tropics.'

She had a point, though. Shooting wasn't cheap, and I wouldn't have been able to do as much as I did without support from indirect sponsors. The sponsors expected in return that I would not only go to the international competitions, but go to them practised and fit: conditions that until very recently I'd been happy to fulfil. I was getting old, I thought. I would be thirty-four in three months.

I drove home without haste and let myself into the quiet house which was no longer vibrant with silent tensions. Dumped my case on the coffee table in the sitting-room with no one to suggest I take it straight upstairs. Unclipped the lock and thought of the pleasant change of being able to go through the cleaning and oiling routine in front of the television without tight-lipped disapproval. Decided to postpone the clean-up until I'd chosen what to have for supper and poured out a reviving scotch.

Chose a frozen pizza. Poured the scotch.

The front doorbell rang at that point and I went to

answer it. Two men, olive skinned, dark haired, stood on the doorstep: and one of them held a pistol.

I looked at it with a sort of delayed reaction, not registering at once because I'd been looking at peaceful firearms all day. It took me at least a whole second to realise that this one was pointing at my midriff in a thoroughly unfriendly fashion. A Walter .22, I thought: as if it mattered.

My mouth, I dare say, opened and shut. It wasn't what one expected in a moderately crime-free suburb.

'Back,' he said.

'What do you want?'

'Get inside.' He prodded towards me with the long silencer attached to the automatic and because I certainly respected the blowing-away power of hand guns, I did as he said. He and his friend advanced through the front door and closed it behind them.

'Raise your hands,' said the gunman.

I did so.

He glanced towards the open door of the sitting-room and jerked his head towards it.

'Go in there.'

I went slowly, and stopped, and turned, and said again, 'What do you want?'

'Wait,' he said. He glanced at his companion and jerked his head again, this time at the windows. The companion switched on the lights and then went across and closed the curtains. It was not yet dark outside. A shaft of evening sunshine pierced through where the curtains met.

I thought: why aren't I desperately afraid? They looked so purposeful, so intent. Yet I still thought they had made some weird sort of mistake and might depart if nicely spoken to.

They seemed younger than myself, though it was difficult to be sure. Italian, perhaps, from the south. They had the long straight nose, the narrow jaw, the black-brown eyes. The sort of face which went fat with age, grew a moustache and became a godfather.

That last thought shot through my brain from nowhere and seemed as nonsensical as a pistol.

'What do you want?' I said again.

'Three computer tapes.'

My mouth no doubt went again through the fish routine. I listened to the utterly English sloppy accent and thought that it couldn't have less matched the body it came from.

'What . . . what computer tapes?' I said, putting on bewilderment.

'Stop messing. We know you've got them. Your wife said so.'

Jesus, I thought. The bewilderment this time needed no acting.

He jerked the gun a fraction. 'Get them,' he said. His eyes were cold. His manner showed he despised me.

I said with a suddenly dry mouth, 'I can't think why my wife said . . . why she thought . . .'

'Stop wasting time,' he said sharply.

'But—'

'*The King and I*, and *West Side Story*,' he said impatiently, 'and *Okla-fucking-homa*.'

'I haven't got them.'

'Then that's too bad, buddy boy,' he said, and there was in an instant in him an extra dimension of menace. Before, he had been fooling along in second gear, believing no doubt that a gun was enough. But now I uncomfortably perceived that I was not dealing with someone reasonable and safe. If these were the two who had visited Peter, I understood what he had meant by frightening. There was a volatile quality, an absence of normal inhibition, a powerful impression of recklessness. The brakes-off syndrome which no legal deterrents deterred. I'd sensed it occasionally in boys I'd taught, but never before at such magnitude.

'You've got something you've no right to,' he said. 'And you'll give it to us.'

He moved the muzzle of the gun an inch or two sideways and squeezed the trigger. I heard the bullet zing past close to my ear. There was a crash of glass breaking behind me. One of Sarah's mementoes of Venice, much cherished.

'That was a vase,' he said. 'Your television's next. After that, you. Ankles and such. Give you a limp for life. Those tapes aren't worth it.'

He was right. The trouble was that I doubted if he would believe that I really hadn't got them.

He began to swing the gun round to the television.

'OK,' I said.

He sneered slightly. 'Get them, then.'

With my capitulation he relaxed complacently and so did his obedient and unspeaking assistant, who was standing a pace to his rear. I walked the few steps to the coffee table and lowered my hands from the raised position.

'They're in the suitcase,' I said.

'Get them out.'

I lifted the lid of the suitcase a little and pulled out the jersey, dropping it on the floor.

'Hurry up,' he said.

He wasn't in the least prepared to be faced with a rifle; not in that room, in that neighbourhood, in the hands of the man he took me for.

It was with total disbelief that he looked at the long deadly shape and heard the double click as I worked the bolt. There was a chance he would realise that I'd never transport such a weapon with a bullet up the spout, but then if he took his own shooter around loaded, perhaps he wouldn't.

'Drop the pistol,' I said. 'You shoot me, I'll shoot you both, and you'd better believe it. I'm a crack shot.' There was a time for boasting, perhaps; and that was it.

He wavered. The assistant looked scared. The rifle was an ultra scary weapon. The silencer slowly began to point downwards, and the automatic thudded to the carpet. The anger could be felt.

'Kick it over here,' I said. 'And gently.'

He gave the gun a furious shove with his foot. It wasn't near enough for me to pick up, but too far for him, also.

'Right,' I said. 'Now you listen to me. I haven't got those tapes. I've lent them to somebody else, because I thought they were music. How the hell should I know they were computer tapes? If you want them back, you'll have to wait until I get them. The person I lent them to has gone away for the weekend and I've no way of finding out where. You can have them without all this melodrama, but you'll have to wait. Give me an address, and I'll send them to you. I frankly want to get shot of you. I don't give a damn about those tapes or what you want them for. I just don't want you bothering me . . . or my wife. Understood?'

'Yeah.'

'Where do you want them sent?'

His eyes narrowed.

'And it will cost you two quid,' I said, 'for packing and postage.'

The mundane detail seemed to convince him. With a disgruntled gesture he took two pounds from his pocket and dropped them at his feet.

'Cambridge main post office,' he said. 'To be collected.'

'Under what name?'

After a pause he said, 'Derry.'

I nodded. 'Right,' I said. A pity, though, that he'd given my own name. Anything else might have been informative. 'You can get out, now.'

Both pairs of eyes looked down at the automatic now on the carpet.

'Wait in the road,' I said. 'I'll throw it to you through the window. And don't come back.'

They edged to the door with an eye on the sleek steel barrel following them, and I went out after them into the hall. I got the benefit of two viciously frustrated expressions before they opened the front door and went out, closing it again behind them.

Back in the sitting-room I put the rifle on the sofa and picked up the Walther to unclip it and empty its magazine into an ashtray. Then I unscrewed the silencer from the barrel, and opened the window.

The two men stood on the pavement, balefully staring across twenty feet of grass. I threw the pistol so that it landed in a rose bush not far from their feet. When the assistant had picked it out and scratched himself on the thorns, I threw the silencer into the same place.

The gunman, finding he had no bullets, delivered a verbal parting shot.

'You send those tapes, or we'll be back.'

'You'll get them next week. And stay out of my life.'

I shut the window decisively and watched them walk away, every line of their bodies rigid with discomfiture.

What on *earth*, I wondered intensely, had Peter programmed onto those cassettes?

CHAPTER FOUR

'Who,' I said to Sarah, 'asked you for computer tapes?'

'What?' She sounded vague, a hundred miles away on this planet but in another world.

'Someone,' I said patiently, 'must have asked you for some tapes.'

'Oh, you mean cassettes?'

'Yes, I do.' I tried to keep any grimness out of my voice; to sound merely conversational.

'But you can't have got his letter already,' she said, puzzled. 'He only came this morning.'

'Who was he?' I said.

'Oh!' she exclaimed. 'I suppose he telephoned. He could have got our number from enquiries.'

'Sarah . . .'

'Who was he? I've no idea. Someone to do with Peter's work.'

'What sort of man?' I asked.

'What do you mean? Just a man. Middle-aged, grey-haired, a bit plump.' Sarah herself, like many naturally slim people, saw plumpness as a moral fault.

'Tell me what he said,' I pressed.

'If you insist. He said he was so sorry about Peter. He said Peter had brought home a project he'd been working on for his firm, possibly in the form of handwritten notes, possibly in the form of cassettes. He said the firm would be grateful to have it all back, because they would have to re-allocate the job to someone else.'

It all sounded a great deal more civilized than frighteners with waving guns.

'And then?' I prompted.

'Well, Donna said she didn't know of anything Peter had in the house, though she did of course know he'd been working on *something*. Anyway, she looked in a lot of cupboards and drawers, and she found those three loose cassettes, out of their boxes, stacked between the gin and the Cinzano in the drinks cupboard. Am I boring you?'

She sounded over-polite and as if boring had been her intention, but I simply answered fervently, 'No, you're not. Please do go on.'

The shrug travelled almost visibly down the wire. 'Donna gave them to the man. He was delighted until he looked at them closely. Then he said they were tapes of musicals and not what he wanted, and please would we look again.'

'And then either you or Donna remembered—'

'I did,' she affirmed. 'We both saw Peter give them

to you, but he must have got them mixed up. He gave you his firm's cassettes by mistake.'

Peter's firm . . .

'Did the man give you his name?' I said.

'Yes,' Sarah said. 'He introduced himself when he arrived. But you know how it is. He mumbled it a bit and I've forgotten it. Why? Didn't he tell you when he rang up?'

'No visiting card?'

'Don't tell me,' she said with exasperation, 'that you didn't take his address. Wait a moment, I'll ask Donna.'

She put the receiver down on the table and I could hear her calling Donna. I wondered why I hadn't told her of the nature of my visitors, and decided it was probably because she would try to argue me into going to the police. I certainly didn't want to do that, because they were likely to take unkindly to my waving a rifle about in such a place. I couldn't prove to them that it had been unloaded, and it did not come into the category of things a householder could reasonably use to defend his property. Bullets fired from a Mauser 7.62 didn't at ten paces smash vases and embed themselves in the plaster, they seared straight through the wall itself and killed people outside walking their dogs.

Firearms certificates could be taken away faster than given.

'Jonathan?' Sarah said, coming back.

'Yes.'

She read out the full address of Peter's firm in Norwich and added the telephone number.

'Is that all?' she said.

'Except . . . you're both still all right?'

'I am, thank you. Donna's very low. But I'm coping.'

We said our usual goodbyes: almost formal, without warmth, deadly polite.

Duty took me back to Bisley the following day: duty and restlessness and dreadful prospects on the box. I shot better and thought less about Peter, and when the light began to fade I went home and corrected the ever-recurring exercise books: and on Monday Ted Pitts said he hadn't yet done anything about my computer tapes but that if I cared to stay on at four o'clock, we could both go down to the computer room and see what there was to see.

When I joined him he was already busy in the small side-room that with its dim cream walls and scratchily polished floor had an air of being everyone's poor relation. A single light hung without a shade from the ceiling, and the two wooden chairs were regulation battered school issue. Two nondescript tables occupied most of the floor-space, and upon them rested the uninspiring-looking machines which had cost a small fortune. I asked Ted mildly why he put up with such cramped, depressing quarters.

He looked at me vaguely, his mind on his task. 'You

know how it is. You have to teach boys individually on this baby to get good results. There aren't enough classrooms. This is all that's available. It's not too bad. And anyway, I never notice.'

I could believe it. He was a hiker, an ex-youth-hosteller, an embracer of earnest discomforts. He perched on the edge of the hard wooden chair and applied his own computer-like brain to the one on the tables.

There were four separate pieces of equipment. A box like a small television set with a typewriter keyboard protruding forward from the lower edge of the screen. A cassette player. A large upright uninformative black box marked simply 'Harris', and something which looked at first sight like a typewriter, but which in fact had no keys. All four were linked together, and each to its own wall socket, by black electric cables.

Ted Pitts put *Oklahoma* into the cassette player and typed CLOAD 'BASIC' on the keyboard. CLOAD 'BASIC' appeared in small white capital letters high up on the left of the television screen, and two asterisks appeared, one of them rapidly blinking on and off, up on the right. On the cassette player, the wheels of the tape-reels quickly revolved.

'How much do you remember?' Ted said.

'About enough to know you're searching the tape for the language, and that CLOAD means LOAD from the cassette.'

He nodded and pointed briefly to the large upright

box. 'The computer already has its own BASIC stored in there. I put it in at lunchtime. Now just let's see . . .' He hunched himself over the keyboard, pressing keys, stopping and starting the cassette player and punctuating his activity with grunts.

'Nothing useful,' he muttered, turning the tapes over and repeating the process. 'Let's try . . .' A fair time passed. He shook his head now and then, and said finally, 'Give me those other two tapes. It must logically be at the *beginning* of one of the sides – unless of course he added it at the end because he had space left . . . or perhaps he didn't do it at all . . .'

'Won't the programs run on your own version of BASIC?'

He shook his head. 'I tried before you came. The only response you get is ERROR IN LINE 10. Which means that the two versions aren't compatible.' He grunted again and tried *West Side Story*, and towards the end of the first side he sat bolt upright and said, 'Well now.'

'It's on there?'

'Can't tell yet. But there's something filed under "Z". Might just try that.' He flicked a few more switches and sat back beaming. 'Now all we do is wait a few minutes while that . . .' he pointed at the large upright box . . . 'soaks up whatever is on the tape under "Z", and if it should happen to be Grantley Basic, we'll be in business.'

'Why does "Z" give you hope?'

'Instinct. Might be a hundred per cent wrong. But it's a much longer recording than anything else I've found so far on the tapes, and feels the right length. Four and a quarter minutes. I've fed BASIC into the Harris thousands of times.'

His instinct proved reliable. The word READY suddenly appeared on the screen, white and bright and promising. Ted sighed heavily with satisfaction and nodded three times.

'Sensible fellow, your friend,' he said. 'So now we can see what you've got.'

When he ran *Oklahoma* again, the file names came up clearly beside the flashing asterisk at the top right of the screen, and although some of them were mysterious to me, some of them were definitely not.

DONCA EDINB EPSOM FOLKE FONTW GOODW HAMIL HAYDK HEREF HEXHM

'Names of towns,' I said. 'Towns with racecourses.'

Ted nodded. 'Which would you like to try?'

'Epsom.'

'OK,' he said. He rewound the tape with agile fingers and typed CLOAD 'EPSOM' on the keyboard. 'This puts the program filed under EPSOM into the computer, but you know that, of course, I keep forgetting.'

The encouraging word READY appeared again, and Ted said, 'Which do you want to do, List it or Run it?'

'Run,' I said.

He nodded and typed RUN on the keyboard, and in

bright little letters the screen enquired WHICH RACE AT EPSOM? TYPE NAME OF RACE AND PRESS 'ENTER'.

'My God,' I said. 'Let's try the Derby.'

'Stands to reason,' Ted said, and typed DERBY. The screen promptly responded with TYPE NAME OF HORSE AND PRESS 'ENTER'.

Ted typed JONATHAN DERRY and again pressed the double-sized key on the keyboard marked 'Enter', and the screen obliged with:

EPSOM: THE DERBY

HORSE: JONATHAN DERRY.

TO ALL QUESTIONS ANSWER YES OR NO AND PRESS 'ENTER'.

A couple of inches lower down there was a question:

HAS HORSE WON A RACE?

Ted typed YES and pressed 'Enter'. The first three lines remained, but the question was replaced with another.

HAS HORSE WON THIS YEAR?

Ted typed NO. The screen responded:

HAS HORSE WON ON COURSE?

Ted typed NO. The screen responded:

HAS HORSE RUN ON COURSE?

Ted typed YES.

There were questions about the horse's sire, its dam, its jockey, its trainer, the number of days since its last run, and its earning in prize money; and one final question:

IS HORSE QUOTED ANTE-POST AT 25–1 OR LESS?

Ted typed YES, and the screen said merely,

ANY MORE HORSES?

Ted typed YES again, and we found ourselves back at

TYPE NAME OF HORSE AND PRESS 'ENTER'.

'That's not handicapping,' I said.

'Is that what it's supposed to be?' Ted shook his head. 'More like statistical probabilities, I should have thought. Let's go through it again and answer NO to ANY MORE HORSES?'

He typed TED PITTS for the horse's name and varied the answers, and immediately after his final NO we were presented with a cleared screen and a new display.

HORSE'S NAME	WIN FACTOR
JONATHAN DERRY	27
TED PITTS	12

'You've *no* chance,' I said. 'You might as well stay in the stable.'

He looked a bit startled, and then laughed. 'Yes. That's what it is. A guide to gamblers.'

He typed LIST instead of RUN, and immediately the bones of the program appeared, but scrolling upwards too fast to read, like flight-information changes at airports. Ted merely hummed a little and typed LIST 10–140, and after some essential flickering the screen presented the goods.

LIST 10–140

10 PRINT 'WHICH RACE AT EPSOM? TYPE NAME OF RACE AND PRESS 'ENTER'

```
20 INPUT A$
30 IF A$='DERBY' THEN 330
40 IF A$='OAKS' THEN 340
50 IF A$='CORONATION CUP' THEN 350
60 IF A$='BLUE RIBAND STAKES' THEN 360
```

The list went down to the bottom of the screen in this fashion, and Ted gave it one appraising look and said, 'Dead simple.'

The dollar sign, I seemed to remember, meant that the Input had to be in the form of letters. Input A, without the dollar sign, would have asked for numbers.

Ted seemed perfectly happy. He typed LIST 300–380 and got another set of instructions.

At 330 the program read: LET A=10: B=8: C=6: D=2: D1=2.

Lines 332, 334, and 336 looked similar, with numbers being ascribed to letters.

'That's the weighting,' Ted said. 'The value given to each answer. Ten points for the first question, which was . . . um . . . has the horse won a race. And so on. I see that 10 points are given also for the last question, which was about . . . er . . . ante-post odds, wasn't it?'

I nodded.

'There you are, then,' he said. 'I dare say there's a different weighting for every race. There might of course be different *questions* for every race. Ho hum. Want to see?'

'If you've the time,' I said.

'Oh sure. I've always got time for TOMS. Love 'em, you know.'

He went on typing LIST followed by various numbers and came up with such gems as:

520 IF N$='NO' THEN GOTO 560: X=X+B

530 INPUT N$: AB=AB+1

540 IF N$='NO' THEN GOTO 560: X=X+M

550 T=T+G2

560 GOSUB 4000

'What does all that mean?' I asked.

'Um . . . well. It's much easier to *write* a program than to read and understand someone else's. Programs are frantically individual. You can get the same results by all sorts of different routes. I mean, if you're going from London to Bristol you go down the M4 and it's called M4 all the way, but on a computer you can call the road anything you like, at any point on the journey, and *you* might know that at different moments I2, say, or RQ3 or B7(2) equalled M4, but no one else would.'

'Is that also what you teach the kids?'

'Er, yes. Sorry, it's a habit.' He glanced at the screen. 'I'd guess that those top lines are to do with skipping some questions if previous answers make them unnecessary. Jumping to later bits of program. If I printed the whole thing out onto paper I could work out their exact meaning.'

I shook my head. 'Don't trouble. Let's try a different race-course.'

'Sure.'

He rewound the tape to the beginning and typed CLOAD 'DONCA', and when the screen said READY, typed RUN.

Immediately we were asked WHICH RACE AT DONCASTER? TYPE NAME OF RACE AND PRESS 'ENTER'.

'OK,' Ted said, pressing switches. 'What about further down the tape? Say, GOODW?'

We got WHICH RACE AT GOODWOOD? TYPE NAME OF RACE AND PRESS 'ENTER'.

'I don't know any races at Goodwood,' I said.

Ted said, 'That's easy,' and typed LIST 10–140. When the few seconds of flickering had stopped, we had:

LIST 10–140

10 PRINT 'WHICH RACE AT GOODWOOD? TYPE NAME OF RACE AND PRESS "ENTER".'

20 INPUT A$

30 IF A$='GOODWOOD STAKES' THEN 330

40 IF A$='GOODWOOD CUP' THEN 340

There were fifteen races listed altogether.

'What happens if you type in the name of a race there's no program for?' I asked.

'Let's see,' he said. He typed RUN, and we were back to WHICH RACE AT GOODWOOD? He typed DERBY, and the screen informed us THERE IS NO INFORMATION FOR THIS RACE.

'Neat and simple,' Ted said.

We sampled all the sides of the three tapes, but the

programs were all similar. WHICH RACE AT REDCAR? WHICH RACE AT ASCOT? WHICH RACE AT NEWMARKET?

There were programs for about fifty racecourses, with varying numbers of races listed at each. Several lists contained not actual titles of races but general categories like STRAIGHT 7 FURLONGS FOR 3 YR OLDS AND UPWARDS, OR THREE MILE WEIGHT-FOR-AGE STEEPLE-CHASE: and it was not until quite late that I realised with amusement that *none* of the races were handicaps. There were no questions at all about how many lengths a horse had won by, while carrying such and such a weight.

All in all, there was provision for scoring for any number of horses in each of more than eight hundred named races, and in an unknown quantity of *un*named races. Each race had its own set of weightings and very often its own set of questions. It had been a quite monumental task.

'It must have taken him days,' Ted said.

'Weeks, I think. He had to do it in his spare time.'

'They're not complicated programs, of course,' Ted said. 'Nothing really needing an expert. It's more organisation than anything else. Still, he hasn't wasted much space. Amateurs write very long programs. Experts get to the same nitty-gritty in a third of the time. It's just practice.'

'We'd better make a note of which side of which tape contains the Grantley Basic,' I said.

Ted nodded. 'It's at an end. After York. Filed under

"Z".' He checked that he had the right tape, and wrote on its label in pencil.

For no particular reason I picked up the other two tapes and briefly looked at the words I had half-noticed before: the few words Peter had pencilled onto one of the labels.

'Programs compiled for C. Norwood.'

Ted, glancing over, said, 'That's the first side you're looking at. Ascot and so on.' He paused. 'We might just as well number the sides properly, one to six. Get them in order.'

Order, to him as to me, was a habit. When he'd finished the numbering he put the cassettes back in their gaudy boxes and handed them over. I thanked him most profoundly for his patience and took him out for a couple of beers; then over his pint he said, 'Will you be trying them out?'

'Trying what out?'

'Those races, of course. It's the Derby next month, some time. If you like we could work out the scores for all the Derby horses, and see if the program comes up with the winner. I'd actually quite like to do it. Wouldn't you?'

'I wouldn't begin to know the answers to all those questions.'

'No.' He sighed. 'Pity. The info must be *somewhere*, but unearthing it might be a bore.'

'I'll ask my brother,' I said, explaining about

William. 'He sometimes mentions form books. I'd guess the answers would be in those.'

Ted seemed pleased with the idea, and I didn't immediately ask him which he was keener to do, to test the accuracy of the programs or to make a profit. He told me, however.

He said tentatively, 'Would you mind very much . . . I mean . . . would you mind if I took a *copy* of those tapes?'

I looked at him in faint surprise and he smiled awkwardly.

'The fact is, Jonathan, I could do with a boost to the economy. I mean, if those tapes actually come up with the goods, why not use them?' He squirmed a little on his seat, and when I didn't rush to answer he went on, 'You know how bloody small our salaries are. It's not fun with three kids to feed, and their clothes, their shoes cost a bomb, and the little devils grow out of them before you've paid for them, practically. I'm never under my limit on my credit cards. Never.'

'Have another beer,' I said.

'It's better for you,' he said gloomily, accepting the offer. 'You've no children. It isn't so hard for you to manage on a pittance. And you earn more anyway, with being a head of department.'

I said thoughtfully, 'I don't see why you shouldn't make copies, if you want to.'

'Jonathan!' He was clearly delighted.

'But I wouldn't use them,' I said, 'without finding out if they're any good. You might lose a packet.'

'I'll be careful,' he said, but his eyes gleamed behind his black-rimmed spectacles and I wondered uneasily if I were seeing the birth of a compulsion. There was always a slight touch of the fanatic about Ted. 'Can you ask your brother where I can get a form book?' he said.

'Well . . .'

He scanned my face. 'You're regretting saying I could copy them. Do you want them for yourself, now, is that it?'

'No. I just thought . . . gambling's like drugs. You can get addicted and go down the drain.'

'But all I want—' He stopped and shrugged. He looked disappointed but nothing more.

I sighed and said, 'OK. But for God's sake be sensible.'

'I will,' he said fervently. He looked at me expectantly and I took the tapes out of my pocket and gave them back to him.

'Take good care of them,' I said.

'With my life.'

'Not that far.' I thought briefly of gun-toting visitors and of much I didn't understand, and I added slowly, 'While you're about it, make copies for me too.'

He was puzzled. 'But you'll have the originals.'

I shook my head. 'They'll belong to someone else. I'll have to give them back. But I don't see why, if copies are possible, I shouldn't also keep what I return.'

'Copies are dead easy,' he said. 'Also they're prudent. All you do is load the program into the computer, from the cassette, like we did, then change to a fresh cassette and load the program back from the computer on to the new tape. You can make dozens of copies, if you like. Any time I've written a program I especially don't want to lose, I record it onto several different tapes. That way, if one tape gets lost or some idiot re-records on top of what you've done, you've always got a back-up.'

'I'll buy some tapes, then,' I said.

He shook his head. 'You give me the money, and I'll get them. Ordinary tapes are OK if you're pushed, but special digital cassettes made for computer work are better.'

I gave him some money, and he said he would make the copies the following day, either at lunchtime or after school. 'And get the form book,' he reminded me, 'won't you?'

'Yes,' I said; and later, from home, I telephoned the farm and spoke to William.

'How's it going?'

'What would you say if I tried for a racing stable in the summer?'

'I'd say stick to farms,' I said.

'Yeah. But the hunters are all out at grass in July and August, and this riding school here's cracking up, they've sold off the best horses, there's nothing much to ride, and there's weeds and muck everywhere. Mr Askwith's taken to drink. He comes roaring out in the mornings clutching the hard stuff and swearing at the girls. There are only two of them left now, trying to look after fourteen ponies. It's a mess.'

'It sounds it.'

'I've been reduced to doing some revision for those grotty exams.'

'Things must be bad,' I said.

'Thanks for the cheque.'

'Sorry it was late. Listen, I've a friend who wants a racing form book. How would he get one?'

William, it transpired, knew of about six different types of form book. Which did my friend want?

One which told him a horse's past history, how long since it had last raced and whether its ante-post odds were less than 25 to 1. Also its sire's and dam's and jockey's and trainer's history, and how much it had won in prize money. For starters.

'Good grief,' said my brother. 'You want a combination of the form book and *The Sporting Life*.'

'Yes, but *which* form book?'

'*The* form book,' he said. '*Raceform* and *Chaseform*. *Chaseform*'s the jumpers. Does he want jumpers as well?'

'I think so.'

'Tell him to write to Turf Newspapers, then. The form book comes in sections; a new updated section every week. Best on earth. I covet it increasingly, but it costs a bomb. Do you think the trustees would consider it vocational training?' He spoke, however, without much hope.

I thought of Ted Pitt's financial state and enquired for something cheaper.

'Hum,' said William judiciously. 'He could try the weekly *Sporting Record*, I suppose.' A thought struck him. 'This wouldn't be anything to do with your friend Peter and his betting system, would it? You said he was dead.'

'Same system, different friend.'

'There isn't a system born,' William said, 'that really works.'

'You'd know, of course,' I said dryly.

'I do read.'

We talked a little more and said goodbye in good humour, and I found myself regretting, after I'd put down the receiver, that I hadn't asked him if he'd like to spend the week with me rather than on the farm. But I didn't suppose he would have done. He'd have found even the drunken Mr Askwith more congenial than the decorum of Twickenham.

Sarah telephoned an hour later, sounding strained and abrupt.

'Do you know anyone called Chris Norwood?' she said.

'No, I don't think so.' The instant I'd said it I remembered Peter's handwriting on the cassette. 'Program compiled for C. Norwood'. I opened my mouth to tell her, but she forestalled me.

'Peter knew him. The police have been here again, asking questions.'

'But what—' I began in puzzlement.

'I don't *know* what it's all about, if that's what you're going to ask. But someone called Chris Norwood has been shot.'

CHAPTER FIVE

Ignorance seemed to surround me like a fog.

'I thought Peter might have mentioned him to you,' Sarah said. 'You always talked with him more than to Donna and me.'

'Doesn't Donna know this Norwood?' I asked, ignoring the bitter little thrust.

'No, she doesn't. She's still in shock. It's all too much.'

Fogs could be dangerous, I thought. There might be all manner of traps waiting, unseen.

'What did the police actually say?' I said.

'Nothing much. Only that they were enquiring into a death, and wanted any help Peter could give.'

'*Peter!*'

'Yes, Peter. They didn't know he was dead. They weren't the same as the ones who came before. I think they said they were from Suffolk. What does it matter?' She sounded impatient. 'They'd found Peter's name and address on a pad beside the telephone. This Norwood's telephone. They said that in a murder investigation they had to follow even the smallest lead.'

'Murder . . .'

'That's what they said.'

I frowned and asked, 'When was he killed?'

'How do I know? Sometime last week. Thursday. Friday. I can't remember. They were talking to Donna, really, not to me. I kept telling them she wasn't fit, but they wouldn't listen. They wouldn't see for ages that the poor darling is too dazed to care about a total stranger, however he died. And to crown it all, when they did finally realise, they said they might come back when she was better.'

After a pause I said, 'When's the inquest?'

'How on earth should I know?'

'I mean, on Peter.'

'Oh.' She sounded disconcerted. 'On Friday. We don't have to go. Peter's father is giving evidence of identity. He won't speak to Donna. He somehow thinks it was her fault that Peter was careless with the boat. He's been perfectly beastly.'

'Mm,' I said noncommittally.

'A man from the insurance company came here, asking if Peter had ever had problems with leaking gas lines and wanting to know if he always started the engine without checking for petrol vapour.'

Peter hadn't been careless, I thought. I remembered that he'd been pretty careful on the canals, opening up the engine compartment every morning to let any trapped vapour escape. And that had been diesel, not petrol: less inflammable altogether.

'Donna said she didn't know. The engine was Peter's affair. She was always in the cabin unpacking food and so on while he was getting ready to start up. And anyway,' Sarah said, 'why all this fuss about vapour? It isn't as if there was any actual *petrol* sloshing about. They say there wasn't.'

'It's the vapour that explodes,' I said. 'Liquid petrol won't ignite unless it's mixed with air.'

'Are you serious?'

'Absolutely.'

'Oh.'

There was a pause: a silence. Some dying-fall goodbyes. Not with a bang, I thought, but with a yawn.

On Tuesday, Ted Pitts said he hadn't yet had a chance to buy the tapes for the copies and on Wednesday I sweet-talked a colleague into taking my games duty for the afternoon and straight after morning school set off to Norwich. Not to see my wife, but to visit the firm where Peter had worked.

It turned out to be a three-room two-men-and-a-girl affair tucked away in a suite of offices in a building on an industrial estate: one modest component among about twenty others listed on the directory-board in the lobby: MASON MILES ASSOCIATES, COMPUTER CONSULTANTS rubbing elbows with DIRECT ACCESS DISTRIBUTION SERVICES and SEA MAGIC, DECORATIVE SHELL IMPORTERS.

Mason Miles and his Associates showed no signs of overwork but neither was there any of the gloom which hangs about a business on the brink. The inactivity, one felt, was normal.

The girl sat at a desk reading a magazine. The younger man fiddled with a small computer's innards and hummed in the manner of Ted Pitts. The older man, beyond a wide open door labelled Mason Miles, lolled in a comfortable chair with an arm-stretching expanse of newspaper. All three looked up without speed about five seconds after I'd walked through their outer unguarded defences.

'Hullo,' the girl said. 'Are you for the job?'

'Which job?'

'You're not, then. Not Robinson, D.F.?'

'Afraid not.'

'He's late. Dare say he's not coming.' She shrugged. 'Happens all the time.'

'Would that be Peter Keithly's job?' I asked.

The young man's attention went back to his eviscerated machine.

'Sure is,' said the girl. 'If you're not for his job, how can we help you?'

I explained that my wife, who was staying in Peter's house, was under the impression that someone from the firm had visited Peter's widow, asking for some tapes he had been working on.

The girl looked blank. Mason Miles gave me a

lengthy frown from the distance. The young man dropped a screwdriver and muttered under his breath.

The girl said, 'None of us has been to Peter's house. Not even before the troubles.'

Mason Miles cleared his throat and raised his voice. 'What tapes are you talking about? You'd better come in here.'

He put down the newspaper and stood up reluctantly, as if the effort was too much for a weekday afternoon. He was not in the least like Sarah's description of a plump grey-haired ordinary middle-aged man. There was a crinkly red thatch over a long white face, a lengthy stubborn-looking upper lip and cheekbones of Scandinavian intensity; the whole extra-tall body being, as far as I could judge, still under forty.

'Don't let me disturb you,' I said without irony.

'You are not.'

'Would anyone else from your firm,' I asked, 'have gone to Peter's house, asking on your behalf for the tapes he was working on?'

'What tapes were those?'

'Cassettes with programs for evaluating racehorses.'

'He was working on no such project.'

'But in his spare time?' I suggested.

Mason Miles shrugged and sat down again with the relief of a traveller after a wearisome journey. 'Perhaps. What he did in his spare time was his own affair.'

'And do you have a grey-haired middle-aged man on your staff?'

He gave me a considering stare and then said merely, 'We employ no such person. If such a person has visited Mrs Keithly purporting to come from here, it is disturbing.'

I looked at his totally undisturbed demeanour and agreed.

'Peter was writing the programs for someone called Chris Norwood,' I said. 'I don't suppose you've ever heard of him?' I made it a question but without much hope, and he shook his head and suggested I ask his Associates in the outer office. The Associates also showed nil reactions to the name of Chris Norwood, but the young man paused from his juggling of microchips long enough to say that he had put everything Peter had left concerning his work in a shoe-box in a cupboard, and he supposed it would do no harm if I wanted to look.

I found the box, took it out, and began to sift through the hand-written scraps of notes which it contained. Nearly all of them concerned his work and took the form of mysterious memos to himself. 'Remember to tell RT of modification to PET.' 'Pick up floppy discs for LMP.' 'Tell ISCO about L's software package.' 'The bug in R's program must be a syntax error in the subroutine.' Much more of the same, and none of it of any use.

There was a sudden noise and flurry at the outer door, and a wild-eyed breathless heavily flushed youth appeared, along with a suitcase, a hold-all, an overcoat and a tennis racket.

'Sorry,' he panted. 'The train was late.'

'Robinson?' the girl said calmly. 'D.F.?'

'What? Oh. Yes. Is the job still open?'

I looked down at another note, the writing as neat as all the others: 'Borrow Grantley Basic tape from GF.' Turned the piece of paper over. On the back he'd written, 'C. Norwood, Angel Kitchens, Newmarket.'

I persevered to the bottom of the box, but there was nothing else that I understood. I put all the scrappy notes back again, and thanked the Associates for their trouble. They hardly listened. The attention of the whole firm was intently fixed on D.F. Robinson, who was wilting under their probing questions. Miles, who had beckoned them all into the inner office, was saying, 'How would you handle a client who made persistently stupid mistakes but blamed *you* for not explaining his system thoroughly?'

I sketched a farewell which nobody noticed, and left.

Newmarket lay fifty miles to the south of Norwich, and I drove there through the sunny afternoon thinking that the fog lay about me as thick as ever. Radar, perhaps, would be useful. Or a gale. Or some good clarifying information. Press on, I thought: press on.

Angel Kitchens, as listed in the telephone directory

in the post office, were to be found in Angel Lane, to which various natives directed me with accuracy varying from vague to absent, and which proved to be a dead-end tarmac tributary to the east of the town, far from the mainstream of High Street.

The Kitchens were just what they said: the kitchens of a mass food-production business, making frozen gourmet dinners in single-portion foil pans for the upper end of the market. 'Posh nosh,' one of my route-directors had said. 'Fancy muck,' said another. 'You can buy that stuff in the town, but give me a hamburger any day' from another, and 'Real tasty' from the last. They'd all known the product, if not the location.

At a guess the Kitchen had been developed from the back half and outhouses of a defunct country mansion; they had that slightly haphazard air, and were surrounded by mature trees and the remnants of a landscaped garden. I parked in the large but well-occupied expanse of concrete outside a new-looking white single-storey construction marked Office, and pushed my way through its plate-glass double-door entrance.

Inside, in the open-plan expanse, the contrast to Mason Miles Associates was complete. Life was taken at a run, if not a stampede. The work in hand, it seemed, would overwhelm the inmates if they relaxed for a second.

My tentative enquiry for someone who had been a

friend of Chris Norwood reaped me a violently unexpected reply.

'That *creep*? If he had any friends, they'd be down in Veg Preparation, where he worked.'

'Er, Veg Preparation?'

'Two-storey grey stone building past the freezer sheds.'

I went out to the car park, wandered around and asked again.

'Where them carrots is being unloaded.'

Them carrots were entering a two-storey grey stone building by the sack-load on a fork-lift truck, the driver of which mutely pointed me to a less cavernous entrance round a corner.

Through there one passed through a small lobby beside a large changing-room where rows of outdoor clothing hung on pegs. Next came a white-tiled scrub-up room smelling like a hospital, followed by a swing door into a long narrow room lit blindingly by electricity and filled with gleaming stainless steel, noisily whirring machines and people dressed in white.

At the sight of me standing there in street clothes a large man wearing what looked like a cotton under-vest over a swelling paunch advanced with waving arms and shooed me out.

'Cripes, mate, you'll get me sacked,' he said, as the swing-door swung behind us.

'I was directed here,' I said mildly.

'What do you want?'

With less confidence than before I enquired for any friend of Chris Norwood.

The shrewd eyes above the beer-stomach appraised me. The mouth pursed. The chef's hat sat comfortably over strong dark eyebrows.

'He's been murdered,' he said. 'You from the press?'

I shook my head. 'He knew a friend of mine, and he got both of us into a bit of trouble.'

'Sounds just like him.' He pulled a large white handkerchief out of his white trousers and wiped his nose. 'What exactly do you want?'

'I think just to talk to someone who knew him. I want to know what he was like. Who he knew. Anything. I want to know why and how he got us into trouble.'

'I knew him,' he said. He paused, considering. 'What's it worth?'

I sighed. 'I'm a schoolmaster. It's worth what I can afford. And it depends *what* you know.'

'All right then,' he said judiciously. 'I finish here at six. I'll meet you in the Purple Dragon, right? Up the lane, turn left, quarter of a mile. You buy me a couple of pints and we'll take it from there. OK?'

'Yes,' I said. 'My name is Jonathan Derry.'

'Akkerton.' He gave a short nod, as if sealing a bargain. 'Vince,' he added as an afterthought. He gave me a last unpromising inspection and barged back through the swing doors. I heard the first of the words he sprayed into the long busy room, 'You, Reg, you get back to work. I've only to take my eyes off you . . .'

The door closed discreetly behind him.

I waited for him at a table in the Purple Dragon, a pub a good deal less colourful than its name, and at six-fifteen he appeared, dressed now in grey trousers and a blue and white shirt straining at its buttons. Elliptical views of hairy chest appeared when he sat down, which he did with a wheeze and a licking of lips. The first pint I bought him disappeared at a single draught, closely followed by half of the second.

'Thirsty work, chopping up veg,' he said.

'Do you do it by hand?' I was surprised, and sounded it.

'Course not. Washed, peeled, chopped, all done by machines. But nothing hops into a machine by itself. Or out, come to that.'

'What, er . . . veg?' I said.

'Depends what they want. Today, mostly carrots, celery, onions, mushrooms. Regular every day, that lot. Needed for Burgundy Beef. Our best seller, Burgundy Beef. Chablis Chicken, Pork and Port, next best. You ever had any?'

'I don't honestly know.'

He drank deeply with satisfaction. 'It's good food,' he said seriously, wiping his mouth. 'All fresh ingredients. No mucking about. Pricey, mind you, but worth it.'

'You enjoy the job?' I asked.

He nodded. 'Sure. Worked in kitchens all my life. Some of them, you could shake hands with the cockroaches. Big as rats. Here, so clean you'd see a fruit fly a mile off. I've been in Veg three months now. Did a year in Fish but the smell hangs in your nostrils after a while.'

'Did Chris Norwood,' I said, 'chop up veg?'

'When we were pushed. Otherwise he cleaned up, checked the input, and ran errands.' His voice was assured and positive: a man who had no need to guard his tongue.

'Er, checked the input?' I said.

'Counted the sacks of veg as they were delivered. If there were twenty sacks of onions on the day's delivery note, his job to see twenty sacks arrived.' He inspected the contents of the pint glass. 'Reckon it was madness giving him that job. Mind you, it's not millionaire class, knocking off sacks of carrots and onions, but it seems he was supplying a whole string of bleeding village shops with the help of the lorry drivers. The driver would let the sacks fall off the lorry on the way here, see, and Chris Norwood would count twenty where there was only sixteen. They split the profits. It goes on everywhere, that sort of thing, in every kitchen I've ever worked in. Meat too. Sides of ruddy beef. Caviar. You name it, it's been nicked.

But Chris wasn't just your usual opportunist. He didn't know what to keep his hands off.'

'What didn't he keep his hands off?' I asked.

Vince Akkerton polished off the liquid remains and put down his glass with suggestive loudness. Obediently I crossed to the bar for a refill, and once there had been a proper inspection of the new froth and a sampling of the first two inches, I heard what Chris Norwood had stolen.

'The girls in the office said he pinched their cash. They didn't cotton on for ages. They thought it was one of the women there that they didn't like. Chris was in and out all the time, taking in the day-sheets and chatting them up. He thought a lot of himself. Cocky bastard.'

I looked at the well-fleshed worldly-wise face and thought of chief petty officers and ships' engineers. The same easy assumption of command: the ability to size men up and put them to work. People like Vince Akkerton were the indispensible getters of things done.

'How old,' I said, 'was Chris Norwood?'

'Thirtyish. Same as you. Difficult to say, exactly.' He drank. 'What sort of trouble did he get you in?'

'A couple of bullies came to my house looking for something of his.'

Fog, I thought.

'What sort of thing?' said Akkerton.

'Computer tapes.'

If I'd spoken in Outer Mongolian, it couldn't have meant less to him. He covered his bewilderment with beer and in disappointment I drank some of my own.

'Course,' said Akkerton, rallying, 'there's a computer or some such over in the office. They use it for keeping track of how many tons of Burgundy Beef and so on they's got on order and in the freezers, stuff like that. Working out how many thousands of ducks they need. Lobsters. Even coriander seeds.' He paused and with the first glint of humour said, 'Mind you, the results are always wrong, on account of activities on the side. There was a whole shipment of turkeys missing once. Computer error, they said.' He grunted. 'Chris Norwood with his carrots and onions, he was peanuts.'

'These were computer tapes to do with horseracing,' I said.

The dark eyebrows rose. 'Now that makes more sense. Every bleeding thing in this town practically is to do with horseracing. I've heard they think the knacker's yard has a direct line to our Burgundy Beef. It's a libel.'

'Did Chris Norwood bet?'

'Everyone in the firm bets. Cripes, you couldn't live in this town and not bet. It's in the air. Catching, like the pox.'

I seemed to be getting nowhere at all and I didn't know what else to ask. I cast around and came up with, 'Where was Chris Norwood killed?'

'Where? In his room. He rented a room in a council house from a retired old widow who goes out cleaning in the mornings. See, she wasn't supposed to take in lodgers, the council don't allow it, and she never told the welfare, who'd been doling out free meals, that she was earning, so the fuss going on now is sending her gaga.' He shook his head. 'Next street to me, all this happened.'

'What *did* exactly happen?'

He showed no reluctance to tell. More like relish.

'She found Chris dead in his room when she went in to clean it. See, she thought he'd have gone to work; she always went out before him in the mornings. Anyway, there he was. Lot of blood, so I've heard. You don't know what's true and what isn't, but they say he had bullets in his *feet*. Bled to death.'

Christ Almighty . . .

'Couldn't walk, you see,' Akkerton said. 'No telephone. Back bedroom. No one saw him.'

With a dry mouth I asked, 'What about . . . his belongings?'

'Dunno, really. Nothing stolen, that I've heard of. Seems there were just a few things broken. And his stereo was shot up proper, same as him.'

What do I do, I thought. Do I go to the police investigating Chris Norwood and tell them I was visited by two men who threatened to shoot my television and my ankles? Yes, I thought, this time I probably do.

'When . . .' My voice sounded hoarse. I cleared my throat and tried again. 'Which day did it happen?'

'Last week. He didn't show up Friday morning, and it was bloody inconvenient as we were handling turnips that day and it was his job to chop the tops and roots off and feed them into the washer.'

I felt dazed. Chris Norwood had been dead by Friday morning. It had been *Saturday afternoon* when I'd flung my visitors' Walther out into the rose bush. On Saturday they had been still looking for the tapes, which meant . . . dear God . . . that they hadn't got them from Chris Norwood. They'd shot him, and left him, and they still hadn't got the tapes. He would have given them to them if he'd had them: to stop them shooting him; to save his life. The tapes weren't worth one's life: they truly weren't. I remembered the insouciance with which I faced that pistol, and was in retrospect terrified.

Vince Akkerton showed signs of feeling it was time he was paid for his labours. I mentally tossed between what I could afford and what he might expect and decided to try him with the least possible. Before I could offer it, however, two girls came into the bar and prepared to sit at the next table. One of them, seeing Akkerton, changed course abruptly and fetched up at his side.

'Hullo, Vince,' she said. 'Do us a favour. Stand us a rum and coke and I'll pay you tomorrow.'

'I've heard that before,' he said indulgently, 'but this friend of mine's buying.'

Poorer by two rum and cokes, another full pint and a further half (for me), I sat and listened to Akkerton explaining that the girls worked in the Angel Kitchens office.

Carol and Janet. Young, medium bright, full of chatter and chirpiness, expecting from minute to minute the arrival of their boyfriends.

Carol's opinion of Chris Norwood was straightforwardly indignant. 'We all worked out it had to be him dipping into our handbags, but we couldn't *prove* it, see? We were just going to set a trap for him when he got killed, and I suppose I should feel sorry for him, but I don't. He couldn't keep his hands off anything. I mean, not anything. He'd take your last sandwich when you weren't looking and laugh at you while he ate it.'

'He didn't see anything wrong in pinching things,' Janet said.

'Here,' Akkerton said, leaning forward for emphasis, 'young Janet here, she works the computer. You ask her about those tapes.'

Janet's response was a raised-eyebrow thoughtfulness.

'I didn't know he had any actual tapes,' she said. 'But of course he was always around. It was his job, you know, collecting the day-sheets from all the departments and bringing them to me. He'd always hang around a bit, especially the last few weeks, asking how the computer worked, you know? I showed him how it came up with all the quantities, how much salt, you know, and things like that, had to be shifted to each department, and how all the orders went through, mixed container loads to Bournemouth or Birmingham, you know. The whole firm would collapse, you know, without the computer.'

'What make is it?' I said.

'What *make*?' They all thought it an odd question, but I'd have gambled on the answer.

'A Grantley,' Janet said.

I smiled at her as inoffensively as I knew how and asked her if she would have let Chris Norwood run his tapes through her Grantley if he'd asked her nicely, and after some guilty hesitation and a couple of downward blushes into her rum and coke, said she might have done, you know, at one time, before they discovered, you know, that it was Chris who was stealing their cash.

'We should have guessed it ages ago,' Carol said, 'but then the things he took, like our sandwiches and such, and things out of the office, staples, envelopes, rolls of sticky tape, well, we *saw* him take those, we were used to it.'

'Didn't anyone ever complain?' I said.

Not officially, the girl said. What was the use? The firm never sacked people for nicking things, if they did there would be a strike.

'Except that time, do you remember, Janet?' Carol said. 'When that poor old lady turned up, wittering on about Chris stealing things from her house. *She* complained, all right. She came back three times, making a fuss.'

'Oh, sure,' Janet nodded. 'But it turned out it was only some odd bits of paper she was on about, you know, nothing like money or valuables, and anyway Chris said she was losing her marbles, and had thrown them away, most like, and it all blew over, you know.'

I said, 'What was the old lady's name?'

The girls looked at each other and shook their heads. It was weeks ago, they said.

Akkerton said he hadn't known of that, he'd never heard about the old lady, not down with his Veg.

The girls' boyfriends arrived at that moment and there was a general re-shuffle round the tables. I said I would have to be going, and by one of those unspoken messages Akkerton indicated that I should see him outside.

'O'Rorke,' said Carol suddenly.

'What?'

'The old lady's name,' she said. 'I've remembered it. It was Mrs O'Rorke. She was Irish. Her husband had just died, and she'd been paying Chris to carry logs in for her fire, and things like that that she couldn't manage.'

'I don't suppose you remember where she lived?'

'Does it matter? It was only a great fuss over nothing.'

'Still . . .'

She frowned slightly with obliging concentration, though most of her attention was on her boyfriend, who was tending to flirt with Janet.

'Stetchworth,' she exclaimed. 'She complained about the taxi fare.' She gave me a quick glance. 'To be honest, we were glad to be rid of her in the end. She was an awful nuisance, but we couldn't be too unkind because of her old man dying, and that.'

'Thanks very much,' I said.

'You're welcome.' She moved away from me and sat herself decisively between her boyfriend and Janet, and Akkerton and I went outside to settle our business.

He looked philosophically at what I gave him, nodded and asked me to write my name and address on a piece of paper in case he thought of anything else to tell me. I tore a page out of my diary, wrote, and gave it to him thinking that our transaction was over, but when I'd shaken his hand, said goodbye and walked away from him he called after me.

'Wait, lad.'

I turned back.

'Did you get your money's worth?' he said.

More than I'd bargained for, I thought. I said, 'Yes, I think so. Can't really tell yet.'

He nodded, pursing his lips. Then with an

uncharacteristically awkward gesture he held out half of the cash. 'Here,' he said. 'You take it. I saw into your wallet in the pub. You're nearly cleaned out. Enough's enough.' He thrust his gift towards my hand, and I took it back with gratitude. 'Teachers,' he said, pushing open the pub door. 'Downtrodden underpaid lot of bastards. Never reckoned much to school myself.' He brushed away my attempt at thanks and headed back to the beer.

CHAPTER SIX

By map and in spite of misdirections, I eventually found the O'Rorke house in Stetchworth. Turned into the driveway. Stopped the engine. Climbed out of the car, looking at what lay ahead.

A large rambling untidy structure; much wood, many gables, untrained creeper pushing tendrils onto the slated roof, and sash window frames long ago painted white. The garden in the soft evening light seemed a matter of grasses and shrubs growing wherever they liked; and a large bush of lilac, white and sweet-scented, almost obliterated the front door.

The bell may have rung somewhere deep inside in response to my finger on the button, but I couldn't hear it. I rang again, and tried a few taps on the inadequate knocker, and when the blank seconds mounted to minutes, I stepped back a few paces, looking up at the windows for signs of life.

I didn't actually see the door open behind the lilac bush, but a sharp voice spoke to me from among the flowers.

'Are you Saint Anthony?' it said.

'Er, no.' I stepped back into the line of sight and found standing in the shadowy half-open doorway a short white-haired old woman with yellowish skin and wild-looking eyes.

'About the fate?' she said.

'Whose fate?' I asked, bewildered.

'The church's, of course.'

'Oh,' I said. 'The *fête*.'

She looked at me as if I were totally stupid, which from her point of view I no doubt was.

'If you cut the peonies tonight,' she said, 'they'll be dead by Saturday.'

Her voice was distinguishably Irish, but with the pure vowels of education, and her words were already a dismissal. She was holding onto the door with one hand and its frame with the other, and was on the point of irrevocably rejoining them.

'Please,' I said hastily, 'show me the peonies . . . so that I'll know which to pick . . . on Saturday.'

The half-begun movement was arrested. The old woman considered for a moment and then stepped out past the lilac into full view, revealing a waif-thin frame dressed in a rust-coloured jersey, narrow navy blue trousers, and pink and green checked bedroom slippers.

'Round the back,' she said. She looked me up and down, but apparently saw nothing to doubt. 'This way.'

She led me round the house along a path whose

flat sunken paving stones merged at the edges with the weedy overgrowth of what might once have been flowerbeds. Past a shoulder-high stack of sawn logs, contrastingly neat. Past a closed side door. Past a greenhouse filled with the straggly stalks of many dead geraniums. Past a wheelbarrow full of cinders, about whose purpose one could barely guess. Round an unexpected corner, through a too-small gap in a vigorously growing hedge, and finally into the riotous mess of the back garden.

'Peonies,' she said, pointing, though indeed, there was no need. Around the ruin of a lawn huge swathes of the fat luxurious blowsy heads, pink, crimson, frilly white, raised themselves in every direction from a veritable ocean of glossy dark leaves, the sinking sun touching all with gold. Decay might lie in the future but the present was a triumphant shout in the face of death.

'They're magnificent,' I said, slightly awed. 'There must be thousands of them.'

The old woman looked around without interest. 'They grow every year. Liam couldn't have enough. You take what you like.'

'Um.' I cleared my throat. 'I'd better tell you I'm not from the church.'

She looked at me with the same sort of bewilderment as I'd recently bent on her. 'What did you want to see the peonies for, then?'

'I wanted to talk to you. For you not to go inside

and shut your door when you learned what I want to talk about.'

'Young man,' she said severely, 'I'm not buying anything. I don't give to charities. I don't like politicians. What do you want?'

'I want to know,' I said slowly, 'about the papers that Chris Norwood stole from you.'

Her mouth opened. The wild eyes raked my face like great watery searchlights. The thin body shook with powerful but unspecified emotion.

'Please don't worry,' I said hastily. 'I mean you no harm. There's nothing at all to be afraid of.'

'I'm not afraid. I'm angry.'

'You did have some papers, didn't you, that Chris Norwood took?'

'Liam's papers. Yes.'

'And you went to Angel Kitchens to complain?'

'The police did nothing. Absolutely nothing. I went to Angel Kitchens to make that beastly man give them back. They said he wasn't there. They were lying. I know they were.'

Her agitation was more than I was ready to feel guilty for. I said calmly. 'Please, could we just sit down . . .' I looked around for a garden bench, but saw nothing suitable. 'I don't want to upset you. I might even help.'

'I don't know you. It's not safe.' She looked at me for a few more unnerving seconds with full beam, and then turned and began to go back the way we had come. I followed reluctantly, aware that I'd been clumsy but still not knowing what else to have done. I had lost her, I thought. She would go in behind the lilac and shut me out.

Back through the hedge, past the cinders, past the cemetery in the greenhouse: but not past the closed side door. To my slightly surprised relief she stopped there and twisted the knob.

'This way,' she said, going in. 'Come along. I think I'll trust you. You look all right. I'll take the risk.'

The house was dark inside and smelled of disuse. We seemed to be in a narrow passage, along which she drifted ahead of me, silent in her slippers, light as a sparrow.

'Old women living alone,' she said, 'should never take men they don't know into their houses.' As she was addressing the air in front of her, the admonishment seemed to be to herself. We continued along past various dark-painted closed doors, until the passage opened out into a central hall where such light as there was filtered through high-up windows of patterned stained glass.

'Edwardian,' she said, following my upward gaze. 'This way.'

I followed her into a spacious room whose elaborate bay window looked out onto the glory in the garden. Indoors, more mutedly, there were deep-blue velvet curtains, good-looking large rugs over the silver-grey carpet, blue velvet sofas and armchairs – and dozens and dozens of seascapes crowding the walls. Floor to ceiling. Billowing sails. Four-masters. Storms and seagulls and salt spray.

'Liam's,' she said briefly, seeing my head turn around them.

When Liam O'Rorke liked something, I thought fleetingly, he liked a lot of it.

'Sit down,' she said, pointing to an armchair. 'Tell me who you are and why you've come here.' She moved to a sofa where, to judge from the book and glass on the small table adjacent, she had been sitting before I arrived, and perched her small weight on the edge as if ready for flight.

I explained about Peter's link with Chris Norwood, saying that Chris Norwood had given what I thought might be her husband's papers to Peter for him to organise into computer programs. I said that Peter had done the job, and had recorded the programs on tape.

She brushed aside the difficult technicalities and came straight to the simple point. 'Do you mean,' she demanded, 'that your friend Peter has my papers?' The hope in her face was like a light.

'I'm afraid not. I don't know where the papers are.'

'Ask your friend.'

'He's been killed in an accident.'

'Oh.' She stared at me, intensely disappointed.

'But the tapes,' I said. 'I do know where those are – or at least I know where copies of them are. If the knowledge that's on them is yours, I could get them for you.'

She was a jumble of renewed hope and puzzlement. 'It would be wonderful. But these tapes, wherever they are, didn't you bring them with you?'

I shook my head. 'I didn't know you existed until an hour ago. It was a girl called Carol who told me about you. She works in the office of Angel Kitchens.'

'Oh, yes.' Mrs O'Rorke made a small movement of embarassment. 'I screeched at her. I was so *angry*. They wouldn't tell me where to find Chris Norwood in all those buildings and sheds. I'd said I'd scratch his eyes out. I've an Irish temper, you know. I can't always control it.'

I thought of the picture she must have presented to those girls, and reckoned their description of her 'making a fuss' had been charitable.

'The trouble is,' I said slowly, 'that someone else is looking for those tapes.' I told her a watered-down version of the visit to my house of the gunmen, to which she listened with open-mouthed attention. 'I don't know who they are,' I said, 'or where they come from. I began to think that so much ignorance might be dangerous. So I've been trying to find out what's going on.'

'And if you know?'

'Then I'll know what *not* to do. I mean, one can do such stupid things, with perhaps appalling consequences, just through not knowing some simple fact.'

She regarded me steadily with the first glimmer of a smile. 'All you're asking for, young man, is the secret that has eluded *homo sapiens* from day one.'

I was startled not so much by the thought as by the words she phrased it in, and as if sensing my surprise she said with dryness, 'One does not grow silly with age. If one was silly when young, one may be silly when old. If one were acute when young, why should acuteness wane?'

'I have done you,' I said slowly, 'an injustice.'

'Everyone does,' she said indifferently. 'I look in my mirror. I see an old face. Wrinkles. Yellow skin. As society is now constituted, to present this appearance is to be thrust into a category. Old woman, therefore silly, troublesome, can be pushed around.'

'No,' I said. 'It's not true.'

'Unless, of course,' she added as if I hadn't spoken, 'one is an *achiever*. Achievement is the saviour of the very old.'

'And are you not . . . an achiever?'

She made a small regretful movement with hands and head. 'I wish I were. I am averagely intelligent, but that's all. It gets you nowhere. It doesn't save you from rage. I apologise for my reaction in the garden.'

'But don't,' I said. 'Theft's an assault. Of course you'd be angry.'

She relaxed to the extent of sitting back into the sofa, where the cushions barely deflated under her weight.

'I will tell you as much as I can of what has happened. If it saves you from chasing Moses across the Red Sea, so much the better.'

To know what *not* to do . . .

I grinned at her.

She twitched her lips and said, 'What do you know about racing?'

'Not a great deal.'

'Liam did. My husband. Liam lived for the horses all his life. In Ireland, of course, when we were children. Then here. Newmarket, Epsom, Cheltenham, that's where we've lived. Then back here to Newmarket. Always the horses.'

'Were they his job?' I asked.

'In a way. He was a gambler.' She looked at me calmly. 'I mean a professional gambler. He lived on his winnings. I still live on what's left.'

'I thought it wasn't possible,' I said.

'To beat the odds?' The words sounded wrong for her appearance. It was true, I thought, what she'd said about categories. Old women weren't expected to talk gambling; but this one did. 'In the old days it was perfectly possible to make a good living. Dozens did it. You worked on a profit expectation of ten per cent on turnover, and if you had any judgement at all, you achieved it. Then they introduced the Betting Tax. It took a slice off all the winnings, reduced the profit margin to almost nil, killed off all the old pros in no time. Your ten per cent was all going into the Revenue, do you see?'

'Yes,' I said.

'Liam had always made more than ten per cent. He took a pride in it. He reckoned he could win one race out of three. That means that every third bet, on average, would win. That's a very high percentage, day after day, year after year. And he *did* beat the tax. He tried new ways, added new factors. With his statistics, he said, you could always win in the long run. None of the bookies would take his bets.'

'Er, what?' I said.

'Didn't you know?' She sounded surprised. 'Bookmakers won't take bets from people who repeatedly win.'

'But I thought that's what they were in business for. I mean, to take people's bets.'

'To take bets from ordinary mug punters, yes,' she said. 'The sort who may win occasionally but never do in the end. But if you have an account with almost any bookie and you keep winning, he'll close your account.'

'Good grief,' I said weakly.

'At the races,' she said, 'all the bookies knew Liam. If they didn't know him to talk to, they knew him by sight. They'd only let him bet in cash at starting price, and then as soon as he'd got his money on they'd tic-tac it round the ring and they'd all reduce the price of that horse to ridiculously small odds, making the starting price very low, so that he wouldn't win much himself, and so that the other racegoers would be put off backing that horse, and stake their money on something else.'

There was a longish pause while I sorted out and digested what she'd said.

'And what,' I said, 'about the Tote?'

'The Tote is unpredictable. Liam didn't like that. Also the Tote in general pays worse odds than the bookies. No, Liam liked betting with the bookies. It was a sort of war. Liam always won, though most times the bookies didn't know it.'

'Er,' I said, 'how do you mean?'

She sighed. 'It was a lot of work. We had a gardener. A friend, really. He lived here in the house. Down that passage where we came in just now, those were his rooms. He used to like driving round the country, so he'd take Liam's cash and drive off to some town or other, and put it all on in the local betting shops, bit by bit, and if the horse won, which it usually did, he'd go round and collect, and come home. He and Liam would count it all out. So much for Dan – that was our friend – and so much for the working funds, and the rest for us. No more tax to pay, of course. No income tax. We went on for years like that. Years. We all got on so well together, you see.'

She fell silent, looking into the gentle past with those incongruously wild eyes.

'And Liam died?' I said.

'Dan died. Eighteen months ago, just before Christmas. He was ill for only a month. It was so quick.' A pause. 'And Liam and I, we didn't realise until after— We didn't know how much we depended on Dan, until he wasn't there. He was so strong. He could lift things . . . and the garden . . . Liam was eighty-six, you see, and I'm eighty-eight, but Dan was younger, not over seventy. He was a blacksmith from Wexford, way back. Full of jokes, too. We missed him so much.'

The golden glow of sunlight outside had faded from the peonies, the great vibrant colours fading to greys in the approaching dusk. I listened to the young voice of the old woman telling the darker parts of her life, clearing the fog from my own.

'We thought we'd have to find someone else to put the bets on,' she said. 'But who could we trust? Some of the time last year Liam tried to do it himself, going round betting shops in places like Ipswich and Colchester, places where they wouldn't know him, but he was too old, he got dreadfully exhausted. He had to stop it, it was too much. We had quite a bit saved, you see, and we decided we'd have to live on that. And then this year a man we'd heard of, but never met, came to see us, and he offered to buy Liam's methods. He said to Liam to write down how he won so consistently, and he would buy what he'd written.'

'And those notes,' I said, enlightened, 'were what Chris Norwood stole?'

'Not exactly,' she said, sighing. 'You see there was

no need for Liam to write down his method. He'd written it down years ago. All based on statistics. Quite complicated. He used to update it when necessary. And, of course, add new races. After so many years, he could bet with a thirty-three per cent chance of success in nearly a thousand particular races every year.'

She coughed suddenly, her white thin face vibrating with the muscular spasm. A fragile hand stretched out to the glass on the table, and she took a few tiny sips of yellowish liquid.

'I'm so sorry,' I said contritely. 'Making you talk.'

She shook her head mutely, taking more sips, then put down the glass carefully and said, 'It's great to talk. I'm glad you're here, to give me the opportunity. I have so few people to talk to. Some days I don't talk at all. I do miss Liam, you know. We chattered all the time. He was a terrible man to live with. Obsessive, do you see? When he had something in his mind he'd go on and on and on with it. All these sea pictures, it drove me mad when he kept buying them, but now he's gone, well, they seem to bring him close again, and I won't move them, not now.'

'It wasn't so very long ago, was it, that he died?' I said.

'On March 1st,' she said. She paused, but there were no tears, no welling distress. 'Only a few days after Mr Gilbert came, Liam was sitting there . . .' She pointed to one of the blue armchairs, the only one which showed rubbed dark patches on the arms and a shadow on its high back. ' . . . and I went to make us some tea. Just a cup. We were thirsty. And when I came back he was asleep.' She paused again. 'I thought he was asleep.'

'I'm sorry,' I said.

She shook her head. 'It was the best way to go. I'm glad for him. We'd both loathed the thought of dying in hospital stuck full of tubes. If I'm lucky and if I can manage it I'll die here too, like that, one of these days. I'll be glad to. It is comforting, do you see?'

I did see, in a way, though I had never before thought of death as a welcome guest to be patiently awaited, hoping that he would come quietly when one was asleep.

'If you'd like a drink,' she said in exactly the same matter-of-fact tone, 'there's a bottle and some glasses in the cupboard.'

'I have to drive home . . .'

She didn't press it. She said, 'Do you want to hear about Mr Gilbert? Mr Harry Gilbert?'

'Yes, please. If I'm not tiring you.'

'I told you. Talking's a *pleasure*.' She considered, her head to one side, the white hair standing like a fluffy halo round the small wrinkled face. 'He owns bingo halls,' she said, and there was for the first time in her voice the faintest hint of contempt.

'You don't approve of bingo?'

'It's a mug's game.' She shrugged. 'No skill in it.'

'But a lot of people enjoy it.'

'And pay for it. Like mug punters. The wins keep them hooked but they lose in the end.'

The same the world over, I thought with amusement: the professional's dim view of the amateur. There was nothing amateur, however, about Mr Gilbert.

'Bingo made him rich,' the old woman said. 'He came here one day to see Liam, just drove up one day in a Rolls and said he was buying a chain of betting shops. He wanted to buy Liam's system so he'd always be six jumps ahead of the mugs.'

I said curiously, 'Do you always think of a gambler as a mug?'

'Mr Gilbert does. He's a cold man. Liam said it depends what they want. If they want excitement, OK, they're mugs but they're getting their money's worth. If they want profit and they still bet on instinct, they're just mugs.'

She coughed again, and sipped again, and after a while gave me the faint smile, and continued.

'Mr Gilbert offered Liam a lot of money. Enough for us to invest and live on comfortably for the rest of our days. So Liam agreed. It was wisest. They argued a bit about the price, of course. They spent almost a week ringing each other up with offers. But in the end it was settled.' She paused. 'Then before Mr Gilbert paid the money, and before Liam gave him all the papers, Liam died. Mr Gilbert telephoned me to say he was sorry, but did the bargain still stand, and I said yes it did. It certainly did. I was very pleased to be going to be without money anxieties, do you see?'

I nodded.

'And then,' she said, and this time with anger, 'that *hateful* Chris Norwood stole the papers out of Liam's office . . . Stole all his life's work.' Her body shook. It was the fact of *what* had been stolen which infuriated her, I perceived, more than the fortune lost. 'We'd both been glad to have him come here, to carry coal and logs and clean the windows, and then I'd begun to wonder if he'd been in my handbag, but I'm always pretty vague about how much I have there . . . and then Liam died.' She stopped, fighting against agitation, pressing a thin hand to her narrow chest, squeezing shut those wide-staring eyes.

'Don't go on,' I said, desperately wanting her to.

'Yes, yes,' she said, opening her eyes again. 'Mr Gilbert came to collect the papers. He brought the money all in cash. He showed it to me, in a briefcase. Packets of notes. He said to spend it, not invest it. That way there would be no fuss with tax. He said he would give me more if I ever needed it, but there was enough, you know, for years and years, living as I do . . . And then we went along to Liam's office, and the papers weren't there. Nowhere. Vanished. I'd put them all ready, you see, the day before, in a big folder. There were so many of them. Sheets and sheets, all in Liam's spiky writing. He never learned to type. Always wrote by hand. And the only person who'd been in there besides Mrs Urquart was Chris Norwood. The only person.'

'Who,' I said, 'is Mrs Urquart?'

'What? Oh, Mrs Urquart comes to clean for me. Or she did. Three days a week. She can't come now, she says. She's in trouble with the welfare people, poor thing.'

Akkerton's voice in the pub floated back: '. . . she never told the welfare she was earning . . .'

I said, 'Was it in Mrs Urquart's house that Chris Norwood lodged?'

'Yes, that's right.' She frowned. 'How did you know?'

'Something someone said.' I sorted through what I had first said to her to explain my visit and belatedly realised that I'd taken for granted she'd known something which I now saw that perhaps she didn't.

'Chris Norwood . . .' I said slowly.

'I'd like to strangle him.'

'Didn't your Mrs Urquart tell you . . . what had happened?'

'She rang in a great fuss. Said she wasn't coming any more. She sounded very upset. Saturday morning, last week.'

'And that was all she said, that she wasn't coming any more?'

'We hadn't been very good friends lately, not with Chris Norwood stealing Liam's papers. I didn't want to quarrel with her. I needed her, for the cleaning. But since that hateful man stole from us, she was very defensive, almost rude. But she needed the money, just like I needed her, and she knew I'd never give her away.'

I looked out towards the peonies, where the greys were darkening to night, and debated whether or not to tell her what had befallen Chris Norwood. Decided against, because hearing of the murder of someone one knew, even someone one disliked, could be incalculably shattering. To thrust an old lady living alone in a big house into a state of shock and fear couldn't do any possible good.

'Do you read newspapers?' I said.

She raised her eyebrows over the oddness of the question but answered simply enough. 'Not often. The print's too small. I've good eyes, but I like big-print books.' She indicated the fat red-and-white volume on her table. 'I read nothing else, now.' She looked vaguely round the dusk-filled room. 'Even the racing pages. I've stopped reading those. I just watch the results on television.'

'Just the results? Not the races?'

'Liam said watching the races was the mug's way of betting. Watch the results, he said, and add them to statistical probabilities. I do watch the races, but the results are more of a habit.'

She stretched out a stick-thin arm and switched on the table-light beside her, shutting the peonies instantly into blackness and banishing the far corners of the room into deep shadow.

On herself the instant effect was to enhance her physical degeneration, putting skin-folds cruelly back where the dusk had softened them, anchoring the ageless mind into the old, old body.

I looked at the thin, wizened yellow face, at the huge eyes that might once have been beautiful, at the white unstyled hair of Liam O'Rorke's widow, and I suggested that maybe, if I gave her the computer tapes, she could still sell the knowledge that was on them to her friend Mr Gilbert.

'It did cross my mind,' she said, nodding, 'when you said you had them. I don't really understand what they are, though. I don't know anything about computers.'

She'd been married to one, in a way. I said, 'They are just cassettes – like for a cassette player.'

She thought for a while, looking down at her hands. Then she said, 'If I pay you a commission, will you do the deal for me? I'm not so good at dealing as Liam, do you see? And I don't think I have the strength to haggle.'

'But wouldn't Mr Gilbert pay the agreed price?'

She shook her head doubtfully. 'I don't know. That deal was struck three months ago, and now it isn't the papers themselves I'm selling, but something else. I don't know. I think he might twist me into corners. But you *know* about these tapes, or whatever they are. You could talk to him better than me.' She smiled faintly. 'A proper commission, young man. Ten per cent.'

It took me about five seconds to agree. She gave me Harry Gilbert's address and telephone number, and said she would leave it all to me. I could come back and tell her when it was done. I could bring her all the money, she said, and she would pay me my share, and everything would be fine.

'You trust me?' I said.

'If you steal from me, I'll be no worse off than I am at present.'

She came with me to the lilac-shrouded front door to let me out, and I shook her thistledown hand, and drove away.

The Red Sea parted for Moses, and he walked across.

CHAPTER SEVEN

On Thursday I trundled blearily round school, ineffective from lack of the sleep I'd forfeited in favour of correcting the Upper V's exercise books. They too, like William, had decisive exams ahead. One of the most boring things about myself, I'd discovered, was this sense of commitment to the kids.

Ted Pitts didn't turn up. Jenkins, when directly asked, said scratchily that Pitts had laryngitis, which was disgraceful as it put the whole Maths department's timetable out of order.

'When will he be back?'

Jenkins gave me a sour sneer, not for any particular reason but because it was an ingrained mannerism.

'His wife telephoned,' he said. 'Pitts has lost his voice. When he regains it, doubtless he will return.'

'Could you give me his number?'

'He isn't on the telephone,' Jenkins said repressively. 'He says he can't afford it.'

'His address, then?'

'You should ask in the office,' Jenkins said. 'I can't

be expected to remember where my assistant masters live.'

The school secretary was not in his office when I went to look for him during morning break, and I spent the last two periods before lunch (Five C, magnetism; Four D, electrical power) fully realising that if I didn't send computer tapes to Cambridge on that very day they would not arrive by Saturday: and if no computer tapes arrived at Cambridge main post office by Saturday I could expect another and much nastier visit from the man behind the Walther.

At lunchtime, food came low on the priorities. Instead I first went out of school along to the nearest row of shops and bought three blank sixty-minute cassettes. They weren't of the quality beloved by Ted Pitts, but for my purpose they were fine. Then I sought out one of Ted Pitts's colleagues and begged a little help with the computer.

'Well,' he said hesitantly. 'OK, if it's only for ten minutes. Straight after school. And don't tell Jenkins, will you?'

'Never.'

His laugh floated after me as I hurried down the passage towards the coin-box telephone in the main entrance hall. I rang up Newmarket police station (via Directory Enquiries) and asked for whoever was in charge of the investigation into the murder of Chris Norwood.

That would be Detective Chief Superintendent

Irestone, I was told. He wasn't in. Would I care to talk to Detective Sergeant Smith? I said I supposed so, and after a few clicks and silences a comfortable Suffolk voice asked me what he could do for me.

I had mentally rehearsed what to say, but it was still difficult to begin. I said tentatively, 'I might know a bit about why Chris Norwood was murdered and I might know perhaps roughly who did it, but I also might easily be wrong, it's just that . . .'

'Name, sir?' he said, interrupting. 'Address? Can you be reached there, sir? At what time can you be reached there, sir? Detective Chief Superintendent Irestone will get in touch with you, sir. Thank you for calling.'

I put the receiver down not knowing whether he had paid extra-fast attention to what I'd said, or whether he had merely given the stock reply handed out to every crackpot who rang up with his/her pet theory. In either case, it left me with just enough time to catch the last of the hamburgers in the school canteen and to get back to class on the dot.

At four, I was held up by Louise's latest grudge (apparatus left out all over the benches – Martin would never do that) and I was fearful as I raced along the corridors the boys were not allowed to run in, and slid down the stairs with both hands on the bannisters and my feet touching only about every sixth tread (a trick I had learned in my far-back youth), that Ted Pitts's colleague would have tired of waiting, and gone home.

To my relief, he hadn't. He was sitting in front of the familiar screen shooting down little random targets with the zest of a seven-year-old.

'What's that?' I said, pointing at the game.

' "Starstrike". Want a go?'

'Is it yours?'

'Something Ted made up to amuse and teach the kids.'

'Is it in BASIC?' I asked.

'Sure. BASIC, graphics and special characters.'

'Can you List it?'

He typed LIST, and Ted's game scrolled up the screen to seemingly endless flickering rows.

'There you are,' Ted's colleague said.

I looked at part of the last section of the program, which was now at rest on the screen:

```
410 RESET (RX, RY): RX = RX – RA: RY = RY – 8
420 IF RY > 2 SET (RX, RY): GOTO 200
430 IF ABS (1 * 8 – RX) > 4 THEN 150
460 FOR Q = 1 TO 6: PRINT @ 64 + 4* Vv, '****';
```

A right load of gibberish to me, though poetry to Ted Pitts.

To his colleague I said, 'I came down here to ask you to record something... anything... on these cassettes.' I produced them. 'Just so they have computer noise on them, and a readable program. They're for, er, demonstration.'

He didn't query it.

I said, 'Do you think Ted would mind me using his game?'

He shrugged. 'I shouldn't think so. Two or three of the boys have got tapes of it. It's not secret.'

He took the cassettes out of my hands and said, 'Once on each tape?'

'Er, no. Several times on each side.'

His eyes widened, 'What on earth for?'

'Um.' I thought in circles. 'To demonstrate searching through file names.'

'Oh. All right.' He looked at his watch. 'I'd leave you to do it, but Jenkins goes mad if one of the department doesn't check the computer's switched off and put the door key in the common-room. I can't stay long anyway, you know.'

He put the first of the tapes obligingly into the recorder, however, typed CSAVE 'A', and pressed 'Enter'. When the screen announced READY, he typed CSAVE 'B', and after that CSAVE 'C', and so on until the first side of the tape was full of repeats of 'Starstrike'.

'This is taking ages,' he muttered.

'Could you do one side of each tape, then?' I asked.

'OK.'

He filled one side of the second tape and approximately half of a side on the third before his growing restiveness overcame him.

'Look, Jonathan, that's enough. It's taken nearer an hour than ten minutes.'

'You're a pal.'

'Don't you worry, I'll hit you one of these days for my games duty.'

I picked up the cassettes and nodded agreement. Getting someone else to do games duty wasn't only the accepted way of wangling Wednesday afternoons off, it was also the coin in which favours were paid for.

'Thanks a lot,' I said.

'Any time.'

He began putting the computer to bed and I took the cassettes out to my car to pack them in a padded envelope and send them to Cambridge, with each filled side marked 'Play this side first.'

Since there was a Parents' Evening that day, I went for a pork pie with some beer in a pub, corrected books in the common-room, and from eight to ten, along with nearly the whole complement of staff (as these occasions involved a three-line whip) reassured the parents of all the fourth forms that their little horrors were doing splendidly. The parents of Paul apple-on-the-head Arcady asked if he would make a research scientist. 'His wit and style will take him far,' I said non-committally, and they said 'He enjoys your lessons', which was a nice change from the next parent I talked to who announced belligerently, 'My lad's wasting his time in your class.'

Placate, agree, suggest, smile: above all, show concern. I supposed those evenings were a Good Thing, but after a long day's teaching they were exhausting.

I drove home intending to flop straight into bed but when I opened the front door I found the telephone on the boil.

'Where have you been?' Sarah said, sounding cross.

'Parents' meeting.'

'I've been ringing and ringing. Yesterday too.'

'Sorry.'

With annoyance unmollified she said, 'Did you remember to water my house plants?'

Hell, I thought. 'No, I didn't.'

'It's so *careless*.'

'Yes. Well, I'm sorry.'

'Do them now. Don't leave it.'

I said dutifully, 'How's Donna?'

'Depressed.' The single word was curt and dismissive. 'Try not to forget,' she said acidly, 'the croton in the spare bedroom.'

I put the receiver down thinking that I positively didn't want her back. It was an uncomfortable, miserable, thought. I'd loved her once so much. I'd have died for her, literally. I thought purposefully for the first time about divorce and in the thinking found neither regret nor guilt, but relief.

At eight in the morning when I was juggling coffee and toast the telephone rang again, and this time it was the police. A London accent, very polite.

'You rang with a theory, sir, about Christopher Norwood.'

'It's not exactly a theory. It's . . . at the least . . . a coincidence.' I had had time to cut my words down to essentials. I said, 'Christopher Norwood commissioned a friend of mine, Peter Keithly, to write some computer programs. Peter Keithly did them, and recorded them on cassette tapes which he gave to me. Last Saturday, two men came to my house, pointed a gun at me, and demanded the tapes. They threatened to shoot my television set and my ankles if I didn't hand them over. Are you, er, interested?'

There was a silence, then the same voice said, 'Wait a moment, sir.'

I drank some coffee and waited, and finally a different voice spoke in my ear, a bass voice, slower, less stilted, asking me to repeat what I'd said to the inspector.

'Mm,' he said, when I'd finished. 'I think I'd better see you. How are you placed?'

School, he agreed, was unavoidable. He would come to my house in Twickenham at four-thirty.

He was there before me, sitting not in a labelled and light-flashing police car, but in a fast four-door saloon. When I'd braked outside the garage he was already on his feet, and I found myself appraising a stocky man with a craggy young-old face, black hair dusting grey, unwavering light brown eyes and a sceptical mouth. Not a man, I thought, to save time for fools.

'Mr Derry?'

'Yes.'

'Detective Chief Superintendent Irestone.' He briefly produced a flip-over wallet and showed me his certification. 'And Detective Inspector Robson.' He indicated a second man emerging from the car, dressed casually like himself in grey trousers and sports jacket. 'Can we go inside, sir?'

'Of course.' I led the way in. 'Would you like coffee – or tea?'

They shook their heads and Irestone plunged straight into the matter in hand. It appeared that what I'd told them so far did indeed interest them intensely. They welcomed, it seemed, my account of what I'd learned on my trek via Angel Kitchens to Mrs O'Rorke. Irestone asked many questions, including how I persuaded the gunmen to go away empty-handed.

I said easily, 'I didn't have the tapes here, because I'd lent them to a friend. I said I'd get them back and post them to them and luckily they agreed to that.'

His eyebrows rose, but he made no comment. It must have seemed to him merely that I'd been fortunate.

'And you'd no idea who they were?' he said.

'None at all.'

'I don't suppose you know what sort of pistol it was?'

He spoke without expectation, and it was an instant

before I answered: 'I think . . . a Walther .22. I've seen one before.'

He said intently, 'How certain are you?'

'Pretty certain.'

He reflected. 'We'd like you to go to your local station to see if you can put together Identikit pictures.'

'Of course, I will,' I said, 'but you might be able to see these men themselves, if you're lucky.'

'How do you mean?'

'I did send them some tapes, but not until yesterday. They were going to pick them up from Cambridge main post office, and I should think there's a chance they'll be there tomorrow.'

'That's helpful.' He sounded unexcited, but wrote it all down. 'Anything else?'

'They aren't the tapes they wanted. I still haven't got those back. I sent them some other tapes with a computer game on.'

He pursed his lips. 'That wasn't very wise.'

'But the real ones morally belong to Mrs O'Rorke. And those gunmen won't come stampeding back here while they think they've got the goods.'

'And how long before they find out?'

'I don't know. But if they're the same two people who threatened Peter, it might be a while. He said they didn't seem to know much about computers.'

Irestone thought aloud. 'Peter Keithly told you that two men visited him on the Wednesday evening, is that right? 'I nodded. 'Christopher Norwood was killed last Friday morning. Eight and a half days later.' He rubbed his chin. 'It might be unwise to suppose it will take them another eight and a half days to discover what you've done.'

'I could always swear those were the tapes Peter Keithly gave me.'

'And I don't think,' he said flatly, 'that this time they'd believe you.' He paused. 'The inquest on Peter Keithly was being held today, wasn't it?'

I nodded.

'We consulted with the Norwich police. There's no room to doubt your friend's death was an accident. I dare say you've wondered?'

'Yes, I have.'

'You don't need to. The insurance inspector's report says the explosion was typical. There were no arson devices. No dynamite or plastics. Just absence of mind and rotten bad luck.'

I looked at the floor.

'Your gunmen didn't do it,' he said.

I thought that maybe he was trying to defuse any hatred I might be brewing, so that my testimony might be more impartial, but in fact what he was giving me was a kind of comfort, and I was grateful.

'If Peter hadn't died,' I said, looking up, 'they might have gone back to him when they found what they'd got from him was useless.'

'Exactly,' Irestone said dryly. 'Do you have friends you could stay with for a while?'

On Saturday morning, impelled, I fear, by Mrs O'Rorke's ten-per-cent promise, I drove to Welwyn Garden City to offer her tapes to Mr Harry Gilbert.

Not that I exactly had the tapes with me as they were still locked up with Ted Pitt's laryngitis, but at least I had the knowledge of their existence and contents, and that should be enough, I hoped, for openers.

From Twickenham to Welwyn was twenty miles in a direct line but far more in practice and tedious besides, round the North Circular Road and narrow shopping streets. In contrast, the architects' dream city, when I got there, was green and orderly, and I found the Gilbert residence in an opulent cul-de-sac. Bingo, it seemed, had kept poverty a long long way from his doorstep, which was reproduction Georgian, flanked with two pillars and surrounded by a regular regiment of windows. A house of red, white and sparkle on a carpet of green. I pressed the shiny brass doorbell thinking it would be a bore if the inhabitants of this bijou mansion were out.

Mr Gilbert, however, was in.

Just.

He opened his front door to my ring and said whatever I wanted I would have to come back later, as he was just off to play golf. Clubs and a cart for transporting them stood just inside the door, and Mr Gilbert's heavy frame was clad appropriately in check trousers, open-necked shirt and blazer. 'It's about Liam O'Rorke's betting system,' I said.

'What?' he said sharply.

'Mrs O'Rorke asked me to come. She says she might be able to sell it to you after all.'

He looked at his watch; a man of about fifty, in appearance unimpressive, more like a minor official than a peddlar of pinchbeck dreams.

'Come in,' he said. 'This way.'

His voice was no-nonsense middle-of-the-road, nearer the bingo hall than Eton. He led me into an unexpectedly functional room furnished with a desk, typewriter, wall maps with coloured drawing pins dotted over them, two swivel chairs, one tray of drinks and five telephones.

'Fifteen minutes,' he said. 'So come to the point.' He made no move to sit down or offer me a seat, but he was not so much rude as indifferent. I saw what Mrs O'Rorke had meant about him being a cold man. He didn't try to clothe the bones of his thoughts with social top-dressing. He'd have made a lousy schoolmaster, I thought.

'Liam O'Rorke's notes were stolen,' I began.

'I know that,' he said impatiently. 'Have they turned up?'

'Not his notes, no. But computer programs made from them, yes.'

He frowned. 'Mrs O'Rorke has these programs?'

'No. I have. On her behalf. To offer to you.'

'And your name?'

I shrugged. 'Jonathan Derry. You can check with her, if you like.' I gestured to the rank of telephones. 'She'll vouch for me.'

'Did you bring these . . . programs with you?'

'No,' I said. 'I thought we should make a deal first.'

'Humph.'

Behind his impassive face, a fierce amount of consideration seemed to be taking place, and at length I had a powerful feeling that he couldn't make up his mind.

I said, 'I wouldn't expect you to buy them without a demonstration. But I assure you they're the real thing.'

It produced no discernible effect. The interior debate continued; and it was resolved not by Gilbert or myself but by the arrival of someone else.

A car door slammed outside and there were footsteps on the polished parquet in the hall. Gilbert's head lifted to listen, and a voice outside the open door called, 'Dad?'

'In here,' Gilbert said.

Gilbert's son came in. Gilbert's son, who had come to my house with his pistol.

I must have looked as frozen with shock as I felt: but then so did he. I glanced at his father, and it came to me too late that this was the man Sarah had described – middle-aged, ordinary, plump – who had gone to Peter's house asking for the tapes. The one to whom she had said, 'My husband's got them.'

I seemed to have stopped breathing. It was as if life itself had been punched out of me. To know what *not* to do . . .

For all my instinct that ignorance was dangerous, I had not learned enough. I hadn't learned the simple fact that would have stopped me from walking into that house: that Mr Bingo Gilbert had a marauding Italian-looking son.

It was never a good idea to pursue Moses across the Red Sea . . .

'My son, Angelo,' Gilbert said.

Angelo made an instinctive movement with his right hand towards his left armpit as if reaching for his gun, but he wore a bloused suede jerkin over his jeans, and was unarmed. Thank the Lord, I thought, for small mercies.

In his left hand he carried the package I had sent to Cambridge. It had been opened, and he was holding it carefully upright to save the cassettes from falling out.

He recovered his voice faster than I did. His voice and his arrogance and his sneer.

'What's this mug doing here?' he said.

'He came to sell me the computer tapes.'

Angelo laughed derisively. 'I told you we'd get them for nothing. This mug sent them. I told you he would.'

He lifted the package jeeringly. 'I told you you were an old fool to offer that Irish witch any cash. You'd have done better to let me shake the goods out of her the minute her old man died. You've no clue, Dad. You should have cut me in months ago, not tell me when it's already a mess.'

His manner, I thought, was advanced son-parent rebellion: the young bull attacking the old. And part of it, I suspected, was for my benefit. He was showing off. Proving that even if I'd got the better of him the last time we'd met, it was he, Angelo, who was the superior being.

'How did this creep get here?' he demanded.

Gilbert either ignored the peacockery or indulged it. 'Mrs O'Rorke sent him,' he said.

Neither of them thought to ask the very awkward question of how I knew Mrs O'Rorke. I'd have given few chances for my health if they'd worked it through. I reckoned that this was one exceptional occasion when ignorance was emphatically the safest path, and that in prudence I should be wholly ignorant of the life and death of Chris Norwood.

'How come he still has the tapes to sell,' Angelo said cunningly, 'if he's already sent them to me?'

Gilbert's eyes narrowed and his neck stiffened, and I saw that his unprepossessing exterior was misleading: that it was indeed a tough bull Angelo was challenging, one who still ruled his territory.

'Well?' he said to me.

Angelo waited with calculation and triumph growing in his eyes and throughout his face like an intoxication, the scarifying lack of inhibition ballooning as fast as before. It was his utter recklessness, I thought, which was to be feared above all.

'I sent a copy,' I said. I pointed to the package in his hand. 'Those are copies.'

'Copies?' It stopped Angelo for a moment. Then he said suspiciously, 'Why did you send copies?'

'The originals belonged to Mrs O'Rorke. They weren't mine to give you. But I certainly didn't want you and your friend coming back again waving your gun all over the place, so I did send some tapes. I had no idea I would ever see you again. I just wanted to be rid of you. I had no idea you were Mr Gilbert's son.'

'Gun?' Gilbert said sharply. '*Gun?*'

'His pistol.'

'Angelo—' There was no mistaking the anger in the father's voice. 'I've forbidden you – *forbidden* you, do you hear, to carry that gun. I sent you to ask for those tapes. To ask. To buy.'

'Threats are cheaper,' Angelo said. 'And I'm not a child. The days when I took your orders are over.'

They faced each other in unleashed antagonism.

'That pistol is for protection,' Gilbert said intensely. 'And it is mine. You are not to threaten people with it. You are not to take it out of this house. You still depend on me for a living, and while you work for me and live in this house you'll do what I say. You'll leave that gun strictly alone.'

God in Heaven, I thought: *he doesn't know about Chris Norwood.*

'You taught me to shoot,' Angelo said defiantly.

'But as a sport,' Gilbert said, and didn't understand that sport for his son was a living target.

I interrupted the filial battle and said to Gilbert, 'You've got the tapes. Will you pay Mrs O'Rorke?'

'Don't be bloody stupid,' Angelo said.

I ignored him. To his father I said, 'You were generous before. Be generous now.'

I didn't expect him to be. I wanted only to distract him, to keep his mind on something trivial, not to let him *think*.

'Don't listen to him,' Angelo said. 'He's only a mug.'

Gilbert's face mirrored his son's words. He looked me up and down with the same inner conviction of superiority, the belief that everyone was a mug except himself.

If Gilbert felt like that, I thought, it was easy to see why Angelo did. Parental example. I would often at school know the father by the behaviour of the son.

I shrugged. I looked defeated. I let them get on with their ill-will. I wanted above all to get out of that house before they started putting bits of knowledge together and came up with a picture of me as a real towering threat to Angelo's liberty. I didn't know if Gilbert would stop his son – or *could* stop him –

if Angelo wanted me dead: and there was a lot of leafy Welwyn Garden City lying quietly in the back garden.

'Mrs O'Rorke's expecting me,' I said, 'to know how I got on.'

'Tell her nothing doing,' Angelo said.

Gilbert nodded.

I edged past Angelo to the door, looking suitably meek under his scathing sneer.

'Well,' I said weakly, 'I'll be going.'

I walked jerkily through the hall, past the attendant golf clubs and out of the open front door, taking with me a last view of Gilbert locking psychological horns with the menace that would one day overthrow him.

I was sweating. I wiped the palms of my hands on my trousers, fumbled open the car door, put a faintly trembling hand on the ignition key and started the engine.

If they hadn't been so busy fighting each other . . .

As I turned out of the drive into the cul-de-sac itself I had a glimpse of the two of them coming out onto the step to stare after me, and my mouth was uncomfortably dry until I was sure Angelo hadn't leapt into his car to give chase.

I had never felt my heart flutter that way before. I had never, I supposed, felt real fear. I couldn't get it to subside. I felt shaky, restless, short of breath, slightly sick.

Reaction, no doubt.

CHAPTER EIGHT

Somewhere between Welwyn and Twickenham, I pulled into a parking space to work out where to go.

I could go home, collect my guns, and drive to Bisley. I looked down at my hands. On present form, I'd miss the target by a yard. No point in wasting money on the ammunition.

It should take a fair while for the Gilberts to discover that they had 'Starstrike' instead of racing programs, but not as long as that to work out that while I had the original tapes, they had no exclusive control of Liam's system. I needed somewhere they wouldn't find me when they came looking. Pity, I thought, that Sarah and I had so few friends.

I walked across the road to a public telephone box and telephoned to William's farm.

'Well, of course, Jonathan,' Mrs Porter said. 'Of course, I'd have you. But William's gone. He got fed up with no horses to ride here and he packed up and went off to Lambourn this morning. He'd a friend there, he said, and he's going straight back to school from there tomorrow evening.'

'Was he all right?'

'So much *energy*!' she said. 'But he won't eat a thing. Says he wants to keep his weight down, to be a jockey.'

I sighed. 'Thanks anyway.'

'It's a pleasure to have him,' she said. 'He makes me laugh.'

I rang off and counted the small stack of coins I had left, and public-spiritedly spent them on the Newmarket police.

'Chief Superintendent Irestone isn't here, sir,' they said. 'Do you want to leave a message?'

I hesitated, but in the end all I said was, 'Tell him Jonathan Derry called. I have a name for him. I'll get in touch with him later.'

'Very good, sir.'

I got back into the car, consulted a slip of paper in my wallet and drove to Northolt to visit Ted Pitts, knowing that quite likely he wouldn't be pleased to see me. When I had finally tracked down the school secretary, he had parted with the requested information reluctantly, saying that the masters' addresses were sacrosanct to save them from over-zealous parents. Ted Pitts, he said, had particularly made him promise not to divulge.

'But I'm not a parent.'

'Well, no.'

I'd had to persuade, but I got it. And one could see, I thought, why Ted wanted to guard his privacy, because where he lived, I found, was in a mobile home on a caravan site. Neat enough, but not calculated to impress some of the social-climbers in the P.T.A.

Ted's wife, who opened the door to my knock, looked surprised but not unwelcoming. She was as earnest as Ted, small, bright-eyed, an occasional visitor to school football matches, where Ted tore up and down the pitches refereeing. I sought for a name and thought 'Jane', but wasn't sure. I smiled hopefully instead.

'How's Ted?' I said.

'Much better. His voice is coming back.' She opened the door wider. 'He'd like to see you, I'm sure, so do come in.' She gestured to the inside of the caravan, where I couldn't yet see, and said – 'It's a bit of a mess. We didn't expect visitors.'

'If you'd rather I didn't—'

'No. Ted will want you.'

I stepped up into the van and saw what she meant. In every direction spread an untidy jumble of books and newspapers and clothes and toys, all the normal clutter of a large family but condensed into a very small space.

Ted was in the minuscule sitting-room with his three little girls, sitting on a sofa and watching while they played on the floor. When he saw me he jumped to his feet in astonishment and opened his mouth, but all that came out was a squeaky croak.

'Don't talk,' I said. 'I just came to see how you are.' Any thoughts I had about cadging a bed from him had vanished. It seemed silly, indeed, to mention it.

'I'm better.' The words were recognisable, but half a whisper, and he gestured for me to sit down. His wife offered coffee and I accepted. The children squabbled and he kicked them gently with his toe.

'Jane will take them out soon,' he said huskily.

'I'm being a nuisance.'

He shook his head vigorously. 'Glad you came.' He pointed to a ledge running high along one wall and said, 'I bought your new tapes. They're up there, with your cassettes, out of reach. The children climb so. Haven't done the copying yet, though. Sorry.' He rubbed his throat as if massage would help, and made a face of frustration.

'Don't talk,' I said again, and passed on William's information about form books. He seemed pleased enough but also subdued, as if the knowledge no longer interested.

Jane returned with one mug of coffee and offered sugar. I shook my head and took a sip of the liquid which looked dark brown but tasted weak.

I said, more to make conversation than anything else, 'I don't suppose either of you know where I could put up for a night or two? Somewhere not too expensive. I mean, not a hotel.' I smiled lopsidedly.

'I've spent so much on petrol and other things this week that I'm a bit short.'

'End of the month,' Ted said, nodding. 'Always the same.'

'But your house!' Jane said. 'Ted says you've got a house.'

'Er . . . um . . . er . . . I haven't been getting on too well with Sarah.' The convenient half-truth arrived just in time and they made small sad noises in sympathetic comprehension. Ted, all the same, shook his head, sorry not to be able to help.

'Don't know of anywhere,' he said.

Jane, standing straight, tucking her elbows into her sides and clasping her hands tightly together said, 'You could stay here. On the sofa.'

Ted looked extremely surprised but his wife very tensely said, 'Would you pay us?'

'Jane!' Ted said despairingly: but I nodded.

'In advance?' she said rigidly, and I agreed again. I gave her two of the notes I'd got from the bank earlier and asked if it was enough. She said yes, looking flushed, and bundled the three children out of the room, out of the caravan, and down towards the road. Ted, hopelessly awkward and embarrassed, stuttered a wheezy apology.

'We've had a bad month . . . they've put the land rent up here . . . and I had to pay for new tyres, and for the car licence. I must have the car and it's falling to bits – and I'm overdrawn . . .'

'Do stop, Ted,' I said. 'I know all about being broke. Not starving broke. Just penniless.'

He smiled weakly. 'I suppose we've never had the bailiffs . . . but this week we've been living on bread mostly. Are you sure you don't mind?'

'Positive.'

So I stayed with the Pitts. Watched television, built bright brick towers for the children, ate the egg supper my money had bought, took Ted for a pint.

The talking couldn't have done his throat much good, but between the froth and the dregs I learned a good deal about the Pitts. He'd met Jane one summer in a youth hostel in the Lake District, and they'd married while he was still at college because the oldest of the little girls was imminent. They were happy, he said, but they'd never been able to save for a deposit for a house. Lucky to have a mobile home. Hire purchase, of course. During the holidays, he looked after the children while Jane took temporary secretarial jobs. Better for the family income. Better for Jane. He still went hiking on his own, though, one week every year. Backpacking. Sleeping in a tent, in hilly country; Scotland or Wales. He gave me a shy look through the black-framed glasses. 'It sorts me out. Keeps me sane.' It wasn't everyone, I thought, who was his own psychotherapist.

When we got back, the caravan was tidy and the children asleep. One had to be quiet, Ted said, going in: they woke easily. The girls all slept, it appeared, in the larger of the two bedrooms, with their parents in the smaller. There was a pillow, a car travelling rug and a clean sheet awaiting me, and although the sofa was a bit short for comfort it was envelopingly soft.

It was only on the point of sleep, far too late to bother, that I remembered that I hadn't called back to Irestone. Oh well, I thought, yawning, tomorrow would do.

In the morning I did call from a telephone box near the public park where Ted and I took the children to play on the swings and seesaw.

Irestone, as usual, wasn't in. Wasn't he *ever* in, I asked. A repressive voice told me the Chief Superintendent was off-duty at present, and would I please leave a message. I perversely said that no, I wouldn't, I wanted to speak to the Chief Superintendent personally. If I would leave a number, they said, he would in due course call me. Impasse, I thought: Ted Pitts had no telephone.

'If I call you at nine tomorrow morning,' I said, 'will Chief Superintendent Irestone be there? If I call at ten? At eleven? At midday?'

I was told to wait and could hear vague conversations going on in the background, and going on for so long that I had to feed more coins into the box, which scarcely improved my patience. Finally, however, the stolid voice returned. 'Detective Chief Superintendent Irestone will be in the Incident Room tomorrow morning from ten o'clock onwards. You may call him at the following number.'

'Wait a minute.' I unclipped my pen and dug out the scrap of paper which held Ted's address. 'OK.'

He gave me the number, and I thanked him fairly coolly, and that was that.

Ted was pushing his tiniest girl carefully round on a sort of turntable, holding her close to him and laughing with her. I wished quite surprisingly fiercely that I could have had a child like that, that I could have taken her to a sunny park on Sunday mornings, and hugged her little body and watched her grow. Sarah, I thought. Sarah – this is the way you've ached, perhaps; and for the baby to cuddle, and the young woman to see married. This is the loss. This, that Ted Pitts has. I watched his delight in the child and I envied him with all my heart.

We sat on a bench a bit later while the girls played in a sandpit, and for something to say I asked him why he'd lost his first intense interest in the racing form-books.

He shrugged, looking at his children, and said in a husky voice which was slowly returning to normal, 'You can see how it is. I can't risk the money. I can't afford to buy the form books. I couldn't even afford to buy a set of tapes for myself this week, to copy the program onto. I bought some for you with the money you gave me, but I just didn't have enough . . . I told you, we've been down to counting pennies for food, and although next month's pay will be in the bank tomorrow I still haven't paid the electricity.'

'It's the Derby soon,' I said.

He nodded morosely. 'Don't think I haven't thought of it. I look at those tapes sitting up on that shelf, and I think, shall I or shan't I? But I've had to decide not to. I can't risk it. How could I possibly explain to Jane if I lost? We need every pound, you know. You can see we do.'

It was ironic, I thought. On the one hand there was Angelo Gilbert, who was prepared to kill to get those tapes, and on the other, Ted Pitts, who had them and set them lower than a dustup with his wife.

'The programs belong to an old woman called O'Rorke.' I said. 'Mrs Maureen O'Rorke. I went to see her this week.'

Ted showed only minor signs of interest.

'She said a few things I thought you'd find amusing.'

'What things?' Ted said.

I told him about the bookmakers closing the accounts of regular winners, and about the system the O'Rorkes had used with their gardener, Dan, going round the betting shops to put their money on anonymously.

'Great heavens,' Ted said. 'What a palaver.' He shook his head. 'No, Jonathan, it's best to forget it.'

'Mrs O'Rorke said her husband could bet with an

overall certainty of winning once every three times. How does that strike you statistically?'

He smiled. 'I'd need a hundred per cent certainty to bet on the Derby.'

One of the children threw sand in the eyes of another and he got up in a hurry to scold, to comfort, to dig around earnestly with the corner of his handkerchief.

'By the way,' I said, when order was restored, 'I took some copies of your game "Starstrike", I hope you don't mind.'

'You're welcome,' he said. 'Did you play it? You have to type in F or S at the first question mark. I haven't written the instructions out yet, but I'll let you have them when I do. The kids,' he looked pleased and a touch smug, 'say it's neat.'

'Is it your best?'

'My best?' He smiled a fraction and shrugged, and said, 'I teach from it. I had to write it so that the kids could understand the program and how it worked. Sure, I could write a far more sophisticated one, but what would be the point?'

A pragmatist, Ted Pitts, not a dreamer. We collected the children together, with Ted brushing them down and emptying sand from their shoes, and drove back to the caravan to home-made hamburgers for lunch.

In the afternoon under Ted's commiserating eyes I corrected the load of exercise books which I happened not to have carried into my house on Friday night.

Five B had Irestone to thank for that. And on Monday morning with Ted's voice in good enough shape, he thought, to quell the monsters in the third form, we both went back to school.

We each drove our own cars. I felt I'd used up my welcome in the caravan and although Jane said I could stay if I liked I could see I was no longer a blessing from heaven. The new pay cheque would be in the bank. There would be more than bread this week, and I would have to think of somewhere else.

Ted stretched up in the last minutes before we left and plucked the six cassettes from the high shelf. 'I could do these at lunchtime today,' he said, 'if you like.'

'That would be great,' I said. 'Then you can keep one set and the others will be Mrs O'Rorke's.'

'But don't you want some yourself?'

'Maybe later I could get copies of yours, but I can't see me chasing round betting shops for the rest of my life.'

He laughed. 'Nor me. Though I wouldn't have minded a flutter . . .' A sort of longing gleamed in his eyes again, and was quickly extinguished. 'Ah well,' he said, 'forward to the fray.' He kissed Jane and the little girls, and off we went.

During the mid-morning break I yet again tried to reach Chief Superintendent Irestone, this time from the coin box in the common-room. Even with the new number, I got no joy. Chief Superintendent Irestone wasn't available at that time.

'This is boring,' I said. 'I was told he would be.'

'He was called away, sir. Will you leave a message?'

I felt like leaving a couple of round oaths. I said, 'Tell him Jonathan Derry called.'

'Very good, sir. Your message timed at ten thirty-three.'

To hell with it, I thought.

I had taken about five paces down the room in the direction of the coffee machine when the telephone bell rang behind me. It was the time of day when masters' wives tended to ring up to get their dear ones to run errands on their way home, and the nearest to the bell answered its summons as a matter of course. My wife, at least, I thought, wouldn't be calling, but someone shouted, 'Jonathan, it's for you.'

Surprised, I retraced my steps and picked up the receiver.

'Hullo,' I said.

'*Jonathan*,' Sarah said. 'Where *have* you been? Where in God's name have you *been*?'

She sounded hysterical. Her voice was high, vibrating with tension, strung higher than I'd ever heard before. Near snapping point. Frightening.

'What's happened?' I asked. I was aware that my voice sounded too calm, but I couldn't help it. It always seemed to come out that way when there was a jumbled turmoil going on inside.

'Oh my *Christ*!' She still had time to be exasperated with me, but no time to say more.

After the shortest of pauses another voice spoke, and this time every hair of my body rose in protest.

'Now you listen to me, creep . . .'

Angelo Gilbert.

'You listen to me,' he said. 'Your little lady wifey's sitting here snug as you like. We tied her to a chair so's not to hurt her.' He sniggered. 'Her friend too, the wet little bird. Now you listen, mug, because you're going to do just what I tell you. Are you listening?'

'Yes,' I said. I was in fact listening with all my might and with one hand clamped over my other ear because of the chatter and coffee cups all around me. It was macabre. It also seemed to have divorced me from any feeling in my feet.

'That was your last runaround, that was,' Angelo said, 'sending us those duff tapes. This time you'll give us the real ones, get it?'

'Yes,' I said mildly.

'You wouldn't like to get your little wifey back with her face all smashed up, would you?'

'No.'

'All you got to do is give us the tapes.'

'All right,' I said.

'And no bloody runaround.' He seemed disappointed that I'd shown so little reaction to his dramatics but even in that dire moment it seemed second nature to use on him the techniques I'd unconsciously developed in the years of teaching: to deflate the defiance, to be bored by the super-ego, to kill off the triumphant cruelty by an appearance of indifference.

It worked on the kids, it worked a treat on Jenkins, and it had already worked twice on Angelo. He should have learned by now, I thought, that I didn't rise to sneers or arrogance: not visibly anyway. He was too full of himself to believe that someone might not show the fear he felt the urge to induce. He might not be ultra-bright, but he was incalculably dangerous.

He held the receiver to Sarah's mouth, and against her I had fewer defences.

'Jonathan . . .' It was half anger, half fright: high and vehement. 'They came yesterday. *Yesterday.* Donna and I have been tied up here all *night*. Where have you damned well *been*?'

'Are you in Donna's house?' I said anxiously.

'*What?* Yes, of *course*. Of *course*, we are. Don't ask such damn silly questions.'

Angelo took the phone back again. 'Now you listen, mug. Listen good. This time there's to be no messing. This time we want the real McCoy, and I'm telling you, it's your last chance.'

I didn't answer.

'Are you there?' he said sharply.

'Sure,' I said.

'Take the tapes to my father's house in Welwyn. Have you got that?'

'Yes. But I haven't got the tapes.'

'Then *get* them.' His voice was nearly a screech. 'Do you hear?' he demanded. 'Get them.'

'It'll take some time,' I said.

'You haven't got time, creep.'

I took a deep breath. He wasn't safe. He wasn't reasonable. He wasn't a schoolchild. I simply couldn't play him too far.

'I can get the tapes today,' I said. 'I'll take them to your father when I get them. It might be late.'

'Sooner,' he said.

'I can't. It's impossible.'

I didn't know exactly why I wanted to delay. It was an instinct. To work things out; not to rush in. This time the Egyptians would have more sense.

'When you get there,' he said, seeming to accept it, 'my father will test the tapes. On a computer. A Grantley computer. Get it, mug? My father bought a Grantley computer, because that's the sort of computer those tapes were written for. So no funny tricks like last time. He'll try the tapes, see? And they'd better be good.'

'All right,' I said again.

'When my father is satisfied,' he said, 'he'll ring me here. Then I'll leave your little wifey and the wet chick tied up here, and you can come and rescue them like a right little Galahad. Got it?'

'Yes,' I said.

'Don't you forget, creep, any funny stuff and your

little wifey will keep the plastic surgery business in work for years. Starting with her nice white teeth, creep.'

He apparently again held the receiver for Sarah because it was her voice which came next. Still angry, still frightened, still high.

'For God's sake, get those tapes.'

'Yes I will,' I said. 'Has Angelo got his pistol?'

'Yes. Jonathan, do as he says. *Please* do as he says. Don't fool about.' It was an order just as much as a prayer.

'The tapes,' I said with an attempt at reassurance, 'are not worth a tooth. Keep him calm if you can. Tell him I'll do what he says. Tell him I've promised you.'

She didn't answer. It was Angelo who said, 'That's all, creep. That's enough. You get those tapes. Right?'

'All right,' I said, and the line abruptly went dead.

I felt pretty dead myself.

The common-room had emptied and I was already going to be late for the Lower VI. I picked up the necessary books mechanically and propelled myself on unfelt feet along the passages to the laboratories.

Get the tapes . . .

I couldn't get them until I could find Ted Pitts, which would probably not be until lunchtime at twelve fifteen. I had an hour and a half until then in which to decide what to do.

The Lower VI were studying radioactivity. I told them to continue the set of experiments with alpha particles that they had started last week and I sat on my high stool by the blackboard from where I often taught, and watched the Geiger counters counting with my mind on Angelo Gilbert.

Options, I thought.

I could yet once again ring the police. I could say an unstable man is holding my wife hostage at gunpoint. I could say I thought it was he who had killed Christopher Norwood. If I did, they might go chasing out to the Keithly house and try to make Angelo surrender – and then Sarah could be a hostage not for three little cassettes, but for Angelo's personal liberty. An escalation not to be thought of.

No police.

What, then?

Give Harry Gilbert the tapes. Trust that Angelo would leave Sarah and Donna undamaged. Do, in fact, precisely what I'd been told, and believe that Angelo wouldn't wait for me to walk into Donna's house and then leave three dead bodies behind when he walked out of it.

It wasn't logically likely, but it was possible.

It would have been better if I could have thought of a good valid logical reason for the murder of Chris Norwood. He hadn't given Angelo the finished computer programs because if he had there would have been no need for Angelo to come to *me*. I had speculated, not for the first time, on exactly what had happened to Liam O'Rorke's original notes, and what had happened to the tapes Peter told me he had sent to the person who had commissioned them. To C. Norwood, Angel Kitchens, Newmarket.

To Chris Norwood, comprehensive thief. Cocky little bastard, Akkerton had said. Vegetable chef Akkerton, feeding his paunch in the pub.

I supposed that Chris Norwood, when first faced with Angelo, had simply said that Peter Keithly was writing the programs and had all the notes, and that Angelo should get them from *him*. Angelo had then gone threateningly to Peter, who had been frightened into giving him programs which he knew were incomplete. By the time the Gilberts discovered they were useless, Peter was dead. Back Angelo must have gone to Chris Norwood, this time waving a gun. And again Chris Norwood must have said Peter Keithly had the programs on tapes. That if he was dead, they were in his house. He would have told him that, I thought, *after* Angelo had shot up the stereo. He would have begun to be really frightened; but he would have still wanted to keep the programs if he could, because he knew they were a meal ticket for life.

Chris Norwood, I guessed, had twice not given Angelo what he wanted; and Chris Norwood was dead.

I also had fooled and obstructed Angelo twice, and I couldn't be sure that I wasn't alive because I'd had a handy rifle. Without his father there to restrain him, Angelo could still be as volatile as the petrol vapour that had killed Peter, even if he thought he finally had his hands on the treasure he'd been chasing for so long.

Some of the Lower VI were getting their nuclei into knots. Automatically I descended from the heights of the stool and reminded them that cloud chambers didn't cloud if one neglected to add dry ice.

No more runarounds, Angelo had said.

Well . . .

What tools did I have, I thought. What skills that I could use?

I could shoot.

I couldn't on the other hand shoot Angelo. Not while he had a Walther to Sarah's head. Not without landing myself in jail for manslaughter at the least.

Shooting Angelo was out.

I had the knowledge that Physics had given me. I could construct a radio, a television, a thermostat, a digital clock, a satellite tracker and, given the proper components, a laser beam, a linear accelerator and an atomic bomb. I couldn't exactly make an atomic bomb before lunch.

The two boys who were using the alpha-particle-scattering analogue were arguing over the apparatus, which consisted of one large magnet bombarded by a host of small ones. One boy insisted that the power of permanent magnets decayed with time and the other said it was rubbish, permanent meant permanent.

'Who's right, sir?' they asked.

'Permanence is relative,' I said. 'Not absolute.'

There was a flash of impermanent electrical activity at that moment in my brain. The useful knowledge was to hand.

God bless all boys, I thought.

CHAPTER NINE

Ted Pitts hunched over the Harris all through lunch-time, making and testing the copies on the new tapes.

'There you are,' he said finally, rubbing his neck. 'As far as I can see they're perfect.'

'Which set do you want?' I said.

He peered at me earnestly through the black frames. 'Don't you mind?'

'Choose which you like,' I said. 'I'll take the others.'

He hesitated, but decided on the originals. 'If you're sure?'

'Certain,' I said. 'But give me the original boxes, *Oklahoma* and so on. It might be better if I hand them over in the right wrappings.'

I slid the copies into the gaudy boxes, thanked Ted, returned to the common-room, and told my four long-suffering lieutenants that I had developed a stupefying sick shivery headache and would they please take my afternoon classes between them. There were groans, but it was a service we regularly did for each other when it was unavoidable. I was going home, I said. With luck, I would be back in the morning.

Before I left I made a detour to the prep room where Louisa was counting out springs and weights for the 2nd form that afternoon. I told her about the headache and got scant sympathy, which was fair. While she took the load of batteries through into one of the laboratories to distribute them along the benches I opened one of her tidy cupboards and helped myself to three small objects, hiding them smartly in my pocket.

'What are you looking for?' Louisa asked, coming back and seeing me in front of the still open doors.

'Nothing particular,' I said vaguely. 'I don't really know.'

'Get home to bed,' she said sighing, casting herself for martyrdom. 'I'll cope with the extra work.'

My absence meant in reality less work for her, not more, but there was nothing to be gained by pointing it out. I thanked her profusely to keep her in a good mood for the others, and went out to the car to drive home.

No need to worry about Angelo being there: he was in the Keithlys' house a hundred miles away in Norfolk.

Everything felt unreal. I thought of the two girls, tied to the chairs, uncomfortable, scared, exhausted. Don't fool about, Sarah had said. Do what Angelo says.

Somewhere in one of the sideboard drawers we had a photograph album, thrust out of sight since we had lost the desire to record our joyless life. I dug it out and turned the pages, looking for the picture I had taken once of Peter, Donna and Sarah standing out on the pavement in front of Peter's house. The sun had been shining, I found. All three were smiling, looking happy. A pang to see Peter's face, no moustache, looking so pleased with himself and young. Nothing special about that photograph: just people, a house, a street. Reassuring to me, however, at that moment.

I went upstairs to my own small room, unlocked the gun cupboard and took out one of the Mauser 7.62s and also one of the Olympic-type rifles, the Anschütz .22. Packed them both into the special suitcase along with some ammunition of both sizes. Carried the case down to the car and locked it into the boot.

Reflected and went upstairs to fetch a large brown bathtowel from the linen cupboard. Locked that also into the boot.

Locked the house.

After that I sat in the car for three or four minutes thinking things out, with the result that I went back into the house yet again, this time for a tube of extra-strength glue.

All I didn't have enough of, I thought, was time.

I started the engine and set off not to Welwyn, but to Norwich.

Propelled by demons, I did the trip in a shorter time than usual, but it was still four-thirty when I reached the city outskirts. Six hours since Angelo had telephoned. Six long hours for his hostages.

I drew up beside a telephone box in a shopping parade not far from Donna's house and dialled her number. Praying, I think, that Angelo would answer: that all would be at least no worse than it had been in the morning.

'Hullo,' he said. Eagerly, I thought. Expecting his father.

'It's Jonathan Derry,' I said. 'I've got the tapes.'

'Let me talk to my father.'

'I'm not at your father's house. I haven't gone there yet. It's taken me all day to get the tapes.'

'Now you listen, creep . . .' He was roughly, nastily angry. 'I warned you . . .'

'It's taken me all day, but I've got them,' I interrupted insistently. 'I've got the tapes. I've got the tapes.'

'All *right*,' he said tautly. 'Now take them to my father. Take them there, do you hear?'

'Yes,' I said. 'I'll go there straightaway, but it'll take me some time. It's a long way.'

Angelo muttered under his breath and then said,

'How long? Where are you? We've been waiting all fucking night and all fucking day.'

'I'm near Bristol.'

'*Where?*' It was a yell of fury.

'It'll take me four hours,' I said, 'to reach your father.'

There was a brief silence. Then Sarah's voice, tired beyond tears, numb with too much fright.

'Where are you?' she said.

'Near Bristol.'

'Oh my God.' She sounded no longer angry, but hopeless. 'We can't stand much more of this . . .'

The receiver was taken away from her in mid-sentence, and Angelo came back on the line.

'Get going, creep,' he said; and disconnected.

Breathing space, I thought. Four hours before Angelo expected the message from his father. Instead of pressure mounting inexorably, dangerously, in that house, there would at worst, I hoped, be a bearable irritation, and at best a sort of defusing of suspense. They wouldn't for another four hours be strung up with a minute-to-minute expectation.

Before getting back into the car I opened the boot, took the telescope and the two rifles out of their non-jolt beds in the suitcase and wrapped them more vulnerably in the brown towel. Put them into the car on the brown upholstery of the back seat. Put the boxes of bullets beside them, also hidden by towel. Looked then at my fingers. No tremors. Not like in my heart.

I drove round into the road where the Keithly house stood and stopped at the kerb just out of sight of the net-curtained window. I could see the roof, part of a wall, most of the front garden – and Angelo's car in the driveway.

There weren't many people in the street. The children would be home from school, indoors having tea. The husbands wouldn't be back yet from work: there was more space than cars outside the houses. A peaceful suburban scene. Residential street, middle-income prosperous, not long built. An uncluttered street with no big trees and no forests of electricity and telegraph poles: new-laid cables tended to run underground for most of their journey, emerging only occasionally into the daylight. In the photograph of Peter's house, there had been one telegraph pole nearby with wires distributing from it to the individual houses all around, but not much else. No obstructions. Near flat asphalt pavements, white kerbstones, tar-and-chipping roadway. A few neat little hedges bordering some of the gardens. A lot of neat green rectangular patches of repressed grass. Acres of net curtains ready to twitch. I-can-see-out-but-you-can't-see-in.

The first essential for pin-point rifle shooting was to know how far one was from the target. On ranges the distances were fixed, and always the same. I was accustomed to precisely three, four, and five hundred yards. To nine hundred and a thousand yards, both of them further than half a mile. The distance affected one's angle of aim: the longer the distance, the further above the target one had to aim in order to hit it.

Olympic shooting was all done at three hundred metres, but from different body positions: standing, kneeling and lying prone. In Olympic shooting also one was allowed ten sighters in each position – ten chances of adjusting one's sights before one came to the forty rounds which counted for scoring.

In that street in Norwich I was not going to get ten sighters. I could afford barely one.

No regular lines of telegraph poles meant no convenient help with measuring the distance. The front gardens, though, I reckoned, should all be of more or less the same width because all the houses were identical, so as inconspicuously and casually as possible I slipped out of the car and paced slowly along the street, going away from Peter's house.

Fourteen paces per garden. I did some mental arithmetic and came up with three hundred yards meaning twenty-two houses.

I counted carefully. There were only twelve houses between me and my target – say one hundred and seventy yards. The shorter distance would be to my advantage. I could reckon in general to hit a target within one minute of a degree of arc: or in other words to hit a circular target of about one inch wide at a hundred yards, two inches wide at two hundred, three inches wide at three hundred, and so on to a ten-inch dinner plate at a thousand.

My target on that evening was roughly rectangular and about four inches by six, which meant that I mustn't be further away from it than four hundred yards. The main problem was that from where I stood, even if I used the telescope, I couldn't see it.

An old man came out of the house against whose kerbstone I was parked and asked if I wanted anything.

'Er, no,' I said. 'Waiting for someone. Stretching my legs.'

'My son wants to park there,' he said, pointing to where my car was. 'He'll be home soon.'

I looked at the stubborn old face and knew that if I didn't move he would be staring at me through the curtains, watching whatever I did. I nodded and smiled, got into the car, reversed into his next-door driveway, and left the street by the way I'd come.

All right, I thought, driving around. I have to come into the street from the opposite end. I have to park where I can see the target. I do not, if possible, park outside anyone's house fully exposed to one of those blank-looking one-way viewing screens. I do not park where Angelo can see me. I count the houses carefully to get the distance right; and above all I don't take much time.

It's a cliché in movies that when an assassin looks through the telescopic sight, steadies the crossed lines on the target and squeezes the trigger, the victim drops dead. Quite often the assassin will perform this feat while standing up, and nearly always it will be with his first shot: all of which makes serious marksmen laugh, or wince, or both. The only film I ever saw that got it right was *The Day of the Jackal*, where the gunman went into a forest to pace out his distance, to strap his rifle to a tree for steadiness, to adjust his sights and take two or three trial shots at a head-sized melon before transferring it all to the place of execution. Even then, there was no allowance for wind – but one can't have everything.

I drove into the top end of Peter's road, with which I was less familiar, and between two of the houses came across the wide entrance gates to the old estate upon which the new estate had been built. The double gates themselves, wrought iron, ajar, led to a narrow road that disappeared into parkland, and they were set not flush with the roadway or even with the fronts of the houses, but slightly further back. Between the gates and the road there was an area of moderately well-kept gravel and a badly weathered notice board announcing that all the callers to the Paranormal Research Institute should drive in and follow the arrows to Reception.

I turned without hesitation onto the gravel area and stopped the car. It was ideal. From there, even with the naked eye, I had a clear view of the target. A slightly sideways view certainly, but good enough.

I got out of the car and counted the houses which stretched uniformly along the street: the Keithlys' was the fourteenth on the opposite side of the road and my target was one house nearer.

The road curved slightly to my right. There was a slight breeze from the left. I made the assessments almost automatically and eased myself into the back of the car.

I had gone through long patches of indecision over which rifle to use. The 7.62 bullets were far more destructive, but if I missed the target altogether with the first shot, I could do terrible damage to things or people I couldn't see. People half a mile away, or more. The .22 was much lighter: still potentially deadly if I missed the target, but not for such a long distance.

In a car I obviously couldn't lie flat on my stomach, the way I normally fired the Mauser. I could kneel, and I was more used to kneeling with the .22. But when I knelt in the car I wouldn't have to support the rifle's weight . . . I could rest it on the door and shoot through the open window.

For better or worse I chose the Mauser. The stopping power was so much greater, and if I was going to do the job, it was best done properly. Also I could see the target clearly and it was near enough to make hitting it with the second shot a certainty. It was the *first* shot that worried.

A picture of Paul Arcady rose in my mind. 'Could you shoot the apple off his head, sir?' What I was doing was much the same. One slight mistake could have unthinkable results.

Committed, I wound down the rear window and then fitted the sleek three-inch round of ammunition into the Mauser's breech. I took a look at the target through the telescope, steadying that too on the window ledge, and what leapt to my eye was a bright, clear, slightly oblique close-up of a flat shallow box, fixed high up and to one side on the telegraph pole: grey, basically rectangular, fringed with wires leading off to all the nearby houses.

The junction box.

I was sorry for all the people who were going to be without telephones for the rest of that day, but not too sorry to put them out of order.

I lowered the telescope, folded the brown towel, and laid it over the door frame to make a non-slip surface. Wedged myself between the front and rear seats as firmly as possible, and rested the barrel of the Mauser on the towel.

I thought I would probably have to hit the junction box two or three times to be sure. 7.62 mm bullets tended to go straight through things, doing most of the damage on the way out. If I'd cared to risk shooting the junction box *through the pole* one accurate bullet would have blown it apart, but I would have to have been directly behind it, and I couldn't get there unobserved.

I set the sights to what I thought I would need for that distance, lowered my body into an angle that felt right, corrected a fraction for the breeze, and squeezed the trigger. Hit the pole, I prayed. High or low, hit the pole. The bullet might indeed go through it, but with the worst of its impetus spent.

7.62 calibre rifles make a terrific noise. Out in the street it must have cracked like a bull whip. In the car it deafened me like in the old days before ear-defenders.

I reloaded. Looked through the telescope. Saw the bullet hole, round and neat, right at the top of the grey junction box casing.

Allelujah, I thought gratefully, and breathed deeply from relief.

Lowered the sight a fraction, keeping my body position unchanged. Shot again. Reloaded. Shot again. Looked through the telescope.

The second and third holes overlapped, lower down than the first, and, maybe because I wasn't shooting at it directly face-on but from a little to one side, the whole casing seemed to have split.

It would have to do. It was all too noisy.

I put the guns and telescopes on the floor with the towel over them and scrambled through onto the front seat.

Started the engine, reversed slowly onto the road and drove away at a normal pace, seeing in the rear-view mirror a couple of inhabitants come out inquiringly into the street. The net curtains must all have been twitching, but no one shouted after me, no one pointed and said 'That's the man.'

And Angelo – what would he think? And Sarah – who knew the sound of a rifle better than church bells? I hoped to God she'd keep quiet.

Going out of Norwich I stopped for petrol and used the telephone there to ring Donna's number.

Nothing.

A faint humming noise, like wind in the wires.

I blew out a lungful of air and wondered with a smile what the repair men would say when they climbed the pole on the morrow. Unprintable, most like.

There were perhaps ways of interfering with incoming calls by technical juggling, by ringing a number, waiting for it to be answered, saying nothing, waiting for the receiver to be put down, and then not replacing one's own receiver, leaving the line open and making it impossible for the number to ring again. I might have trusted that method for a short while, but not for hours: and with some exchanges it didn't work.

Further along the road I again stopped, this time to tidy and reorganise the car. I returned the Mauser and the telescope to their beds in the suitcase in the boot, along with the 7.62 mm ammunition; then broke all my own and everyone else's rules and loaded a live .22 round into the breech of the Anschütz.

I laid the towel on the back seat and rolled the Olympic rifle in it lengthways, and then stowed it flat on the floor behind the front seats. The towel blended well enough with the brown carpet, and I reckoned that if I didn't accelerate or brake or corner too fast, the gun should travel without moving.

Next I put four extra bullets into my right-hand pocket, because the Anschütz had no magazine and each round had to be loaded separately. After so many years of practice I could discharge the spent casing and load a new bullet within the space of two seconds, and even faster if I held the fresh bullet in my right palm. The two rifles were physically the same size, and I'd have taken the Mauser with its available magazine if it hadn't been for its horrific power in a domestic setting. The .22 would kill, but not the people in the next house.

After that I juggled around a bit with the cassettes and their boxes and the glue and the bits I'd pinched from school, and finally drove on again, this time to Welwyn.

Harry Gilbert was expecting me. From the way he came bustling out of his house the moment I turned into his driveway he had been expecting me for a long time and had grown thoroughly tired of it.

'Where have you *been*?' he said. 'Did you bring the tapes?'

He had come close to me as I emerged from the car, thrusting his chin forward belligerently, sure of his power over a man at a disadvantage.

'I thought you didn't approve of Angelo threatening people with your pistol,' I said.

Something flickered in a muscle in his face.

'There are times when only threats will do,' he said. 'Give me the tapes.'

I took the three tapes out of my pocket and showed them to him; the three tapes themselves, out of their boxes.

I said, 'Now ring Angelo and tell him to untie my wife.'

Gilbert shook his head. 'I try the tapes first. Then I ring Angelo. And Angelo leaves your wife tied up until you yourself go to release her. That is the arrangement. It's simple. Come into the house.'

We went again into his functional office, which this time had an addition in the shape of a Grantley computer sitting on his desk.

'The tapes.' He held his hand out for them, and I gave them to him. He slotted the first one into the recorder which stood beside the computer and began to fumble around with the computer's typewriter-like keys in a most disorganised fashion.

'How long have you had that computer?' I said.

'Shut up.'

He typed RUN, and not surprisingly nothing happened, as he hadn't fed the program in from the cassette. I watched him pick up the instruction book and begin leafing through it, and if there had been all the time in the world I would have let him stew in it longer. But every minute I wasted meant one more dragging minute for Donna and Sarah, so I said, 'You'd better take lessons.'

'Shut *up*.' He gave me a distinctly bull-like glare and typed RUN again.

'I want Angelo out of that house,' I said, 'so I'll show you how to run the tapes. Otherwise we'll be here all night.'

He would have given much not to allow me the advantage, but he should have done his homework first.

I ejected the tape to see which side we'd got, then re-inserted it and typed CLOAD 'EPSOM'. The asterisks began to blink at the top right hand corner as the computer searched the tape, but at length it found 'EPSOM', loaded the Epsom program, and announced READY.

'Now type RUN and press "Enter",' I said.

Gilbert did so, and immediately the screen said:

WHICH RACE AT EPSOM?

TYPE NAME OF RACE AND PRESS 'ENTER'.

Gilbert typed DERBY, and the screen told him to type the name of the horse. He typed in 'ANGELO', and made the same sort of fictional replies Ted Pitts and I had done. Angelo's win factor was 46, which must have been maximum. It also said quite a lot about Gilbert's estimate of his son.

'How do you get Ascot?' he said.

I ejected the tape and inserted the first side of all.

Typed CLOAD 'ASCOT', pressed 'Enter', and waited for READY.

'Type RUN, press "Enter",' I said.

He did so, and at once got WHICH RACE AT ASCOT? TYPE NAME OF RACE AND PRESS 'ENTER'.

He typed GOLD CUP and looked enthralled by the ensuing questions, and I thought that he'd played with it long enough.

'Telephone Angelo,' I said. 'You must surely be satisfied that this time you've got the real thing.'

'Wait,' he said heavily. 'I'll try all the tapes. I don't trust you. Angelo was insistent that I don't trust you.'

I shrugged. 'Test what you like.'

He tried one or two programs on each of the sides, finally realising that CLOAD plus the first five letters of the racecourse required, inserted between inverted commas, would unlock the goodies.

'All right,' I said at length. 'Now ring Angelo. You can run the programs all you like when I've gone.'

He could find no further reason for putting it off. With a stare to which his own natural arrogance was fast returning he picked up one of the telephones, consulted a note pad beside it, and dialled the number.

Not surprisingly he didn't get through. He dialled again. Then, impatiently, again. Then, muttering under his breath he tried one of the other telephones with ditto nil results.

'What is it?' I said.

'The number doesn't ring.'

'You must be dialling it wrong,' I said. 'I've got it here.'

I fished into my pocket for my diary and made a show of fluttering through the leaves. Came to the number. Read it out.

'That's what I dialled,' Gilbert said.

'It can't be. Try again.' I'd never thought of myself as an actor but I found it quite easy to pretend.

Gilbert dialled again, frowning, and I thought it time to be agitated and anxious.

'You *must* get through,' I said. 'I've worried and rushed all day to get those tapes here, and now you *must* ring Angelo, he *must* leave my wife.'

In experience of command he had tough years of advantage, but then I too was accustomed to having to control wily opponents, and when I took a step towards him it was clear to both of us that physically I was taller and fitter and quite decisively stronger.

He said hastily, 'I'll try the operator,' and I fidgeted and fumed around him in simulated anxiety while the operator tried without success and reported the number out of order.

'But it can't be,' I yelled. '*You've got to ring Angelo.*'

Harry Gilbert simply stared at me, knowing that it was impossible.

I cut the decibels a shade but looked as furious as I could, and said, 'We'll have to go there.'

'But Angelo said . . .'

'I don't give a damn what Angelo said,' I said

forcefully. 'He won't leave that house until he knows you've got the tapes, and now it seems you can't tell him you have. So we'll bloody well have to go there and tell him. And I'm absolutely fed up with all this buggering about.'

'You can go,' Gilbert said. 'I'm not coming.'

'Yes you are. I'm not walking up to that house alone with Angelo inside it with that pistol. He said I was to give the tapes to *you*, and that's what I've done, and you've got to come with me to tell him so. And I promise you,' I said threateningly, warming to the part, 'that I'll take you with me one way or another. Knocked out or tied up or just sitting quietly in the front seat beside me. Because you're the only one Angelo will listen to.' I snatched up the cassettes lying beside the computer. 'If you want these tapes back you'll come with me.'

He agreed to come. He hadn't much choice. I pulled the cases for the tapes out of my pocket and showed him the labels, *Oklahoma, The King and I, West Side Story.* Then I ejected the cassette which was still in the recorder and put all three of the tapes into their cases. 'And we'll take these,' I said, 'to prove to Angelo that you have them.'

He agreed to that also. He came out with me to my car, slamming his own front door behind him, and sat in the front passenger seat.

'I'll hold the tapes,' he said.

I put them, however, on the glove shelf out of his

immediate reach and told him he could have them once we got to Norwich.

It was a strange journey.

He was a far more powerful man than I would normally have thought of opposing, yet I was discovering that I had probably always thought of myself as being weaker than I was. For the whole of my life I had gone in awe of headmasters; as a pupil, as a student, as a teacher. Even when I'd disagreed or despised or rebelled, I'd never tried actively to defeat. One could easily be chucked out of school and out of college and out of the better jobs in physics.

Harry Gilbert couldn't chuck me out of anything, and perhaps that was the difference. I could face his belief in his own superiority and not be intimidated by it. I could use my wits and my muscles to get him to do what I wanted. It was heady stuff. Have to be careful, I reflected, not to develop delusions of grandeur of my own.

Angelo, I thought suddenly, feels just as I do. Feels the spreading of the wings of internal power. Feels he can do more than he realised. Sees his world isn't as constricting as he thought. Angelo too was emerging into a new conception of ability . . . but in him there were no brakes.

'There is someone there with Angelo,' I said. 'My

wife said "they".' I spoke neutrally, without aggression.

Gilbert sat heavily silent.

'When Angelo came to my house,' I said, 'there was another man with him. Very like Angelo in looks. Did what Angelo told him.'

After a pause Gilbert shrugged and said, 'Eddy. Angelo's cousin. Their mothers were twins.'

'Italian?' I said.

Another pause. Then, 'We are all Italian by descent.'

'But born in England?'

'Yes. Why do you ask?'

I sighed. 'Just to pass the journey.'

He grunted, but gradually a good deal of his resentment of my behaviour subsided. I had no idea whether or not he considered it justified.

Anxiety on my part didn't need to be acted. I found myself drumming my fingers on the steering wheel when stopped by red lights and cursing long lorries which delayed my passing. By the time we got to Norwich, it would be over the four hours I'd warned Angelo to expect, and of all things that I didn't want, it was Angelo ballooning into premature rage.

'Will you pay Mrs O'Rorke anything for these tapes?' I said.

A pause. 'No.'

'Not even without Angelo knowing?'

He gave me a fierce sideways glare. 'Angelo does

what I tell him. Whether I pay or don't pay Mrs O'Rorke is nothing to do with him.'

If he believed all that, I thought, he was deluding himself. Or perhaps he still wanted to believe what had so far been true. Perhaps he truly didn't see that his days of domination over Angelo were ticking away fast.

Just let them last, I thought, for another two hours.

CHAPTER TEN

The long lingering evening was slowly dying by the time we reached Norwich, though it wouldn't be totally dark for another hour. I drove into the Keithlys' road from the direction that would place Gilbert nearest to the house when I pulled up at the kerb: Angelo had seen my car at his father's house as I had seen his, and the sight of it would alarm him.

'Please get out of the car as soon as I stop,' I said to Gilbert. 'So that Angelo can see you.'

He grunted, but when I pulled up he opened the door as I'd suggested, and gave any watchers from behind the curtains a full view of his lumbering exit from the front seat.

'Wait,' I said, standing up on my own side and talking to him across the top of the car. 'Take the tapes.' I reached across the top of the car and gave them to him. 'Hold them up,' I said, 'so that Angelo can see them.'

'You give too many orders.'

'I don't trust your son any more than he trusts me.'

He gave me a bullish stare of fully revived confidence, but he did in fact turn and lift the tapes, showing them to the house.

Behind his back I leant down and picked up the towel-wrapped rifle, holding it longways with the stock to my chest and the flap of my jacket falling over it.

Angelo opened the front door, shielding himself half behind it.

'Go in,' I said to Gilbert. 'This street is full of people watching through the curtains.'

He gave an automatically alarmed look at being spied on and began to walk towards his son. I slid round the car fast and walked close behind him, almost stepping on his heels.

'Explain,' I said urgently.

His head lifted ominously, but he said loudly to Angelo, 'Your telephone's out of order.'

'*What?*' Angelo exclaimed, opening the door a fraction wider. 'It can't be.'

Gilbert said impatiently, 'It is. Don't be a fool. Why else would I come all this way?'

Angelo turned away from the door and strode into the sitting-room, which was where the telephone was located. I heard him pick up the receiver and rattle the cradle, and slam the instrument down again.

'But he brought the tapes,' Gilbert said, walking to the sitting-room door and showing the bright cases. 'I tried them. All of them. This time they're the real thing.'

'Come in here, you creep,' Angelo called.

I propped the wrapped rifle, barrel downwards to the carpet, against the small chest of drawers which stood within arm's reach of the sitting-room door, and showed myself in the doorway.

The sitting-room furniture was all pushed awry. Sarah and Donna sat back-to-back in the centre of the room, with their wrists and ankles strapped to the arms and legs of two of the chairs from the dining room. To one side stood Angelo, holding the Walther, with, beyond the two girls, his look-alike, Eddy. There were glasses and plates sprinkled about, and the smell of long hours of cigarette smoke.

Sarah was facing me.

We looked at each other with a curious lack of emotion, I noticing almost distantly the dark smudges under her eyes, the exhausted sag of her body, the strain and pain round her mouth.

She said nothing. No doubt she considered I was showing too little concern and was too calm as usual: the message on her face wasn't love and relief but relief and disgust.

'Go home,' I said wearily to Angelo. 'You've got what you wanted.'

I prayed for him to go. To be satisfied, to be sensible, to be ruled by his father, to be approximately normal.

Harry Gilbert began to turn from his son back

towards me, saying, 'That's it, then, Angelo. We'd best be off.'

'No,' Angelo said.

Gilbert stopped. 'What did you say?' he said.

'I said, no,' Angelo said. 'This creep's going to pay for all the trouble he's put me to. You come here, creep.'

Gilbert said, 'No, Angelo.' He gestured to the girls. 'This is enough.'

Angelo pointed his pistol with its bulbous silencer straight at Donna's head. 'This one,' he said viciously, 'has been screaming at me for hours that they'll report me to the police, the stupid little bitch.'

'They won't,' I said quickly.

'Dead right they won't.'

Even to Gilbert his meaning was clear. Gilbert made movements of extreme disapproval and active fear and said, 'Put down the gun. Angelo, put it down.' His voice thundered with parental command and from long long habit Angelo began to obey. Even in the same second he visibly reversed his instinct; and I knew that for me it was then or never.

I stretched out my right arm, thrust my hand down into the towel and grasped the stock of the rifle. Swung the towel off the barrel and in the same fluid movement stood in the doorway with the barrel pointing straight at Angelo and the safety catch unlocking with a click.

'Drop it,' I said.

They were all utterly astounded but perhaps Angelo most of all because I'd twice played the same trick on him. The three men stood there as if frozen, and I didn't look at Sarah, not directly.

'Drop the pistol,' I said. He was still pointing it towards Donna.

He couldn't bear to drop it. Not to lose that much face.

'I'll shoot you,' I said.

Even then he hesitated. I swung the barrel to the ceiling and squeezed the trigger. The noise crashed in the small room. Pieces of plaster fell from the ceiling. The sharp smell of cordite prevailed over stale cigarette, and all the mouths were open, like fish. The rifle was pointing back at his heart with the next round in the breech almost before he'd moved an inch, and he looked at it with dazed disbelief.

'Drop the pistol,' I said. '*Drop it.*'

He was still undecided. I'll have to hit him, I thought despairingly. I don't want to. Why won't he drop the bloody thing, there's nothing he can gain.

The air seemed to be still ringing with the aftermath of explosion, but it was into silence that Sarah spoke. With a sort of sullen ferocity, which seemed as much directed at me as at Angelo, she said loudly, 'He shot in the Olympic Games.'

Angelo's eyes developed doubt.

'Drop the pistol,' I said quietly, 'or I'll shoot your hand.'

Angelo dropped it.

His face was full of fury and hate and I thought him capable of flinging himself upon me regardless of consequences. I looked at him stolidly, showing no triumph, showing nothing to inflame.

'You've got the tapes,' I said. 'Get in the car, all three of you, and get out of my life. I'm sick of your faces.' I stepped back a pace into the hall and nodded with my head towards the front door.

'Just get out,' I said. 'One at a time. Angelo first.'

He came towards me with dark eyes like pits in the olive face, the light too dim now to give them wicked life. I stood back a few steps further and followed his progress to the front door, as in my own house, with the black barrel.

'I'll get you,' he said.

I didn't answer.

He pulled open the door with the force of rage and stepped outside.

'Now you,' I said to Harry Gilbert.

He was almost as angry as his son, but perhaps it was fanciful of me to guess that there was also some recognition that I'd been able to stop Angelo where he couldn't, and that that had been a good thing.

He followed Angelo out onto the driveway and I saw them both opening the doors of Angelo's car.

'Now you,' I said to Eddy. 'You pick up Angelo's gun. Pick it up by the silencer. Do you know how to unload it?'

Eddy the carbon-copy nodded miserably.

'Do it, then,' I said. 'Very very carefully.'

He looked at the rifle and at Angelo getting into the car, and shook the bullets out of the clip, letting them drop on the carpet.

'Right,' I said. 'Take the pistol with you.' I gestured with the rifle barrel and jerked my head towards the open front door, and of the three of them it was Eddy who left with the least reluctance and the most speed.

From inside the hall I watched Angelo start the engine, slam the gears into reverse and make a rough exit into the road. Once there he deliberately side-swiped my car, damaging his own rear wing in the process, and accelerated down the street as if to prove his superior manhood.

With a feeling of terrible tension I closed the front door and went into the sitting-room. Crossed to Sarah, looked at the rubber straps which fastened her wrists and unbuckled them.

Unbuckled those round her ankles. Then those round Donna.

Donna started crying. Sarah shoved herself stiffly off the chair and collapsed onto the softer contours of the sofa.

'Do you realise how long we've been sitting there?' she demanded bitterly. 'And before you damned well ask, yes, they did untie us now and then for us to go to the bathroom.'

'And to eat?'

'I hate you,' she said.

'I really wanted to know.'

'Yes, to eat. Twice. He made me cook.'

Donna said between sobs, 'It's been awful. Awful. You've no idea.'

'They didn't . . . ?' I began anxiously.

'No they didn't,' Sarah said flatly. 'They just sneered.'

'*Hateful*,' Donna said. 'Called us mugs.' She hobbled across the carpet and lowered herself gingerly into an armchair. 'I hurt all over.' Tears trickled down her cheeks. I thought of Angelo's description of 'wet chick' and stifled it quickly.

'Look,' I said, 'I know you don't feel like it, but I'd be much happier if you'd stuff a few things into a suitcase and we all left this house.'

Donna helplessly shook her head, and Sarah said 'Why?' with mutiny.

'Angelo hated having to go. You saw him. Suppose he comes back? When he thinks we're off guard . . . he might.'

The idea alarmed them as much as me and also angered Sarah. 'Why did you give them the pistol?' she demanded. 'That was *stupid*. You're such a *fool*.'

'Are you coming?'

'You can't expect us . . .' Donna wailed.

I said to Sarah, 'I have to make a phone call. I can't do it from here.' I indicated the dead telephone. 'I'm going away in the car to do it. Do you want to come, or not?'

Sarah took stock of that rapidly and said that yes, they were coming, and despite Donna's protests she drove her stiffly upstairs. They came down a few minutes later carrying a holdall each, and I noticed that Sarah had put on some lipstick. I smiled at her with some of the old pleasure in seeing her resurfacing briefly, and she looked both surprised and confused.

'Come on, then,' I said, and took the hold-alls from them to put in the boot. 'Best be off.' I fetched the rifle, once again wrapped loosely in the towel to confuse the neighbours, and stowed it in the suitcase. Checked that Donna had brought the door keys: shut the front door; drove away.

'Where are we going?' Sarah asked.

'Where would you like?'

'What about *money*?'

'Credit cards,' I said.

We drove a short way in a silence broken only by Donna's occasional sniffs and sobs, going along now with lights on everywhere and the long soft evening turning to full dark.

I pulled up beside a telephone box and put through a reversed charge call to the Suffolk police.

'Is Detective Chief Superintendent Irestone there?' I said. Hopeless question, but had to be asked.

'Your name, sir?'

'Jonathan Derry.'

'One moment.'

I waited through the usual mutterings and clicks, and then a voice that was still not Irestone's said, 'Mr Derry, Chief Superintendent Irestone left instructions that if you telephoned again, your message was to be taken down in full and passed on to him directly. Chief Superintendent Irestone asked me to say that owing to . . . er . . . a hitch in communications he was not aware that you had tried to reach him so often, not until this afternoon. I am Detective Inspector Robson. I came to your house with the Chief Superintendent, if you remember.'

'Yes,' I said. A man nearing forty, fair-headed, reddish skin.

'If you tell me why you rang, sir?'

'You'll take notes?'

'Yes, sir. And a recording.'

'Right. Well – the man who came to my house with a pistol is called Angelo Gilbert. His father is Harry Gilbert, who runs bingo halls all over Essex and north-east London. The man who came with Angelo is his cousin Eddy – don't know his last name. He does what Angelo tells him.'

I paused and Inspector Robson said, 'Is that the lot, sir?'

'No, it isn't. At this moment all three of them are travelling from Norwich in Angelo's car.' I told him the make, the colour, the number, and that it had a bashed-in nearside rear wing. 'They are probably going to Harry Gilbert's house in Welwyn Garden City. I think Angelo also lives there, but perhaps not Eddy.' I gave him the address. 'They should arrive there in about an hour and a quarter to an hour and a half. In the car there is a Walther .22 pistol with a silencer. There may or may not be bullets in it. It may or may not be the pistol which Angelo waved at me, but it looks identical. It might be the pistol which killed Christopher Norwood.'

'That's very useful, sir,' Robson said.

'There's one more thing...'

'Yes?'

'I don't think Harry Gilbert knows anything at all about Chris Norwood's death. I mean, I don't think he even knows he's dead. If you go to arrest Angelo, Harry Gilbert won't know why.'

'Thank you, sir.'

'That's all,' I said.

'Er,' he said, 'the Chief Superintendent will be in touch with you.'

'All right, but—' I hesitated.

'Yes, sir?'

'I'd be glad to know...'

'Just a minute, sir,' he interrupted, and kept me hanging on through some lengthy unintelligible background talk. 'Sorry, sir, you were saying?'

'You remember I sent Angelo some computer tapes with games on?'

'Yes, I do. We went to Cambridge main post office

and alerted the man whose job it was to hand out letters-to-be-called-for, but unfortunately he went for his tea-break without mentioning it to anyone, and during that short period your package was collected. A girl clerk handed it over. We didn't find out until it was too late. It was . . . infuriating.'

'Mm,' I said. 'Well, Angelo came back with more threats, demanding the real tapes, and I've just given them to him. Only . . .'

'Only what, sir?'

'Only they won't be able to run them on their computer. I think when they get home they might try those tapes straight away, and when they find they don't work they might . . . well, they might set out to look for me. I mean—'

'I know *exactly* what you mean,' he said dryly.

'So, er, I'd be glad to know if you plan to do anything about Angelo this evening. And if you think there's enough to hold him on.'

'Instructions have already gone off,' he said. 'He'll be picked up tonight as soon as he reaches the house in Welwyn. We have some fingerprints to match . . . and some girls who saw two men arrive at Norwood's. So don't worry, once we've got him, we won't let him go.'

'Could I ring up to find out?'

'Yes.' He gave me a new number. 'Call there. I'll leave a message. You'll get it straight away.'

'Thank you,' I said gratefully, 'very much.'

'Mr Derry?'

'Yes?'

'What's wrong with the tapes this time?'

'Oh, I stuck magnets into the cases.'

He laughed. 'I'll see you later, perhaps,' he said. 'And thanks. Thanks a lot.'

I put the receiver down smiling, thinking of the three powerful Magnadur magnets distorting the programs on the tapes. The permanent magnets which were black and flat; two inches long, three-quarters of an inch wide, three-sixteenths of an inch thick. I'd stuck one into the inside of each case, flat on the bottom, black as the plastic, looking like part of the case itself. I'd taken the tapes and the cases separately to Harry Gilbert's – the tapes in the one pocket, the cases in another – and only after he'd played them had I married them all together. Sandwiching electromagnetic recording tapes between such magnets was like wiping a blackboard roughly with a wet sponge: there would be traces of what had been recorded there, but not enough to make sense.

It might take Angelo all the way home to see what I'd done, because the magnets did look as if they belonged there.

Or it might not.

I drove wearily in the direction of home. I seemed to have been driving for ever. It had been a very long day. Extraordinary to think it was only that morning that I'd set out from Ted Pitts's.

Both of the girls went to sleep as the miles unrolled, the deep sleep of release and exhaustion. I wondered briefly what would become of us in the future, but mostly I just thought about driving and keeping my own eyelids apart.

We stayed in a motel on the outskirts of London and slept as if dead. The alarm call I'd asked for dragged me from limbo at seven in the morning and, yawning like a great white shark, I got through to the number Inspector Robson had given me.

'Jonathan Derry,' I said. 'Am I too early?'

It was a girl's voice which answered, fresh and unofficial. 'No, it's not too early,' she said. 'John Robson asked me to tell you that Angelo Gilbert and his cousin Eddy are in custody.'

'Thank you very much.'

'Any time.'

I put the receiver down with a steadily lightening heart and shook Sarah awake in the next bed.

'Sorry,' I said, 'but I've got to be in school by nine o'clock.'

CHAPTER ELEVEN

There was a period when Sarah went back to work and Donna drooped around our house trying to come to terms with the devastation of her life. Sarah's manner to her grew gradually less over-protective and more normal, and when Donna found she was no longer indulged and pampered every waking minute she developed a pout in place of the invalid smile, and went home. Home to sell her house, to collect Peter's insurance money, and to persuade her Probation Officer to take Sarah's psychological place.

On the surface, things between myself and Sarah continued much as before: the politeness, the lack of emotional contact, the daily meetings of strangers. She seldom met my eye and seemed only to speak when it was essential, but I slowly realised that the deeply embittered set of her mouth, which had been so noticeable before the day we set off to Norwich, had more or less gone. She looked softer and more as she had once been and although it didn't seem to have altered her manner towards me it was less depressing to look at.

In my inner self a lot had changed. I seemed to have stepped out of a cage. I did everything with more confidence and more satisfaction. I shot better. I taught with zest. I even found the wretched exercise books less of a drag. I felt that one day soon I would stretch the spreading wings, and fly.

One night as we lay in the dark, each in our frostily separate cocoon, I said to Sarah, 'Are you awake?'

'Yes.'

'You know that at the end of term I'm going to Canada with the rifle team?'

'Yes.'

'I'm not coming back with them.'

'Why not?'

'I'm going to the United States. Probably for the rest of the school holidays.'

'Whatever for?'

'To see it. Perhaps to live there, eventually.'

She was silent for a while: and what she said in the end seemed only obliquely to have anything to do with my plans.

'Donna talked to me a lot, you know. She told me all about the day she stole that baby.'

'Did she?' I said noncommittally.

'Yes. She said that when she saw it lying there in its pram, she had an overpowering urge to pick it up and cuddle it. So she did. She just did. Then when she had it in her arms she felt as if it belonged to her, as if it was hers. So she carried it to her car, which was just there, a few steps away. She put the baby on the front seat beside her and drove off. She didn't know where she was going. She said it was a sort of dream, in which she had at last had the baby she'd pined for for so long.'

She stopped. I thought of Ted Pitts's little girls and the protective curve of his body as he held his smallest one close. I would have wept for Sarah, for Donna, for every unwillingly barren parent.

'She drove for a long way,' Sarah said. 'She got to the sea and stopped there. She took the baby into the back of the car and it was perfect. She was in utter bliss. It was still like a dream. And then the baby woke up.' She paused. 'I suppose it was hungry. Time for its next feed. Anyway it began to cry, and it wouldn't stop. It cried and cried and cried. She said that it cried for an hour. The noise started driving her mad. She put her hand over its mouth, and it cried harder. She tried to hug its face into her shoulder so that it would stop, but it didn't. And then she found that its nappies were dirty, and the brown stuff had oozed down the baby's leg and was on her dress.'

Another long pause, then Sarah's voice, 'She said she didn't know babies were like that. Screaming and smelly. She'd thought of them as sweet and smiling at her all the time. She began to hate that baby, not love it. She said she sort of threw it down onto the back seat in a rage, and then she got out of the car and just left it. Walked away. She said she could hear the baby crying all the way down the beach.'

This time the silence was much longer.

'Are you still awake?' Sarah said.

'Yes.'

'I'm reconciled now to not having a child. I grieve . . . but it can't be helped.' She paused and then said, 'I've learned a lot about myself these past weeks, because of Donna.'

And I, I thought, because of Angelo.

After another long while she said, 'Are you still awake?'

'Yes.'

'I don't really understand, you know, all that happened. I mean, I know that that hateful Angelo has been arrested for murder, of course I do, and that you have been seeing the police, but you've never told me exactly what it was all about.'

'You seriously want to know?'

'Of course I do, otherwise I wouldn't ask.' The familiar note of impatience rang out clearly. She must have heard it herself because she immediately said more moderately, 'I'd like you to tell me. I really would.'

'All right,' I said, and I told her pretty well everything, starting from the date that Chris Norwood set it all going by stealing Liam O'Rorke's notes. I told her events in their chronological order, not in the jumbled way I learned of them, so that a clear pattern emerged of Angelo's journeyings in search of the tapes.

When I'd finished, she said slowly, 'You knew all through that day when he had us tied up that he was a murderer.'

'Mm.'

'My God.' She paused. 'Didn't you think he might kill us? Donna and me?'

'I thought he *might*. I thought he might do it any time after he knew his father had the tapes. I thought he might kill all of us, if he felt like it. I couldn't tell . . . but couldn't risk it.'

A long silence. Then she said, 'I think, looking back, that he did mean to. Things he said . . .' She paused. 'I was glad to see you.'

'And angry.'

'Yes, angry. You'd been so *long* . . . and Angelo was so bloody *frightening*.'

'I know.'

'I heard the rifle shots. I was in the kitchen cooking.'

'I was afraid you might tell Angelo you heard them.'

'I only spoke to him when I absolutely had to. I loathed him. He was so *arrogant*.'

'You shook him,' I said, 'telling him I'd shot in the Games. It was the clincher.'

'I just wanted to . . . to kick him in the ego.'

I smiled in the darkness. Angelo's ego had taken quite a pummelling at the hands of the Derrys.

'Do you realise,' I said, 'that we haven't talked like this for months?'

'Such a lot has happened. And I feel . . . different.'

Nothing like a murderer, I thought, for changing one's view of the world. He'd done a good job for both of us.

'Do you want to come, then,' I said, 'to America?'

To America. To go on together. To try a bit longer. I didn't really know which I wanted; to clear out, cut loose, divorce, start again, remarry, have children, or to make what one might of the old dead love, to pour commitment into the shaky foundations, to rebuild them solid.

It was Sarah, I thought, who would have to decide.

'Do you want us to stay together?' I asked.

'You've thought of divorce?'

'Haven't you?'

'Yes.' I heard her sigh. 'Often, lately.'

'It's pretty final, being divorced,' I said.

'What then?'

'Wait a bit,' I said slowly. 'See how we go. See what we both really want. Keep on talking.'

'All right,' she said. 'That'll do.'

INTERVAL

Letter from Vince Akkerton to Jonathan Derry.

Angel Kitchens,
Newmarket.
July 12th

Dear Mr Derry,

You remember you were asking about Chris Norwood, that day back in May? I don't know if you're still interested in those computer tapes you were talking about, but they've turned up here at the Kitchens. We were clearing out the room we change from outdoor clothes in, prior to it being repainted, you see, and there was this bag there that everyone said didn't belong to them. So I looked in it, and there were a lot of old papers of writing and three cassettes. I thought I'd give them a run on my cassette player, because they didn't have any labels on saying what was on them, but all that came out was a screeching noise. Well, a mate of mine who heard it said don't throw them away, because I was going to, that's computer noise, he said. So I took the tapes in to Janet to see what she could make of them, but she said the firm has got rid of their old computer, it wasn't big enough for all it was having to do, and they've now got a company computer or something with disc drives, she says, and it doesn't use cassettes.

So, anyway, I remembered about you all of a sudden, and I found I'd still got your address, so I thought I'd ask you if you thought this was what you were talking about. I threw the pages of writing into the rubbish, and that's that, they're gone, but if you want these tapes, you send me a tenner for my trouble and you can have them.

Yours truly,
Vince Akkerton

Letter from the executors of Mrs Maureen O'Rorke to Jonathan Derry.

September 1st

Dear Sir,

We are returning the note you wrote to Mrs O'Rorke, together with your enclosure of three cassettes.

Unfortunately Mrs O'Rorke had died peacefully in her sleep at home three days before your gift was posted. In our opinion, therefore, the contents of the package should be regarded as belonging to yourself, and we herewith return them.

We are,
Yours faithfully,
Jones, Pearce and Block, Solicitors

Letter from the University of Eastern California selection board to Jonathan Derry.

London
October 20th

Dear Mr Derry,

Subsequent to your interview in London last week we have pleasure in offering you a three-year teaching post in the Department of physics. Your salary for the first year will be Scale B (attached) to be reviewed thereafter. One full semester's notice to be given in writing on either side.

We understand that you will be free to take up the post on January 1st next, and we await your confirmation that you accept this offer.

Further details and instructions will be sent to you upon receipt of your acceptance.

Welcome to the University!
Lance K. Barowska, D.Sc.
Director of Selections, Science Faculty,
University of Eastern California

Letter from Harry Gilbert to Marty Goldman Ltd, Turf Accountants.

October 15th

Dear Marty,

In view of what has happened, I'm asking you to release me from the transfer that we had agreed. I haven't the heart, old friend, to build any more kingdoms. With Angelo jailed for life, there's no point in me buying all your betting shops. You knew, of course, that they were for him – for him to manage, anyway.

I know you had some other offers, so I hope you won't be coming after me for compensation.

Your old friend,
Harry

Excerpt from a private letter from the Governor of Albany Prison, Parkhurst, Isle of Wight to his friend the Governor of Wakefield Prison, Yorkshire.

Well, Frank, we're letting Angelo Gilbert out on parole this week, and I wish between you and me that I felt better about it. I'd like to have advised against it, but he's served fourteen years and there's been a lot of pressure from the Reformers group on the Home Sec. to release him. It's not that Gilbert's actively violent or even hostile, but he's been trying hard to get this parole so for the last two years there's been no breath of trouble.

But as you know with some of them they're never stable however meek they look, and I've a feeling Gilbert's like that. You remember, when you had him about five years ago, you felt just the same. It isn't on the cards, I suppose, to keep him locked up for life, but I just hope to God he doesn't go straight out and shoot the first person who crosses him.

See you soon Frank,
Donald

PART TWO

WILLIAM

CHAPTER TWELVE

I put my hand on Cassie's breast, and she said 'No, William. No.'

'Why not?' I said.

'Because it's never good for me, twice, so soon. You know that.'

'Come on,' I said.

'No.'

'You're lazy,' I said.

'And you're greedy.' She picked my hand off and gave it back to me.

I replaced it. 'At least, let me hold you,' I said.

'No.' She threw my hand off again. 'With you, one thing leads to another. I'm going to get some orange juice and run the bath, and if you're not careful, you'll be late.'

I rolled onto my back and watched her walk about the bedroom, a tall thin girl with too few curves and very long feet. Seen like that in all her angular nakedness, she still had the self-possessed quality which had first attracted me; a natural apartness, a lack of cling.

Her self-doubts, if any, were well hidden, even from me. She went downstairs and came back carrying two glasses of orange.

'William,' she said, 'stop staring.'

'I like to.'

She walked to the bathroom to turn on the taps and came back brushing her teeth.

'It's seven o'clock,' she said.

'So I've noticed.'

'You'll lose that cushy job of yours if you're not out on the gallops in ten minutes.'

'Twenty will do.'

I rose up, however, and pinched the bath first, drinking the orange juice as I went. Count your blessings, I said to myself, soaping. Count Cassandra Morris, a better girl than I'd ever had before; seven months bedded, growing more essential every day. Count the sort of job that no one could expect to be given at twenty-nine. Count enough money, for once, to buy a car that wasn't everyone's cast-off held together by rust and luck.

The old ache to be a jockey was pretty well dead, but I supposed there would always be regret. It wasn't as if I'd never ridden in races; I had, from sixteen to twenty, first as an amateur, then a professional, during which time I'd won eighty-four steeplechases, twenty-three hurdle races, and been wretchedly cursed by unstoppably lengthening body. At six foot one I'd broken my leg in a racing fall, been imprisoned in traction for three months, and grown two more inches in bed.

It had been practically the end. There *had* been very tall jump jockeys in the past, but I'd progressively found that even if I starved to the point of weakness I couldn't keep my weight reliably below eleven stone. Trainers began saying I was too tall, too heavy, sorry lad, and employing someone else. So at twenty I'd got myself a job as an assistant trainer, and at twenty-three I'd worked for a bloodstock agent, and at twenty-six on a stud farm, which kept me off the race-course too much. At twenty-seven I'd been employed in a sort of hospital for sick racehorses which went out of business because too many owners preferred to shoot their liabilities, and after that there had been a spell of selling horse cubes, and then a few months in the office of a bloodstock auctioneer, which had paid well but bored me to death; and each time between jobs I'd spent the proceeds of the last one in wandering round the world, drifting homewards when the cash ran out and casting around for a new berth.

It had been at one of the points of no prospects that Jonathan had sent the cable.

'Catch the next flight. Good job in English racing possible if you interview here immediately. Jonathan.'

I'd turned up on his Californian doorstep sixteen hours later and early the next morning he had sent me off to see 'a man I met at a party'. A man, it transpired, of middle height, middle years and middling grey hair: a man I knew instantly by sight. Everyone in racing, worldwide, knew him by sight. He ran his racing as a big business, taking his profits in the shape of bloodstock, selling his stallions for up to a hundred times more than they'd earned on the track.

'Luke Houston,' he said neutrally, extending his hand.

'Yes, sir,' I said, retrieving some breath. 'Er ... William Derry.'

He offered me breakfast on a balcony overlooking the Pacific, eating grapefruit and boiled eggs and giving me smiling genial glances which were basically as casual as X-rays.

'Warrington Marsh, my racing manager in England, had a stroke four days ago,' he said. 'Poor guy, he's doing well – I have bulletins every a.m. – but it is going to be some time, a long time, I'm afraid, before he'll be active again.' He gestured to my untouched breakfast. 'Eat your toast.'

'Yes, sir.'

'Tell me why I should give you his job. Temporarily, of course.'

Good grief, I thought. I hadn't the experience or the connections of the stricken revered maestro. 'I'd work hard,' I said.

'You know what it entails?'

'I've seen Warrington Marsh everywhere, on the racecourse, at the sales. I know what he does, but not the extent of his authority.'

He cracked his second egg. 'Your brother says you've gotten a lot of general know-how. Tell me about it.'

I listed the jobs, none of which sounded any more impressive than they had in fact been.

He said, 'College degrees?' pleasantly.

'No, I left school at seventeen, and didn't go to university.'

'Private income?' he said. 'Any?'

'My godfather left some money for my schooling. There's still enough for food and clothes. Not enough to live on.'

He drank some coffee and hospitably poured me a second cup.

'Do you know which trainers I have horses with in the British Isles?'

'Yes, sir. Shell, Thompson, Miller, and Sandlache in England and Donavan in Ireland.'

'Call me Luke,' he said. 'I prefer it.'

'Luke,' I said.

He stirred sweetener into his coffee.

'Could you handle the finance?' he said. 'Warrington always has full responsibility. Do millions frighten you?'

I looked out at the vast blue ocean and told the truth. 'I think they do in a way, yes. It's too easy in the upper reaches to think of a nought or two as not mattering one way or another.'

'You need to spend to buy good horses,' he said. 'Could you do it?'

'Yes.'

'Go on,' he said mildly.

'Buying potentially good horses isn't the problem. Looking at a great yearling, seeing it move, knowing its breeding is as near perfect as you can predict, and being able to afford it, that's almost easy. It's picking the excellent from among the second rank and the unknowns, that's where the judgment comes in.'

'Could you guarantee that every horse you bought for me, or advised my trainers to buy, would win?'

'No, I couldn't,' I said. 'They wouldn't.'

'What percentage would you expect to win?'

'About fifty per cent. Some would never race, others would disappoint.'

He unaggressively, quietly, slowly and without pressure asked me questions for almost an hour, sorting out what I'd done, what I knew, how I felt about taking ultimate powers of decision over trainers who were older than myself, how I felt about dealing with the racing authorities, what I'd learnt about book-keeping, banking and money markets, whether I could evaluate veterinarian and nutritive advice. By the end I felt inside out; as if no cranny of my mind stayed gently unprobed. He would choose someone older, I thought.

'How do you feel,' he said finally, 'about a steady job, nine to five, weekends off, pension at the end of it?'

I shook my head from deep instinct, without thinking it out. 'No,' I said.

'That came from the heart, fella,' he observed.

'Well . . .'

'I'll give you a year and a ceiling beyond which you're not to spend. I'll be looking over your shoulder, but I won't interfere unless you get in a fix. Want to take it?'

I drew a deep breath and said, 'Yes.'

He leaned smilingly forward to shake my hand. 'I'll send you a contract,' he said, 'but go right on home now and take over at once. Things can fall apart too fast with no one in charge. So you go straight to Warrington's house, see his wife Nonie, I'll call her you're coming, and you operate from the office he's gotten there until you find a place of your own. Your brother told me you're a wanderer, but I don't mind that.' He smiled again. 'Never did like tame cats.'

Like so much else in American life the contract, when it swiftly followed me over the Pond, was in complete contrast to the relaxed approach of the man who offered it. It set out in precise terms what I must do, what I had discretion to do, what I must not do. It stated terms of reference I'd never have thought of. He had given me a great deal of freedom in some ways and none at all in others; but that, I supposed, was fair enough. He wouldn't want to stake his whole British operation on an unknown factor without enforceable safeguards. I took it to a solicitor who read it and whistled and said it had been drawn up by corporation lawyers who were used to munching managers as snacks.

'But do I sign it?' I said.

'If you want the job, yes. It's tough, but as far as I can see, fair.'

That had been eight months ago. I had come home to widespread and understandable disbelief that such a plum should have fallen my way. I had survived Nonie Marsh's resentment and Warrington's incoherent unhelpfulness; had sold several of Luke's unpromising two-year-olds without great loss, had cajoled the trainers into provisionally accepting me and done nothing sweat-makingly disastrous. Despite all the decisions and responsibility, I'd enjoyed every minute.

Cassie appeared in the doorway.

'Aren't you going to get out of that bath?' she demanded. 'Just sitting there smiling.'

'Life's good.'

'And you'll be late.'

I stood up in the water and as she watched me straighten she said automatically, 'Mind your head.' I stepped out onto the floor, and kissed her, dripping down her neck.

'For God's sake, get dressed,' she said. 'And you need a shave.' She gave me a towel. 'The coffee's hot, and we're out of milk.'

I flung on a few clothes and went downstairs, dodging beams and low doorways on the way. The cottage we'd rented in the village of Six Mile Bottom (roughly six miles south of Newmarket) had been designed for seventeenth-century man, who hadn't suffered the dietetic know-how of the twentieth. And would seven feet, I wondered, ducking into the kitchen, be considered normal in the twenty-fifth?

We had lived in the cottage all summer and in spite of its low ceilings it suited us fine. There were apples now in the garden, and mists in the mornings, and sleepy wasps trying to find warm cracks in the eaves. Red tiled floors and rugs downstairs, dining-room surrendered to office, sitting-room cosy round an as yet untried hearth; red-checked curtains, rocking chairs, corn dollies and soft lights. A townspeople's country toy, but enough, I sometimes thought, to make one want to put down roots.

Bananas Frisby had found it for us. Bananas, long-time friend, who kept a pub in the village. I'd called in there one day on my way back to Newmarket and told him I was stuck for somewhere to live.

'What's wrong with your old boat?'

'I've grown out of it.'

He gave me a slow glance. 'Mentally?'

'Yeah. I've sold it. And I've met a girl.'

'And this one,' he suggested, 'isn't ecstatic about rubbing down dead varnish?'

'Far from.'

'I'll keep it in mind,' he said, and indeed he called me a week later at Warrington's house and said there was a tarted-up cottage down the road from him that I could go and look at: the London-based owners didn't want to sell but could do with some cash, and they'd be willing to let it to someone who wouldn't stay for ever.

'I told them you'd the wanderlust of an albatross,' he said. 'I know them, they're nice people, don't let me down.'

Bananas personally owned his almost equally old pub, which was very slowly crumbling under his policy of neglect. Bananas had no family, no heirs, no incentive to preserve his worldly goods; so when each new patch of damp appeared inside his walls he bought a luxurious green potted plant to hide it. Since I'd known him, the shiny-leafed camouflage had multiplied from three to eight: and there was a vine climbing now through the windows. If anyone ever remarked about the dark patches on the walls, Bananas said the plants had caused them, and strangers never realised it was the other way round.

Bananas' main pride and joy was the small restaurant, next door to the bar, in which he served *cuisine minceur* of such perfection that half the passing jockeys of England ate there religiously. It had been over his dried, crisp, indescribable roast duck that I'd first met him, and like a mark well hooked had become an addict. Couldn't count the *délices* I'd paid for since.

He was already up as usual when I waved to him on my way to the gallops: sweeping out, cleaning up, opening his windows wide to get rid of the overnight fug. A fat man himself, he nonetheless had infinite energy, and ran the whole place with the help of two women, one in the bar and one in the kitchen, both of whom he bossed around like a feudal lord. Betty in the kitchen cooked stolidly under his eagle eye and Bessie in the bar served drinks with speed bordering on sleight-of-hand. Bananas was head-waiter and every other sort of waiter, collecting orders, delivering food, presenting bills, cleaning and relaying tables, all with a deceptive show of having all day to chat. I'd watched him at it so often that I knew his system; he practically never wasted time by going into the kitchen. Food appeared from Betty through a vast serving hatch shielded from the public view, and dirty dishes disappeared down a gentle slide.

'Who washes up?' I'd said once in puzzlement.

'I do,' Bananas said. 'After closing time I feed it all through the washer.'

'Don't you ever sleep?'

'Sleep's boring.'

He needed, it seemed, only four hours a night.

'And why work so hard? Why not have more help?'

He looked at me pityingly. 'Staff cause as much work as they do,' he said. And I'd found out later that he closed the restaurant every year towards the end of November and took off to the West Indies, returning in late March when the Flat racing stirred back to life.

He hated the cold, he said: worked at a gallop for eight months for four months' palm trees and sun.

That morning on the Limekilns, Simpson Shell was working his best young prospect and looking smug. The eldest of Luke Houston's five trainers, he had been resigned to me least and still had hang-ups which showed on his face every day.

'Morning, William,' he said, frowning.

'Morning, Sim.' I watched him with the rangy colt upon whom the Houston hope of a classic next season was faintly pinned. 'He's moving well,' I said.

'He always does.' The voice was slighting and impatient. I smiled to myself. Neither compliments nor soft soap, he was saying, were going to change his opinion of the upstart who had overruled him in the matter of selling two two-year-olds. He had told me he disagreed strongly with my weeding-out policy, even though I'd put it to him beforehand and discussed every dud to be discarded. 'Warrington never did that,' he'd thundered, and he'd warned me he was writing to Luke to complain.

I never heard the result. Either he'd never written or Luke had backed me up; but it had consolidated his Derry-wards hostility, not least because although I had saved Luke Houston a stack of pointless training fees I had at the same time deprived Simpson Shell. He was waiting, I knew, for the duds to win for their new owners so that he could crow, and it was my good luck that so far they hadn't.

Like all Luke's trainers, he trained for many other owners besides. Luke's horses at present constituted about a sixth of his string, which was too high a percentage for him to risk losing them altogether: so he was civil to me, but only just.

I asked him about a filly who had had some heat in her leg the previous evening, and he grumpily said it was better. He hated me to take a close interest in his eight Houston horses, yet I guessed that if I didn't, another letter would be winging to California complaining that I was neglecting my duties. Sim Shell, I thought ruefully, couldn't be pleased.

Over in the Bury Road, Mort Miller, younger, neurotic, fingers snapping like firecrackers, told me that Luke's ten darlings were eating well and climbing the walls with eagerness to slaughter the opposition. Mort had considered the sale of three no-gooders a relief, saying he hated the lazy so-and-sos and grudged them their oats. Mort's horses were always as strung up as he was, but they certainly won when it mattered.

I dropped in on Mort most days because it was he, for all his positive statements, who in fact asked my opinion most.

Once a week, usually fitting in with race meetings, I visited the other two trainers, Thompson and Sandlache, who lived thirty miles from each other on the Berkshire Downs, and about once a month I spent a couple of days with Donavan in Ireland. With them all, I had satisfactory working arrangements, they on their part admitting that the two-year-olds I'd got rid of were of no benefit to themselves, and I promising that I would spend the money I'd saved on the training fees on extra yearlings in October.

I would be sorry, I thought, when my year was over.

Driving home from Mort's, I stopped in the town to collect a radio I'd been having repaired, and again to fill up with petrol, and again at Bananas's pub to pick up some beer.

Bananas was in the kitchen prodding some marinating veal. Opening time still lay an hour ahead. Everything in the place was gleaming and fresh and the plants grew damply in their pots.

'There was a fellow looking for you,' Bananas said.

'What sort of fellow?'

'Big man. Didn't know him. I told him where your cottage was.' He scowled at Betty, who was obliviously peeling grapes. 'I told him you were out.'

'Did he say what he wanted?'

'Nope.'

He shed an apron and took his bulk into the bar. 'Too early for you?' he said, easing behind the counter.

'Sort of.'

He nodded and methodically assembled his usual breakfast; a third of a tumbler of brandy topped up with two scoops of vanilla-walnut ice cream.

'Cassie went off to work,' he said, reaching for a spoon.

'You don't miss much.'

He shrugged. 'You can see that yellow car a mile off, and I was out front cleaning the windows.' He stirred the ice cream into the brandy and with gourmand enjoyment shovelled the first instalment into his mouth. 'That's better,' he said.

'It's no wonder you're fat.'

He merely nodded. He didn't care. He told me once that his size made his fat customers feel better and spend more, and that his fat customers in search of a miracle outnumbered the thin.

He was a natural eccentric, himself seeing nothing unusual in anything he did. In various late-night sessions, he'd unbuttoned a little of his inner self, and under the surface geniality I'd had glimpses of a deep pessimism, a moroseness which looked with despair at the inability of the human race to live harmoniously on the beautiful earth. He had no politics, no god, no urge to agitate. People, he said, were known to starve on rich fertile tropical earth; people stole their neighbours' lands; people murdered people from racial hate; people tortured and murdered in the name of freedom. It sickened him, he said. It had been going on from pre-history, and it would go on until the vindictive ape was wiped out.

'But you yourself seem happy enough,' I'd once said.

He looked at me darkly. 'You're a bird. Always on the wing. You'd be a sparrowhawk if you hadn't such long legs.'

'And you?'

'The only option is suicide,' he said. 'But right now it's not necessary.' He'd deftly poured himself another brandy, and lifted the glass in a sort of salute. 'Here's to civilisation, damn it.'

His real fore-names, written over the pub doorway, were John James, but his nickname was a pudding. 'Bananas Frisby', a hot fluffy confection of eggs, rum, bananas and orange, was an item nearly always on his menu, and 'Bananas' he himself had become. It suited his outer persona well, but his inner, not at all.

'You know what?' he said.

'What?'

'I'm growing a beard.'

I looked at the faint shadow on the dark jaw. 'It needs compost,' I said.

'Very funny. The days of the big fat slob are over. What you see is the start of the big fat distinguished innkeeper.' He took a large spoonful of ice cream and drank some of the liquid as a chaser, wiping the resulting white moustache off on the back of his hand.

He wore his usual working clothes: open-necked shirt, creaseless grey flannels, old tennis shoes. Thinning dark hair scattered his scalp haphazardly, with one straight lock falling over an ear, and as Frisby in the evenings wasn't all that different from Frisby in the mornings I couldn't see a beard transforming the image. Particularly not, I thought interestedly, while it grew.

'Can you spare a tomato or two?' I said. 'Those Italian ones?'

'For your lunch?'

'Yeah.'

'Cassie doesn't feed you.'

'It's not her job.'

He shook his head over the waywardness of our domestic arrangements, but if he had had a wife I wondered which one of them would have cooked. I paid for the beer and the tomatoes, promised to bring Cassie to admire the whiskers, and drove home.

Life for me was good, as I'd told Cassie. Life at that moment was a long way from Bananas' world of horrors.

I parked in front of the cottage and walked up the path juggling radio, beer and tomatoes in one hand and fishing for keys with the other.

One doesn't expect people to leap out of nowhere waving baseball bats. I had merely a swift glimpse of him, turning my head towards the noise of his approach, seeing the solid figure, the savagery, the raised arm. I hadn't even the time to think incredulously that he was going to hit me before he did it.

The crashing blow on my moving head sent me dazed and headlong, shedding radio, beer cans, tomatoes on the way. I fell half on the path and half on a bed of pansies and lay in a pulsating semi-consciousness in which I could smell the earth but couldn't think.

Rough fingers twined themselves into my hair and pulled my head up from its face-down position. As if from a great distance away from my closed eyes a harsh deep voice spoke nonsensical words.

'You're not—' he said. '*Fuck it.*'

He dropped my head suddenly and the second small knock finished the job. I wasn't aware of it. In my conscious mind, things simply stopped happening.

The next thing that impinged was that someone was trying to lift me up, and that I was trying to stop him.

'All right, lie there,' said a voice. 'If that's how you feel.'

How I felt was like a shapeless form spinning in a lot of outer space. He tried again to pick me up and things inside the skull suddenly shook back into order.

'Bananas,' I said weakly, recognising him.

'Who else? What happened?'

I tried to stand up and staggered a bit, trampling a few more long-suffering pansies.

'Here,' Bananas said, catching me by the arm, 'come into the house.' He semi-supported me, and found the door was locked.

'Keys,' I mumbled.

'Where are they?'

I waved a vague arm, and he let go of me to look for them. I leant against the doorpost and throbbed. Bananas found the keys and came towards me and said in anxiety, 'You're covered in blood.'

I looked down at my red-stained shirt. Fingered the cloth. 'That blood's got pips in,' I said.

Bananas peered at my chest. 'Your lunch.' He sounded relieved. 'Come on.'

We went into the cottage where I collapsed into a chair and began to sympathise with migraine sufferers. Bananas searched in random cupboards and asked plaintively for the brandy.

'Can't you wait until you get home?' I said without criticism.

'It's for you.'

'None left.'

He didn't press it. He may have remembered that it had been he, a week ago, who'd emptied the bottle.

'Can you make tea?' I said.

He said resignedly, 'I suppose so,' and did.

While I drank the resulting nectar, he told me that he'd seen a car driving away from the direction of the cottage at about eighty miles an hour down the country road. It was the car, he said, of the man who'd asked for me earlier. He had been at first puzzled and then disquieted, and had finally decided to amble down to see if everything was all right.

'And there you were,' he said, 'looking like a pole-axed giraffe.'

'He hit me,' I said.

'You don't say.'

'With a baseball bat.'

'So you saw him,' Bananas said.

'Yeah. Just for a second.'

'Who was he?'

'No idea.' I drank some tea. 'Mugger.'

'How much did he take?'

I put down the tea and patted the hip pocket in which I carried a small notecase. The wallet was still there. I pulled it out and looked inside. Nothing much in there, but also nothing missing.

'Pointless,' I said. 'What did he want?'

'He asked for you,' Bananas said.

'So he did.' I shook my head which wasn't a good idea as it sent little daggers in all cranial directions. 'What exactly did he say?'

Bananas gave it some thought. 'As far as I can remember, he said, "Where does Derry live?" '

'Would you know him again?' I asked.

He pensively shook his head. 'I shouldn't think so. I mean, I've a general impression – not young, not old, roughish accent – but I was busy, I didn't pay all that much attention.'

Oddly enough, though I'd seen him for only a fraction of the time Bananas had, I had a much clearer recollection of my attacker. A freeze view, like a snapshot, standing framed in my mind. A thick-set man with yellowish skin, greyish about the head, intent eyes darkly shadowed. The blur on the edge of the snapshot was the downward slash of his arm. Whether the memory was reliable, or whether I'd know him again, I couldn't tell.

Bananas said, 'Are you all right to leave?'

'Sure.'

'Betty will finish those grapes and stare into space,' he said. 'The old cow's working to rule. That's what she says. Working to rule, I ask you. She doesn't belong to a union. She's invented her own bloody rules. At the moment rule number one is that she doesn't do anything I don't directly tell her to.'

'Why not?'

'More pay. She wants to buy a pony to ride on the Heath. She can't ride, and she's damn near sixty.'

'Go on back,' I said smiling. 'I'm OK.'

He semi-apologetically made for the door. 'There's always the doctor, if you're pushed.'

'I guess so.'

He opened the door and peered out into the garden. 'There are beer cans in your pansies.'

He went out saying he would pick them up, and I shoved myself off the chair and followed him. When I got to the door he was standing on the path holding three beer cans and a tomato and staring intently at the purple and yellow flowers.

'What is it?' I said.

'Your radio.'

'I've just had it fixed.'

He looked up at me. 'Too bad.'

Something in his tone made me totter down the path for a look. Sure enough, my radio lay in the pansies: what was left of it. Casing, dials, circuits, speaker, all had been comprehensively smashed.

'That's nasty,' Bananas said.

'Spite,' I agreed. 'And a baseball bat.'

'But *why*?'

'I think,' I said slowly, 'that maybe he thought I was someone else. After he'd hit me, he seemed surprised. I remember him swearing.'

'Violent temper,' said Bananas, looking at the radio.

'Mm.'

'Tell the police,' he said.

'Yeah.'

I took the beer from him and sketched a wave as he walked briskly up the road. Then I stared for a while at the shattered radio thinking slightly disturbing thoughts: like what would my head have looked like if he hadn't stopped after one swipe.

With a mental shiver, I went back indoors and applied my concussion to writing up my weekly report sheet for Luke Houston.

CHAPTER THIRTEEN

I never did get around to consulting the doctor or calling the police. I couldn't see anything productive coming from spending the time.

Cassie took the whole affair philosophically but said that my skull must be cracked if I didn't want to make love.

'Double ration tomorrow,' I said.

'You'll be lucky.'

I functioned on two cylinders throughout the next day and in the evening Jonathan rang, as he sometimes did, keeping a long-distance finger on little brother's pulse. He had never grown out of the *in loco parentis* habit and nor, to be honest, did I want him to. Jonathan, six thousand miles away, was still my anchor, my most trusted friend.

A pity about Sarah, of course. I would have seen more of Jonathan if I could have got on better with Sarah. She irritated me like an allergy rash with her bossiness and her sarcasm, and I'd never been able to please her. I'd thought at one time that their marriage was on the way to the cemetery and I hadn't grieved much, but somehow or other they'd retreated from the brink. She certainly seemed softer with Jonathan nowadays, but when I was around the old acid rose still in her voice, and I never stayed long in their house. Never staying long in one place was in fact, according to her, one of my least excusable faults. I ought to buckle down, she said, and get a proper job.

She was looking splendid these days, slender as a girl and tawny with the sun. Many, I supposed, seeing the fair hair, the good bones, the still tight jawline, the grace of movement, would have envied Jonathan his young-at-forty-five wife. And all, as far as I knew, without the plastic surgeon's knife.

'How's Sarah?' I said automatically. I'd been asking after her religiously most of my life, and not caring a jot. The truce she and I maintained for Jonathan's sake was fragile; a matter of social form, of empty politeness, of unfelt smiles, of asking after health.

'She's fine,' he said. 'Just fine.' His voice after all these years had taken on a faint inflection and many of the idioms of his adopted country. 'She sends you her best.'

'Thanks.'

'And you?' he said.

'Well enough considering some nutter hit me on the head.'

'What nutter?'

'Some guy who came here and lay in wait, and took a bash at me.'

'Are you all right?'

'Yeah. No worse than a racing fall.'

'Who was he?' he asked.

'No idea. He asked for directions from the pub, but he'd got the wrong man. Maybe he asked for Terry . . . it sounds much the same. Anyway, he blasted off when he found he'd made a slight error, so that's that.'

'And no harm done?' he asked insistently.

'Not to me, but you should see my radio.'

'What?'

'When he found I was the wrong guy, he took it out on my radio. I wasn't awake, mind you, at that point. But when I came round, there it was, smashed.'

There was a silence on the other end, and I said, 'Jonathan? Are you still there?'

'Yes,' he said. 'Did you see the man? What did he look like?'

I told him: fortyish, greyish, yellowish. 'Like a bull,' I said.

'Did he say anything?'

'Something about me not being who he expected, and fuck it.'

'How did you hear him if you were knocked out?'

I explained. 'But all that's left is a sore spot for the hair brush,' I said, 'so don't give it another thought.'

We talked about this and that for the rest of our

customary six minutes, and at the end he said, 'Will you be in tomorrow night?'

'Yes, I should think so.'

'I might call you back,' he said.

'OK.' I didn't bother to ask him why. He had a habit of not answering straightforward questions with straightforward answers if it didn't suit him, and his noncommittal announcement told me that this was one of those times.

We said amicable goodbyes and Cassie and I went to bed and renewed our normal occupation.

'Do you think we'll ever be tired of it?' she said.

'Ask me when we're eighty.'

'Eighty is impossible,' she said, and indeed it seemed so to us both.

Cassie went to Cambridge every day in her little yellow car to spend eight hours behind a building society desk discussing mortgages. Cassie's mind was full of terms like with-profits endowment and early redemption charges, and I thought it remarkable, sometimes, that she'd never suggested a twenty-five year millstone round my own neck.

I'd once before tried living with someone: nearly a year with a cuddly blonde who wanted marriage and nestlings. I'd felt stifled and gone off to South America and behaved abominably, according to her parents. But Cassie wasn't like that: if she wanted the same things she didn't say so, and maybe she realised, as I did, that I always came back to England, that the homing instinct was fairly strong. One day, I thought, one *distant* day . . . and maybe with Cassie . . . I might, just perhaps, and with all options open, buy a house.

One could always sell it again, after all.

Jonathan did telephone again the following evening, and came straight to the point.

'Do you,' he said, 'remember that summer when Peter Keithly got killed in his boat?'

'Of course, I do. One doesn't actually forget one's own brother being tangled up in a murder.'

'It's fourteen years ago,' he said doubtfully.

'Things that happen when you're fifteen stay sharp in your mind for ever.'

'I guess you're right. Anyway, you know who I mean by Angelo Gilbert.'

'The bumper-off,' I said.

'As you say. I think the man who hit you on the head may be Angelo Gilbert.'

A great one, my brother, for punching the air out. On a distinctly short breath I said, 'You sound very calm about it.' But then of course he would. He was always calm. In the scariest crisis it would be Jonathan who spoke and acted as if nothing unusual was happening. He'd carried me out of a fire once as a small child and I'd thought that somehow nothing was the matter, nothing was really wrong with the flames and the roaring and crashing all around us, because he'd looked down at me and smiled.

'I checked up,' he said. 'Angelo Gilbert got out of prison seventeen days ago, on parole.'

'Out—'

'It would take him a while to orientate himself and to find you. I mean, if it was him, he would have thought you were me.'

I sorted my way through that and said, 'What makes you think it was him?'

'Your radio, really. He seemed to enjoy destroying things like that. Televisions. Stereos. And he'd be forty now, and his father reminded me of a bull. What you said took me right back.'

'Good grief.'

'Yes.'

'You really think it was him?'

'I'm afraid it's possible.'

'Well,' I said, 'now that he knows he got the wrong guy, maybe he won't bother me again.'

'Monsters don't go away if you don't look at them.'

'What?'

'He may come back.'

'Thanks very much.'

'William, take it seriously. Angelo was dangerous in his twenties and it sounds as if he still is. He never did get the computer programs he killed for, and he didn't get them because of me. So take care.'

'It might not have been him.'

'Act as if it was.'

'Yeah,' I said. 'So long, Professor.' The wryness in my voice must have been plain to him.

'Keep off horses,' he said.

I put the receiver down ruefully. Horses, to him, meant extreme risk.

'What's the matter?' Cassie said. 'What did he say?'

'It's all a very long story.'

'Tell it.'

I told it on and off over the next few hours, remembering things in pieces and not always in the order they'd happened, much as Jonathan had told it to me all those years ago. Before going off to Canada to shoot he had collected me straight from school at the end of that summer term and we'd gone to Cornwall, just the two of us, for a few days' sailing. We'd had great holidays there two or three times before, but that year it blew a gale and poured with rain continuously, and to amuse me while we sat and stared through the dripping yacht club windows waiting for the improvement which never came, he'd told me about Mrs O'Rorke and Ted Pitts and the Gilberts, and how he'd stuck magnets in the cassettes. I'd been so fascinated that I hadn't minded missing the sailing.

I wasn't sure that I'd been shown every alley of the labyrinth; my quiet schoolmasterly brother had been reticent in patches and I'd always guessed that it was because probably in some way he'd used his guns. He never would let me touch them, and the only thing I ever knew him to be scared of was having his precious firearms certificate taken away.

'So there you are,' I said finally. 'Jonathan got Angelo tossed into clink. And now he's out.'

Cassie had listened with alternating alarm and amusement, but it was doubt that remained in the end.

'So what now?' she said.

'So now, if Angelo's on the rampage, hostilities may be resumed.'

'Oh no.'

'And there are certain disadvantages that Derry number two may have to contend with.' I ticked them off on my fingers. 'One, I can't shoot. Two, I know practically nothing about computers. And three, if Angelo's come charging out of jail intending to track down his lost crock of gold, I've no idea where it is or even if it still exists.'

She frowned. 'Do you think that's what he wants?'

'Wouldn't you?' I said gloomily. 'You spend fourteen years in a cell brooding over what you lost and dreaming of vengeance and yes, you're going to come out looking for both – and a small detail like having attacked the wrong man isn't going to put you off.'

'Come to bed,' Cassie said.

'I wonder if he thinks the way he used to.' I looked at her increasingly loved face. 'I don't want him busting in here to hold you hostage.'

'With no Jonathan to cut the telephone wires and send for the posse? Come to bed.'

'I wonder how he did it?'

'What?'

'Cut the wires. It isn't that easy.'

'Climbed the pole with a pair of scissors,' she said.

'You can't climb a pole. There aren't any footholds except at the top.'

'Why are you wondering about it after all these years? Come to bed.'

'Because of a bang on the head.'

She said, 'Are you really anxious?'

'Uneasy.'

'You must be. I've mentioned bed three times and you're still sitting down.'

I grinned at her and rose to my feet – and at that moment an almighty crash on the front door burst it open with splintering wood and a broken lock.

Angelo stood in the gap. Stood for less than a second regaining his balance from the kick which had brought him in, stood with the baseball bat swinging and his face rigid with ill intent.

Neither Cassie nor I had time to protest or yell. He waded straight in, laying about him, smashing anything near him, a lamp, some corn dollies, a vase, a picture . . . the television. Like a whirlwind demented, he devastated the pretty interior, and when I leapt at him I met a fist in the face and a fast knee which missed my groin, and I smelled his sweat and heard his breath rasp from exertion and took in what he was grittily saying: and it was just my name and Jonathan's, over and over.

'Derry – Derry – Fucking *Derry.*'

Cassie tried to help me, and he slashed at her with the heavy wooden bat and connected with her arm. I saw her stumble from the pain of it and in a fury I put one of my own arms round his neck and tried to yank his head back, to hurt him enough to make him drop his weapon and probably if the truth were told to throttle him. But he knew more about dirty fighting than I'd ever learned and it took him about two elbow jabs and a scrunching backhand jerk of my fingers to prise me loose. He shook me off with such force that I half fell, but still clung to his clothes with octopus tentacles, not wanting to be thrown clear so that he could get another swing with that bat.

We crashed around the broken room with me sticking to him with at least his equal ferocity and him struggling to get free; and it was Cassie, in the end, who finished it. Cassie who had grabbed the brass coal scuttle from the hearth by its shining handle and swung it in an arc at arm's length, aiming at Angelo's head. I saw the flash of its gleaming surface and felt the jolt through Angelo's body: and I let go of him as he fell in a sprawl on the carpet.

'Oh, God,' Cassie was saying. 'Oh, God.' There were tears on her face and she was holding her left arm away from her body in a way I knew all too well.

Angelo was visibly breathing. Stunned only. Soon to awake.

'Have to tie him,' I said breathlessly. 'What've we got?'

Cassie painfully said, 'Washing line,' and before I could stop her she'd vanished into the kitchen, returning almost at once with a new line still in its package. Wire wrapped in plastic, the bright label said. Strong enough, indeed, for a bull.

While I was still uncoiling it with unsteady fingers, there was the sound outside of someone thudding up the path and I had time for a feeling of absolute despair before I saw who it was.

Bananas came to the dark doorway with a rush and there stood stock still taking in the ravaged scene.

'I saw his car come back. I was just closing up . . .'

'Help me tie him,' I said, nodding at Angelo, who was stirring ominously. 'He did all this. He's coming round.'

Bananas turned Angelo onto his face and held his hands together behind his back while I built knots around the wrists, and then continued with the job himself, leading the line down from the wrists to join it to two more knots round the ankles.

'He's broken Cassie's arm,' I said.

Bananas looked at her and at me and at Angelo, and walked purposefully over to where the telephone stood miraculously undamaged on its little table.

'Wait,' I said. 'Wait.'

'But Cassie needs a doctor. And I'll get the police . . .'

'No,' I said, 'not yet.'

'But you must.'

I wiped my nose on the back of my hand and looked remotely at the resulting smear of blood. 'There's some pethidine and a syringe in the bathroom,' I said. 'It'll do a lot to stop Cassie hurting.'

He nodded in understanding and said he would fetch it.

'Bring the box marked "Emergency". It's on the shelf over the bath taps.'

While he went and came back with his ever-surprising speed, I helped Cassie to sit on a chair and to rest her left arm on a cushion which I put on the telephone table. It was the forearm, I found, which was broken: both bones, probably, from the numb uselessness of her hand.

'William,' she said whitely, 'don't. It hurts. Don't.'

'Darling . . . darling . . . It has to have support. Just let it lie there. Don't fight it.'

She did mutely what I said and looked paler than ever.

'I didn't feel it,' she said. 'Not like this . . . not at first.'

Bananas brought the emergency box and opened it. I tore the syringe out of its sterile package and filled it from the ampoule of pethidine. Pulled Cassie's skirt up high over the sun-browned legs and fed the muscle-relaxing pain-killer into the long muscle of her thigh.

'Ten minutes,' I said, pulling the needle out and rubbing the place with my knuckles. 'A lot of the pain will go. Then we'll be able to take you to the casualty department of Cambridge hospital to get it set. Nowhere nearer will be open at this time of night.'

She nodded slightly with the first twitch of a smile, and on the floor Angelo started trying to kick.

Bananas again walked towards the telephone and again I stopped him.

'But, William—'

I looked around at the jagged evidence of a passionate need for revenge; the explosion of fourteen years of pent-up hate.

I said, 'He did this because my brother got him jailed for murder. He's out on parole. If we call the police he'll be back inside.'

'Then, of *course*,' Bananas said, picking up the receiver.

'No,' I said. 'Put it down.'

He looked bewildered. Angelo on the floor began mumbling as if in delirium; a mixture of atrocious swear words and loud incomprehensible unfinished sentences.

'That's stir talk,' said Bananas, listening.

'You've heard it before?'

'You hear everything in the end in my trade.'

'Look,' I said. 'I get him sent back to jail and then

what happens? It wouldn't be so long next time before he was out, and he'd have a whole new furious grudge to avenge. And by that time he might have learned some sense and not come waving a piece of wood and going off half-cock, but wait until he'd managed to get a pistol, and sneak up on me one day three, four years from now, and finish me off. This . . .' I waved a hand, 'isn't an act of reason. I'm only Jonathan's brother. I myself did him no harm. This is anger against life. Blind, colossal, ungovernable rage. I can do without him focussing it all on me personally in the future.' I paused. 'I have to find a better . . . a final solution. If I can.'

'You can't mean . . .' Bananas said tentatively.

'What?'

'To . . . to . . . No, you couldn't.'

'Not that final solution, no. Though it's quite a thought. Cement wellingtons and a downwards trip in the North Sea.'

'Tankful of piranhas,' Cassie said.

Bananas looked at her with relief and almost laughed, and finally put the telephone receiver back in its cradle.

Angelo stopped mumbling and came fully awake. When he realised where he was and in what condition, the skin, which had until then been pale, became redly suffused: the face, the neck, even the hands. He rolled halfway over onto his back and filled the room with the intensity of his rage.

'If you start swearing,' I said, 'I'll gag you.'

With an effort he said nothing, and I looked at his face squarely and fully for the first time. There wasn't a great deal left of the man whose picture I had once pored over in a newspaper; not youth, not black hair, not narrow jaw, not long thin nose. Age, heredity, prison food, all had given him fatty deposits to blur the outlines of the head and bulk the body.

Average brains, Jonathan had said. Not clever. Relies on his frightening-power, and gets results from that. Despises everyone. Calls them creeps and mugs.

'Angelo Gilbert,' I said.

He jerked, and looked surprised, as if he had thought I wouldn't know him: and nor would I have, if Jonathan hadn't called.

'Let's get it straight,' I said. 'It was not my brother who sent you to prison. You did it to yourself.'

Cassie murmured, 'Criminals in jail are there voluntarily.'

Bananas looked at her in surprise.

'My arm feels better,' she said.

I stared down at Angelo. 'You chose jail when you shot Chris Norwood. Those fourteen years were your own fault, so why take it out on *me*?'

It made no impression. I hadn't really thought it would. Blaming one's troubles on someone else was average human nature.

Angelo said, 'Your fucking brother tricked me. He stole what was mine.'

'He stole nothing of yours.'

'He did.' The words were bass-voiced, fierce and positive, a growl in the throat. Cassie shivered at the menace Angelo could generate even tied up in ignominy on a cottage floor.

The crock of gold, I thought suddenly, might have its uses.

Angelo seemed to be struggling within himself but in the end the words tore out of him, furious, frustrated, still bursting with an anger that had nowhere to go. '*Where is he?*' he said. 'Where's your fucking brother? I can't find him.'

Saints alive . . .

'He's dead,' I said coldly.

Angelo didn't say whether or not he believed me but the news did nothing for his general temper. Bananas and Cassie displayed a certain stillness, but thankfully kept quiet.

I said to Bananas, 'Could you watch him for a minute while I make a phone call?'

'Hours if you like.'

'Are you all right?' I asked Cassie.

'That stuff's amazing.'

'Won't be long.' I picked the whole telephone off the table beside her and carried it into the office, closing the door as I went.

I called California, thinking that Jonathan would be anywhere but home, that I'd get Sarah, that it would be siesta time under the golden sun. But Jonathan was in, and he answered.

'I just had a thought,' I said. 'Those tapes that Angelo Gilbert wanted, have you still got them?'

'Good grief,' he said. 'I shouldn't think so.' A pause while he reflected. 'No, we cleared everything out when we left Twickenham. You remember, we sold the furniture and bought new out here. I got rid of pretty well everything. Except the guns, of course.'

'Did you throw the tapes away?'

'Um,' he said. 'There was a set I sent to Mrs O'Rorke and got back again. Oh yes, I gave them to Ted Pitts. If anyone still has them it would be Ted. But I shouldn't think they'd be much use after all these years.'

'The tapes themselves, or the betting system?'

'The system. It must be long out of date.'

It wouldn't matter too much, I thought.

'There are a lot of computer programs out here now for helping you win on horses,' Jonathan said. 'Some of them work, they say.'

'You haven't tried them?'

'I'm not a gambler.'

'Oh yeah?'

'What do you want the tapes for?' he said.

'To tie Angelo up in knots again.'

'Take care.'

'Sure. Where would I find Ted Pitts?'

He told me doubtfully to try the East Middlesex

Comprehensive, where they'd both been teaching, but said it was unlikely he was still there. They hadn't been in touch with each other at all since he'd emigrated. Perhaps I could trace Ted through the Schoolmasters Union, who might have his address.

I thanked him and disconnected, and went back into the sitting-room, where everyone looked much as I'd left them.

'I have a problem,' I said to Bananas.

'Just one?'

'Time.'

'Ah. The essence.'

'Mm.' I stared at Angelo. 'There's a cellar under this cottage.'

Angelo had no fear: one had to give him that. I could see quite clearly that he understood I meant not to let him go, yet his only reaction was aggressive and set him struggling violently against the washing line.

'Watch him,' I said to Bananas. 'There's some stuff in the cellar. I'm going to clear it out. If he looks like getting free, give him another bash on the head.'

Bananas looked at me as if he'd never seen me before; and perhaps he hadn't. I put a quick apologetic hand on Cassie's shoulder as I went, and in the kitchen opened the latched wooden door which led to the steps to the cellar.

Down there it was cool and dry: a brick-lined room with a concrete floor and a single light bulb swinging from the ceiling. When we had come to the cottage we had found the garden chairs stacked in there, but they were now outside on the grass, leaving only oddments like a paraffin stove, some tins of paint, a step-ladder and a stack of fishing gear. I carried everything in relays up the steps and dumped it all in the kitchen.

When I'd finished there was nothing in the cellar to help a captive; yet I would still have to keep him tied because of the nature of the lockless door. It was made simply of upright planks with bracing bars across the top, centre and bottom, the whole screwed together with the screwheads thankfully on the kitchen side. Across near the top there were six thumbsized holes, presumably for ventilation. A good enough barrier against most contingencies, but not to be trusted to withstand the sort of kick with which the enemy had battered his initial way in.

'Right,' I said, going back into the sitting-room. 'Now you, Angelo, are going into the cellar. Your only alternative is an immediate return to jail, as all this . . .' I indicated the room ' . . . and that . . .' Cassie's arm ' . . . will cancel your parole and send you straight back behind bars.'

'You bloody can't,' he said furiously.

'I bloody can. You started this. You damn well take the consequences.'

'I'll get you *busted*.'

'Yeah. You try it. You got it wrong, Angelo. I'm not my brother. He was clever and wily and he tricked you silly, but he would never use physical force; and I will, you mug, I will.'

Angelo used words that made Bananas wince and glance apprehensively at Cassie.

'I've heard them before,' she said.

'You've a choice, Angelo,' I said. 'Either you let my friend and me carry you carefully down the steps without struggling, or you struggle and I pull you down by the legs.'

The loss of face in not struggling proved too much. He tried to bite me as I bent down to put my arms under his armpits, so I did what I'd said; grasped the line tying his ankles and dragged him feet foremost out of the sitting-room, through the kitchen and down the cellar steps, with him yelling and swearing the whole way.

CHAPTER FOURTEEN

I tugged him well away from the stairs, let go of his legs and returned to the kitchen. He shouted after me blasphemously and I could still hear him when the door was shut. Let him get on with it, I thought callously; but I left on the single light, whose switch was outside on the kitchen wall.

I wedged the latch shut by sliding a knife handle through the slot, and for good measure stacked the step-ladder, the table and a couple of chairs into a solid line between the refrigerator and the cellar door, making it impossible for it to open normally into the kitchen.

In the sitting-room and without hustling, I said, 'OK. Decision time, mates.' I looked at Bananas. 'It's not your fight. If you'd rather, you can go back to your dishwashing and forget this ever happened.'

He looked resignedly round the room. 'I promised you'd leave this place as you found it. Practically pledged my soul.'

'I'll replace what I can. Pay for the rest. And grovel. Will that do?'

'You can't manage that brute on your own.' He shook his head. 'How long do you mean to keep him?'

'Until I find a man called Pitts.' I explained to him and Cassie what I wanted to do and why, and Bananas sighed and said it seemed fairly sensible in the circs, and that he would help where he could.

We shoe-horned Cassie gently into my car and I drove her to Cambridge while Bananas in his effective way set himself to tidy the sitting-room. There wasn't a great deal one could do at that point about the splintered and unclosable front door, and he promised to stay in the cottage until we got back.

In the event it was only I who returned. I sat with Cassie through the long wait in the silent hospital while they tried to find someone to X-ray her arm, but it seemed that after midnight the radiology department was firmly shut, with all the radiologists asleep in their own homes, and only the direst surgical emergency would recall them.

Cassie was given a careful splint from shoulder to fingernails and also another pain-killer and a bed: and when I kissed her and left she said, 'Don't forget to feed the bull,' which the nurses put down to drug-induced light-headedness.

Bananas was asleep when I got back, flat out on the sofa and dreaming I dare say of palm trees. The mess I'd left behind was miraculously cleared with every broken fragment out of sight. There were many things missing but overall it looked more like a room the owners would recognise. Gratefully I went quietly into the kitchen and found my barricade altered and strengthened with four planks which had been lying in the garage, the door now wedged shut from top to bottom.

The light switch was up. Except for whatever dim rays were crawling through the ventilation holes, Angelo was lying in the dark.

Although I'd been quiet I'd woken Bananas, who was sitting up pinching the bridge of his nose and blinking heavy eyelids open and shut.

'All the pieces are in the garage,' he said. 'Not in the dustbin. I reckoned you might need them, one way or another.'

'You're great,' I said. 'Did Angelo try to get out?'

Bananas made a face. 'He's a horrible man, that.'

'You talked to him?'

'He was shouting through the door that you'd stopped his circulation by tying his wrists too tight. I went to see, but you hadn't, his fingers were pink. He was halfway up the stairs and he tried to knock me over. Tried to sweep my legs from under me and make me fall God knows what he thought it would achieve.'

'Probably to scare me into letting him go.'

Bananas scratched himself around the ribs. 'I came up into the kitchen and shut the door on him, and switched his light off, and he went on howling for ages about what he'd do to you when he got out.'

Keeping his courage up, I thought.

I looked at my watch. Five o'clock. Soon be light. Soon be Friday with all its problems. 'I guess,' I said yawning, 'that a couple of hours' shut-eye would do no harm.'

'And that one?' He jerked his head towards the kitchen.

'He won't suffocate.'

'You're a revelation to me,' Bananas said.

I grinned at him and I think he thought me as ruthless as our visitor. But he was wrong. I was fairly sure that Angelo that night had come back to kill, to finish off what he had earlier started, knowing by then who I was and not expecting a Cassie. I was soft compared with him.

Bananas walked home to his dishwasher and I took his place on the sofa, feeling the bedroom too far away out of touch. Despite the hectic night I went to sleep immediately and woke with mind-protesting reluctance to switch off the alarm clock at seven o'clock. The horses would be working on the Heath. Simpson Shell had set up a trial of two late-developing three-year-olds, and if I wasn't there to watch he'd be writing to Luke Houston to say I was a shirker . . . and I wanted anyway, Angelo or no Angelo, to see how those horses went.

I loved the Heath in the early mornings with the

manes blowing under the wide skies. My affection for horses was so deep and went back so far that I couldn't imagine life without them. They were a friendly foreign nation living in our land, letting their human neighbours tend them and feed them, accepting them as servants as much as masters. Fast, fascinating, essentially untamed, they were my landscape, my old shoes, the place to where my heart returned, as necessary to me as the sea to sailors.

Even on that morning they lifted my spirits and I watched the trial with a concentration Angelo couldn't disrupt. One of the three-year-olds finished most decisively fast and Simpson said with careful civility that he hoped I would report to Luke how well the colt was looking.

'I'll tell Luke you've done wonders with him. Remember how unbalanced he looked in May? He'll win next week, don't you think?'

He gave me the usual ambivalent stare, needing my approbation but hating it. I smiled internally and left him to drive the short distance to where Mort was directing his string.

'All OK?' I asked.

'Well, yes,' Mort said. 'Genotti's still shaping up well for the Leger.' He flicked his fingers six times rapidly. 'Can you come back to the house for breakfast? The Bungay filly is still not eating well, and I thought we might discuss what we could do. You sometimes have ideas. And there's Luke's bill. I want to explain one or two items before you query them.'

'Mort,' I interrupted him regretfully, 'could we postpone it for a day or two? Something's come up that I'll have to deal with first.'

'Oh? Oh.' He sounded put out, because I'd never refused him before. 'Are you sure?'

'Really sorry,' I said.

'I might see you this afternoon,' he said, fidgeting badly.

'Um, yes. Of course.'

He nodded with satisfaction and let me go with good grace, and I doubted whether I would in fact turn up on Newmarket racecourse for that day's programme, even though three of Luke's horses were running.

On my way through the town I stopped at a few shops which were open early and did some errands on my prisoner's account, buying food and one or two small comforts. Then I rocketed the six miles to the village and stopped first at the pub.

Bananas, looking entirely his usual self, had done the dishes, cleaned the bar, and put Betty's back up by saying she was too old to start learning to ride.

'The old cow's refusing to make the celery mousse for lunch. Working to her stupid rules.' He disgustedly assembled his breakfast, adding chopped ginger as a topping to the ice cream and pouring brandy lavishly over the lot. 'I went down to the cottage again. Not a peep from our friend.' He stirred his mixture with anticipation. 'You can't hear him from outside, however loud he yells. I found that out last night. You'll be all right if you keep any callers in the garden.'

'Thanks.'

'When I've finished this, I'll come and help you.'

'Great.'

I hadn't wanted to ask him, but I was most thankful for his offer. I drove on down to the cottage and unloaded all the shopping into the kitchen, and Bananas appeared in his tennis shoes while I was packing food into a carrier. He looked at the small heap of things I'd put ready by the door.

'Let's get it over,' he said. 'I'll carry this lot.'

I nodded. 'He'll be blinded at first by the light, so even if he's got himself free we should have the advantage.'

We began to remove the barricade from against the door, and when it would open satisfactorily I took the knife out of the latch, picked up the carrier, switched on the cellar light and went into the cage.

Angelo was lying face down in the middle of the floor, still trussed the way we'd left him: arms behind his back, white clothes line leading slackly between tied wrists and tied ankles.

'It's morning,' I said cheerfully.

Angelo barely moved. He said a few low words of which 'turd' was the only one distinguishable.

'I've brought you some food.' I dumped in one

corner the carrier bag which in fact contained two sliced loaves, several cartons of milk, some water in a plastic bottle, two large cooked chickens, some apples and a lot of various candy bars and chocolate. Bananas silently dumped his own load which consisted of a blanket, a cheap cushion, some paperback books and two disposal polystyrene chamber pots with lids.

'I'm not letting you out,' I said to Angelo, 'but I'll untie you.'

'Fuck you,' he said.

'Here's your watch.' I had slipped it off his wrist the evening before to make the tying easier. I took it out of my pocket and put it on the floor near his head. 'Lights out tonight at eleven,' I said.

It seemed prudent at that point to search Angelo's pockets, but all he was carrying was money. No knives, no matches, no keys: nothing to help him escape.

I nodded to Bananas and we both began to untie the knots, I the wrists, Bananas the ankles, but Angelo's struggles had so tightened our original work that it took time and effort to remove it. Once Angelo was free we coiled the line and retreated up the stairs, from where I watched him move stiffly into a kneeling position with his arms loose and not yet working properly.

The air in the cellar had seemed quite fresh. I closed the door and fixed the latch and Bananas restacked the barricade with methodical thoroughness.

'How much food did you give him?' he asked.

'Enough for two to four days. Depends on how fast he eats it.'

'He's used to being locked up, there's that about it.'

Bananas, I thought, was busy stifling remaining doubts. He shoved the four planks into place between the cellar door and the refrigerator, casually remarking that during the night he'd sawn the wood to fit.

'More secure that way,' he said. 'He'll not get out.'

'Hope you're right.'

Bananas stood back, hands on hips, to contemplate his handiwork, and indeed I was as sure as one could be that Angelo couldn't kick his way out, particularly as he would have to try it while standing on the stairs.

'His car must be here somewhere,' I said. 'I'll look for it after I've phoned the hospital.'

'You phone, I'll look,' Bananas said, and went on the errand.

Cassie, I was told, would be having her arm set under anaesthetic during the morning. I could collect her at six that evening if all went well.

'May I speak to her?'

'One moment.'

Her voice came slowly and sleepily onto the line. 'I'm pie-eyed with pre-med,' she said. 'How's our guest?'

'Happy as a kangaroo with blisters.'

'Hopping . . . mad?'

'That pre-med isn't working,' I said.

'Sure is. My body's floating but my brain's fizzing along in zillions of sparks. It's weird.'

'They say I can fetch you at six.'

'Don't . . . be late.'

'I might be,' I said.

'You don't love me.'

'Yeah.'

'Sweet William,' she said. 'A pretty flower.'

'Cassie, go to sleep.'

'Mm.'

She sounded infinitely drowsy. 'Goodbye,' I said, but I don't think she heard.

I telephoned next to her office, told her boss she'd fallen down the cellar steps and broken her arm, and that she'd probably be back at work sometime the next week.

'How irritating,' he said. 'Er . . . for her, of course.'

'Of course.'

Bananas came back as I was putting down the receiver and said that Angelo's car was parked harmlessly at the top of the lane where the hard surface petered out into muddy cart track. Angelo had left the keys in the ignition. Bananas dumped them on the table.

'Want anything, shout,' he said. I nodded gratefully and he padded off, a power-house in a suit of blubber.

I set about the task of finding Ted Pitts, telephoning first to Jonathan's old school, the East Middlesex Comprehensive. A female voice there crisply told me that no one of that name was presently on the staff, and that none of the present staff could help me as they were not there: the new term would not start for another week. The only master who had been teaching in the school fourteen years ago would be, she imagined, Mr Ralph Jenkins, assistant headmaster, but he had retired at the end of the summer term and in any case it would be unlikely that any of his past assistants would have kept in touch with him . . .

'Why not?' I asked curiously.

After the faintest of hesitations the voice said levelly, 'Mr Jenkins himself would have discouraged it.'

Or in other words, I thought, Mr Jenkins had been a cantankerous old bastard. I thanked her for as little as I had realistically expected and asked if she could tell me the address of the Schoolmasters Union.

'Do you want their number as well?'

'Yes please.'

She told me both, and I put through a call to their offices. Ted Pitts? Edward? I suppose so, I said. Could I wait? Yes, I could.

The answering voice, a man's this time, shortly told me that Edward Farley Pitts was no longer a member. He had resigned his membership five years previously. His last known address was still in Middlesex. Did I want it? Yes please, I said.

Again I was given a telephone number along with the address. Another female voice answered it, this time with music and children's voices loud in the background.

'What?' she said, 'I can't hear you.'

'Ted Pitts,' I shouted. 'Can you tell me where he lives?'

'You've got the wrong number.'

'He used to live in your house.'

'What? Wait a minute . . . shut up, you lousy kids. What did you say?'

'Ted Pitts . . .'

'Terry, shut off that bleeding stereo. Can't hear myself think. Shut it off. Go on, shut it off.'

The music suddenly stopped.

'What did you say?' she said again.

I explained that I wanted to find my lost friend, Ted Pitts.

'Guy with three daughters?'

'That's right.'

'We bought this house off of him. Terry, you knock Michelle's head on that wall one more time and I'll rattle your teeth. Where was I? Oh yes, Ted Pitts. He gave us an address to send things on to but it's years ago and I don't know where my husband put it.'

It was really important, I said.

'Well, if you hold on I'll look. Terry, *Terry*!' There was the sound of a slap and a child's wail. The joys of motherhood, I thought.

I held on for an age listening to the scrambled noise of the squabbling siblings, held on so long that

I thought she had forgotten all about me and simply left me off the hook, but in the end she did come back.

'Sorry I've been so long, but you can't put your hand on a thing in this house. Anyway, I've found where he moved to.'

'You're a doll,' I said, writing it down.

She laughed in a pleased fashion. 'Want to call round? I'm fed up to the teeth with these bloody kids.'

'School starts next week.'

'Thank the Lord.'

I disconnected and tried the number she had given me, but to this one there was no reply. Ten minutes later, again no reply.

I went to the kitchen. All quiet from the cellar. I ate some cornflakes, padded restlessly about and tried the number again.

Zilch.

There was something, I thought, looking at it, that I could immediately do about the front door. It wouldn't at the moment even fit into the frame, but given a chisel and some sandpaper . . . I fetched them from the tool-rack in the garage and reduced the sharply splintered patches to smooth edges, shutting the door finally by totally removing the broken lock. It looked all right from the outside but swung inward at a touch: and we had sweet but inquisitive neighbours who called sometimes to sell us honey.

I again dialled Ted Pitts's possible number. No reply.

Shrugging, I tugged a small chest of drawers across inside the front door and climbed out through the dining-room window. Drove down to the pub: told Bananas the way in.

'Do you expect *me*—?'

'Not really. Just in case.'

'Where are you going?' he asked.

I showed him the address. 'It's a chance.'

The address was in Mill Hill on the northern outskirts of London. I drove there with my mind resolutely on the traffic and not on Cassie, unconscious, and Angelo, captive. Crunching the car at that point could be the ultimate disaster.

The house, when I found it, proved to be a middle-sized detached affair in a street of trees and somnolence; and it was empty.

I went up the driveway and looked through the windows. Bare wall, bare floors, no curtains.

With sinking spirits I rang the bell of the house next door, and although it was clearly occupied there was no one in there either. I tried several more houses, but none of the people I spoke to knew anything more of Ted Pitts than yes, perhaps they had seen some girls going in and out, but of course with all the shrubs and trees one was shielded from one's neighbours, which meant, of course, that also one couldn't see them.

It was in one of the houses obliquely opposite, from where only a corner of the Pittses' front garden was visible, that in the end I found some help. The front door was opened a foot by a large woman in pink hair rollers with a pack of assorted small dogs roaming round her legs.

'If you're selling, I don't want it,' she said.

I exercised on her the story I had by then invented, saying that Ted Pitts was my brother, he'd sent me his new address but I'd lost it, and I wanted to get in touch with him urgently. After six repetitions, I almost believed it.

'I didn't know him,' she said, not opening the door any wider. 'He didn't live there long. I never even saw him, I don't think.'

'But, er, you noticed them move in . . . and out.'

'Walking the dogs, you see.' She looked fondly down at the pack. 'I go past there every day.'

'Do you remember how long ago they left?'

'It must be ages. Funny your brother didn't tell you. The house was for sale for weeks after they'd gone. It's only just been sold, as a matter of fact. I saw the agents taking the board down just last week.'

'You don't happen to remember,' I said carefully, 'the name of the agents?'

'Goodness,' she said. 'I must have walked past it a hundred times. Just let me think.' She stared at her pets, her brow wrinkled with concentration. I could still see only half of her body but I couldn't tell whether the forbidding angle of the door was designed to keep the dogs in or me out.

'Hunt bleach!' she exclaimed.

'What?'

'Hunt comma B L E A C H.' She spelled it out. 'The name of the agents. A yellow board with black lettering. You'll see it all over the place, if you look.'

I said fervently, 'Thank you very much.'

She nodded the pink rollers and shut herself in, and I drove around until I found a yellow board with Hunt, Bleach's local address: Broadway, Mill Hill.

The brother story brought its by now familiar crop of sympathetic and/or pitying looks, but finally gained results. A slightly sullen-looking girl said she thought the house had been handled by their Mr Jackman who was now away on his holidays.

'Could you look in the files?'

She took advice from various colleagues, who doubtfully agreed under my urging that perhaps in the circumstances she might. She went into an inner office, and I heard cabinet drawers begin to open and shut.

'Here you are, Mr Pitts,' she said, returning, and it took me a fraction to realise that of course I too would be Pitts. 'Ridge View, Oaklands Road.'

She didn't give me a town. I thought: he's still *here*.

'Could you tell me how to get there?' I said.

She shook her head unhelpfully, but one of the colleagues said, 'You go back up the Broadway, right round the roundabout until you're pointing towards London, then first left, up the hill, turn right, that's Oaklands Road.'

'Terrific.' I spoke with heartfelt relief which they

took as appropriate, and I followed their directions faithfully and found the house. It looked a small brown affair; brownish bricks, brown tiled roof, a narrow window each side of an oak front door, bushes screening much else. I parked in what seemed an oversized driveway outside a closed double garage, and doubtfully rang the doorbell.

There was no noise from inside the house. I listened to the distant hum of traffic and the nearer hum of bees round a tub of dark red flowers, and pressed the bell again.

No results. If I hadn't wanted to find Ted Pitts so much I would have given up and driven away at that point. It wasn't even the sort of road where one could enquire at a neighbour's: there were houses only on one side, with a steep wooded hillside rising on the other, and the houses themselves were far-spaced and reclusive, drawing themselves back from public view.

I rang a third time out of indecisiveness, thinking that I could wait, or come back, or leave a note begging Pitts to call me.

The door opened. A pleasant-looking girl-woman stood there; not young, not yet middle-aged, wearing a loosely flowing green sundress with broad straps over suntanned shoulders.

'Yes?' she said enquiringly. Dark curly hair, blue eyes, the brown glowing face of summer leisure.

'I'm looking for Ted Pitts,' I said.

'This is his house.'

'I've been trying to locate him. I'm the brother of an old friend of his. A friend he had years ago, I mean. Could I see him, do you think?'

'He isn't here at the moment.' She looked at me doubtfully. 'What's your brother's name?'

'Jonathan Derry.'

After the very slightest pause her face changed from watchfulness to welcome; a smile in remembrance of time past.

'Jonathan! We haven't heard from him for years.'

'Are you . . . Mrs Pitts?'

She nodded. 'Jane.' She opened the door wide and stepped back. 'Come in.'

'I'm William,' I said.

'Weren't you . . .' she frowned, 'away at school?'

'One does tend to grow.'

She looked up at me. 'I'd forgotten how long it was.' She led me across a cool dark hall. 'This way.'

We came to a wide stairway of shallow green-carpeted steps leading downwards, and I saw before me what had been totally invisible from the higher roadway, that the house was large, ultra-modern, built into the side of the hill and absolutely stunning.

The stairs led directly down to a huge room whose ceiling was half-open to the sky and whose floor was partly green carpet and partly swimming pool. There were sofas and coffee tables nearest the stairs and lounging chairs, bamboo with pink, white and green cushions, dotting the far poolside, out in the sun; and on either side wings of house spread out protectively, promising bedrooms and comfort and a life of delight. I looked at the spectacular and pretty room and thought no schoolmaster on earth could afford it.

'I was sitting over there,' Jane Pitts said, pointing to the sunny side. 'I nearly didn't answer the doorbell. I don't always bother.'

We walked around there, passing white trellised alcoves filled with plants and cushioned bamboo sofas with bathing towels casually thrown down. The pool water looked sea-green and peaceful, gleaming and inviting after my trudging search.

'Two of the girls are around somewhere,' Jane said. 'Melanie, our eldest, is married, of course. Ted and I will be grandparents quite soon.'

'Incredible.'

She smiled. 'We married at college.' She gestured to the chairs and I sat on the edge of one of the loungers while she spread out voluptuously on another. Beyond the house the lawn sloped grassily away to a wide sweeping view over northwest London, the horizon lost in misty purples and blues.

'This place is fantastic,' I said.

She nodded. 'We were so lucky to get it. We've only been here three months, but I think we'll stay for ever.' She pointed to the open roof. 'This all closes over, you know. There are solar panels that slide across. They say the house is warm all winter.'

I admired everything sincerely and asked if Ted

were still teaching. She said without strain that he sometimes taught University courses in computer programming and that unfortunately he wouldn't be home until quite late the following evening. He would be so sorry to have missed me, she said.

'I would quite urgently like to talk to him.'

She gently shook her head. 'I don't honestly know where he is, except somewhere up near Manchester. He went this morning, but he didn't know where he'd be staying. In a motel somewhere, he said.'

'What time would he be back tomorrow?'

'Late. I don't know.'

She looked at the concern which must have shown plainly on my face and said apologetically, 'You could come early on Sunday, if you like, if it's that important.'

CHAPTER FIFTEEN

Saturday crawled.

Cassie wandered around with her plastered arm in a sling and Bananas jogged down to the cottage three or four times, both of them worried by the delay and not saying so. It had seemed reasonable on Thursday night to incarcerate Angelo with his handiwork still appalling us in the sitting-room and Cassie in pain, but by Saturday evening she and Bananas had clearly progressed through reservations and uneasiness to downright anxiety.

'Let him go,' Bananas said when he came late after closing time. 'You'll be in real trouble if anyone finds out. He knows now that you're no pushover. He'd be too scared to come back.'

I shook my head. 'He's too arrogant to be scared. He'd want his revenge, and he'd come back to take it.'

They stared miserably at each other. 'Cheer up,' I said. 'I was ready to keep him for a week – two weeks – as long as it took.'

'I just don't know,' Bananas said, 'how you could calmly go to the races.'

I'd gone uncalmly to the races. Also to the gallops in the morning and to Mort's for breakfast, but no one I had seen could have guessed what was going on at home. Behind a public front I found it was fairly easy to hide an ongoing crime: hundreds of people did it, after all.

'I suppose he's still alive,' Cassie said.

'He was up by the door swearing at four o'clock.' Bananas looked at his watch. 'Nine and a half hours ago. I shouted at him to shut up.'

'And did he?'

'Just swore back.'

I smiled. 'He's not dead.'

As if to prove it Angelo started kicking the door and letting go with the increasingly familiar obscenities. I went into the kitchen and stood close to the barricade, and when he drew breath for the next verbal onslaught I said loudly, 'Angelo.'

There was a brief silence, then a fierce furious growling shout: '*Bastard*.'

'The light's going out in five minutes,' I said.

'I'll kill you.'

Maybe the heavily savage threat should have raised my goose bumps, but it didn't. He had been murderous too long, was murderous by nature, and I already knew it. I listened to his continuing rage and felt nothing.

'Five minutes,' I said again, and left him.

In the sitting-room Bananas was looking mildly piratical in his open-necked shirt and his sneakers and his four days' growth of harsh black beard, but he himself would never have made anyone walk the plank. The gloom and doom in his mind deplored what I was doing even while he condoned it, and I could almost sense him struggling anew with the old anomaly that to defeat aggression one might have to use it.

He sat on the sofa and in short order drank two stiff brandies with his arm round Cassie, who never minded. He was tired, he'd said, of us being out of his favourite tipple: he'd brought the bottle himself. 'Have some ice-cream with it?' Cassie had suggested, and he'd said seriously, 'What flavour?'

I gave Angelo his five minutes and switched off the light, and there was a baleful silence from the cellar.

Bananas gave Cassie a bristly kiss, said she looked tired, said every plate in the pub needed washing, said 'Barbados!' as a toast, and tossed back his drink. 'God rest all prisoners. Good night.'

Cassie and I watched his disappearing back. 'He's half sorry for Angelo,' she said.

'Mm. A fallacy always to think that because you feel sorry for the tiger in the zoo he won't eat you, given the chance. Angelo doesn't understand compassion. Not other people's for him. He feels none himself. In others he sees it as a weakness. So never, my darling, be kind to Angelo expecting kindness in return.'

She looked at me. 'You mean that as a warning, don't you?'

'You've a soft heart.'

She considered for a moment, then found a pencil and wrote a message to herself in large letters on the white plaster.

REMEMBER TIGERS.

'Will that do?'

I nodded. 'And if he says his appendix is bursting or he's suffering from bubonic plague feed him some aspirins through the ventilation holes, and do it in a roll of paper, and not with your fingers.'

'He hasn't thought of that yet.'

'Give him time.'

We went upstairs to bed but as on the previous night I slept only in brief disturbed snatches, attuned the whole time to any noise from the cellar. Cassie slept more peacefully than before, the cast becoming less of a problem as she grew used to it. Her arm no longer hurt, she said; she simply felt tired. She said play would be resumed when the climate got better.

I watched the dark sky lighten to streaks of navy-blue clouds across a sombre orange glow, a strange brooding dawn like the aura of the man downstairs. Never before, I thought, had I entered a comparable clash of wills; never tested so searchingly my willingness to command. I had never thought of myself as a leader, and yet, looking back, I'd never had much stomach to be led.

In recent months I had found it easier than I'd expected to deal with Luke's five trainers, the power seeming to develop as the need arose. The power to keep Angelo in the cellar, that too had arisen, not merely physically, but also in my mind. Perhaps one's capacity always expanded to meet the need: but what did one do when the need was gone? What did generals do with their full-grown hubris when the war was over? When the whole world no longer obeyed when they said jump?

I thought: unless one could adjust one's power-feelings perpetually to the current need, one could be headed for chronic dissatisfaction with the fall of fate. One could grow sour, power-hungry, despotic. I would shrink back, I thought, to the proper size, once Angelo was solved, once Luke's year was over. If one saw that one had to, perhaps one might.

The fierce sky slowly melted to mauve-grey clouds drifting over a sea of gold and lingeringly then to gentle white over palest blue, and I got up and dressed, thinking that the sky's message was false: the problems didn't fade with the sun and Cain was still downstairs.

Cassie's eyes, when I left, were saying all that her tongue wasn't. Hurry. Come back. I don't feel safe here with Angelo.

'Sit by the telephone,' I said. 'Bananas will run.'

She swallowed. I kissed her and drove away, burning up the empty Sunday-early roads to Mill Hill. It was still only eight-thirty when I turned into Oaklands

Road, the very earliest that Jane Pitts had said I could arrive, but she was already up and in a wet bathing dress to answer the doorbell.

'Come in,' she said. 'We're in the pool.'

'We' were two lithely beautiful teenage girls and a stringy man going bald who swam without splashing, like a seal. The roof was open to the fair sky and a waiting breakfast of cereals and fruit stood ready on one of the low bamboo tables, and none of the Pittses seemed to mind or notice that the new day was still cool.

The stringy man slithered out onto the pool's edge in a sleek economical movement and stood shaking the water from his head and looking approximately in my direction.

'I'm Ted Pitts,' he said, holding out a wet hand. 'I can't see a damn thing without my glasses.'

I shook the hand and smiled into the unfocussed eyes. Jane walked round with some heavy black frames which converted the brown fish into an ordinary short-sighted mortal, and he dripped round the pool beside me to where his towel lay on a lounging chair.

'William Derry?' he said, blotting water out of his ears.

'That's right.'

'How's Jonathan?'

'Sends his regards.'

Ted Pitts nodded, towelled his chest vigorously and

then stopped abruptly and said, 'It was you who told me where to get the form books.'

All those years ago . . . information so casually given. I glanced around the amazing house and asked the uppermost question. 'The betting system on those tapes,' I said. 'Did it really work?'

Ted Pitts's smile was of comprehensive contentment. 'What do you think?' he said.

'All this—'

'All this.'

'I never believed in it,' I said, 'until I came here the other day.'

He towelled his back. 'It's fairly hard work, of course. I shunt around a good deal. But with this to come back to . . . most rewarding.'

'How long . . .' I said slowly.

'How long have I been gambling? Ever since Jonathan gave me the tapes. That first Derby . . . I borrowed a hundred quid with my car as security to raise some stake-money. It was madness, you know. I couldn't have afforded to lose. Sometimes in those days we had hardly enough to eat. It was pretty well desperation that made me do it, but of course the system looked mathematically OK and it had already worked for years for the man who invented it.'

'And you won?'

He nodded. 'Five hundred. A fortune. I'll never forget that day, never. I felt so sick.' He smiled vividly, the triumph still childlike in its simplicity. 'I didn't tell anybody. Not Jonathan. Not even Jane. I didn't mean to do it again, you see. I was so grateful it had turned out all right, but the *strain* . . .' He dropped the damp towel over the arm of a chair. 'And then, you know, I thought, why not?'

He watched his daughters dive into the pool with their arms round each other's waists. 'I only taught for one more term,' he said calmly. 'I couldn't stand the head of the Maths department. Jenkins, his name was.' He smiled. 'It seems odd now, but I felt oppressed by that man. Anyway, I promised myself that if I won enough during the summer holidays to buy a computer, I would leave at Christmas, and if I didn't, I'd stay and use the school's computer still, and be content with a wager now and then.'

Jane joined us, carrying a pot of coffee. 'He's telling you how he started betting? I thought he was crazy.'

'But not for long.'

She shook her head, smiling. 'When we moved out of our caravan into a house – bought it outright with Ted's winnings – then I began to believe it would last, that it was safe. And now here we are, so well off it's embarrassing, and it's all thanks to your dear brother Jonathan.'

The girls climbed dripping out of the pool and were introduced as Emma and Lucy, hungry for breakfast. I was offered bran flakes, natural yoghurt, wheat germ and fresh peaches, which they all ate sparingly but with enjoyment.

I ate as well, but thought inescapably of Angelo and of Cassie alone with him in the cottage. Those planks would hold . . . they'd kept him penned in for two whole days. No reason to think they'd fail this morning . . . no reason, just a strong feeling that I should have persuaded her to wait with Bananas.

It was over coffee, when the girls were again swimming and Jane had disappeared into the house, that Ted said, 'How did you find me?'

I looked at him. 'Don't you mean why?'

'I suppose so. Yes.'

'I came to ask you to let me have copies of those tapes.'

He breathed deeply and nodded. 'That's what I thought.'

'And will you?'

He looked at the shimmering pool for a while and then said, 'Does Jonathan know you're asking?'

'Yeah. I asked him where the tapes were now, and he said if anyone knew, you would. You and only you, he said.'

Ted Pitts nodded again and made up his mind. 'It's fair. They're his, really. But I haven't any spare tapes.'

'I brought some,' I said. 'They're out in the car. Can I fetch them?'

'All right.' He nodded decisively. 'I'll change into dry clothes while you're getting them.'

I fetched the computer-type tapes I'd brought for the purpose, and he said, 'Six? You'll only need three.'

'Two sets?' I suggested.

'Oh. Well, why not?' He turned away. 'The computer's downstairs. Would you like to see it?'

'Very much.'

He led the way into the body of the house and we went down some carpeted stairs to a lower floor. 'Office,' he said succinctly, leading the way into a normal-sized room from which one could see the same wide view of London as upstairs. 'It's a bedroom really. Bathroom through there,' he pointed. 'Spare bedroom beyond.'

The office was more accurately a sitting-room with armchairs, television, bookshelves and pinewood panelling. On an upright chair by one wall stood a pair of well-used mountain climbing boots, with the latest in thermal sleeping bags still half in its carton on the floor beside them. Ted followed my glance. 'I'm off to Switzerland in a week or two. Do you climb?'

I shook my head.

'I don't attempt the peaks,' he said earnestly. 'I prefer walking, mostly.' He pulled open a section of the pine panelling to reveal a long counter upon which stood a host of electronic equipment. 'I don't need all this for the racing programs,' he said, 'but I enjoy computers . . .' and he ran his fingers caressingly over the metal surfaces with the ardour of a lover.

'I've never seen those racing programs,' I said.

'Would you like to?'

'Please.'

'All right.' With the speed of long dexterity he fed a tape into a cassette recorder and explained he was putting the machine to search for the file 'Epsom'. 'How much do you know about computers?' he said.

'There was one at school, way back. We played "Space Invader" on it.'

He glanced at me pityingly. 'Everyone in this day and age should be able to write a simple program. Computer language is the universal tongue of the new world, as Latin was of the old.'

'Do you tell your students that?'

'Eh . . . yes.'

The small screen suddenly announced 'READY?' Ted pressed some keys on the keyboard and the screen asked 'WHICH RACE AT EPSOM?' Ted typed DERBY, and the screen in a flash presented:

EPSOM: THE DERBY.

NAME OF HORSE?

He put in his own name and randomly answered the ensuing questions, ending with:

TED PITTS. WIN FACTOR: 24

'Simple,' I said.

He nodded. 'The secret is in knowing which questions to ask, and in the weighting given to the answers. There's nothing mysterious about it. Anyone could evolve such a system, given the time.'

'Jonathan says there are several of them in the United States.'

Ted nodded. 'I've got one of them here.' He opened a drawer and brought out what looked like a pocket calculator. 'It's a baby computer with quite elegant programs,' he said. 'I bought it out of curiosity. It only works on American racing of course, because one of its bases is that all tracks are identical in shape, left-handed ovals. It is geared chiefly to prize money. I understand that if you stick to its instruction book religiously you can certainly win, but of course like Liam O'Rorke's system you have to work at it to get results.'

'And never back a hunch?'

'Absolutely not,' he said seriously. 'Hunches are hopelessly unscientific.'

I looked at him curiously. 'How often do you go to the races?'

'To the races themselves? Practically never. I watch them, of course, on television, sometimes. But you don't need to, to win. All you need are the form books and objectivity.'

It seemed to me a dry view of the world where I spent my life. Those beautiful creatures, their speed, their guts, their determination, all reduced to statistical probabilities and microchips.

'These copies of yours,' he said, 'do you want them open, so that anyone can use them?'

'How do you mean?'

'If you like, you can have them with passwords, so

that they wouldn't work if anyone stole them from you.'

'Are you serious?'

'Of course,' he said, as if he were never anything else. 'I've always put passwords on all my stuff.'

'Er, how do you do it?'

'Easiest thing in the world. I'll show you.' He flicked a few switches and the screen suddenly announced 'READY?'

'You see that question mark,' Ted said. 'A question mark always means that the computer operator must answer it by typing something. In this case, if you don't type in the correct sequence of letters the program will stop right there. Try it. See what happens.'

I obediently typed EPSOM. Ted pressed the key marked 'Enter'.

The screen gave a sort of flick and went straight back to 'READY?'

Ted smiled. 'The password on this tape is QUITE. Or it is at the moment. One can change the password easily.' He typed QUITE and pressed 'Enter' and the screen flashed into WHICH RACE AT EPSOM?

'See the question mark?' Ted said. 'It always needs an answer.'

I thought about question marks and said I'd better not have passwords, if he didn't mind.

'Whatever you say.'

He typed BREAK and LIST 10–80, and the screen suddenly produced a totally different-looking format.

'This is the program itself,' Ted said. 'See Line 10?'

Line 10 read INPUT A$: IF A$='QUITE' THEN 20 ELSE PRINT 'READY?'

Line 15 read GO TO END.

Line 20 read PRINT 'WHICH RACE AT EPSOM?'

'If you don't type QUITE,' Ted said, 'you never get to line 20.'

'Neat,' I agreed. 'But what's to prevent you looking at the program, like we are now, and seeing that you need to type QUITE?'

'It's quite easy to make it impossible for anyone to List the program. If you buy other people's programs, you can practically never List them. Because if you can't List them you can't make copies, and no one wants their work pinched in that way.'

'Um,' I said. 'I'd like tapes you *can* List, and without passwords.'

'OK.'

'How do you get rid of the password?'

He smiled faintly, typed 10 and then pressed 'Enter'. Then he typed LIST 10–80 again, but this time when the program appeared on the screen there was no Line 10 at all. Line 20 was the first.

'Elementary, you see,' he said.

'So it is.'

'It will take me quite a while to get rid of the passwords and make the copies,' he said. 'So why don't you go and sit by the pool. To be honest. I'd get on faster on my own.'

Pleased enough to agree, I returned to the lazy bamboo loungers and listened to Jane talking about her daughters. An hour crawled by before Ted reappeared bearing the cassettes, and even then I couldn't leave without an instructional lecture.

'To run those tapes, you'll need either an old Grantley personal computer, and there aren't many of them about nowadays, they're obsolete, or any type of company computer, as long as it will load from a cassette recorder.'

He watched my incomprehension and repeated what he'd said.

'Right,' I said.

He told me how to load Grantley BASIC, which was the first item on Side 1 of the tapes, into a company computer, which had no language of its own built in. He again told me twice.

'Right.'

'Good luck with them,' he said.

I thanked him wholeheartedly, and Jane also, and as quickly as decently possible set off on the drive home.

Half a mile down the road, compelled by a feeling of dread, I stopped by a telephone box and called Cassie. She answered at the very first ring and sounded uncharacteristically shaky.

'I'm so glad it's you,' she said. 'How long will you be?'

'About an hour.'

'Do hurry.'

'Is Angelo . . .?'

'He's been banging ever since you left and wrenching at the door. I've been in the kitchen. He's shaking those planks, he'll have the door off its hinges if he goes on and on. I can't strengthen the barricade. I've tried, but with one arm—'

'Cassie,' I said. 'Go up to the pub.'

'But—'

'Darling, go. Please do.'

'What if he gets out?'

'If he gets out I want you safe up the road with Bananas.'

'All right.'

'I'll see you,' I said, and disconnected. Drove like the furies towards home, taking a chance here and there and getting away with it. Across Royston Heath like a streak, weaving through pottering Sunday-outing traffic. Through the town itself; snarling down the last stretch crossing the M11 motorway, and finally branching off the main road into Six Mile Bottom village.

Wondering all the way what Angelo would do if he did get free. Smash up the cottage? Set fire to it? Lie in wait somewhere for me to return?

The one thing he would not do was to go meekly away.

CHAPTER SIXTEEN

I walked carefully up the path to the lockless front door which we now no longer guarded with the chest because Cassie found climbing through the window too difficult.

The birds were singing in the garden. Would they sing if Angelo were among them, hidden in the bushes? No they wouldn't. I reached the door and pushed it open.

The cottage lay silent as if long deserted, and with spirits sinking I went through to the kitchen.

Angelo had ripped away one of the main timbers of the door and had dislodged two of the extra planks which had been wedging it shut. The door in fact was still closed, but the knife had gone from the latch.

The hole in the door was large enough to shove an arm through, but not to allow the passage of a grown man. The table and chairs and the two lowest planks hadn't shifted, but with the progress he'd made their stopping power was temporary. I had come not a minute too soon.

'Angelo,' I said.

He appeared almost instantly at the hole in the door, scowling furiously at my return. He put both hands into the gap and violently tried to wrench away the wood from each side, and I saw that he had already been bleeding from his exertions.

'I'm going to let you out,' I said. 'You can save your strength.'

'I'll get you.' The deep growl again. The statement of intent.

'Yeah,' I said. 'I dare say. Now listen, because you'll want to hear.'

He waited, eyes black with ferocity in the shadows.

I said, 'You believe that my brother cheated you out of some computer tapes. They weren't yours to start with, but we'll not argue about that. At this moment *I* have those tapes. They're here in the cottage. It's taken me a good while to get them, which is why you've stayed here this long in the cellar. I'll give you those tapes. Are you listening?'

He wouldn't say so, but his attention was riveted.

'You spent fourteen years brooding over the fortune you lost. I'll give it to you. Fourteen years swearing to kill my brother. He's dead. You came here to do violent damage, and for that you could lose your parole. I'm prepared not to report you. In return for the computer tapes and for your continued freedom you can clear out of here and henceforward leave me strictly alone.'

He stared through the door with little change of expression; certainly without joy.

I said, 'You may have been brooding over your revenge for so many years that you can't face not having the prospect of it there any longer to keep you going. You may fall apart from lack of purpose.' I shrugged. 'But *if* I give you liberty and the treasure you want, I'll expect the slate to be wiped clean between you and me.' I paused. 'Do you understand?'

He still said absolutely nothing.

'If you agree that what I'm offering is OK,' I said, 'you can throw out that knife you took from the door latch, and I will give you the three tapes and the keys to your car, which is still where you left it.'

Silence.

'If you choose not to accept that offer,' I said, 'I'll telephone to the police to come and fetch you, and they'll hear about you breaking my friend's arm.'

'They'll have you for keeping me in here.'

'Maybe. But if they do, you'll never get those tapes. And I mean it. *Never*. I'll destroy them immediately.'

He went away from behind the door but after a long minute he reappeared.

'You'll trick me,' he said. 'Like your brother.'

I shook my head. 'It's not worth it. I want you out of my life altogether and permanently.'

He made a fierce thrusting movement with his unshaven chin, a gesture which could be taken as assent.

'All right, then,' he said. 'Hand them over.'

I nodded. Turned away from him. Went into the sitting-room and sorted out one copy of each tape, shutting the three spares into a chest drawer. When I returned Angelo was still standing by the door; still suspicious, still wary.

'Tapes.' I showed him. 'Car keys.' I held them up. 'Where's the knife?'

He raised his hand and let me see it: a dinner knife, not very sharp, but destructive enough to be counted.

I laid the three cassettes on a small tray and held it out to him, and he put his arm through the hole to snatch them up.

'Now the knife,' I said.

He dropped it out onto the tray. I slid it into my hand and replaced it with the keys.

'All right,' I said. 'Go down the steps. I'll undo the barricade. Then you can come up and go out. And if you've any thoughts of rushing me, just remember your parole.'

He nodded sullenly.

'Have you still got that computer you bought fourteen years ago?'

'Dad smashed it. When I got sent down. Out of rage.'

Like son, like father . . . 'The tapes are still in the same computer language,' I said. 'Grantley Basic. The language itself is there, on Side 1. You'll need to know that.'

He scowled. Beyond him entirely to be placated, let alone pleased.

'Go on,' I said. 'I'll unbar the door.'

He disappeared from the impromptu window and I tugged away the effective planks and pulled the table and chairs from their stations, and stood finally out of his arms' reach behind them.

'Come up,' I called. 'Undo the latch and be on your way.'

He came out fast, clutching the cassettes in one bloodstained hand and the keys in the other: gave me a brief hard stare which nonetheless held little of the former menace, and disappeared through the sitting-room towards the front door. I followed and watched him go down the path, first quickening his step and almost running as he turned into the lane and then fairly sprinting out of sight towards where he'd left his car. In a short time he came blasting back again, driving as if he feared I would still somehow stop him; but in truth all I did want was to be rid of him once and for all.

The empty cellar stank like a lair of an animal.

I looked into it briefly and decided it was a job for a shovel, a hose, a broom and some strong disinfectant, and while I was collecting those things Bananas and Cassie walked anxiously along from the pub.

'We saw you come,' she said, 'and we saw him go. I wanted to be here but Bananas said it might snarl things up.'

'He was right.' I kissed her soundly, both from love and tension released. 'Angelo hates to lose face.'

'You gave him the tapes?' Bananas asked.

'Yeah.'

'And may they choke him,' Cassie said.

I smiled. 'They may not. I'd guess Ted Pitts is worth a million.'

'Really?' Her eyebrows shot up. 'Then why don't *we*—?'

'It takes time and work. Ted Pitts lives right at the London end of the M1, half a mile off the country's biggest artery. I'll bet he spends countless days beating up that road to towns in the north, traipsing round betting shops, sucking his honey. It's what I guess he does, anyway. He was near Manchester yesterday, his wife said. A different town every day, so that no one gets to know him.'

'What difference would that make?' Bananas said.

I explained what happened to constant winners. 'I'll bet there isn't a single bookie who knows Ted Pitts by sight.'

'If *you* did it,' Bananas said thoughtfully, 'I suppose they'd know you at once.'

I shook my head. 'Only on the racecourse. Round

the backstreet betting shops in any big town I'd be just another mug.'

They both looked at me expectantly.

'Yeah,' I said. 'I can just see me spending my life that way.'

'Think of the loot,' Bananas said.

'And no tax,' said Cassie.

I thought of Ted Pitts's splendid house and of my own lack of amassed goods. Thought of him walking the upper slopes of Swiss mountains, restoring his spirit, wandering but coming home. Thought of my lack of a settled life-pattern and my hatred of being tied down. Thought of the way I'd enjoyed the past months, making decisions, running a business, knowing all the time it was just for a year, not a lifetime, and being reassured by such impermanency. Thought of spending hot summer days and wet winter afternoons in betting shops, playing the percentages, joylessly, methodically making a million.

'Well?' Bananas said.

'Maybe one day, when I'm hungry.'

'You've no sense.'

'You do it then,' I said. 'Give up the pub. Give up the cooking. Take to the road.'

He stared at me while he thought about it, then grimaced and said, 'There's more to life than making money. Not a lot, but some.'

'One of these days,' said Cassie with sweet certainty,

'you'll both do it. Not even a saint could sit on a goldmine and be too lazy to pick up the nuggets.'

'You think it's just lazy—?'

'I sure do. Where's your buccaneering heart? Where's the glint of piracy? What about the battlecry of those old north-country industrialists – where there's muck there's brass?' She looked alight with enthusiasm, a glow I guessed derived as much from Angelo's absence as from the thought of an available fortune.

'If you feel the same when I've finished for Luke Houston,' I said, 'I'll give it a trial. Just for a while.'

'Picky,' she said. 'That's what you are.'

All the same it was in better spirits that I set about cleaning the cellar and making it fit for fishing gear to live in; and in the later afternoon, all three of us sat in the sun on the cottage grass while Cassie and Bananas discussed how they would spend the lolly they thought I would inevitably chase.

They already felt as I did that Angelo's revengeful lust had been at last dissipated, and they said he had even done us a favour as without his violent attack I would never have sought out Ted Pitts.

'Good can come of bad,' Cassie said with satisfaction.

And bad of good, I thought. Jonathan's conjuring tricks had trapped Angelo thoroughly and made it certain that he would be convicted empty handed. Had ensured that for fourteen years Angelo would be unable to kill anyone else. But that particular good sequence of actions which had seemed so final at the time had proved to be only a plug for a simmering volcano. The psychopathic young man had at length erupted as a full-blown coarsened thug, no longer as Jonathan had described him, occasionally high on the drug of recklessness, but more plainly, comprehensively, violent.

Time changed perspectives. From disasters could come successes, and from successes, disasters. A pity, I thought, that one could never perceive whether to weep or cheer at the actual event.

Our lives gradually quietened to sensible proportions. Cassie went back to work in a sling and Bananas invented a new delight involving liquid spiced beef: and I began a series of forays to stud farms to take preliminary peeks at the yearlings soon to be offered at the sales, all too aware that the climax of my year was approaching, the test by which Luke would judge me, looking back. To buy young stock that would win would be satisfactory; to buy a colt to sire a dynasty would be luck. Somewhere between the two lay an area in which judgment would turn out to have been good, indifferent or absent, and it was there that I hoped to make as few mistakes as possible.

For about a week I mosied around all over the place with detours to race meetings and to Luke's two trainers in Berkshire, and spent every spare waking minute with the Stud Book. Sim Shell said severely that he wished to be present and in full consultation whenever I bought anything for him personally to train, and Mort with every nerve twitching asked for Sir Ivor, Nijinsky and Northern Dancer, all at once, and at the very least.

Cassie came with me to the evening session on the first day of the sales, roaming about on the forever legs and listening engrossed to the gossip. Every year Newmarket sale ring saw fortunes lost quicker than crashing stock markets, but the talk was all of hope and expectation, of slashing speed and breeding potential, all first-day euphoria and unspent cheques.

'What excitement,' Cassie said. 'You can see it in every face.'

'The joy of acquisition. Disillusion comes next week. Then optimistic gloom. Then, if you're lucky, complacent relief.'

'But today . . .'

'Today,' I nodded. 'There's still the chance of buying the winner of the Derby.'

I bought two colts and a filly on that evening for staggering sums, reassured to a point by having competed against top echelons of bloodstock agents but pursued by the sapping fear that it was I who had pressed on too far, not they who had stopped too soon.

We stayed to the end of the programme, partly

because of Cassie's fascination with a new world but also because it was when the big buyers had gone home that a bargain sometimes arose, and I did in fact buy the last lot of the day, a thin-looking pony-like creature, because I liked his bright eyes.

The breeder thanked me. 'Is it really for Luke Houston?'

'Yes,' I said.

'He won't be sorry. He's intelligent, that little colt.'

'He looks it.'

'He'll grow, you know,' he told me earnestly. 'His dam's family are all late growers. Come and have a drink. It isn't every day I sell one to Luke Houston.'

We went back, however, to drink and eat with Bananas, and from there to the cottage, where I sent off a telexed report to Luke, for whom our midnight was three in the afternoon.

Luke liked telexes. If he wanted to discuss what I'd sent he would telephone after his evening dinner, catching me at six in the morning before I left for the gallops, but more normally he would reply by telex or not at all.

The dining-room was filled with equipment provided by Luke: a video-disc recorder for re-watching and analysing past races, a print-out calculator, photocopier, a row of filing cabinets, an electric typewriter, the telex machine and a complicated affair which answered the telephone, took messages, gave messages, and recorded every word it heard, including my own live conversations. It worked on a separate line from the telephone in the sitting room, a good arrangement which most simply divorced our private calls from his business, allowing me to pay for one and him the other. All he hadn't given me – or had had me collect from an unwilling Warrington Marsh – was a computer.

When I came down the following morning I found the telex had chattered during the night.

'Why didn't you buy the Fisher colt? Why did you buy the cheap colt? Give my best to Cassie.'

He had never actually met Cassie but only talked to her a few times on the telephone. The politeness was his way of saying that his questions were simply questions, not accusations. Any telexes which came without 'best to Cassie' were jump-to-it matters.

I telexed back. 'Two private owners who detest each other, Schubman and Mrs Crickington, beat each other up to three hundred and forty thousand for the Fisher colt, way beyond its sensible value. The cheap colt might surprise you yet. Regards, William.'

Cassie these days was being collected and brought back by a slightly too friendly man who lived near the pub and worked a street away from Cassie in Cambridge. She said he was putting his hand on her knee instead of the steering wheel increasingly often and she would be extremely glad to be rid of both him and the plaster. In other respects than driving the cast had been accommodated, and our night-time activities were back to their old joy.

By day we slowly repaired or replaced everything which had been smashed, using as references the pieces Bananas had stacked in the garage. Television, vases, lamps, all as near as possible to the originals. Even six corn dollies hung again in their mobile group, dollies freshly and intricately woven from the shiny stalks of the new harvest by an elderly ethnic-smock lady who said you had to cut the corn for them specially nowadays by hand, because combine harvesters chopped the straw too short.

Bananas thought that replacing the corn dollies might be going too far, but Cassie said darkly that they represented pagan gods who should be placated – and deep in the countryside *you never knew.*

I carpentered new pieces into both the damaged doors and fitted a new lock to the front. All traces of Angelo gradually vanished, all except his baseball bat which lay along the sill of the window which faced the road. We had consciously kept it there to begin with as a handy weapon in case he should come back, but even as day after peaceful day gave us a growing sense of ease we let it lie: another hostage to the evil eye, perhaps.

Jonathan telephoned me one evening and although I was sure he wouldn't approve of what I'd done I told him everything that had happened.

'You kept him in the *cellar*?'

'Yeah.'

'Good God.'

'It seems to have worked.'

'Mm. I can't help being sorry that Angelo has that system after all.'

'I know. I'm sorry too, after all you did to keep it from him. I really hated giving it to him. But you were right, he's dangerous, and I don't want to vanish to California, the life I want is right here on the English turf. And about the system . . . Don't forget, it isn't enough just to possess it, you'd have to operate it discreetly. Angelo knows just about nothing about racing, and he's impetuous and undisciplined, not cunning and quiet.'

'He may also,' Jonathan said, 'think that the system gives a winner every time, which it doesn't. Old Mrs O'Rorke said it steadily gave an average of one winner in three.'

'Angelo versus the bookies should be quite a match. And by the way, I told him you were dead.'

'Thanks very much.'

'Well, you didn't want him turning up one day on your sunny doorstep, did you?'

'He'd never get a visa.'

'You can walk across the Canadian border,' I said, 'without anyone being the wiser.'

'And the Mexican,' he agreed.

I told him in detail about Ted Pitts's house, and he

sounded truly pleased. 'And the little girls? How are they?'

'Grown up and pretty.'

'I envied him those children.'

'Did you?' I said.

'Yes. Well . . . there you are. It's the way life turns out.'

I listened to the regret in his voice and understood how much he himself had wanted a daughter, a son . . . and I thought that I too would regret it one day if I didn't . . . and that maybe it would be terrific fun if Cassie . . .

'Are you still there?' he said.

'Yeah. If I get married, will you come over to the wedding?'

'I don't believe it.'

'You never know. I haven't asked her yet. She might not want to.'

'Keep me posted.' He sounded amused.

'Yeah. How's Sarah?'

'Fine, thanks.'

'So long,' I said, and he said, 'So long,' and I put down the receiver with the usual feeling of thankfulness that I had a brother, and specifically that he was Jonathan.

More days passed. By the end of the first week's sales I'd bought twelve yearlings for Luke and lost five more to higher bidders, and I'd consulted with Sim until he was sick of it and given Mort a filly that was on her toes if not actually a dancer, and spent two evenings in the Bedford Arms with the Irish trainer Donavan, listening to his woes and watching him get drunk.

'There's more good horses in Ireland than ever come out,' he said, wagging an unsteady finger under my nose.

'I'm sure.'

'You want to come over, now. You want to poke around them studs, now, before you go to the sales.'

'I'll come over soon,' I said. 'Before the next sales, two weeks from now.'

'You do that.' He nodded sagely. 'There's a colt I have my eye on, way down below Wexford. I'd like to train that colt, now. I'd like for you to buy that little fella for Luke, that I would.'

In that particular year, as a trial, the first Newmarket Yearling Sales had been held early, at the beginning of September. The Premium Sales, when most of the bluest-blooded youngsters would come under the hammer, were as usual at the end of the month. The colt Donavan had his eye on was due to be sold two weeks ahead, but unfortunately not only Donavan had his eye on it. The whole of Ireland and most of England seemed also to have their optics swivelled that way. Even allowing for Irish exaggeration, that colt seemed the best news of the season.

'Luke would want that fella, now,' Donavan said.

'I'll bid for it,' I said mildly.

He peered boozily into my face. 'What you want to do, now, is to get Luke to say there's no ceiling. No ceiling, that's the thing.'

'I'll go to Luke's limit.'

'You're a broth of a boy, now. And it's write to Luke I did, I'll admit it, to say you were as green as a pea and no good to man nor horse, not in the job he'd given you.'

'Did you?'

'Well now, if you get me that little colt I'll write again and say I was wrong.' He nodded heavily and half fell off the bar stool. He was never drunk on the gallops or at the races or indeed by the sale-ring itself, but at all other times – probably. The owners didn't seem to mind and nor did the horses: drunk or sober, Donavan produced as many winners year by year as anyone in Ireland. I didn't like or dislike him. I did business with him before ten in the morning and listened intently in the evenings, the time when through clouds of whisky he spoke the truth. Many thought him uncouth, and so he was. Many thought Luke would have chosen a smoother man with tidier social manners, but perhaps Luke had seen and heard Donavan's intimate way with horses, as I now had, and preferred the priceless goods to a gaudier package. I had come to respect Donavan. Two solid days of his company were quite enough.

When the flood of purchasing trainers and agents and go-it-alone owners had washed out of the town temporarily, Sim gave a brown short-necked filly a final work-out and afterwards rather challengingly told me she was as ready as could be to win the last race on St Leger day, on Saturday.

'She looks great,' I said. 'A credit to your care.'

Sim half scowled. 'You'll be going to Doncaster, I suppose?'

I nodded. 'Staying up there, Friday night. Mort's running Genotti in the St Leger.'

'Will you help me saddle mine up?' Sim said.

I tried to hide my astonishment at this olive branch of epic proportions. He usually attempted to keep me as far from the runners as possible.

'Be glad to,' I said.

He nodded with customary brusqueness. 'See you there, then.'

'Good luck.'

He was going up on the Wednesday for the whole of the four-day meeting but I didn't particularly want to, not least because Cassie still found it difficult to manage on her own with the rigid arm. I left her on the Friday, though, and drove to Doncaster, and almost the first person I saw as I walked through the racecourse gates was Angelo.

I stopped abruptly and turned aside, willing him not to spot me, not to speak.

He was buying two racecards from one of the booths near the entrance, holding up the queue while he sorted out coins.

I supposed it was inevitable I would one day see him if he took to racegoing at all often, but somehow it was still a shock. I was glad when he turned away from the booth in the opposite direction to where I stood: there might be a truce between us but it was fragile at best.

I watched while he barged his way through the swelling crowd with elbows like battering rams and thighs like rocks: he was heading not to anywhere where he could place a bet but towards the less populated area near the rails of the track itself, where supporters had not yet flocked to see the first race. Reaching the rails, he stopped beside an elderly man in a wheelchair and unceremoniously thrust one of the racecards into his hands. Then he turned immediately on his heel and bulled his way purposefully towards the serried ranks of bookmakers inside the stands, where I lost sight of him, thankfully, for the rest of the day.

He was back, however, on the Saturday. Although I seldom bothered with gambling, I decided to have a small bet on Genotti in the St Leger, infected no doubt by Mort's fanatical eagerness, and as I stood near a little Welsh bookmaker whom I'd long known, I saw Angelo, thirty feet away, frowning heavily over a small notebook.

'Genotti,' my bookmaker friend said to his clerk who wrote down (in the book) every transaction, 'three tenners at fives, William Derry.'

'Thanks, Taff,' I said.

Along the row Angelo began arguing about a price on offer, which was apparently less than he thought fair.

'Everyone else is at five to one.' His voice was a growl which I knew all too well.

'Try someone else, then. It's fours to you, *Mister* Gilbert.'

With half my mind I was satisfied that Angelo was indeed rushing in stupidly with the system where Liam O'Rorke and Ted Pitts had taken care not to tread, but also I was uneasy that he should be arousing opposition so soon. I positively needed for him to win for a while. I'd never envisaged him sticking to the anonymous drudgery required for long-term success, but the honeymoon period should not already have been over.

Taff-the-bookmaker glanced over his shoulder at the altercation and gave his clerk an eyes-to-heaven gesture.

'What's all the fuss about?' I asked.

'He's a right git, that man.' Taff divided his comment impartially between him, his clerk, and the world in general.

'Angelo Gilbert.'

Taff's gaze sharpened on me directly. 'Know him, do you?'

'Somebody pointed him out . . . he murdered somebody, years ago.'

'That's right. Just out of jug, he is. And *stupid* – you wouldn't credit it.'

'What's he done?'

'He came up to York last week with a fistful of banknotes, laying it about as if there were no tomorrow, and us not knowing who he was at that moment. And there's us thinking we were all taking lollipops off a baby when whammo, this outsider he'd invested about six big ones on comes cantering in from nowhere and we're all paying out and wincing and scratching our heads over where he got the info, because the trainer hadn't had as much as a quid on, as far as we knew. So Lancer, that bloke along there arguing with this Gilbert, he asks this geezer straight out who'd put him onto the winner, and the stupid git smirked and said Liam O'Rorke did.'

Taff peered at my face, which I felt must have mirrored my feeling of inner shock, but apparently it merely looked blank because Taff, who was a good sixty-plus, made a clicking sound with his mouth and said, 'Before your time, I suppose.'

'What was?'

Taff's attention was torn away by several customers who crowded to place bets, and he seemed vaguely surprised to see me still there when they'd gone.

'Are you that interested?' he asked.

'Got nothing else to do.'

Taff glanced along to where Angelo had been, but Angelo had gone. 'Thirty years ago. Thirty-five. Time does go quick. There was this old Irishman, Liam O'Rorke, he'd invented the only system I ever knew that would guarantee you'd win. Course, once we'd cottoned to him we weren't all that keen to take his bets. I mean, we wouldn't be, would we, knowing he had the edge on us somehow. Anyway, he would never part with his secret, how he did it, and it went with him to the grave, and good riddance, between you and me.'

'And now?'

'And now here's this geezer rocking us back on our heels with this huge win at York and then he's sneering at us and calling us mugs and saying we don't know what's hit us yet, and what he's using on us is Liam O'Rorke's old system resurrected, and now he's all indignant and complaining that we won't give him a good price. Acting all hurt and angry.' Taff laughed contemptuously. 'I mean, how stupid can you get?'

CHAPTER SEVENTEEN

Genotti won the St Leger by an easy four lengths.

Mort's excitement afterwards seemed to levitate him visibly off the ground, the static electricity about him crackling in the dry September sunshine. He wrung my hand with bone-scrunching enthusiasm and danced round the unsaddling enclosure giving rapturous responses to all who congratulated him, reacting with such uncomplicated delight to his victory that he had all the crowd smiling. It was easy, I reflected, to think of Mort as simple through and through, whereas, as I had gradually discovered, he traversed mental mazes of tortuous routes where pros battled cons like moves on a chessboard, and the plans and solutions which seemed so obvious once they had turned out to be right were the fruits of the mazes.

I collected my winnings from Taff, who gloomily said he would never have given anyone five to one if he'd known beforehand that Genotti was Angelo Gilbert's fancy.

'Did Angelo win?' I asked.

'Of course he did. He must have had a grand on. None of us would take his money at the finish.'

'So he didn't get fives?'

'More like evens,' he said sourly.

At evens, Angelo would still have doubled his money, but for Angelo that might not be enough. Grievance, I could see, might raise a very ugly head.

'No system could win every single time,' I said. 'Angelo won't.'

'I dare say not,' Taff said with obstinacy. 'But you can take it from me that no bookie on the racecourse will in future give that arrogant so-and-so much more than evens, even if what he's backing is lame on three legs, carrying two stone overweight and ridden by my old dad.'

'At evens, he wouldn't win over all,' I said.

'So who's crying? We're not in the loving-kindness business, you know.

'Fleece the mugs?'

'You got it.'

He began paying out other successful punters with the rapidity of long practice but it was seldom that he would go home from a racetrack with less cash than he'd brought. Few bookmakers were gamblers at heart and only the good mathematicians survived.

I drifted away from him and drank some champagne with the similarly fizzing Mort and a little later helped Sim to saddle the filly, who made it another hooray-for-Houston day by a short head. Sim took it more calmly than Mort, but with a satisfaction at least as deep, and he seemed to be admitting and acknowledging at last that I was not an ignorant bossy upstart but a well-meaning colleague and that all Luke's successes worked for our joint good. I wasn't sure how or why his attitude had changed, I knew only that a month earlier a friendly drink together in a racecourse bar to celebrate a Houston winner would have been unthinkable.

Thinking more of Mort and Sim and the horses than of the still active spectre of Angelo, I drove from Doncaster to collect Cassie, and from there to a late dinner with Bananas. He too, it appeared, had backed Genotti, more than doubling my own winnings.

'I had a hundred on,' he said.

'I didn't know you ever bet.'

'On the quiet, now and then. Hearing all I do, how could I not?'

'So what did you hear about Genotti?'

He looked at me pityingly. 'Every time you've seen that colt work on the gallops, you've come back like a kid with tickets to the Cup Final.'

'More to the point,' Cassie said, 'if you'd used Liam O'Rorke's system, would it have come up with Genotti?'

'Ah.' I read Bananas's new menu and wondered what he meant by Prisoner Chicken. Said casually, 'Angelo Gilbert backed him.'

'*What?*'

I explained about Angelo, the bookmakers, and stupidity in general.

'He's blown it,' Cassie said, not without satisfaction.

I nodded. 'Into fragments.'

Bananas looked at me thoughtfully. 'What's it going to do for the dear man's temper?'

'It's not William's fault,' Cassie said.

'That trifle didn't stop him before.'

Cassie looked frowningly alarmed. 'What's Prisoner Chicken?' I said.

Bananas smirked. 'Breast of chicken marinated in lemon juice and baked under match-stick thin bars of herb pastry.'

'It sounds dry,' I said with jaundice.

'Bread and water are optional extras.'

Cassie laughed and Angelo retreated a little. We ate the Prisoner Chicken which was predictably a delight of juice and flavour and reminded us not at all of its inspiration.

'I'm going to Ireland tomorrow,' I said to Cassie. 'Like to come?'

'Ireland? There and back?'

I nodded. 'To see a man about a horse.'

'What else?'

So we spent some of my winnings on her fare, and went down south of Wexford to see the colt all the world wanted: and half the world, it seemed, was there on the same errand, standing around an untidy stable yard with blank faces all carefully not expressing identical inner thoughts.

Cassie watched as the beautifully coupled brown yearling skittered around under the calming hands of the stud groom and unprofessionally pronounced him 'sweet'.

'A money machine on the hoof,' I said. 'Look at the greed in all those shuttered faces.'

'They just seem uninterested to me.'

'Enthusiasm puts the price up.'

One or two of the bored-looking onlookers advanced to run exploratory hands down the straight young bones, stepping back with poker-playing noncommittal eyes, the whole procedure hushed as if in church.

'Aren't you going to feel its legs?' Cassie asked.

'Might as well.'

I took my turn in the ritual, and found like everyone else that the young limbs were cool and firm with tendons like fiddle strings in all the right places. There was also a good strong neck, a well-shaped quarter and most importantly a good depth of chest. Quite apart from his pedigree, which resounded with Classic winners, one couldn't, I thought, even imagine a better-looking animal: all of which meant that the bidding at the sale on Wednesday would rise faster than Bananas Frisby.

We flew thoughtfully back to England and I sent a telex to Luke. 'Bidding for the Hansel colt will be astronomical. I've seen him. He is without fault. How high do you want me to go?'

To which, during the night, I received a reply. 'It's your job, fella. You decide.'

Ouch, I thought. Where is the ceiling? How high is disaster?

Newmarket filled up again for the new week of sales, the most important programme of yearling sales of the whole season. Everyone in racing with money to spend brought determination and dreams, and the four-legged babies came in horse-boxes from just up the road, from Kent and the Cotswolds, from Devon and Scotland, from across the Irish Sea.

The Hansel colt from Wexford was due to be sold at the prime time of seven-thirty on the Wednesday evening and by seven the high-rising banks of seats of the sale ring were invisible under a sea of bodies, Cassie somewhere among them. Down near the floor in the pen reserved for probable bidders, Donavan was breathing heavily at my elbow as he had been all afternoon, determinedly sober and all the gloomier for it.

'Now you get that little colt, now, you get him for me.' If he'd said it once he'd said it a hundred times, as if repetition of desire could somehow make the purchase certain.

They brought the colt into the ring in the sudden hush of a host of lungs holding back their breath all at once, and the light gleamed on the walking gem and he did in truth look like a prince who could sire a dynasty.

The bidding for him started not in thousands but in tens of thousands, leaping in seconds to the quarter million and racing away beyond. I waited until the first pause and raised the price by a giant twenty-five thousand, to be immediately capped by a decisive nod from an agent along to my right. I raised another twenty-five and lost it as quickly, and another, and another: and I could go on nodding, I thought, until my head fell off. Nothing easier in the world than spending someone else's money as fast as noughts running through the meter on a petrol pump.

At eight hundred thousand guineas I just stopped. The auctioneer looked at me enquiringly. I didn't blink. 'Against you, sir,' he said.

'Go on,' said Donavan, thinking I'd merely overlooked that it was my turn. 'Go on, go on.'

I shook my head. Donavan turned and literally punched me on the arm in an agony of fear that my dithering would lose him the colt. 'Go on, it's you. Bid, you bugger, bid.'

'Any more, sir?' the auctioneer said.

I again shook my head. Donavan kicked my leg. The auctioneer looked around the silent sale ring. 'All done, then?' he said; and after a lifetime's pause his gavel came down sharply, the clap of opportunity gone for ever. 'Sold to Mr O'Flaherty. Next lot, please.'

Under the buzz of comment that followed the

super-colt out of the ring, Donavan thrust a furious purple face towards mine and yelled uninhibitedly, 'You buggering *bastard*. Do you know who bought that colt?'

'Yes I do.'

'I'll kill you, so I will.'

Shades of Angelo . . .

'There's no reason,' I said, 'why Luke should pay for your feud with Mick O'Flaherty.'

'That colt will win the Derby.'

I shook my head. 'You're *afraid* it will.'

'I'll write to Luke, so I will. I'll tell him it's you who's afraid. Bloody English. I'd kill the lot of you.'

He stalked away with rage pouring visibly from every pore, and I watched him with regret because I would indeed have liked to buy him his little fellow and seen him croon over him to make him a champion.

'Why did you stop?' Cassie asked, taking my arm.

'Does it worry you?'

She blinked. 'You know what they're saying?'

'That I didn't have the nerve to go on?'

'It was just that I heard . . .'

I smiled lopsidedly. 'My first big battle, and I retreated. Something like that?'

'Something.'

'O'Flaherty and Donavan hate each other so much it curdles their judgment. I meant to go as far as seven hundred and fifty thousand guineas and I thought I'd get the colt, I really did, because that's an extremely high price for any yearling. I went one bid higher still, but it wasn't enough. O'Flaherty was standing behind his agent prodding him in the back to make him carry on. I could see him. O'Flaherty was absolutely determined to buy the colt. To spite Donavan, I think. It isn't sense to go on bidding against someone compelled by raw emotion, so I stopped.'

'But what if he *does* win the Derby?'

'About ten thousand thoroughbred colts were born last year in the British Isles alone. Then there's France and America too. *One* colt from that huge crop will win the Derby the year after next, when he's three. The odds are against it being this one.'

'You're so cool.'

'No,' I said truthfully. 'Bruised and disgruntled.'

We drove home and I sent the telex to Luke. 'Regret under-bidder at eight hundred and forty thousand pounds excluding tax for Hansel colt. Donavan's deadly rival Mick O'Flaherty successful at eight hundred and sixty-six thousand two fifty. Donavan furious. Sack me if you like. Regards, William.'

The return message came within an hour. 'If the colt wins the Derby you owe me ten million pounds otherwise you are still employed. Best to Cassie.'

'Thank God for that,' she said. 'Let's go to bed.'

Two busy days later I dropped her at work and drove on south-westwards to Berkshire to visit Luke's other trainers during the morning and to go on to see three of their horses race at Newbury in the afternoon; and there again on the racecourse was Angelo.

This time he saw me immediately before I had time to dodge: came charging across a patch of grass, took roughly hold of my lapel, and told me the betting system didn't work.

'You sold me a pup. You'll be sorry.' He looked quickly around as if hoping to find us both on deserted moorland, but as there was only concrete well populated, he smothered his obvious wish to slaughter me there and then. He was physically tougher, I thought. Less pale, less puffy; the effects of long imprisonment giving way to a healthy tan and tighter muscles, the bull-like quality of the body intensifying. The black eyes . . . cold as ever. I looked at his re-emerging malevolence and didn't like it a bit.

I pulled his hand off my lapel and dropped it. 'There's nothing wrong with the system,' I said. 'It's not my fault you've been tramping all over it like a herd of elephants.'

His voice came back in the familiar bass register. 'If I'm still losing by five tomorrow, I'll *know* you've conned me. And I'll come after you. That's a promise.'

He turned away abruptly and strode off towards the stands, and in a while I went in search of Taff among the bookmakers.

'The latest on Angelo Gilbert?'

He looked down at me from his raised position on an inverted beer crate. 'He's nuts.'

'Are you still offering him rotten odds?'

'Look you, Mr Derry, I'm too busy to talk now.' He was indeed surrounded by eager customers holding out cash. 'If you want to know, buy me a pint after the last race.'

'Right,' I said, 'it's a deal.' And at the end of the afternoon he came with me into the crowded bar and shouted the unexpected news into my attentive ear.

'That man Angelo's gone haywire. He won big money at York, like I told you, and a fair amount at Doncaster, but before York it seems he lost a packet at Epsom and last Monday he kissed goodbye to a fortune at Goodwood, and today he's plunged on two horses who finished out of sight. So we're all back to giving him regular odds. Old Lancer – he works for Joe Glickstein, Honest Joe, you must have seen his stands at all the tracks?' I nodded. 'Well, Old Lancer, he took a thousand in readies this afternoon off that Angelo on Pocket Handbook, what couldn't win if it started yesterday. I mean, the man's a screwball. He's no more playing Liam O'Rorke's system than I'm a bleeding fairy.'

I watched him drink his beer, feeling great dismay that Angelo couldn't manage the system even to the extent of letting it find the right horses. He had to be guessing some of the answers to the multifarious questions instead of looking them up accurately in the form books: skipping the hard work out of laziness and still trusting the scores which the computer returned. But a computer couldn't advise him, couldn't tell him that omitting an answer here and an answer there would upset all those delicately balanced weightings and inevitably distort the all-important win factors.

Angelo was dumb, dim, stupid.

Angelo would think it was my fault.

'They say his father's getting tired of it,' Taff said.

'Who?'

'That Angelo person's father. Old Harry Gilbert. Made a packet out of bingo halls, they say, before he got struck.'

'Er, struck?'

Taff brought a lined brown outdoor face out of the beer mug. 'Struck down with arthritis, I think it is. He can't hardly walk, anyway. Comes to the races sometimes in a wheelchair, and it's him what has the cash.'

Enlightened, I thought back to the previous week at Doncaster, seeing in memory Angelo giving a racecard to an elderly chairbound man. Angelo's father, still indulgent, still supportive, still paying for his deadly middle-aged son.

I thanked Taff for his information. 'What's this Angelo to you?' he said.

'A long-time no friend of my brother's.'

He made an accepting motion with his head, looked

at his watch and finished his beer at a gulp, saying he'd left his clerk looking after the day's takings and he'd be happier having his mitts on them himself. 'We've all had a good day,' he said cheerfully, 'with those two odds-on favourites getting stuffed.'

I drove homewards and collected Cassie who was waiting at the hospital after what they had called a progress assessment.

'Plaster off next week,' she complained. 'I wanted it off this afternoon, but they wouldn't.'

The plaster was by then itching badly, the 'Remember tigers' was fading, Cassie was insisting that her arm *felt* mended and impatience had definitely set in.

We again went to the sales: I seemed to have spent half a lifetime round that sale ring, and Luke now owned twenty-eight yearlings he had not yet seen. I had signed cheques on his behalf for nearly two million pounds and was tending to dream about it at night. There was only the Saturday morning left now, an undistinguished programme according to the catalogue, the winding-down after the long excitements of the week. I went early by habit and with only short premeditation bought very cheaply the first lot of the day, an undistinguished-looking liver chestnut colt whose blood lines were sounder to the inspection than his spindly legs. One couldn't have foretold on that misty autumn morning that *this* was the prince who would sire a dynasty, but that in the end was what happened. My mind, as I signed for him and arranged for him to be sent along the road to Mort's stable, was more immediately on the conversation I'd had with Jonathan on the telephone the evening before.

'I want to talk to Angelo's father,' I said. 'Do you remember where he lived?'

'Of course I do. Welwyn Garden City. If you give me a minute, I'll find the street and the number.' There was a pause while he searched. 'Here we are. Seventeen, Pemberton Close. He may have moved, of course, and don't forget, William, he won't be in the least pleasant. I heard he was threatening all sorts of dire revenges against me after Angelo was convicted, but I didn't hang around long enough for him to get going.'

'Angelo seems to depend on him for cash,' I said.

'That figures.'

'Angelo's making a right balls-up of the betting system. He's losing his father's money and he's blaming me for it, and stoking up again towards volcanic eruption with me as the designated target for the lava flow.'

'He's an absolute pest.'

'He sure is. How does one rid oneself of a monster that won't go away? Don't answer that. Engineering Angelo back into jail permanently is all I can think of, and even then I would need to do it so that he didn't know who'd done it, and would it even on the whole be fair?'

'Provocation? Put a crime in his way and invite him to commit it?'

'As you say.'

'No, it wouldn't exactly be fair.'

'I was afraid you wouldn't think so,' I said.

'Nothing much short of murder would put him back inside for the whole of his life. Anything less and he'd be out breathing fire again, as you said before. And however could you line up a living victim?'

'Mm,' I said, 'it's impossible. I still think the only lasting solution is to make Angelo prosper, so I'll see if I can persuade his old dad to that effect.'

'His old dad is an old rattlesnake, don't forget.'

'His old dad is in a wheelchair.'

'Is he?' Jonathan seemed surprised. 'All the same, remember that rattlesnakes don't have legs.'

I reckoned that on that Saturday afternoon Angelo would still be blundering around the bookies on Newbury racecourse and that his father might have stayed at home, so it was then that I drove to Welwyn Garden City, leaving Cassie wandering around the cottage with a duster and an unaccustomedly domestic expression.

The house at number seventeen Pemberton Close proved to be inhabited not by Harry Gilbert but by a stockbroker, his chatty wife and four noisy children on roller skates, all of them out in the garden.

'Harry Gilbert?' said the wife, holding a basket of

dead roses. 'He couldn't manage the stairs with his illness. He built himself a bungalow full of ramps.'

'Do you know where?'

'Oh, sure. On the golf course. He used to play, poor man. Now he sits at a window and watches the foursomes go by on the fourteenth green. We often wave to him, when we're playing.'

'Does he have arthritis?' I asked.

'Good Lord, no.' She made a grimace of sympathy. 'Multiple sclerosis. He's had it for years. We've seen him slowly get worse . . . We used to live four doors away, but we always liked this house. When he put it up for sale, we bought it.'

'Could you tell me how to find him?'

'Sure.' She gave me brisk and clear instructions. 'You do know, don't you, not to talk about his son?'

'Son?' I said vaguely.

'His only son is in prison for murder. So sad for the poor man. Don't talk about it, it distresses him.'

'Thanks for warning me,' I said.

She nodded and smiled from a kind and unperceiving heart and went back to tidying her pretty garden. Surely goodness and mercy all thy days shall follow thee, I thought frivolously, and no monsters who won't go away shall gobble thee up. I left the virtuous and went in search of the sinner, and found him, as she'd said, sitting in his wheelchair by a big bay window, watching the earnest putters out on the green.

The wide double front doors of the large and still

new-looking one-storey building were opened to me by a man so like Angelo at first sight that I thought for a fearsome moment that he hadn't after all gone to the races; but it was only the general shape and colouring that was the same, the olive skin, greying hair, unfriendly dark eyes, tendency to an all-over padding of fat.

'Eddy,' a voice called. 'Who is it? Come in here.'

The voice was as deep and harsh as Angelo's, the words themselves slightly slurred. I walked across the polished wood of the entrance hall and then across the lush drawing room with its panoramic view, and not until I was six feet away from Harry Gilbert did I stop and say I was William Derry.

Vibrations could almost be felt. Eddy, behind me, audibly hissed from the air leaving his lungs. The much older version of Angelo's face which looked up from the wheelchair went stiff with strong but unreadable emotions, guessed at as anger and indignation, but possibly not. He had thinning grey hair, a grey moustache, a big body in a formal grey suit with a waistcoat. Only in the lax hands was the illness visible, and only then when he moved them; and from his polished shoes to the neat parting across his scalp it seemed to me that he was denying his weaknesses, presenting an outwardly uncrumbled façade so as to announce to the world that authority still lived within.

'You're not welcome in my house,' he said.

'If your son would stop threatening me, I wouldn't be here.'

'He says you have tricked us like your brother.'

'No.'

'The betting system doesn't work.'

'It worked for Liam O'Rorke,' I said. 'Liam O'Rorke was quiet, clever, careful and a statistician. Is Angelo any of those things?'

He gave me a cold stare. 'A system should work for everyone alike.'

'A horse doesn't run alike for every jockey,' I said.

'There's no similarity.'

'Engines run sweetly for some drivers and break down for others. Heavy-handedness is always destructive. Angelo is trampling all over that system. No wonder it isn't producing results.'

'The system is wrong,' he said stubbornly.

'It may,' I said slowly, 'be slightly out of date.' Yet for Ted Pitts it was purring along still: but then Ted Pitts too was quiet, clever; a statistician.

It seemed that I had made the first impression upon Harry Gilbert. He said with a faint note of doubt, 'It should not have changed with the years. Why should it?'

'I don't know. Why shouldn't it? There may be a few factors that Liam O'Rorke couldn't take into account because in his time they didn't exist.'

A depressed sort of grimness settled over him.

I said, 'And if Angelo has been hurrying through the

programs, skipping some of the questions or answering them inaccurately, the scores will come out wrong. He's had some of the answers right. You won a lot at York, so I'm told. And you'd have won more on the St Leger if Angelo hadn't scared the bookmakers with his boastfulness.'

'I don't understand you.' The slur in his speech, the faint distortion of all his words was, I realised, the effect of his illness. Articulation might be damaged but the chill awareness in his eyes said quite clearly that his intelligence wasn't.

'Angelo told all the bookmakers at York that he would henceforth fleece them continually, because it was he who possessed Liam O'Rorke's infallible system.'

Harry Gilbert closed his eyes. His face remained unmoved.

Eddy said belligerently, 'What's wrong with that? You have to show people who's boss.'

'Eddy,' Harry Gilbert said, 'you don't know anything about anything and you never will.' He slowly opened his eyes. 'It makes a difference,' he said.

'They gave him evens on the St Leger winner. The proper price was five to one.'

Harry Gilbert would never thank me: not if I gave him lifesaving advice, not if I helped him win a fortune, not if I kept his precious son out of jail. He knew, all the same, what I was saying. Too much of a realist, too old a businessman, not to. Angelo in too many ways was a fool, and it made him more dangerous, not less.

'What do you expect me to do?' he said.

'I expect you to tell your son that if he attacks me again, or any of my friends or any of my property, he'll be back behind bars so fast he won't know what hit him. I expect you to make him work the betting system carefully and quietly, so that he wins. I expect you to warn him that the system guarantees only one win in three, not a winner every single time. Making the system work is a matter of strict application and careful persistence, not of flamboyance and anger.'

He stared at me expressionlessly.

'Angelo's character,' I said, 'is as far different from Liam O'Rorke's as it's possible to get. I expect you to make Angelo aware of that fact.'

They were all expectations, I saw, that were unlikely to be achieved. Harry Gilbert's physical weakness, though he disguised it, was progressive, and his imperfect control of Angelo would probably only last at all for exactly as long as Angelo needed financing.

A tremor shook his body but no emotion showed in his face. He said however with a sort of throttled fury, 'All our problems are your brother's fault.'

The uselessness of my visit swamped me. Harry Gilbert was after all only an old man blindly clinging like his son to an old obsession. Harry Gilbert was not any longer a man of reason, even if he had ever been.

I tried all the same, once more. I said, 'If you

had paid Mrs O'Rorke all those years ago, if you had bought Liam's system from her, as you had agreed, you would legally have owned it and could have profited from it ever since. It was because you refused to pay Mrs O'Rorke that my brother saw to it that you didn't get the system.'

'She was too old,' he said coldly.

I stared at him. 'Are you implying that her age was a reason for not paying her?'

He didn't answer.

'If I stole your car from you,' I said, 'would you consider me justified on the grounds that you were too ill to drive it?'

'You prattle,' he said. 'You are nothing.'

'Mug,' Eddy said, nodding.

Harry Gilbert said wearily, 'Eddy, you are good at pushing wheelchairs and cooking meals. On all other subjects, shut up.'

Eddy gave him a look which was half-defiant, half-scared, and I saw that he too was dependent on Harry for his food and shelter, that it couldn't be all that easy out in the big cynical world for murderers' assistants to earn a cushy living, that looking after Harry wasn't a job to be lightly lost.

To Harry Gilbert I said, 'Why don't you do what you once intended? Why don't you buy Angelo a betting shop and let the system win for him there?'

I got another stretch of silent unmoving stare. Then

he said, 'Business is a talent. I have it. It is, however, uncommon.'

I nodded. It was all the answer he would bring himself to make. Certainly he wouldn't admit to me of all people that he thought Angelo would bankrupt any sensible business in a matter of weeks.

'Keep your son away from me,' I said. 'I've done more for you in getting you that system than you deserve. You've no rights to it. You've no right to demand that it makes you a fortune in five minutes. You've no right to blame me if it doesn't. You keep your son away from me. I can play as rough as he does. For your own sake, and for his, you keep him off me.'

I turned away from him without waiting for any sort of answer, and walked unhurriedly out of the room and across the hall

Footsteps pattered after me on the polished wood.

Eddy.

I didn't look round. He caught up with me as I opened the front door and stepped outside, and he put his hand on my arm to make me pause. He looked back guiltily over his shoulder to where his uncle sat mutely by his splendid window, knowing the old man wouldn't approve of what he was doing. When he saw Harry was looking out again steadfastly to the golf, he turned on me a nasty self-satisfied smirk.

'Mug,' he said, speaking with prudent quietness, 'Angelo won't like you coming here.'

'Too bad.' I shook his hand off my sleeve. He sneered back in a poisonous mixture of slyness and malice and triumph, and half-whispered his final enjoyable words.

'Angelo's bought a pistol,' he said.

CHAPTER EIGHTEEN

'Why are you so thoughtful?' Cassie asked.

'Uneasy.'

We were sitting as so often at a table in Bananas' dining room with him moving about light-footedly in his sneakers seeming never to hurry yet keeping everyone fed. The plants grew with shining healthy leaves in the opulent gloom of his designedly intimate lighting, glasses and silverware gleaming in candlelight and mould spreading slowly in the dark.

'It's not like you,' Cassie said.

I smiled at her thin sun-tanned uncomplicated face and said that I didn't want above all things a return visit from Angelo.

'Do you really think he'd come?'

'I don't know.'

'We'd never get any more corn dollies,' she said. 'It's too late now for decent straw.'

Her arm in its plaster lay awkwardly on the table. I touched the bunched fingertips peeping out. 'Would you consider leaving me for a while?' I asked.

'No, I wouldn't.'

'Suppose I said I was tired of you?'

'You're not.'

'Are you so sure?'

'Positive,' she said contentedly. 'And anyway, for how long?'

I drank some wine. For how long was an absolute puzzle. 'Until I get Angelo stabilised,' I said. 'And don't ask me how long, because I don't know. But the first thing to do, I think, is persuade Luke he needs a computer right here in Britain.'

'Would that be difficult?'

'It might be. He has one in California . . . he might say he didn't need two.'

'What do you want it for, the betting system?'

I nodded. 'I think,' I said, 'that I'll try to rent one. Or some time on one. I want to find out what the winners should be according to O'Rorke, and what Angelo's doing wrong. And if I can put him right, perhaps that will keep him quiet.'

'You'd have thought just giving him the tapes would be enough.'

'Yes, you would.'

'He's like a thistle,' she said. 'You're sure you've got rid of him and he grows right back.'

Thistles, I thought, didn't go out to buy guns.

Bananas reverently bore his eponymous soufflé to the people at the next table, the airy peaks shining light and luscious and pale brown. The old cow, whose skill had produced it, must have stopped working to rule: Bananas himself, joining us later for coffee, gloomily admitted it. 'She took an hour to shred carrots. Did them by hand. Ten seconds in the processor. She said processors were dangerous machinery and she'd have to negotiate a new rate for all jobs with machinery.'

Bananas' new beard had grown curly which was unforeseen in view of the lank straight locks further up but seemed to me to be in accord with the doubleness of his nature.

'Historically,' he said, 'it's seldom a good idea to appease a tyrant.'

'The old cow?'

'No. Angelo Gilbert.'

'What do you suggest, then?' I asked. 'Full-scale war?'

'You have to be sure you'll win. Historically, full scale war's a toss-up.'

'The old cow might leave,' Cassie said, smiling.

Bananas nodded. 'Tyrants always want more next time. I dare say next year she'll turn to motor racing.'

'I suppose you don't know anyone who has a computer you can feed any language into?' I said.

'Turkish? Indo-Chinese? That sort of stuff?'

'Yeah. Gibberish, double-speak, jargonese and gobble-de-gook.'

'Try the sociologists.'

I tried, however, Ted Pitts, early the following morning, and reached Jane instead.

'Ted isn't here,' she said. 'I'm afraid he's still in Switzerland. Can I help?'

I explained I wanted to borrow a good computer to run a check on the racing programs and she said sadly that she couldn't really lend me Ted's, not without him being there; she knew he was working on a special program for his classes and if anyone touched the computer at present his work could be lost, and she couldn't risk that.

'No,' I agreed. Did she know of anyone else whose computer I could use?

She thought it over. 'There's Ruth,' she said doubtfully. 'Ruth Quigley.'

'Who?'

'She was a pupil of Ted's. Actually he says there's nothing he can teach her now, and when she comes here I can't understand a word they say to each other, it's like listening to creatures from outer space.'

'Would she have a computer of her own?'

'She's got everything,' Jane said without envy. 'Born rich. Only child. Only has to ask, and it's hers. And on top of that, she's brainy. Doesn't seem fair, does it?'

'Beautiful as well?'

'Oh.' She hesitated. 'Not bad. I don't really know. It's not the sort of thing you *notice* about Ruth.'

'Well, um, where could I find her?'

'In Cambridge. That's why I thought of her, because she lives over your way. She writes programs for teaching-machines. Would you like me to ring her? When do you want to go?'

I said 'Today', and half an hour later I'd had my answer and was on my way, seeking out a flat in a modern block on the outskirts of the town.

Ruth Quigley proved to be young: very early twenties, I guessed. I could see also what Jane meant about not noticing her looks, because the first, overpowering and lasting impression she gave was of the speed of her mind. There were light eyes, light brown extra-curly hair and long slender neck, but mostly there was an impatient jerk of the head and a stumblingly rapid diction as if to her utter disgust her tongue couldn't speak her thoughts fast enough.

'Yes. Come in. Did you bring your tapes?' She wasted no precious words on any other greeting. 'This way. Old Grantley Basic, Jane said. You've got the language with you. Do you want to load it, or shall I?'

'I'd be glad if—'

'Hand them over, then. Which side?'

'Er, first program on Side 1.'

'Right. Come along.'

She moved with the same inborn rapidity, disappearing down a short passage and through a doorway before I'd even managed a step. She must always find, I thought, that the rest of the world went along intolerably in slow motion.

The room into which I finally followed her must originally have been designed as a bedroom, which it now in no way resembled. There was a quiet, felt-like pale green floor covering, track-lighting with spotlights, a roller blind at the window, matt white walls – and long benches of machines more or less like Ted Pitts's, only double.

'Workroom,' Ruth Quigley said.

'Eh, yes.'

It was cooler in there than out on the street. I identified a faint background hum as air-conditioning, and remarked on it.

She nodded, not lifting her eyes from the already almost completed job of loading Grantley Basic into a machine that would accept it. 'Dust is like gravel to computers. Heat, damp, all makes them temperamental. They're thoroughbreds, of course.'

Racing programs . . . thoroughbred computers. Excellence won. Pains taken gave one the edge. I was beginning to think like her, I thought.

'I'm wasting your time,' I said apologetically.

'Glad to help. Always do anything for Jane and Ted. They know that. Did you bring the form books? You'll need them. Simple programs, but facts must be right. Most teaching-machines, just the same. They bore me quite often. Multiple-choice questions. Then the child takes half an hour to get it right and I put it in a bright remark like, "Well done, aren't you clever."

Nothing of the sort. Encouragement, they say, is all. What do you think?'

'Are they gifted children?'

She gave me a flashing glance. 'All children are gifted. Some more so. They need the best teaching. They often don't get it. Teachers are jealous, did you know?'

'My brother always said it was intensely exciting to have a very bright boy in the class.'

'Like Ted, generous. There you are, fire away. I'll be in and out, don't let me disturb you. I'm working on a sort-listing of string arrays. They said it was taking them eighteen minutes, I ask you. I've got it down to five seconds, but only one dimension. I need two dimensions if I'm not to scramble the data. I'm poking a machine-language program into the memory from BASIC, then converting the machine code into assembly-language economics. Am I boring you?'

'No,' I said. 'I just don't understand a word of it.'

'Sorry. Forgot you weren't like Ted. Well, carry on.'

I had brought in a large briefcase the tapes, the racing form books, all sorts of record books and all the recent copies of a good racing paper, and with a feeling that by Ruth Quigley's standards it was going to take me a very long time I set about working out which horses were *likely* to have won according to Liam O'Rorke, and checking them against those which had actually reached the post first. I still needed a list of the horses which Angelo had backed, but I thought

I might get that from Taff and from Lancer on the following day: and *then* I might be able to figure out where Angelo had messed everything up.

FILE NAME?

CLOAD DONCA, I typed. Pressed the 'Enter' key, and watched the asterisks; waited for READY. Pressed 'Enter' again and got my reward.

WHICH RACE AT DONCASTER?

ST LEGER, I typed.

DONCASTER: ST LEGER. TYPE NAME OF HORSE AND PRESS 'ENTER'.

GENOTTI, I typed. Pressed 'Enter'.

DONCASTER: ST LEGER.

GENOTTI.

ANSWER ALL QUESTIONS YES OR NO WITH A NUMBER AND PRESS 'ENTER'.

HAS HORSE WON AS A TWO YEAR OLD?

YES, I typed. The screen flashed a new question leaving the headings intact.

HAS HORSE WON AS A THREE YEAR OLD?

YES, I typed.

HOW MANY DAYS SINCE HORSE LAST RAN?

I consulted the daily newspaper which always gave that precise information, and typed in the number which had appeared there on St Leger day: 23.

HAS HORSE WON OVER DISTANCE: ONE MILK SIX FURLONGS?

NO, I typed.

HAS HORSE RUN OVER DISTANCE: ONE MILE SIX FURLONGS?

NO.

TYPE LONGEST DISTANCE IN FURLONGS OVER WHICH HORSE HAS WON.

12.

HAS HORSE RUN ON COURSE?

NO.

TYPE IN PRIZE MONEY WON IN CURRENT SEASON.

I consulted the form books and typed Genotti's winnings, which had been fairly good but not stupendous.

HAS HORSE'S SIRE SIRED WINNERS AT THE DISTANCE?

I looked it up in the breeding records, which took much longer, but the answer was YES.

DAM ditto?

YES.

IS HORSE QUOTED ANTE-POST AT TWELVE TO ONE OR LESS?

YES.

HAS JOCKEY PREVIOUSLY WON A CLASSIC?

YES.

HAS TRAINER PREVIOUSLY WON A CLASSIC?

YES.

ANY MORE HORSES?

YES.

I found myself back at the beginning and repeated the program for every horse which had run in the race. The questions weren't always precisely the same, because different answers produced alternative queries, and for some horses there were far more questions than for others. It took me a good hour to look everything up, and I thought that if I ever did begin to do it all seriously I would make myself a whole host of more easily accessible tables than those available in the record books. When I at last answered NO to the final question ANY MORE HORSES? I got the clear reply that left no doubt about Liam O'Rorke's genius.

Genotti headed the win factor list. An outsider turned up on it in second place, with the horse that had started favourite in third: and the St Leger result had been those three horses in that order exactly.

I could hardly believe it.

Ruth Quigley said suddenly, 'Got the wrong result? You look flummoxed.'

'No – the right one.'

'Disturbing.' She grinned swiftly. 'If I get the results I expect, I check and check and check. Doesn't do to be complacent. Like some coffee?'

I accepted and she made it as fast as she did everything else.

'How old are you?' I said.

'Twenty-one. Why?'

'I'd have thought you'd have been at the university.'

'Degree at twenty plus one month. Nothing unusual. Cheated my way in, of course. Everything's so slow nowadays. Forty years ago, degrees at nineteen or less were possible. Now they insist on calendar age. Why?

Why hold people back? Life's terribly short as it is. Masters degree at twenty plus six months. Did the two courses simultaneously. No one knew. Don't spread it around. Doing my doctorate now. Are you interested?'

'Yes,' I said truthfully.

She smiled like a summer's day, come and gone. 'My father says I'm a bore.'

'He doesn't mean it.'

'He's a surgeon,' she said, as if that explained much. 'So's my mother. Guilt complexes, both of them. Give to mankind more than you take. That sort of thing. They can't help it.'

'And you?'

'I don't know yet. I can't give much. I can't get jobs I can do. They look at the years I've been alive and make judgments. Quite deadly. Time has practically nothing to do with anything. They'll give me the jobs when I'm thirty that I could do better now. Poets and mathematicians are best before twenty-five. What chance have they got?'

'To work alone,' I said.

'My God. Do you understand? You're wasting time, get on with your programs. Don't show me what I should do. I've got a research fellowship. What do I seek for? What is there to seek? Where is the unknown, what is not known, what's the question?'

I shook my head helplessly, 'Wait for the apple to fall on your head.'

'It's true. I can't contemplate. Sitting under the

apple trees. Metaphorical apple trees. I've tried. Get on with your nags.'

Philosophically I loaded YORK and worked through the three races for which there were programs, and found that in two of them the highest-scoring horse had won. Three winners from the four races I'd worked through. Incredible.

With a feeling of unreality I loaded EPSOM and went painstakingly through the four races for which there were programs; and this time came up with no winners at all. Frowning slightly I loaded NEWBU for Newbury and from a good deal of hard accurate work came up with the win factors of the race in which Angelo had backed the absolute no-hoper Pocket Handbook.

Pocket Handbook, who had finished exhausted and tailed-off by at least thirty lengths, was at the top of the win-factor list by a clear margin.

I stared distrustfully at the rest of the scores, which put the race's actual winner second from the bottom with negligible points.

'What's the matter?' Ruth Quigley said, busy at her own machine and not even glancing my way.

'Parts of the system are haywire.'

'Really?'

I loaded GOODW and sorted through five races. All the top scorers were horses which in the events had finished no nearer than second.

'Are you hungry?' Ruth said. 'Three-thirty. Sandwich?'

I thanked her and went with her into her small kitchen where I was interested to see that her speed stopped short of dexterity with slicing tomatoes. She quite slowly, for her, made fat juicy affairs of cheese, chutney, tomatoes and corned beef which toppled precariously on the plate and had to be held in both hands for eating.

'Logical explanations exist,' she said, looking at my abstracted expression. 'Human logic's imperfect. Absolute logic isn't.'

'Mm,' I said. 'Ted showed me how easy it is to add and delete passwords.'

'So?'

'It would be pretty easy, wouldn't it, to change other things besides?'

'Unless it's in ROM. Then it's difficult.'

'ROM?'

'Read only Memory. Sorry.'

'He showed me how to List things.'

'You've got RAM, then. Random Access Memory. Change what you like. Kids' stuff.'

We finished the sandwiches and returned to the keyboards. I loaded the Newbury file, chose the Pocket Handbook race and listed the program piece by piece.

LIST 1200–1240 I typed, and in front of the resulting screenful of letters, numbers and symbols sat figuring out the roots of trouble.

```
1200 PRINT 'TYPE IN PRIZE MONEY IN CURRENT SEASON'
1210 INPUT W: IF W < 1000 THEN T = T + 20
```

1220 IF W < 1000 THEN T = T: IF W < 5000 T = T

1230 IF W < 10000 THEN T = T: IF W < 15000 THEN T = T

1240 GOSUB 6000

Even to my ignorant and untutored eyes it was nonsense. Liam O'Rorke wouldn't have meant it, Peter Keithly wouldn't have written it, Ted Pitts would never have used it. In plain language, what it was saying was that if the season's winnings of a horse were *less* than one thousand pounds, the win factor score should be increased by 20, and if they were *more* than one thousand, and however much more, the win factor score would not increase at all. The least successful horses would therefore score most highly on that particular point. The weighting was topsy-turvy and the answers would come out wrong.

With the hollow certainty of what had happened staring me in the face, I loaded the Epsom file and searched the Lists of the programs for the four races on which Angelo had lost. In two cases the weightings for prize money were upside down.

Tried Goodwood. In three of the five listed races, the same thing.

Depressed beyond measure, I loaded the files for Leicester and Ascot, where races were to be held during the week ahead. Typed in the names of all the races to be run there and found there were programs for eight of them: one at Leicester, seven at Ascot. Listed each of the eight programs in sections, and found that in four of them the score for amassing much prize money was nought, and the score for prize money of under one thousand pounds was anything up to 20.

There were programs for some races at all the tracks which I knew for a certainty were not fourteen years old. Modern races, introduced since Liam O'Rorke had died.

The programs were no longer pure O'Rorke, but O'Rorke according to Pitts. O'Rorke updated, expanded, renewed. O'Rorke, on these particular tapes, interfered with, falsified, mangled. Ted Pitts – one had to face it – had wrecked the system before he'd handed it to me . . . and had delivered me defenceless to the wrath of Angelo Gilbert.

I thanked the frustrated and brilliant Miss Quigley for her day-long patience and drove home to Cassie.

'What's the matter?' she said immediately.

I said wearily, 'The ess aitch I tee has hit the fan.'

'What do you *mean*?'

'Angelo thinks I've tricked him. That the betting system I gave him is wrong. That it produces too many losers. Well, so it does. Normally it must be all right but on these tapes it's been altered. Ted Pitts has rigged so many of the programs that anyone using them will fall flat on his greedy face.' And I explained about the reversed scores for winning, which produced scatty results. 'He may also have changed some of the other weightings to get the same effect. I've no way of knowing.'

She looked as stunned as I felt. 'Do you mean Ted Pitts did it on *purpose*?'

'He sure did.' I thought back to the time he'd taken to make me 'copies'; to the hour I'd spent sitting by his pool talking to Jane, leaving him, at his own request, to work alone.

'But why?' Cassie said.

'I don't know.'

'You didn't tell him, did you, what you wanted the tapes for?'

'No, I didn't.'

She said doubtfully, 'Perhaps it might have been better if you'd said how vital they were.'

'And perhaps he wouldn't have given them to me at all if he'd known I had Angelo locked in the cellar. I mean, I thought he might not want to be *involved*. Most people wouldn't, with something like that. And then, if he was like Jonathan, he might have changed the weightings anyway, just to prevent Angelo from profiting. You never know. Jonathan himself would somehow have tricked Angelo again. I'm sure of it.'

'You don't think Ted Pitts asked Jonathan what he should do, do you?'

I thought back and shook my head. 'It was before nine in the morning when I went to the Pitts's house. That would make it about one a.m. in California. Even if he had his number, which I doubt, I don't think he would have telephoned Jonathan in the middle of the night . . . and Jonathan anyway sounded truly disappointed when I told him I'd given Angelo the tapes. No, Ted must have done it for his own reasons, and by himself.'

'Which doesn't help much.'

I shook my head.

I thought of the certainty with which I'd gone to Harry Gilbert's house on the previous day. Hell's teeth, how wrong could one be, how naïve could one get?

If I warned Angelo not to use the tapes in the week ahead he would be sure I had tricked him and was scared to death of his revenge.

If I didn't warn him not to use the tapes, he would most likely lose again and be more sure than ever that I'd tricked him . . .

If I wrung the right answers out of Ted Pitts and told them to Angelo, he would still think I had deliberately given him useless tapes – on which he had already lost.

Ted Pitts was in Switzerland walking up mountains.

'Would you care,' I said to Cassie, 'for a long slow cruise to Australia?'

CHAPTER NINETEEN

Jane Pitts on the telephone said, 'No, terribly sorry, he moves about and stops in different places every night. Quite often he sleeps in his tent. Is it important?'

'Horribly,' I said.

'Oh dear. Could I help?'

'There's something wrong with those tapes he made for me. Could you by any chance lend me his own?'

'No, I simply can't. I'm frightfully sorry but I don't know where he keeps anything in that room and he positively hates his things being touched.' She thought for a few minutes, puzzled but not unwilling, friendly, anxious to help. 'Look, he's sure to call me one day soon to say when he'll be home. Would you like me to ask him to ring you?'

'Yes please,' I said fervently. 'Or ask him where I can reach him, and I'll call him. Do tell him it's really urgent, beg for me, would you? Say it's for Jonathan's sake more than mine.'

'I'll tell him,' she promised, 'as soon as he rings.'

'You're unscrupulous,' Cassie said as I put down the receiver. 'It's for your sake, not Jonathan's.'

'He wouldn't want to weep on his brother's grave.'

'*William!*'

'A joke,' I said hastily. 'A joke.'

Cassie shivered, however. 'What are you going to do?'

'Think,' I said.

The basic thought was that the more Angelo lost, the angrier he would get, and that the first objective was therefore to stop him betting. Taff and the others could hardly be persuaded not to accept such easy pickings, which left the source of the cash, Harry Gilbert himself. Precisely what, I wondered, could I say to Harry Gilbert which would cut off the stake money without sending Angelo straight round to vent his rage?

I could tell him that Liam O'Rorke's system no longer existed: that I'd got the tapes in good faith but had been tricked myself. I could tell him a lot of half-truths, but whether he would believe me, and whether he could restrain Angelo even if he himself were convinced, of those imponderables there was no forecast.

Realistically there was nothing else to do.

I didn't particularly want to try to trap Angelo into being sent back to jail: fourteen years was enough for any man. I only wanted, as I had all along, for him to leave me alone. I wanted him deflated, defused . . . docile. What a hope.

A night spent with my mind on pleasanter things produced no cleverer plan. A paragraph in the *Sporting Life*, read over a quick breakfast after an hour with the horses on the Heath, made me wish that Angelo would solve my problems himself by bashing someone else on the head: about as unlikely as him having a good week on the system. Lancer the bookmaker, said the paper, had been mugged on his own doorstep on returning from Newbury races on Friday evening. His wallet, containing approximately fifty-three pounds, had been stolen. Lancer was OK, police had no leads: poor old Lancer, too bad.

I sighed. Who, I wondered, could I get Angelo to bash?

Besides, of course, myself.

On account of the knee-groper, I was driving Cassie to work whenever possible, and on that morning after I'd dropped her I went straight on to Welwyn Garden City, not relishing my prospects but with not much alternative. I hoped to persuade both Harry Gilbert and Angelo that the havoc the years had caused to the O'Rorke system couldn't be undone, that it was blown, no longer existed, couldn't be recovered. I was going to tell them again that any violence from Angelo would find him back in a cell; to try to make them believe it . . . to fear it.

I was taller than Angelo and towered over a man in a wheelchair. I intended slightly to crowd them, faintly to intimidate, certainly to leave a physical impression that it was time for them to back off. Even on Angelo, who must have known how to frighten from childhood, it might have some effect.

Eddy opened the front doors and tried at once to close them again when he saw who had called. I pushed him with force out of my way.

'Harry isn't dressed,' he said fearfully, though whether the fear was of me or of Harry wasn't clear.

'He'll see me,' I said.

'No. You can't.' He tried to bar my way to one of the wide doors at the side of the entrance hall, thereby showing me which way to go, and I walked over there with Eddy trying to edge me out of my path by leaning on me.

I thrust him again aside and opened the door, and found myself in a short passage which led into a large bedroom which was equipped first and most noticeably with another vast window looking out to the golf.

Harry Gilbert lay in a big bed facing the window, ill and growing old but still in some indefinable way not defenceless, even in pyjamas.

'I tried to stop him,' Eddy was saying ineffectually.

'Take this tray and go away,' Harry Gilbert said to him, and Eddy picked off the bedclothes the half-eaten breakfast which I had interrupted. 'Shut the door.' He waited until Eddy had retreated and then frostily to me said, 'Well?'

'I've discovered,' I said with urgency, 'that Liam O'Rorke's betting system has the equivalent of smallpox. It should be treated like the plague. It'll bring trouble to all who touch it. The old system has been through too many hands, been adulterated by the years. It's gone bad. If you want to save your cash, you'll stop Angelo using it, and it's pointless getting angry with me on any counts. I got the system for you in good faith and I'm furious to find it's useless. Bring Angelo in here and let me tell him.'

Harry Gilbert stared at me with his usual unreadable face, and it was without any visible consternation that he said in his semi-slurred way, 'Angelo isn't here. He is cashing my cheque at the bank. He is going to Leicester races.'

'He will lose,' I said. 'I didn't need to warn you. I'm warning you. Your money will be lost.'

Thoughts must have traversed the brain behind the cold eyes but nothing much showed. Finally, and it must have been with an inner effort, he said, 'Can you stop him?'

'Stop the cheque,' I said. 'Call the bank.'

He glanced at a clock beside him. 'Too late.'

'I can go to Leicester,' I said. 'I'll try to find him.'

After a pause he said, 'Very well.'

I nodded briefly and left him, and drove towards Leicester feeling that even if I had managed to convince Harry, which was in itself uncertain, I was facing the impossible with Angelo. The impossible all the same had to be tried: and at least, I thought, he wouldn't actually attack me on a busy racecourse.

Leicester races on that cold autumn day turned out to be as busy as a well-smoked beehive, with only a scattering of dark-coated figures trudging about doggedly, head down to the biting wind. As sometimes happened on city-based tracks on weekdays, the crowd was thin to the point of embarrassment, the whole proceedings imbued with the perfunctory and temporary air of a ritual taking place without fervour.

Taff was stamping about by his beer crate, blowing on his fingers and complaining that he would have done better business if he'd gone to the day's other meeting at Bath.

'But there's the Midlands Cup here,' he said. 'It'll be a good race. I thought it would pull them – and look at them, not enough punters to sing auld lang syne round a tea-pot.' The Welsh accent was ripe with disgust.

'What are you making favourite?' I said smiling.

'Pink Flowers.'

'And what about Terrybow?'

'Who?'

'Runs in the Midlands Cup,' I said patiently. Terrybow, the computer's choice, top of the win factors. Terrybow with a habit of finishing tenth of twelve, or seventh of eighth, or fifteenth of twenty: never actually last but a long way from success.

'Oh, Terrybow.' He consulted a notebook. 'Twenties, if you like.'

'Twenty to one?'

'Twenty-five then. Can't say fairer than twenty-five. How much do you want?'

'How much would you take?'

'Whatever you like,' he said cheerfully. 'No limit. Not unless you know something I don't, like it's stuffed to the eyeballs with rocket dust.'

I shook my head and looked along the row of cold disgruntled bookmakers who were doing a fraction of their usual trade. If Angelo had been among them I would have seen him easily, but there was no sign of him. The Midlands Cup was the fourth race on the programme and still an hour ahead, and if Angelo was sticking rigidly to the disaster-laden system, Terrybow would be the only horse he would back.

'Have you seen Angelo Gilbert here today, Taff?' I asked.

'No.' He took a bet from a furtive-looking man in a raincoat and gave him a ticket. 'Ten at threes, Walkie-Talkie,' he told his clerk.

'How's Lancer?' I asked. 'Can't see him here.'

'Cursing muggers and rubbing a lump.' He took another tenner from a purposeful woman in glasses. 'Ten at eights, Engineer. Some kids rolled old Lancer on his own doorstep. I ask you, he carries thousands around the racecourse, pays it in to his firm at the end of the day, and then goes and gets himself done for fifty quid.'

'Did he see who robbed him?'

'One of Joe Glick's other boys who's here says it was a bunch of teenagers.'

Not Angelo, I thought. Well, it wouldn't have been. But if only he *would* . . .

I looked speculatively at Taff, who worked for himself and did carry his takings home at the end of the day. Pity one couldn't catch Angelo in the act of trying to retrieve his stake money after Terrybow had lost . . . pity one couldn't arrange for the police to be on hand when Angelo mugged Taff on the way home.

I'm down to fantasies, I thought: it's depressing.

The time passed and Angelo, who had been so ubiquitous when I had been trying to avoid him, was nowhere to be seen. I walked among the bookmakers and asked others besides Taff, but none of them had seen Angelo at all that afternoon, and there was still no sign of him during the run-up to the Midlands Cup. If he had gone to Bath after all, I thought, I was wasting my time – but the only race that day on the O'Rorke tapes was the Midlands Cup; its only designated horse, Terrybow.

With less than five minutes to go, when the horses were already cantering down to the start, a tremendous burst of tictac activity galvanised the men with white gloves high on the stands who semaphored changes of odds. With no direct link like telephones or radio the bookmakers relied on tic-tac to tell them if large sums had been placed with their firms on any particular horse, so that they could bring down the offered price.

Taff, watching his man signalling frenziedly, rubbed out the 20 written against Terrybow on his blackboard and with his piece of chalk wrote in 14. Along the row all the other bookies were similarly engaged. Terrybow fell again to 12.

'What's happening?' I said to Taff urgently.

He cast an abstracted eye in my direction. 'Someone down in the cheap ring is piling a stack on Terrybow.'

'*Damn*,' I said bitterly. I hadn't thought of looking for Angelo anywhere but round his usual haunts: certainly not in the comfortless far enclosure away down the course where the entrance fee was small, the view of the races moderate, and the expectation of the few bookmakers trading there modest to the point of not being worth standing in the cold all afternoon. And even if I'd thought of it I wouldn't have gone there, because it would have meant risking missing Angelo in the paddock. Damn and blast, I thought. Damn Angelo today and all days and for the whole of his life.

'You knew something about this Terrybow,' Taff said to me accusingly.

'I didn't back it,' I said.

'Yeah, that's right, so you didn't. So what's going on?'

'Angelo Gilbert,' I said. 'He's betting where he isn't known in case you wouldn't give him a good price up here.'

'What? Really?' He laughed, rubbed out the 12

against Terrybow and replaced it with 20. A small rush of punters resulted and he took their money with relish.

I went up on the stands and watched in a fury while Terrybow ran true to his form and drifted in twelfth of fifteen. Ted Pitts, I thought bleakly, might as well have shoved me under the wheels of a truck.

I did see Angelo that afternoon, and so did practically everyone else who hadn't gone home before the sixth race.

Angelo was the angrily shouting epicentre of a fracas going on near the weighing-room; a row involving several bookmakers, a host of racegoers and some worried-looking officials. Disputes between bookmakers and clients were traditionally dealt with on that spot by one particular Jockey Club official, the Ring Inspector. Angelo appeared to have punched him in the face.

The milling crowd parted a little and shifted and I found myself standing near the front of the onlookers with a clear view of the performance. The Ring Inspector was holding his jaw and trying to argue round his winces, six bookmakers were declaring passionately that money once wagered was lost for ever, and Angelo, waving his hard bunched fist, was insisting they gave it back.

'You tricked me,' he shouted. 'The whole bloody lot of you, you stole my cash.'

'You bet it fair and square,' yelled a bookmaker, wagging a finger forcefully in Angelo's face.

Angelo bit the finger. The bookmaker yelled all the harder.

A man standing next to me laughed but most of the on-lookers had less objectively taken sides and it seemed that a general brawl needed only a flashpoint. Into the ugliness and among the angrily gesturing hands and violent voices walked two uniformed policemen, both very young, both slight, both looking poor opponents in size and in forcefulness for the prison-taught Angelo. The Ring Inspector said something to one of them which was inaudible to me in the hubbub and to his immense and visible surprise Angelo suddenly found himself wearing, on the wrist he happened not to be waving in the air at that moment, a handcuff.

His bellow of rage fluttered the pigeons off the weighing-room roof. He tugged with his whole weight and the boy-policeman whose own wrist protruded from the other cuff was jerked off his feet onto his knees. It looked not impossible that Angelo could pick him up bodily and simply run off with him, but the second constable came to his rescue, saying something boldly to Angelo and pulling his radio-communicator out of the front of his uniform jacket to bring up reinforcements.

Angelo looked at the ring of spectators through

which he had little real hope of pushing and at his unexpectedly adroit captor, now rising from his knees, and at the seething book-makers who were showing signs of satisfaction, and finally straight at me.

He took a step towards me with such strength that the half-risen policeman lost his balance again and fell on his back, his arm twisting awkwardly over his head, stretching in the handcuff. There was about Angelo suddenly such an extraordinary growth of menace, something so different from a mere racecourse argument, that the thronging voices fell away to silence and eyes looked at him with age-old fright. The monstrous recklessness seemed to swell his whole body, and even if his words were banal his gritty voice vibrated with a darkness straight out of myth.

'You,' he said deliberately, 'you and your fucking brother.'

There was an awareness in his face of the attentive crowd of witnesses around us and he didn't say aloud what was in his mind, but I could hear it as clearly as if he'd woken the sleeping hills.

I'll kill you. *I'll kill you.*

It was a message not so much new as newly intense. More than ever implacable. A promise, not a threat.

I stared back at him as if I hadn't heard, as if it wasn't there looking at me out of his eyes. He nodded however as if savagely satisfied and turned with a contemptuous shrug to the rising policeman, jerking him the last few inches upright; and he went, after that, without fighting, walking away between the two constables towards a police car which was driving in through the gates. The car halted. They put him in the back seat between them and presently rolled away, and the now strangely quiet crowd began to spread open and disperse.

A voice in my ear, the Welsh voice of Taff, said, 'You know what set all that off?'

'What?' I asked.

'The bookies down in the cheap ring told Angelo he was a right mug. They were laughing at him, it seems. Joshing him, but friendly like to start with. They said they'd be happy to keep on taking his money because if he thought he'd bought Liam O'Rorke's old system he'd been robbed, duped, bamboozled, made a fool of and generally conned from here to Christmas.'

Dear God.

'So then this Angelo sort of exploded and started trying to get his stake back.'

'Yes,' I said.

'Well,' Taff said cheerfully. 'It all makes a change, though I reckon those goons in the cheap ring would have done better to keep their mouths shut. That Angelo was a bit of a golden goose and after this he won't lay no more golden eggs.'

I drove home with a feeling that the seas were closing over my head. Whatever I did to try to disentangle myself from Angelo it seemed that I slid further into the coils.

He was never, after this, going to believe that I hadn't tricked him on purpose. Even if I could at last get him the real correct system, he wouldn't forgive me the bets lost, the sneers of the bookmakers, the click of those handcuffs.

The police might hold him overnight, I thought, but not much longer: I doubted if one punch and a few yells would upset his parole. But to the tally in his mind would be added a night in the cells to rankle with those in my cellar – and if he'd come out of prison angry enough to attack me with nothing against me but the fact of my being Jonathan's brother, how much more would he now come swinging.

Cassie had long been home when I finally got there and was buoyantly pleased with the prospect of having the plaster off her arm on the following afternoon. She had arranged a whole day off from work and had thanked the groper for the last time, confident that she would be able to drive more or less at once. She was humming in the kitchen while I cooked some spaghetti for supper and I kissed her abstractedly and thought of Angelo and wished him dead with all my heart.

Before we had finished eating, the telephone rang and, most unexpectedly, it was Ted Pitts calling from Switzerland. His voice, on the whole, was as cool as the Alps.

'Thought I'd better apologise,' he said.

'It's kind of you.'

'Jane's disgusted with me. She told me to ring you at once. She said it was urgent. So here I am. Sorry, and all that.'

'I just wondered,' I said hopelessly, 'why you did it.'

'Mashed up the weightings?'

'Yes.'

'You'll think I'm mean. Jane says I'm so mean she's ashamed of me. She's furious. She says all our wealth is due to Jonathan, and I've played the most rotten trick on Jonathan's brother. She's hardly speaking to me she's so cross.'

'Well . . . *why?*' I said.

He did at least seem to want me to understand. He spoke earnestly, explaining, excusing, telling me the destructive truth. 'I don't know. It was an impulse. I was making those copies and I suddenly thought I don't want to part with this system. I don't want anyone else to have it. It's mine. Not Jonathan's, just mine. He didn't even want it, and I've had it to myself all these years, and I've added to it and made it my own. It belongs to me. It's *mine.* And there you were, just asking for it as if I would give it to you as of right, and I suddenly thought why should I? So I just quickly changed a lot of the weightings. I didn't have time to test them. I had to guess. I altered just enough, I thought, but it seems I did too much. Otherwise you wouldn't have checked . . . I intended that when you used the system, you wouldn't win enough to think it worth all the work, and you'd get tired of it.' He paused. 'I was jealous of you having it, if you really want to know.'

'I wish you'd told me . . .'

'If I'd said I didn't want to give it to you, Jane would have made me. She says I must now. She's so cross.'

'If you would,' I said, 'you might save me a lot of grief.'

'Make your fortune, you mean.' The apology, it seemed, hadn't come from the heart: he still sounded resentful that I should be learning his secrets.

I thought again about telling him about Angelo but it still seemed to me that he might think it the best reason for *not* giving me the system that I could devise, so I said merely, 'It could work for two people, couldn't it? If someone else had it, it wouldn't stop you yourself winning as much as ever.'

'I suppose,' he said grudgingly, 'that that's true.'

'So . . . when do you come home?'

'The week after next.'

I was silent. Appalled. By the week after next heaven knew what Angelo would have done.

Ted Pitts said with half-suppressed annoyance, 'I suppose you've betted heavily on the wrong horses and lost too much, and now you need bailing out a lot sooner than the week after next?'

I didn't dispute it.

'Jane's furious. She's afraid I've cost you more than you can afford. Well, I'm sorry.' He didn't truly sound it.

'Could she find the tapes to give to me?' I said humbly.

'How soon do you need them?'

'More or less at once. Tonight, if possible.'

'Hmph.' He thought for a few moments. 'All right. All right. But you can save yourself the journey, if you like.'

'Er, how?'

'Do you have a tape recorder?'

'Yes.'

'Jane can play the tapes to you over the telephone. They'll sound like a lot of screeching. But if you've a half-way decent recorder the programs will run all right on a computer.'

'Good heavens.'

'A lot of computer programs whiz round the world on telephones every day,' he said. 'And up to the satellites and down again. Nothing extraordinary in it.'

To me it did seem extraordinary, but then I wasn't Ted Pitts. I thanked him with more intensity than he knew for his trouble in ringing me up.

'Thank Jane,' he said.

I did thank her, sincerely, five minutes later.

'You sounded in such *trouble*,' she said. 'I told Ted I'd sent you to Ruth because you'd wanted to check the tapes, and he *groaned*, so I asked him why . . . and when he told me what he'd done I was just *furious.* To think of you wasting your precious money when everything we have is thanks to Jonathan.'

Her kindness made me feel guilty. I said, 'Ted said you could play the real tapes to me over the telephone – if you wouldn't mind.'

'Oh yes, all right. I've seen Ted do it often. He and Ruth are always swopping programs that way. I've got the tapes here beside me. I made Ted tell me where to find them. I'll go and get the recorder now, if you'll hang on, and then I'll play them to you straight away.'

I had called her from the office because of the message-recorder already fitted to that telephone, and when she returned I recorded the precious programs on Luke's supply of fresh unused tapes which might not have been of prime computer standard but were all the same a better lot, I reckoned, than trying to record new machine language on top of old.

Cassie came into the office and listened to the scratchy whining noises running on and on and on.

'Horrible,' she said: but to me, sweet music. A ransom to the future. Passport to a peaceful world. In a sudden uprush of optimism entirely at variance with the gloom of my drive home from Leicester, I convinced myself that this time, now that we had the genuine article, our troubles would come to an end. The solution was still, as it had always been, to make Angelo rich, and at last it could be done.

'I'll give these tapes to Angelo,' I said, 'and we'll

go away from the cottage for just a while, a few weeks, just until he's won enough not to want his revenge. And we'll be free of him at last, thank God.'

'Where shall we go?'

'Not far. Decide tomorrow.'

When three tapes were full and the noises fell quiet I switched off the recording part of the machine and spoke again to Jane.

'I'm very grateful,' I said. 'More than I can say.'

'My dear William, I'm so sorry . . .'

'Don't be,' I said. 'You've saved my life.' Quite literally, probably, I thought. 'Everything,' I said, 'will be all right.'

One shouldn't say such things. One really shouldn't.

CHAPTER TWENTY

Cassie came with me in the early morning to see the horses work on the Heath, shivering a little in boots, trousers and padded husky jacket, but glad, she said, to be alive in the free air and the wide spaces. Her breath, like mine, like that of all the horses, spurted out in lung-shaped plumes of condensing vapour, chilled and gone in a second and quickly renewed, cold transformed to heat within the miracle of bodies.

We had already in a preliminary fashion left the cottage, having packed clothes and necessaries and stowed the suitcases in my car. I had also brought along a briefcase containing the precious tapes and a lot of Luke's paperwork and had rerouted my telephone calls by a message on the answer-system, and it remained only to make a quick return trip to pick up the day's mail and arrange for future postal deliveries to be left at the pub.

We hadn't actually decided where we would sleep that night or for many nights to come, but we did between us have a great many friends who might be cajoled, and if the traditional open-house generosity of the racing world failed us, we could for a while afford a hotel. I felt freer and more light-hearted than I had for weeks.

Sim was positively welcoming on the gallops and Mort asked us to breakfast. We shivered gratefully into his house and warmed up with him on toast and coffee while he slit open his letters with a paperknife and made comments on what he was at the same time reading in the *Sporting Life*. Mort never did one thing at a time if he could do three.

'I've re-routed my telephone messages to you,' I told him. 'Do you mind?'

'Have you? No, of course not. Why?'

'The cottage,' I said, 'is at the moment uninhabitable.'

'Decorators?' He sounded sympathetic and it seemed simplest to say yes.

'There won't be many calls,' I promised. 'Just Luke's business.'

'Sure,' he said. He sucked in a boiled egg in two scoops of a spoon. 'More coffee?'

'How are the yearlings settling?' I asked.

'Come and see them. Come this afternoon, we'll be lunging them in the paddock.'

'What's lunging?' Cassie said.

Mort gave her a fast forgiving smile and snapped his fingers a few times. 'Letting them run round in a big circle on the end of a long rein. Gives them exercise. No one rides them yet. They've never been saddled. Too young.'

'I'd like that,' Cassie said, looking thoughtfully at the plaster and clearly wondering about the timing.

'Where are you staying?' Mort asked me. 'Where can I find you?'

'Don't know yet,' I said.

'Really? What about here? There's a bed here, if you like.' He crunched his teeth across half a piece of toast and ate it in one gulp. 'You could answer your own phone calls. Makes sense.'

'Well,' I said. 'For a night or two . . . very grateful.'

'Settled then.' He grinned cheerfully at Cassie. 'My daughter will be pleased. Got no wife, you know. She scarpered. Miranda gets bored, that's my daughter. Sixteen, needs a girl's company. Stay for a week. How long do you need?'

'We don't know,' Cassie said.

He nodded briskly. 'Take things as they come. Very sensible.' He casually picked up the paperknife and began cleaning his nails with it, reminding me irresistibly of Jonathan who throughout my childhood had done his with the point of a rifle bullet.

'I thought I'd go to Ireland at the weekend,' I said, 'and try to make peace with Donavan.'

Mort gave me a blinding grin, 'I hear you're a turd and an ignorant bastard, and should be dragged six times round the Curragh by your heels. At the least.'

The telephone standing on the table by his elbow

rang only once, sharply, before Mort was shouting 'Hullo?' down the receiver. 'Oh,' he said, 'Hullo, Luke.' He made signalling messages to me with his eyebrows. 'Yes, he's here right now, having breakfast.' He handed over the receiver, saying. 'Luke rang your number first, he says.'

'William,' Luke said, sounding relaxed and undemanding. 'How are the new yearlings?'

'Fine. No bad reports.'

'Thought I'd come over to see them. See what you've gotten me. I feel like a trip. Listen, fella, do me a favour, make me some reservations at the Bedford Arms for two nights, fourteenth and fifteenth October?'

'Right,' I said.

'Best to Cassie,' he said. 'Bring her to dinner at the Bedford on the fourteenth, OK? I'd sure like to meet her. And fella, I'll be going on to Dublin. You aiming to go to the Ballsbridge Sales?'

'Yeah, I thought to. Ralph Finnigan died . . . they're selling all his string.'

Luke sounded appreciative. 'What would you pick, fella? What's the best?'

'Oxidise. Two years old, well bred, fast, a prospect for next June's Derby and bound to be expensive.'

Luke gave a sort of rumbling grunt. 'You'd send it to Donavan?'

'I sure would.'

The grunt became a chuckle. 'See you, fella, on the fourteenth.'

There was a click and he was gone. Mort said, 'Is he coming?' and I nodded and told him when. 'Most years he comes in October,' Mort said.

He asked if we'd like to see the second lot exercise but I was anxious to be finished at the cottage so Cassie and I drove the miles back to the village and stopped first at the pub. Mine host, who had been invisible earlier, was now outside in his shirtsleeves sweeping dead leaves off his doorstep.

'Aren't you cold?' Cassie said.

Bananas, perspiring in contrast to our huskies, said he had been shifting beer barrels in his cellar.

We explained about going away for a while, and why.

'Come inside,' he said, finishing the leaves. 'Like some coffee?'

We drank some with him in the bar but without the ice cream and brandy he stirred into his own. 'Sure,' he said amiably. 'I'll take in your mail. Also papers, milk, whatever you like. Anything else?'

'How absolutely extravagantly generous are you feeling?' Cassie said.

He gave her a sideways squint over his frothy mugful. 'Spill it,' he said.

'My little yellow car is booked in today for a service and its road test, and I just wondered . . .'

'If I'd drive it along to that big garage for you?'

'William will bring you back,' she said persuasively.

'For you, Cassie, anything,' he said. 'Straightaway.'

'Plaster off this afternoon,' she said happily, and I looked at her clear grey eyes and thought I loved her so much it was ridiculous. Don't ever leave me, I thought. Stay around for ever. It would be lonely now without you . . . It would be agony.

We all went in my car along to the cottage and left it out in the road because of Cassie wanting Bananas to back her little yellow peril out of the garage onto the driveway. She and he walked towards the garage doors to open them and I, half watching them, went across to unlock the front door and retrieve the letters which would have fallen on the mat just inside.

The cottage lay so quiet and still that our precautions seemed unnecessary, like crowd barriers on the moon.

Angelo is unpredictable, I told myself. Unstable as Mount St Helens. One might as well expect reasonable behaviour from an earthquake, even if one does ultimately wish him to prosper.

REMEMBER TIGERS.

There was a small banging noise out by the garage. Nothing alarming. I paid little attention.

Six envelopes lay on the mat. I bent down, picked them up, shuffled through them. Three bills for Luke, a rate demand for the cottage, an advertisement for books and a letter to Cassie from her mother in

Sydney. Ordinary mundane letters, not worth dying for.

I gave one final glance round the pretty sitting-room, seeing the red check frills on the curtains and the corn dollies moving gently in the breeze through the door. It wouldn't be so long, I thought, before we were back.

The kitchen door stood open, the light from the kitchen window lying in a reflecting gleam on the white paint: and across the gleam a shadow moved.

Bananas and Cassie, I thought automatically, coming in through the kitchen door. But they couldn't. It was locked.

There was hardly time even for alarm, even for primaeval instinct, even for rising hair. The silencer of a pistol came first into the room, a dark silhouette against the white paint, and then Angelo, dressed in black, balloon-high with triumph, towering with malice, looking like the devil.

There was no point in speech. I knew conclusively that he was going to shoot me, that I was looking at my own death. There was about him such an intention of action, such a surrender to recklessness, such an intoxication of destructiveness, that nothing and no one could have talked him out of it.

With a thought so light-fast that it wasn't even conscious, I reached out to the baseball bat which still lay on the window sill. Grasped its handle end with the dexterity of desperation and swung towards Angelo in one continuous movement from twisting foot through legs, trunk, arm and hand to bat, bringing the weight of the wood down towards the hand which held the pistol with the whole force of my body.

Angelo fired straight at my chest from six feet away. I felt a jerking thud and nothing else and wasn't even astonished and it didn't even a fraction deflect my swing. A split second later the bat crunched down onto Angelo's wrist and hand and broke them as thoroughly as he'd broken Cassie's arm.

I reeled from the force of that impact and spun across the room, and Angelo dropped the gun on the carpet and hugged his right arm to his body, yelling one huge shout at the pain of it and doubling over and running awkwardly out of the front door and down the path to the road.

I watched him through the window. I stood in a curious sort of inactivity, knowing that there was a future to come that had not yet arrived, a consequence not yet felt but inexorable, the fact of a bullet through my flesh.

I thought: Angelo has finally bagged his Derry. Angelo has taken his promised revenge. Angelo knows his shot hit me straight on target. Angelo will be convinced that he has done right, even if it costs him a lifetime in prison. In Angelo, despite his smashed wrist, despite his prospects, there would be at that moment an overpowering, screaming, unencompassable delirium of joy.

The battle was over, and the war. Angelo would be satisfied that in every physical, visible way, he had won.

Bananas and Cassie came running through the front door and looked enormously relieved to see me standing there, leaning a little against a cupboard but apparently unhurt.

'That was Angelo!' Cassie said.

'Yeah.'

Bananas looked at the baseball bat which lay on the floor and said, 'You bashed him.'

'Yeah.'

'Good,' Cassie said with satisfaction. 'His turn for the dreaded plaster.'

Bananas saw Angelo's gun and leaned to pick it up.

'Don't touch it,' I said.

He looked up enquiringly, still half bent.

'Fingerprints,' I said. 'Jail him for life.'

'But—'

'He shot me,' I said.

I saw the disbelief on their faces begin to turn to anxiety.

'Where?' Cassie said.

I made a fluttery movement with my left hand towards my chest. My right arm felt heavy and without strength, and I thought unemotionally that it was because some of the muscles needed to lift it were torn.

'Shall I get an ambulance?' Bananas said.

'Yes.'

They didn't understand, I thought, how bad it was. They couldn't see any damage, and I was concerned mostly about how to tell them without frightening Cassie to death.

It wasn't that at that point it felt so terrible, but I still knew in a detached fashion that it soon would be. There was an internal disintegration going on like the earth shifting, like foundations slipping away. Accelerating, but still slowly.

I said, 'Ring Cambridge hospital.'

It all sounded so calm.

I slid down, without meaning to, to my knees, and saw the anxiety on their faces turn to horror.

'You're really hurt,' Cassie said with spurting alarm.

'It's . . . er . . . er . . .' I couldn't think what to say.

She was suddenly beside me, kneeling, finding with terrified scarlet fingers that the entry wound that didn't show through the front of my padded husky jacket led to a bigger bleeding exit at the back.

'Oh my *God*,' she said in stunned absolute shock.

Bananas strode over for a look and I could see from both their faces that they did know now, there was no longer any need to seek the words.

He turned grim-faced away and picked up the telephone, riffling urgently through the directory and dialling the number.

'Yes,' he was saying. 'Yes, it's an emergency. A man's been shot. Yes, I did say shot . . . through the chest . . . Yes, he's alive . . . Yes, he's conscious . . . No, the bullet can't be in him.' He gave the address or the cottage and brief directions. 'Look, stop asking damn fool questions . . . tell them to shift their arse . . . Yes, it does look *bloody* serious, for God's sake stop wasting time . . . *My* name? Christ Almighty, John Frisby.' He crashed the receiver down in anger and said, 'They want to know if we've reported it to the police. What the hell does it matter?'

I couldn't be bothered to tell him that all gunshot wounds had to be reported. Breathing, in fact, was becoming more difficult. Only words that needed to be said were worth the effort.

'That pistol,' I said. 'Don't put it . . . in a plastic bag. Condensation . . . destroys . . . the prints.'

Bananas looked surprised and I thought that he didn't realise I was telling him because quite soon I might not be able to. I was beginning to feel most dreadfully ill, with clamminess creeping over my skin and breaking into a sweat on my forehead. I gave a smallish cough and wiped a red streak from my mouth onto the back of my hand. An enveloping wave of weakness washed through me and I found myself sagging fairly comprehensively against the cupboard and then half lying on the floor.

'Oh, William,' Cassie said. 'Oh *no*.'

If I'd ever doubted she loved me, I had my answer. No one could have acted or feigned the extremity of despair in her voice and in her body.

'Don't . . . worry,' I said. I tried a smile. I don't suppose it came off. I coughed again, with worse results.

I was trying to breathe, I thought, through a lake. A lake progressively filling, fed by many springs. It was happening faster now. Much faster. Too fast. I wasn't ready. Who was ever ready?

I could hear Bananas saying something urgent but I didn't know quite what. My wits started drifting. Existence was ceasing to be external. I'm dying, I thought, I really am. Dying too fast.

My eyes were shut and then open again. The daylight looked odd. Too bright. I could see Cassie's face wet with tears.

I tried to say, 'Don't cry,' but I couldn't get the breath. Breathing was becoming a sticky near-impossibility.

Bananas was still talking, distantly.

There was a feeling of everything turning to liquid, of my body dissolving, of a deep subterranean river overflowing its banks and carrying me away.

Dim final astringent thought . . . I'm drowning, God damn it, in my own blood.

CHAPTER TWENTY-ONE

Cassie's face was the next thing I saw, but not for more than a day, and it was no longer weeping but asleep and serene. She was sitting by a bed with me in it, surrounded by white things and glass and chromium and a lot of lights. Intensive care, and all that.

I woke by stages over several hours to the pain I hadn't felt from the shot, and to tubes carrying liquids into and away from my log of clay and to voices telling me over and over that I was lucky to be there; that I had died and was alive.

I thanked them all, and meant it.

Thanked Bananas, who had apparently picked me up and put me in my own car and driven me at about a hundred miles an hour to Cambridge because it was quicker than waiting for the ambulance.

Thanked two surgeons who it seemed had worked all day and then again half the night to staunch and tidy the wreckage of my right lung and stop blood dripping out of the drainage as fast as the transfusions flowed into my arm.

Thanked the nurses who clattered about with deft hands and noisy machinery, and in absentia thanked the donors of blood type 'O' who had refilled my veins.

Thanked Cassie for her love and for sitting beside me whenever they'd let her.

Thanked the fates that the destructive lump of metal had missed my heart. Thanked everyone I could for anything I could think of in gratitude for my life.

The long recurring dreams that had come during unconsciousness faded, receded, seemed no longer to be vivid fact. I no longer saw the Devil pacing beside me, quiet but implacable, the master waiting for my soul. I no longer saw him, the Fallen Angel, the Devil with Angelo's face, the yellow face with frosted hair and black empty holes where the eyes should have been. The Presence had gone. I was back to the daft real enjoyable world where tubes were what mattered, not concepts of evil.

I didn't say how close I had been to death because they were saying it for me, roughly every five minutes. I didn't say I had looked on the spaces of eternity and seen the everlasting Darkness and had known it had a meaning and a face. The visions of the dying and the snatched-from-death were suspect. Angelo was a living man, not the Devil, not an incarnation or a house or a dwelling place. It was delirium, the confusion of the brain's circuits, that had shown me the one as the other, the other as the One. I said nothing for fear of ridicule: and later nothing from feeling that I had in truth been mistaken and that the dreams were indeed . . . merely dreams.

'Where is Angelo?' I said.

'They said not to tire you.'

I looked at the evasion in Cassie's face. 'I'm lying down,' I pointed out. 'So give.'

She said reluctantly, 'Well . . . he's here.'

'*Here?* In this hospital?'

She nodded. 'In the room next door.'

I was bewildered. 'But why?'

'He crashed his car.' She looked at me anxiously for signs I supposed of relapse, but was seemingly reassured. 'He drove into a bus about six miles from here.'

'After he left the cottage?'

She nodded. 'They brought him here. They brought him into the emergency unit while Bananas and I were waiting there. We couldn't believe it.'

It wasn't over. I closed my eyes. It was never ever going to be over. Wherever I went, it seemed that Angelo would follow, even onto the slab.

'William?' Cassie said urgently.

'Mm?'

'Oh. I thought . . . '

'I'm all right.'

'He was nearly dead,' she said. 'Just like you. He's still in a coma.'

'What?'

'Head injuries,' she said.

I learned bit by bit over the next few days that the hospital people hadn't believed it when Bananas and Cassie told them it was Angelo who had shot me. They had fought as long and hard to save his life as mine, and apparently we had been placed side by side in the Intensive Care Unit until Cassie told them I'd have a heart attack if I woke and found him there.

The police had more moderately pointed out that if it was Angelo who woke first he might complete the job of murdering me: and Angelo was now in his unwaking sleep along the hallway, guarded by a constable night and day.

It was extraordinary to think of him being there, lying there so close. Unsettling in a fundamental way. I wouldn't have thought it would have affected me so badly, but my pulse started jumping every time anyone opened the door.. Reason said he wouldn't come. The subconscious feared it.

Bodies heal amazingly quickly. I was free of tubes, moved to a side ward, on my feet, walking about within a week: creeping a bit, sure, and stiff and sore, but positively, conclusively alive. Angelo too, it seemed, was improving. On the way up from the depths. Opening unseeing eyes, showing responses.

I heard it from the nurses, from the cleaners, from the woman who pushed a trolley of comforts, and all of them watched me curiously to see how I would take it. The piquancy of the situation hit first the local paper and then the national dailies, and the constables guarding Angelo started drifting in to chat.

It was from one of them that I learned how Angelo had lost control of his car while going round a roundabout, how a whole queue of people at a bus stop had seen him veer towards the bus as if unable to turn the steering wheel, how he'd been going too fast in any case, and how he had seemed at first to be *laughing*.

Bananas, when he heard it, said trenchantly, 'He crashed because you broke his wrist.'

'Yes,' I said.

He sighed deeply. 'The police must know it.'

'I expect so.'

'Have they bothered you?'

I shook my head. 'I told them what happened. They wrote it down. No one has said much.'

'They collected the pistol.' He smiled. 'They put it in a paper bag.'

I left the hospital after twelve days, walking slowly past Angelo's room but not going in. Revulsion was too strong even though I knew he was still lightly unconscious and wouldn't be aware I was there. The damage he had caused in my life and Cassie's might be over but my body carried his scars, livid still and still hurting, too immediate for detachment.

I dare say I hated him. Perhaps I feared him. I certainly didn't want to see him again, then or ever.

*

For the next three weeks I mooched around the cottage doing paperwork, getting fitter every day and persuading Bananas at first to drive me along to the Heath to watch the gallops. Cassie went to work, the plastered arm a memory. My blood had washed almost entirely off the sitting-room carpet and the baseball bat was in the cellar. Life returned more or less to normal.

Luke came over from California, inspected the yearlings, met Cassie, listened to Sim and Mort and the Berkshire trainers, visited Warrington Marsh, and went off to Ireland. It was he, not I, who bid for Oxidise at Ballsbridge and sent the colt to Donavan, and he who in some way smoothed the Irish trainer's feelings.

He came back briefly to Newmarket before leaving for home, calling in at the cottage and drinking a lunchtime scotch.

'Your year's nearly through,' he said.

'Yeah.'

'Have you enjoyed it?'

'Very much.'

'Want another?'

I lifted my head. He watched me through a whole minute of silence. He didn't say, and nor did I, that Warrington Marsh was never going to be strong enough again to do the job. That wasn't the point: the point was permanence . . . captivity.

'One year,' Luke said. 'It's not for ever.'

After another pause I said, 'One year, then. One more.'

He nodded and drank his drink, and it seemed to me that somewhere he was smiling. I had a presentiment of him coming over again the next year and offering the same thing. One year. One year's contract at a time, leaving the cage door open but keeping his bird imprisoned: and as long as I could go, I thought, I might stay.

Cassie, when she came home, was pleased. 'Mort told him he'd be mad to lose you.'

'Did he?'

'Mort likes you.'

'Donavan doesn't.'

'You can't have everything,' she said.

I had quite a lot, it was true; and then the police telephoned and asked me to see Angelo.

'No,' I said.

'That's a gut reaction,' a voice said calmly. 'But I'd like you to listen.'

He talked persuasively for a long time, cajoling again every time I protested, wearing down my opposition until in the end I reluctantly agreed to do what he wanted.

'Good,' he said finally. 'Wednesday afternoon.'

'That's only two days—'

'We'll send a car. We don't expect you to be driving yet.'

I didn't argue. I could drive short distances but I

tended to get tired. In another month, they'd said, I'd be running.

'We're grateful,' the voice said.

'Yeah . . .'

I told Cassie and Bananas, in the evening.

'How awful,' Cassie said. 'It's too much.'

The three of us were having dinner alone in the dining-room as the restaurant didn't officially open these days on Mondays: the old cow had negotiated Mondays off. Bananas had done the cooking himself, inventing a soufflé of white fish, herbs, orange and nuts to try out on Cassie and me: a concoction typically and indescribably different, an unknown language, a new horizon of taste.

'You could have said you wouldn't go,' Bananas said, heaping his plate to match ours.

'With what excuse?'

'Selfishness,' Cassie said. 'The best reason in the world for not doing things.'

'Never thought of it.'

Bananas said, 'I hope you insisted on a bullet-proof vest, a six-inch-thick plate glass screen and several rolls of barbed wire.'

'They did assure me,' I said mildly, 'that they wouldn't let him leap at my throat.'

'Too kind,' Cassie murmured.

We poured Bananas's exquisite sauce over his soufflé and said that when we had to leave the cottage we would camp in his garden.

'And will you bet?' he asked.

'What do you mean?'

'On the system.'

I thought blankly that I'd forgotten all about that possibility: but we did have the tapes. We did have the choice.

'We don't have a computer,' I said.

'We could soon pay for one,' Cassie said.

We all looked at each other. We were happy enough with our own jobs; with what we had. Did one always, inevitably, stretch out for more?

Yes, one did.

'You work the computer,' Bananas said, 'and I'll do the betting. Now and then. When we're short.'

'As long as it doesn't choke us.'

'I don't want diamonds,' Cassie said judiciously, 'or furs, or a yacht . . . but how soon can we have a pool in our sitting-room?'

Whatever Luke said to my brother when he got home to California I never knew, but it resulted in Jonathan telephoning that night to say he would be arriving at Heathrow on Wednesday morning.

'What about your students?'

'Sod the students. I've got laryngitis.' His voice bounced the distance strong and healthy. 'I'll see you.'

He came in a hired car looking biscuit-coloured from the sun and anxious about what he would find, and although I was by then feeling well again it didn't seem to reassure him.

'I'm alive,' I pointed out. 'One thing at a time. Come back next month.'

'What exactly happened?'

'Angelo happened.'

'Why didn't you tell me?' he demanded.

'I'd have told you if I'd died. Or someone would.'

He sat in one of the rockers and looked at me broodingly.

'It was all my fault,' he said.

'Oh, sure.' I was ironic.

'And that's why you didn't tell me.'

'I'd probably have told you one day.'

'Tell me now.'

I told him, however, where I was going that afternoon, and why, and he said in his calm positive way that he would come with me. I had thought he would: had been glad he was coming. I told him over the next few hours pretty well everything which had happened between Angelo and me, just as he had told me all those years ago in Cornwall.

'I'm sorry,' he said, at the end.

'Don't be.'

'You'll use the system?'

I nodded. 'Pretty soon.'

'I think old Mrs O'Rorke would be glad. She was proud of Liam's work. She wouldn't want it wasted.'

He reflected for a bit and then said, 'What make of pistol, do you know?'

'I believe . . . the police said . . . a Walther .22?'

He smiled faintly. 'True to form. And just as well. If it had been a .38 or something like that you'd have been in trouble.'

'Ah,' I said dryly. 'Just as well.'

The car came for us as threatened and took us to a large house in Buckinghamshire. I never did discover exactly what it was: a cross between a hospital and a civil service institution, all long wide corridors and closed doors and hush.

'Down there,' we were directed. 'Right along at the end. Last door on the right.'

We walked unhurriedly along the parquet flooring, our heels punctuating the silence. At the far end there was a tall window, floor to ceiling, casting not quite enough daylight; and silhouetted against the window were two figures, a man in a wheel-chair with another man pushing him.

Those two and Jonathan and I in due course approached each other, and as we drew nearer I saw with unwelcome shock that the man in the wheelchair was Harry Gilbert. Old, grey, bowed, ill Harry Gilbert who still consciously repelled compassion.

Eddy, who was pushing, faltered to a halt, and Jonathan and I also stopped, we staring at Harry and Harry staring at us over a space of a few feet. He looked from me to Jonathan, glancing at him briefly at first and then looking longer, more carefully, seeing what he didn't believe.

He switched to me. 'You said he was dead,' he said.

I nodded slightly.

His voice was cold, dry, bitter, past passion, past hope, past strength to avenge. 'Both of you,' he said. 'You destroyed my son.'

Neither Jonathan nor I answered. I wondered about the genetics of evil, the chance that bred murder, the predisposition which lived already at birth. The biblical creation, I thought, was also the truth of evolution. Cain existed, and in every species there was survival of the ruthless.

It was only by luck that I had lived; by Bananas's speed and surgeons' dedication. Abel and centuries of other victims were dead: and in every generation, in many a race, the genes still threw up the killer. The Gilberts bred their Angelos for ever.

Harry Gilbert jerked his head back, aiming at Eddy, signalling that he wanted to go; and Eddy the look-alike, Eddy the easily led, Eddy the sheep from the same flock, wheeled his uncle quietly away.

'Arrogant old bastard,' Jonathan said under his breath, looking back at them.

'The breeding of racehorses,' I said, 'is interesting.'

Jonathan's gaze came round very slowly to my face. 'And do rogues,' he asked, 'beget rogues?'

'Quite often.'

He nodded and we went on walking along the corridor, up to the window, to the last door on the right.

The room into which we went must once have been finely proportioned but with the insensitivity of government departments it had been hacked into two for utility. The result was one long narrow room with a window and another inner long room without one.

In the outer room, which was furnished only by a strip of mud-coloured carpet on the parquet leading to a functional desk and two hard chairs, were two men engaged in what looked like unimportant passing of the time. One sat behind the desk, one sat on it, both fortyish, smallish, smooth, bored-looking and with an air of wishing to be somewhere else.

They looked up enquiringly as we went in.

'I'm William Derry,' I said.

'Ah.'

The man sitting on the desk rose to his feet, came towards me, shook hands, and looked enquiringly at Jonathan.

'My brother, Jonathan Derry,' I said.

'Ah.'

He shook hands with him too. 'I don't think,' he said neutrally, 'that we'll need to bother your brother.'

I said, 'Angelo is more likely to react violently to Jonathan than to me.'

'But it was you he tried to kill.'

'Jonathan got him jailed . . . fourteen years ago.'

'Ah.'

He looked from one of us to the other, his head tilted slightly back to accommodate our height. We seemed to be in some way not what he'd expected, though I didn't know why. Jonathan did certainly look pretty distinguished, especially since age had given him such an air of authority, and he had always of the two of us had the straighter features; and I, I supposed, looked less a victim than I might have. I wondered vaguely if he'd been expecting a shuffling little figure in a dressing gown and hadn't reckoned on clothes like his own.

'I think I'll just go and *explain* about your brother,' he said at last. 'Will you wait?'

We nodded and he opened the door to the inner room parsimoniously and eeled himself through the gap, closing it behind him. The man behind the desk went on looking bored and offered no comment of any sort, and presently his colleague slid back through the same sized opening and said they were ready for us inside and would we please go in.

The inner room was lit brightly and entirely by electricity and contained four people and a great deal of electrical equipment with multitudinous dials and sprouting wires. I saw Jonathan give them a swift sweep of the eyes and supposed he could identify the lot, and he said afterwards that they had all seemed to be standard machines for measuring body changes – cardiograph, encephalograph, gauges for temperature, respiration and skin moisture – and there had been at least two of each.

One of the four people wore an identifying white coat and introduced himself quietly as Tom Course, a doctor. A woman in similar white moved among the machines, checking their faces. A third person, a man, seemed to be there specifically as an observer, since that was what he did, without speaking, during the next strange ten minutes.

The fourth person, sitting in a sort of dentist's chair with his back towards us, was Angelo.

We could see only the top of his bandaged head, but also his arms, which were strapped by the wrists to the arms of the chair.

There was no sign of any plaster on the arm I'd broken: mended no doubt. His arms were bare and covered sparsely with dark hair, the hands lying loose, without tension. From every part of his body it seemed that wires led backwards to the machines, which were all ranked behind him. In front of him there was nothing but a stretch of empty brightly lit room.

Dr Course, young, wiry, bolstered by certainties, gave me an enquiring glance and said in the same quiet manner, 'Are you ready?'

As ready, I supposed, as I ever would be.

'Just walk round in front of him. Say something. Anything you like. Stay there until we tell you it's enough.'

I swallowed. I had never wanted to do anything less

in all my life. I could see them all waiting, polite, determined, businesslike . . . and too damned understanding. Even Jonathan, I noticed, was looking at me with a sort of pity.

Intolerable.

I walked slowly round the machine and the chair and stopped in front of Angelo, and looked at him.

He was naked to the waist. On his head, below a cap of fawn crêpe bandage, there was a band of silvery metal like a crown. His skin everywhere gleamed with grease and to his face, his neck, his chest, arms and abdomen were fastened an army of electrodes. No one, I imagined, could have been more comprehensively wired; no flicker of change could have gone unmonitored.

He seemed as well-fleshed and as healthy as ever, despite his earlier two weeks in a coma. The muscles looked as strong, the trunk as tank-like, the mouth as firm. The hard man. The frightener. The despiser of mugs. Apart from his headdress and the wires he looked just the same. I breathed a shade deeply and looked straight into his black eyes, and it was there that one saw the difference. There was nothing in the eyes, nothing at all. It was extraordinary, like seeing a stranger in a long-known face. The house was the same . . . but the monster slept.

It was five weeks all but a day since we had last faced each other; since we had brought each other near to death, one way or another. Even though I had been prepared, seeing him again affected me powerfully. I could feel my heart thudding: could actually hear it in the expectant room.

'Angelo,' I said. My tongue felt sticky in my dry mouth. 'Angelo, you shot me.'

In Angelo, nothing happened.

He was looking at me in complete calm. When I took a pace to one side, his eyes followed. When I stepped back he still watched.

'I am . . . William Derry,' I said. 'I gave you . . . Liam O'Rorke's betting system.' I said the words slowly, clearly, deliberately, trying to control my own uneven breath.

From Angelo there was no reaction at all.

'If you hadn't shot me . . . you'd have been free now . . . and rich.'

Nothing. Absolutely nothing.

I found Jonathan standing beside me and after a pause Angelo's gaze wandered from me to him.

'Hullo, Angelo,' Jonathan said. 'I'm Jonathan, do you remember? William told you I was dead. It wasn't true.'

Angelo said nothing.

'Do you remember?' Jonathan said. 'I tricked you sideways.'

Silence. A dull absence of all we had endured for so long. No fury. No sneers, no threats, no towering hurricane of hate.

Silence, it seemed to me, was all that was appropriate. Jonathan and I stood there together in front of the shell of our enemy and there was nothing in the world left to say.

'Thank you,' Tom Course said, coming round the chair to join us. 'That should do it.'

Angelo looked at him.

'Who are you?' he said.

'Dr Course. We talked earlier, while we were fixing the electrodes.'

Angelo made no comment but instead looked directly at me.

'You were talking,' he said. 'Who are you?'

'William Derry.'

'I don't know you.'

'No.'

His voice was as deep and as gritty as ever, the only remnant, it seemed, of the old foe.

Dr Course said heartily, 'We'll take all those wires off you now. I expect you'll be glad to get rid of them.'

'Who did you say you are?' Angelo said, frowning slightly.

'Dr Course.'

'Who?'

'Never mind. I'm here to take the wires off.'

'Can I have tea?' Angelo said.

Dr Course left the taking-off of the wires to his woman colleague and led us round to look at the results on the machines. The observer, I noticed, was also consulting them acutely, but Course paid him scant attention.

'There we are,' he said, holding out a yard long strip of paper. 'Not a flicker. We had him stabilised for an hour before his visitors came. Breathing, pulse rate, everything rock steady. Quiet in here, you see. No interruptions, no intrusions, no noise. That mark, that's the point at which he saw *you*,' he nodded at me, 'and as you can see, nothing altered. This is the skin temperature chart. Always rises if someone's lying. And here . . .' He moved across to a different machine. 'Heart rate unchanged. And here . . .' to another. 'Brain activity, very faint alteration. He couldn't have seen *you*, his hated victim, suddenly and unexpectedly standing in front of him, and yet show no strong body or brain changes, not if he'd known you. Absolutely impossible.'

I thought of my own unrecorded but pretty extreme responses, knew that it was true.

'Is this state permanent?' Jonathan asked.

Tom Course gave him a swift look. '*I* think so. It's *my* opinion, yes. See, they dug pieces of skull out of his brain tissue. Brilliant repair job on the bone structure, have to hand it to them. But there you are, you can see, no memory. Many functions unimpaired. Eat, talk, walk, he can do all that. He's continent. He'll live to be old. But he can't remember anything for longer than about fifteen minutes, sometimes not even that. He lives in the absolute present. Loss of capacity for memory is not all that rare, you know, after severe brain damage. But with this one, there were *doubts.* Not *my* doubts, official doubts. They said he was faking, that he knew he'd go to a hospital, not a prison, if he could persuade everyone he'd lost his memory.'

Tom Course waved a hand around the machines. 'He couldn't have faked today's results. Conclusive. Settle the arguments once and for all. Which is why we're all here, of course. Why they gave us this facility.'

His woman colleague had taken the silver band off Angelo's forehead and the straps off his wrists, and was wiping the grease from his skin with pieces of cotton wool.

'Who are you?' he said to her, and she answered, 'Just a friend.'

'Where will he go?' I said.

Tom Course shrugged. 'Not my decision. But I'd be careful. I'm not a civil servant. My advice, I don't suppose, will be taken.' His remark was clearly aimed at the observer, who remained obstinately impassive.

I said slowly, 'Could he still be violent?'

Tom Course gave me a swift sideways glance. 'Can't tell. He might be. Yes, he might be. He looks harmless. He'll never *hate* anyone, he can't remember anyone long enough. But the sudden impulse . . .' He shrugged again. 'Let's say, I wouldn't turn my back on him if we were alone.'

'Not ever?'

'How old is he? Forty?' He pursed his mouth. 'Not for another ten years. Twenty perhaps. You can't tell.'

'Lightning?' I said.

'Just like that.'

The woman finished wiping the grease and was holding out a grey shirt for Angelo to put on.

'Have we had tea?' he said.

'Not yet.'

'I'm thirsty.'

'You'll have tea soon.'

I said to Tom Course, 'His father was outside ... did Angelo see him?'

Course nodded. 'No reaction. Nothing on the machines. Conclusive tests, the whole lot of them.' He looked slyly at the observer. 'They can stop all the arguing.'

Angelo stood up out of the chair, stretching upright, seeming strong with physical life but fumbling with the buttons of his shirt, moving without total coordination, looking around vaguely as if not quite sure what he should be doing next.

His wandering gaze came to rest on Jonathan and me.

'Hullo,' he said.

The doors from the outer room opened wide and two whitecoated male nurses and a uniformed policeman came through it.

'Is he ready?' the policeman said.

'All yours.'

'Let's be off, then.'

He fastened a handcuff round Angelo's left wrist and attached him to one of the nurses.

Angelo didn't seem to mind. He looked at me uninterestedly for the last time with the black holes where the eyes should have been and walked as requested to the door.

Diminished, defused . . . perhaps even docile.

'Where's my tea?' he said.